THE
CHILDREN OF LYR
Book III

MOTHER

OF THE

MOON

LINA C. AMAREGO

Lina C. Amarego

For information contact: LCamarego@gmail.com or www.silverwheelpress.com

Cover Design by COVERDUNGEONRABBIT

ISBN: 9781734826593

First Edition: DECEMBER 2022

CONTENT WARNING:
This book contains mature themes, including brief moments of violence, torture, suicidal ideation and actions, memory loss, manipulation, and sexual content. This book is not suitable for readers under the age of 14. Reader discretion is advised.

Mother

of the

Moon

Lina C. Amarego

BOOK III
OF
THE CHILDREN OF LYR

SILVER WHEEL PRESS
FANTASY WORLDS, HUMAN STORIES

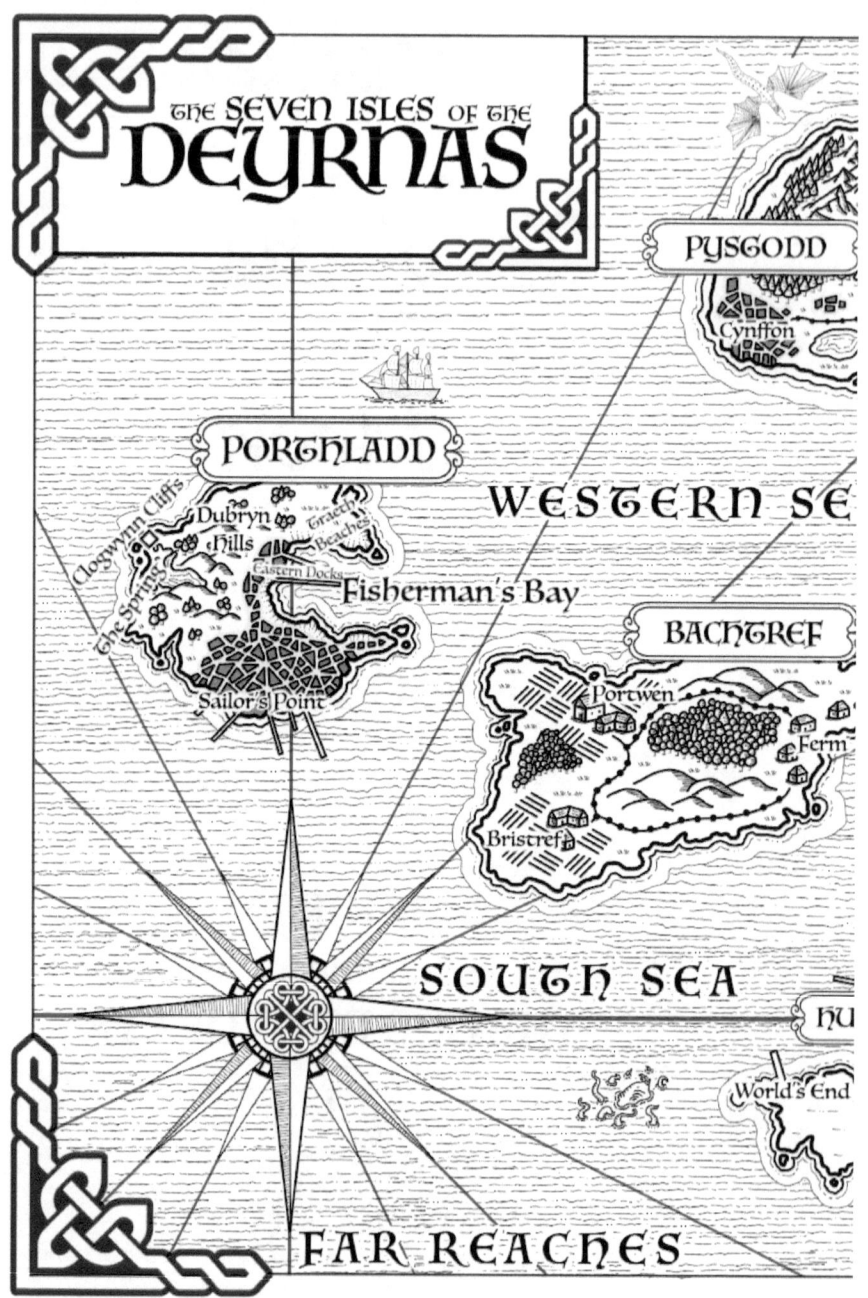

THE SEVEN ISLES OF THE
DEYRNAS

PYSGODD

Cynffon

PORTHLADD

WESTERN SE

Clogwyn Cliffs
Dubryn
Hills
Graeth
Beaches
Eastern Docks
The Strips
Fisherman's Bay

BACHTREF

Portwen

Ferm

Sailor's Point

Bristref

SOUTH SEA

HU

World's End

FAR REACHES

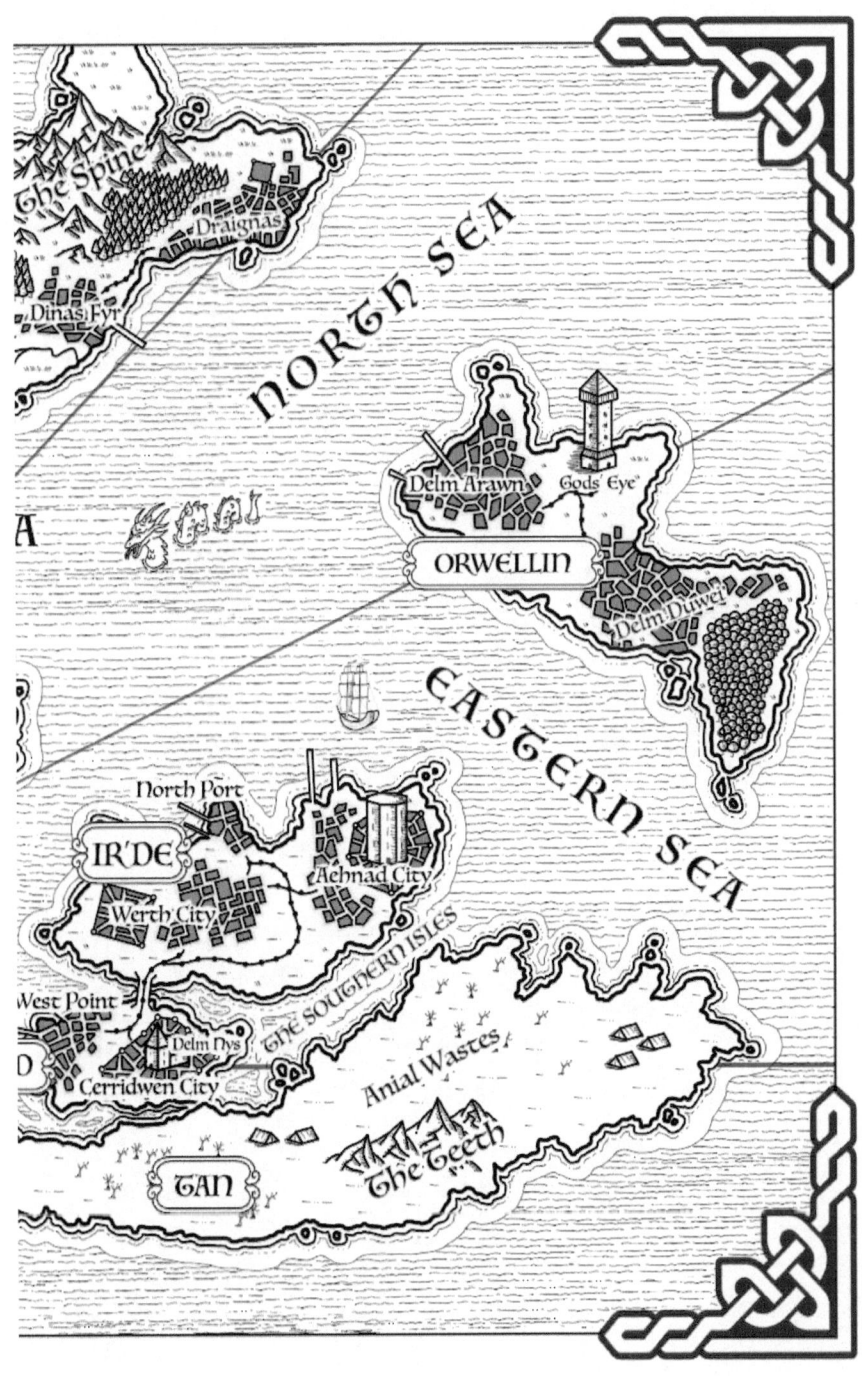

To Mom,
For demonstrating what true strength & sacrifice looks
like.
And for those in need of unconditional love.

I

Legends and Leads

RONAN

The day my wife died, a legend was born. Every corner of the Deyrnas sang the mourning song turned battle cry. Word of her departure spread faster than lightning through dry kindling. It took less than a week, and every hungry belly and broken heart, every fatherless child and loveless widow—they all added her name to their nightly prayers.

They did not pray for her. They prayed *to* her.

But to the chagrin of those who knew her best, it was not Keira's name on their lips. Nor the Rydha, the liberator.

Bren Ariannad.

The day my wife died, an idea was born. A vision for a new world, one made from the same sea-salt and sincerity that Keira lived by. A dangerous desire for more, shared by every Deyrnasian who'd ever felt lost or forgotten, every outcast and outlaw.

The day my wife died, a revolution began.

And on every flag, her crest. A compass embedded in a silver wheel beneath a crescent moon. A defiant cry for all of those who dared steer their course against the tide.

Bren Ariannad.

Queen of the Silver Wheel.

Queen of the Lost.

Queen of the Deyrnas.

Queen of the Otherworld.

In the few months since Porthladd's fall, the story grew and carried, as untamable and vicious as the plague. Mama used to warn me that a single story held more power than an entire army. When I was a child, it was a comfort. I'd listen at her feet with stars in my eyes, the fire in my chest alight with wonder and mystery. I devoured her stories, let them make me, teach me, cultivate me. Her stories could cure all ills, could fix all problems.

Now, I knew the truth. I saw stories for the empty promises they were: mist and smoke in a world of iron and steel. If the Deyrnasians wanted to, they could live in the safe embrace of whatever story brought them comfort in the dark.

I no longer cared for stories. I cared only for my wife and child.

And I would weave whatever story I needed to get them back. I would tell the tale and play my part, would pay in whispers instead of gold if it got me closer to finding her.

The magicka and medics of Hud had always valued mist and riddles as currency. Unlike Ir'de, where jewels and silks made a man into a master, Hud dealt in shadows and secrets.

I waited in the clay and stone alley in the middle of Cerridwen City, the hazy fog of morning masking my hiding spot against an abandoned crate, ready to don my role. If Keira was the Queen of the Lost, I was the King of the Lonely, a phantom waiting in the wings.

Griffin's intel had never failed before, but as the sun rose higher, shrinking the shadows into mere slivers, I doubted my first mate. I'd been waiting for an hour for one of Katrin's little snakes to arrive, bringing whatever chapter of the story we were meant to try and rewrite today. Even if I had given up on the Deyrnas, they still needed me. Needed the Serpent Prince and his crew of snakes to fight Locasta's tyranny. Needed the war criminals brave enough to kill a Councilman. Needed the disciples of the Rydha willing to lay down their lives to free Bachtref and Porthladd from death's grip.

I stuffed my hands in my pockets, cold despite the hot southern sun bearing down. I had no intention or desire to free the whole world. It was simply collateral salvation.

My impatience grew as the scent of dried herbs and the busy sounds of morning rose from the nearby shops and stone front buildings. They baked the bread and brewed the trouble they'd need for the day. If I waited any longer, I might be diced and stirred into a poultice or potion. Several of the magicka I'd met relentlessly bargained for even one of my scales.

Finally, a form took shape in the shadows. She was young, maybe a year younger than Saeth and Tarran, round-eyed and innocent. Dull brown hair framed her face before swooping back into a bun at the nape of her slender neck, accentuating both the simple pleasantness and *plainness* of her unremarkable face. Her frock was not made of sheer southern gossamer, but instead of stiff black cotton, and she tugged at the high neck as her direct gaze pierced my skin. Tiny droplets of sweat gathered at her brow, the only measure of her discomfort.

A spy in saint's clothing, she looked like she was born and bred Orwellin.

All talented storytellers needed a good costume.

She stepped forward first, producing a small scroll from the inside of her long black sleeve. Doe eyes narrowed into daggers as she cleared her throat. "You look lost, traveler. In need of a compass?"

I nodded once. She was well-trained, using the code even though my face was enough proof of who I was. "In need of a miracle," I responded accordingly, unsheathing my hands and tossing her a few gold crowns. "For your time and effort."

She caught the coins with ease, the corner of her lips tugging upwards as she shed the skin of her disguise. "Aye, *Ddraig Aur*." She sauntered forward with the Ir'desian grace she was born with before tucking the scroll into my breast pocket. "My mistress says hello."

I winced at both the title and the mention of her employer. I hated the name, *Golden Dragon*, like I was some sort of prized beast to be displayed. And it was starting to become a hassle to avoid Katrin's advances while maintaining my mask. But Katrin was a businesswoman first and foremost. If she wanted to treat me like a jewel in her collection, fine. I needed her wealth and access to pay my debts.

After all, we all had our parts to play. I hoped my wife would forgive the faked flirtations so long as they led me back to her.

I'll wait for you in the Otherworld.

I pressed an empty kiss to the girl's knuckles, my smirk serpentine. "Give your mistress my best."

The girl may have blushed, but I didn't stay long enough to find out. I'd wasted enough time, the sun yawning higher into Nef's territory with every breath and step.

My wife was waiting.

I took back paths, the hood of my long black cloak masking my signature blond curls as I dodged in and out of alleys, avoiding the crowded streets. My face was too recognizable for main roads. If I was seen by friends, it would be even longer until I could get back to the inn where my crew waited with an important guest. I'd been swarmed two days ago making my way to the western market, a pack of devotees to *Ariannad's* throne sobbing as they tried to get a glimpse of the *Ddraig Aur* himself, living proof of *Ariannad's* miracles.

If I was seen by the enemy, I'd be forced to unsheathe my fangs.

Neither option seemed like a good way to start my morning. Especially when I had urgent meetings to attend.

The inn was called the *Black Cauldron*, a fitting name for the debauchery and drudgery brewed in its walls. Like all buildings in Hud, it was made of dusky stone and clay, which was probably the only reason it still stood despite the nightly duels and dealings. Ivy clung to its side like the scent of Trouble, covering the name above the door, the perfect hiding spot for folks like us who preferred not to be found. We'd forfeited luxury when we'd turned on the High Council.

I breezed through the rundown wood door, nearly tearing it from its hinges. I wasn't quite used to the siren strength coursing through my veins, my wife's potent and precious gift. Saeth attempted to behead me last week when I crushed her favorite dagger while trying to clean it.

Ellian sat at the first oak table, long brown curls covering his face as he used a stack of parchment for a pillow. He startled as the door slammed against the stone wall, snarling under his breath, sending the stack of letters flying.

"Where are the others?" I bit my cheek to stifle the laugh as he scrambled.

Ellian shot me a warning look as he righted himself, tucking his oversized green tunic back into his waistband. "Most of them are asleep or in the courtyard training. The rest are upstairs in your quarters with our guest of honor."

So she was already here, then. Something hungry and cruel growled in the pit of my stomach, ready to sink its fangs into her. I had a bone to pick.

But it would have to wait. Wars were not won with perseverance and power alone. They were not only fought with strength and steel.

I swallowed hard, finally taking out the scroll to read. This was true power. *Information.*

Katrin's writing was muddled, but thorough. I ignored the first half entirely, her musings about her day and little hearts drawn in red ink, skimming the letter for the knowledge I needed most. I found the paragraph halfway down the page.

According to our friend Councilman Renfried, there is no change in Orwellin. Ivette said Councilmen and women from across the Deyrnas are hiding there. Locasta has them convinced that their lives are at risk, and that she is the only one that can protect them from the 'radicals.' They have plenty of supplies stored in God's Eye stocks to stay there while we all starve. It's well protected. Orwellin men are still in control of Porthladd and Bachtref. My girl Jessa said the guards are all of the same strange sort that sacked Porthladd. Practically lifeless. They look like men, but they barely talk and aren't swayed by any of my little snakes' advances. So either they are all eunuchs, or they are spellcast.

I thought of the swarms of guards from the night my wife died. They'd been enchanted then, whatever dark gift Locasta possessed propelling them into unthinking action. And when Connor fell, so did they, like puppets whose strings had been cut.

The thought both comforted and disturbed. On one hand, the idea of an enemy that was unafraid made my blood run cold. Stomach sinking, I remembered the way they came for us, unconcerned for their own lives and bodies, driven only by the bloodlust. Keira used to say the more one cared, the more they had to lose. Only now did I understand. The advantage in a fight always came with a cost.

But oppositely, there was a deep, lightning-hot hope burning in my core. Perhaps, if we cut off the head, the body would fall too. If we could stop Locasta, or, more importantly, the Dark God...

I forced myself to read on, unwilling to entertain the wish even in the privacy of my mind.

Please visit Ir'de again. Hud is so dark and depressing even during the warmest days. I'm so glad you're taking your stand in the south, but wouldn't you want to stay somewhere nicer? My establishment has plenty of room for you and your crew. I'd even let you share my quarters. The silk sheets are fit for a ki. . .

"What's the word today, Captain?" Ellian saved me from more of Katrin's rambling as he reached for the letter.

"If you insist on calling me that, *Councilman*, we are going to have trouble." I handed him the scroll, ready to be rid of it.

"More trouble than being hunted by a demon woman wearing a skin suit?" He raised an eyebrow, smoothing back his hair with his free hand to tame the wild locks in a high knot atop his head so he could read clearly.

He'd been wearing his hair longer ever since Reagan had taken to braiding it. I didn't have the heart to make fun of him for it. The little dragon had tamed him, as she had the rest of us.

Besides, he was one of the few people she spoke to. I'd grow a beard and dye my hair green if it got her to say even a word to me. She was probably outside with Griffin now, sharpening her daggers, imagining my heart as the target.

I stuffed my hands back in my pockets and pushed the thought of my littlest cousin's scorn away. I only had room for one heartbreak at a time. Ellian's emerald eyes raked over the letter, bronze skin flushing as he too cringed at Katrin's attention to particular details. I cleared my throat, summing it up to spare him the embarrassment, "No change from Orwellin. My assumption is whatever faction of the guard that participated in the revolt before is either dead, or laying low."

Ellian nodded, sitting back down into the stiff chair, fingering through a stack of papers and brandishing a different note. "But most of the Bachtreffian and Porthladdian refugees arrived safely in Ir'de and Pysgodd."

I scanned this letter with less contempt than the last, Councilwoman Tommins' chicken scrawl a welcome change from

Katrin's swirling script. "The old wolf in the North says they have room for more, if we need it."

Ellian scoffed. "I'll send word, but no one will want to go to that frozen wasteland with fall approaching."

"Remind them it's better to be frozen than dead," I answered, but the venom was gone from my tongue. "And write another letter to the Tannians. We need reinforcements, and every assassin has a price. Figure out what theirs is."

I didn't care if everyone in Porthladd froze to death or fell to an army of puppet soldiers. Didn't care if they wanted to burn on the sands of Tan or die by the spears of the warriors there. They could choose whichever fate suited them best. They'd abandoned us, let my wife lay down her life for them while Connor stole everything from us.

And yet, here I was, ensuring their safe passage. Dealing with devils to secure their future. Following in my wife's footsteps like a loyal dog. Not for them, but for her. Protecting the things she was willing to die for. I ran a hand over my face, reapplying my mask, readying myself for the task ahead.

"Let's go talk to our guest, shall we?"

I took the steps two at a time, my boots echoing with determination against the stone. Ellian wouldn't be far behind, one loyal pup after another.

At the top of the steps and down the first corridor, the most stalwart pet of all stood watch in front of my door, her fangs already bared.

I hadn't expected Siobhan to stay—or any of the sirens. The moment the guards fell in Porthladd, I thought they'd be off, their gemstone tails breaching the water the last we'd ever see of them, at least in this lifetime. Hiraeth wasn't just their home—it was their everything.

And yet. Every last one of them pledged their aid to my wife. To her cause. To her crew, too, it would seem. They hadn't faltered since.

It was still strange to see her in Huddian garb, a breezy burnt orange tunic tucked into cotton pants and a sword belt. It was even stranger to see two daggers strapped to her hip and one to her thigh, as if she needed steel when she was made of something far more deadly.

Her grin went lethal as she saw us approach, her teeth exposed. "Good, you *do* know how to play fetch." She ruffled Ellian's hair, tearing curls from the knot. Despite being twice her size and just as feral, he winced like a kicked mutt. Siobhan rolled her eyes, tired of playing with her food. "You're dismissed, shifter."

Ellian stood taller, his hackles raised. "Who put you in charge?"

"Do you want to challenge it?" Siobhan stepped closer with a low chuckle. "I promise my fangs are sharper than yours."

I rubbed my temples. I might have been made of god-stuff now, but my crew still had the supernatural ability to give me a headache from the Otherworld. As deeply grateful as I was for the sirens' continued presence in my life, I didn't have time for their bickering. "Do me a favor, Ellian. Go spar with Reagan."

The air shrank from the room, Siobhan and Ellian's faces both drawing tight. Both had Tannian blood and claws to rival any predator's, yet even they knew better than to tempt the little dragon's fury. Ellian clapped me on the shoulder. "That's your mess, brother."

I shrugged him off. I didn't need the reminder. "Then go train with her so she doesn't hurt herself or Griffin."

Ellian offered a grim smile before turning to go. Siobhan focused her topaz glare on me, the banter and barking falling away, leaving only her true bite. "She's inside waiting for you, Ro. They've already started questioning her."

The beast in my chest stretched and yawned, shaking off the shackles of sleep. I was hungry for this, hungrier than I'd ever been for the spring.

The day my wife died, a dragon was born. And if old Madame Hedd wanted to stand in my way, I'd swallow her whole.

I opened the door without knocking, pushing past where Laureli and Marina stood at the other side of the entrance. The stone walls baked us in the mid-morning heat that poured through the dingy windows. The deep-colored drapes snuffed out the sun's persistent rays. Drab, dirt-caked oak furniture absorbed the light and life from the room. More like a dungeon than an inn, the room scraped the tender flesh under my scales.

Still, I took the empty, high-backed, straw-woven chair at the room's center. It may have looked like a prison, but I would make it my throne room. Keira used to say the key to a good negotiation was to ask for what you wanted like it already belonged to you. I would not ask to take up space anymore; I would demand it.

"Look who decided to join us." Madame Hedd sat on the chair opposite me, her salt-and-pepper hair as unraveled as the fraying upholstery beneath her. But the gleam in her eye shone like a newly polished stone, as if not a day or deed had passed since our last meeting. She greeted me with a vicious grin, drinking me in like a brewer tasting their prized barrel. "I remember you, traveler. Though I see you've changed quite a bit."

I tucked my hands in my pockets, this time, to hide the claws that threatened to unsheathe themselves. "You haven't. What's your secret?"

A scoff as she rapped her crooked fingers against the wooden armrest. "Ye don't want to know."

"But there is something you can tell us. How do we send a message to her?" Laureli shifted forward, a single claw drawing itself from her pointer finger. She dragged it across the discolored stone of the nearest wall, the resulting screech like steel against glass. Madame Hedd grimaced as Laureli breathed a deep chuckle. "I'm disappointed, Beatrice. You owe me quite a bit, if I recall correctly."

Irritation prickled under my skin, but I hid it beneath a crooked brow. "You know each other?"

Laureli nudged the edge of Hedd's chair with the heel of her boot, and I swore I saw the old crow wince. "I taught this hag everything she knows back when she was still a little street urchin."

"Then ye should be able to see where to go yourself." Madame Hedd snorted, but her nostrils flared, the beat of her heart quickening. The siren in my soul blinked awake, sniffing the blood in the water. Madame Hedd was afraid of Laureli. Not only because she was a siren, but for what she was *before*. "Ye've gotten weak, Laureli." It sounded like a wish, not a fact.

The dull insult barely glanced off Laureli. "And you've gotten old. Is that why your memory needs refreshing?" Marina bit her lip to stop from laughing, but the humor fell from Laureli's expression. "I can only see things on this side of the veil, you know that. You, on the other hand...you were always very talented in that department."

Madame Hedd crossed her arms but squared her shoulders, preening her feathers with the flattery. "Summon her. Ye claim she's a goddess, right?" Her ivy-and-clay stare was ancient and all-knowing. My stomach knotted, as if she'd reached down my throat and started twisting my insides with that look. "Summon her like ye would any of the others."

I opened my mouth to tell her just how many times we'd tried, how many times I sat kneeling at the edge of my bed, praying like a fool, hoping that my Goddess Ariannad might grace me with her favor for one moment. But before the vulnerable truth could slide out of my traitorous lips, Marina cut me off with a warning glance. She sauntered to the threadbare bed shoved against the nearest wall, falling into it with a dramatic huff. She flipped her long auburn hair over her shoulder, pouting at Madame Hedd like a child begging for candy. "We've tried. But she's in Arawn's keep. She has a contract with him."

Madame Hedd's lips twisted into a grimace. "I remember. *Melthith* spot. She should've just had a baby and been rid of it."

I'd never been quick to rage, but the fire that lit my insides was hotter than the Southern Sun.

My wife. My *baby*.

"Watch your tongue, woman," My grin masked the dragon's fangs I was dying to sink into her flesh. I allowed a single claw to slip from my forefinger, the brief, flashing pain of the shift nothing in comparison to the agony of her words. "I'm not nearly as civilized as I used to be."

Madame Hedd's gaze fell to my talon, greed swimming in their emerald hue. "Oh, but ye'r far more interesting now, boy." Quickly, she reached out a hand across the rickety table that separated us, pricking her finger on the sharp edge before I pulled it back. A droplet of blood formed at the tip of her digit, scenting the air with the familiar, sweetened iron aroma. My stomach growled, the most primal and predatory pieces of me already clawing their way up my gullet. The muscles in my jaw worked hard to cover my desire with the dullest mask I owned. Hedd drew the wound into her mouth and sucked away the spot. "Did your missus do this to ya? Her work is excellent. Better than her mother's, I'd say."

I picked an invisible speck of dirt from beneath my claw. I was my wife's deadliest design, not some child's toy to be played with. If Madame Hedd wanted the Golden Dragon, I'd give it to her. "I've had enough. Marina?"

Marina didn't need further coaxing, a devil's grin snaking across her face as she sauntered to Hedd. Dainty fingers clasped around the crone's wrist in one fast motion, Marina shuddering once as her signature power scented the air. Humans couldn't smell it, but the burnt lilac-and-whiskey mixture accosted my nostrils, intoxicating as the siren who wielded it.

"Madame Beatrice Hedd. Threat level five of ten. Seer and *Saranaid*." Truths tumbled from her mouth as she clutched the woman tighter, readying for the harder part. "This won't hurt."

Madame Hedd remained unbothered, like stone in a rainstorm. "Won't work, either. Ye can compel me to tell my truths, but ye can't force me to look into someone else's."

"Then name your price," I said as my father's only son, as the boy who learned to swindle before he learned to spell. I kicked my boots up on the table, falling into the role with ease. "I promise my offer will be better than Morwyn Locasta's. Because once she finds out we came to you, whether or not you tell us anything, she'll want a word, too."

Hedd's expression fell, disinterest dissolving into disgust. Thin lips trembled as the scent of her fear mingled with Marina's magic, turning the sweet concoction bitter.

"Here's your truth." The woman turned her glower to Marina, the mockery gone from the crinkles in her eyes. "That woman could offer me the entire Deyrnas and I wouldn't accept. I don't make deals with devils."

Marina lifted her gaze to me and nodded once before dropping her hold.

Truth.

The beast in my chest roared with the small victory, the first spark of hope catching fire. Perhaps this gods-forsaken island was magick-blessed after all.

"Then help us instead, Bea," Laureli cooed, one witch using her spellcraft over the other. "We're on the same side."

Madame Hedd paused, chewing the inside of her cheek as she waited. Decided. After a sharp exhale through her nose, she finally answered, "I can't contact your wife. Not a chance. If she has a contract with Arawn, he'll know, and he'll come for me too. I'm not sacrificing my soul."

The tide shifted again, hope souring into frustration once more. I gripped the edge of the table, something dark and deadly stirring in my depths. "Then give us something. A lead, a crumb…" My voice strained as I fought the ugly, festering thing in my pit, the heat of the room suddenly suffocating. "Anything that puts us a step ahead of Morwyn."

Laureli and Marina both shifted their weight, concerned, but I ignored them, my gaze fixed on the crone that held the keys to the Otherworld. Madame Hedd rubbed her temple with a gnarled knuckle. "I can't contact yer wife, because my soul is at risk. But sirens and shifters…ye don't have souls, not anymore. Not in the same way. Ye've already died and come back. Ye paid the ritual's price, and ye've made contracts with other gods that Arawn has no claim to."

As if it was summoned, the dragon in my gut stretched its wings. Somehow, I knew what she was saying was true, like it had been stitched into the fabric of my being. Like *she* had been stitched there, an artist leaving her signature, an author of life signing her name to the bottom. I'd paid the price twice over, but my heart and soul belonged to my goddess. My *Bren Ariannad.*

My Keira.

The contract was signed and dotted the day she saved my life from Arawn's clutches, or perhaps when she turned me into a siren. But it was drawn before that, on the day I said my vows as her husband. Drafted earlier still, the day I first saw her, wild as the sea, staring out at the horizon, claiming everything the sky touched as her own, myself included.

"That's reassuring. I always knew you were a soulless witch, Laurie." Marina snorted, ignoring Laureli's pointed glare.

I blinked, refocusing on the task at hand. At the plan weaving itself together, the plot unfolding before me like a good read. *Bren Ariannad* and her siren servant. "How does it help us?"

"I can't send *messages*, but ye folk…" Hedd sat back into the chair, the old wood creaking like the woman's bones. But her lips pursed with lethal curiosity. "Ye can cross the veil yourselves."

Marina's jaw dropped as my heart did. "You mean physically *go* to the Otherworld?"

My chest constricted, the hope that flooded my veins too rich to withstand.

Body and soul. Both of which belonged to her. To my wife.

I'll wait for you in the Otherworld.

"Aye." Madame Hedd confirmed, the single syllable so sweet I barely heard the warning that followed. "Though I've heard it's not a pleasant trip."

I'll wait for you in the Otherworld.

I was going to save her. It didn't matter if the way was dark and fiery. I'd walk through flame, through wind and storm and sorrow. I'd fight Arawn's hounds with my bare hands, leash them with my own rage. I'd go to hell and back, and I would carry my wife home myself, with the claws and fangs and fury she gave me.

Laureli folded her arms in apprehension, but I saw the sparkle of daring in the corner of her eye. "We won't get stuck?"

"The gate might still have a price, but it can't ask you for your lives," Hedd cautioned, mischief in the tilt of her head.

I didn't care about the price. I'd pay it, gates be damned. Arawn could ask for my scales, my strength, my soul. I'd give it all up for Keira. For the precious life inside of her.

I stood, ready to set the dragon free. "Pack your bags, ladies. We have a long swim ahead of us."

The *Black Cauldron* was not built for our numbers, a fact apparent when fifteen of us tried to cram ourselves into my quarters that evening for a meeting. But we needed privacy, so we piled into the stone room, some sitting on the floor, others on the furniture. Siobhan and Laureli stood watch out in the corridor, but the rest of us squirmed and elbowed each other as we fought for even an inch more of space.

I tried not to dwell on how keenly it resembled the inside of a mausoleum, bodies wrapped and packed tightly. Hopefully, it wasn't an omen for what was to come. Still, the crew and the sirens all stared at me in varied levels of shock, as if I told them I had wings and ate stars for breakfast.

"You're shitting kittens," Griffin spoke first, a hysterical laugh breaking free. "Does the siren thing make you stupid?"

Only Saeth looked something other than surprised, her dagger-sharp eyes filled with something far worse.

Determination.

"This isn't fair," she growled. Sandwiched between Griffin and Tarran on the floor, her wiry frame looked even more diminutive, but as she twirled the repaired *Wynd Dant* in her fingers, I knew her rage could outmatch either of her mountain-sized kin. She turned her cold stare on Nelle. "Make me a siren too, then."

There was no softness left in her gaze–those parts had hardened and sharpened since Finna's death. Since Keira. Without her cousins' warmth and light, she was all edges and ice.

The Frozen Queen.

I shuddered as I imagined her with a real set of teeth and claws. Her will was so powerful, there were moments I thought I could smell it on her, the same magick and mist that made the sirens and I *other*. I had no doubt she could freeze over hell itself with a single look.

But luckily for every living creature on the face of the earth, it was a possibility we'd never have to witness.

Nelle's violet gaze fell to her lap as she shifted closer to Marina, for protection or comfort or both. "You know I can't do that."

No, luckily for all the mortals involved, Nelle could not turn Saeth. Only Keira and Danura had that power, and neither of them could do anything now. We hadn't heard anything from Danura since they left the island, and none had been able to find Hiraeth since, a troubling development. Still, Saeth opened her mouth, a protest ready on her forked tongue.

"You're not coming, Saeth," I interjected before she could filet Nelle and serve her for dinner. "None of you can. Only the sirens and shifters. So Ellian, that means you."

"Sounds like an adventure." Ellian stood against the door, substantial physique blocking out the entrance. He nodded once, expression drawn. I knew he'd much rather stay behind, to defend Porthladd, to defend the Deyrnas. But he knew as well as I that Keira was our greatest asset in that fight. And he knew we needed a *blaidd* if the stories about Arawn's hounds were more than myths.

When I was a child, I used to pray to Lyr that the stories my mother told me would come true. Mama warned me to be careful what I wished for.

An adventure, indeed. One I'd live in, not just read about. One I desperately wished would all fade away.

Vian, who'd perched himself on the stone sill, tore his gaze from the window, charcoal eyes brimming with the foolishness of a boy not yet afraid of wishing. "I can come, too. My contract is with Nef, not the Dark God."

"Not a chance, little bird." Marina answered before I could, a hand planted on her generous hip. The sirens all had the same fondness for the boy Keira shared, their time in Hiraeth a secret I'd never fully understand. "Even my gifts haven't quite figured out your true nature yet."

"And yer only a boy," Vala added from the old chair she rested in, looking at the crumpled handkerchief in her hands, unable to look directly at him. My aunt-in-law's face lacked color, her curls dry and drained of their buoyancy. Had she any tears left to spare, they might have welled in her eyes. "Ye have too much life yet to live to bet it on maybes."

Her words scented the air with death, rotted and sorrowful, everything she wasn't saying loud in the silence. Cramped as we were in the tiny room, any one of us would've given everything to be even more crowded. Would've cried with joy just to have a few more warm bodies in the room, their voices among the chorus.

Cedric. Owen. Lochlan. Alina. Roland. Finna. Baby Owen. Reina. Keira.

Even the betrayers, the names we left off our nightly prayers…

So many of those midnights, I wished I could turn back time. To go back to before, back to when I was a silly boy who believed in stories and wishes, to when Keira was a girl, not a goddess, who still possessed an Otherworldly spirit. To when our families were unfractured and unburdened. To when even the barest of rooms were crowded with those that we loved, our lives simple.

"She needed me last time." Vian broke the silence, bringing us back to the moment. To the land to the living, where a room of mostly new friends waited to avenge all we'd lost.

There was no turning back the tides of time. But we could do better going forward.

"I know." I acknowledged the boy, the little brother I never would have met if my wife hadn't accepted her adventures with grace and courage. The boy that still would be rotting in a cage beneath Delm Arawn had she not rescued him.

The boy that saved her when I couldn't. The one willing to do it again.

But I would not fail this time. And I would not cage him to the Dark God's realm instead. "But the others need you now. You and Gennevieve will stay back, help keep the crew safe."

Without another word, Vian turned his attention back outside the window, captured again by whatever the wind whispered. In between Cassryn and Willow, Genni fiddled with her gloves, blonde fringe falling in her face in the way that made her look so young. "Why me?"

Cassryn looked over to her twin, a rare smile on her stony face, before they answered in unison, "You're the strongest."

And the youngest. They didn't need to say it, but the message was there. Genni didn't know exactly how long she'd been on Hiraeth, or how many years had passed since she left her home in Bachtref. But her soul was youthful despite her dangerous gift, and she did not belong anywhere near the Dark God's keep.

And she *was* the strongest. A single touch from her finger was instant death. If we were leaving my family behind, I'd need her to look after them, even the ones who thought they were strong enough on their own.

Never let them have your queen.

My queen might have been gone, but I still had my knights, armed and ready to defend the tower.

"I don't like this." Griffin's leg bounced, a bold move in such tight quarters. "Lyr's left nut, you're talking about the *Otherworld*, not a quiet sail to Bachtref! And what in Lyr's name are we supposed to do, sit around with our thumbs up our arses until you get back?"

Marina snorted, one master of mischief challenging another. "Exactly that, if it suits your fancy."

Rhett echoed Griffin, leaning back onto the stone wall as his baritone filled the room. "This is madness, Ronan. There has to be a better plan."

"Maybe one that doesn't spew us across the four seas." Tarran nodded in agreement, my crew rallying together once more.

I wanted to believe it, too. Believe them. Believe that Keira wasn't all the way in the Otherworld, but just outside the door, a dagger in her hand and a plan in her head.

Nelle sighed, anchoring us all back to reality before hope could fill our sails and take us too far from shore. "Only a god can kill a god. Morwyn Locasta is only a figurehead. If we're going to defeat Arawn, we need Keira."

"We work better together." Tarran's complaint was feeble as his freckles. It was a wonder the boy hadn't lost his will to fight, hadn't lost that little piece of sunshine he kept close to his heart. It warmed my own, even if I had little use for the daydreams and determination.

Ellian cleared his throat, the Councilman, not the blacksmith, leaning into his natural authority. "The Deyrnas need people here, too. Good people. Keeping an eye on Locasta, making sure the refugees get to their destinations safely."

"The Deyrnas can rot," a small voice chimed in, so much darker than the last time I'd heard it.

I'd been avoiding looking at her the whole time. I was aware of her tiny shape in the corner of the bed, of her knees pulled to her chest. Of the heat and hatred in her glare, oppressive as she trained its full weight on me.

Every time our eyes met, earth against sea, something cracked within me. Something that might never be repaired. Despite how wonderfully my tail worked, that ocean of heartbreak seemed too vast, too deep to swim across. I didn't even know where to dive in.

Rhett reached across when I couldn't, placing his broad hand on our young cousin's knee. "You don't mean that."

"Oh, but I do." Reagan smacked him off, standing. She climbed off the bed, stepping on Tarran's hand as she did, but still, her focus never shifted from me, a dragon marking its prey. A cruel, wicked smile carved her face, one I'd taught her. One that held nothing of the sweet girl who begged for stories. One that showed only her most hateful, rotten parts. "And Keira can rot too."

Her words cleaved angrily between my gills, suffocating as they were sharp. And like a beast backed into a corner, the frayed strands of my civility snapped. The anger I'd buried beneath layers of ash rose to the surface, ready to explode. "If that's what you think, then leave."

She tilted her chin, readying for the sparring match we'd be dancing around. A humorless laugh escaped her mouth, "Where would you have me go, hmm? Home to Porthladd, to my mother?"

The blame in her tone peeled back my scales and sliced the quivering underbelly. The day my wife died, so did my aunt. They did not sing Reina Mathonwy's name across the Deyrnas. They did not mourn her life.

Reagan did. Reagan remembered. And Reagan raged, ready to blame the true monsters who sent her there. If I had a soul to give, I'd offer it in a heartbeat to bring Reina back. But I couldn't. Mortals could not return from Arawn's realm.

But Keira could. And I would not let my cousin's suffering stand in the way of our salvation.

I spat the words out like they were on fire. "If you want to act like a spoiled child, you can go pout outside while the adults figure out a plan."

My arrow struck as she winced, and for a flicker of a moment, I wanted to take it back. Wanted to wrap her in my arms and kiss her forehead like I did when she was little. Wanted to be the hero in her story instead of the villain she'd made me.

But she wasn't little anymore. It had only been months, but there were years hidden in the lines of her face. Decades in the tilt of her chin. Lifetimes in the hard shells of her eyes.

Eyes that narrowed with stone-cold contempt as she delivered the last lethal blow. "Great. Who are you going to get killed this time, hmm?"

Her hellfire scorched the last parts of me that were mine. And from the ashes, the creature in my core clawed its way out, snapping and snarling.

"I wasn't the one out of place on the deck, and I wasn't the one that *missed*," the creature spoke with my voice.

The air vanished from the room as my message struck. Words that were true. Words that were cruel. The second they flew from my fangs, regret tamed the beast once more, heavy as chains. Reagan blinked back tears I wished would drown me.

Her hatred was unbearable. Her disappointment was worse. Her throat bobbed once before the reproach tilted her lips in a frown. "No, Ronan. You did absolutely *nothing*."

She stormed out of the room, not looking back. Vian hopped off the ledge and followed after her, offering me a pity-steeped look before closing the door behind them.

The serpent in my stomach twisted in a vicious sadness. Reagan was right. The day my wife died, I did nothing. I'd been frozen in fear as I let my aunt and wife sacrifice themselves to save us all. Reagan had been reckless, but she'd *tried.*

My words would no longer be weightless.

I'll wait for you in the Otherworld.

Twelve sets of eyes trained themselves on the very interesting floorboards, polite coughs the only sound as they tried to clear the discomfort in the room like a scratchy throat.

Saeth spoke first, the outermost layer of ice thawing as she looked at the door, wishing her friend might come back through it. "Ronan, that was too—"

"I know." I stopped her, whether to save her from saying it or myself from hearing it, I didn't know. "I'm—it's been a long day. I'll go apologize later."

Griffin did not afford me the same mercy. "You need to fix this mess, Ro. I'm done being the stand-in." His swords poked out from behind him, reminding me of the truths I'd been avoiding. Ignoring.

The day my wife died, so did a part of my youngest cousin, the part that believed in my stories. The part that believed in Keira, in me. Perhaps while I was there, I could fetch that part from the Otherworld, too.

2

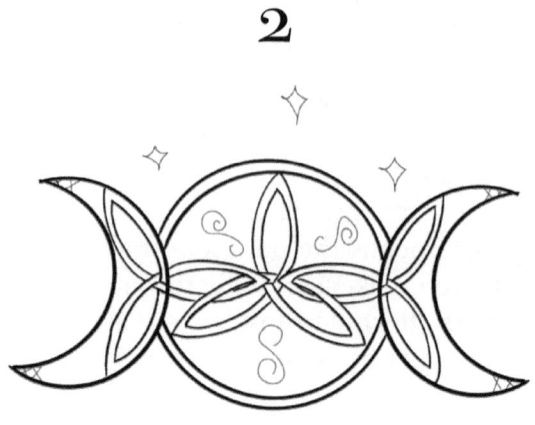

Death and Defiance

KEIRA

The Otherworld was not the paradise of legends. It was a wasteland. It was ice and numbness. It was nothing.

I was nothing.

Miles and miles of white, cold ice stretched out before me, the only contrast a black blot in the distance that looked like some kind of building, hidden behind fields of icy mist. Trapped in the tundra, my body was too frozen to feel anything. *If I even still had a body.* It was too cold to be sure. The only part of myself I was certain of was my arm, black and rotted as it was, the odious color stark against the blinding white landscape of my prison.

The Otherworld was nothing but unyielding, restless light.

I couldn't feel the arm. I couldn't feel anything anymore.

My mind, however, was still excruciatingly sharp.

Today, Death came to me in white robes. Frost encased his marble-cut form, every muscle and line made of the same ornate elegance. Darkness–sweet, delicious darkness–swirled around him, a welcomed respite from the garish white light.

As it did every day, his beauty stole my breath.

"Goodday, Ariannad, my darling," he purred, plucked-cherry lips caressing the sounds with care. Tiny snowflakes rested on the tips of his coal-black lashes, softer and more tender than a mother's kiss.

If time existed in Arawn's realm, it passed in a seamless blur. The only semblance of day came with his repeated presence, a "goodday" and a perfect smile before I was plunged into the torture.

As I did every day, I did not answer him.

"Precious girl, you know if you don't answer, I can't let you go." He clicked his tongue, stroking my cheek with his long, bone-white fingers. He smelled of pine and snow, like yuletides long forgotten and secrets taken to the grave. The obsidian of his round eyes bore into mine as he searched for the answer to his unending torment.

I wanted to lose myself in them. To swim in the inky pools and let them envelop me in lightless rapture.

Such beauty in those cruel eyes.

I swallowed back the words that threatened to spill from the untamed place within me.

"I wish you wouldn't do this to yourself," he sighed, running a hand through the silken midnight hair that fell to his broad shoulders. A single strand fell into his face, like a misplaced prayer floating in front of his pained eyes. "I want to save you, Ariannad. The things we could do together, girl…" Eyes burned like coal on fire amidst the ice. "We could rearrange the stars to our liking."

I shut my eyes to his beauty, as I did every day when he proposed the same thing.

It would be so deliciously easy to say yes. To end it all. Those *eyes*, dark and deep enough to swallow me whole. Strong arms, sturdy enough to hold my broken pieces together. His bed, perhaps, warm enough to thaw my frozen soul. What was one tortuous eternity for another? If Death himself wanted to comfort me, who was I to resist his gentle embrace?

Ronan.

The last spark of my gift whispered it inside me, no louder than the sound of a feather falling.

Ronan.

Ronan.

Ronan.

When my eyes opened again, I was filled with his name and his name alone, a riotous cry echoing through my empty, frozen shell.

No, not today. One more day, I'd wait. One more nightmare. I could hang on. I would, for Ronan.

Ronan.

Ronan.

The Dark God frowned as he stood. Such sadness and longing in those eyes. Such regret. "As you wish, *Caraid*."

I was dragged into blissful darkness.

Ronan's arms around me. So warm. So real.

Not real. The harsh reminder pulsed through my mind. *Not real, not real, not real.*

"What's the matter, Mrs. Mathonwy?" The velvet tenor swathed me in fondness. He pulled my chin up so I could see the mirage of sapphire blue, the tumultuous ocean of his eyes. "Bad dream?"

"Go away," I managed to say, but it lacked the usual venom.

I was tired. So tired. I just wanted him to hold me forever.

Not real.

"Keira girl, I'm here for you." The honeyed lie was sweet as he pressed a kiss to my forehead.

I was expecting the gunshot, but I flinched all the same.

Then he was on the ground, bleeding. Crying. "Keira, please, save me. Please."

Not real. Not real.

Still, I knelt beside him, my hands stanching the wound. The pale flesh in absence of the darkness of my cursed hand was a reminder that this was still the dream, the vision. But I couldn't help myself as the tears slid down my face, the screams caught in my throat.

"Please, no. Not again."

I was frozen.

The light left his eyes. His body rotted before me. It might have been hours or days, but I watched it decompose. Watched as skin fell away from bones, as eyes sank further to the earth, as flesh shriveled up into plant food.

"Keira?" Reagan's voice called from behind me. Chestnut eyes filled with horror as she took in Ronan's corpse.

Another decaying body splayed before me. Bloated, pale, fish-eaten. Shark's teeth razor sharp in his mouth. Chestnut hair tangled as sailor's knots.

Lochlan.

"Papa?" Reagan choked the word out as she fell to her knees beside him. Again, I watched as his mutilated form fell apart in her hands, like sea foam against the shore. As it dissolved, another cadaver in its place, one that wore my coat, my hair. Everything but my face.

Reina's dead walnut eyes—the same color as Reagan's—stared empty into the frozen wasteland. Red pooled across the white ground, like rose-petals on a burial shroud.

Reagan lifted her chin, focusing her endless rage on me. On the true culprit. On the murderer, the *Melthith*, the demon responsible for both of her parents' demise. "I trusted you. How could you?"

My response stuck in my throat, the same as it did every time. My guilt choked me, stealing the breath from my frozen lungs. Reagan—*no, not Reagan*—ripped the dagger from my belt. Eyes wide and feral, she let loose a howl before plunging it into her small frame.

I felt it. I felt the pain, the searing heat as the blood pooled in her middle.

I watched helplessly as chestnut hair turned to crimson. Dark eyes melted to green. The little girl's frame filled and morphed into womanhood.

Finna stared back, lips red with blood. An unbridled laugh tore from her middle, blood spraying. I sank to my knees, hands frenzied to stop the bleeding. To save her, save Owen. Her shrill laughter pierced the air, drowning out my sobs.

"No, Finna, please," I begged, hands stained red. I shut my eyes, finding the small, dormant piece of my magick, coaxing it to the surface. I would make her stronger. I would give her claws and fangs to match her dagger-sharp wit. I would make her more.

Darkness instead. There was no saving her. Not here, not ever.

Not real, not real, not real.

Real.

Real.

It was all too real. Too fresh. Each death a reminder of my failure. Each memory a truth I could never escape. The Carthu couldn't cleanse me here. Water forgot, cleaned, forgave.

Ice remembered.

I was frozen.

But against the frosted, blinding wasteland of my prison, a figure appeared on the horizon.

Shadow morphing into color, soft edges sharpening into clear lines, the body took life. Hair like citrus and sunset, dappled with silver streaks. A coat bluer than the sea, clinging to a work-worn, whiskey-fond frame. Hazel eyes squinted at me as he stumbled closer, eyes that I'd know even in the darkest, coldest of hells. "Keira girl?"

This was a new trick.

Not real, not real, not real.

"Oh, my poor girl." Papa rushed toward me, swaddling me in a hug. "This isn't possible." His beard tickled my cheek as he murmured against it, whiskey-and-wet-wood scent calling every single memory I had of him to the surface.

Not real, not real.

I couldn't stop myself from hugging him back.

The Dark God was *learning.* He knew my weakness.

Desperate and lonely, I took the bait.

"Papa," I cried, holding him tighter. He was so blissfully warm, like the first spring day after a long winter, and my chilled limbs ached to be held. This wasn't real, but I wanted it to be, more than I wanted air in my lungs or life in my veins. I just wanted Papa. Wanted him to be the one holding me as I succumbed to the Dark God once and for all. "I missed you so much. Please, help me end this."

"Small victories, little one," he hummed, stroking my hair. I felt so small, so safe in his embrace, like not even the Dark God's cold could reach me here. His deep voice rumbled through his chest as he spoke my favorite words of wisdom: "What do you want first?"

What did I want?

A honeyed smirk and sapphire eyes. Warm hands and velvet-smooth laughter.

Ronan.

Ronan.

Ronan.

It should have been the only answer. It wasn't. Another voice sang above all.

Death.

Death.

Death.

I wanted it all to *stop*. But there was no sweet release in death anymore. I'd already passed through the veil. This was my eternity. The Otherworld was the final destination.

"I want it to end, Papa."

"Come now, Keira girl." Papa pulled back to look at me, sunset eyes stern, and I missed the heat of him like a fish missed water. "I didn't raise ye to give up, not like that. Ye'll teach yer daughter the same."

Confusion clouded my mind, like fog during low tide. The forgotten daydream of a golden-haired girl with silver eyes flashed through me and left faster than a bullet from a gun.

The Dark God's ruse was cruel. He no longer taunted me with my past alone. Now, he toyed with the future I'd never get to have.

"I don't have a daughter," I sneered at my false father, the mirage too perfect, the freckles painted with a god's careful brush.

He frowned, gaze filling with an unnamable sadness I hoped I'd never know. "Not yet, Keira girl. Not yet."

I opened my mouth to answer, but Papa faded away in a wave of mist and smoke.

I was back in my cage of ice. The Dark God stood before me, his form the only structure in the field of mist and ice.

I was frozen.

Death's eyes held tears, the ebony now stained glass. "I've been watching you since you were a girl, Ariannad. So fiery, even then. So strong and selfless. You're all of the good parts of *her* without any of the spite or greed." A tender hand reached out and tucked the wild strand of hair behind my ear. "When will you see that it hurts me to do this? Why won't you let me stop?"

He said the same thing every day.

Normally, I stayed silent.

Today was different.

Today he played with Papa.

Today I said, "Fuck off."

3

Runaways and Remembrances

GRIFFIN

The stone walls of the *Black Cauldron* reminded me of the brig of the Ceffyl, but without any of the familiarity I'd found in the bowels of my family's ship. The *Cauldron* was cold and unfeeling. Impersonal as a harlot's affection. A haven for the heartless, a den of misdeeds and delinquents.

A month ago, I might have loved it. Lyr's left ass cheek, I would've *savored* it, the lowlight that painted every bad decision in a favorable shade, the seedy patrons and watered down whiskey. I would've made it my castle, fit for the carefree King without a conscience.

Now it was a prison, made of mortar and mischief.

Or maybe the prison was internal, a cage of my own making.

Either way, I served my sentence as I always did, with my drink in one hand and my dick in the other. Which worked wonders most of the time. It was easier to forget at the bottom of the bottle or on top of a brawny blond. Easier to *breathe*.

But as of late, the blond in my bed didn't disappear in the morning. Like a hangover, he lingered, long eyelashes brushing his tawny cheek in a way that made my stomach clench. The threadbare linens did little to cover the vast planes of his strong back, his heavy arm stretched across my chest. But for a broody bastard, his face was serene in sleep, even with the jagged scar across the left eye.

A scar he earned saving my sister. Or trying to, at least.

I was the last of my mother's children now, the only man not yet made a martyr. Unlike me, martyrs never lived long enough to let her down.

Rhett started that way—another fling intended to disappoint dear old Vala. Or perhaps to distract me from the countless ways I'd already sullied her sight of me.

I didn't know when I let him catch me without my armor. Maybe it was in the forest of *Hiraeth*, the night death breathed down my neck with little *neid* bites on my arm. Or maybe the first day in the brig together, when his hair matched the soft hay, when I saw a glimpse of the boy beneath the brick wall.

But now, like a bad case of the scratches, he was entirely under my skin.

The thought did more to disturb than it did to comfort. I wanted him. Not just in the ways I already had him—though, *that* was always a great way to pass the time. Rhett was a snake by name, but a lion in bed. All instinct, no inhibition. And Lyr's freckled fart-box, I wanted more. Wanted him to see me. Wanted him to know me.

But wanting was dangerous. Wanting was weakness.

Wanting led to refugees stuck in run-down inns with itchy sheets and cheap whiskey. Wanting led to jackasses who played pirate, pretending to be something more and barely handling the pressure.

Wanting led to sisters and unborn nephews dying on the fucking street, their blood on your hands matching the red of your betrayer father's.

I didn't know if it was the thought or the hangover, but the contents of my stomach swished. All I wanted now was a drink or something greasy to settle my gut.

I tried to remove myself from the stiff mattress without disturbing the sleeping prince at my side, first lifting his arm off me. But one shift, and the entire frame of the mattress groaned. Rhett stirred, blinking his stupidly long lashes.

"Griff?" Eyes met mine, one blue and white, one pure silver.

It was jarring at first, the metallic creation that Nelle had shoved into my lover's face. Ellian fashioned the orb from the finest silver he could find, the work of a true craftsman. But it was the healer and her raven-haired witch friends, Laureli and Neirida, who made it *work*. Now, it swiveled in unison with its flesh-made partner, reading my face with the blend of scrutiny and sincerity only Rhett Mathonwy could perfect.

"How's the eye?" I asked before he could comment at my current state, my finger tracing the scar that marred his pretty skin.

"Better than my real one. No idea how they did it, but it's excellent." Rhett smiled, scar crinkling.

"That's nice." I threw on a hapless grin as I sat up, donning my shirt. I thanked Lyr for the scar, for the strange eye it framed. They were reminders of what I could lose if I let myself want more.

Of what Rhett would lose if he continued to court Trouble like me.

"You seem tired." Rhett rose, running a hand through his unruly hay-colored locks. "Did you sleep?"

No. I hadn't slept in weeks.

A white nightdress stained red. A swollen stomach punctured and poured out like a skin of wine. My hands, covered in it. A scream in the distance. My scream? A blue eye, rolling across the cobblestone, my fingers fumbling to catch it, to hold on, to put it all back...

Life was easier to live when the dead stayed buried or burned. And yet, here I was, wanting and wishing like a fool. I stretched my arms above my head so he wouldn't see the blood rush from my face as a wave of nausea rolled through my gut. *It's just a hangover.* I chose a smirk instead. "I slept like a whore in a Councilman's bed."

Rhett's deep sigh rumbled through his chest like thunder, his reproach even sharper now that his glare was made of metal. "You don't have to do that."

"Do what?"

"Lie."

I swallowed down the curses I wanted to fire off. None of them were truly meant for him. "Then what would you have me say?"

Silver softened, both sober and sweet as he looked at me like I was something worthy of his affection. "Tell me the truth." He brushed a curl behind my ear, coarse fingertips delicate as Ir'desian silk. "Tell me the nightmares are getting worse. Tell me what you see when you close your eyes...where you go when you get quiet…"

I wanted so badly to tell him. To give the broken, forgotten part a voice. To shatter the bottle of my emotions and let it all pour out, messy as it was. I wanted to fall into his arms and sob like a child, like I would cry into my mother's skirts as a boy.

Wanted to tell him he loved a broken man. Wanted to tell him how much I hated myself for not saving my sister.

Wanting was dangerous.

I corked the bottle before it could explode.

"Where do I start?" I crossed my arms, my armor made of steel and sarcasm, my two greatest weapons aside from Truth and Triumph. I pitched my voice higher, the mockery that used to make Keira furious. "Perhaps with the fact my cousin, my best friend, is missing and held hostage by the God of Death?"

"I'm sorry, I–" Rhett started, but I cut him off with swordlike precision.

"Or how about that now, her husband thinks he's going to go save her! Or wait, no, is it the fact that it's my father's fault? That his last dying deed was a betrayal?" The words fell out like coins from a gambler's purse, just as reckless and raw. "No, that's not it, is it, Rhett? Perhaps it's the fact that my sister, my *fucking sister*–"

Crimson against ivory, blood against stone.

I'd always been Trouble's whore, but now I was its torturee. Its plaything to be ruined and discarded, just as Fate had toyed with my sister. My father. My nephew…

I shoved it all down, into the pit where I jailed my conscience. I wouldn't. Couldn't.

Rhett's throat bobbed as he floundered for the words to make it right, as if such poetry existed. "I was just trying to–"

My answering glare silenced him. "Don't ask questions you can't handle the answer to."

Like a match striking a wick, rage ignited in his expression. "Then start handling your own business, Griffin. If not with me, fine. But I don't need a magic eye to see that you're hiding." His muscled jaw clenched as he bit back harsher words I knew I deserved.

Hurt. Clear as day on the horizon. But it was easier to hurt him now than let Trouble have its way with him. Easier to keep him at arm's length than have him ripped from my embrace. My armor was made of smirks and insincerity as I ran a hand through my hair. "Listen, I know we have fun together, but–"

"You think this is just for fun?" He cut me off, voice rising like a storm over the water. "That I lost my eye for a bit of *fun?*"

Guilt climbed up my throat, burning like last night's whiskey. "I didn't mean it like that."

Rhett stood, chest rising and falling in heavy breaths as he looked down at me. He waited, bad decisions warring in his good eye. Finally, "I meant what I said. That night in Porthladd. I don't know what you think this is, but I lo—"

"I can't do this now." The words came as the panic flashed through my veins. I stood, shoving my feet into my boots, looking anywhere but at him, at the intensity of his love, his blazing affection…

Wanting was weakness.

Loving was lethal.

"Where are you going?" His voice sounded so far away as I gathered my swords and made for the door, like he'd retreated all the way behind the wall I'd built.

I owed him more. I owed him a 'sorry' or a 'thank you' or the three words he wanted to hear most. Words I wanted to say.

"To spar," was all I gave him before rushing out of the door and into the cool hallway.

Despite the damp, dusty rugs and moss on the stone walls, it was easier to breathe in the corridor. Easier to breathe without the blond-haired, blue-eyed devil trying to commit the unforgivable sin of loving me.

I buttoned my trousers and straightened my tunic, as if it did anything to stop the unraveling. I fell back onto the wall, letting the cool stone ground me to myself.

Breathe in. Breathe out. Repeat.

"What has your panties in a twist?" Saeth punctured my sails with her needled tongue as she turned the corner and sauntered down the hall.

I scoffed, crossing my arms before my cousin could catch me with my emotional cock out. "If that guard had taken his tongue instead of his eye, I'd be in a much better mood."

Her jade gaze narrowed—*so similar to Finna's, in both color and contempt*—as she stuck her first to her hip. "Right. Because then he couldn't remind you that he's way too good for you."

Scrawny as she was, Saeth hit with the bluntness of a battle axe. "Was there another meeting I missed?" I pushed off the wall, towering over the little goblin. "Where everyone got together and said 'Hey, Griffin seems to be in a shitty mood, why don't we all gang up on him today?'"

Saeth tilted her chin up to meet my gaze, but she wore the smirk of a creature thrice her size. "No, but that's a good suggestion. I'll send out formal invitations next time."

The insult woke the part of me that fought first and cared second. I needed it, the fire and fight. Needed a sharp-edged sparring partner like Saeth to distract and disarm me. I rolled my shoulders back. "Do you wanna go out in the yard and put your money where your mouth is?"

"As much as kicking your ass would thrill me, no." She patted my chest and rolled her eyes, a cat done playing with its food. "Ronan has a laundry list of supplies he needs before setting sail tomorrow."

The fire sputtered out as my disappointment settled in. I didn't want to think about Ronan and his newest death wish before breakfast. Didn't need a reminder of the hollow desperation in his eyes, or my part in putting it there. I'd been avoiding him like a gambler avoids debt collectors, dodging my guilt.

Silver eyes, ushering the unspeakable command in our silent language. A nod in return when I should've protested.

I shrugged off the gut-punch of a memory, cracking my neck and focusing on the cousin in front of me instead of the one clawing at the back of my mind. I ruffled her hair, baiting the brat I knew still lived beneath the layers of ice and insolence she wore. "And you're his lackey now?"

The edge in Saeth's tone went from teasing to biting. "Yes, since you've been slacking, *first mate*." She spat my title at me like it tasted foul. In my ear, *Truth* rang, the familiar twinkling sound I both relied on and detested. Saeth had petitioned for the role twice since Ronan became the official Captain, and there was no denying she would be better at it than I was.

Uncle Cedric used to say titles were as easy to take away as they were to say, a lesson Saeth liked to remind me of daily. I knew I deserved her reproach more than I deserved my position, but Ronan was either too stubborn or distracted to care. And I clung to it, too desperate to let go.

Without my position in the crew, I had nothing. No siblings left to call me brother, no father left to call me son. The crew were the only ones I had left to disappoint.

"Give me a break, Captain Cranky-pants," I whined as I nudged her arm, surrendering the last shreds of my pride.

The fire in her gaze dimmed. She sighed, conceding the battle, knowing she'd win the war. "Reagan is still out in the yard. Maybe you two can go sulk together."

Saeth walked away without another word, ready to pick up the pieces everyone else dropped. Maybe one day, I'd thank her. One day, I'd tell her how much we all needed her...loved her, even.

Loving was lethal.

I stalked off down the stone steps and outside to the courtyard. I needed to hit something. To fight, if only to stop myself from falling apart. If a teenager with an attitude problem was my only option, I would take it. Uncle Cedric used to say beggars couldn't be choosers.

Sticky and suffocating, the Huddian heat was oppressive to most. But the moment I stepped into the morning warmth, I relished the way the humidity licked my skin, the sweat beading at my neck almost instantly. I squinted against the sun, my eyes adjusting and muscles relaxing with every warm ray of light that soaked into my freckled flesh.

Old tables and empty barrels cluttered the courtyard. Perhaps it was once an oasis in the middle of the Huddian squalor, but now it was as abandoned and unloved as the rest of the *Black Cauldron*.

It was the perfect hiding spot for those of us who wanted to abandon ourselves for a bit.

I closed my eyes and inhaled the stale air like it was Madame Katrin's finest perfume. Breathe in. Breathe out. Repeat. Let the sun and sweat help me forget. Let the clutter and chaos hide me from the truth.

A dagger whizzing past my ear shattered the calm as it lodged into a nearby crate with a perfect *thwack*. My eyes flew open, and I reached instinctively for my swords, searching for the assailant that dared slight the Swordsinger.

Arms crossed, the tiny tyrant looked at me through narrowed eyes. "Are you here to spar, or are you coming to lecture me too?"

I'd seen that look before, on another teenager's face. Agony hiding behind anger. Grief underneath layers of granite indifference. Reagan was a tad younger than Keira had been, but the defiant tilt of the little dragon's head was an uncanny match for my missing cousin. Two orphans who learned to sheathe their hearts instead of their daggers.

I'd never been one to pity. Pity was like a dry handjob from a scullery maid's calloused palms. It never satisfied the real need. I'd much rather be pissed off, and I had a feeling Reagan might feel similarly.

"If it's all the same to you, I'd feel a lot better with steel in my hand." I pulled Truth and Triumph from my back. The cool metal of Truth's graceful hilt kissed my palm, completing my arm. With a taunting smile, I tossed Triumph to Reagan.

"Good." She caught the precious sword with ease. "Square off, old man."

I twirled Truth once, loosening my wrist as the fire fueled me. I was a blade meant to be brandished, no matter how tiny the opponent. Fights were easy. Fights, I won. "Are you sure you can handle it, Shrimpy?"

I knew my mistake the second the endearment slipped, pain flashing in Reagan's eyes. "Don't you dare call me that."

Better to be pissed off than pitied. "I'll stop calling you Shrimpy if you win."

Reagan moved faster than I expected her to, swiping low and aiming for my knees. For all the time she spent distancing herself from Keira's legacy, our captain's signature was written in every one of Reagan's movements. I shuffled back out of her reach, kicking the sword from her hand and letting it clatter on the cobblestone. She swore under her breath as she scrambled for the blade on all fours.

I crouched down to meet her level, the fight and fire now in full flare. "You'll have to do better than that, *Shrimpy*. I saw that one coming from a league away."

She gripped the hilt of Triumph again, a saccharine smirk crawling over her face. "See this, then."

I had no time to react as the dirt flew in my eyes. I fell back, blind for a moment, when Triumph's hilt smacked my cheek, forcing the air from my lungs.

"You little shit," I coughed and sputtered as I wiped my eyes, fumbling to find my feet beneath me. It had been years since I tasted my own blood. I blinked through the remaining dirt, Reagan's smile serpentine as she fell back into a ready stance again.

"Let's go, old man. This is fun."

I tightened my hold on Truth. As much as she had my cousin's fire, she was born a Mathonwy. If Keira pulled a trick like that, Uncle Cedric would've handed her her ass on a platter. But Reagan wasn't afraid to sip from Trouble's cup. And Lyr's ass, was it fun to fight with someone who wasn't afraid to play dirty.

She met my next jab well, the song of steel breaking the morning peace. I didn't hold back, didn't slow myself to meet her pace. Instead I unleashed, and to my delight and surprise, the little dragon met every parry and strike.

Breathe in. Breathe out. Repeat.

This is what I was. Rage and ruination, steel and savagery. I didn't need to think about all of the wrong I'd done, all of the pain I'd caused. The people I'd hurt. The ones I failed to protect.

The little dragon had her own demons to exorcize, and despite her stature, each blow hit harder and harder. I took every lump and bruise she delivered with glee, her unfiltered fury feeding the greedy God of War that owned my soul.

Together, spinning around and knocking over crates and barrels in the small courtyard, we let Truth and Triumph sing the song of our rage and hurt. Until our breath was labored and our backs ached and the taste of metal coated our tongues.

Breathe in. Breathe out. Repeat.

"I'm done," Reagan gasped for air after the third or fourth go, leaning on Triumph for support. "You win."

I fell back on one of the stone columns, the sweat coating my back sticking me to the spot. "No, you did. You're still standing after four rounds with the Swordsinger." I unfastened the skin of water on my belt, tossing it to her for the first swig. "You're getting good."

She uncorked the leather pouch with her teeth and guzzled back a few greedy glugs, dribbles coming out the side of her mouth in her sheer exhaustion. When she'd had her fill, she handed it back, a peace offering. "I've learned my lesson."

"That makes one of us." I sat as I drank, letting the cool water rinse away the taste of blood and stifle the rage still brewing in my gut. "I'm nearly twice your age, and I still can't manage to learn when to shut my mouth."

"Better than picking fights you can't win," she sighed as she plopped down next to me, turning her face to the rising sun that bathed the courtyard in warmth. Her face was relaxed in the tentative peace that only pure fatigue afforded. "What's got your goat today, old man?"

My chest squeezed again, as it had when Rhett asked earlier. But I was too tired to stop it, too tired to shield anyone from the tidal wave anymore.

"It's almost October." I squinted up at the southern sun, so warm and bright here. Back home in Porthladd, leaves would already be falling from trees as the autumn chill settled in. I could almost see what could have been, Fate fucking with my head. The markets selling scarves from Ir'de and pumpkins for the harvest. My mother fussing about, trying to buy enough fabric to make everyone new coats for the coming winter. My father haggling with Mr. Marlins for a discount on his famous apple-and-cinnamon spiced whiskey, since we were such good customers.

Finna carrying the little one in her arms as everyone gathered around to ogle him and count his freckles.

"Finna's boy would've been due any day now. And no one else seems to notice." The words tumbled out, Truth still in my hand buzzing at the admission. Reagan was quiet for a moment, like she could see it too, the daydream that broke my heart and kicked me in the nuts every day. Her small hand covered mine.

"My mama would have noticed." Chestnut eyes filled with tears. She blinked them back before they could betray her. "She would've sewn a shroud or made you ginger cookies or something silly."

I chuckled humorlessly as Reina's soft smile entered the illusion, my masochistic mind imagining her teaching Finna how to properly rock the baby. I reached for the other flask I kept at my hip, washing away the vision with a deep dreg of it. The whiskey burned my throat, mixing with the guilt and regret.

Reagan snatched the flask from me and took a swig, daring me to say something with a look that could straighten my curls. "Drinking won't bring Finna back."

The rumble of Trouble sounded through my gut again. "Blaming Keira won't bring your Ma back."

She stared back, and for a moment, I thought I could see the fire die out before it engulfed us both once more. She crossed her arms.

"Then maybe everyone shouldn't be so concerned about bringing *her* back. What if she deserves what she got?"

Not even the God of War could win in a fight with the little demon before me. But because I was Trouble's cuckold, I leaned in, baiting the dragon again. "Your mother forgave her."

"I'm not like my mother." Her voice was quiet, but I could hear the roar beneath it. She snatched Triumph again, running her small finger across the sharp blade, drawing a thin line of red from the tip. "If I was, I'd be dead."

A laugh escaped me as I took the blade from her slowly. "You are like Keira, though." She opened her mouth to protest, but I squished her mouth together, too tired to listen to the whining. "You're made of the same salt. The wit, the fearlessness. The *rage*."

She smacked my hand away and spat at my feet. "Rage feels better than grief."

I shrugged, letting the sun warm my face as I looked away. "I know, I'm not lecturing you. Just don't let it eat you alive, little dragon. Take it from someone who knows."

We sat in silence for a few long moments, all the witty retorts and rebuttals as dead as our missing family. We no longer needed sparring partners. Just friends to witness each other's pain in silence.

Reagan broke the quiet, the first mourner to leave the funeral. She stood and brushed off the seat of her pants before extending a hand to me. "We should do something to remember them. Finna and Owen. And Mama."

My whole chest swelled with gratitude, an ache nearly as uncomfortable as guilt. But still, despite the piece of Trouble in me that whispered for me to run, I took her outstretched hand. "What do you have in mind?"

"Hold still." Nelle's stern command echoed in the bare stone room that served as her makeshift workshop. I stilled at her order, the air kissing the exposed flesh of my chest as I sat on the edge of the oak worktable. The room smelled of mold and herbs, the decaying stone in stark contrast with the fragrant life Nelle's medicines breathed into every space she occupied.

"Like the view?" I waggled my eyebrows at her as I gestured to my torso, earning a laugh from Reagan, who watched on.

Nelle lips thinned into a fine line. She rubbed her pale hands together before placing them on my chest. "This will only hurt for a second."

"I'm no stranger to pain," I started before the light flashed, but cut off as searing heat shot across my chest, sending a string of vile curses tumbling from my lips. Reagan laughed again, and I shot her a dirty look as I rubbed the tender spot.

"It's perfect." A broad smile crossed Nelle's face as she admired her handiwork. She held up a small, silver-framed mirror, angling it so I could ogle my own half-naked body. "Care for a look?"

My stomach did a somersault. Perched above my left pec, the larger fox stared back in the mirror, her fur the same color as the faint hair of my chest, her jade green gaze somehow piercing even in ink. Tucked into the crook of her tail, the smaller fox's eyes were closed, peaceful as he nestled into his mama's side.

The air rushed from the small room. I ran a finger over the tender flesh, never so enamored with a part of my own skin.

Reagan smiled brightly as she nudged my side, pulling me back to reality. "Move, big guy. My turn."

I hopped off the chair, swallowing down the tears that rose from their cage. Reagan took the seat, holding out her arm for Nelle.

"Aye, sit tight." Nelle held the little dragon's bicep, blowing a strand of black hair out of her face as she focused. Another flash, a small hiss from Reagan, and then it was done. "There. Not so bad, right?"

The white snake wrapped itself all the way from the base of her wrist to the top of her bicep, its chocolate-colored eyes resting at the edge of her shoulder. Reagan sat silent, staring at the way the iridescent scales contrasted the honey of her skin, just as gentle and loving as the woman who once wore them.

"Your mother would've killed me for this." I cleared my throat, offering my friend a hand, a mooring line back to the land of the living, just as she had for me. "But it suits you."

Tears lined the chestnut of her eyes, but she smiled, the warmest I'd seen her in ages. "I know. Thank you, Nelle."

The siren placed a quick kiss on Reagan's forehead before turning her violet stare on me. "How's Rhett's eye? Need any tinkering before I set off with Ronan?"

The warmth that filled my middle washed away faster than cheap lip stain off a harlot's mouth. *Rhett.* I'd run away from my mess for long enough, it seemed, and Trouble wouldn't forget the debt I owed him. I sighed as I pulled my sweat-soaked shirt back over my head, wishing I could somehow disappear in it. "He's fine. Thank you for that, too."

"I'm good at healing flesh wounds." Nelle pointed to the mark that now covered my chest, the corners of her sharp mouth softening. "Wounds of the heart are harder."

I opened my mouth to try and express the wellspring of gratitude I felt, but the door to the workroom banged open, carrying with it the scent of Trouble born on a warm breeze.

"Ah good! You're both here!" Vian panted as he stumbled inside, shutting the door behind him with clumsy hands. Somehow, the little whirlwind seemed even more frantic than usual, a feat that should've been impossible by human standards. Dark eyes locked on Reagan and me. "I have an urgent proposal for you. Nelle, cover your ears."

Nelle chuckled as she crossed her arms. "Why does this feel like a bad idea?"

"Because it is." A devilish grin that could rival my own flashed across the young boy's angular face. "Do us both a favor, pretend you're not here."

Nelle rolled her eyes, but turned around to fuss with some of the herbs on her worktable, unbothered by the boy and his antics. In the short time we'd all known him, we'd gotten used to Vian's particular brand of strange. But the hair at the back of my neck stood at attention, Truth buzzing something wicked and wild in my ear.

"What is it?" Reagan's voice was low, as if she could sense the sword's whispers, too.

Something dangerous danced in Vian's obsidian eyes, the beginnings of an idea that might make even the God of Mischief sweat. "The wind has a plan. But I need your help."

4

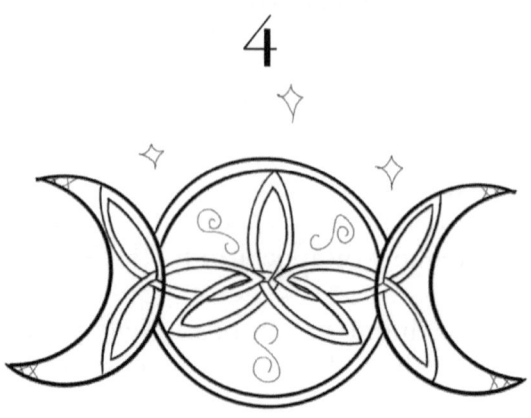

Dreams and Dresses

KEIRA

Black smoke against white flesh. Devouring me from the inside out. Clawing its way up my arm. Red hair against stone streets, blood the same color. A body disintegrating to ash as the light burned...my light. Chestnut eyes, lifeless as the bloodstained deck of the ship. Screaming that pierced the night. Mama, no. Mama, please. *A daughter made orphan, with hate in her gaze and fire in her veins.*

Another little girl, with her daddy's sea-glass stare. With her mother's raven hair.

Just out of reach. Terror in her voice as her screams joined the chorus. Mama, no. Mama, please. *A daughter not yet born, already bearing the weight of the world.*

Not real.

Not real.

Not real.

Cold burned like sunfire as the vision cleared, the torment of my mind giving way to the unending light once more. Fixed to my cage of ice, the world spun around me at a nauseating angle, shapes blurring in and out of focus.

The illusions had been so much *worse*. Another one of Death's cruel tricks. Sometimes the little girl looked like Papa, with strawberry-blonde curls and freckles like stars. Sometimes, she looked like Ronan, with a deviled grin and hair like sunlight on the horizon. Sometimes, she looked like Death, his ebony stare and rosebud lips on her small face.

On the worst days, she looked like me. My mirror in both beauty and pain as she screamed for me.

Today, Death's dark eyes tinted my favorite shade of blue. Like an ocean of shadow-swallowed sapphires, the garish light softer in the crystal of his gaze. Tears gathered in the corners, threatening to spill with just one blink of his thick coal lashes.

It was a dirty trick, to wear my colors. *His* colors. To remind me of what I could never have again.

To tempt me to look longer. To forget the unborn possibilities and instead rapture in the guaranteed bliss.

Ronan.

Ronan.

Ronan.

"Good morning, *Caraid*." His throat bobbed as he tucked a strand of my hair behind my ear, sea-deep voice strangled with sadness.

Despite the ice, it took considerable effort to freeze my lips together. To stop them from traitorously parting with one solemn cry of surrender.

I was tired. So tired.

Death.

Death.

Death.

Cherry-stained lips pressed into an immeasurably thin line. "Silent again, I see."

At that, the wick lit, the flicker of starfire left in the deepest parts of me small but rebellious. I cleared my throat, hoarse with disuse. "Do you prefer 'fuck off'?"

Death blinked back, the blue in his eyes fading again to obsidian. A feeble, hesitant smile tugging at the corner of his mouth. "I do." He stood, towering over me like God's Eye, casting me in the warmth of his shadow. He gripped my chin between gentle fingers, holding me like I was delicate as falling snow. Like if he let go, I'd vanish. "I can handle your anger. I understand it, your hurt, your confusion. I will gladly take it on the chin if it opens you up."

The words awakened a forgotten part of me, the memory of a honeyed voice in a dusty shack ringing clear as springwater in my ears.

Anything but the silence, Keira. I can't do a lifetime of silence.

Ronan.

Ronan.

Ronan.

"I'm not confused or angry," I lied. The ghost of the NightMare of the Four Seas spoke, the thought of Ronan's vulnerability steeling over the last frayed threads of my resilience. For him, I could withstand the cold. For him, I could hang on. "I don't care."

Surprise lifted Death's dark brows before the lines of his face relaxed into an easy smile. Arawn dropped my chin and stood straighter as he beamed at me. "You don't care, yet you speak. Even the coldest winter eventually thaws for a chance to greet the coming spring. I can bear your iciness if it means the blossoming of something new."

When I was little, I loved the cold. Every winter, my family would make our last trek to Pysgodd before the waters froze. My uncles, burly as they were, would shiver belowdecks, wrapped in furs. But I would stand on the bow of the *Ceffyl*, letting the bitter cold bite my cheeks to rosiness, letting Nef's northernmost wind tussle and tie my hair into sailor's knots. Winter had been nothing more than an impish playmate, calling to my most wild parts.

Now, I'd give anything for a taste of spring. For the balmy kiss of a warm rain. For the humid hug of the first bloom.

Again, I said nothing, gnawing my lower lip. Not out of pride or strength, but out of fear. Fear that if I started speaking again, I'd never be able to stop. That if I admitted my thawed edges, I'd melt entirely into the springtime of Death's embrace.

The smile faded from Death's red lips. A sigh rocked his sturdy frame. "I hate it when you hurt." He clutched his chest above his heart, boldly assuming he had one. "I feel it too. I feel the pain as you hold your kin, as you say goodbye–"

My gut churned, the words too raw, too hateful to hear aloud. The air rushed from my throat, like a wave pulling back from the shore before it slammed into me again.

Too many loved ones lost, too many to try and hold, to save. And again and again, they fell, bleeding out in my hands. Too many goodbyes. The air swirled in my chest like a hurricane, this time destroying the walls within. I had nothing left, no barriers or boundaries. Nothing to stop the deep, soul-shattering ache as it spread through my limbs.

Sunset eyes and ginger beards, twin in appearance. Bullet holes and blade marks, sullied red. Shipwrecks and crashing thunder.

"Stop it." I wasn't sure it was my voice that spoke, but Death's eyes widened as they locked onto mine. Another pathetic, mewling sob escaped my traitorous lips: "Stop torturing me."

He stepped close again, cradling my face in his palms. I saw my pain mirrored in his dark eyes as they searched mine. "*Caraid*, this isn't my doing. The dreams, the visions…" He paused to stroke my hair, his throat bobbing as he swallowed back the emotion rising to his lips. "The Otherworld only sees us as we see ourselves. When will you forgive yourself, hmm?"

Pain gave way to rage, phantom fire in my veins thawing the ice that shielded my heart.

The Otherworld only sees us as we see ourselves.

There was a part of me deep down that knew he was right. A forgotten part that remembered all of Papa's lessons, a part that couldn't forget if I tried.

I'd lost sight of myself. I no longer knew who or *what* Keira was, if she existed at all. I only saw the murderer, the kin-killer. The prisoner in ice and sorrow.

"This isn't my fault!" I snarled at Death, or maybe at myself. I couldn't bear the burden of my own guilt. The abandoned part of me glared at him, the last spark of Papa's light I had left. "You're the one keeping me here. Stop playing with your food and either let me go, or fuck off."

Dark tendrils swirled around Death's frame as my words struck. "Trapped, yes." He tapped the ice with the tip of his long finger. I yelped as a hissing sound rose from where they touched, the frost slowly melting. "For your safety, and for mine. I can see the hatred in your eyes. But are you in pain? Have I harmed a single hair on your head?"

A harsh scoff escaped my hoarse throat. "So I should thank you for that?"

A laugh rumbled in Arawn's chest, but it had an edge of hurt. "No, I don't deserve your thanks, but I do hope for your understanding. Haven't you ever judged someone for their family?"

Blond hair, the same as his snake father's. A serpent smile on his face, a traitor's crest on his breast pocket...

Ronan.

Ronan.

Ronan.

"I–" I started, but halted. The ice thawed further, my chest and elbows free now, but I was still frozen, my regret a prison in itself. So many wasted moments with Ronan, spent hating him when I could've listened. Could have tried to see things clearly. So many lives lost to my ignorance and prejudice.

When I looked back up, Death's brow knotted, his eyes searching mine for absolution. "Your mother...she was a trickster. Never honest, not as a wife or a queen."

My heart shuddered to a stop for a moment at the mention of the silver queen, the siren queen that claimed the title *Mother*. It still felt strange to say. I'd never had a mother before, never knew how to accept her as a reality.

But now Arawn knew Danura? No, he was *married* to her?

In the dark recesses of my mind, the words of one of Ronan's stories found me, as if my husband wanted me to remember something, someone...

Donn, the keeper of light, queen of the heavens...

Was the *Serenhi* more than she claimed to be? Did the queen of the sirens once wear a heavier crown? Despite the ice, something hot churned in my gut, a reminder of the otherness of my mother, the piece of her I shared. It seemed impossible. Yet, here I was, staring Death in his glorious face, my heart still thundering in my chest.

He banished her to the isle of the lost and struck her name from all the world...

Realization slammed into me before a darker thought rumbled in my chest. If Danura was his queen, *his wife*...what did that make me?

"I could see your good intentions, but I was wary." Arawn's voice broke, like ice shattering against stone. "I promise I don't intend to keep you there for long. It is my greatest wish to set you free, to unleash you. But I had to make sure you wouldn't try to run or kill me the second I let you out."

"How do you know I won't?" I stretched my rotten shoulder, moving as the ice thawed from my frame. I was stiff and sore, but it was better than numb. Better than nothing. I relished the proof of my corporeality. It didn't matter who or what my mother was, not if I still had life in my veins. Death watched me, fingers twitching at his side, a strange mix of eagerness and worry in the tension of his frame.

Arawn exhaled. "I know you well enough now."

My hands free of the restraints, I clenched my fists at my side, desperate to hang onto the flickering rage in my core. "You know nothing."

"Then tell me. I want to know everything." A broad, bright smile as he stepped closer, gingerly taking my frozen hand in his. His skin was so warm, so inviting, that no matter how strong my resentment, I couldn't help the sigh of relief that escaped my lips. "Over dinner, perhaps."

"I'd rather freeze," I spat at Death's feet as I jerked my hand away, despite every instinct in my body that begged me to hold tighter, to embrace the warmth.

"Why?" The single, lonely word held centuries of sadness in it, his voice soft as he stared at his rejected hand. "Am I so hideous and terrible?"

I watched Death for a moment, his broad chest rising and falling as his breathing quickened. Watched the god before me, the keeper of war and pain. The minstrel of death, the minister of darkness. Watched the husband who cast out my mother, jealous and scorned. The man who stared at me like I was his only hope.

The snowmelt finally dripped around my ankles, the feeling returning to my numb legs. I staggered, limbs weak with disuse, but I was free. Weak, and tired. But free. And that freedom was mine to wield as I wished. I could rush at him, attack. I had no plan or strength, but I also had nothing to lose. Or worse, I could run *to* him. Could fall into his arms, trading a cage of ice for the prison of his touch.

"You're a monster," I reminded myself, before I could make the mistake of seeing him as anything other.

Arawn's face fell, shoulders slack, as my insult hit him. Still, he stared at me as if he knew me, better than I might have ever known myself. "We all are monsters, *Caraid*. Some of us just chose not to hide our true nature."

Monsters and murderers, living on borrowed time.

The truth, plain but lethal, sliced through my most vulnerable parts. If Death was a monster, so was I. I had done as much harm as he had, had scorned my family, cast out my friends. Had brought pain and ruination to everything and everyone I'd ever touched. I was a curse made whole, a monster with no more righteousness than the Dark God.

At least he didn't pretend to be anything other. He didn't ruin lives while claiming to save them.

We're all the same when we're dead.

I had no more energy to hide my monstrous parts. I took one wobbling, traitorous step toward him. "What do you want from me?"

"Dinner." Arawn's grin went feral as he extended his hand to me, a monster closing in on its fallen prey. "That's all."

The front door to Death's domain was not covered in ice, as I imagined it would be. Instead, it looked like an abandoned Orwellin temple, the black marble stairs scuffed and cluttered with debris, the tall, looming columns entangled by dying ivy.

We'd walked for what felt like an eternity across the ice, the mist hugging my still-numb form as we trudged deeper. But Death led, and I followed, until through the haze, the black structure I'd seen from afar jutted toward the sky. It loomed over me as I stood on the first step, the tall, onyx doors opening by their own will.

Death sauntered in, and again, I trailed behind, my cold feet desperate for respite against the elements.

I blinked away my surprise as I took in my surroundings, ignoring the chill than ran up my spine as the heavy doors clicked shut behind me. The interior was more of the same. No decorations adorned the walls, no signs of life. Not even smudges in the layers of dust to indicate it had been given any attention in years. Just dark floors and black walls, all painted in a thick layer of unloved staleness.

Here, the stench of rot and regret was all that was real. It was a tomb without a corpse to keep it warm. A mausoleum without any memory.

Arawn's hand found the small of my back as he pushed me a step further into the room. His cheeks reddened as his eyes fell to the unloved floor. "Not what you expected?"

My chest clenched. I pitied Death. A slanderous smile caught the corner of my mouth. "It's not cold."

Death's eyes met mine again, hope brimming in the impossible black. Like the ice, his frame melted, tension dissolving from his broad shoulders. He cleared his throat, gesturing towards the dusty staircase that occupied the center of the room. "Your quarters are up the stairs and to the left."

A familiar panic fluttered in my chest. This was not the first manor I'd entered, expecting one thing and finding another entirely. My heart ached as I imagined the white marble and gold frames hanging across the wall, the deep red velvet curtains dusty and drawn.

Ronan.

Ronan.

Ronan.

My worldview had shifted that day, my entire foundation rearranged to accommodate my husband and his kin, even if I didn't mean for it to happen. My fingers twitched at my side, steadying myself before Death could change me yet again. "Why are you being like this?"

"Darling girl, what about my behavior has suggested anything otherwise?" As if he was a window to my past, Death stuck his hands in the pockets of his tailored white suit. Something vicious and painful squeezed my chest tighter, a viper taking hold around my heart, protecting me from Arawn's mimicry. No, he was not my husband. Not Ronan. This was not Mathony Manor, and I was not the same narrow-minded fool I'd once been. Still, as he stepped closer, dark eyes trained on me with burning intensity. His pine and snow scent quickened my pulse. "I've been begging you to let me help you since that first day. I simply needed you to talk to me."

I stepped back, one defiant, brave step into the girl I remembered. The Keira who loved her husband and her kin above herself, the Keira who was not swayed by pretty words and potent stares. "I don't understand any of this."

Undeterred, Arawn nodded to the staircase once more. "Go get dressed in something more appropriate. The servants will help. We'll talk when you're ready."

Death disappeared into a mist before I could refuse, before I could listen to the dark pit in my stomach telling me to run and never look back.

"Mistress Ariannad," a woman's voice called from the top of the stairs, and I spun to it, nearly toppling over in my surprise.

Not a woman, a girl.

"What—"

The child couldn't have been older than Reagan. She was short, her form barely clearing the onyx wood banister at the top of the landing. Her hair, dark as Death's, was smoothed back into a careful bun, one to compliment the crisp black cotton smock dress she wore. She waved at me frantically, as if we were old friends, not total strangers, a bright smile across her cherubic features. "Come, Mistress Ariannad! Cythie is here to get you dressed."

I should've run. She was just a girl, no match for me, even in my state of distress. I should've fled while I had the chance, even if it meant freezing in the cold, frozen wasteland of the Otherworld.

And yet.

Another little girl, brown ringlets instead of black, but the same warm grin. Another lost soul, a sister in snake's skin. Another family found in the walls of another manor.

It was all a farce, a trap meant to ensnare me with my own weak wishes.

And yet.

Was it selfish to submit to simple pleasures? I'd chosen my fate that day on the *Ceffyl*, with Reagan's hateful glare and Connor's blade. I'd fired the gun myself, and I hadn't regretted it for one moment since. The torturous nightmares, the frozen, endless days...I would do it for a thousand years if it meant keeping my loved ones safe. I deserved the consequences of my own chaos.

Death.

Death.

Death.

But what would happen if I chose dinner instead of denial? Was it wrong to allow myself to rest in peace instead? Did I deserve rest at all?

The Otherworld only sees us as we see ourselves.

"Cythie?" I repeated the strange name, unable to ignore the desperate, festering, need in my softest parts. And like the monstrous thing I was, I climbed the steps. "Sorry, you scared me. I didn't think anyone else was here."

Cythie bounced excitedly, grabbing my wrist with cold, clammy hands. "Many servants like Cythie live in the palace. We are only seen when wanted."

The thought chilled me as she led me through the hallway. The rest of the estate was in a similar state of disrepair, paintings hanging from the walls at odd angles, curtains ripped and torn, everything covered in a thin layer of cobwebs. If there were servants, why was this place a wreck?

"What happened to this place?" The thought escaped my lips before I could recant it.

Cythie slowed, her heels echoing across the obsidian floor cracking the stiff silence. She stared at her toes. "He won't let us fix it. Says it's his punishment."

The Otherworld only sees us as we see ourselves.

Again, perfidious pity strangled my heartstrings. Death, maker of misery and malice, a prisoner in his own paradise.

Cythie straightened her shoulders and pulled me onward, into a room down the east corridor. She pushed open the heavy wooden door, a loud creak echoing through the emptiness. The shadows of the conversation before shooed from her face as she smiled again, eyes crinkling at the corners. "Your quarters, Mistress Ariannad. Come on in, Cythie will bathe you."

"I can bathe myself," I chuckled as I pushed past, but the laughter stole from my chest as I took in the room. The space was pristine, not a single cobweb or dust bunny in sight. The decor was sparse, but tastefully so, the simplicity welcome. At the center, a large four poster bed stood proud, sea-blue sheets covering it, with half a dozen-white pillows that looked softer than clouds strewn across. The curtains swayed as a fresh, salt-air breeze drifted into the room, sunlight pouring onto the spotless wood floor. A fire crackled in the hearth, warm and woody, as a pot of something that smelled suspiciously like Reina's stew simmered.

Sorrow slammed into my stomach like a cannonball. My breath fled, my heart sinking to my toes. I needed air. I flew to the window, to the sea that awaited outside.

Nothing. Frozen, icy nothing.

"Mistress Ariannad, is the room not to your liking?" Cythic placed a hand on my back, her touch gentle but still cold as ice. It steadied and sobered me, reminding me of who and *where* I was.

This place looked and smelled like paradise. Like home. But the otherworld was not the paradise of legends. It was not home. It was hell. It was carefully crafted torture, designed to deceive and deflect.

Not real. Not real.

No, this was not home. This was not Mathonwy Manor, not my ship. Cythie was not Reagan, not my strong-willed cousin. And Arawn was nothing like my husband, no matter how expertly he pretended.

"It's fine." I threw on a Mathonwy mask, a smile that didn't reach my eyes, as I tucked away my heart once more. I would not let Arawn have it, no matter what promises of paradise he offered. "Perfect."

Cythie smiled back, none the wiser as she flitted into the second room through an arched doorway, and I followed her through. A large, black ceramic tub sat in the center, an elegant crane-necked faucet made of sparkling brass pouring already warm water into it. Cythie produced a small vial from one of her dress pockets, pouring it into the bath. Lavender scented the room as she stirred the contents with her fingers, the rising steam beckoning. "Here, Mistress. Enjoy."

She dipped into a curtsey then fled the small room. I listened to her heels carry her out the door before I peeled off the stiff white tunic I'd been stuck in. The garish, festering black of my arm stood in stark contrast, the only proof of my reality.

Real. Real. Real.

I would not fall for this pretense. But I would play along. And Lyr below, I needed a bath more than I needed my pride. I lowered myself into the warm tub, the hot water chasing all remnants of the frozen chill from my limbs. I let it wash away my worries, let the scented soap and steam scrub away my sorrow.

I was far from home, and I'd left my family yet again to fend for themselves. But I had done enough feeling sorry for myself to last a lifetime. No, I would not submit, but I would not succumb to my own torturer either.

The Otherworld only sees us as we see ourselves.

If I truly was the orchestrator of my own suffering, then I would see to it that it meant something. I would not waste time feeling sorry. Instead, I would dance with Death himself if it got me closer to victory. If it saved my family from whatever hell on earth I'd left behind.

I finished my bath and my musings, feeling more like myself. Like the woman I thought I'd killed on the *Ceffyl*. Cythie left a black silk robe on the edge of the tub, and I wrapped it around my shoulders quickly, tying the waist tightly like armor. As I returned to the bedroom, I saw it for the battleground it was. This was not comfort, this was a cage. Death had freed me from the ice only to ensnare me in a far more dangerous trap.

Cythie reappeared from the same black mist, nearly startling me twice. She held a gown in her hand, the same obsidian as Death's eyes, the material sparkling with gems that looked like stars. She laid it down on the bed before ushering me to sit. "Mistress Ariannad is so lovely, but so tired. We need to get you dressed, but let Cythie fix your hair first."

I complied, playing my part in this game. Auntie Vala once told me it was better for my enemies to see me as weak, as a blushing bride, rather than the half-wild pirate I truly was.

I was no longer half wild. No, now I was truly feral, a *blaidd* unleashed. But I would paint on a pretty mask, I would don a dress and dance in it if it tricked Death into submission.

Papa used to say it was better to know your enemy than have them know you.

"A braid is fine," I instructed Cythie as I sat on the plush edge of the mattress, my back to her. She sat behind me, cold fingers working through my wet hair with ease. I suppressed a shiver as she worked.

"His Holiness is fond of braids," she mused, finishing her work fast, letting the long plait fall over my shoulder.

"Good."

Cythie continued, a worker bee that knew her place in the hive. She fanned out the dress, letting the skirts breathe as she helped me step into it. "This dress will look lovely on Mistress Ariannad's skin."

"Captain Keira, Cythie," I corrected as I pulled the heavy material over myself, my costume complete. I would dress up and play Death's game, but no matter what they put me in, I would not forget myself. Never again. "I'm a Captain. Or a Madame. I'm married."

"None of that matters in the Otherworld, Mistress Ariannad." Cythie waved me off, but her lips pursed slightly. "Let Cythie do your laces."

Another flash of dark smoke, and a second servant appeared. "I can help with those."

My heart sank to the bottom of Lyr's keep before soaring.

She wore the same stiff uniform as Cythie, her hair tied in a bun, but her blonde locks were a welcome contrast against the black of Arawn's palace.

Chestnut eyes, lifeless as the bloodstained deck of the ship. Screaming that pierced the night. Mama, no. Mama, please. *A daughter made orphan, with hate in her gaze and fire in her veins.*

Not real. Not real. Not real.

Another phantom, torturing me from the recesses of my mind. Another fiction meant to punish me. But this time, my black mark still marred my flesh. This time, she wasn't bleeding out on the deck. She wasn't lifeless, her daughter crying over her unmoving form. Chestnut eyes met mine, a warning in them to stay quiet.

Real.

My voice caught in my throat, my guilt a noose. "Rei–"

"Cythie can do it." The young girl stuck her hands to her hips and jutted her lip out in a pout.

"I know ye can. Ye've done well. Let me earn my keep." As I'd seen her do a thousand times, Reina smiled softly at the girl, smoothing a palm over her dark hair. "Can ye find something fer her hair? A broach, perhaps, to make it look nice?"

"Cythie will be right back," Cythie nodded, her smile returning, before she flashed again into a dark cloud of smoke and secrets.

As soon as she was gone, Reina's smile fell, an all-too-familiar concern in the sharp angles of her slender shoulders.

I stood still in the center of the room, the dress sitting awkward and unlaced off my shoulders, too startled or scared to move. My stomach flipped, hope and guilt warring inside of it. "Is it–are you real?"

Chestnut eyes, lifeless as the bloodstained deck of the ship.

"Stay quiet, Keira girl." Reina gripped my arms, the same gentle hold she always employed, her eyes searching mine frantically. "Listen carefully."

I shuddered in her embrace, in the kindness and warmth of it, even here, even in death. If this was another of Arawn's tricks, it was the most convincing yet, Reina's steady grace impossible to replicate. *Real.* The churning feeling rose up my throat, words spilling in a tidal wave. "I'm so sorry, Rei, I couldn't–"

"Not now, love." She pressed a finger to my lips, silencing the storm within. If she was a ghost, she certainly *felt* real, the careworn skin of her hand just as I remembered. Her voice dropped, urgent as the current. "Nothing here is what it seems. Stay alert, but don't let him know that ye've seen me."

Nothing here is what it seems.

No, it wasn't. This was a world of smoke and mirrors, a lie crafted of my own truths, meant to burn me from within. The clever part of me knew this had to be another of the Otherworld's tricks. I'd seen her face so many times in my terrors, seen her smile and heard her scream. Seen her in her kitchen, rushing around as she made a meal. Seen her bleed out, over and over and over again, my coat her burial shroud.

And yet. This felt different. Felt like home. Like hope.

Real.

"How do I know this is real?" I whispered, scanning her stare for the tell, for the slight imperfection that gave away the ruse. I found none, only the specific sorrow of the first Mathonwy to embrace me as kin.

"Ye don't," she sighed, rubbing small circles over my shoulder. "But I need you to trust me. I've been waiting for him to bring you here, but we don't have time to waste if we are going to fix this."

I nodded, my blood rushing through my ears as I struggled to understand. As she had many times before, she swiveled around to tighten the laces of the gown, tying me into the black fabric. Her fingers moved quickly, and her soft words rushed with equal fervor. "No one else can know what I'm about to tell you, and I don't know if I'll have time to come again. Do you understand?"

"Yes," I whispered, compliant under her touch, the only lifeline I had back to myself.

Reina paused, finishing the lacing, turning me to face her once more. Her brow knotted, the pain of truth resting heavy on it. A gentle hand caressed my cheek, and the outline of a smile danced across her face. "Keira, you're pregnant."

The world stopped spinning, and my stomach rolled. "What?"

Another little girl, with her daddy's sea-glass stare. With her mother's raven hair.

A daughter not yet born, already bearing the weight of the world.

I opened my mouth to protest, to deny it. It couldn't be true. I was dead, a soul wandering the Otherworld. I'd given up my life the day Connor slit my throat, forfeited any chance of a future.

And yet.

Something both dark and light rumbled deep in my core, an answer to a question that I didn't know I was asking. A truth that had been written far before me, and that would still hold strong long after me. A power born with the making of the universe itself, crafted from the same chaos.

"You have to–" Reina started, but another mist cut through the tension of the moment. I swayed as the world started turning again, like I'd come back to life.

"Cythie found a pretty tiara for Mistress Ariannad!" Cythie beamed as she held up a crystal diadem, obsidian stones set in swirling, delicate silver. "You may go now, Miss Reina."

Reina nodded to the girl, but didn't move her eyes from mine. "Good evening, Mistress Ariannad. Wear that crown carefully."

5

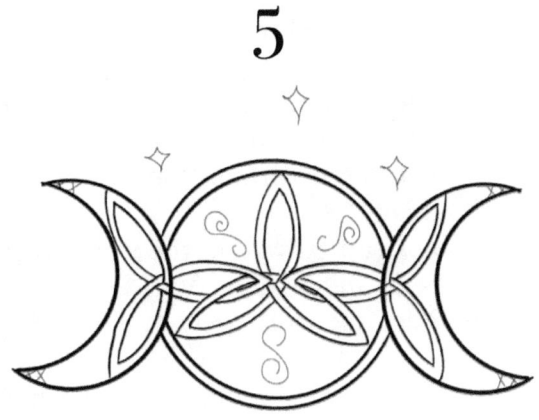

Dinners and Delusions

KEIRA

Death tasted like honey and ginger. A perfect blend of bitter and sweet, glazed over melt-in-your-mouth roasted quail. I'd never tasted anything so exquisite in my life.

Funny, that death somehow felt more vivid.

When Arawn invited me to dinner, this was not what I was expecting. We sat on the stone patio at the back of the palace, and unlike the rest of the estate, it was not dismal with disuse. Instead, it overlooked the most impressive garden I'd ever seen. Tall, trimmed hedges that reached skyward, covered with bright, blood-red roses in full bloom. It'd been hidden from me in the mist, tucked away behind the imposing figure of the palace. But now, it captivated the view, hundreds of rows extending well past where my eyes could see, a glorious sea of green and red stark against the light and ice I'd come to know.

Reagan would have loved it.

I pushed the thought from my mind before it could rip open the festering wound in my gut. I tore my gaze away from the garden and back toward the fare before me. Dishes intimately piled the table, making it hard to admire the delicate swirling roses carved into the thick wrought-iron surface. But I didn't mind, my mouth watering at the selection. A bird roasted in an exquisite demi-glace, pies and pastries fresh-baked and steaming. A mountain of mashed potatoes garnished with something green I'd never tried before. Fresh-picked berries filling obscenely large ceramic bowls. A meal to die for, perhaps, if I wasn't already dead.

No, not dead. Stuck somewhere in the in-between. Trapped in the Otherworld, my heart still beating. My lungs still sucking in air.

And in my middle, life still grew, new and powerful and terrifying.

I swallowed the food I gnawed on, my stomach sloshing at the thought.

Could Reina be trusted? Was she even *real?* Had my guilt-ridden psyche finally snapped, my mind giving me a respite to help me escape my unending torment?

No, not real. Another trick. Another lie.

But if it was real...if I was truly *pregnant*...

"Is the food to your liking?" Arawn cleared his throat, pulling me back to the moment. To his obsidian gaze. To the furrowed brow that waited for an answer.

"It's delicious. I forgot—" I stumbled, my tongue still in sailor's knots. It was so easy to forget. Who I was. *Where* I was. I looked down at the plate of food. It looked and smelled and tasted so real. "I didn't think I could still do this here."

"Do what?" Arawn squeezed a ripe berry in between his finger and thumb before popping it between his already-stained lips.

"Eat. Breathe..." I gestured to the table before us. If it was trickery, it was truly remarkable. And tempting. "Live."

Live as though I hadn't killed so many loved ones with my own recklessness. Enjoy a meal as if the Deyrnas wasn't starving because of the monster before me.

Tears stung my eyes. It was so easy to follow Death deeper and deeper into my denial. To forget all that I'd left behind. The damage, the victory. My family. My husband.

Ronan.

Ronan.

Ronan.

I would not forget again. This charade was mine. I could pretend to be the person he saw me as, a queen wrapped in a silken gown, wearing the crown intended for my mother. But it was nothing more than a costume, a little girl playing dress-up in her mama's closet, trying to distract and disarm Death.

"This could be paradise if you chose it." Arawn spoke quietly, voice thick with something I couldn't name. "You're the mistress of your own fate, after all."

I painted on a smile, but I couldn't keep the edge from my voice. "And yet, every choice I made still landed me here."

Landed my family in deep waters. If I was truly the mistress of my own fate, I was a masochistic monster. If this was my doing, I deserved to rot for it. I pushed my plate away, unwilling to feed the beast.

"Is it so terrible?" Arawn nudged my plate back to me, his hair brushing over his shoulders as he leaned forward. I could smell his breath again, somehow still fresh and sweet despite the meal. "Perhaps this is what you were born for."

"Perhaps." I stared back at Death, at the ice and stone of his posture. Perhaps I was meant to be with him, my destruction and ruination a match for his. Perhaps my fate was this prison of ice, not the warm embrace of my husband's arms.

"I know your pain," Arawn sighed, stretching a large hand toward me and gripping my fingers tightly.

Heat surged through my middle, burning and riotous. Then, a flash of bright light from the spot where we touched.

My power, same as it had been in Porthladd. No longer air and sea, but white-hot light.

I flinched, attempting to pull away, but Death held tighter. Slowly, his shadows crept along the edges, blissful dark devouring the burning starfire.

For a moment, I watched where they mingled. Where the soft, gentle darkness caressed the harsh, raging light. Where the two danced, a perfect balance, as right and true as the very foundations of the universe.

Midnight and moonlight. Pain and joy. Death and life.

I tore my hand away before it could swallow me whole. The light disappeared, retreating back inward, tangling once more in the uncomfortable pit in my stomach. "I'm sorry—I don't—"

"Don't be sorry for what you are," Arawn interrupted, still staring at my hand as his shadows evaporated. A small, careful smile broke across his face. "That power is a glorious gift. It should be celebrated, not shamed."

In response, the primordial thing in my middle shifted and twisted, begging to be released again. I swallowed hard, willing it back into its cage. "It's not mine. I don't know how to use it."

No, it wasn't mine. I'd found it at the bottom of the river in *Hiraeth*, had taken it to replace what I'd lost. But it was greater than me, a piece of the cosmic puzzle I couldn't possibly claim ownership of.

No, instead, it would own *me* if I let it.

Arawn gripped my chin gently, pulling my eyes to him. I swatted him away on instinct, but I held his gaze, the soft blackness inviting me in. He spoke with the same tenderness, his voice a cool breeze on a blistering summer day. "They have taught you to fear your gift. That it is wicked and wrong. But you are perfectly made."

Panic prickled at the back of my neck, images flashing across my mind.

Light, searing and hot, bursting forth from my palm. Connor's puppet, crumpling to the ground, melting into screams. Ronan's sapphire stare, clouded with unmistakable fear. Not devotion, or love, or awe.

Raw, unadulterated horror. At what I'd done. At who I was.

No, I was not perfect. I was rotten and wicked and ruined. And this thing inside of me would rule me if I gave it any room.

Arawn leaned back in his proud chair, interrupting my dark spiral. "Your gift will be inconsistent until you learn to embrace it, to trust it. If you'd like, I can teach you to control it before it consumes you."

One of Papa's lessons clanged like a warning bell in the back of my mind.

A good Captain doesn't seek to control others, but themselves.

So strange, to hear something so similar from Death's lips. But a deep, frightened part of me, the part that was a sailor and a soldier, knew he was right. Knew that if I didn't learn how to properly leash this thing inside of me, it would be my own ruining.

Then again, maybe that was best for everyone. Maybe if I went down, I could take this rotten place with me.

"Why?" I voiced aloud, steeling myself to the parts of me that were salt and sea. "If I learn to use it, what's going to stop me from using it against you to get myself out of here?"

The lie tasted sweet on my tongue. I knew there was no getting out of the Otherworld. There was no crossing back, no matter how many stories Ronan told about those who did. But for a moment, I let myself believe it. Let myself dare to imagine.

Death's eyes widened, amusement lifting his dark brows. "If you chose to try and ruin me, I'd gladly accept." Loneliness edged his dry laugh in a way I knew all too well. Pity sat heavy in my gut. But when his eyes found mine again, something light shone in their depths. His hand slid toward mine. "But I do hope—a dangerous thing, hope, I know—but nonetheless, I do desperately wish that you chose to stay. To make this your home."

Home.

A good sailor needs a home to come back to.

I had a home. Had a husband. Had a life. Had something to hope for, a future worth seeing through.

Keira, you're pregnant.

The cruel trick sliced through my vulnerable underbelly, sharper than steel. The Otherworld had tired of taunting me with my past. Now, it was taunting me with the future I'd forsaken. With the home I'd never get to have.

It was my fault, my *fate* that led me to the Otherworld. But Death had played his hand, too. I was a fool to pity him, to let his pretty words pamper and soothe. If I was cursed to this hell for a reason, so was he.

"I already had a home," I spat at Death, a familiar rage filling me. "You took me from it."

Hurt flashed across Arawn's expression as he recoiled. "Was that place really your home?" He scoffed, softness hardening to ice once more. His voice was equally cold as he lashed back, "They othered you as a child, made you feel alone, made you withhold your gift. Then they blamed you for everything that went wrong, limited you, asked you to sacrifice your freedom for theirs."

There's more than one way to sacrifice a life.

He was right. No one had ever embraced my gift, other than Ronan. But even he had turned from me, *feared* me. I had made him more, made him a *siren*, and he saw me as a stranger. And I'd shouldered the blame for all of my family's troubles since I was sixteen. My father's death, my uncle's betrayal, my family's downfall.

"And I'd do it all again." I tilted my chin up at Death as I laid bare my truth, the last remnants of Captain Keira surging to the surface. "They are my family."

Arawn watched me for a long moment, embracing the hatred and heat I poured into my stare. "I had a family once, too. What I wouldn't give to have them back…"

A dark chord echoed through me. None of the legends ever mentioned Arawn's family. They spoke of his wife, of *Danura*, of his betrayal…but I had learned well enough that legends were just well-spun lies. Had there been more? I let myself picture it, picture the people that Death called kin. A daughter, perhaps, with Danura's white-blonde hair and his cherry-plucked grin. Or a son, with an obsidian stare and a pine-scented smile.

I shook off the thought, not daring to see Death as a doting father. "I'm sorry for your loss."

He softened, ice melting again into sweet springtime. "I find your loyalty admirable. You truly are a goddess of generosity and goodness."

Heat rushed to my cheeks, betraying my resolve. I could play cool all I wanted, but underneath it all, I was still a child desperate for any validation. "I'm not a goddess. I'm just a girl."

This time, Death laughed aloud, the sound warm as it was broad. "You have never been just a girl. You are so much more, and you always have been. I've seen you. Seen the wild, free spirit. Seen the joy and pain and light. You're not a monster, you're a miracle."

War raged in my veins, my sensible and wild parts battling for the higher ground. I didn't want him to see me, to know me. To read me like a book. And yet, his words stirred something ancient. Something that begged to be noticed, to be understood.

You were never just a little girl. Little sea monster, maybe.

A sharp pang of fresh hurt shot through me. Ronan had said it at the spring, right after our wedding. I had wanted to kill him, to bury all my guilt and grief with him.

I'd been wrong then. Perhaps I was wrong now, too. If Death deemed me a miracle, perhaps I could let myself see him as a saint. But it was betrayal to the man I loved, to the boy I left behind.

Sensing my wavering resolve, Arawn pushed back from the table and stood, towering over me like God's Eye. He held out a hand.

"What are you doing?"

A flash of light in his pitch-black eyes. "Dance with me."

Again, my heart beat like a wardrum. "I don't dance."

"Yes, you do." He took my hand and pulled me effortlessly from my seat. My traitorous heart let him, the beating stopping for a moment as he drew me close, into his pine and rose scent. My skirts caught the light, shimmering like starlight as they swayed.

I should've shoved him back, should've kicked him in the shin and run away. But I didn't. Instead, I froze, trapped in the scaffold of his sturdy arms. My voice quivered, weak as my will. "I don't dance with men who aren't my husband."

Ronan.

Ronan.

Ronan.

"Your vows ended the day you crossed into the Otherworld." Arawn's free hand slid across the plane of my back, settling between my shoulder blades. A gentleman's hold, but his eyes burned like frostbite. "But I'm not a fool. I'm not asking for your love, *Caraid*. Not yet. Just a dance."

Death.

Death.

Death.

"And if I say no?" A brave hand—the last brave part of me—settled on his chest, pushing slightly. "Will you trap me in the ice again?"

"It hurts that you think me so cruel, but I hope to change that perspective." His chin dipped, and a single strand of silken hair fell across his face, masking the pain in his gaze. His face was a mere inch from mine, his balmy breath reddening my already scarlet cheeks as he sighed, "No, if you don't wish to dance, you may head back to your room. You can even bring more of the food with you. I'll leave you to yourself for a peaceful night. You've earned it."

Death held his breath as he harbored me, waiting. *Wanting.*

A dangerous part of me—a part I hated more than any other—wanted it, too. Wanted a peaceful night, coddled by Death's dark dance. I didn't want him, necessarily. I didn't know him. But an escape from the cold, the loneliness...I could use a friend in the Otherworld.

"I can't dance with you." I pressed against his strong frame, putting much-needed distance between us. My mind might have wanted to slip into darkness, to swim in the respite of his inky eyes.

But my heart was not weak. My heart was not *mine*. It had not come with me to the Otherworld, and it would not succumb to the ice.

Ronan.

Ronan.

Ronan.

"So be it." Death wore a sad smile as he let go, fingers brushing across my palm as they lingered just a moment longer. "Rest well." He turned to the table, his back straight as a blade, grip tight on the edge. Waiting for me to retreat. I hesitated for a moment, torn. Between temptation and triumph. Between liberation and loyalty. Head and heart.

Sheathing my emotions once more, I started toward the patio doors, desperate to be back inside. Back into the cage of my room, the last safe place away from Arawn. Away from temptation. But as my palm caressed the cold handle to the door, temptation drew me back, like a fish on the hook.

"Why me?" I spun around, anger flashing through me. Anger towards him, for seducing me, for using me. Anger towards myself for falling for it. I let it erupt, a geyser against the glacier of this prison, an outpouring of all the pain and suffering I'd been buried under. "Because of my mother? I've met her once, and I don't think she cares very much for me. If you're trying to bait her or use me to get to her...you've got the wrong girl."

His head whipped to me again, silver tears lining the pools of endless black. "I only noticed you because of Donn...Danura, yes." He swallowed hard, proud throat bobbing with emotion. He spoke again, voice soft as a rose petal. "But you are not bait, *Caraid*, nor are you the prize. You are the key to paradise."

You are the key to paradise.

Before his words could unlock a part of me I refused to unleash, I ran inside, shutting Death out.

I slammed the door of my bedroom behind me, sinking against the sturdy wood. The unlit lamps abandoned me to darkness, a pool of moonlight in front of the open window was the only witness to my shame.

I knew Arawn probably had servants lurking in the shadows, hidden from sight like Cythie had been. But for a moment, I pretended that it was only me and the moonlight. Two lonely, cold rocks floating through the blackness.

My head fell into my hands. Lyr below, what was I *doing?* Or, not doing, for that matter. I was a fighter, a warrior, a Captain. I should have been stronger, should've fought tooth and nail to free myself. I was not so easily seduced by a pretty man with sad eyes.

No, not a man. A god. Death himself, danger and darkness embodied.

I was a fool, a shrimp swimming straight into a shark's maw, asking him to devour me. This was a trap, and I was walking into it without so much as a thought. If my husband, or worse, *my father* could see the weak-willed witch I'd become…

A burst of black smoke, and lanternlight filled the room. I startled to my feet, ready to strike.

Reina materialized from the same blackness, holding the lantern in one hand, and a steaming bowl in the other. She wore the same stiff black dress, but this time, her smile was unguarded. "Yer finally back."

Not real, not real, not real.

A torture of my own doing, punishment for my foolishness. My reward for courting Death.

I braced against the door, the world spinning as I unraveled. "No, no, I won't do this, not tonight. You've all tortured me enough. I've earned rest for once."

And for once, it wasn't a lie. I knew I deserved my demise, but it could wait until the morning. Tonight, I needed to sit a little longer in the lazy river of denial, to let the moon absolve me of my sin, to let it all wash away with the evening tide.

"I don't know that I'd call serving ye a hot plate of stew torture, but so be it." Reina's eyes narrowed as she stepped closer, lips pursed. She set the bowl and lantern on the wooden table next to the bed, sticking her freed hands to her hips. "Ye all right, Keira dear?"

No, I was not all right. Nothing would ever be truly all right again.

Not real.

Not real.

Before I could spit that at the ghost, another burst of smoke, right next to her. The swirling blackness solidified, the form much taller than Reina.

"Well, hello!" Floppy, honey-brown curls materialized first, blending into bronze skin. The ghost smiled warmly and offered a hand. "We've only met a few times, but I've heard how ye've helped my little girl."

I'd seen that smile, spiked with shark teeth. That same hand, reaching out, ready to drag me into the deep. His skin, pale and bloated and fish-bitten. His large frame, falling from a mast, a dark spot against my soul.

Lochlan.

My first kill. My deepest regret.

Not real. Not real.

Real.

Real.

Real.

"No. Not you," I gasped, legs shaking beneath me. Lochlan's brow furrowed as his hand fell along with his smile, so similar to Reagan when she was deep in thought. I waited for the dream to shift, for his grin to become a growl, for he and his wife to tear me apart or crumple dead to the ground.

This time, the phantoms just stared back, looking at me like *I* was the ghost. Perhaps I was, only a shadow of who I'd been before.

The Otherworld sees us as we see ourselves.

"Keira, this is real." Reina took a hesitant step closer, rubbing my arm gently. Her palm was colder than death, but as cracked and work-worn as I remembered it. "I'm here."

I opened my mouth to say something, my hand, still black with my mark, reaching out to touch her. But before I could, the room plunged into shadows, darkness eating at the lanternlight for a long moment. I screamed as the mist took form, my nightmares corporeal in front of me.

Three bodies materialized, all burly and strong, wearing the same dark, stiff waistcoats instead of their normally bright colors.

"Wow, you were right, she's so grown now," the tallest demon said as he nudged the one next to him. He wore my cousin Owen's soft smile as his disguise. His freckles were exactly as I remembered, the ponytail of red hair just as neat as he always kept it. It had been nearly four years since I'd seen him, but the Otherworld had captured the memory better than I could have. "I've missed you, Shrimpy."

The second phantom nudged my cousin back, Roland's voice just as grating as it had been in life, his boyish smirk still so out of place on his wrinkled visage. "I'll tell ye, she's the best Captain I'd ever sailed under. Clever girl somehow managed to tame my grump of a son."

"Well, your son tamed my mess of a brother, so we're all even," Owen said, and the two shared a laugh, Reina's soft giggle joining the chorus. It was a gut-wrenching trick, but not the cruelest. Not the one that brought ugly, burning tears to the corner of my eye.

It was the third imposter that held my gaze, that made my heart ache with impossible sadness. He stroked his salt-and-ginger beard, one wiry eyebrow raised, looking at me with a gaze that always meant business. Instead of laughing with the phantoms of my family, he leaned on the corner of the bed, patting the soft blue duvet next to him. "Sit down, Keira girl. We need to chat."

"Papa." I stood frozen for another breath. I wanted so desperately for him to be real. The man that always made it right. The man whose advice had cradled me on my darkest nights. I took a staggering step toward him.

Not real, not real, not real.

Real.

Real.

Real.

Real in the specificity of his freckles, real in the way his left shoulder tilted higher than his right, the result of an old injury. Real in the way he fiddled with the edge of his coat sleeve, even though it was the wrong color, black instead of brilliant blue.

Papa's lips pulled down, his famous disappointed frown so perfect. *So real.* "We don't have a lot of time, but Reina made sure the little girl tending to ye will be occupied for a while."

Reina straightened out her dark skirt, brushing off the stiff fabric with a smirk. "Cythie is handling a very stubborn stain."

"Poor little girl," Roland chuckled again, the sound like a ship bottom scraping the rocks. "Lochlan, yer wife is an evil genius."

Lochlan grinned and puffed his chest out, tucking Reina to his side. "She was your sister first."

No, not Lochlan and Reina and Roland. Shadows and mist. Demons and delusions, wearing their faces. Illusions, manifestations of my twisted imagination, dreams that I wanted to desperately be reality.

The Otherworld sees us as we see ourselves.

Tonight, they didn't torture me. They were here to comfort me, a desperate girl's need for love fueling the forgery of my family. But sweet as it was, it was a lie, an empty likeness. It would never be enough, never be *real*.

"This isn't real," I choked out, my throat closing over. "Please."

"Keira girl, listen closely." Papa rose and took a few broad steps toward me, sunset gaze clouded with worry. He squeezed my shoulder, the sensation *so real* as he smiled. "We are here. All of us. Here for you."

"It can't...I won't–" The air rushed from my lungs, my legs wobbling beneath me. I wanted it to stop, for the daydreams to disappear back into dust. Wanted the dead to stay dead, wanted my mind to stop meddling with my memory. My heart threatened to burst, too fragile to withstand the torment.

Not real, not real.

Death.

Death.

Death.

Another flash of black, the smoke so close it nearly filled my lungs. A hand appearing first, reaching out, reaching toward me...

A sharp slap straight across the face. My cheek stung, but the world righted itself as the pain grounded me.

Pain was real. Pain was a reminder of my body, of its weakness. Of its vitality.

"Feel real yet?" Finna tossed her crimson hair over her shoulder, smug smile crawling across her perfect porcelain face. "If not, I'm happy to do it again."

I stared silently at my cousin as she folded her arms. She was not the fragile, frantic woman I'd last seen. Not the bleeding, bawling mess that haunted my every nightmare. No, this Finna stood straight, her chin tilted with her signature brand of demure defiance. This Finna watched me like a countess, subtle strength and cleverness her crown.

This was the Vixen Queen I remembered. Finna, not sent to comfort or console, but to command. Her jade eyes stared at me with candied contempt, daring me to question her corporeality. Insisting that I see her as more than an imitation.

"Still petty, even in death." Owen shook his head before pulling his sister back. "Sorry, Shrimpy, I tried to teach her right."

Finna shrugged her eldest brother off, not shifting her gaze from me. "It helped, didn't it?"

I scanned the faces of my family. Lochlan and Reina, holding each other tight, both watching me with concern. Owen and Roland, flanking Finna, benevolent and obedient as always, waiting for a task. Finna herself, sporting a full-lipped smile as shadows danced in her gaze.

Papa, biting his lip to hold back a laugh, waiting for me to catch on, as always.

Real.

Real.

Real.

My heart swelled, light threatening to burst from my fingertips, joy seizing my limbs.

There were so many things I wanted to say. Apologies that'd strangled me for years. Questions that taunted me for ages. Thank yous that I'd carried my whole life.

"You're—" I stuttered, too afraid to speak any of my truths aloud. "You're all—"

"Real as the gills on a fish, aye," Papa let go of the laugh he was holding, the sound like waves slapping against the hull of a ship. He reached out, stroking my cheek with his whiskey-and-wood scented palm, rubbing the sore spot Finna left. "Don't worry. We're gonna get ye out of this place. The rest of ye, clear off. I'd like a word with my Keira girl."

6

Plans and Parting Gifts

RONAN

When I was still a deckhand on his ship, Captain Cedric used to say there were only a few moments in life that turned a boy into a man. Said it wasn't gradual, like the way the shore slowly dissolved into the sea, one grain of sand at a time.

"Only a handful of moments, boy," he'd say, his hazel eyes a mirror to the sunset as he stared out at the horizon. "That's all ye get, a few choices, and suddenly yer grown, and those choices define who ye are. Those actions speak louder than any words ye'd ever say."

"How will I know when those moments come?" I'd ask, hanging on his every word, but still absolutely lost to their meaning.

"Ye'll know, Ronan. Ye'll know."

Standing on the docks of West End in Cerridwen City, supervising nearly two dozen crewmembers as they busied themselves, I knew this was one of those moments. After today, after this choice, none of us could ever be the same. When I returned–if I returned at all–there would be nothing left of the boy who loved stories, of the deckhand that clung to his Captain's words. No, there would only be the man left, the Captain carrying the weight of his own choices.

But he'd also have his wife. His child. His future.

The massive shadows of the *Madyn*, the *Ddraig*, and the *Ceffyl Dwr* cast us in darkness, the early morning sun just yawning past the horizon line. When she rose, we'd be off, three ships headed for three different ports, carrying the weight of the world in our cargo holds.

One ship headed to hell itself.

Ellian stood beside me, a nervous shake in his leg. Neither of us spoke, content in our quiet as we watched the crews load the ships, the last details of our desperate plan weaving together. We'd been as careful as we could, and now there was no more waiting. No more backhanded deals done in dark alleys, no more coded letters read by lanternlight. We'd run out of time and luck.

"Is there anything else ye need, *Captain?*" Greyson Leary approached us as my third crew finished packing the *Ddraig* first, wincing as he addressed my title. I knew it was a reflex from the life he lived before. He straightened out his gray long coat, stuffing his pride back into its expensive pockets. My father shuffled behind him, his own crimson threads sitting haphazard on his shoulder.

Two men, making choices that didn't suit their fancy, but instead served a greater good.

"No, thank you, Grey. Your sacrifice is much appreciated." I clapped him on the shoulder, offering a genuine smile. Once upon a time, on a dock much like this one, I might have instead parried with a smirk and a snide remark about Connor's hand up his arse.

We'd both lost too much to this war to give a shit anymore.

"What good is a ship without a crew?" Greyson echoed my thoughts with a humorless laugh. "Besides, I'm for anything that puts those fuckers back into the abyss they came from."

All of his men had died in the fall of Porthladd, Connor's cronies turning on him the second Finna was gone. All he had left was his crest and his cutter. A ship without a crew, a flag without a cause. He rolled back his shoulders, vengeance fueling the burning embers in his amber eyes.

I nodded, the beast in my middle incensed by his anger. His pain. We were both hungry for blood. For revenge. For the true monsters to pay for the lives lost with their own.

"That's the plan." I stuffed my hands in my pockets, hoping he couldn't smell the bluff. In truth, there wasn't a plan, not really. Just a hunch. A dangerous attempt driven by desire and desperation.

There was no *Ddraig Aur*, no *Bren Ariannad* granting wishes to wayward whisperers. There were no miracles, no legends driving us forward. We were emptyhanded and unarmed, actors playing pretend on a grand stage. Plans and prayers were for people with the privilege of hope. Of time.

I had something more potent. I had purpose, and no soul left to sacrifice. Nothing left to lose, everything to gain. To take back.

Ellian shot me a sideways glare, like my partner in crime could smell my thoughts. Perhaps he could, his shifter's nose almost as sharp as my siren scent. He cleared his throat, his Councilman's mask the only disguise we had left. "I sent another letter to Councilwoman Tommins in Pysgodd. She knows you both are coming with the supplies, and that the *Ceffyl* is coming up in a week with more from Ir'de."

Leary nodded, offering some overdue respect for his former colleague. My father, however, hadn't learned that trick yet.

"Aye, *Councilman*. The *Ddraig* knows her way around," Reese grumbled, crossing his arms. He'd been obedient, the serpent subdued and charmed. But he was still a Mathonwy, still made of venom and vulgarity. He raised an eyebrow, cobra fangs still sharp despite their disuse. "But do we have to take the sea-witch?"

I rolled my eyes, my inner dragon huffing smoke. "Neirida has contacts on all the islands, and she's a talented smuggler. Let her help you. Besides, Vala will be on the *Ddraig* too to help keep an eye on her."

A Branwen, accompanying Reese Mathonwy on the *Ddraig*, to escort a siren smuggler and supplies to Pysgodd. In another time, another life, it might have been the most ridiculous story I could tell. But now, it was cold reality, and I had no concern to spare for the ghosts of a feud long finished.

"Aye, aye, I hear ye." My father held up his hands in false surrender, the scar over his eye crinkling as he squinted at me. "I'll just sleep with my eyes open so the witches can't dice me up and sell me at the market."

My patience wavered, his sarcasm scraping beneath my scales. Perhaps a younger version of myself might have laughed along, might have simpered and snickered at the snide strike. I had no love for Neirida. She was the least agreeable of the sirens, and selfish as she was sneaky. But she was also useful, her skill unmatched. My father was only as good as his ship, and his ability to shut his trap.

"Be safe, Captain Mathonwy." I brushed past him before my fangs poked out.

"Come back home, boy." He grabbed my elbow, his voice low. For a moment, I could see the worry in his wrinkles, the kindred concern beneath the conman. His throat bobbed. "That's not a request, it's an order."

I softened, fangs retreating. I was a son before I was a siren. A boy before a beast. My father had been a pain in the arse, but he stayed. He *tried.* "Take care of yourself, Pa."

I didn't wait for a reply before setting toward the next ship. Time slipped through my fingers faster than sand, and I had none left to waste. Ellian followed at my heels, nodding a pleasant goodbye to my father before scurrying after me.

The *Madyn* was the smallest cutter in the harbor, but her sleek gray paint stood sharp against the worn wooden dock. The *Ceffyl* was faster, but we needed something more easily handled by an inexperienced crew. The *Madyn* was a tame mare in comparison to the wild, unbridled stallion of the *Ceffyl*'s rigging. The sirens were not sailors, despite their scales. I'd be the only shipman worth their salt on the vessel, a part I never imagined myself playing.

Ye'll know, Ronan. Ye'll know.

I'd also never imagined the inhabitants of *Hiraeth* abandoning their homes to sail at my side. And yet, they were my only hope, inexperienced and out of place as they were.

The sirens gathered at the base of the gangway, flopping around like fish out of water as they scrambled to load the ship. Griffin and Rhett had pitched in earlier, already stowing the heavy cargo. But still, there were sacks of silk and bundles of Lyr-knew-what to be carried, full of souvenirs from their excursion in the realms of men. Marina, saucy as ever, brought a wardrobe fit for any weather, featuring the most expensive Ir'desian silk and Pysgoddian fur that money and her crimson smile could buy. Nelle sorted through enough dried herbs and tinctures to cure half of the Deyrnas if she needed to, a feat I desperately hoped she wouldn't have to attempt. And Laureli had seven bags to herself, a feral smile on her face as she took inventory of all the poultices and enchanted items she'd snagged from the best shops in Hud.

They packed as if they'd gone on holiday. Like they were about to set out for another.

As if they planned on living long enough to keep their belongings.

"Now, remember everything I taught you, all right?" Nelle reminded Gennevieve, tucking the girl's blue tunic into the waistband of her trousers as she rambled. "What is the best remedy for nausea?"

Genni sighed, swatting Nelle's hands away. "Peppermint leaves or ginger root."

Viperous sadness squeezed my chest as I watched the two. They weren't kin, but they were family, two sisters sewn together by the tides of Fate. And here I was, tearing at that seam, asking them to sacrifice their safety and stability for a chance at mine.

The boy who washed up on *Hiraeth*'s shore a few years ago, the boy who loved stories, might have felt guilty. Might have tried to weave a tale together to make them smile, to numb the pain of loss and regret. The man searching for his wife, the Siren Prince she'd made, did not. I felt only gratitude, wrapped in my vicious greed.

"Thank you again, Genni." I ruffled her blonde fringe. Her round cheeks reddened, nose wrinkling in a sweet smile. "For keeping my kin safe."

"Will you stop fussing over her?" Marina whined as she sauntered up the gangway, an enormous silk sack strapped to her back. She stuck a hand to her hip. "You should be more worried for us! What if the whiskey runs out on our way?"

"Don't even joke like that, Marina." Cassryn snapped her head up, pulled from a conversation with her twin over the details of a chart, stone face set and reinforced with steel. Still, her skin paled. "I'm already sick to my gills."

Willow snickered. "A siren that's afraid of sailing, who would have thought."

"I'm not afraid of sailing, you twit, I'm afraid of sailing *sober*." Cassryn snatched the chart from her twin's hands before storming up the gangway. "Keep talking and you'll eat scales."

I bit back a laugh, the last remnants of hope swelling in my stomach. The sirens were not sailors, but they were survivors. They'd all endured their own personal trials and tribulations, and had made *Hiraeth*, the land of the lost and wild, their home. We might be headed to our deaths, fools chasing phantoms on the word of a phony, but at least we'd be entertained. If we were to greet our demise on this voyage, it vanquished the edge of nervousness in my veins to know it would be with a laugh and a belly full of whiskey.

"All sirens on deck," Siobhan commanded, voice carrying across the harbor. The crew fell silent, noting their heavily armed first mate with the regard and respect she deserved. She was not a sailor, but Siobhan knew how to run a tight ship. "Except Neirida and Genni."

The laughter dissipated from the air, no more time left to banter over booze or bicker. This chapter of the story had closed, and there were no lines left for any of us to stall before the climax.

The sirens sucked in a collective breath, a unified chorus taking their last moment of harmony before fracturing into their own melodies. Eyes darted to each other, stares swimming with the things none of them had the salt left to say. The goodbyes they would swallow rather than speak into existence.

Tears lined Gennevieve's eyes, turquoise shimmering blue with sapphire-strong resolve. She grabbed the worn leather bag Nelle had packed for her, the little healer's first tool kit, strapping it to herself like a lifeline in a storm. "I'll keep everyone here safe, I promise."

"We know, little duck." Laureli stepped forward, offering Gennevieve a small, perfectly round orb the size of an orange. She folded it into the younger girl's hands, a seed planted in soft earth. "Hang on to this, and we'll see you soon."

The beast in my middle winced as the soft moment sliced through my center, reminding me of pain I hadn't parted with. Of another young girl whose bright eyes used to gaze at me with wonder. Of the hurt I'd be leaving behind.

Who are you going to get killed this time, hmm?

"Get the ladies settled," I mumbled to Ellian, turning away from the sirens and toward the ship that tugged at one of my last, frayed heartstrings. One I could never cut, even if I wanted to be untethered to the tiny tyrant. "I'll escort Genni and see the rest off."

"Sure thing, Captain," Ellian grunted, shooting me a curious look before huffing up the gangway. He didn't need wolf ears to hear the ulterior motive in my tone.

"Come on, furball." Siobhan nudged his side as she hustled onto the ship. "Let's see how good you are at herding."

I tugged Genni's slim arm, tearing the guppy from the group before I lost my resolve. With one last long stare, she turned, waddling after my long-legged steps to keep up.

Captain Cedric used to say a few choices made a boy a man. A man didn't run from his little cousin, hiding behind his scales to avoid her scorn. A man didn't leave without saying goodbye, even if it was met with more guilt.

I would no longer be the little boy that survived off of stories and secrets. I would choose to be the man my family needed. To be *more*, as my wife made me.

I led Gennevieve up the gangway of the *Ceffyl*, relishing the familiar creak of the wood as we boarded. If this were to be my last moment as one of its crew, I'd face it with the courage I knew Keira had carved into my scales.

Gennevieve planted a peck on my cheek before running across the deck and into the cabin below, presumably to settle her things and let herself cry in private.

"Ahh, look who came crawling back to us." Griffin watched me board from his perch on the portside rail, Trouble already in the tilt of his head as he assessed me. But I could smell the sourness of fear and uncertainty in his scent, the concern his confidence masked. "Are you backing out already, Captain?"

A wish, not a criticism.

The rest of the crew stopped their tasks. Rhett dropped the heavy crate he held, Saeth going still as steel in the rigging, Vian peeking over the edge of the crow's nest, Tarran casually leaning against the mop in his hand instead of scrubbing the deck like he should have been.

A wish shared. One last spark of hope, fizzling on dying embers.

I wished I could say yes. Wished it were that easy, to stay, to somehow summon Keira another way. Wished I could be the boy that fired back with a smart remark, wished I could tell my crew it was all an elaborate ruse, another one of the Sea Snake's tricks.

But a wish was as useful as a bandage on a bullet hole. It was a comfort, but did little more than contain the bleeding. It did nothing to heal the festering wound underneath, nothing to stitch the skin back together.

I had my role to play, my choices to make. And Griffin had his.

"You're the Captain now, Griffin." I saluted my brother in arms, my fist over my heart. "Keep them safe until I get back, aye?"

Griffin blinked twice at me, sitting up straighter, his mask of indifference slipping as I let mine fall. For a whisper of a moment, we both let the boys we once were say farewell before we had to welcome in the men we would become. He let loose a long, heavy breath, and saluted me back. "Aye, brother. I will."

Rhett wrapped a strong arm over Griffin's shoulder, a rare smile hanging awkwardly on his face. He rolled his metallic eye. "Don't worry, it's just a quick stop in Ir'de for us, then on to Pysgodd. I'm here to make sure none of them cause too much trouble."

My chuckle was genuine, the last laugh offered to whatever gods would protect my kin. "Then it's you I'm really worried about."

Saeth slid down the mizzenmast, the wraith's expression drawn. She was made of metal, but there was mist in her eye, the last smoky remnants of the girl she'd melted down to forge her blade. "Bring her home, okay?"

"And the rest of them, too." Tarran threw down his mop and stood behind his twin. Like sunshine glinting off steel, the two of them together shone somehow brighter. "We need you all safe."

Vian dangled fully over the ledge of the crow's nest, long black hair waving like a flag. "The wind wishes you luck."

Reflective hope billowed beneath my breast, my heart swelling with pride. I might have been a boy playing pretend, a silly storyteller chasing substance, but these people, my crew, my family...they were mere people playing the games of gods, but they would not be puppets. They weren't children waiting for choices to be made for them. The weavers of destiny, they forged their own fate, with steel and steadfast loyalty their only weapons.

They didn't need me as a Captain. The world needed *them*.

"I'm not very good with goodbyes." I stuffed my hands in my pockets, as if it covered the raw vulnerability in my voice. "But I wanted to thank you all, for—"

"Don't talk to us like you're not coming back." Saeth cut me off. "This isn't goodbye."

Griffin puffed out his chest, tapping Truth's hilt where it rested against his back. "We'll see you soon, brother."

No, it wasn't goodbye. I would not fail. I couldn't.

"Aye," I managed, despite the final 'see you later' stuck in my throat. I looked to the cabin door, to where I could smell her hiding, her rose-scented rage clear as crystal. "Where is...?"

I trailed off, still too much of a coward to say her name, one last attempt to delay the inevitable heartbreak. The crew cast their eyes down, weight shifting as the air scented with regret and reconciliations left unrequited.

"She won't come up." Vian graciously saved me as he somersaulted down the rigging, lithe body somehow landing upright on the deck. The sprite stood tall, sorrow in his dark eyes. "I tried. I'm sorry."

Though I'd anticipated it, the truth still stung like a bullet to the gut. I couldn't push her, couldn't beg for her forgiveness. Not when I didn't deserve it. Yet somehow, there was still a part of me, part of the boy who loved stories, that hoped this one might have a different ending. That perhaps I could die the hero, not the villain.

"No, don't be sorry, Vian, it's not your fault. Tell her I love her, all right?"

The boy nodded twice. "She knows."

"You should go. We're wasting the tide." Saeth cleared her throat, her sharp tone a salvation. But her coldness wasn't cruelty; it was kindness. It was better than the pity I could smell in everyone's quickened pulse.

I took one last long look at my people, at the enemies turned brothers, at the cousins turned confidants. I couldn't care less about the rest of the Deyrnas, about the world I was leaving behind. But I would sell my scales to fix it if it meant repaying them for their goodness.

I tore my gaze away before the boy inside could linger any longer. I needed the beast if I was going to *survive* for them. "Right then, I'm off."

I made it halfway down the gangway before a fall breeze carrying the scent of roses stopped me in my tracks, followed by an equally sweet soprano voice that called to my most sincere parts. "Ronan! Wait!"

I swiveled on my heel, too fast, like a dog chasing its tail. I caught my balance as I stared up at her, catching my snake's mask before it could fall off entirely. "Yes?"

Reagan panted at the top of the plank, fists clenched to her sides, her face made of marble as she went to war with herself. With the parts of her that hated me, and the parts that were still the little girl who used to sit on my knee to savor my stories. Choosing which parts were in control.

No, Reagan's choice to remain a child had been stolen from her. Only fourteen, she held the weight of womanhood on her shoulders, her girlhood crushed under the mountain of grief. Grief I had done nothing to help heal.

Sucking in a breath, I braced myself for impact, for whatever final fire she'd fling at me. A cruelty I no doubt deserved.

Her voice was soft when it finally found its footing. "Don't forget Airid."

Surprise stole my breath, the air rushing from my sails. "I—" I stuttered, the Serpent Prince's suavity abandoning me entirely. I took a stumbling step forward. "I have time for a quick story, if that's—"

"No, I just mean—" she interrupted, voice wobbly as my confidence. Tears welled in her eyes, refreshing as rain against dry, cracked soil. "If you want to get to Keira, you need to raise some hell. Show the Dark God what you're made of. Make him regret it."

Ye'll know, Ronan. Ye'll know.

Fortified by my cousin's kindness, by her *courage*...I knew without any sliver of a doubt. For Reagan, for Keira...there would be no going back. No retreating to the comfortable confines of who I once was.

I was no longer a boy, no longer a Captain. I was a hell-bringer, a harbinger of the end, fueled by the potent potion of hope and hatred combined. By my cousin's choice to love despite her loss.

For her, I would kill the Serpent Prince, and from his ashes, rise the *Ddraig Aur*.

"Aye, little dragon. That I can promise you."

The true dragon stared down at me over the bridge of her nose, her proud chin tilted skyward. She folded her arms, the white snake tattoo coiling around her bicep a permanent reminder. "And then bring her back. I need to have a word with her."

I opened my mouth to respond, but she whipped around and stalked off, back onto the *Ceffyl*, to the crew, without another word.

I let myself mourn for a moment, mourn the soul-crushing hug I might never get, mourn the little girl that might never look up to me again.

Then I set off toward the *Madyn*, ready to raise the dead.

7

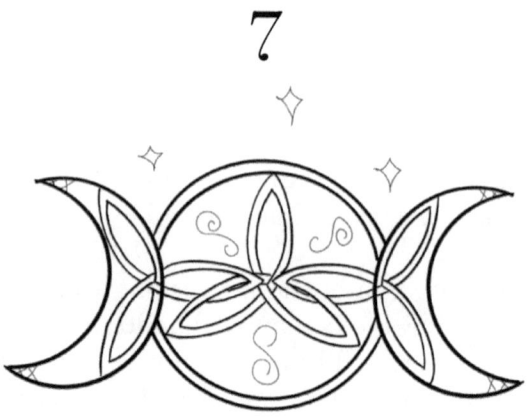

Fathers and Faults

KEIRA

Misty tears blurred my eyes as I stared at my father, my voice strangled by the emotion in my throat.

Papa. The man who taught me to sail and think and love. Sitting on the edge of my bed, like he had every night when I was a girl, to tell me stories and teach me lessons that would fuse to my very bones.

He had the same look in his eyes tonight.

Real.

Real.

Real.

He patted the seat next to him. "I'd say you look like ye've seen a ghost, but I suppose ye have."

My feet carried themselves to my seat, the obedient little girl in me biting at the bit for another chance to make my father proud.

Not that I'd earned it. In the years since we'd parted, I'd become someone my father would've despised. A wretched, wicked monster that had failed nearly every task I'd been given.

The Otherworld sees us as we see ourselves.

Would my father see the same thing?

"It doesn't feel real." The admission left my lips unbidden. I'd never been able to lie to my father, and it seemed the years apart had done nothing to improve the skill. Even if he was just an illusion. "None of it does."

I looked at the floorboards, avoiding the all-knowing glint in his gaze.

"Ye said the same thing back when Eleri Mathonwy died, ye know." He cleared his throat, settling into the routine we both knew so well. Teacher and student, parent and child. "It was the first funeral ye'd ever been to, and ye held on the whole time, didn't cry even a single drop. Ye were strong for yer friend that day."

Vague flashes of memory stirred in my mind's eye. I remembered the halls of Mathonwy Manor, decked in black, as we gathered in somber silence. Remembered the scent of ash on Traeth Beach later that day, as the funeral pyre floated off to sea. Remembered Ronan's cries as he bade farewell to his mama.

Remembered feeling nothing at all.

"Is she here? His ma?" My voice sounded far away, still stuck in the memory.

Papa nodded. "Aye, but she's faded now."

At that, my attention snapped back to the present. "Faded?"

Papa stroked his beard, a frown pulling his features. "Like Cythie. She doesn't remember who she was before. It happens over time, apparently. It takes a strong will to stay present."

For a moment, I let myself imagine the rapture of forgetting. Was I strong enough to stay as myself, to remain as Keira Branwen-Mathonwy as the NightMare of the Four Seas?

The Otherworld sees us as we see ourselves.

But I already was nothing, a faded after-image of the girl I'd used to be.

"I don't feel strong anymore." The tears I didn't shed in life before stung the back of my eyes. I'd long abandoned the ability to quell them. "I'm sorry."

Papa patted my back, a chuckle shaking his frame. "Strength isn't always about holdin' it in, Keira girl. Sometimes, it's about lettin' it out."

At that, I looked up, something unlocking within me.

I'd always hidden behind walls of stone and salt and steel, my emotions enemies to be fought and forced into submission. Only rage had been allowed an outlet, the guard to the prison of pain in my heart.

But I'd already made my final sail beyond the veil, and there was nothing left to protect. No duty to carry out, no vulnerability to shield. No identity.

I was tired. So tired.

Tired of choking it down and wrestling for control. Tired of hiding and holding. I'd let go once before, in the *Hiraethean* river, and come out stronger. I'd drowned my walls and risen reborn.

It was time to let go. Time to move on, if not in rebirth, in Death.

I flung myself into Papa's arms, letting the little girl free of her imprisonment. Her tears stained rivers across my face, water ready to cleanse, to forget. To forgive.

To fade.

"I miss him. Miss home. I've missed you, too. So much."

Papa wiped the tears from my cheeks with his stiff sleeve. "I'm right here now. I'm sorry Aidan and I left ye to fend with this mess all on yer own."

My stomach did a flip like I was a new sailor again. I'd seen Aidan several times in my illusions, his bullet wound oozing black blood, the same shade scarring my arm as I accepted the god's curse...

"Is he here?" I swallowed hard, not knowing if I could face the kin I'd killed. "Aidan?"

Papa shrugged, taking my hand in his. The rope-burned pads of his fingers were somehow still gentle, mooring me back to the bedroom. "No one has seen him. Or Weylin or Donnall."

I exhaled a breath of relief. I was just as much at fault as my uncles for how our family's name had been sullied. They'd betrayed the Branwen crest, but I had too. Still, I was the true coward, unable to look them in the eyes. Unable to admit my wrongdoings to their faces.

We're all monsters. Some of us just hide it better.

"But enough about us old farts," Papa continued, ever the Captain leading us on, not letting me linger in my own self-pity for too long. I blinked at him as a smile tugged at his features, the expression plucked straight from a memory. "I'm sure yer dyin' to get back to that lad of yers and to go start yer family right."

Again, parts of me warred. I'd spent the last—however long I was here—pining over a future I'd never see. Regretting the past I hadn't made the most of.

But I was tired, so tired. So *faded*, my edges blurred by the blackness of Death's shadows.

Ronan.

Ronan.

Ronan.

Death.

Death.

Death.

My heartbeat slowed, tired too, as I sighed, "But there is no going back, Papa."

No, there was no use pretending like I had a choice. Imagining a different outcome. That would be the most ridiculous delusion of all, more than my dead family members somehow made real, more than the conjured nightmares of my past that tortured my mind.

"Maybe not fer a mere mortal," Papa mused, a lilt in his tone that used to mean adventures on the horizon. His hazel stare bore beneath my skin, Captain Cedric in full form tonight. "But that's why I have a job fer my good luck charm, if yer up for it, Captain."

A tempest of emotion swirled through me, the breath catching in my chest.

Papa called me *Captain*. Needed *me* to help him, instead of the other way around for once. I was a smudge on the Branwen name, but Papa still looked at me like I was the center of his universe, still called me his lucky charm and let me fight at his side.

I managed a nod, words evaporating from my mouth.

Some Captain I was.

"Arawn wants something from ye. Find out what." Papa's crescent smile matched the moonlight seeping through the curtains. He twisted his whiskers as he spoke, the old sailor spinning his plan. "I've heard about him, from yer Ma. She painted a very…dark picture, one I'm sure might have been a bit exaggerated thanks to her personal problems with the fellow. But whether or not she's right about his heart, there are things we've all learned here that aren't adding up."

Papa had always been my compass. A needle pointing north, even when the rest of the world was topsy-turvy. And like always, he was right. Nothing here made sense. Nothing felt *real*, except for him at my side. His unvanquishable presence, strong and bright even in the decay and dismay of the Otherworld.

It was hard to trust anything here. Anyone.

But Papa had never failed me. Never led me astray.

Even his shadow was trustworthy.

"Tell me more."

Papa stood, his lopsided shoulders accentuated as he tucked his hands behind his back. His gaze drifted far away, like a Huddian fortune-teller reading a crystal ball as his mind sorted through the details.

"Yer the first he's ever interacted with directly. He doesn't like seeing his servants, makes us all do our work cloaked in shadows so he can pretend he's alone." I hung on his every word, just like the little girl who used to wrap herself around his legs and let him drag her around the *Ceffyl*. "And he makes no secret that he's been interested in ye for a long time. He's mentioned yer name for years, before even I got here. But no one knows why. He keeps it all private."

My stomach clenched.

You're not a prize. You're the key to paradise.

I don't know what I did to earn Death's attention. But I'd seen it for myself in the inky pools of his eyes, in the icy possession of his touch. And when his power called to mine, when the shadows in his veins coaxed forward those slivers of moonlight from me…

There was a sick, sad part of me that craved the attention.

"He told me he wants to train me…to teach me to use my powers." I swallowed the lump in my throat and watched Papa's black boots worry tracks into the floorboards.

He nodded as he paced, ideas racing behind the hazel of the mapmaker's eyes. "That's a good start. I dunno what he wants to gain from teaching ye, but my guess is it isn't good. But, at the very least, it will give ye a chance to get stronger, and to get closer. It's better to know yer enemy."

My enemy.

The Dark God was my jailor. He'd used his puppets to drown me in the Otherworld, had trapped me in ice and snow and a sorrow of my own making for what felt like weeks. Months, maybe.

My enemy.

But then again, he'd fed me and clothed me in the finest satin imaginable. He'd held my hand and whispered promises of paradise in my ear, had given me a choice in how I spent my eternity.

My hands clenched in the soft-as-feathers fabric of the blue duvet, another kindness from the king of cruelty.

"He's not…" My voice wobbled as the admission seared my tongue. "He's not what I imagined."

Arawn was an enigma. A manipulative monster one moment, then a lonely-hearted hermit the next. The ice of his touch could both freeze and caress. The darkness of his stare could menace and soothe.

But was he my *enemy*?

Papa stopped his pacing for a moment to stroke his beard as he assessed me. I knew that look like I knew my own name, the careful, contemplative reproach of a father-made-legend. My skin crawled under its gravity, his judgment more important to me than I'd ever wanted to admit.

The Otherworld sees us as we see ourselves.

How would Papa see me?

"No, it seems he defies all expectations." He exhaled after a long moment, his grin matching the uneven slant of his shoulders. "Except for with ye. With *ye*, he lets down his walls, ever so slightly. Even if he thinks he's in control…ye can get inside that head of his, and get something out of it."

There he was, Captain Cedric Branwen, ever the brilliant businessman, his crest and contract the small victories he swore by. There was always an angle to be worked, always a negotiation to win.

What do ye want first, and how do ye get it?

"I don't even know what I want," I answered aloud, letting the truth tumble through my fingertips for the first time ever. My goals had always aligned with his, Papa the compass and I the wheel that turned us to wherever he pointed. But I had no one left to steer me. No motivation or desire outside of the sleep that called to me, the mattress I sat on begging me to dive into its depths. To rest.

Papa kneeled in front of me, meeting my faraway gaze. The judgment in his was softened by something pure, a love that predated the Otherworld itself. A selflessness only a parent had the capacity for.

"I'll tell ye what *I* want fer ye. I want yer freedom, Keira girl. For ye and my little granddaughter." He patted my knee, mist gathering in his lashes, ready to spill. I'd only seen my father cry a handful of times in my life, and it was never any less shocking. My throat constricted as he spoke, his words warbled by the tears he held back. "Or at least a way to free the Deyrnas from Locasta. There are Branwens still above that need us. Need *ye*."

I stayed silent, guilt and greed fighting for purchase in my chest. I wanted my family to be safe more than anything. Ronan and Griffin, Saeth and Vian and Reagan and the others...they deserved happiness beyond a shadow of a doubt, and I knew they still faced threats in the world above that could darken that. I'd taken Connor with me, but Locasta still lived. Still plotted and puppeted, all in the Dark God's name.

My enemy.

But I didn't have a life to sacrifice for them anymore. My lease on martyrdom had expired when I sent myself to this icy grave. And even though I still breathed in the world below, I had no power over what happened above.

And I was tired.

So, so tired.

Papa took my silence for submission, soldiering on with the details of his mutiny against Death. "I don't know if Arawn knows what his devotees are doing in his name...but I do know he didn't keep Connor around. He eviscerated him, body and soul. There is Death, and then there is true absence, Keira. Whether that was to protect ye, or to silence him from speaking to the rest of us about what he knew..."

I blinked, my heartrate doubling. "Connor is *gone?*"

"Not even a shadow of him left." Papa nodded, darkness creeping across his expression. "You have a mighty task, Keira girl. This is no small victory. This could mean the whole war."

Connor Yorath was not just dead, but gone. Disappeared into nothingness by the God of Death himself.

The thought made the hungry, primordial thing in my middle swirl with a sick glee, a victory over a man who'd brought me nothing but sadness. But a dread crept along my spine, sending shivers up it.

If Arawn could erase Connor, could he do the same to me? To my family, servants to his ruined estate, if he found out we'd been working against him?

A darker thought I'd never voice aloud followed it.

Did I *want* him to erase me? To finally finish what Connor had started and silence me?

Keira, you're pregnant.

Not real.

Not real.

I inhaled as the air thinned around me, Papa's warm hand on my knee the only anchor. The only *real*, as it always was.

"How do I know this isn't a trap?" I cried, my armor slipping again. I wasn't the NightMare of the Four Seas anymore, wasn't a saltborn sailor who lived by her sword. No, I was just a confused, lonely little girl desperate for her father's approval. Begging for him to save her from the nightmare instead. "How do I know you're not just a delusion meant to get my hopes up and torture me?"

At that, Papa laughed, the sound plucked straight from my childhood, and all doubts vanished. Even in the worst of my nightmares, that laugh had never been replicated, too bright and real to mimic. This was the man who kissed every scraped knee and soothed every heartache. The man who chased bugs from my bedroom and cleared the shadows from my worried head. Papa stood and stuck his hands to his hips. "How do ye know the sky is blue and that grass is green? Have a little faith, kid. We are real, and we want to help. All of us. We're placing all our bets on ye."

Papa was real. Here, and ready to captain this crew to victory once more. My faith in him was as sure as the blood in my veins running Branwen blue, through and through.

But it wasn't Papa I didn't trust.

The Otherworld sees us as we see ourselves.

No, I was the blemish to this plan, the illusion. Everyone always saw me as my father's daughter, just as strong and sure as he was. But I wasn't. I was his shadow, the absence of light that followed him around and rode his accomplishments as my own. And if I really was pregnant, if this was *real*, the only thing I could ever offer my own child was disappointment.

I hung my head in my hands, everything too heavy to bear. "Everyone that puts their faith in me gets hurt."

The bed shifted as Papa sat again, his arm around me a far more welcome weight. He tucked me to his side, his balmy voice wrapping me up in layers of protection to keep me from crumbling. "Oh, my poor girl. Bad things happen only when ya lose faith in *yerself*. But I'm here to make sure ye don't forget again. I was too hard on ye growing up. I put so much pressure on ye to do the right thing all the time, to follow in my footsteps. And I'm so proud of the woman ye are now, but ye don't see yerself clearly, and that's my fault."

I jerked upright, gratitude and shame playing tug of war with my wayward heart.

Papa was proud of me. Proud of who I was. The thought alone could give me wings and fly me all the way to the distant moon.

But like my mirror, he blamed himself for the mistakes written below my name. For the blood on *my* hands.

"No. No, it's not your fault. I'm the one who stopped living with honor. I'm the one who's been messing it all up—"

"Listen, honor has no place down here," Papa interrupted, his tone low as the nighttime tide. His gaze burrowed holes straight into my soul, reawakening the slumbering thing with his intensity. "There is no code among the dead, no soul to save. Whatever we have to do, this time, we hold no punches. Here, the only thing that matters to me or any of us is *ye*. Yer safety, and yer future. Yer made of sea and stars. Not even Death himself can stop ye."

I inhaled a deep breath, letting the cedar scent and solid presence of him settle the inner child. She could rest now, her part done, her father's favor finally won.

But there were other parts of me that needed tending. Other versions of myself that needed my father's strength to set things right. Maybe one day, I could rest, could sleep in the oblivion of Death's soft mattress and wait for the end of the world.

But today, my Captain had a plan. For me, and for my daughter. And even if I had no honor left to my name, even if I had to lie and steal and cheat death to accomplish my goals, I would see it through.

"Tell me what happens next, Captain."

8

Captains and Confessions

GRIFFIN

I was born to be Trouble's puppet, not the *Ceffyl's* Captain. Sitting on the starboard rail, watching Hud shrink into the horizon as we pointed the old ship north, I knew I was out of my league.

Vian stood next to me, balancing precariously on the ledge as the wind tousled his ebony locks, a slap-happy smile on his face as he finished laying out his master plan. The crew waited quietly in front of us, scraping their jaws off the ground. Tarran stood rigid in front of the cabin, frozen in either shock or awe or both. Saeth leaned against the mizzenmast, feigning disinterest as she used her little knife to pick dirt from her nails, but her sharp eyes flicked to us every few seconds, betraying her intrigue. Rhett rubbed his temples as he sat on the third step up to the gallery, Gennevieve next to him strangling her sewing work like it owed her money. But all four sets of eyes stared at Vian like he was a virgin in a whorehouse. Only Reagan relaxed, a sly smile on her round face as she sat crisscrossed on the wooden deck.

If Vian's scheme proved anything, it was that this little nymph was made of something both wild and wicked. At first, I'd wondered what drew Keira to the wind-whisperer, this shrimp of a boy with no experience and very few skills to name; but now it was clear as fine-made glass.

They were both crazy.

"You're mad," Tarran voiced my thoughts aloud. "You know that? Absolutely nuts."

For once in his gods-forsaken life, my freckled fool of a cousin was right. The plan was nothing short of feverish, the kind of insanity that I'd only seen in men after three too many mugs of ale and a few too many hands lost. That pitiful, powerful place where desperation and dauntlessness mixed.

I'd always flirted with Trouble, but I'd never taken it to bed, not like this. I wasn't brewed with the same ingredients as Keira and Vian, the same potency. I was like cheap ale or an ugly harlot—*available*, but never quite as satisfying as the expensive stuff.

But I'd do the job if you were in a quick fix. Which, as trouble would have it, we were.

Only a god could kill a god.

Any god would do.

So we'd set our course, defying Ronan and Ellian's command to go westward first. Forsaking valuable supplies from Ir'de for a chance at something even more precious. Something worth risking everything for.

"I like it," Saeth said after a long moment as she twirled her newest dagger in her fingers. The setting sun cast her light skin in bronze, emphasizing her sharp, metallic edges. I let loose a breath, somehow lighter with her approval. If Saeth was a whiskey, she'd be top-shelf. "Who came up with it?"

"The wind," Vian boasted, hopping off the ledge and landing lightly. He crossed the sun-soaked deck in a few long strides to offer a hand to Reagan, hoisting her up from where she lounged on the deck. "And Reagan and I helped."

Reagan shrugged, an uncharacteristically sheepish smile spreading across the little dragon's maw. She fiddled with the end of her earth-colored braid. "I had a small hand in it."

'Small,' my left-ass cheek. The moment Vian had burst into Nelle's makeshift workroom, the little dragon had spread her wings. She'd already had the details of our mutiny worked out in her head, her hatred for her cousin a fire in her belly, stoked by Vian's request.

Find the other gods in case Ronan fails to bring back Keira. In case the Deyrnas needs divine intervention to avoid disaster.

It was clear that the God of Mischief had a plan for Reagan Mathonwy, his signature written in the crooked tilt of her grin.

"I want to be on board with this, but..." Rhett ran a hand through his honeyed hair, slick with saltwater and sweat, his shoulders slumping. The old wood creaked as he shifted his weight. "But the *gods*...if they even exist in the first place...they aren't going to just be sitting in the nearest harbor waiting for us."

The wind picked up, a balmy breeze carrying the scent of salt and brine with it. I tilted my head back, letting the warm sun bake my skin. At my back, the familiar ringing buzzed through me, drowning out the discordant screeches of gulls overhead.

Truth.

Rhett was right. If this harebrained scheme was even possible, it wouldn't be easy. If the gods *did* exist, they had a cruel sense of humor. If they had the ability to help, why had they been hiding all this time, watching us rot and ruin everything we touched? If they had the power to stop this madness, to stop Locasta from taking over, to stop people from dying...

Crimson against ivory. Blood against stone.

My hands shook with rage, chasing away the remnants of my worry. If the gods existed, they were either pretenders, or they were cowards. If they had the power to save people, to save my sister, and they didn't...they were heartless. And if they didn't have the power...I'd have no use for them.

Either way, I wanted answers. Wanted justice, for my sister, for Keira, for my bastard father...

Or revenge, if that was what Trouble brought. Perhaps that would be enough to soothe the guilt sloshing around in my gut like the churning waves slapping against the hull of the *Ceffyl*.

Pissed off was better than pity. Anger was better than anguish.

I was not cut to be Captain, but I was forged as a blade. And if it was my duty to mow down the despicables that stood in my crew's way, I'd gladly accept.

"It's worth a shot. Even if the others do find Keira..." My eyes shot to Reagan, to my partner in fury and foolishness. If she needed me to be the first to strike, so be it. "Let's not leave everything to her for once. These gods have been hiding, sitting on their godly asses for centuries, doing nothing. It's time they earned their titles."

"The wind's message was clear," Vian piped up as the ship rocked, the sea breeze hastening into a bold gust.

"Lyr's ass, this again." Tarran hung his head. The yellow-bellied brat was the only sensible one of us left. "What did the 'wind' say, hmm? Did it give us explicit instructions on how to find ancient, unidentified gods and topple an evil regime?"

Vian bobbed his head, leaning back on the rail with the smug swagger of the bird that caught the worm. "Aye. She said, 'Come find me.'"

As the tension on deck shifted, another gale of wind swayed the ship, cold and cutting as it bit my cheeks, sending a shiver down my spine. I prayed to Trouble that it was an invitation, not a warning.

Come find me.

"Lyr's bollocks, we're screwed," Rhett sighed, pinching the bridge of his nose. His silver-and-blue eyes squinted at me, seeing past my suit of armor like he always did, scratching the vulnerable skin beneath. "Griffin, you need to think this through. Say somehow we do find the gods. What if they don't like us barging in and demanding they fight? What if they decide to use their gifts against *us?*"

A stone sank down my stomach.

Fights were easy. Fights, I won. Or at least, I used to.

I was named the Swordsinger for a reason. My swords and I knew battle better than I knew my own ass. But even I had lost against Locasta and her witchcraft. Enchanted swords or not, what good was I against a god?

"We have a Gennevieve." Vian shrugged, nodding to where the blonde girl and her gloved hands nervously sewed ribbons. Poor girl had been a mess since we left port, dissolving into crying fits every other hour. Vian and Tarran took turns settling her, the only task I had no qualms about delegating as Captain. I had no idea how to handle tears, to handle anyone's emotions really, not without a bottle of whiskey or a busty blonde in my bed. And while the little duckling made stew that could rival my mama's, she was little more than a dainty decoration to brighten the ship.

But then again, I'd seen the power that rested in her littlest finger. Seen a grown man dissolve into dust in front of my eyes, seen the fangs that could tear flesh and the claws that could cut deeper than my steel.

Her big blue eyes shot up from her work, her entire frame shaking like a flag during a hurricane. "I—I don't know if my curse works against gods."

"Don't worry, we're here to help you." Tarran offered a lopsided smile, as if she wasn't the most lethal creature on this ship. As if she was a lamb, not a siren, soft and in need of someone to herd her home.

I rolled my eyes out of pity for the poor pissant. He wasn't the first Branwen to be bested by a blond beauty. It was our family's curse, to be wooed into thinking we could grow gills and fight Lyr himself for a single kiss.

I stared off to the horizon, refusing to meet Rhett's penetrating gaze, feeling it burn holes through my britches. "We will deal with how to convince them when we get there."

"Get *where*, again?" Tarran huffed as he plopped down next to Genni, the little shit resigned to follow our fool's chase.

I pulled out Uncle Cedric's compass from my coat pocket. Sunlight glinted off the worn metal, light pooling in my palm like magic. Ronan had entrusted it to me, saying it belonged in Branwen hands. But despite the way my large paws enveloped the old thing easily, I still felt small. Unworthy. I watched the arrow spin, waiting for it to point to anything tangible. Anything that could ease the nerves in my gut or clear my head. "First problem to solve: where do we start looking? Do we have any leads aside from the wind?"

"We know where one god is." Saeth cleared her throat, sauntering to me without a care and snatching the compass from my grip with a quick strike. She dangled the dial from its long gold chain, swinging it back and forth like a Huddian fortune teller at a fair. "If you can't remember what it is you've lost, I suggest going to the isle where all is found. Keira's mom is a goddess, right? Danura? Maybe she can lead us to the rest."

Come find me.

At my back, Truth practically giggled with shrill delight, a clear confirmation.

Keira was made of something special, distilled and refined into a brew both potent and powerful. But perhaps it was time to sip straight from the source.

Reagan swiped the trinket from her friend, lips pulling back to expose a feral grin. "Let's get lost."

A gunshot, ringing in the cavernous dungeon, echoed by Mama's screams. A pool of betrayer's blood on the stone floor—Papa's blood. Phantom limbs, choking me as I thrashed against them. Demons laughing in the dark.

A white nightdress stained red. I cover her stomach with my hand, trying to hold back the flood, to turn back time.

"What did you do?" I breathe, air ragged in my lungs.

A swollen stomach punctured and poured out like a skin of wine. My hands, covered in it.

A scream in the distance. My scream? A burst of light, the scent of burnt flesh and boiled blood.

A ship deck, swarming with black cloaks. Demons snatching and swiping, pulling me down. A blue eye, rolling across the cobblestone, my fingers fumbling to catch it, to hold on, to put it all back...

Dark, clawed hands, grabbing me, holding me down, shaking my shoulders...

"Griffin, please, wake up." Not claws, but fingers, digging into my shoulders as he shook me. My eyes fluttered open to soft lantern light, not blinding darkness. I jolted upright, pushing my assailant back, tumbling out of the bed we shared...

The bed, not the deck. Not the bloodstained streets of Porthladd.

I inhaled sharply as the world righted itself and my pulse slowed. Strong hands again on my frame, one silver and one blue eye, gaze laced with concern.

Breathe in, breathe out. Repeat.

I registered my surroundings, my breath grounding me back to the room. Uncle Cedric's old cabin. The Captain's Quarters. It was the widest room in the *Ceffyl*, the bed large enough for both Rhett and I to spread out. The frame was harder than rocks, but it beat the hammocks and cots in the thinner cabins. Blue sheets from Ir'de, still soft after years of use. Charts covering the wooden walls, filled with red marks, reminders of journey's sailed under friendlier skies. My swords hanging on the iron hooks, gold hilts shimmering in the light, within arm's reach and ready if I needed them.

I was not meant to be the *Ceffyl's* Captain. But as far as I was concerned, this room was the safest place in the entire Deyrnas.

Breathe in, breathe out. Repeat.

"Hey, hey...I'm here." Rhett's thumb worked gentle circles into the bare flesh of my arms as he held me upright. Carefully, like I was a baby and not a brawler, he lowered us both back to seated, eyes still scanning mine for signs of crazy. "I'm here."

I let his stare steady me, let the bright blue and dull silver chase away the crimson and smoke that haunted my dreams.

I swallowed down the last urge to scream, biting it back like a shot of cheap gin. "I'm sorry–" I stuttered, my voice hoarse. My screams must have been real this time. I cleared my throat, offering a weak grin. "I'm fine."

Rhett sighed, letting go of me as he fell back onto the worn pillows. "No, you're not fine." He rubbed his temples with the heels of his hands, deep voice rumbling in his chest with an exhaustion that was both physical and mental. "You're not fine, Griffin. None of us are fine."

My gut lurched again, a sharp pang of guilt like a punch to the gut. I knew my armor had been wearing thin, knew that I'd been spreading my sickness to the rest of the crew. I had to keep my walls up, to keep Rhett out not for my sake, but for his. Loving was lethal. "I must've had too much to drink last night. I'm–"

"Stop." Rhett's bare chest rose and fell in uneven breaths. He removed his hands from his eyes, palms stained with tears. "Please. We can't keep doing this. I can't keep–"

"I know," I admitted, and I could hear Truth's faint buzz from where she hung across the room. The words bubbled out faster than I could catch them, like a drink straight from the tap. "Shit, Rhett, I know. But what am I supposed to do? We are running to find gods, Rhett. *Gods.* What in Lyr's name can I do against the makers of the cosmos?"

I was a man, not a myth. Not the Swordsinger or a Godslayer.

I had a bad habit of losing bets. And I had an even worse habit of losing loved ones. If I took this bet, if I put the crew in harm's way to play hero, for a slim chance at salvation...I ran the risk of losing everything I had left. The only hope the Deyrnas had, too.

I stared at the charts on the wall, waiting for one of them to tell me what to do, where to go. Perhaps the ghosts of Captains past had left wisdom there, something even a fool like me could latch onto. A safe bet instead of a gamble.

"I don't know, Griffin," Rhett finally spoke, shaking his head. Long, silk hair fell in front of his face. On instinct, I reached out, pushing the soft blond strands away. He swallowed hard before continuing. "None of us know. But I do know drinking yourself to death and ignoring the people who love you...it doesn't make any of it easier."

Another jab beneath my battered armor. One that stabbed deep.

Crimson against ivory, blood against stone.

Another bet I lost. Another risk too steep.

Breathe in, breath out, repeat.

Except this time, the air still burned as it rushed in and out, scraping my lungs from the inside. Panic and pain, demanding to be felt, demanding I finally pay up on my losses. My chest tightened, the last resistance to the reckoning I knew I deserved.

"I'm not trying to make it easier." My voice came out in pathetic bursts between breaths, shaky and shameful. "I deserve to feel it. The guilt, the grief. It's my *fault*."

There it was, the ugly truth. The bullshit behind the bluff. The hidden rust beneath the gilded paint. I didn't need Truth buzzing at my back to see it for myself.

Papa, Finna, Keira...

I'd begged them to go save Mama. I'd walked right into my father's traitorous trap. I put them all in that dungeon, and I did nothing to get them out.

I let Finna die on the street, alone and afraid. I let Keira sacrifice herself instead. Let her pay for my losing hand.

Let the Deyrnas pay for losing her.

I had no power this time to stop the tidal wave as it escaped my lips in harsh, shaking sobs, no armor left to hide the piteous truth: "Lyr's ass, Rhett, it's my *fucking fault*. It's all my fucking fault."

Another cry tore through me, vicious as a northern wind in winter, burning cold as it seared all the way from my stomach to my throat. I sank into the bed, curling in on myself, my limbs heavier than stone. I wished I could sink into Lyr's keep, wished it wasn't too late for me to take Keira's place, or Finna's, or Pa's....

Rhett shifted to kneeling, sitting back against his heels like a devotee at an altar. Slowly, and just as reverently, he reached out a hand, stroking my cheek. "No, it's not, Griffin."

I smacked him away, the whirlwind suffocating, stealing the air from the room, dragging me deeper down. "Stop, I—"

"No, say it. It's not your fault." Rhett grabbed my face in between his warm palms and leaned closer, pressing his forehead to mine.

The whirlwind stopped, and all I could see was him, the light blue of his one eye, like the sky after a storm. I smelled the sleep on his breath as it tickled my face, gentle against the caustic burning in my lungs. The warmth of his hands fought back the cold as they entwined with my shaky fingers. "Griffin, say it."

Breathe him in. Breathe him out. Repeat.

"It's not my fault." I repeated, the words as tricky on my tongue as a foreign language.

Rhett squeezed my hands, stare unbroken, silver-and-blue as strong as steel and sea. "Again. It's not your fault."

"It's not my fault." This time, it didn't feel as feeble. Or as untrue.

As if she was listening, or perhaps laughing at me, I swore I heard Truth murmur from her perch across the room.

"We are mortals playing with gods, Griff. This mess is not our fault." Our foreheads pressed together, our breaths intertwined. His voice was barely more than a whisper, a prayer to whatever bastard god may be listening. "But that doesn't mean we can give up. Even if we want to. As a wise man once said, our families are so fucked anyway, what's the harm in trying?"

For a moment, we weren't hunting gods or licking our wounds. Instead, we were the two lonely, second-born sons that bonded in the brig of the *Ceffyl* on that first fateful voyage together. Two headstrong, heartsick kids who needed a friend in the darkness, needed someone to bet on them despite the odds stacked against.

What's the harm in trying?

I had a bad habit of losing bets. I was not luck's friend, I was Trouble's pawn.

It didn't matter. We had no other hands to play, no hidden cards up our sleeves. We had one last, desperate chance, a way to either double our winnings or lose our last coin. And it didn't matter if I wanted to or not. Rhett was right. We had to take it, win or lose.

But I wouldn't let anyone else pay up for me this time. No more I-Owe-You's, no more creditors taking my place.

"I have a tendency of letting people down. Even when I don't want to." I sat up, pulling away from him, allowing my armor to slip back between us again. Wanting him, loving him...it was dangerous. For me, and for him. For the people counting on us not to screw this up. "I don't want to hurt you, Rhett."

I attempted to untangle my fingers from his, but he squeezed tighter. "Only I decide what hurts me. And what heals me." He stared at our hands, bare torso shimmering with a sheen of sweat, but the corner of his mouth tilted upwards. "Griffin, you are a mess and a menace, but that doesn't change how I feel."

"Ow, was that one supposed to make me feel better?" I cracked, the instinct a defense to the danger stirring in his dilated pupils.

"Shut up," he grumbled, his smile widening, that swirling, reckless thing simmering in it. "Listen, I didn't know how to be myself before I met you. Didn't even know who I was. Lyr's ass, I thought I was going to run away with Maddox Pultain, the bastard. You didn't let me down, you lifted me up. Like you do for everyone on this ship."

For another brief, fleeting moment, I let myself remember the boy I met in the brig, with two bright blue eyes instead of one. No scars to tell the story of his suffering. He was naive then, ready to risk it all for a cheat and a liar, his faith both blind and somehow beautiful.

He'd grown since. No longer naive, grief teaching him the hard lessons of the heart. Life had kicked us both in the crotch enough times since then to remind us how to guard ourselves.

But he'd never lost that faith, even when everyone else waivered. It was no longer blind, his new silver stare laced with hell-honed scrutiny. Still, Rhett Mathonwy had the power to make even mortal men feel like a god. His whole-hearted hope was enough to fortify even the weakest of wills. If Rhett Mathonwy believed in you, you had to be worth something.

I had to be worth something.

"You didn't need me to find who you were." I allowed the outermost layer of my armor to slip. "You're the one that lifts everyone up. You do it quietly, and without thanks. But you keep us all together."

A full-bodied smile lit the room, almost bright enough to make a wayward wash-up like me believe in miracles. My heart somersaulted in my chest, the excruciating ache of something I couldn't run from or drown in a drink seizing every fiber that was mine.

"I know you're not ready to say it back, and that's all right. I'm patient." Rhett's voice was tight as a sail in a windstorm, but full of something just as intangible and powerful. "But I meant it in Porthladd, and I need you to know I love you. Your grit, your humor, your loyalty...all of it. All of *you*. I love you, and I'm here for you when you're ready to let me in."

Rhett Mathonwy was not a gambler.

His father had been. Roland was a crafty old bastard, his rocky laugh the perfect cover for every bluff. He had a knack for swindling silver pieces and a taste for trouble I could admire.

But Rhett hadn't inherited his father's talent for trickery. His tells were written plainly across his face, the way his nose scrunched when he bluffed or the way he bat his stupidly long lashes whenever he lied.

I'd seen it first the day of Keira's wedding, when he threatened to fight me for stepping on his toe. His jaw had clenched and his fists were ready, but his scrunched little nose told a different story. Gave me a glimpse at the gullible, good-hearted boy beneath the bluff. The boy who fought for a whore's honor, who wept at his father's funeral, who lost an eye and still stood and fought for his former foe's freedom.

I waited for his nose to scrunch, for him to blink twice. Waited for him to tell me it was a joke, that someone as good and pure and kind and selfless as he was could never love a bastard like me.

He didn't. He just stared back at me, a soft, open smile on his pink mouth and a silver tear in the silver corner of his eye.

"Shut up," I said with a grin, swallowing down the ball of emotion lodged in my throat, gulping back the words I might have spilt otherwise.

His scar crinkled as his smile turned mischievous. "Make me."

I was not a holy man. I was Trouble's cuckold, a crass, irreverent fool who'd been challenging the gods' wrath his whole life. But as I took Rhett's face in my hands, as I held his faintly stumbled cheeks in my palms, as I covered his cracked lips with mine, I offered a silent prayer to any of the fuckers listening.

They better bet their asses that this time, I was coming for them. This time, I wouldn't lose.

I pushed Rhett back, lowering his head to the pillow, pressing into him. Every place where our bodies connected, every scrape of his skin against mine, every point of perfect pressure sent lightning coursing through me. Our kiss deepened, his mouth opening with a deliciously deep moan, allowing me in, opening the doors to his temple. I let my mouth explore, traveling down his neck, his jaw, desperate for a taste of every inch of him.

Gods needed faithful followers to exist. Without faith, they were like smoke without fire. Just stories and whispers, mist and misplaced arrogance.

I was just a man, a simple fool that flirted with Trouble. But I had one last ace up my sleeve, one last truly powerful thing fueling the fire in my belly. And as I kissed him in the lanternlight, as I tasted the power of his love and devotion on my tongue, more intoxicating than any drink I'd ever had, I prayed that the gods were ready for me.

Sex, like whiskey, used to be my favorite sleep aid. Better than any belladonna the magickas in Hud sold, a good romp through the hay used to settle me on even the stormiest nights at sea.

Yet, despite how delightfully satisfying this particular session had been, despite how peacefully Rhett snored next to me, his long hair a tangled bird's nest against the pillow, I tossed and turned like a dingy during a thunderstorm.

Maybe that was the difference between fucking and making love. One satisfied a primal need, the other only created a deeper longing, like a drunk going through withdrawal.

The boat rocked gently, Lyr cradling the *Ceffyl* like a babe, but we might as well have sailed right into a typhoon with how much my head swirled.

I stared at the ceiling of my uncle's old cabin, tracing the deep lines in the wood's face. It was my last resort against the whirlwind of thoughts that swam in the darker depths of my mind, like sharks on the hunt, ready for me to stumble in.

Crimson against ivory. Blood against stone.
Silver eyes, speaking in our silent language.
Gods and gargoyles, waiting for me at the edge of the world.

I love you, Griffin Branwen. All of you.

I didn't know where my feet would carry me, but it didn't matter. I couldn't sit here like chum in a bucket, ready for one of those vicious thoughts to take a bite of me. I pushed out of bed, throwing my discarded shirt over my head with little grace or care.

I looked back at my bedmate, at the boy brave enough to love a bastard. He deserved someone capable of saying it back, and perhaps if I survived this suicide mission, I'd give him what he wanted. His face buried in the pillow, I couldn't see the scar, only the red marks across his back from our much more pleasurable encounter. Softly, I planted a kiss on the angriest mark before covering him with the deep blue sheet. Rhett huffed once with a slight twitch at the contact, but did not stir, breath heavy and even.

I bit back a laugh and headed out the door, out to the balmy summer air of the topdeck. The moon was a thin smile in the sky, grinning at me like a bitch with a secret, but the night was clear, the starlight enough to bathe the deck in soft white. Still, I lit a lantern, the single kerosene flame the only protection I had against the true dark.

Nighttime on the *Ceffyl Dwr* had always been a different brand of creepy. While the old girl creaked and cracked, the ghostly woosh of the waves against the hull sounded even spookier in the relative silence of the stars. Keira used to say they whispered to her like old friends. I had no interest in whatever they had to say, a chill running down my spine at the thought despite the tepid air.

When I was a boy, I hated it. Whenever I was assigned nighttime lookout, I would swab the deck myself twice a day or clean out the chamberpots, trading duties with whichever uncle would pity me most. I used to lie and say it was to make sure I got plenty of beauty sleep, as the only Branwen that had any looks to his name. But my family knew the truth—knew I hated the dark and danger that lurked in the deep. And on nights I couldn't bargain or bet my way out of it, I'd sit up in the crow's nest with my back against the mizzenmast, scanning the open sea for ships, for sharks—or phantoms—jumping at even the slightest shift in the wind.

As if the ghosts were already waiting for me, a hammock swayed between the mizzenmast and the wheel, the white canvas harsh against the inky night. There was no wind to warrant the movement, the sky sleepy. Yet the white fabric tipped and moved, out of time with the rhythm and pitch of the waves.

A cannonball sank through my toes, and for the second time that night, I muttered a prayer to whatever god would pity me.

"K-Keira?" I took a shaky step forward, ice running through my veins.

The hammock shifted again, and this time, an arm popped out. I tripped back, stumbling over myself as I swallowed a scream.

But as the phantom hammock moved, a head emerged. Pin-straight ginger hair instead of midnight black. Sharp, skinny features instead of lean muscle. Green eyes instead of silver.

"Lyr's hairy arse, Saeth, you scared the shit out of me." I exhaled, shoulders releasing as the corked bottle of tension in my gut popped.

My cousin sat up, holding onto the sides of the hammock for dear life, her face paler than usual. "Sorry, I just figured I'd see what the fuss was about. But this thing is the worst."

"Move over, then," I grumbled as she swung her legs out of the damned thing, sitting in it like a swing. I set the lantern down and shuffled in next to her. It took a minute of adjusting, my arm around her bony frame and her sharp elbow in my side, but after a moment, we were both able to sit upright.

We hadn't been this close physically since we were little, when I used to throw her on my back and let her steer me where to go like a plowhorse. She'd giggle like a fiend, shrill and sharp even then, a Mad Queen happy to have a faithful servant.

It stopped when she was a bit older than Reagan's age now, when Auntie Alina died. When the fire burned away the last of her softness.

"Can't sleep?" I dug my heels into the deck to give us a push, tucking my steel-made little cousin into my side despite the discomfort. The hammock tilted, the fabric groaning before settling into an even swinging rhythm.

A bitter laugh, harsh as ever from her lips, but she settled closer. "Haven't slept for weeks. Why start now?"

Guilt nibbled at my gut. I stared out to the dark horizon, imagining the demons that chased Saeth. She'd been so strong, so sharp even when the rest of us unraveled. Ronan had been maniacally focused, and I'd been useless. I was still just the stupid, selfish prick I'd always been, ready to swab the deck and pass off my duties to whatever Branwen would bet with me.

Keira once said I sounded like Uncle Cedric. It might have been true, his advice easy to mimic and spit out. But I didn't act like him. I had none of his leadership or courage. And as he used to say, a true Branwen let their actions do the talking.

I gathered my courage, ready to let my actions finally speak. "It should be you, Saeth. You're the Captain now."

A real, shrill laugh pierced the night quiet, and Saeth doubled over, her whole form shaking.

I hadn't heard that laugh in years, the Mad Queen's cackle. While it stung to have it pointed at me, a part of my gut unlocked, a pressure fizzing out. After a moment, my laugh joined hers, just as real and free and frenzied.

"Griffin, I'm not a Captain," she gasped between laughs, smacking my thigh as she steadied herself. When the fit had finally passed, she swiveled to face me, narrowed gaze serious once more. "I'm a cutlass. Point me in the right direction, and I'm useful. But the wrong direction…I'm too cold. Jaded. I don't have your heart."

A thin finger prodded my chest, right where the alleged organ rested.

"I'm the Swordsinger. If either of us are weaponry, it's me." I nudged her side, waggling my eyebrows at her, hoping for another of those rare laughs. Anything instead of the ice that set back in, the frozen steel that we'd all seen since Finna–

"You know what I mean." Saeth interrupted that particularly painful thought before it could slice me open. Her jaw clenched and unclenched as she picked her words carefully. "You're just…*good*. You see the best in people and bring it out of them. Like Uncle Cedric used to."

You're wise, sometimes, you know that? Like Papa used to be.

"That's so everyone ignores the worst in me," I scoffed, leaning back into the fabric, tearing myself away from my cousin and her sharp-eyed scrutiny. "It's a good trick, I'll teach it to you."

Saeth rolled her eyes before staring out to the horizon again. The first rays of sunlight were finally peeking out from the water, streaks of purple and gold kissing the vast black. We sat there in silence for a few minutes, watching the sun rise, watching it chase away the demons and ghosts lurking in the shadows.

"Sometimes I feel like...I don't know, like I'm part shark. Like I'm cold blooded," Saeth said after a long moment, gaze trained on the sun. Her voice was soft as silk, again the steel sword setting down her weaponry. Her throat bobbed, the admission stuck in it. "I forget I'm human sometimes, forget to care...and it scares me."

I wasn't born a Captain, but I had to try. For once in my life, it was my turn to be brave. My turn to be the lookout, even if the ghosts and gods and goblins came after me instead.

This time, I'd be ready for them.

Until then, I could only do what I did best.

"Yikes, Saeth, that's intense." I flicked her nose, and she swatted me away. I didn't know *how* I was going to fight the gods, didn't know how I'd save the dead or defeat Death himself. But I'd be damned if I couldn't make my family laugh in the face of fear, if I couldn't keep them safe from their own insecurities. My voice dipped low. "Listen, if you choose to eat anyone...I nominate Tarran."

Saeth still stared out to sea, but the corner of her mouth twisted upwards. "Oh, don't worry, he's first on the menu."

Trouble roared with victory in my chest, happy to have the Mad Queen as a playmate. I lounged back, nearly tipping the hammock as it swayed. "I imagine he'd be best fried. Maybe baked."

Saeth went stiff as a board, her back rigid and her face frozen. "Shut up."

I recoiled and shrugged, ignoring the tinge of guilt that bit at my heels. "Too far? Fair enough."

Ice melted into sheer, unadulterated joy. A wicked, unfettered smile broke across her face, exposing all her teeth. She raised her arm, pointing to a thin line against the hazy pink horizon. "No, Griffin, look. Is that familiar?"

I squinted against the rays of sunlight as they reflected against the water. Sure as shit, jutting up from the water, an island silhouette surrounded by thick, swirling mist.

Hiraeth.

I didn't need Truth on my back to confirm my suspicion.

"Unfortunately." I hopped out of the hammock, hoping I could pull one last trick out of my sleeve before Trouble dragged me in to pay my debt. "Let's go god-hunting, Sharky."

9

Searches and Sirens

RONAN

The world beneath the waves was quiet.

Down below, where the light was sparse and dim, where my scales cooled to match the bone-deep chill, the only sound was the eerie woosh of water filtering through my gills.

Below, I was a pure predator. No mask to maintain, no ruse to uphold. I was not Captain or Serpent Prince, not cousin or friend or any of the other roles I managed. I was just the wicked beast of my wife's making. Just the deep drag of my gills and the streamlined speed of my tail and the sharp edges of my claws.

I dove deeper into the abyss, the icy water biting at my exposed skin. Down in the depths, the world was simple. No expectations to meet, no tasks to juggle. Just the hunt.

We'd been scouring the four seas for three weeks now with no luck. Nearly a whole month, and not a single clue, not even an overturned seashell to point us in the right direction. Laureli hovered over her crystal ball day and night, eyes bloodshot and glossed over, the only wheel steering us at all. The old witch was tougher than nails, but it was taking its toll on her. The rest of us, taking shifts, searched the ocean floor for any signs of the gates to the Otherworld. And every minute spent below the waves, every minute I used my gills instead of my lungs, my tail instead of my legs…

I felt the parts of me that *cared* crack, the water washing away what was human. All that was left was the desperate need, the frenzied addiction gnawing at the edges of every nerve.

I'll wait for you in the Otherworld.

Over the ridge, serrated rocks jutted up from the seafloor, framing the mouth of a deep cavern, the darkness within impenetrable. I squinted as I slowed my swim, even my siren eyes struggling against the blackness.

We'd seen places like this before, dark and dangerous and unrefined. If hell was truly at the bottom of the sea, as all of the legends suggested, one of these holes in the floor of the world had to be the gate.

A chill ran down my spine all the way to the tip of my golden tail. I inched further, a blackness within me calling to the unending dark of the cave. I blinked, and the dark shifted, moving with the water, a tangible, twisting thing that if I reached out, I could touch....

"We should head back," a distorted voice called from behind me, pulling me from the cavern.

I whipped around, fangs bared and claws ready, putting the darkness at my back. I could feel it watching me, the hair at the nape of my neck standing at attention.

Siobhan folded her arms across her chest as she flicked her citrine fin at me with an annoyed swoosh. "Don't you dare point those things at me."

I inhaled, letting the taste of salt and brine steady me, and then exhaled, tension rolling off my shoulders as my gills discarded the water.

"Sorry," I muttered, my human parts swimming again to the surface. I was not just siren, but sailor, too. Captain and confidant, not just claws and chaos. I nodded to the darkness again, the preternatural tug at my center worsening. "This could be it, Sio."

Siobhan swam closer, brassy skin glistening in the filtered light. She narrowed her eyes with expert scrutiny, not just a predator assessing its prey, but a warrior sizing up her opponent.

"If it is, we need the others." The water did little to mute the apprehension in her tone. She sucked at her fangs before speaking again, weighing her options. "You know the rules—mark any suspicious places, and then come back with reinforcements."

The beast in my gut grumbled, animal arrogance churning in my chest. "I made the rules, Siobhan, you don't have to quote me," I seethed through clenched teeth, shoving back the siren call and instead focusing on my human parts. Down below, it was difficult to not let those parts drown. "We're running out of time. I can feel it. She's slipping away…"

Not just Keira, but me. As if the longer I was away from my maker, *my wife*, the less and less of the man there was to tame the beast. She'd given me life when the spring could not, and yet it felt like I'd traded one dependency for another. Just as the cravings had set in whenever I denied myself a soak, I felt it clawing at my middle, angry and wild and blinded by desire. Begging me to give in to the frenzied cold, to the delicious, detached rage that killed without thought. Without her here, without her light and life by my side…

The beast beneath my skin stirred again, daring me to finish the thought as he licked his lips.

"Then that's all the more reason to go back to the surface and check in with the others, Ronan." Siobhan's hand on my shoulder dragged me back to the present, her touch warm despite the chill. It was not an intimate gesture, but an anchor back to my body, to my reality. Her face softened, the ever-present scowl relaxing into an attempt at a smile. "I understand what you're going through…but this is a team effort. The girls need your guidance, and you need our help, too."

"Fine. But we're coming back here. I have a strange feeling." I stared back at the cavern, at the engrossing dark within, at the whispers I could hear but couldn't quite make out. The dragon within purred and flexed with intrigue, a dangerous call to *come and see* beckoning through my veins...

Siobhan's fingers traced down my arm before linking through mine. She squeezed, swimming around me so her face blocked my view of the cave. An eyebrow raised, she learned forward, touching her forehead to mine. "Hey, come back, Ro. It's marked. Now let's go, you stubborn ass."

Marina was the one with the gift of truth, but Siobhan had a gift for sniffing out bullshit. I sighed, leaning back into her, her siren's touch somehow reengaging my human heart. I had fangs and fins, but I also had friends counting on me. Friends who saw my ferocious parts and still swam at my side, friends willing to follow me to the

Otherworld to find my wife. Friends that needed me to keep my head on straight. Friends that needed the Serpent Prince, the *Ddraig Aur*. Their Captain.

"Thanks." I gave my friend's hand a parting kiss across the knuckles before letting go, gunning back to the surface as fast as my fins would carry me.

As soon as the *Madyn* was in sight, I shifted back. Blinding heat seared through me, the pain both intense and instant as flesh tore and restitched itself. As I sheathed my scales and forgot my fins, the world dimmed. Colors softened, and the chill of the ocean seeped deeper into my skin. Still, I relished the ache and incompetence of my human form, the strain of my muscles and the shiver in my bones as I swam the last few yards to the cutter with my legs and lungs.

Marina was there first to fish me out of the water, throwing a rope over the side for me to climb up. I dragged myself over the rail, dripping onto the painted gray deck, ignoring the way Marina ogled my nude form with a feral smirk. "Well, *hello*, Captain Mathonwy."

I snatched my dry trousers from where they were folded on a crate, stepping into them with inhuman speed, shooting the sea-wench a dark glare as I fumbled with the brass buttons. "Any luck on your end?"

"Nothing but fish," Marina sighed, supple curves dissolving into the crate she leaned against with a dramatic sway. Based on how dry her auburn locks were, my guess was she hadn't looked too hard. The girl was as lazy as she was lusty.

Willow, her dark curls still dripping wet, scurried over with a grand smile, a reluctant Cassryn on her heels. "Actually, Captain, there was an interesting reef further south. I've never seen that species of coral—the skeletal structure was discular."

"Good work, girls." Siobhan tucked her fresh tunic into her brown trousers as she approached before strapping her weapons back to her strong thighs. I hadn't seen her come aboard, but she was already there and dressed, the first mate stepping easily back into her role as commander.

I stood straighter, remembering the role I was set to play. The *Ddraig Aur*, the Golden Dragon, proud as I was powerful. Not the heartless, harsh beast of the blue that whispered to the darkness. "Did you map it out?"

"*Did we map it out,*" Cassryn mocked with an eye roll, sweeping her wet hair back into a tight bun. "No, we just waved at it and swam away."

The dragon within snarled, spiked tail raised and fire rushing up my throat, ready for me to spew it at Cassryn. She might have been made of stone, but even granite melted under enough heat, and I had plenty to spare. "Watch your tongue–"

"Aye, let's be kind," Nelle interrupted as she and Ellian swished through the cabin door, her violet eyes trained on me though she addressed the whole crew. Her brow furrowed, giving me a reproachful glare that would've made my aunt Reina proud. "We're all a bit worse for wear."

I bit my forked tongue, swallowing back the fire. It burned as it sank through my throat, but I threw on my best serpent smile to stifle the discomfort.

"Half an hour's rest, then we go again," I called out to the crew, shoving my hands in my pockets to hide the claws threatening to unsheathe themselves. "I saw a cavern three leagues north that had a strangeness to it."

A collective groan echoed through the group, all but Siobhan and Nelle doing little to mask their displeasure. Cassryn rubbed her temples while Willow's mouth twisted into a worried knot. Marina kicked a peg of the portside rail, hands fisted in the skirts of her deep burgundy dress. She pursed her lips at me like a toddler throwing a tantrum. "I liked you better when you were human. So much less demanding then."

"I like you better when you're silent," I snapped back. Marina blinked at me, crimson eyes reddening with rage, but I pushed past her, headed belowdecks to fetch a shirt and perhaps a drink. Maybe that would satisfy the simmering need sloshing around in my stomach.

I knew it wouldn't. Knew the pangs of this hunger all too well. Knew the tight pull of the headache resting beneath my brow, the prickling itch beneath my skin too deep to scratch, even with my claws.

"Laureli needs you first." Nelle grabbed my arm as I passed, stopping me in my tracks.

At that, my human parts perked up. The seer only called for me when she had something, and I was in desperate need of *any* news, good or bad. "I'll see her right away."

I pulled to go, but Nelle squeezed tighter, giving me a quick once-over. The healer's eyes too keen to miss the bruised bags beneath mine, her mouth flattened, and she shared a long, knowing look with Siobhan at my side. "And then you both should rest. Or *feed*. When was the last time?"

She didn't mean slurping a bowl of stew or hunking into a loaf of fresh sourdough. No, a different lust scraped my insides; the carnivorous desires of my other form needed quelling. Sirens required a more...*sanguineous*...source of nutrition to survive, preferably raw and sipped straight from a vein.

It was no different than enjoying a steak dinner, I told myself. It didn't matter what brand of libations we savored, animal or...otherwise...it did the trick all the same.

My stomach growled at the thought, the predator drooling, ready to sink his fangs in.

If I didn't offer the beast a scrap soon, I'd go belly-up. But with every drop of blood, whether it was fish or chicken or cow, the lines blurred red. Every sip, and the siren got stronger, devouring another part of the man I'd once been.

"Aye, thank you, Nelle." I cleared my throat, grasping at the strands of the Serpent Prince, the storyteller and swindler. "I'll eat before we head out again."

Nelle pursed her lips, but didn't pursue it further. Grateful for her mercy, I fled into the cabin, Siobhan still at my right.

I was running out of time. I needed to find Keira. Needed my wife back, needed her steady presence and sturdy power...before it wasn't *me* hunting for her.

"Captain, you think it's best to keep at it like this?" Ellian followed us, his footsteps heavy behind mine, the stiff wood of the *Madyn* creaking beneath him.

"It's necessary. The Deyrnas is waiting for us." The half-truth tasted like sand on my tongue. The Deyrnas would wait. Keira would wait.

I couldn't any longer.

I quickened my pace, shimmying down the first ladder to the second level, beelining down the corridor for my bunk. I needed to be dressed, to be in boots and a shirt and whatever other costume helped me feel more like a man than a monster.

Ellian pinched his nose as he pursued. "I just think—"

"No one's asking you to think, Ellian." I shot him down with the pinpoint precision of the pistol that put us in this position in the first place. "You're here to help us *hunt*."

"Yeah, furball. Sit." Siobhan snorted as Ellian blinked twice, the double-edged insult wedging between his ribs. "Good boy."

"I disagree with Marina. I like you both better when you're underwater," he mumbled, hurt flashing across his bronze features.

"Funny, I don't like you at all," Siobhan huffed at him, a cat playing with its food.

Normally, the banter would've been the perfect remedy for my malady, a surefire way to summon the Sea-Snake from the depths. He'd never been one to pass up a chance at a snarky remark. But now, their bickering grated on every exposed nerve, shredding the last strands of my decency into ribbons.

"If the two of you are quite finished, might I suggest silence. You only have twenty-eight minutes left," the dragon roared with my voice. I walked through the door to my bunk, shutting it halfway. "Find another place to flirt or fight or...*whatever* you're doing."

Siobhan froze, mouth hanging open in disbelief, unblinking eyes screaming with disdain. But Ellian ducked his head into the opening before I could slam it shut, large palm splayed against the door, the *blaidd* sniffing out my bluff.

"You know, the first thing my father taught me as a blacksmith...even steel can snap if you overwork it." He shoved the door in another inch, and despite the siren strength in my veins, it gave, demonstrating the sheer force behind the *faoladh*'s facade. But his emerald stare softened, my friend the Councilman peeking out from beneath his long lashes. "The girls need a break. You need a break, brother. You're no good to Keira if you're exhausted."

I gnawed my bottom lip, fighting back the guilt and hunger battling in my middle. I knew I didn't have much time. I felt myself unraveling like the frayed edges of a worn coat, the Storyweaver coming apart at the seams. But I knew the girls would roast me alive if I kept pushing them.

One more night, then. One last search.

I'll wait for you in the Otherworld.

I hoped my wife had more patience than I did.

"Fine," I sighed, shoulders releasing as I gave in. "We try again at dawn. Tell everyone to get some rest."

Ellian patted my shoulder with his sizable hand before scampering off like a good dog, ready to herd the rest of them into bed for the night. Siobhan hesitated for a moment, hands clasped behind her back, the scent of sadness wafting from her citrine stare. "You too, Ro."

I managed a nod before I shut the door, leaning against the coarse wood for support.

The space was more akin to a closet than a Captain's quarters, walls so close I could touch either side if I stood in the middle. But Laureli needed space for her workshop, so Leary's old haunt went to her instead. Not that I minded. The small cot and my old velvet rucksack were all I needed now. Here, in the cramped cabin two floors belowdecks, the world was quiet. There was nothing but the gentle kiss of the water against the hull, the baritone groan of the ship as she swayed.

Here, I could be nothing at all. Not captain, not predator, not siren or serpent.

Perhaps here, I was just a man, hungry for rest. A husband, lonely for his lost wife.

I shut my eyes, shoving it all back, letting the quiet snuff out the last of the dragon's fire.

One more night. One last search.

I grabbed my clean tunic off the cot, pulling it over my head and tucking it in. Soft gray, it hugged my skin, soothing the inescapable itch ever so slightly. Here, I didn't need to sport my family's colors, or my wife's. It didn't matter anymore. Mathonwy or Branwen, Serpent or Sea-horse...

I was too desperate to give a shit anymore. We all were.

Desperate for answers. For anything.

With another deep breath, I strapped my pistol to my hip and headed back out of the room, abandoning the quiet to satisfy a different sort of starvation.

We were hundreds of miles east of Hud, but somehow, stepping into Laureli's room transported me back to the streets of Cerridwen City. The gray walls of the cabin were covered with thick, woven tapestries, jewel-toned designs both vibrant and intricate. Littered across the floor, plush pillows of every color under the sun brightened the dull space. Delicate gold candlesticks lit the room, wax dripping over the sides as the flames danced. Laureli sat in the center, surrounded by the finery, stacks of gold bracelets clanking as she stared into the crystal orb, studying the swirling secrets hidden in the mist.

"Please tell me you've got more than we do, old friend." I fell into a nearby pillow the color of deep wine, the feathered softness a welcome respite from the stiff stretch of my cot.

Glassy eyes snapped up, as if noticing my presence in the room for the first time. Her brow furrowed, deepening the already-etched lines on her forehead. She passed me a tall, silver goblet, the tentacles of a sea beast carved into the side, its grip unrelenting. Red liquid sloshed over the side. "Here, drink."

I took a sniff, noting the fruity bouquet of the plum wine...and the hint of metal and salt beneath. My belly grumbled with hunger, but I wrinkled my nose and set the goblet back down before the kraken could restrain me.

"I'm fine without one." I spat out the lie as I swallowed down the desperate desire, my throat catching on the sticky sweet scent of it.

Laureli sniffed once, smelling the hunger on me like an unwashed coat. I knew she could hear my pulse quicken, knew she could see through my facade even without her crystal ball.

"I'm not," she sighed, lifting the goblet to her lips and taking a long dreg. I ignored the way my mouth watered, ignored the sharp sting of my fangs as they slid from their sheaths. Setting down the goblet in front of me again, she wiped her mouth with the back of her hand, red staining her pale skin.

Before she could finish the glass herself, or before I started drinking her instead, I chugged the contents. Keira used to tell me a true warrior knew which fights they needed to concede. I let the thick liquid coat my tongue, my throat, the inside of my belly, drowning down the hunger that clawed its way up my gullet. If I needed to concede this battle to win the war, it was a wager I was willing to make.

When the beast was satiated, smug in its small victory, my mind freed itself from the cage. I sat straighter, finally back in control, the siren within too distracted by its gluttony to care.

"What do you have for me?" I cleared my throat, ready to sink my teeth into the task at hand. Wars were won battle by battle, day by day, and I needed a small victory more than I needed air in my lungs.

The flickering candles cast Laureli's drawn expression in shadows. "This isn't easy, boy. It's like isolating a single grain of sand on a beach, or a specific drop of water in this entire sea."

Disappointment sat heavy in my chest, squeezing like the kraken's snare. "So you have nothing."

"I said it wasn't easy." Laureli shot back, her fangs peeking from beneath her thin lips. Then, a ferocious grin. "I didn't say I had nothing."

My heart skipped a beat, the fresh dewdrop of hope satisfying a different thirst. "I always knew you were my favorite."

"Flattery won't get you far, you cad." Laureli swatted my arm before leaning over the crystal ball again. The garish yellow eye blinked and flashed before vanishing into the vapors. Laureli grabbed my hands, planting them on the opposite side of the smooth glass surface. "Anyway, I keep seeing a gate. Two giant doors at the bottom of the sea, carved from the same stone as God's Eye. There are drawings carved into it, telling a story...I can't quite decipher it."

As she spoke, the image floated into the fog. Obsidian doors, larger than any I'd ever seen, with careful figures scored into the stone. Pictures of demons and devils, with horns and snouts and fangs and wings, crushed beneath the feet of three imposing figures. Two men, broad and brawny, arms outstretched and heads back in rapturous joy. In between them, a woman, her form supple and soft, her hands clasped in front of her, her head hanging.

"Certainly hard to miss," I mused, committing the image to memory. "Any idea where?"

Laureli shook her head, but answered, "It feels a lot like Hiraeth."

"It's in *Hiraeth*?" I hissed, whisking my hands back. "And you didn't think to mention that earlier?"

"No, you arse, I mean, it feels different every time." The old seer tightened her grip on the crystal, eyes clouding with the same haze. "Sometimes it's by a reef, others by a cavern, once so deep I could barely make it out..."

My thoughts wandered to the devouring dark of the cavern I'd seen this morning, the strange pull within...had it been there, waiting in the shadows? Would it still be there next time we went?

We'd been close before, I could feel it in my bones. There had been a few times when we felt the tug, the gate taunting us with the sweet scent of death and darkness...only for it to disappear as soon as we got close.

"It moves." No, Laureli was right. This was not meant to be easy. Like plucking a strand of hair from a lion's mane or a scale from a dragon's back. The gate to the Otherworld was a predator playing with its food, taunting us closer and closer, but never letting us set our traps.

Laureli shook her head again, gaze clearing like the sky after a storm, clouds rolling out as quickly as they'd appeared. "I think it's *called*."

No, the gate was not the predator. It was the bait.

And we were the fools frenzied for a bite.

"By who?" I asked, knowing the answer somewhere deep in the parts of me that were siren. The parts that could recognize another shark in the water, that could calculate my competition before it could sink its teeth into me.

"We've long suspected this, the girls and I..." Laureli sat back onto the pillows, bracelets clinking. "I have a theory that the reason Danura can't leave Hiraeth is that it needs substantial power to stay present. That if she left, it would all crumble."

"So we need a god to call the gates of the Otherworld." I voiced the thought aloud, the dragon within growling at the thought. For once, perhaps our goals were aligned, serpent and siren, two animals on the hunt for the same game. The same vengeance.

"Aye. Or a soul to sacrifice would be my guess."

"That's just peachy," I chuckled, the sound humorless and harsh. "Too bad we're all short on souls and gods right now."

Again, another job I'd need my wife for. Another task I couldn't complete on my own, despite my fangs and fury and foresight.

"We'll think of something," Laureli assured me, but the words were soaked in the scent of dishonesty.

No, there was no "something" to quench this thirst. No substitute for the true power we needed, watered down wine no match for the blood of a god.

The blood of a god.

The idea rippled through me, the last sharp parts of the Serpent Prince latching on.

We didn't have the means to trap our prey, gods too big of a game for a few half-fish like us. However, if we couldn't be hunters, we could be scavengers. We could swoop in and steal the spoils of someone else's success, like sirens scouring a shipwreck. And there was one god that had been trapped for ages, her cage made of the same magick we needed to manipulate to save my wife.

"I know I couldn't summon Keira because Arawn has her in his keep," I mused, the last threads of my tapestry weaving themselves into place. "But what would I need to summon my mother-in-law?"

"Whatever it is will have to wait," A cold, stiff voice said by way of greeting, banging into the small space with reckless abandon. Cassryn filled the doorway with her stony stance, arms crossed tightly. "There's trouble from the crew. Marina is leading a mutiny against your orders up on the deck, and I'm afraid it's bad."

"She's what?" I gaped, frustration filling my middle once more. I shot to my feet, ready to wring Marina's pretty neck. "Has anyone been hurt?"

Cassryn shook her head, a rare, wry smile fighting its way onto her marble expression. "Worse. She's declared we're playing Truth or Dare."

IO

Plays and Parries

KEIRA

When I was eleven years old, Ronan forced me to participate in a play he wrote for the *Ceffyl's* crew. It was a ridiculous farce of some long-forgotten myth—something about a lass who spoke to dragons— but being the only girl on the ship, Ronan had made me the lead role, taking the mantle of the Dragon King for himself.

We'd spent hours belowdecks going over his grand design, rehearsal stealing me away from my duties as a deckhand. I didn't mind getting out of the hard labor, but it meant subjecting myself to being Ronan's doll for the day. He'd dressed me in a white gown and used some of the cosmetics from Ir'de to paint my face, to help me 'get into character,' while he taped fake scales to his arms made from old scraps of a torn sail.

Despite being the lead, my role was very small. Ronan, the Storyweaver, also gave himself the honor of narrator, his boisterous telling sending the whole crew roaring with laughter. It was a performance to rival that of any troupe in Ir'de, Ronan dancing about like a puppet on a string, weaving in and out of his roles with expert precision.

He'd only entrusted one line to me, near the climax. A single sentence, to be delivered after the Dragon King offered the girl his horde. Yet when the time came, despite the vigorous rehearsal I'd been subjected to, I was so entranced in Ronan's performance, a captivated spectator, that I forgot. I stood awkwardly for a moment, forgetting how to speak, forgetting what to say, so wrapped up in the frenzied dance that was Ronan Mathonwy.

I wished I could forget the role I had to play now. Wished Ronan was here to sweep me up in one of his stories and carry me away like the tide. Wished I could wipe off my makeup and strip back my costume and step back into the life I knew and craved.

You have a task, Keira girl. This is no small victory. This could mean the whole war.

Papa's words were meant to inspire. As he had so many times, he'd sat me down last night, imparting his wisdom while ushering his well-calculated command. I wanted to make it work, to give Papa something to be proud of one last time.

But I did not know if I could see it through. This was not a simple job for a deckhand, nor was it one of Ronan's plays. This farce was a dangerous, deadly game meant for an actress far more skilled than I.

"You look nervous," Death said as he cracked his knuckles, a devastating smile on his crimson lips. His black, form-hugging tunic emphasized the carefully carved shape of him, simple and seductive in comparison to the delicate white robes he normally wore. He dropped into a grappler's stance, black leather trousers straining at the effort.

My costume was far more comfortable than the dress I'd been in last night. My own black tunic and trousers were soft as a mother's kiss, wrapping my muscles like a tight hug. Had I been on the ship, it would've been perfect to spar in, both moveable and tight enough to not get in the way.

Yet despite the leisurely attire, my lungs ached like they'd been strapped tightly in a corset, air spinning fast in my chest like a hurricane. Out in the cold, my breath swirled in front of my face.

Never thought I'd see the day when Keira Branwen was nervous, my husband had teased the first night at the shack, the last time I felt out of place in my own skin. I laughed to myself, imagining how that version of me could never have predicted the current moment. That nervousness was child's play in comparison to the electricity in my veins now.

Nervous or exhilarated, I couldn't tell which.

"Would it be wrong if I was?"

"No." Arawn stood straight and took a purposeful step toward me. Shadows licked his heels, rolling over the icy terrain. As he stopped in front of me, his misted breath mixing and twisting with mine, the shadows enveloped us, blocking out the bright blemish of the light against the ice. "Allow me to help."

As if answering a distant call, the moonbeams in my veins stirred, warmth spreading down my arms and to my fingertips. It oozed from my palms, a single white spark defiant against the Dark God's gift.

"Why does it do that?" I exhaled, remembering my role, fearfully clinging to the simple lines I'd been given.

He wants something from you. Find out what.

Papa's instructions had been clear. No one had ever heard of Arawn taking a live prisoner to the Otherworld before. None of the servants who Reina and Finna had pulled gossip from in their new positions. None of the laborers or gardeners who Papa, Owen, and Lochlan had surveyed.

All of the souls in the Otherworld *served* him. To his credit, the work was not cruel or unusual. But everyone had a purpose. A position. And he had a *plan*.

I was not his servant. But it was foolish to assume I didn't have a part to play in his performance.

Arawn chuckled, the sound rumbling like thunder in his chest. "What do you know about your gift?"

My gift. His curse. My eyes fell to the black spot marring my hand. It used to annoy me, to summon shadows and whispers I didn't want to hear. Now, it gave me no discomfort, instead wrapping itself around me like an old friend.

But before, there had been something else. A different whisper, a watery tug from the deepest parts of me.

"It used to be like breathing," I answered, my muscles still remembering the echo of that bubbling lightning. "The water used to call back to me, and when I would get angry...the storms would come in."

For a moment, I let myself slip back into that role. The heartbroken little girl who burned for her father's vengeance. The homesick sailor shipwrecked on an island of her own grief, sinking into the abyss of her sadness. The fire-forged fighter, made of steel and salt, sharpened into a blade, fueled by precious, vicious rage. The sea-blessed battle-axe. The storm made woman.

"Our emotions are very powerful things." Arawn's hand drifted to my middle, large palm pressing against my abdomen. Where we connected, that same blistering heat condensed, pressure and power building like a canon ready to fire. The light in my palm doubled in size, a full moon rebellious against the dark. "Gods are channels for the universe. The power, the energy stored in us, it mimics the energy in the world around us. And when we get emotional, good or bad, we release that energy. It's only natural that the world reacts."

The primordial piece I found in *Hiraeth* expanded in my center, in both breadth and depth, like a sail caught in a storm. Heat coursed through me, simmering and swelling, ready to be released.

"The water doesn't react anymore," I admitted, missing the gentle buzz instead of the burn. "Even if I'm upset. The light does, though. When I feel…"

Love. Loss.

My husband, pale and sickly, melting beneath the Ir'desian sun. Sunken eyes and skin slick with sweat. Heartbeat faint and lifeforce fluttering.

Fear, fury.

My cousin, bruised and bleeding, her life spilling onto the stone-laid street. Frenzied laughter and my knife still buried inside her. Regret and rage fighting for dominance in her final farewells.

"No, that's not light, Ariannad darling." Arawn removed his hand, and his shadows retreated. The shining orb in my palm flickered once before huffing out. But Arawn's dark gaze lingered where the light had been, voice quiet in a reverence I'd only heard from an Orwellin priest. "It's far more powerful than that. You don't just call forth the energy that already exists. *You* get it in its pure form, the True Fire, and you get to *decide* what it becomes."

You control your own fate.

Decisions came with freedom, but also consequence. Decisions meant having the power to shift the outcome, but not always being able to predict the impact it had on those around you.

Perhaps this time, I'd choose the right path. This time, I could turn the tides in my favor.

You have a task, Keira girl. This is no small victory. This could mean the whole war.

"How do you do it?" I whispered to Death.

"My gift is the opposite." A stray shadow materialized in front of him, the blackness beckoning my light once more. "I do not call forth energy...mine is the absence of it. Death. Darkness. The void that's left after energy is released back to the universe."

Death and Life. Emptiness and Energy.

Find out what he wants.

Perhaps it was as simple as this. Something to bring light back into his dark world. A friend to fill the void.

"Which is why my magic manifests as light when you use your shadows." I watched carefully as our gifts mixed and merged, two sides of the same coin. "It balances it."

"Very perceptive. And also why when you were a young sailor, it manifested as storms and lightning and water. It was what you needed most to balance you." Arawn grinned as he sucked in the shadows, the darkness disappearing once more. He stepped back, cracking his neck before falling back into his deep stance. "But you don't need my powers to bring yours out. This time, I want you to call it yourself. Try again."

I folded my arms across my chest, unsure if I wanted to wrestle with Death himself today. "And why are we sparring for that?"

"Your gifts used to best answer when you were in danger," Death simpered with a hint of menace. "I thought we'd recreate the environment."

He did not hesitate before lunging at me.

Impact, harder than a cannonball to the gut.

His broad shoulder knocked the air out of my sails as he splayed me flat on my back. The world tilted, dizzying as it spun.

"What the hell was that?" I sputtered back to standing, the world swaying again.

Death already stood over me with a smug smirk on his cherry lips. "Training. Come on, Ariannad darling. We go again."

Something spurred to life within, a forgotten fury that waited in the depths. Perhaps it was hearing my father's old commands on his tongue, perhaps it was the grin, so similar to my husband's snake smile, or perhaps it was simply my body's reminder of pain, proof again of my corporeality...

But Keira Branwen rose from the dead, her fists clenched and her teeth bared, ready for a fight.

He attacked again, even faster, this time swooping low for my legs. Instincts kicking in, I somersaulted over him, catching myself on my palms and rolling out. My wrists stung from the impact, but my heart beat wildly in my chest, the familiar pace filling me with an old sense of purpose.

Death shot back to his feet, but I was already on mine, legs sturdy beneath me. I settled into a ready crouch, savoring the sensation of stiff muscles loosening.

This was not a role I had to think about playing. I knew this choreography well, the mechanics and style, the technique and performance. This was Keira Branwen, the NightMare of the Four Seas, the sailor and swordsmith.

A razor-edged smirk sliced across my face. "You're not going to like me when I'm mean."

This time, I moved first, shooting low to sweep his legs from under him. Death tumbled to the ground as I took out his knee. As he hit, I grabbed his arm, hooking my legs around it and leaning back. It was a maneuver Griffin taught me, one that used to have him howling in pain with a dislocated shoulder whenever we went too far. I sank into the hold, grip firm on Arawn's smooth skin.

"I think I like you better this way," Arawn said through gritted teeth. But the God of Death was not easily bested. Instead of whining 'uncle,' he hoisted my whole body up with his one arm before slamming me back to the ground. I winced as I smacked the ice, my grip faltering, and he reared back up to his feet.

I scurried to mine, relishing the biting ache in my ribs. I'd be bruised and bloodied by the end of this, but I was not a stranger to pain. Pain was real. Pain I could feel.

Pain was power.

I narrowed my eyes at Arawn as I spat on the ground, a small spot of blood staining the snow-laden floor. "I think your lips would look even prettier if you shut them."

"So you think I'm pretty?" Death's brow's lifted, wrinkling the smooth plane of his forehead, surprise and delight dancing in his dark eyes. "I'll shut up if you make me. Are you even *trying* to use your gift?"

A flame lit in my veins, ancient and angry. It waited just below my fingertips, ready for me to call it, but I wouldn't. I didn't want to feel the burning, the power that clouded my eyes and numbed my heart. I wanted this, the bone-deep bruises and the fire in my lungs as I gasped for air. Wanted the NightMare of the Four Seas, free and ferocious, not the prisoner of Death.

"*Pretty* useless. Are you trying to get your ass kicked?"

I knew these lines like the back of my hand, no rehearsal needed. If this was the role I had to play, the version of myself that I needed to resurrect to accomplish my mission, so be it.

Find out what he wants.

I would after I flattened him.

I charged again, aiming at his head this time. He was bigger than I was, and stronger, too, much like Griffin, so I'd have to use my speed against him. I jumped up, ready to bring my foot to his temple, but he caught my ankle, spinning me over his shoulder.

I hit the ground again, hard, my knees crashing into the ice, sending shockwaves of agony up my legs. I hissed and doubled over, more red pooling against white as my skin sliced open.

"Get up," Arawn commanded as he stood over me. The humor and delight dashed from his expression, lips now drawn in a tight line. "A goddess kneels to no one."

He offered a hand, and I took it, letting him hoist me back to standing. My legs shook beneath me, but he held tight, steady as a mizzenmast amid a storm.

I didn't feel like a goddess. I felt like a girl, silly and stubborn. Like a child playing dress up on her father's ship, her costume too large for her, her lines muddled.

"Let's go again," I gritted through my teeth, pushing away from him and squaring up once more. I would not let Death pity me, would not let him see me weak and wanting. I was not the goddess he summoned, but I had to play my part, had to see my duty through to the end.

But Death shook his head, running his hand through his long mane of hair. "No, this isn't working. You need to clear your head. Think of things that made you feel your gift before."

At his command, it winked again within me, dominant and demanding to be felt.

Love. Loss.

My husband, fighting alongside my family, darkness encroaching. My cousins, battered and beaten, still struggling against the hive of puppet soldiers. My friend, wearing my colors, my name, dead in my stead.

Fear, fury.

My enemy, holding a silver pistol, trained on my kindred spirit. Her rage, bubbling up in her brown eyes, the blame entirely mine. My life, the only thing I had left to offer, the only shield against Death himself.

Death, who watched me now, obsidian stare filled with subtle wonder. Death, who ensnared me in ice, but set me free of my failures. Death, who only saw me as I saw myself.

Perhaps my gift could only share that perspective. Perhaps it only answered those who knew their own voice, knew how to decide their own fate.

"I can't."

I shoved back the bright light, burying it again beneath the ice. No, I couldn't feel those things, not anymore. Without the mirror of my family, without their perspective, I only saw myself as I saw the Otherworld.

A vast, frozen nothingness. A reflection, fading in the darkness. An echo of what used to be, the phantom of what might have been.

A little girl, playing pretend. A compass without true north.

Arawn gritted his jaw, an uncharacteristic urgency woven into his baritone. "Why not?"

Something unlocked as I allowed myself one admission, one truth amidst lines and lies. "I don't want to feel those things without the people I love. Without them loving me, too."

Death's whole frame deflated like I'd pierced him with my dagger. "You mean Ronan."

Ronan.

Ronan.

Ronan.

"Yes."

Without his direction, without him to write my lines and tell my story, I was nothing. I had family here. Had Reina and Owen and Finna. Had Papa. Had so many loved ones who'd I'd missed with my whole soul, who I used to depend on for guidance and grit.

But without Ronan, it was meaningless. Without his sea-blue stare and snake-skinned snark, I was not the NightMare of the Four Seas. Without his golden heart and his steadfast presence, I wasn't goddess or girl. Without Ronan, it all meant nothing.

I was nothing.

"Do you..." Death chewed his bottom lip, his massive form somehow small, the sweet sadness in his eyes shrinking him. "Do you need to see him?"

Ronan.

Ronan.

Ronan.

My pulse doubled, heart threatening to leap from my chest. The thing inside me burned bright, begging to be released. Aching for my husband. For my Ronan.

"Yes."

Again, I forgot my place, my lines. Captivated in the story that was Ronan Mathonwy, my heart and head set on him and him alone. It didn't matter what Death wanted from me. Only what I could get from *him*.

Death stood before me, long black lashes dusting with fresh tears. But again, he offered a hand, sturdy and sure despite the wind that shook his frame. "Then follow me, *Caraid*."

II

Truths and Tonics

RONAN

Every conman worth his salt needed to know two things above all else; how to stack the odds in his favor, and how to talk his way out of trouble if things went belly-up. I'd played many high-stakes games in my life, the Mathonwy legacy of cunning and craftiness steeped deep in my bones. We did not balk from a challenge; but we would cheat and lie and trick to ensure our victory. My uncle Roland had been the best at it, his sleight of hand made of lopsided smiles. My father's trickery had less tact, his poker face flawed with tells–but he could provoke his opponent to their wits' end, a snake charmer made to bait and switch.

I'd mastered both techniques. I could hide my feelings and stoke others', could weave my own narrative of lies that lured even the fastest of flies to my honey.

But nothing prepared me for the prospect of playing Truth or Dare with a ship full of drunk sirens.

Cassryn had called Laureli and I to the galley after the rest had already busted open a barrel of rum, cups full and spirits high. They lounged around the long wooden table, a chorus of laughter greeting us as we entered.

Despite the clawing, festering pit of impatience in my chest, I knew I had to give them this. Knew that without a respite and some rest, they would not survive the war to come.

And neither would I. Running on the last fumes of regret and rage, there was little left to burn. A hollowness settled in the cage of my ribs, the beast within even lumbering back to whatever deep, sleepy cave it dwelled in.

Summoning Danura and knocking on Death's front door would have to wait another night. Rest demanded a toll be paid first. But it was clear that my definition of rest and theirs were sorely mismatched.

Lanternlight warmed already rosy cheeks, the scent of stale liquor and mixed herbs swirling with each breathy laugh. Another night, it might have been a comfort, the clinging coziness of eight bodies packed into this wooden pocket of peace. But the harsh back of my chair only poked at open sores, my body still on alert. Laureli's drink had soothed the serrated edges of my hunger, but nothing but deep, endless sleep could satiate my tired soul.

We sat in a circle around the table, Ellian to my left, stiff as a board, his dark brown locks tied up in a lopsided bun. Nelle to my right giggled as she swirled her generous mug with a cinnamon stick. Marina, the mischief maker herself, Cassryn, Willow, Laureli, and Siobhan all lounged about, even the deadliest of the sirens taking the night to enjoy and explore.

Marina explained the game, holding her very full glass, a risky glow radiating from her crimson stare. The premise was innocent enough; going around in a circle, we'd either offer a personal truth, or submit to a dare. But I knew these women—*these water demons*—and there would be nothing innocent about any game the truth-witch invented.

"Playing is mandatory, or I'll eat you all alive, got it?" Marina chuckled, fangs peeking from her bow-shaped lips. "If you can't play a turn, sip your drink."

The most important skill every Mathonwy man learned was when to fold. To know when the con was up, when there was no trick up our tailored sleeves left to play. A skilled cheat was one that could walk away before they stayed long enough to turn the fool.

If I stayed, I'd either be siren food by morning's light, or they'd all be dragon-bait.

I dragged a tired hand through my too-long hair, fingers tugging through the matted curls. Lyr below, I needed a long scrub and my cot, not to flirt with Marina's fire. I pushed up from my seat, cracking my stiff neck. "You all have fun. I think I need some sleep."

Laureli scooted her chair back, blocking my path to the door, an eyebrow raised. "Too good for us now?"

Impatience scratched down my back like a rusted fork, creating a deeper itch than it satisfied. My skin fit too tightly, my siren parts swimming uncomfortably close to the surface. Keira used to say the beast you feed is the one that grows, and after my generous sips of blood this afternoon, it wouldn't take much prodding to go fully feral.

"Come on, Captain." Cassryn stuck a muscled leg out to trip me, the stone sentry keen on playing guard tonight. Her dark curls bounced as she wagged her head, rum washing her marbled mask with an uncharacteristic whimsy that usually belonged to her sister. "When did you get so boring?"

Untamed parts of me snarled at the insult, tugging at the leash to be let free. "When my wife died."

And so did all the decent, fun parts of me. The parts that could laugh over a game with friends, that could drink and be merry with my kin. My wit and charm, my cleverness and cunning, all gone. All that was left was the *Ddraig Aur*, the Golden Dragon ready to bear its fangs and set the world on fire to save his wife. That creature had no tolerance for useless truths told around a table.

The gemstone stares all studied me, some colored with the distinct tint of contempt, others soaked in wretched pity. The scent accosted the air, cloyingly sweet like burnt caramel. Silence wrapped the room like an itchy wool blanket, warm in the worst, sweat-soaked way.

"Please don't leave me alone with them," Ellian pleaded, shrugging off the quiet, voice tender in a way I rarely heard from the boisterous blacksmith.

Something twisted in my middle, the shifter triggering a hidden transformation in my deepest parts. Snakes and dragons were loners, instinct driving them to think only for themselves. But *blaidds* were pack animals, safety not just in their strength, but in their solidarity.

I looked around the table again, to the expectant faces peeking up from the rims of their cups. Sirens always swam better in schools. I couldn't swarm Arawn's keep without them. Couldn't save my wife with my desperation alone. I owed them a drink and a dare at the very least.

Didn't mean I had to like it.

"One round," I ground out through clenched teeth, stalking back to my seat. I stifled the urge to jump ship and swim right into the Otherworld singlehandedly to avoid whatever scheme Marina had concocted.

Then again, if they wanted to play dares with a dragon, they'd better be prepared to taste my fire.

Marina wasted no time, bouncing in her chair the second my backside hit mine, a master predator lunging for her first innocent fish. "Nelle, you first. Truth, or dare?"

"Truth." Nelle held her mug close for emotional support, sipping the spirits off the top. "But go easy on me."

The rest of the girls—and Ellian—leaned in, all ready for Marina's first strike.

The siren basked in the undivided attention like a cat soaking up sun on a windowsill. She crossed her arms against her supple chest, seduction even in the most harmless of gestures, the Ir'desian dancer always performing. Her ruby stare stilled on Nelle. "What's the most reckless thing you've ever done?"

A piece of me I hadn't remembered winked awake, my head whipping to watch Nelle's crimson blush deepen. As loathe as I was to admit it, it was an excellent question. The Violet Dove had always been a healer first, but we'd all glimpsed the sharp edges beneath her sage-and-jasmine smile.

"Back before we even had Caden, Idris..." her veiled grin widened as she swirled the contents of her glass, "*my husband* and I went on a trip to Ir'de to gather supplies for our practice. While we were there, this woman in the market followed us, and she kept making eyes at Idris. It didn't bother me at first, but eventually, while I was away grabbing something from a different stall, she convinced him to come into her shop."

The pungent scent of Nelle's jealousy, acidic and bitter, mulled the air, intense now despite the decades of diffusion. The sting of soured memories surged through my veins. I bit back the shot of rum someone had poured for me, letting it cleanse the aftertaste of forgotten envy from my tongue.

"What did you do next, cry at her?" Cassryn jabbed, leaning her chin on her folded hands, pulling me back to Nelle's story.

Nelle sucked back a deep dreg of her spirits, wincing as the liquid burned down her throat. "No. I walked in, saw her trying to make a pass at him, and before I could think, I threw a whole vial of peppercorn at her head."

Siobhan nearly spat out her sip, choking on the liquid. "Wow. I always knew you had a set of claws on you *before* the shift."

I bit my lip to stifle a laugh. Perhaps we all were beasts even before our goddesses gave us fins and fangs and fury. I, for one, had always been a wicked, rotten snake, as evidenced by my venomous mood tonight.

Nelle shrugged, pulling the cinnamon stick from her drink and chewing on the tip. "I did give her a free headache remedy after. But I'm also pretty sure that's the night we conceived our son. Turns out, my husband was happy to feel like a damsel in distress who needed rescuing."

At that, the beast in my belly perked its ears up. Memories floated up, reminding me of another lovesick man happy to be rescued by his jealous, courageous wife.

The blaring light of the hazardous Ir'desian sun, the smell of sex and regret wafting from the brothel behind me, the noisy market bludgeoning my ears…all washing away in an instant, my northern star returned to the sky.

"You came back."

She'd come to rescue me, again and again.

This time, I would return the favor.

A lump formed in my throat, made of my stupid pride and anguish. I scanned the rosy faces around the table, siren and shifter alike, newfound gratitude swelling in my lungs. Nelle and Siobhan had been the ones to follow her then, had helped her save me in Katrin's bathhouse where I almost died the *third* time. Ellian and I'd come a long way from trading insults in *The Dancing Raven*. We'd been two devotees at Ariannad's altar, both vying for her attention and favor. But now he fought with us tooth and nail, had sailed to *Hiraeth* and back, even after Keira rejected him. The rest of the sirens had saved me in *Hiraeth*, when I'd been a lonely, broken soul washed up on their sands. And they'd saved all of Porthladd when they'd showed up for us, risking their lives and their secrets to save a world that'd abandoned them.

Every Mathonwy man knew how to con and cheat, knew when to fold and when to flee…but the best of us knew when to settle our debts.

I owed these people my life three times over. My wife's life, too. And I could never pay them what I owed. There was no sum in the universe vast enough to settle the score. But I could at the very least play a few hands with them, show them a little more appreciation and mercy.

Sirens always swam better in schools. I wouldn't stray from mine any longer.

"Your husband sounds like a good man." I coughed around the vicious lump of my shame. Keira always said desperation made men monsters. Mine had made me the biggest rutting ass in this world and the next.

And yet, Nelle smiled at me like I was the sun, squinting through the tears that lined her violet stare. "He was. Thank you."

Good job, boy.

A familiar, ethereal voice rumbled deep in the back of my mind. The ship swayed and bobbed, as if the sea was patting me on the back, too.

Marina winked at me once, so fast I almost missed it, before letting loose a fake retch, sticking her pointer finger in her mouth for emphasis.

"*Blech*, you're so sappy. My turn." She stretched back, curves almost freeing themselves from the gauzy dress hanging loosely from her shoulders. "I choose dare, so someone give me something good. Or dirty."

A thousand thorned suggestions rattled through my head, the Sea-Snake chomping at the opportunity, but Cassryn beat me to it.

"I dare you to shut up," she scoffed, tossing her mess of curls over her shoulder.

I didn't have Marina's gift for truth-seeing, but I did know how to spot the signs when a player bluffed too close to the sun.

Marina went eerily still, limbs tense like a lithe panther crouching in the grass, ready to strike. A vicious grin exposed her fangs. "Deal. But what else should I do with my lips if they're not talking?"

Cassryn winked, puckering her lips and making mocking kissing sounds, but Marina would not be bested. She pounced, so much faster than one would imagine from a woman of her stature, smacking a loud, wet kiss right on Cassryn's half-open mouth.

"Marina!" Willow squealed as the siren smooched her sister, Cassryn knocking over the remnants of her mug on herself as she gently shoved Marina off her with a laugh.

Laughter broke across the room like cracked ice, a small fracture first, then fissures in every direction. Nelle let loose a tiny snort, then the rest joined in, a dam breaking loose.

A traitorous chuckle bubbled up from my own throat, reedy and hoarse with disuse. Marina thumbed the side of her lip, fixing the smudges of her scarlet lip-stain, half of which had been transferred all over Cassryn's. Marina shrugged, the picture of innocence, but then pretended to sew her lips shut, completing Cassryn's dare.

"Don't try to beat Marina at her own game," I said before I could catch myself, a long dormant part of me finally cresting to the surface.

Cassryn fired an arrow-sharp look at me while wringing the spilled rum out her damp black tunic like it was my neck, but a smirk crawled onto her stained lips. "I think I won that round."

Marina cut in again. "Your turn, Cass."

"Truth."

The siren waggled her brows at her, still not done playing with her food. "Okay, here's an easy one; did you like our little lip lock?"

Cassryn tucked her arms under her pits, re-armoring herself, but even the stony soldier had a soft spot for Marina. "The best I had in a while, though I'd imagine it'd be better if I didn't get my clothes wet."

The scarlet witch's eyes raked over the wet tunic. "Maybe it'd be better with no clothes at all, Cassie."

"Moving on before Cassryn and Marina need to get a room..." Laureli huffed between full-bodied giggles.

Ellian nudged my side, shoulders shaking with silent laughter of his own as the two sirens flirted with their fangs out. "This is going to get ugly quick, isn't it?"

I clinked my mug against his, two men stupid enough to venture into the sirens' den. "You bet your furry arse."

We made our way around the circle, each of Marina's machinations undoing layer after layer of tension in the room, inhibitions freeing themselves from chains as the truth-witch tended to each of our unspoken desires. Warmth stirred in my middle and in my cheeks as I drank and laughed, the coiled ball of wired anxiety I kept in my own gut unwinding with each new act. After Laureli rattled off–in *explicit* detail–the best lay she ever had, and Willow drank three shots mixed with some foul-smelling potion Nelle had in her arsenal, it was Siobhan's turn.

"Truth." She nodded once, sitting straighter as she braced herself–a much safer bet from a woman used to weathering long battles.

But Marina knew how to hit hard and fast–and decidedly below the belt. She licked her lips. "Interesting. All right…who would you rather bed tonight, Ellian or Ronan?"

She might have doused me in oil and set me aflame the way my whole body instantly burned with shame. "Marina, don't push too far."

Siobhan had been a comfort to a long-forgotten, broken-hearted boy. But while I did not regret our mutually pleasurable escape, it had left scars on her, harbored feelings now festering wounds she hid beneath her hard exterior.

Her face blanched before she spat her next words syllable by syllable, a general ready to strike down insubordination. "Nope. Dare instead."

"You can't change your mind, it's against the rules," Willow whined, drunk and dumb enough to miss the way the air in the room shifted to a chilled standstill.

"I said dare." Siobhan's jagged tone left no room for argument.

Willow's eyes blew wide, but Marina's narrowed, sniffing the discomfort like chum in the water. "Fine. I dare you to plant one on Ellian."

Siobhan's whole build went taut as a wind-blown sail, murderous rage simmering in her scent.

"Marina, come on," I hedged, remembering my role as stand-in Captain. My crew needed rest and recreation–not a death-match brawl between two demons of the deep. "She doesn't need that."

"What, am I so unappealing?" Ellian snorted, covering the distinct metallic scent of insecurity that rose from his copper skin.

Siobhan twisted to him, coiled braids whipping around with her speed. "No, it's not–"

"Kiss him or drink one of Nelle's concoctions." Marina's ultimatum sliced through whatever protest Siobhan had on her tongue. "Your choice, hon."

Siobhan hurtled one last dark look Marina's way before shifting her gaze to Ellian's mouth. She gripped his chin tightly in her hands, pulling his face to her. "Fine. Pucker up, pooch."

The sirens echoed a dog-whistle as Siobhan's lips crashed into Ellian's. As his hand—*reflexively*—cupped the side of her face. As the tension in her stiff back unraveled, sinking deeper into the kiss.

Several *long* moments passed, the cheers ending before Siobhan ripped away and plopped back into her seat, facing away suspiciously.

"Um…truth. Or dare. Whichever," Ellian stammered, swallowing hard. He did not pivot—staring after Siobhan with burning intensity.

I didn't need to study them closely to smell the rippling want between them, desire clear as daybreak. I fought the smile working its way on my lips. Maybe even the deepest scars could fade with the right remedy. Another Marina miracle.

"Truth," Ellian repeated with more surety, shaking his head, coming out of his trance.

"I think we already got our truth, based on that blush. You get a pass, shifter." Marina winked at him, tossing her long auburn locks over her shoulder. "Anyway, Ronan…truth or dare?"

"Dare." I didn't particularly feel like parting with any truths tonight. Those chips I'd keep tucked away in the dark cage of my heart, the beast protecting its horde. "But I warn you not to give me anything you wouldn't want my wife to hear about when we rescue her."

I was pretty certain the only person in this room Keira wouldn't mind me kissing was Ellian, and the poor oaf had suffered enough excitement for one night.

Marina nodded, message thankfully received. Even she wouldn't tempt a goddess's wrath. "Then I dare you to tell us your favorite story."

Despite all I heard tonight, that request was the most shocking. "What?"

"Oh, please!" Willow clapped frantically, wild curls flying with the action. Next to her, Cassryn nodded, still licking her wounds.

"It's been forever since we've heard you narrate, and there's only so many of Marina's tall tales we can tolerate." Nelle twirled the tip of her dark braid with a drunken grin. Marina whacked her arm, sending them both into another fit of giggles.

"Besides, I think we should shift course anyway." Siobhan cleared her throat, eyes flicking to Ellian, and then to me in a rare silent plea. "This game could get more dangerous than any of us are willing to venture tonight. Tell a story, Ro."

My mind reeled, searching for a short story to tell, one that would satisfy their hunger and let me leave shortly. I didn't know what time it was, but the ache settling into my muscles reiterated my body's deep need for a warm bath and my soft cot.

But despite my years of practice, only one narrative came to mind. One that felt too close to the truth. Too painful.

Perhaps it was exhaustion, or the rum, or the weight of the debt I owed these friends, but the tale came rattling from my mouth anyway.

"Before Lyr split the isles of man, the Deyrnas was ruled by one emperor, a man named Maskin. He was kind and generous, and watched over his people well. He was so focused on others, he forgot himself, and never bothered to take a wife despite his devilish good looks."

"I volunteer if he's still single." Marina waggled her eyebrows, earning another laugh from the crowd, albeit this one less hearty. The sirens all leaned forward, listening closely to Maskin's eulogy.

I continued, a forgotten voice replacing mine, one born of the Storyweaver, the Sea-Snake who lived off riddles and fairy tales. "After the split, Maskin did everything he could to keep the Deyrnas safe, even establishing small councils to advise him from the different isles so he could stay in the capitol as the leader they all needed. But one night, a woman came to him in a dream. She had a voice like starlight, and when she sang his name, something in his soul awakened. When he woke to find her gone, he vowed to find her no matter the cost."

I paused, swallowing back the lump lodged soundly in my throat. I shoved away thoughts of my favorite silver-eyed, star-dusted face. Of the vow I still honored in every crevice of my soul.

My voice carried over the expectant silence that settled, stronger now, like a prayer intended to my long-off love. "So he scoured the kingdom, journeying to every far corner to find his bride. Everywhere he went, he offered homage to the locals, giving out gifts, listening to their needs. And in turn, they helped him find his love—a woman named Mira living all the way in what would one day be Bachtref."

"I love happy endings," Willow breathed a dreamy sigh, leaning her head on her fist. Cassryn glared at her for the interruption, but even her statuesque posture loosened.

Unfortunately, not all endings were happy. Not yet.

If it's not all right, it's not the end.

"But while Maskin wooed his soon-to-be-wife, finally feeling whole, the councils he set up planned a coup. They swarmed the abandoned capitol and unseated him from his throne. And though he was loved by the people, and had only given more and more of himself to them, Maskin refused to ask them to fight. He would not risk Mira's safety, or the lives of his people, for a throne."

"I spoke too soon," Willow pouted, earning a full-bodied snort from Laureli.

A chuckle worked its way out of my mouth, the next breath of the story carried on its back. "Maskin did live happily—since he could not return to Orwellin, he made a happy home in Bachtref, tending to the land and selling his crops to feed the kingdom in a different way. And he and his wife lived long, full lives, with many healthy children, all of whom ventured out into the world and made names for themselves."

And that's why this story was my favorite. No gods or monsters, no magic or mysteries. Just mortals, living fulfilling lives. Just a king sacrificing a throne for his heart. A happy ending born not from spells or riddles, not from lies or well-made cons, but from love and loyalty. From true hearts and good intentions.

Nelle placed a gentle hand on my forearm, thumb rubbing asymmetrical circles. "See? Gods are not the only ones who can change the world for the better."

A flash of light where we touched, and a surge of blinding pain. I hissed through my teeth, but then she pulled away, revealing the black lines of ink that made a home under my skin.

A proud dragon, wings unfurled, wrapped around a crescent moon. Protecting its most prized treasure. Its heart.

Tears welled in my eyes, blurring the lines of my newest tattoo.

"We can do this, Ronan." Marina's voice held an uncharacteristic softness, but every syllable had the weight of the truth-teller's certainty. "We'll save her, and after we've stopped Arawn, you two can go make babies and plant corn until you're old and wrinkly."

I contemplated each and every one of them seated around the table again with new vision. Nelle, a healer, not just of sores and scrapes, but of heartbreak. Marina, who understood not just the truth of what we said, but all the words we couldn't. Cassryn and Willow, light and dark sides of the same coin, sisters that could balance even the most uneven odds. Laureli, a seer who saw not just the path forward, but the path within. Siobhan, not just a spear, but a shield to protect those she held close. And Ellian, a loyal brother, born not of blood but of bravery and choice.

For them, I could be the beast my wife made. A dragon, ready to take to the skies, to burn down the world and rebuild it in their image.

I was tired of playing the long con. Tired of underhanded trades and desperate lies. Instead, I would be like Maskin. Would lay all my chips on the table and let them fall where they may. Would find good in the small victories, miracles in the mundane.

"We do need one god, though." I discarded the sorrow that wrapped around my heart, instead standing firm in the pocket of power I'd found in my friends' love. We had a purpose, and I had a wife to save. But first, we needed someone else's support. "A goddess, in fact. Right Laureli?"

The seer nodded, the air in the galley shifting.

Marina perked up, stretching once before her smile dissolved into something sharp-edged and sinister. "I was hoping tonight would end in an orgy, but I'll take a summoning ritual instead."

I smirked. "Tomorrow night, we summon Danura."

12

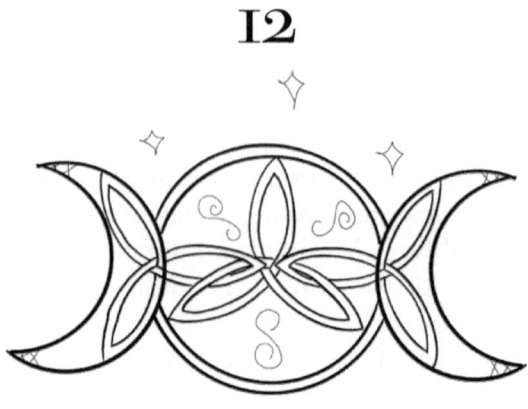

Mirrors and Misery

KEIRA

My reflection stared back at me in the black ice, Arawn standing behind her as his hand rested on her shoulder. The girl in the mirror wore my face; silver eyes and ebony hair, speckled freckles across the bridge of her nose, full brows casting shadows in the hollows beneath her eyes.

But she was missing something, a vitality I couldn't name, a spark I hadn't seen or felt since I'd been below. Perhaps it had been snuffed out when she earned the angry, puckered scar across her throat, the pink line the only remembrance of the blade that felled her. Or perhaps she'd been consumed by the mark devouring the pale skin of her shoulder, the reminder of the sentence she served.

Yet something brighter sparkled in my middle, something even Death couldn't squash. The promise of seeing Ronan dangled in my face, so close I could almost reach out and catch it.

The sheet of ice stretched from the ground all the way to the dark ceiling, the entire wall made of the cold, smooth glacier. It was the first room aside from my own in Death's mansion that wasn't littered with signs of neglect, the stone floor polished and the black candelabras on the other walls free of cobwebs and dust. Even the single, high-backed chaise that stood in the center of the room had fresh roses in a vase on the table next to it, those blood-red petals the only spot of color in the black room.

But my eyes didn't move from the ice, the harsh white the only thing I cared to notice.

"How does this work?" The reflection's lips moved as mine did.

Arawn grinned, but it didn't meet his eyes. He reached out, touching the ice with his bare palm. "You can only see things as they are happening. It does not tell the future and cannot look into the past."

As he spoke, our reflections in the ice disappeared, engulfed by billowing shadows.

"But can you see anyone?" I asked again, scanning the shadows for any hint of blond or spark of blue, for a crooked nose and sideways smile...

"Yes." Death crossed to the chair in three long strides before falling into it. One leg dangled over the side as he leaned his head back into the soft fabric, covering his eyes with his arm. "Would it make you uncomfortable to know I've spent most of my time watching you?"

I tore my gaze away from the shadows to give him a long look. It was the most relaxed I'd seen him, his limbs loosely draped across the chaise, his long hair falling freely over the cushion. But beneath his arm, his pale cheeks burned red, his ears peeking from his hair a similar scarlet. And instead of his normally intense, direct stare, he hid his eyes, too afraid or ashamed to look up.

Death was *embarrassed*.

Like when Auntie Vala used to hide in the kitchen whenever guests came to call, waiting until they'd tasted the food before she'd come and sit and laugh along. Or like Finna, hiding her nightgowns in my closet whenever she snuck a suitor into her chambers, pretending her wash basket full of dirty clothes was mine.

This was his safe space. His home. The only place he could be himself, perhaps. Where he allowed himself to want. To wonder what waited beyond the gates.

But no one hid from Death. No home was safe from his snare. I ran an absentminded finger across my scar, the raised flesh a reminder of that very thing.

"Yes," I answered honestly, imagining the large wall painted with my image, with me running around my father's ship, or fighting with my family. Or worse, with me and Ronan together, our intimate moments on display…

But I shook off the thought, instead remembering what I needed.

Ronan.

Ronan.

Ronan.

"But I'm asking you to help me stalk my husband," I continued before he could respond, offering him a piteous smile. "So I'm not any better. We're all monsters, right?"

We were all monsters, some of us just hid it better. If I had to hide my monstrous parts to distract Death, to see my husband one last time…

At that, his arm fell. His lips parted and dark eyes shone with disbelief. A pang of guilt shot through me for my dishonesty, but I brushed it off, turning back to the wall, waiting with bated breath.

"I'll turn around to give you some privacy, but I'm here if you need me," Death said, and the chaise creaked as he shifted his weight. I stifled a scoff at the irony of privacy now of all times, but I didn't question Death's newfound sense of boundaries. After a long pause, he finally uttered the command I'd been waiting for: "Show her Ronan Mathonwy."

The shadows in the ice churned for a moment longer, tendrils twisting into shapes before fading away into a clear picture. It was more precise than any painting I'd seen from the masters in Ir'de, vivid in its excruciating detail.

My heart sank to my toes, heavier than an ocean of ice as the image moved.

He was underwater, his glorious golden tail flicking behind him, his sapphire eyes somehow sparkling in the dark deep. His curls floated freely, in desperate need of a cut, but he looked healthy, vibrant in his siren form. Strong and sure. Purposeful.

So close, like I could reach out and touch him if I tried. Perhaps if I broke the ice, he would spill into the room, like a goldfish in a glass bowl.

My legs gave out, my knees hitting the marble floor again, cuts ripping open. But I didn't care. Didn't feel it. Only urgency tugged at my center, the pang of cold beneath my fingertips as I clawed at the wall. The air fled the room, as if I was on top of a mountain, not in the lowest chambers of Death's domain.

"Ronan." I choked on the word, on the single prayer, my shaking hands tracing his form in the ice. "Ronan, can you hear me?"

"No, he can't, nor can you hear him," Death answered, reminding me of my audience. Of the ice between us. Of the prison he built me. "But if you watch long enough, you'll learn to read lips."

I watched him dive deeper, his muscled form cutting through the water like a ship on a clear day. If I could not reach out and touch him, if I could not run back through the veil between life and death and swoop him up in my arms, I would gladly watch from afar, a spectator to his triumphs and tribulations.

Ronan swam up to a dark cave, the shadows inside nearly as dark as Death's door. I held my breath, something clenching in my gut. Ronan stared into the blackness, his smooth chest heaving as he breathed it in, his gills stretching at the effort.

I knew that face, though I'd never seen it in siren form. Knew the wanting. The waiting. The adder in the grass, calculating when to strike. The shark in the water, latching on to the scent of blood.

I stiffened, waiting, wanting. For what, I didn't know. But the thing inside me jerked and pulled, a rope ready to be tossed like a lifeline in a storm, waiting to be yanked tight...

Another predator in the water cut through the connection like it was a single thread. Her warm skin and orange tail nearly as bright as my husband's, her form just as clear in the icy mirror.

The anchor in my gut sank lower, threatening to pull me through the floor and down into the abyss.

Siobhan's hands traced down his arm before twining with his fingers. Pulling him back from the darkness. The thing in my middle stretched before snapping, and I doubled over as it recoiled, hitting me like a punch to the gut.

"Ronan?" His name was no longer a prayer, but a cry for help.

Siobhan leaned her forehead against his, a soft smile sweeping across her warm features. Ronan leaned into the touch, the tip of his long fin brushing against hers. They stayed there for a moment, mouths moving with whispered words I'd never hear. Promises I'd never be a part of.

I knew that face on him, too. Knew the wanting. The waiting. Knew the boy behind the mask who smiled back at her, knew the fear and loneliness swimming in the sapphire of his gaze.

A feather-soft kiss grazed the back of her hand.

I slammed my fist against the ice, knuckles breaking as my heart did. The ice did not budge, only showed them swimming upward, back to the surface, back to the life they'd live together...

"This is a trick, isn't it?" I stumbled to my feet, voice cracking like shattered glass.

Arawn shuffled from his seat, brow knit. "No, I assure you..."

"Prove it!" I shouted, banging my fist against the wall again. My blood splattered across the image, and fresh shadows spurred, marring the image of my husband just as he broke the surface of the water. Sapphire dissolved into darkness once more. I scratched at the mirror again, desperate for another taste of my own poison. "Prove it *right now!*"

Arawn stepped between me and the mirror, his mass casting a shadow. Gently, he placed one hand on the ice, voice infused with sorrow. "Show me Keira Branwen-Mathonwy."

The mist moved, and my image reappeared. Not my reflection, but my back, the mess of knots snagged in my hair, the untucked tail of my tunic, as if the shadows watched us from behind.

Not real.

Not real.

Not real.

"That proves nothing," I snarled, the feral and furious parts of me the only unbattered bits I had left. My chest heaved as sobs worked their way up my throat, burning like the power in my veins.

"Fine," Death sighed, shifting his hand again across the ice. "Show me Morwyn Locasta."

A new image emerged from the shadows, a woman dressed in a stiff black frock, her dark hair pulled in a tight bun that accentuated the skeletal edge of her cheekbones. She sat in a high-backed chair at a black desk, spindled fingers sorting through paperwork, shadows of her own dancing over the page. A faceless guard approached, and she tilted her gaze up from the parchment, a single eyebrow raised in annoyance.

Not real.

Not real.

Not real.

"Rancid bitch." A fresh wave of fury washed through me, a storm raging in my chest. The force in my center transformed again, molding into something new, something mean. Fire, not light. My control slipped, the scorching flame fleeing to my fingertips, red sparks spilling from them. I slapped my hand against the ice, wishing it would all melt away, wishing I could burn the whole palace to the ground...

"Show me Saeth Branwen," Death demanded, covering my hand with his, and the blackness stirred again, morphing and twisting until the new picture painted itself across the ice.

The fire died in my chest, the smoke clearing from my mind.

Saeth sat in my hammock, swinging gently in the night breeze. Soft silver tears streamed down her sharp cheeks as she stared at the stars, arms folded across her chest, hugging herself.

In my whole life, I'd never seen Saeth cry. Not a single sob shed at her mother's funeral, not a whisper of a whimper as Finna bled out onto the streets of Porthladd. Saeth suffered only in silence, her steel and ice impervious to saltwater tears.

Uncle Aidan always said the best lies were ones based in truth. That if they were too strange, it was a dead giveaway for the deception. I had no doubt that Arawn was an excellent liar. The God of Death knew how to hide his monstrous parts well, buried beneath sheets of ice, stuffed away behind fragrant beds of roses.

But this moment, this rare glimpse into my cousin's sorrow...

There was no faking her tears, no imagining the wobble in her normally sturdy lower lip, no conjuring the gentle shake of her slim shoulders.

I looked away, looked instead at Arawn, at the frown tugging his mouth down, at the dark hair sweeping in front of his face to hide the pity I knew waited in his gaze.

Real.

Real.

Real.

No, this was not an illusion. This was my personal torture, tangible and terrible and real. A tidal wave of fresh tears rose up faster than a hurricane wind, shaking my whole frame as they spilled over.

Ronan.

Ronan.

Ronan.

I'll wait for you in the Otherworld.

I never deserved him in the first place, his golden heart. But I had waited, secretly hoping that even if it took him an eternity to join me, even if he had a long, healthy, happy life ahead of him, that when his scales lost their shine and his bones crumbled to dust, that he'd swim home to me.

I'll wait for you in the Otherworld.

I had waited. He hadn't.

No, that wasn't right. I was overthinking. After everything Ronan and I had been through, every miscommunication and misstep, every triumph and tribulation, he wouldn't have moved on this fast.

But Siobhan could offer him something I could not. Something he—something *I*—desperately needed.

A friend. A comforting touch. An anchor.

"What…" Arawn's broad hands claimed my shoulders as my world shattered around me. He leaned down, blissfully dark eyes scanning mine. "What can I do to ease your pain?"

"Nothing, I'm—" I stuttered, desperate to disappear into the darkness, for anything that stopped the cracking in my soul. "He's…."

He's gone.

What had I expected? Did I expect him to chase after me, to defy death itself to cross the veil and come save me? No, I'd rather die a thousand deaths than see him forfeit his life for mine.

Had I expected him to then live out his life in mourning and misery? Expected him to stay chaste, expected him to wistfully wait for me until his time came, alone and unloved? Perhaps one day his friendship with Siobhan would turn to more, or perhaps another woman would walk into his life that could make him happy. Did I want him to deny that part of himself? To sit and wallow in frozen misery just like I was?

No, that was a fate worse than death. One I'd wish on my worst enemies, not the one man I loved more than life itself. Not on the boy who wore the sun in his smirk and the stars in his heart.

Still, the lonely pit sank deeper in my stomach, realization heavy on my shoulders. My husband would not spend eternity alone.

But I would.

Death inhaled sharply before wrapping his arms around me. I stiffened for a moment, the hard planes of his chest cold as ice, his heartbeat somehow far away. These were not the arms I craved, not the touch that soothed. But his deep voice buzzed through me as he spoke. "I'm so sorry you had to see that."

At that, I softened, melting into his frame, my arms captaining themselves to twine around his waist. He was not my husband, not the person I had given my heart. But perhaps even Death could greet me like a friend, could offer a sympathetic hug to warm the chill.

Even the coldest winters eventually gave way to glorious spring. If this was my fate, if my husband had chosen his...was it so wrong to embrace Death? To live out my eternity in the springtime of his strong arms?

I'd been sitting on the precipice of this choice for so long, staring out over the cliff's edge, imagining what it would be like to jump. But now, I no longer needed to choose. The road behind me was wiped away, no going back. I'd come too far, and all that was left were the waters below, waiting for me to dive in.

After all, a part of my soul had belonged to him long before the *Melthith* spot marked me. The day I sent Lochlan to his watery grave, the day I'd used my gifts as a curse, the day I'd first courted Death by doing his dirty work...I'd sent a part of my soul, too.

"It's not your fault," I croaked, breathing in Death's scent, the pine and snow, mixed with patience and sorrow. So foreign to the citrus and sea I loved most, but a cheap comfort nonetheless. "I'm... I'm glad he's not alone."

It wasn't a lie, though it stung like acid as it left my mouth. If one of us had to be the lonely and broken-hearted, I preferred it be me. The day of my wedding, I chose to lay down my future for the folk I loved. This was no different, no less painful or important.

Papa used to say there was more than one way to sacrifice a life. Perhaps there would be victory in surrendering my soul to Death. Adventure in my sacrifice.

"You don't have to be alone either," Death mumbled into my hair, his cheek pressed against my head. He squeezed tighter, pressing me closer into the consoling cage of his broad chest. "We could...we could try..."

My gut clenched at the thought of anyone other than Ronan, but I I closed my eyes to picture it, to imagine what waited beyond the cliff's edge. But instead of obsidian and pine, instead of snow-white skin and rosebud lips and prayers unanswered and secrets unshared...

Citrus-scented hands and gold scales, sun-kissed tan and sapphire smiles, tales still being written and truths still believed...

Death.
Death.
Death.
Ronan.
Ronan.
Ronan.

"I can't." I pushed against Arawn' chest gently, detaching myself enough to look up at him. "I think I need some time."

Time. An eternity, perhaps, to mourn my marriage.

A flash of reckless hope scattered across his expression, lips parted slightly as he tucked a strand of my wild hair behind my ear. "The Otherworld is patient, *Caraid.*" His fingers trailed down my cheek and to my neck, to where the scar blemished my fair skin, all the way to where his mark painted my pale shoulder in his crest. "Here, everything eventually forgets."

His icy touch lingered, goosebumps spreading like wildfire where we met.

I didn't want to forget. I wanted to reach through the mirror, to steer the wheel of my own life, to run to my husband and never look back. But if forgetting was the only way, perhaps I could let myself bask in the pool of blissful ignorance.

"I need some rest."

Rest. Reflection. A moment to breathe, a moment to find my lungs again after they'd been ripped out. A second to stare out over the cliff, a small drop of eternity to decide how I would endure it.

The Otherworld sees us as we see ourselves.

How did I see myself without Ronan? Without my family and friends, without my home and my husband...what purpose did I have?

Arawn nodded, his gaze steeped in sympathy, before pressing a soft kiss to my forehead. I froze at the touch, at the gentle brush of his smooth mouth against my skin, but he pulled away before I could reject him. "I'll be waiting when you're ready."

He breezed by as he made his way up the stairs, leaving me alone.

For a moment, I sucked in the solitude, letting it fuel my tears anew. Death's touch was not painful as I'd imagined. It was compassion against the cold tundra of our cage, a small victory in a sea of failures. It put an end to a restless ache, the sweet respite of nothingness in his frozen fingertips.

But it was not the paradise of my husband's love.

I didn't know if I deserved the mercy of a friend to fend off the loneliness.

My feet carried me absentmindedly to my quarters, like a ghost wandering through Death's estate, an unresolved spirit stuck to my surroundings. I pushed through the door, the scent of the sea breeze slamming into my senses as it wafted from the false window, another reminder of what I could no longer claim. It smelled of voyages unsailed, of shanties unsung, of life unlived. Of laughs long left behind, of tears soaked deep into the *Ceffyl's* sails.

But mixed with the scent of the ocean was lavender and foxglove, the unforgiving floral mixture dominating the space.

On the large bed, my cousin sat with legs crossed, hands folded on her knees. Her foot bounced with impatience. "Finally. What took you so long?"

Here, everything eventually forgets.

I'd forgotten my one mission, my only purpose pushed to the back of my mind to make room for smoke and mirrors. I'd forgotten my task, assigned by Papa, my Captain. Forgotten who I was supposed to be, the role I was given.

For a flash of a second, relief washed over me, the pit in my stomach unwinding. It might have shattered me to see his honeyed gaze dull ever so slightly, to see the almost imperceptible slump in his shoulders. If I had any small victories left, it was that I was so very accomplished at disappointing my father, even in Death.

Find out what he wants from ye.

I'd forgotten, but I didn't care. Not anymore.

Here, everything eventually forgets.

If only I could forget my heartbreak. My husband.

"I can't do this," I snapped at Finna as I stormed into the adjacent washroom. I turned on the long spout to the tub, letting the liquid fill the onyx basin. Perhaps the water would wash it all away, would let me drown my sorrows in its silken caress. I sat on the edge, considering the bliss of falling in and never coming out.

"Keira?" Finna's heels clacked across the marble floor as she entered, arms folded across her supple chest. "What happened?"

While I was grateful that Papa would not bear witness to my shame, irritation prickled at the back of my neck, and I bit my cheek. Of all the people waiting for me, of all the faces I craved, of course it had to be Finna here to watch me lick my wounds. Finna, with her superior blend of scorn and sarcasm. Finna, with her perfect posture, her head always held high enough to look down at me. Finna, with enough fight in her to flatten an army with a single feathered insult. "Go away."

"Not until you tell me what's going on," she huffed, sitting stiff-backed on the edge of the tub, sticking a hand in the now-tepid water. She swirled an elegant finger in the soup before flicking a drop of water at me. "Start talking."

Anger surged in my stomach, gratefully filling the emptiness. If Finna wanted a fight, I could oblige. Could play that role instead of the miserable martyr I was now.

"I can't hurt him."

Finna rolled her eyes, coughing up a humorless laugh. "I know it's intimidating, he's the God of Death after all, Keira, but you have to—"

"No, I know what he is." I cut her off, my blood boiling in my veins. "He doesn't deserve to be hurt like that. Like *this*."

No, no one deserved this ache. This cold. Not even the God of Death. Not even the king of monsters, with his endless stare and icy touch. Even he earned respite from an empty eternity. And even if he insisted on seeing himself as a monster, even if he hid in shadows and self-loathing, I would not be the one to torture him further. I would not spit salt in his wounds or kick him while he was down. No, for once in my Lyr-forsaken life, I would not make things worse.

Finna's disdain twisted the corner of her mouth into a frown. "What in Lyr's name are you talking about?"

The fire extinguished again. The shadows shapeshifted in my mind's eye, a memory now etched into my soul no matter how desperately I wanted to forget. My mouth went dry, the truth ash on my tongue. "Ronan and Siobhan...I saw them together. In Death's magic mirror. And while I'm sure it was just friendly, it made me realize there is no going back. He has to live his life, and I no longer have mine. Our future, our plans...they're gone."

Gold and citrine against the sunken blue. Sapphire and amber, staring into each other's souls. Citrus and sage, a perfectly balanced blend.

Finna shot up faster than an arrow from a crossbow, her focus just as pointed. "Another illusion?"

"No. At least, I don't think so." I stared into the bath, the water reflecting my distorted image back to me. My cheeks seemed paler, like my life force had washed away with every tear that streamed down my face. "It wasn't a trick, it was a window."

And I was on the outside, looking in. A spectator to my own sorrow.

Something clenched and churned in my gut, a pity I had no name for. Was this what it was like for Arawn, watching me from the sidelines my whole life, an outcast to the world he helped forge?

"*And?*" My cousin whined as she tapped her foot, the single word grating against my nerves like steel against glass.

"And it *hurt*, Finna," I hurled back, my voice dredging up from my battered lungs, hoarse from tears. My breath turned ragged, the pain fresh. "It hurts. To imagine him one day moving on, to see him live his life without me... I didn't think I could still feel here, not like this..."

Not like sunset smiles and salted laughter. Not like two creatures carved from the same mold, two sirens floating in the seafoam. Two friends with futures ahead.

Finna's thin brows knotted. "And what does any of that have to do with the Dark God?"

Saeth might have been the blunt one, but at least her attacks were direct hits. Finna's brand of brutality was far more covert, a knife buried deep between your ribs before she twisted and teased. We were all monsters, and my cousin was the cleverest cutthroat of us all.

But I didn't want to be a monster, not anymore. I wanted no one else's blood on my hands, no matter how black it stained.

"It has to do with me." I sank my hands into the warm tub and closed my eyes. Water forgave and forgot. Water washed and cleansed and carried it all away. "I won't hurt him, too. I've caused enough misery."

I kept my eyes closed, relishing the darkness beneath my lids. No, no more misery. Only the tender caress of endless night. The cold kiss of frozen forgetfulness. The opposite of misery and destruction was not joy or creation. It was death, absence. Apathy. The empty void, expansive enough to fall forever into.

"I thought I was the selfish fool."

I expected Finna's clever remark, her snide smirk.

I didn't expect the water splashed across my face.

Eyes flying open, I coughed as it went up my sinuses. Panic flooded my veins as I slipped and hit the granite floor, pain shooting up my palms and reverberating through my aching elbows. With a gut-wrenching heave, I cleared the obstruction from my airways, snorting it back onto the marble floor.

Water cleansed and forgave, but it also could drown and burn.

"What the hell, Finna?" I finally sputtered, crawling to the edge of the tub and hoisting myself back to standing on shaky legs.

Finna's nostrils flared as she stared down the bridge of her upturned nose. "Keira, that man is a god. He has had *eternity* to perfect his ruse. To paint himself as the wise, wounded man willing to risk his kingdom for a girl." Her voice brushed carefully over her words, quiet as silk dragging across a bare floor. Crimson curls bobbed as she lowered her chin, gaze fixing on the dark marble. "Take it from me. From my mistake. You warned me about Connor, and I didn't listen. But Connor was just a pawn. Arawn is not your friend. He is the king, and he'll use you until you're just as dried up and dead as I am."

The warning was soft, but it still slashed through my vulnerable parts with the precision of a dagger.

Connor had hidden his villainy from Finna, had cloaked it in careful competence and stiff logic. He did not bear his fangs or claws, but instead his fury and cruelty were both quiet. Covert. And in the end, it had felled us both, Finna and I falling prey to the same predator disguised as a pansy.

Arawn's pine-scented pity, his rose-kissed lips and shadow-soft sincerity... they weren't monstrous to the eye. Everything about him invited and entranced, the enchanting darkness of his stare, the sturdy fortress of his embrace...

But that did not make him harmless. Snakes didn't need to be big to be venomous.

Denial and desolation warred in my mind, the words stuttering from my battle-battered lips. "He wouldn't—"

"He wouldn't, what, *hurt you?*" Finna's shrill, soulless laugh slashed the quiet. She scrutinized me through thin slits, the intensity sharp enough to peel my skin off. "He already has. He knew what he was doing, showing you Ronan and Siobhan. He knew *exactly* which wound to pour salt into. He's been watching you, and you're playing right into his trap. Just like I did."

He'd been watching me since I was a girl, studying me like a scroll, my wishes and fears laid bare on his grand, icy display. A bloodhound, latching on to my scent and stalking me with predatory precision.

No one hid from Death. No home was safe from his snare.

My heart thudded violently against my ribs in a painful, persistent rhythm. When did it end? When did the fight stop? If Arawn was truly the king of monsters, if he did plan on chewing me up and spitting out my brittle bones after he'd picked them clean...what did I care? I looked back at my mirrored visage in the water, soulless silver eyes meeting mine.

"Finna, what's the point?" I whispered, the last embers of the light inside finally forfeiting to the ferocity of the darkness that seeped into my soul through my *Melthith*-blackened skin. "What do you *care?* You said it yourselves, you're all stuck here anyway. Papa, Reina, you...you're all dead, if you're even real. What do you care if I stay and spend my days doing something selfish for once? I'm tired of being everyone else's martyr."

The truth stunned me as it sputtered out, the emptiness creeping back into the space it had stolen in my spirit.

We were all monsters. Selfish and stupid. Hungry and hateful. What was the use of hiding it any longer? When my husband no longer needed me to be his hero, his silver wheel to guide his course, his *Ariannad*, his goddess...

Why not be the NightMare instead? Why not dine with darkness and dance with Death while I waited for my day of deliverance?

"What's the *point?*" Finna hissed, taking two long steps toward me. She'd always been a few inches shorter, but even as she sucked in a deep breath and stared up at me, I felt smaller than an ant beneath her heeled boot. A delicate hand found my middle, covering the same spot Death's fingers caressed earlier, just below my navel. "*This.* This is the point. This *baby* is the fucking point, Keira. This life. Not yours, not mine. *Your daughter's.*"

Here, everything eventually forgets.

I'd forgotten, had buried that truth in the ice, beneath layers of self-importance and sorrow. Beneath obsidian stares and selfish longing. Beneath shame and pity and pine-scented placations. Beneath hurt and sadness and citrus-stained specters.

Keira, you're pregnant.

The world swayed again as reality crashed back into me with the force of a cannonball. It slammed into my center, into the parts that held and grew and carried, into the womb that watered the seed.

Finna pressed closer, tears brimming and spilling onto her porcelain cheek. "I don't care what you want, or what Uncle Cedric wants, or what I want. I care about this baby."

My heart raced as the word rumbled through me, true and triumphant and terrifying.

Baby.

"Finna—" I clutched her slender shoulders to stop myself from falling, to stop the world from spinning out from under me.

"I had a choiceless choice." Her throat bobbed and she swallowed the wave of tears that threatened to drown us both. Her hand drifted from my middle to her own, cradling a phantom wound I could not see, but knew was there. "If I didn't...if I didn't end things the way I did, Connor would've used me, used my son as his plaything. The Dark God would have used him against me. And I wasn't a goddess that could fight him off."

I gaped at her, tongue dry as a desert. I had no words, no justification for my uselessness. Finna Branwen was the Queen of Silk and Sadness, a mother made martyr. And even though my cousin had never seen battle in her life, even though she was never a leader or a fighter...

She had been willing to sacrifice herself instead of letting her son be a pawn. She made herself a monster so her baby never would be.

"But you do have a choice," she continued, jade stare steeling over, hard as diamond. "Don't screw it up."

We're all monsters.

I was the most vicious, selfish one of all. But perhaps I did have the choice to be something else. Something that created instead of destroyed. Someone who stayed. Who cared. Who had a purpose. Or if I didn't have any chances left, maybe my daughter would be better. Could *choose* better.

A name rattled through me, loud and riotous. Not Ronan. Not Death.

Ariannad.

Ariannad.

Ariannad.

And then, louder still. Brighter. Stronger.

Rhiannon.

Rhiannon.

Rhiannon.

An answer to a question. A destination to a journey.

I was a rotten, wicked monster, made to challenge the God of Death himself, made to be a burning, blazing light in the darkness. Destruction and determination. Creation and chaos. And my daughter would be something even greater. Something even more defiant and wonderful, something made of sea and salt and star. She would be the best of her Branwen name and her Mathonwy lineage. She would take the power Danura had blessed me with and the wisdom Papa gifted me, and make it something more. She would have Saeth's sharpness and Finna's cleverness. Griffin's grit and Owen's kindness. Reina's softness and Reagan's rebellion.

And she would have her father's heart, even if I didn't anymore. If he chose to give his love to Siobhan, or some other lucky lady, so be it. I would still put her first. I would fight the tricky bitch of Fate one-handed if it meant giving my daughter a chance.

My daughter. My *Rhiannon.*

Death could have my soul, too black to save. But he could not have hers. And I would set the whole Otherworld on fire, would melt the ice and defy Death to set my daughter free.

I was nothing.

She would be everything.

"What if I can't fix it?" I allowed myself one last human moment, one last admission of vulnerability before sacrificing myself to my monstrous parts. I reached for Finna's hand, the same little girl I'd always been, chasing after my brave, beautiful older sister. "You said it yourself, Arawn knows exactly how to play me."

She placed her hand over mine, cold fingers giving mine a tight squeeze. Sister to sister. Mother to mother. "Find out why you, why *now*. If you don't, I won't be the only one around here mourning an unborn child."

13

Reunions and Regrets

GRIFFIN

I'd never cared for pretty things. Perhaps it was because I was a sailor, and anything nice I ever owned would be salt and sweat-soaked after one day at sea. Or maybe it was because I was an idiot and didn't have the patience for it. What did I care if I wore Ir'desian silk or Bachtreffian burlap as long as my arse was covered?

My sister and ma loved life's finery, both of them frolicking about in the markets week after week, always searching for whatever fine new import would accentuate their beauty.

They would've loved *Hiraeth*. The effortless, intoxicating beauty of the island. The danger and desire in every unique flower, petals softer than satin. The sweet-scented air that surrounded us, more fragrant than any perfume they'd ever purchased. The bright colors, richer than any dye they'd used, the low-hanging, plump fruit juicier than anything Porthladd's market had ever seen.

It all made me want to vomit.

My stomach churned as the crew and I hacked through the greenery, making our way inland. Foreign branches scratched the exposed skin of my arms and calves, my sleeves rolled up to my elbows, my trousers hiked to my knees. The tropical warmth licked at the back of my neck, even with my curls knotted in a nub at the crown of my head.

We'd been at this for hours, all of us trekking through the unmarred terrain, journeying deeper and deeper down *Hiraeth's* gullet, waiting for the island to swallow us whole. Gennevieve carved a path, the little duck carefully waddling through the thick foliage. Her blonde ringlets were swept up in a messy plait, sweat matting her fringe to her brow. Without her siren's gifts, the rest of us were even less put-together. Saeth had ripped the sleeves off her old gray tunic, tying one around her forehead to sop up the moisture. Rhett and Tarran had both abandoned their shirts entirely, the first glistening like a god in the sparkling *Hiraethean* light, his stone-cut form as rugged as the terrain, the latter red and bloated as the harsh sunlight burned him. Only Vian moved unbothered, whatever cool winds he summoned for himself wiping away the proof of his effort.

"Are we there yet?" Reagan groaned as she brought up the rear, curls wild with frizz while she dragged her feet through the leafy debris.

"Almost, I think." Gennevieve pouted and stuck her hands to her hips, round eyes drinking in the next treeline. "I never worked on the patrol team, and the island is a bit different already."

Another surge of bile coursed up my stomach, and I bit it back. We'd trusted Gennevieve out of necessity, not choice. Not that she hadn't been trying her best, but unless she was willing to start turning all these trees to ash with that curse of hers, we'd be screwed if we didn't move faster.

In my left hand, Triumph murmured a warning that Trouble was not far away.

"This is ridiculous." Reagan stomped her foot, acting more like a toddler than a trouble-tested teen. I shot her a look harsher than piss in whiskey.

"This was your idea, kid," I grumbled, slashing Truth through another thick vine that blocked our path forward, my back aching at the effort. This was what I got for letting a rage-fueled, egomaniac little girl and a half-wild, formerly imprisoned sprite make the decisions. "Hush, or Rhett's carrying you back to the ship."

"Pssh, he could try," Reagan snorted, sauntering past us and to the front with Genni.

"Don't tempt me with a good time," Rhett said, offering a glance that told me *exactly* whose fault this was. As Captain, my crew's crazed judgements were my responsibility now. No wonder Keira and Ronan both decided to fuck off to let us fend for ourselves.

"I said hush," I muttered, sounding more and more like my disposed cousins. I was usually the one being told to stay quiet, not the one giving the order.

Reagan quirked a brow, the little shit almost as talented as I was at raising trouble. She tossed her chestnut braid over her shoulder with a head swish that would've made my sister proud. "Why? Scared of a little snake bite, Griffin?"

A flash of fear ran down my spine, remembering the whispers of the slimy *neid* as they sank their fangs into my flesh. Rhett stole another glance back at me, this one tinted with a shade of concern. He knew the horror of *Hiraethean* nightfall just as terribly as I did. We'd barely survived that night in the jungle. Without Keira here now, who knew if we'd be so lucky. I opened my mouth, ready to tell Reagan where my sword would bite if she didn't shut her trap, but Vian cut me off, the long-limbed boy twirling in between us like an Ir'desian dancer.

"*Hiraeth* is friendly." He tugged the end of Reagan's braid as he skipped around her, mischief in the tilt of his scrunched-nose smirk. "Follow me, it'll be fine."

I didn't need Triumph's warning or Genni's direction to know that we were headed straight for danger. With these two leading the charge, it was a miracle from Lyr himself that we hadn't already shipwrecked or died.

Then again, the day was young, the sun only just reaching her apex in the sky. There was still plenty of time for us to run shit out of luck. Especially as we crawled deeper into the land of the lost, her hearty treeline hiding all sorts of terrors. If I let myself listen, the *neid's* whispers were waiting just around the next bend.

"Friendly? This place gives me the creeps." Tarran again voiced my thoughts aloud as he blocked the sun from his eyes. He scanned the greenery to our right. I didn't know what he looked for, but I couldn't blame him for being alert. I'd been acquainted with enough attractive men and women in my time to know pretty things were often poisonous. *Hiraeth's* beauty was only a flowered disguise for its most monstrous inhabitants.

"Shut up," Saeth snapped at her twin, stance straightening like the fine edge of my sword. Tarran pouted, but stayed quiet as he took in his twin's grave expression. Saeth halted, sharp focus trained on a spot to our left. "Everyone, quiet, I think I saw something."

I held my hand up, signaling the crew to stop. I followed her gaze to a patch of chest-high cattails twenty paces to our left. The eerie plants lined a small, murky pool, ripples disrupting the muddy water.

I sucked in a breath as I squinted, heart beating against my breastbone. The cattails swayed, joining the chorus of birdsong with their eerie *woosh*. I stilled, waiting for whatever lurked in the water, my hands tightly wrapped around Truth and Triumph, their voices in harmony.

Between the reeds, two red eyes met mine.

"Found him!" Vian shattered the stillness before I could sound the retreat, running toward the water and splashing into the pool with reckless abandon. "How have you been, old boy?"

As he charged, the beast raised his head, long tendrils of his weed-like mane dripping with dark mud, his blue-tinted skin slick with the slime.

A *ceffyl dwr*. In the flesh.

My heart dropped to my arse, panic pouring liquor through my veins and setting it on fire.

"Get away!" My instincts kicked in as the boy reached out to the beast with a stupid smile slapped across his face. Dropping Triumph to the mossy floor, I grabbed Vian's wrist, dragging him away from the monster before it could sink its teeth into him.

"Don't worry, he's harmless." A gentle voice lilted through the canopy of the trees, somehow drowning out the music of *Hiraeth's* mischief. I whirled around to find the sound, my crew's heads darting about in unison. The *ceffyl* snorted, taking a single webbed step out of the muck and mire before bowing at the knee. I dipped quickly to retrieve my weapon.

From behind a gnarled, vine-wrapped cedar, a woman clothed in a white gossamer gown stepped into the small clearing. Her silver hair hung loose around her shoulders, haloing her pale face in its luminescent glow. She floated across the ground, feet not making any sound against the crunchy debris. A delicate hand stroked the *ceffyl's* bowed head. "You are all a long way from home. Welcome back, Vian."

The boy bowed at the waist, black hair flopping forward, mimicking the *ceffyl's* reverent stance. The woman smiled, a perfect row of white teeth revealing themselves from behind her ruby-stained lips.

I'd never cared for pretty things, but I did have a proclivity towards pretty *people*. Yet despite the woman's undeniable beauty, my stomach recoiled, Triumph screaming her warning in my palm.

Of all the dangerous creatures that lurked in the darkness, this was the deadliest one. This woman, dressed in silk and starshine, was just as poisonous as she was pretty.

"*Serenhi!*" Gennevieve's lip wobbled before she flung herself at the master predator, wrapping her arms around the woman's waist and burrowing her head into the crook of her shoulder.

The woman laughed like windchimes and stroked the little duck's hair away from her face. "Welcome home, Genni."

The crew exhaled a collective breath, their relief vocal and visible. Tarran stopped shaking, running a hand over his face—most likely to whip away stray tears. Rhett's hand stopped twitching toward his sword, his arms folding instead across his broad chest in well-honed, feigned disinterest. Saeth's eyes narrowed at the woman, but her stance surrendered as she sank her weight into her hip. Reagan let loose a smile, accomplishment splayed across her features. The *ceffyl dwr* even seemed to relax, nipping the edge of Vian's tunic playfully.

But my instincts still prickled at the back of my neck, Triumph practically shouting at me to stay alert. A lifetime as Trouble's personal plaything taught me when to breathe and when to hold.

"Danura," Vian addressed the woman as he ran his fingers through the *ceffyl's* mane, the wind whisperer a fan of flirting with Trouble. "These are my friends."

Danura. Keira's mother. Goddess of Light and Love, Author of Life and Liberty.

I didn't need Truth in my hand to recognize her. Her silver eyes, a match for my cousin's. The subtle danger that dressed her from head to toe, proof enough of her power.

A chill ran down my back.

"I know who you are." Danura's metallic stare—so similar to Keira's in both tint and intensity—widened as she drank us all in. "Where is Keira?"

Tension rolled through the crew like thick mist once more, stealing our breath. Heavy shame rumbled low in my stomach. I looked to Rhett, my partner's lips thinning into a severe grimace just as mine did.

If Keira were here, we wouldn't be.

"In the Otherworld." Saeth pierced the shrill silence, chin high in indignant rage. "Rotting."

Danura clutched her stomach as if Saeth had stabbed her, silver eyes welling with tears. The goddess's pain was likely a well-practiced facade. After all, she'd been absent most of my cousin's life. It was hard to believe Keira's death would matter much now. But my own gut clenched, the painful reminder branding my heart like a hot iron.

If Keira were here, we would be safe.

Before I could dwell further on the pain and grief, before I could further question Danura's tears, another figure joined the fray, and my sorrow was lapped up by shock and curiosity.

Out of all the pretty things I might've stumbled upon in the Land of the Lost, Colonel Drystan Farchos was not one of the ones I'd expected. The handsome guard looked just as refined as he had when we left him last. He no longer wore his guard's uniform, instead donning simple, crème-colored linens that only deepened the dark bronze of his skin. But his warm curls were still smoothed into a bun at the nape of his neck, and his stubble trimmed straighter than a sword's edge. He didn't need a broadsword or a black cloak to radiate the same stalwart energy steeled to his very bones.

He stumbled over a root before he straightened, flattening his tunic. His gold eyes clamped onto me first, and a dazzling smile broke across his bronze face. "Oh, by the gods, you made it!"

I wondered if he still was sore about us leaving him in the bowels of Delm Arawn, knocked out and hogtied.

"Drystan?" Reagan spat his name out first, blushing at the sight of him. Not that I blamed her. I knew my own jaw hung slack as I tried—and failed—to ignore the little somersault my stomach did. He was both pretty and poisonous, that was for sure. Or at least, Rhett's venom would be if my bedmate caught me staring for too long.

Only I decide what hurts me.

As if he could hear my thoughts, Rhett tensed behind me, his silver eye barely a slit as he stared the unarmed guard down. "Oh, great, *you* again. You're right, Tarran, this place does give me the creeps."

A wash of shame trailed down my back. Rhett knew I was far from a maiden when I first met him, and I'd never felt like I needed to explain my past before. Except when it came to the Colonel. Our flirtation was little more than that—just two strangers in a brothel who found each other for a night instead of being proper, paying patrons. And yet, something about Drystan scraped underneath Rhett's skin like a rusty dagger.

Admittedly, seeing him here in *Hiraeth* infected me with corroded unease.

My throat ran dry. Tarran opened his mouth to speak, but he was interrupted by Vian, whose dark eyes burned like coal as they bore into his former jailor's skull. "Are you here as a guest, or a captive?"

My personal history with the guard became instantly secondary as everyone's attention snapped to the boy. I'd never seen the wind-sprite so still, his wiry frame taut as a bowstring. Tension rippled from him, the breeze shifting into a gale as it rustled through the trees.

I knew Drystan as a handsome stranger in a seedy escape, and as a guard with a gilded sense of justice.

Vian knew him only as a warden.

"A friend. I only wish to help, if you'll let me." Drystan raised his hands in surrender, looking to Danura. I tensed again, the surprise wearing off as Triumph murmured another warning in my ear. We weren't out of the forest of foes yet, and a friendly face did not negate the questions and concerns swirling in my chest.

Drystan had helped us escape Delm Arawn with our lives. But he had also been complicit to the horrors that hid beneath the Nightless City. And only Lyr knew what his business was here, in *Hiraeth*.

The thought was dashed by the next surprise lurking in the shadows, one that sent fury blazing through my pit. Shocked gasps rippled through the crew, all of us seeing the ghost at the same time. My fingers clenched tighter around Triumph, if only to stop me from smacking the smirk off the old man's ginger-bearded face.

Weylin fucking Branwen.

Hiraeth was not only the land of the lost, but the prison of the found.

"I'm here as a friend too, if ye'll have me." He walked into the clearing, arms crossed, his normally-scowling brow relaxed in something that might have resembled shame.

Saeth's jaw dropped first, and she took a stumbling step forward. She might have been part shark, but even she could fall prey to bait on a hook. "*Weylin?*"

"Papa," Tarran echoed, his voice breaking over the more affectionate title. "Is that you?"

"Aye, boy. Ye both look well." Weylin stared back at his children, at the crew. Weylin, somehow living and breathing, eyes crinkling around the edges as he smiled. He wore the same simple tan linens as Drystan, clean and wrinkle-free, a stark contrast to his normally disheveled attire.

But he was here. In *Hiraeth. Alive.*

Weylin, who had run off in Orwellin when we needed him, choosing his fancy guns over his crew, his kin.

Weylin, whose murder was the pawn Connor Yorath needed to frame Keira at Finna's wedding.

Weylin, who was supposed to be dead.

Weylin, the last of the Branwen brothers.

Weylin, who I wanted to kill myself for all the ways he'd screwed us over.

"What the hell are you still doing alive, old man?" I must have asked the question aloud, as his head swiveled from his daughter to me. My heart thundered in my chest, not fear or panic driving the beat faster, but pure rage.

The rage that he was alive, *breathing*, when my father and sister were not. That he was here, *free*, when Keira had paid the price twice over for his death.

"It's a long story." The old man pitched an eyebrow before casting a fond look at both Drystan and Danura.

"I think perhaps we all should sit and chat." Danura's honeydew voice was sickeningly sweet. Her glittering silver eyes traced over all of us with a hint of amusement that made my skin crawl. "It seems we have quite a bit of catching up to do."

As Trouble's personal toilet-brush, I'd seen my fair share of standoffs and hostile negotiations. I was cut out for them, in fact. Being built like a horse had its advantages—I never had to do much other than exist to command attention and respect. Since the time I was sixteen, grown men—sea-tested and salt-forged sailors, no less—would shrink when I entered a room, their wary gazes tracing my every move like a wild bear that stumbled into their campsite.

It was a gift my uncles used to exploit, one I'd taken advantage of one too many times for Trouble's liking.

Late afternoon sunlight spilled onto the colorful stones of the patio, and for the first time in my life, I felt small. Danura stared at me with a faint look of amusement from her spot across the generously sized bamboo table, as if I were not a mountain of a man, but a little boy dressed in his uncle's captain coat.

They'd led us to the compound under the banner of friendship, Genni insisting this would be a lovely chat. And while the setting was nothing short of breathtaking—the trimmed flowers and woven huts quaintly designed—Truth and Triumph still sang the chorus of Trouble in my ears.

My crew were all seated by my side, armed and at the ready, yet I had never felt so naked and stripped bare. Rhett at my right bounced his leg nervously underneath the table, his anxiety just as palpable. Saeth to my left twirled her favorite dagger between her fingers, envy-green gaze locked on her father's ruddy face, while Tarran sat between them as a human shield. Reagan perched on Rhett's right, a practiced smirk pitched on her face, Trouble's favorite assistant ready to poke the real bear.

"After we freed the cages you'd missed, that's when Officer Leath and I ran into your uncle here," Drystan spoke, his velvet voice echoing through the empty clearing. "We were setting traps all over Orwellin for a few months, trying to uproot some of the other Council members and alert the common people to the horrors right below their feet. But Locasta closed in on us. Those puppet guards of hers are fierce as they are freaky."

"We know firsthand." Tarran shuddered.

I took a long swig of the goblet of fruity wine Genni had placed in front of me, wishing it were something much stronger. Strong enough to drown out the memory of the puppeted guards, the memory of their unseeing eyes and desperate bloodlust.

Crimson against ivory.

Silver eyes, uttering an unspoken command.

Drystan continued, voice thickening, "Leath went back to Porthladd to warn you all, but I guess he didn't make the trip."

I granted the Colonel a nod, the vague memory of the young officer coloring my mind's eye. He was barely older than Saeth and Tarran, a boy not yet made a man. A boy who gave his life to try and warn us before it was too late.

I hoped my family would be there to greet him in the Otherworld. Like Weylin should have been.

I stared at the old man again, at the familiar wrinkles and hazel stare fixed on his hands.

"That still doesn't explain what you two are doing together, or what brought you here." Rhett voiced my thoughts for me, leg bouncing so aggressively I thought he'd knock over the table if it kept up. I placed a palm on his thigh, and he quieted beneath my touch. He sighed, shoulders unknotting, but he didn't tear his eyes from Drystan.

"That day in the dungeons—you all woke me up to the damned coward I'd been. I knew I had to do *something*. From there, it was your uncle who had the bright idea of tracking Danura down and seeing if she could help stop Locasta." Drystan nodded to Weylin, who offered a sheepish grin. I scoffed, swallowing down the instinct to flash the old bastard my favorite finger, instead focusing on the hidden bit of information that clanged through me like a warning bell.

"You'd been to *Hiraeth* before?" I gaped at Weylin, blinking as if the old man was not in fact the old, surly gunner I knew, but an imposter wearing his ugly face. That theory seemed more likely than any fantasy we'd been presented with yet.

He shook his head, gaze falling to his coarse hands. "No. But my brothers had been. And..." he paused to swallow, daring a peek at Saeth's harsh features. "So had my wife. Long ago."

"Brothers? Plural?" My stomach flipped, the weak wine turning to worry as a new parade of questions churned in my gut. "And *Auntie Alina* was here?"

I searched Weylin for any sign of familiarity, but he was not the man I thought I knew. Nor was anyone in my family, the legend of the Branwen brothers a facade for the betrayers and liars they truly were.

Weylin gnawed his lower lip. "Donnall still didn't tell ye?"

Papa's name slammed into me like a bullet from Weylin's fancy pistol.

Please, I did what you asked, let Finna and Vala go—

Bullet holes and bloodied stone. Echoing screams and black smoke.

"Didn't get the chance." Fruity wine mixed with bile and threatened to surge back up my throat. I choked it down, spitting my next words instead. "Pa's dead. Connor slit his throat after he betrayed us to save my Ma."

Weylin paled, fist tightening around the bamboo table. "Oh gods. I'm sorry, boy. Is Vala…?"

"Alive. Safe, for now, in Pysgodd with Reese Mathonwy." Rhett linked his fingers through mine, his warmth rescuing me from grief's icy chokehold.

Rhett wasn't a betting man, but he'd taken a chance on me. Had decided to stay through my pain, decided to stake his life saving mine.

I would no longer be a coward hiding behind him. I'd be the captain he'd bet on.

"But Finna died in Porthladd." I mustered the courage to say it myself, hating the way the words tasted on my tongue. I squeezed Rhett's hand for strength and rubbed the remembrance of her on my chest. I wished it worked like a genie lamp, and somehow, if I prayed hard enough, she too would pop out from the treeline like a magical mist. Not dead, just another traveler lost to *Hiraeth.*

No, Finna was gone. Wanting was dangerous. Especially in this island hell.

Weylin's head dipped, revealing a patch of scalp amidst the ginger and silver. Running made us all older, it seemed. After a long moment, he looked up at Drystan, silver tears lining his hazel eyes. "I told ye, we should've found another way to get off this damned island."

"What happened to your ship?" Reagan tilted her head, the little dragon stirring. I'd seen that look on her face all too frequently, the narrowed eyes and thin-pressed lips.

I shuddered. When Reagan wanted a fight, her wish often came true.

Then again, better a fight than my uncle's crocodile tears. Better a brawl than a parade of 'should haves' and 'would haves' that carved deep gouges in my own patience.

I crossed my arms, rallying to Reagan's side, the fight brewing in my britches the only thing potent enough to chase away grief. "Yeah, how did you manage to get here and lose your only way out?"

Drystan sighed, rubbing his faint beard. "No idea. It was here, and then it was gone."

A goblet clattered to the ground. Heads whipped to the sound, purple wine staining the dirt as it pooled at Vian's feet. Genni swooped down with a cloth napkin to clean the mess, but my sight drifted to his quivering hands.

The boy had been quiet for some time, which was never a good sign in his case, but his eyes widened as if he'd seen a ghost. Then again, he might have, on this gods-forsaken island. I stiffened in my seat, listening closely for Truth and Triumph's warning.

"The *Awelymor*," Vian whispered, lanky frame trembling.

Realization crashed into me like a ship wrecking in the shallows.

The Awelymor. Keira's stolen schooner, the one we left in Ir'de.

Pieces fell into place, horror gripping my middle. We'd all been trying to complete this particular puzzle separately, wondering why it didn't all fit, only to see now that we'd been hoarding the wrong bits.

Drystan's jaw clenched tighter than a pulled crossbow, gold eyes flashing with something dark as he confirmed my suspicion. "How did you know that name?"

A stone sank down to my toes. The rebels in Orwellin that had suddenly dropped off the face of the earth, the mysterious black-painted ship…Drystan and Weylin had been on our side, in the shadows, the whole time. Until Keira accidentally stranded them here.

Until I'd convinced her to sail right into Locasta's trap.

"I'm so sorry, Griffin." Vian pushed back from the table, runaway tears streaking down his pale cheeks. "We thought it was a wash-up."

Guilt stabbed me through the heart, sharper than any blade. If Keira were here, she'd know what to say to soothe his pain. She'd tell him he wasn't to blame. Because he wasn't, nor was Weylin, as much as I wanted to skewer him.

I was the one that got in the way, Trouble's fucktoy at it again.

It was my fault.

I gaped at Vian, grasping for words as the weight of my failures fumbled my tongue. Reagan fought my fight instead, slipping her hand into Vian's. "If you weren't with us, we wouldn't have saved Vala, and you couldn't have saved me from Connor."

Truth sang in my ear.

Of course, the youngest was the wisest yet again. Vian had done nothing but protect and save. He brought Keira home to us in one piece. He risked himself in the dungeon to carry my mother to safety. He was the one to push Reagan out of Connor's grasp so Keira could strike.

He was a hero.

And I was the fool that ruined it all.

My fault.

I dug my fingers into Rhett's thigh to keep from crumbling.

"We all make our choices, Vian," Danura addressed the boy, but her silver stare was trained on me, a harsh reminder of my failure. I shrank beneath it, again a man made mouse. "We can't always predict the outcome. I don't blame you or Keira for leaving the way you did. I only blame myself that I didn't help you more. So if this is anyone's fault, it's *mine*. I should've armed you both with the truth and a better way out."

Danura lifted her chin skyward, a queen's challenge laid at my feet. She would not let me shoulder the blame on my own, a gauntlet for responsibility thrown like a true Captain. For a moment, I wondered if she had the gift of mindreading, or if a simpleton like me was an easy guess.

Weylin grabbed an empty goblet and poured fresh wine into it, pushing it across the table to Vian. A peace offering. "We all wish we'd helped more."

Wishing and wanting, dangerous games.

Vian fell back into his seat, wiping his tears with the back of his free sleeve, his other hand still twined with Reagan's. Her thumb traced circles across the back of his.

I sucked in a breath, re-armoring myself. I was not built a captain, but if a guard like Drystan could turn revolutionary, if a goddess like Danura could admit mistakes, if an old goat like *Weylin* could change…

Perhaps a fool like me could find his footing. Or at least play pretend long enough to get Danura on our side.

"If you really wanted to help, Weylin, you could've just stayed on the *Ceffyl*." Saeth slashed through the tentative peace with brutal efficiency, stealing the air from the clearing. Chair clattering to the ground, she stood, towering over Tarran to stare down her father. "But no. You abandoned us for your own selfish gain. Like usual. Like you abandoned us after Mama—"

"Watch yer words," Weylin grunted, fist clenching.

The rest of us went silent, none brave enough to swim in the way of two sharks circling each other.

My cousin never cried, but I swore I saw the sheen of a rebel tear stuck in her eye. For a moment, her throat bobbed as she swallowed back the last parts of her that were daughter. The last parts that were little girl. Then she stood taller, any trace of emotion freezing over, her voice ice cold when she spoke again. "Why, so you can forget how you were never enough for her? So you can blame everyone else for her death, instead of the fact you were never there to protect her? To protect *us?*"

As usual, Saeth struck true.

Before, Weylin might have raged. Might have stood and pointed a thick finger in his daughter's face, might have yelled and cursed and screamed to Lyr a thousand hateful words. Might have banged his chest and defended his honor.

Today he did not. Today he simply stared back, jaw slack, shock and sorrow battling for purchase on his wrinkled expression.

"Saeth, please. That is going too far." Tarran winced, placing a broad hand on his twin's arm.

"Stop protecting him from his shame, Tarran." Saeth slapped him away, going in for the killing blow. A cruel smile snaked its way across her face as she bared her razor teeth. "I'm glad Mama's gone. That way she doesn't have to be disappointed in the coward you turned out to be."

Weylin opened and shut his mouth. Once, twice.

"You look like her." The words came not from his gob, but the full lips of the Goddess of Life herself.

"What?" Saeth snapped her head in Danura's direction, the shark scenting her next prey.

Silence deepened, the rest of the crew not daring even a breath as the two pretty predators locked in on each other. The thought occurred to me that perhaps, as Captain, I should intervene.

But I held no rank in this standoff of queens. Ice and starfire, steel and silver. I'd be eviscerated before I had the time to draw Truth from her sheath.

Danura nodded, swirling the wine in her goblet before drinking deep. "Not the hair, obviously, but the nose. The sharp features. The eyes." Lips pulled into a soft smile, as if she didn't possess the most venomous tongue on the island. "Alina was one of my dearest friends. Do you have any of her gifts? She had a brilliant sense of smell. It made her the best tracker of our group before Siobhan."

Saeth went preternaturally still.

Another puzzle piece fell into place. Saeth's cold demeanor, Weylin's knowledge of this place, Alina's hazy history…

My aunt had been here because she was *from* here.

A siren. Both pretty and poisonous.

Heads around the table ducked, staring groundward, no one daring to get caught in the crossfire. Even Reagan shifted in her seat, closer to Vian, as if she would be his shield when the tension finally exploded.

Saeth breathed in twice, nostrils flaring with the action. Then she struck, faster than a viper. "No, I don't. And whatever gift she had couldn't protect her from the fire. She's been dead for more than three years. That seems to be a trend with people who befriend you."

She did not wait to be dismissed, stalking off into the *Hiraethean* jungle on her own without a final word.

I sank back into my chair, stomach sloshing with unease. "Genni, please go make sure she's safe."

The little duck blanched, but nodded. "Aye, Captain."

I doubted she was afraid of what lurked beyond, but of Saeth herself. I didn't blame her. Part siren or not, Saeth was made of something far more lethal than whatever *Hiraeth* could throw at us. She stood, and Tarran pushed back from his seat to follow.

Rhett rubbed a calloused palm across my back, melting my tension away. I offered a small smile to my companion before finding my strength, turning my grin to Danura. "Please don't mind Saeth, she's—"

"She's absolutely right." Danura waved the justification off like a stray fly, a glorious silver smile lighting her features. "I've done very little to help anyone, lately. Griffin, isn't it? Let's you and I take a stroll."

14

Gardens and Gods

GRIFFIN

I'd been utterly and truly screwed far too many times to count in my short life, but there were only a handful of moments where I knew I'd gone too far. Knew that the lines I crossed were marked in permanent ink. Knew the scars I'd carved were unhealable.

First time, when Owen died. I carried him back home myself, strapping my brother's lifeless body to my back, dragging him to the *Ceffyl* on my own. But I hadn't truly understood the weight of my actions, of my *grief*, until I saw my mother, sitting ramrod straight at the kitchen table of Branwen Townhouse. Saw the deep, vicious rivers tears had etched into her cheeks. Saw the dull, sunken gaze that stared unseeing at the grooved wood. Saw her lips move, muttering a sentence I'd never outlive:

Your fault. It should've been you.

She wasn't wrong. Sharp as it stung, I couldn't fault her for blaming me. If I'd had the chance to go back, I would've swapped places in less than a heartbeat. Death was better than living in the shadow of a martyr.

A smarter man might have learned from his blunders right then and there. But I'd always been as smart as I was subtle—which I was decidedly not.

As I followed Danura through rows of woven huts, the setting sun filtering the clearing with a kaleidoscope of color, I couldn't help the itch in my britches that told me I'd ventured too far once again. That I'd made a mess I might never see clean.

Triumph whispered unheeded warnings in my ear, confirming my suspicion.

The rest of my crew stayed behind, finishing supper and catching up with Drystan and Weylin. Rhett would keep them safe. The real potential threat was with me, anyway. I didn't know if she planned on killing me off or cutting me loose, but neither option sounded pleasurable. I trudged two steps behind her at all times, as if staying out of arm's reach was defense enough against a goddess.

"You remind me of your uncle." Danura twirled on her heel, stopping me in my tracks to give me a long once-over.

I caught my balance before I could fall on my face. I fashioned a grin that made harlots blush, hoping it was thick enough armor to cover my blundering. "Certainly not the grump sitting at your table."

The goddess threw her head back and laughed, a twinkling sound that tickled the back of my neck like a gentle breeze. Lyr below, I was in for it. Danura's shoulders shook as she glided away, her pace slower this time. "No, you remind me of Cedric, actually. Has anyone ever told you that you bear a striking resemblance to him?"

Something cleaved in my chest, a family wound I hid deep. I'd always admired Uncle Cedric–everyone did. It was hard not to, with the leadership and love that graced his every word like honey. We lived off it. Ma and Auntie Alina especially, the way they doted on Keira for him.

But there was no question that his brothers resented him for it. *Killed* him for it. Aidan might've held the dagger, but I'd heard my Pa and Weylin mutter enough jealous curses under their breaths to know they harbored their own hatred for the man.

Hatred for themselves, really, for never measuring up.

Your fault. It should've been you.

"My pa might've mentioned it to my mother during a few drunken spats," I admitted, surrendering a slice of my soul to the goddess. I might've looked a bit too much like my uncle for my envious father's liking, a truth I never dared to peek into. But I carried Pa's legacy in rank and role: a second-born son destined to disappoint.

Danura slowed, silver eyes scrutinizing every damned freckle on my face like they were a map to my past. "It's not just the looks, though for a moment, you made an old woman swoon." She winked, nearly knocking me on my arse with it. "But you have his presence."

My heart fluttered for a moment, flattery fanning a flame I'd long let fade. Keira had said it before too, in some of our most tender moments.

You remind me of Papa sometimes.

But Keira was gone, because of my choices. My string of uncorrected mistakes. Her faith had been as misplaced as a fish in a forest.

"That's where you're wrong, Your Majesty. I'm a flirt and a fuck-up." I shrugged, focusing instead on the compact dirt path beneath my feet. Truth didn't need to tell me what I was not. "I'm not my uncle. Cedric was steady."

I could still feel the heat of her gaze, though I was too chicken to greet it. "When I knew him, Cedric was a mischievous cad with a craving for trouble and a look that could melt a goddess's broken heart."

At that, I looked up, the mere mention of Trouble stoking the curiosity I had no control over. I raised a brow, daring her to deny the obvious lie. "You and I must be talking about very different people." Cedric was the center. The constant. The Captain. Not a good-for-nothing bastard like me.

"I met him when he crashed his ship racing his brothers."

"What?"

"Aye." She nodded, strolling alongside me now. "He and young Aidan both landed here and nearly burnt it to the ground in the process."

Like she was in on the secret, teasing me, Truth sang in my ear.

I stopped in my tracks, trying to tie together the strings of the tall tale Danura offered. I rubbed the sweat from the back of my neck, the tropical heat not the only discomfort tingling beneath my skin.

My uncles, washed up on *Hiraeth*. I remembered the first journey we made here, where Keira found the photo on her father's ship… and then Alina, apparently a resident of this magical fuckery.

Nothing I thought certain was even remotely right or real. Fancy swords or not, I knew nothing of the secrets my seniors had silenced.

The path widened into another clearing, a babbling river coursing through the center. It was broad enough to swim, though the depth was hard to decipher. But the water had an inviting air to it, a tranquility blanketing the area. It was probably an omen I should stay away, but fortunes were wasted on fools. I stumbled over and plopped down at its bank, pulling my favorite flask from my belt loop.

"Listen, lady, if I'm going to process all of this, I'm going to need a drink."

Danura chuckled, gracefully lowering herself next to me, "You and I both."

She reached into the water, cupping her hands to scoop a generous sip. She shut her eyes, and a moment later the liquid turned blood red, the faint aroma of fermented grapes scenting the already fragrant air. Danura drank, a tiny driblet of the sweet wine running down her chin. She flashed a radiant smile, her lips stained crimson.

Lyr's left nut, I was in over my head. Pretty and inviting as she was, I had no doubt that this woman—no, this *goddess*—could rip me to bits before I had the sense to cry uncle. I gulped back the fear that filled my mouth, feigning unflappability. "Neat trick. Are you gonna pull a rabbit out of my arse next?"

Her gaze narrowed as she stared out over the river, no doubt debating whether or not to drown me in it. "When are you going to tell me the bad news? Why are you here?"

Another moment where Trouble bested me. Another mistake I had no hope of fixing on my own.

I took a deep swig of my flask, letting whiskey wash away the last of my pride. "Keira's in the Otherworld. Ronan is headed to save her."

A long beat, the only sound the river's song. Danura sat still, ancient agony rippling over her features for a brief moment before it vanished. She'd had centuries to learn to hide her heart away, a gift I wished I could imitate. Then, after a sharp inhale, "They'll be all right. Arawn is tough, but she's stronger."

A piteous anchor sank in my gut, though I had no place to judge. I'd spent enough of the last few months wasting away at the bottom of a bottle to know the delicious draw of denial firsthand. But despite my rather fervent exploration, I hadn't found the answers I needed in any spirit known to man or god. And Danura deserved the truth; not as the goddess I needed her to be, but as the mother she was.

Keira's ma, I reminded myself, before I could mistake the enchantress as anything other. I covered her hand with mine where it rested delicately on her knee. "Stronger than the God of Death?"

Something shifted in the air as her head snapped to face me; something darker and deeper than a mortal like me was meant to understand. Her voice rumbled low in her chest, a laugh like a hurricane brewing. "You have no idea who she is, do you? Cedric and his good-for-shite brothers armed you with *nothing*."

Truth and Triumph both echoed her words, a warning clanging in my skull.

I was in too deep already, yet I knew I was only standing at the edge of the abyss. One more step, and I'd sink to the very bottom of the world. Perhaps all the way down to Arawn's keep. At least there, I'd be in good company.

A smarter man would've turned back before the point of no return. Would've swam to the surface, hopped on his ship, and sailed away. Would've let the monsters and gods do their own bidding and bargaining. Perhaps there was still a chance. Rhett and I could pack everyone back on the *Ceffyl*, set ourselves full tilt to Pysgodd. We could forge a new home, stuck in the mountains, drinking whiskey to keep ourselves warm. We could spend our days chopping firewood and fucking like animals, not worrying about anything more than weathering the long winter months.

I wasn't a smart man. And I hated the cold. Almost as much as I hated minding my own damn business.

I tossed my head back, squinting up at the purple-bruised sky. Then, I took another step, ready to dive into the deep. "Do this idiot a favor and spell it all out for me. How is my cousin strong enough to beat Arawn?"

Danura leaned forward, twirling her hands in the water. The river swirled around her, the bubbling building as soft, silver light radiated from the tips of her fingers. "Gods are immortal, but we are not indestructible. We are conduits for our power." She scanned my face for understanding, and I nodded, fighting back the fear crawling around in my clenched asshole. Danura stroked the water again, the river running deep red. "For example, I can shape life and change it.

Turn water to wine, make soil rich enough to sustain a harvest, give a woman claws and a fin instead of fingers and toes. But contrary to popular belief, I do not create it outside of the natural way."

Danura cupped the red liquid in both hands again, lifting the liquid to my lips. Daring me to drink straight from Trouble's cup.

First-class fool I was, I opened my mouth, drinking down my dose of the goddess's potion. Both sweet and bitter, there was no mistaking the true transformation I'd just witnessed. I let the wine run down my throat, hoping it would remake me into someone equipped to handle this. Perhaps it would give me gills, too, a much-needed accessory to breathing in the abyss.

"Point deliciously made." I wiped the excess from my chin, letting the heat that flared in my gut fuel me. "How does Arawn's work? And Keira's?"

Danura ran her hands along her dress, silver gossamer staining a macabre red. I wondered how many battles she'd fought and won, how many shades of blood she'd worn and tasted. Her gaze stretched worlds away, perhaps lost in a similar violent memory.

"Arawn does not decide who dies. He only shapes what death looks like, and he can harness the darkness of it, the fear." Her voice dipped to a whisper then, worry washed away by wonder. Her face lit up as she stared up to the sunshine, her constellation of freckles basking in the warmth. "But Keira—Keira *is* untapped potential. Her gift is different from any other I've seen. I harness life force, Arawn fear and shadows. Nef the wind and skies, Lyr the seas and storms. But from the moment Keira was born, the first moment I held her in my arms—Fate itself kneeled to her. She can harness energy, and her power has a *pull* to it. If she learns to use it, she could be the mother of the moon and stars, controlling the tides of destiny to her whim."

Truth and Triumph rang again, and this time it sounded like a hymn. A prayer to the Goddess Ariannad, to the keeper of Fate and Fortune.

I knew what Danura said was true even without magick. I'd felt it too, the tug at the center of my being that anchored around Keira. Following her as a child, wild and unbridled, it was like getting caught in a riptide. She led, and we trailed behind, trying our best to keep from drowning.

And the older she got, the more she grew—seas and storms and serpents of the deep obeyed her command. Light and dark both danced on the tips of her fingers. Power, pure and raw, in the silver of her stare. In the proud tilt of her chin.

She was a goddess, one even the authors of life and death would succumb to.

But she was also just a girl, raised with mortal emotions and moods. A woman with worries and wants like any other.

A cousin who needed me to stand strong. A captain who needed her crew.

I stood up, no longer willing to waste away on a riverbank while my best friend waited for me. While my future niece waited. "She's pregnant."

A beat, as the truth broke like a crashing wave.

"*What?*" Danura scrambled to her feet, grace replaced with panic. She grabbed the fabric of my tunic, pulling me toward her with surprising strength. A snarl ripped from her throat: "Does she know? Does *he?*"

"I have no clue," I said gently as I untangled my shirt from her grip. I stepped back, standing straighter, mimicking Keira's brand of Captain's confidence. I had a mission, and for once in my Lyr-forsaken life, I'd see it through to the end. "But we need your help. Morwyn Locasta, his lackey, has control over the entire Deyrnas. She wiped out half of Porthladd just trying to get to Keira, and there's famine in Bachtref thanks to her. Refugees are flocking to Pysgodd to wait out the winter where she won't come for them. But we think they're preparing for the Dark God to do something, we just don't know what. But we do know that the Deyrnas needs a deity, one that she can't kill."

She shook her head, eyes wide. "I can't."

"What?" Disappointment crashed through me, harsher than any blow I'd ever taken in battle. Wanting was weakness, yet again. I'd been a fool to get my hopes up, to put my faith in another washed-up goddess. A growl grew in my throat, guttural and harsh. "*Why?*"

Danura dismissed me and stalked out of the clearing, back toward the huts. "I have to go to Keira. If he gets his hands on that baby…" she called over her shoulder, not slowing her frantic charge, "it would be so much worse."

Unease stalled my limbs, legs turning lead. I had no idea what I was doing, what I'd gotten into. But I couldn't quit now. No turning back. I chased after, willing my feet forward. I caught up to her in six long strides, my fire stoked by both stupidity and duty.

"My crew and I are not enough to save the world." I grabbed her arm, pulling her to a halt. She shot me a look that could boil water, but I did not balk beneath it. I could not run from my responsibility anymore, and neither would she. "You built it. It's yours to protect."

She inhaled, breathing me in, looking through long lashes as she weighed my words. My *worth*.

A smarter sailor might have run. Might have tucked his tail between his legs and scampered away before she could strike him down.

I was not smart. But I was steady. Or at least, I would be. For my crew. For Keira. I rose to my full height, unflinching as the Queen came to her decision.

"*That's* the Cedric in you." She raised her hand, and I braced for a slap. But instead, her warm palm caressed my cheek, wistfulness whispering in her dimpled smile. She blinked it back, taking a careful step away before re-armoring herself. "Pysgodd."

I dropped her arm, her deflection dizzying. "Lyr's tits, what about Pysgodd?"

She did not wait for me to catch on, careening straight out down the dirt path back to the open refectory. "Get your crew and go, *now*. Nef and Gwynn are in Pysgodd. Cerridwen too, maybe, though I haven't heard from that little brat in a few centuries. They will help you with Locasta while I deal with Arawn."

"They're real? *Alive?*" I called after, stumbling behind. Again, just a man caught in the current of the cosmos, fighting to stay afloat.

"Aye, hurry. Tell them their mother sent you."

15

Visions and Voices

RONAN

Fingers trailed aimlessly along my chest, tracing the bold lines of my tattoo as she had a thousand times before. Breath shuddered from my lips, misty in the cold morning of the spring.

"I've missed you," she whispered as silver eyes peered from heavy-lidded lashes. Oh, gods above and below, she was everything I remembered and more. She waded closer in the water, pale skin luminant in the moonlight. Or perhaps it was just her, glowing from within, my very own star made woman.

I reached out slowly—carefully—not wanting to see her wash away like ripples in a pool. Fingertips brushed along her cheek, down the long line of her neck, across the graceful curve of her shoulders.

"I've missed you more." My heartbeat doubled, slamming within my chest like the strong cadence of a dragon's wings as I took flight.

A smile shattered across her face, dazzling at it was dizzying.

Then she kissed me. Lips crashed together like a violent storm against the shore, desperate and dangerous in our need. My arms snaked around her waist as she hoisted herself up, body pressed flush against mine. A moan broke free from my mouth, and I pulled her tighter, our kiss deepening.

Like tasting the raindrops after years of drought, each fluid movement of our mouths together revived my cracked heart. Each inch where our naked skin connected restored my famished soul. Keira nipped my lip, fingers twining in my hair as her legs circled my center. The weight of her in my arms felt so right, my inner dragon roaring with triumph as I held her close.

The spring vanished, melting away as we molded together.

Then the rocking of the Ceffyl greeted us, swaying with our bodies as we continued our exploration. I laid her down on the bed—our bed—her midnight hair sprawling across the pillow like gentle night. For a moment, our kiss broke, and I looked down on her, my goddess incarnate, my wife.

"Welcome home, Mrs. Mathonwy."

Keira's answering smile undid the last fraying strands of my restraint. "You are my home."

There was no waiting, no teasing or taunting. Hovering just above her, I slid into her, my most vulnerable parts finding salvation in hers. We moved together, slowly at first, then all at once, chasing our mutual pleasure, an oasis in the desert.

She sang a soft symphony of whimpers as we crescendoed closer and closer to our final notes. Then, with a wicked smirk, she twisted, flattening me on my back with ease. I sank into the soft mattress, hands planted into the supple flesh of her upper thigh as she sat atop me, a queen on her throne.

"My turn," she giggled, before setting her hips to motion once more. Slow, taunting strokes set my skin afire, my hips involuntarily bucking upwards to meet her languid pace.

"I love you." The words hurried from my lips. "I love you so much." Nothing would ever satisfy me like she did, no substance ever enough to quench the unending hunger I had for her presence.

Another mocking grin as she continued her teasing pace. Her hands splayed across my chest for support, nails digging slightly into my skin. I didn't care—I relished the pain and pleasure of her touch. I gripped her hips tighter, dragging them up and down my length, begging with my body for the release we both craved. A generous goddess, she granted my wish, bouncing faster. I bit my lip to stifle a moan.

Her smile grew, and her hands traveled up, wrapping around my neck.

"Don't stop," she commanded, and I obeyed, her faithful servant, driving the pace harder with deep thrusts.

Her chokehold tightened, air thinning. A flash of panic shot through me, but dashed as the ecstasy rose, a slow, excruciatingly delicious build towards climax.

"Keira, I'm—" My speech cut off as her grip became a cobra's hold, crushing my windpipe and stealing the breath from my lungs. I gasped, my hands flying to her wrists in reflex, but she squeezed harder.

"Stop, Keira, it hurts—" I coughed, black spots clouding my vision.

A dark chuckle bit through my fear.

Not hers.

Deep, male. Ancient.

Total blackness, and then the Ceffyl *disappeared.*

Ice, cold and sharp, pressed against my back. A much larger form, clothed in black robes, kneeled on my stomach, crushing my ribcage. His hair–almost the same ebony as Keira's–framed his face in shadows. Pain flashed as his massive hands choked me tighter.

"You will never have her again, not even in dreams, boy," the ancient voice growled, rage so palpable it smothered me. I kicked and thrashed, but he held strong, pressing me further into the frost. "She belongs to me now. She's mine.*"*

My claws shot from my fingertips, skewering his wrists. He howled, darting off me, blood staining the blue ice with crimson.

I scattered to my feet, spitting on the ground. "She belongs to no one."

"It's all mine." A smile and snarl stirred into one expression, lips red as the gore around us. Death stood straighter, his hair falling from his face. Obsidian eyes burned like coal, and his arms fell to his sides, blood pouring freely from his wounds. "You and your kin will have nothing left. I will bring ruin to your front door, and she will stand by my side, my queen, as I lay waste to you and your pathetic world."

"She could never love a monster like you." My voice was hoarse, but my conviction strong. My goddess, my wife, was good. The monster before me reeked of rot and ruin, of death and despair. Keira would see right through it, would cut him down in an instant...

"You're wrong, Ronan." The air froze, and my heart stopped beating. Keira strode across the ice, silver eyes shining cold as metal. Her black dress trailed through the blood as she laced an arm through Death's. "I already do."

Then, with a triumphant smile, he grabbed her face and kissed her, claiming her mouth with his.

A scream tore from the depths of my soul, ice cracking around me. I fell, the pits of the Otherworld swallowing me whole, devouring my shattered soul...

"Ronan?" A voice–*familiar*–yelled my name. My eyes flew open, a different face hovering over me, concern knitting his brow instead of contempt. "Ronan, are you all right, brother?"

My eyes adjusted to the low lamplight, breath rushing in rapid gasps. "He was here, he–he had her–"

"Who? Who was here?" Ellian asked, curls messy with sleep, his white tunic rumpled.

Nighttime. It was night. I'd gone to bed just a while ago, right after the last round of our game and the stroke of midnight...

My eyes drank in my surroundings, the familiar gray wood of my little cupboard, my red coat hanging on the back of the single chair. Sweat coated my frame, my cot...

My cot was torn to shreds, clawmarks littering the burlap.

"It was a nightmare," I croaked out, willing my heart to slow its wardrum's beat. I was not in the spring, or the *Ceffyl*, or the Otherworld. I was still on the *Madyn*, in my now-ruined quarters.

Keira was gone. Arawn still had her.

The dragon roared, vowing another vengeance on the Dark God's name. I brushed my matted hair from my forehead, meeting Ellian's green-eyed stare. "I saw Keira." My voice broke as her name poured from my lips. "And then the Dark God, he was...taunting me...threatening me."

"You were screaming. Woke half the ship." His copper face blanched, focus dropping to my neck. "Shit, what happened to your throat?"

On instinct, my fingers flew to the spot. I pressed my Adam's apple, and a tenderness answered. I stood, crossing to the small, dingy mirror that hung crooked on the wall. I cursed through grit teeth. Sure enough, a necklace of angry, red welts curled around my neck, a visceral reminder of Arawn's threat.

"Not a dream. A visit." I sucked in my reflection. My skin wasn't as pale as it had been earlier, Laureli's gift of blood and a few drinks with the sirens reinstating the rouge to my pallor. But my eyes still read as hollow, sapphire dark and muddy with a plague that was far from physical.

My vision had been clear. Nothing would truly feed me until I had my wife back. Until Keira wore the mantle of Captain once more. Until I could hold her in my arms and keep her truly safe.

Until I had Arawn's head on a spike.

"Things must not be going as he wants them to if the Dark God is willing to get his own hands dirty for once. He's getting desperate." A serpent smirk slithered across my face as I turned back to Ellian, the beast in my chest licking its lips. Soon, we'd feast on the spoils of war. "But so am I. He played his hand; now it's our turn."

"Do you have a plan, Captain?" Ellian squared his stance, the wolf answering a call. Perhaps he could smell it too, the change in the tide, the lingering rot in the air that signaled Arawn's slipping surety.

We were close. So seductively close.

All we needed now was a little divine intervention.

"Wake the rest of the crew and tell Nelle to brew some hangover remedies for anyone who isn't already stirring after my outburst." I clapped my comrade on the shoulder, rage readying my resolve. "No more waiting. We summon Danura before the sun rises."

Wind howled a war cry, the frigid night air scraping the flesh from our rosy cheeks. Morning was just around the corner, the sky its darkest before the first stretches of dawn. Skin prickled into goosebumps as the chill caressed our naked forms—all ready to jump in the blue if this worked the way we needed it to. But the fire Arawn lit under our asses was enough to keep even a crew of cold-blooded sharks warm, the sirens all rallied and ready within minutes.

Laureli outlined the finer details of the ritual belowdecks—emphasizing the risk failure would bring to our minds and bodies. Summoning a goddess would take all of the power we had. But none of the sirens balked—they simply stripped down and filtered onto the gray-stained deck, ready to sacrifice themselves if the need presented.

The single sliver of the famished moon above us was the only light we creatures of the deep and dark needed to see. Our perfect circle took little space on the small craft as the sirens stood hand in hand, our shoulders pressed together to form an impenetrable barrier. Laureli and Nelle to my left both sported grave masks, the witch and the healer understanding the crushing cost if we failed. Willow and Cassryn stood sentry directly across from me, both sisters ready for whatever the night brought. Even Marina lacked the lackadaisical charm she'd sported only hours ago, the siren's posture straight and severe as she flanked Siobhan's left. All eyes focused on me, personalities shed to make way for the primal magic that made us all. Siobhan nodded, squeezing my hand once for support.

A buzzing lit my spine as the ship swayed, a strange and seductive call resonating deep in my gut. Not the beast I'd been battling in my chest, not the remnants of my wife's starfire burning in my heart, but something *other*. Something untapped.

Something I'd make mine.

I lifted my chin to the waning moon, daring it to bear witness to our first stand against the Dark God's endless night. "Laureli, begin the incantation."

"We call on you, ancient mother of life." Laureli's rich voice chanted the first words, rhythmic and raw. A tingling set my fingertips ablaze where I held her hand, her magic pulsing through me. The circle of sirens swayed together as the spell traveled, a low hum in the back of our throats as we harmonized with Laureli's descant. "We, your faithful followers, are desperate for your love. Shower us in your presence like starshine, Donn."

"Donna, *Serenhi*, come to us," we sirens sang in unison, eyes tilting skyward.

The tingling surged to a searing heat, but I held on tighter to both Laureli and Siobhan. The ancient thing in the depths of me writhed with discomfort, begging to be let free.

Laureli sang on, brow beading with sweat, rich voice straining hoarse. "We ask for your favor, your guidance. Materialize before us, inexhaustible as the full moon. Danura, mother of all, deliver us from the darkness."

Power crested again, hot and heavy as it surged through every nerve. The unmistakable scent of charred scales sullied the crisp air, the spell trying to force us all to turn. The familiar tearing sensation ran up my legs, flesh struggling to be ripped and restitched. I fought the urge to tear my hand away from Laureli, instead grasping firmer still.

We would not fail. Could not.

This time, the sirens shouted our verse, pain coloring our song as the burning grew in our palms. "Donn, *Serenhi*, come to us."

"Is it working?" Siobhan gritted out, her whole form shaking. Bright orange scales carved her hips, the transformation tugging even the strongest of us. The others began to wilt as the throbbing charged through their limbs, but hands stayed clasped together. Hearts stayed strong.

Laureli's claws bit into my skin as she held on; drops of my crimson blood spilled between my fingers. Her song became a cry as she lifted my bleeding hand to the heavens. "Author of life. We offer up the sacrifice of our blood to bring you, body and soul, to greet us with the light of your face."

As my blood hit the deck, something within crashed to my toes.

Agony shot through my bones with the force of a bullet, molten heat lacerating my veins. A grunt worked its way up my throat, hotter than dragon's fire. I swallowed it back. Let it feed the primordial predator in my pit.

"Something is wrong," Nelle groaned, face contorted in her torture, fangs poking through. "We should at least hear her whispers...or *something*."

Nothing. No response, only pain. Only the magic forcing us to be *other* once more. The sirens crumpled beneath it, still hand in hand, but sunken faces and twisted postures begged for relief.

Laureli stared at me, a heartbeat shared between us.

She broke hold first, and the pain snuffed out instantly, leaving only a phantom ache as if it had only been a cruel trick of the mind, not a true bodily affliction. Willow's knees hit the deck, and Cassryn crawled on wobbly limbs to tend her sister.

"It must be Arawn's curse," Marina muttered, leaning onto Siobhan's sturdy frame for support.

A deeper pain set in, one fashioned of disappointment and desperation. I rubbed the tender bruises across my neck, barely there but far more of a wound than any lingering cost of the magic.

I needed Danura. Needed my wife, before it was too late. I trusted Keira. She would never willingly betray me. But a faint fear stuck in the back of my mind like footprints in snow.

You're wrong Ronan. I already do.

Had she already fallen for his trap? Or worse, had she given herself to him? I knew all too well what she was willing to sacrifice to keep us safe.

Nelle broke my trance, tears lining her striking violet stare. "I'm sorry, Ronan, but I suspected this much. She's bound to the island."

The deep thing that stirred suddenly snarled and snapped, a new beast baring its fangs. I was done with apologies and excuses. Done with disavowed gods and unbroken curses. "What good is the goddess if she can't break her own spells? Doesn't she have her own power?"

"Yes, but it's scattered. Weak." Siobhan's self-conscious arm covered her exposed chest as she stepped forward. The others had already shuffled into their clothes, heads hanging to avoid my gaze. I didn't think the sirens knew shame; though perhaps it was less about their nudity and more about the vulnerability of our failure here tonight. What it meant for us all.

"I'm sorry, Ronan," Laureli echoed, voice still cracked and dry from the effort of her song. "I thought we could try."

And she had. I knew they all had. I saw the pain in their faces, the effort written into their harsh cries. The disappointment now in the slack of their normally proud postures.

We, too, were scattered. Frayed. Just the forgotten relics of the gods that made us, previews of the power that had been dashed across the darkness.

I ran my hand over my face, cruel resignation settling beneath my scales.

But the beast my wife made was not content with concession. Inside, it roared, daring me to weave the strings of success back together. To use the scales and claws and fangs my maker gave me to forge a new fate.

"That's it. Scattering power…" I sucked in a breath as realization reignited the fire.

It was a risk, one I would bear the burden of, but I had to try. Had to trust the gold my wife gilded me in.

I focused inward, sacrificing myself to the Siren Prince. I winced as the flesh at my hip cleaved and reconstructed, several golden scales glittering in the darkness. Biting my cheek, I unfurled a claw, and sliced.

I held up the single scale, thin as paper but strong as diamond, ignoring my bleeding hip. "I need one of each of your scales."

"*What?*" Marina stuck a hand to her side, staring at me as if I had six tails. Maybe I did. I didn't recognize the creature clawing its way up from my belly, captaining the vessel of my body. But I trusted it, heart and soul.

Laureli must have sensed my resolve, or perhaps could smell the magick rolling off me in waves of citrus and starlight. She winced once and ripped an aquamarine scale from her calf, handing it to me. "Do it."

I placed it in my palm on top of my gold one. A flash of silver light as they touched, signaling a response, and my chest swelled.

Small victories, indeed.

I closed my eyes, pouring every ounce of focus and fury into the buzzing of my palms. Into the parts of me that were both siren and storyteller. Into the ancient truth fused to my bones, one married to the novel power coating my scales.

Then I sang, the melody bubbling up from that part of me. The part that already knew the answers I'd sought, the part that begged me to remember.

"Long ago, in ages past.
Three gods ruled in harmony.
Donn, Arawn, and Lyr,
Their power strong in solidarity."

"Ronan, what are you doing?" Siobhan hissed, sinking into a defensive stance, ready to pounce if this went south.

It wouldn't. Certainty coursed through my veins like a powerful potion, a self-fulfilling prophecy authored by the thing pulsating within. It coated my tongue with truth, each word of my song weighty under the magick that caressed them.

A song of past and present. A song of curses and cures.

A song long forgotten and remembered by all.

A song of caution and triumph.

I sank to my knees, bowing before the truth, offering my song to the universe that made both monsters and men.

"But a crew divided cannot sail,
And as the bonds of love did break,
Donn, Arawn, and Lyr,
Their fortitude did shake."

"Quick, give him the scales," Nelle commanded this time, her amethyst scale added to the pile. Then citrine and ruby, onyx and ivory, as the others added their offering to the altar. Fragments glowed as they fused together, starshine radiating from my outstretched hands.

The sirens gasped, surrounding me as the spell transformed. As the gift my wife gave me and the power I'd been born with came together, creating something terrible and great. My voice carried, echoing across the empty ocean.

"Lyr split his fortune across four seas,
In springs and ceffyl's stares.
Arawn cast his across the realms,
In hounds, weapons, and wares.

Humming again, as the siren chorus lent their voices to mine, our call clanging through the endless night.

"Donn's lot was taken,
Tossed across the skies,
But some was saved and remade,
In siren scales and eyes."

"Brilliant." Laureli flashed a smile, as the scales created a crystal in my hand, the light—no, the *star*—trapped within.

A piece of Danura's power, stolen from the life she gave all of us. Repurposed from the power she'd given Keira, and by extension, me. A fragment of what she once wielded, only the whisper of what she'd been before.

But enough.

Laureli gripped my shoulder, and we sang the final verse in unison, the Seer and Storyweaver both filling the duties we were crafted for.

"We call you now, O mother blessed,
This gift of power given to thee.
No longer fractured, but united,
Grant us your presence be."

The star burned, light blinding us. I dropped it to the deck as it singed my hands, shielding my eyes as it exploded into sunlight, into pure power and dazzling radiance—

Into a woman, her outline wavering for a single second before solidifying. Into silver eyes and a stern chin, into ethereal power and effortless grace.

Into surprisingly *dark* hair, woven with natural strands of silver instead of its normal brilliant white.

Into a face smeared with shock, eyes alight with panic and lip trembling in terror.

"No, no!" Danura stumbled forward, crashing to her knees, fresh tears sliding down her freckled cheeks. "What did you just *do?*"

16

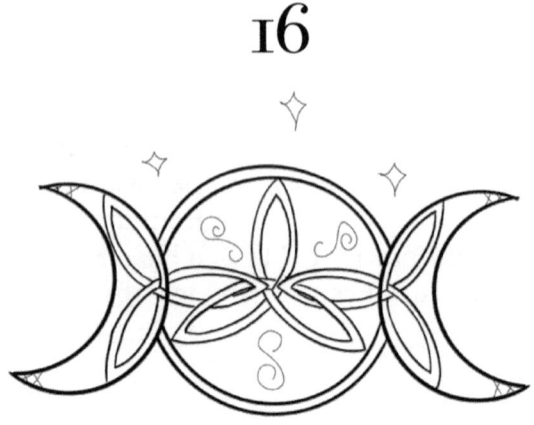

Crowns and Conspiracy

KEIRA

Papa used to say no Branwen was ever left behind. I was no longer Branwen or Mathonwy. No longer Captain or cutlass. Not daughter or wife. I had only one role left to play, one last part of me a defiant light against the darkness of the Otherworld.

Mother.

And yet, though I had forsaken my names and my titles, given them to the grave, I was not alone.

No Branwen left behind, not even in the Otherworld.

Reina and Finna stood behind me, braiding my hair into intricate plaits, the two working in synchronized silence. Matching in their stiff black uniforms, they fashioned uninterested faces as Cythie flitted across the room in a frenzy, none the wiser to my cousins' ruse. Finna chewed her bottom lip, the only indication of her worry.

Of the dangerous game we prepared to play.

I watched their ghostly reflections dancing in the vanity mirror, but it wasn't the living dead haunting me. I could place my fate in their nimble fingers, and yet a looming sense of dread swam in my core.

If I failed my task, what would happen to them? Would they be wiped from existence, just as Connor was?

Death didn't take too kindly to betrayal, it seemed.

But I wouldn't leave my kin behind, either. Branwen or Mathonwy.

Finna finished braiding first, picking up the obsidian diadem resting on the vanity in front of me. Her practiced whine brought me back to the present. "Cythie, could you polish this tiara? It's simply filthy."

The little girl's nose scrunched up like she could smell Finna's flowered horseshit. "Miss Finna, a reminder that Miss Cythie does outrank you." Cythie folded her arms across her chest, sending Finna a look that could rival Saeth's sharpness. "Just because you're older than me doesn't mean you can boss me 'round."

I stiffened in my seat, pressing my back into the wood chair for support. If we couldn't get rid of the kid, we would be dead in the water before we even hoisted anchor.

"Would ye really mind, Cythie?" Reina lilted as she fashioned a warm smile, another Mathonwy mask made of sunlight and sincerity. "I would do it, but ye've got such a good eye for it. It always sparkles like stars whenever ye shine it."

The tension in my shoulders dissolved quickly as it came, a wave of gratitude crashing into me. The White Snake was enigmatic as ever. Even in the black and white of Death's domain, she could sell a colorful story better than any Ir'desian peddler.

Cythie eyed the diadem, blush rising to her pale cheeks. "Well, I—"

"Please Cythie, for me?" I tried to mimic Reina's sugary tone, sweeter than any pastry she ever made. "I want to look special tonight."

Special, like a present wrapped up just for Death. Like a dagger disguised in a dress. I'd hide my monstrous parts if it meant keeping the more delicate parts safe.

Rhiannon.

Rhiannon.

"Cythie would be most pleased." The little girl snatched the diadem from Finna's fingers and tilted her chin up, matching my cousin's candied contempt with ease. "Finna, you can finish the dusting in here while Cythie is gone."

In a flash of black, she vanished.

The three of us released a collective breath, tension dissolving from the room like the shadows Cythie disappeared into. A tiny, dangerous bud of hope blossomed in my middle, like an early sign of spring amidst a snow-covered frost. Perhaps tonight would go as we planned and make way for the rest of this frozen hell to melt.

"Annoying little git," Finna grumbled, but a smile lit her features. Did she smell it too? The dizzying, dangerous flower that had taken root?

"She's a sweet girl, takes her work seriously," Reina giggled while pinning my braids up, even the White Snake tipsy on the daydream laid before us.

"How does it work, exactly?" I stared at the open space where Cythie had been not a moment before. I'd been so caught up in my personal hell that I hadn't thought to explore the inner workings of the Otherworld. If it only saw us as we saw ourselves, how did so many end up in Death's service? "Who tells you what to do?"

Reina stilled, nibbling her bottom lip. "We aren't quite sure. When we first came...well, it's the same at first for everyone. You see parts of yourself that aren't so flattering. Moments from your life."

The Otherworld sees us as we see ourselves.

A trail of ice ran down my spine, as if Death himself breathed down my neck. I was all too familiar with the living nightmares. The distorted flashbacks that death favored to torture his prisoners. Or rather, that we all tortured ourselves with.

Black smoke against white flesh. Devouring me from inside out. Clawing its way up my arm. Red hair against stone streets, blood the same color. A body disintegrating to ash as the light burned, my light. Chestnut eyes, lifeless as the bloodstained deck of the ship. Screaming that pierced the night. Mama, no. Mama, please. *A daughter made orphan, with hate in her gaze and fire in her veins.*

Not real.

Not real.

No, Reina and Finna were no longer bleeding out in Porthladd. They were here, real. Safe. Reina's gentle fingers wound in my hair, Finna's practiced scowl clear in the mirror.

"We all have regrets." Finna's absentminded hand drifted to her middle.

I gave her other hand a light squeeze. No Branwen left behind, not now, not ever. "You're not alone, Finn."

Jade eyes misted as she squeezed back. "I know."

"Some souls get trapped in that cycle." Reina's voice took on new heaviness, her usual lilt weighed with a husky sorrow only the Otherworld knew. A stray thought drifted to Donnall, Aidan, and Weylin. Could they be stuck in that whirlwind of their own terror and regret? I made a mental note to look into it as Reina finished the pins in my hair, gesturing to her black uniform like it had always been there. "But the ones that break free are given a place. It's like waking up, and we sort of just...know what to do? Where to go."

A sadness crept up my chest, lodging itself in my throat. No Branwen left behind, and yet even in Death, I'd been given so much more than the rest of my family. None of them had any say in what their lives looked like now. It was either an eternity of self-inflicted sorrow, or service to the Dark God's destitute domain.

I had a choice. I had since the first day Death chose to visit me, since his first "Good morning." And day after day, I chose to wallow in my misery instead of doing something. Forever a selfish monster, I'd let my family wait, stuck in this gilded prison while I toyed with my woe and Death's feelings for me.

After Papa died, I'd been a slave to my own impulse, making my choices and not caring about the consequences. But since I'd become Captain, it'd been the opposite. I let my inaction lead, let my fear and indecision rule me.

Now I knew the price. Knew how actions spoke volumes above pretty words.

I wouldn't pay twice. Tonight, I would act. Tonight, the Dark God would submit and serve *my* whim. Tonight, I'd trudge forward, burning a path for my future daughter to walk straight out of the Otherworld.

And I wouldn't leave my family behind.

"I promise, I'll make it right."

"Aye, we know ye will." Reina stroked my cheek, leaning closer to wink at me in the mirror. "Ye sure look the part."

She was right. I took a long look at the girl in the mirror. She was no longer the NightMare of the Four Seas, a feral sailor dressed in her uncle's oversized long-coat. No longer Death's sunken doll either, no frilly ballgown made of stars and sad smiles.

The woman staring back was something entirely *other*. Silver eyes shone with moonlight, not born of hope, but of vengeance. Raven hair glistened as it framed her face like a crown, not given by Death, but taken by force. The vivid scar on her neck was not a mark of pain, but power, a symbol of the lengths she'd go to in order to ensure her family's safety. At first glance, her silk dress appeared black, but beneath the soft light, hints of wine-red cut through, smoldering beneath like lava ready to flow. It cut low on her chest, emphasizing how soft her frame had gotten, hugging each curve closer than the secrets she kept beneath.

Fury and femininity. Destruction and divinity. Monster and mother both.

"You look like a goddess," Finna breathed, and for once in our lives, I agreed.

Tonight, I would turn the silver wheel of fate myself to save my daughter, even if it meant Death's damnation.

"May I interrupt? I have flowers fer the lady." Papa's ginger beard poked through the doorway, and I jumped to my feet. It was still so strange to have him close, like the last five years were simply a blink in time. Our eyes met, and for a moment, all I wanted was to shrink back to the version of myself that was daughter before all else. Wanted to run to him and wrap myself in his hug, and pretend that my biggest problems were sparring practice and deckhand duties.

But that girl had died when he did.

Papa crossed his arms as he took me in. "Oh, Keira girl, ye look—"

"Like Arawn's worst nightmare," I finished for him, forcing myself to stand straighter. *Think tall, you'll be tall.*

I was a fucking giant.

A wry smile twisted my father's face, eyes dancing with mischief meant for a much younger man. Not that I blamed him. I could feel it too, the taunt of a small victory so close. "Ye clear on the plan this time, girl?"

"A stroll through the garden, tell him my choice. Then dinner and a dance. Find out more about what he needs from me."

Papa nodded, my recitation perfect. "Aye, we need to know more about what's happenin' up top if we have any chance of getting ye there."

The last words soured the air, fear sprinkling across the back of my neck. I wasn't trapped in ice anymore, but Death's invisible shackles still weighed around my wrists. "I'm still not so sure I can get out. No one can. Not even him, I think."

Papa shrugged, plopping onto the corner of my bed like he owned the room. "If there is a way in, there's a way out. Simple as that." He stroked his beard, an old habit practiced whenever he needed to think. "The boys are in place. They'll be keeping an eye on ye at dinner in case ye need them."

The boys. My sunken crew. Lochlan and Roland, Papa and Owen. Branwen and Mathonwy both.

No one left behind, above or below.

"I need to get us access to the mirror again. I'll ask Arawn, but perhaps you could do some digging with the servants," I said, no longer a deckhand, but a deity. "Last time, he showed me Locasta. She didn't seem to be doing anything nefarious, but I want to make sure everyone topside is safe too."

Finna went rigid, lips tightening into a deep frown. "Before I...well, before I kicked the bucket, I overheard things Morwyn and Connor were saying." Her gaze flicked up to me, panic surging in her dilated pupils. "It might be relevant."

My own heart sped in response, an itch of worry crawling beneath my skin. I never thought to assume they wanted anything other than my life that night. I was their primary target, but perhaps I was only one part of the larger plan. "What did they say?"

"There was a ritual they wanted to perform with...with the baby. And my Pa's betrayal," Finna stuttered, the Vixen Queen quivering. Reina placed a steadying hand on her elbow, concern knitting her delicate brows together. Finna breathed a shaky breath, continuing through chattering teeth, "They needed... betrayer's blood, the soul of the innocent...and the heart of the god?"

Papa shot up from the bed, urgency animating his limbs. Sunset eyes found mine. "I remember a story from long ago. Yer ma mentioned it, back when we first met. Before I believed what she was. About blood spells. I think it's how he trapped her..."

A different story swarmed my senses, one once told by my favorite bard, on the deck of our ship...

Arawn's jealousy knew no bounds. In a fit of rage, he took his spear and drove it through his wife's heart. He took her power and scattered it across the sky, banishing her to the island of the lost...

Dread pooled deep in my gut as I cursed myself, wishing I could remember the details of Ronan's story.

"Heart of a god…" Reina murmured, clutching the fabric of her black frock. She'd been there that night on the ship, when talks of gods and monsters were little more than just scary bedtime stories. When our biggest fears were Finna's wedding and banishments. Chestnut eyes shot to me as she recalled the fragments I could not. "That would explain why he wants Keira to fall for him. There's more than one way to possess a heart. But what does he want to do with the spell?"

I shuddered at the possibilities. I'd thought sacrificing myself to Arawn's keep would be enough to clear my debt. Thought that my soul was the only part of me I had to sell to the Otherworld. But instead of clearing my ledger, I'd only put myself, and possibly my whole crew, at greater risk.

Finna paced as she tried to calculate the cost of my blunder. "When I took matters into my own hands, I ruined the whole blood of an innocent thing for him." She stopped in her tracks, gaze falling to my middle. Color ran from her face. "You can't tell him about her. No matter what."

Horror flooded my senses, limbs turning led beneath me.
Blood of an innocent.
A child, Mrs. Mathonwy.
It had been the goal all along. Connor's and Locasta's.
Arawn's.

Madame Hedd had warned me back in Hud, back when I was trying to lay my debt on any fool that would pay it for me. No soul was innocent, except for one not yet tainted by life. By experience.

Rage lit like a candle in an inferno, turning fear to ash in my veins. I wouldn't pay that price then, or now. If Death came for my daughter, I would burn the whole Otherworld to cinders, burying him beneath the debris. "I would never."

"Yer a sailor and a soldier, Keira girl. But ye've always been so much more." Papa brushed a knuckle across my cheek, tearing me back to the moment. To the *plan*. "Ye'll be yer own good luck charm tonight, my little Silver Wheel. Tell him what he wants to hear, and see if we can squeeze something outta him too."

I nodded once. I knew the part I had to play. The Goddess Ariannad. Weaver of Fate, I would spin whatever lies I needed to in order to craft my web, a black widow setting her trap. I would not be Arawn's puppet or his prey.

I'd be his doom.

Black burst in the room, the sand in our hourglass run out. Cythie materialized, the black tiara radiant in her tiny hands, a proud tilt to her chin. "Isn't it shiny now—oh, Mr. Cedric? What are you—"

"Hiya, Cythie!" Papa interrupted, patting the girl's head with easy fondness. I'd seen this version of him a thousand times before, knew how warm his smile could make someone feel. A simple target, Cythie beamed as Papa took the tiara to inspect her expert work. "Wow, brighter than a crow's feather. Would ye and Miss Reina mind giving me a hand, actually? The kitchen has some silver that could use a shine like this before dinner tonight."

"What a grand idea!" Reina bounced on her toes, the White Snake effortlessly playing her part in Papa's ruse. "The Master will be so pleased."

My family knew their roles tonight as well. No one left behind, they'd all rally and roll with me, no matter the risk. We were past the point of life or death. Tonight, we played for real keeps: salvation, or oblivion.

I would not let my family down.

"Thank you, Cythie. It's perfect." I took the diadem from Papa's grasp, placing it atop my braids.

I would take this crown first. Then I'd take Death's throne.

Papa's hazel eyes glinted gold. He stared at me, a father looking at his daughter one last time before she became something else. Something *other*. "Goodday, Miss Keira. Glad ye like the flowers, though they are nothing compared to yer beauty."

"Goodday, Mr. Cedric. Ms. Reina." I swallowed the lump lodged in my throat, pushing past the part of me that wanted to stay a little girl following in her father's oversized footsteps.

They disappeared into blackness without another word. I turned to Finna, ready to fight the battle ahead.

"I swear, lying runs in that man's blood." My cousin quirked an eyebrow as she fanned out the base of my skirt for me. "Hopefully you inherited that gift."

"I think it's a talent all Branwens have. Our track record isn't as clean as we used to believe."

Honor has no place down here.

Finna stopped fiddling with my hemline. "Be careful, Keira. I know I've been harsh, but if anything were to happen—"

"You haven't been harsh, you've been honest." There were so many things I could have said to my sister, to the girl made of cleverness and beauty, but they all died on my tongue. I only hoped I could steal some of her gifts for tonight, too. "Thank you."

Finna stared at the ground, an uncharacteristic shyness in her diverted gaze. "Is it awful of me to be jealous? I made my choices, but part of me is sad that you're going to get out of here, going to save everyone while I'm a prisoner in a palace. Again."

My heart raged against the cage of my ribs. No Branwen left behind, and yet, even if I did find a way out, I had no guarantee I could take them with me. Mortals only crossed out of Arawn's domain in Ronan's happiest stories.

I took her delicate hands in mine, squeezing once. "I've always been jealous of you. You're so effortlessly... perfect. Pretty and clever and enticing. I don't know what's supposed to come out of this, or how long it will be until I see you all again if things go well...but I want my daughter to know you. Even if it's just my stories about you. Hopefully then, she'll be better than me."

Finna and I had always been two sides of the same coin. Women in a world of men that would devastate us if we let them, wielding the weapons we knew best. Sisters in a clan that let ambition break our bonds, holding the fraying threads of our family together in our limited fingers. I had a long list of regrets in my life, many of which could trap me in a cycle of nightmares for eternity. But none compared to the way I'd let life cleave a gap between my eldest cousin and I.

I would not make the same mistake in death. My daughter would know the legend of Finna Branwen and learn from our collective mistakes.

Finna's lower lip wobbled for a moment before she steeled herself over. The Vixen Queen once more, she pecked my cheek once, the gentle act fortifying me with the strength I needed. "Don't you forget you are a Branwen. We were born of something far more potent than Death."

"Knock knock, my *Caraid*." The velvet voice preceded his body as he misted into the room, Death needing no invitation.

I jumped, shifting in front of Finna as he materialized, before he could recognize her. "Arawn, I–"

"Your maid must have been frightened," he laughed, his towering frame corporeal once more. Tonight, his long hair was tied back in a knot that emphasized the icy sharpness of his cheeks and jaw. The corner of his wide mouth tugged up in a grin, further spotlighting the hard planes of his face. "I rarely come to this wing, and my reputation is a bit much sometimes. Please give my apologies to her later."

"Of course." I let loose a sigh of relief. Finna must have shadowed out before he caught a glimpse of her.

I focused instead on the myth in front of me and the task ahead. Even knowing more of the truth, it was hard not to gawk at him like the handsome god he was. Tonight, Death dressed the part, a blood red suit lined with gold trim accentuating his marble-cut form. It was both seductive and dangerous, as if he knew the game of cat and mouse we were about to play and was determined to be the predator.

But tonight, I was ready. I smoothed the front of my dress, remembering my purpose. In an intentionally slow, fluid movement, I offered him my hand. "I'm ready when you are, *Your Highness.*"

Death's brows lifted as he filtered his fingers through mine. With painful languidness, he raked his eyes over me, greedily studying each and every curve of the silk dress across my body, all the way from the tip of my crown to my toes. Obsidian eyes darkened, his smile turning wolfish. "I see you mean to ruin me tonight in that dress."

I met his smile with my own. If only he knew how right he was.

I was no longer Branwen or Mathonwy. No longer Captain or cutlass. Not daughter or wife.

Tonight, I'd become Queen Mother of the Otherworld.

17

Spells and Scales

RONAN

Danura stared me down from across the gnarled wood table with a look that could bend steel. But despite the fire in her expression, she shivered beneath the shawl Nelle wrapped around her. Her gossamer gown–stained with suspicious red–was far better suited for *Hiraethean* heat than the frigid eastern sea. But the chill had little to do with her attire, and far more to do with the dark hair that framed her freckled face, the pale sheen that coated her normally radiant skin.

In the dim light of the *Madyn's* galley, Danura looked entirely *mortal*.

"We needed your help, *Serenhi*," Nelle broke the silent standoff, hiding her hands in her work apron. She stood awkwardly next to me, torn between her former queen and current captain, eyes darting between both. "We've been so close, but only a god can open the gates…"

"Then you should've come to *Hiraeth* instead of summoning me," Danura hissed, though the normally stern edge to her voice had eroded into exhaustion, the deep blue bags beneath her eyes an echo of it.

"You don't think we tried that?" Siobhan pushed off from where she leaned in the doorway, pulling out the chair next to her former leader and straddling it. Dark knuckles turned white as she gripped its back, strange tears welling in the molten amber of her eyes. "We couldn't come back."

It had been the first tactic we tried, sending the sirens back to Danura for reinforcements. When they'd washed back up on Ir'de's southern shore after searching the seas for five days straight, exhaustion and panic painted in vivid color across their expressions...

It had nearly crippled the whole crew.

"Impossible." Danura pulled the blanket tighter around her shoulders, a shield against truths she refused to accept. She stuck her chin up at me, the ghost of the queen she once was staring down the bridge of her nose. "Your crew managed. I'd just sent them on their way to Pysgodd before you ripped me from my home like some washed-up genie."

"My crew was in *Hiraeth*?" Nothing could damper the surprise in my voice, the hitch of hope in my sharp intake of breath.

I'd sent them to Pysgodd, to ferry supplies and watch over the refugees. It was no small task, our supply chain one of the only lifelines keeping the Deyrnas from the edge of total famine, but it was clearly safer than a voyage to hell. But if they'd gone to *Hiraeth*, to the land of lost wishes and forgotten miracles...

Had they figured out something I hadn't? Had Griffin and Rhett revealed some piece of the puzzle I'd overlooked?

Danura shot through my billowing sails like a cannon, leaving me dead in the water. "They were there for the same reason you summoned me. To ask for my help, and to tell me you managed to let Arawn take Keira and the baby."

Every bone in my body threatened to crack under the rockslide of guilt and rage that buried me. Of the truth that would crush my will into dust.

I let Connor take her. I stood by and did nothing, a reality that would haunt me long after the world stopped its spinning.

But at least I'd been there. At least I watched her lift the gun, watched her lifeblood rain on the deck, watched her body dissolve into a mist of smoke and shadows.

My tongue forked, the wicked snake striking true. "Fine accusations coming from the goddess that sent a school of fish to fight her battles."

Danura rocketed from her seat. "Keira only left *Hiraeth* to save *you*. If she stayed, I could have protected her."

A snarl burrowed through my clenched teeth. "Keep my wife's name out of your mouth."

"She was my daughter before she was your wife, *boy*."

"And you were *his* wife before you were her mother," I thundered, my voice clanging around the small room. Silence filled the space, both sirens gaping at me. Danura only blinked, barely registering the shock. The dragon's fire coated my tongue again, unsatisfied without quivering prey to chase. "None of this would've happened if you, Lyr, and Arawn hadn't made a mess of it all and abandoned the Deyrnas. Abandoned *Keira*."

At that, Danura sat, the force knocking her back into the chair. The muscles in her jaw struggled as she swallowed back whatever arrow-tipped accusation she'd cocked her bow with, a knowing frown instead seated on her mouth.

"Blame will get us nowhere." Nelle cleared her throat, but it did nothing to wash the strain still hanging in the air. Her fists balled tighter in the hideaway of her apron. "We have a purpose, *Serenhi*. We've managed to find Arawn's gate a few times. We just cannot open it without a god."

"Without you," Siobhan echoed with a comforting squeeze to Danura's arm, latent loyalty undetachable from the warrior's composition. I tried not to roll my eyes at how easily they rolled over for her.

I had no loyalty left for Danura, despite our history together. She was a means to an end. To my wife.

Danura ran a shaking hand over her face, the action so human, my gut clenched for a fraction of a moment. She sighed, an ancient fatigue filling the sound. "You really have no idea what you've done. The spell you used wasn't just a summoning, it was a binding. You used the scales to trap my power and tie it to you directly."

Silver eyes—no, too dull to be silver, but a flat gray—stared past the defense of my rage, past the masks I'd been wearing.

In all honesty, I had no idea what I had done. No idea where the spell came from, or where I'd even heard the story. I'd just followed the tugging in my gut, the cord that connected me to my maker, to Fate itself.

A misty memory, one I wasn't entirely sure was even mine, rattled down my spine. Whispered words, feverish and powerful. Flesh ripping and remaking, heat and light and darkness and danger.

Not just a siren, but more. A man, with the breadth to hold the sea itself in his arms. A god, one no mortal inconvenience like time or distance or weakness could threaten.

I shook free of the thought. Wherever the incantation had come from, it was a necessary choice. I leashed another snarky comment, instead biting out something closer to sincerity. "I'm sorry if it's inconvenient. But we need you to get to Keira."

Danura nodded, resigned in the slump of her shoulders, so slender beneath her shawl. "The problem is that *Hiraeth* was also a binding spell. Without me there, the island is gone."

Both Siobhan and Nelle inhaled sharply. Nelle covered her mouth against the sob that rocked out of her. A warning churned in my gut like oil spilled in water, unsettled, yet too slippery to undo. Once upon a time, *Hiraeth* was just a fairytale, a legend whispered to warn children not to stray too far from home. But the myth had been very real, to me and my people. A place where things weren't lost, but found. The thought of it gone was even harder a story to swallow.

Danura's lips flattened into a thin line. "Worse off, now that my new vessel is a few siren scales instead of a whole island teeming with life, my powers are significantly reduced."

I hedged my next question carefully, afraid of the sting of disappointment. "Can you still open the gate?"

"I don't know. But I have no other option." She shrugged, leaning further back in her chair. A humorless laugh shook her frame. "You should've let me handle this."

All pity or penitence I might have felt in the moment before dried and shriveled up, replaced by a flood of fury that demanded retribution. "You have had centuries to handle it and didn't."

I stood from my chair, chin tilted skyward. Whatever my wife had made me, siren or dragon, demon or god, I would use it to turn stories and spells into reality. "We will open the gate. If your power is tied to ours now, your vessel isn't just a few scales, but seven cold-blooded, near-immortal sirens. We'll do it together."

Danura met my gaze, silver stars clashing against golden scales, primordial power against fresh potential. An absentminded hand ran through her salt-streaked black hair, a reminder of what happened to gods robbed of their gifts. "There will still be a price."

"I've made my peace. Whatever it demands, I'll pay it. Will you?"

My challenge sat unanswered for a long pause, Danura's breath held as she counted the cost for herself. Then, an exhale.

"We are wasting time. We should go now, before whatever power I have left fades." She looked to Siobhan, a silent command to her favored general.

But Siobhan turned to me, swinging her leg over the chair and standing at attention, a soldier expecting an order. "Captain?"

For once, I didn't wince at the title. "Get the girls ready, and tell Laureli to get Ellian into that breathing apparatus. We leave at daybreak."

I strode from the table, past Danura, before the price of my mistakes could nip at my ankles. But I paused at the door, offering her one last mortal courtesy before I stepped through the gate to godhood. "Get some rest. You'll need it."

18

Dances and Desire

KEIRA

I followed Death down a deserted corridor, heeled shoes echoing across the marble floor like a battle cry. My armor was made of silk and secrets instead of steel, but I didn't need my weapons. Tonight, my beauty would be my blade.

It was a role a younger version of me might have scoffed at—I'd always been a sailor first and a lady second. But femininity was a weapon like any other in my arsenal, and I was a warrior before all else.

I'm trying to make you look like a blushing bride. Someone the Council won't see as a threat.

"Where are we headed?" I twined my arm through his, the first arrow in my quiver. He stiffened before melting beneath my touch, muscles unwinding.

Dark eyes shimmered as he halted, stopping in front of towering black doors of smooth, matte stone. He let loose a smile, one so bright it might've pierced my armor had I not been ready. "I had the servants tidy up the ballroom. It's been far too long since I've used it."

Gently slipping out of my grip, he pushed the doors open together, light pouring through the crack. He stepped over the threshold, extending a hand to me with a bow, inviting me forward.

I took it, reminding myself that while tonight might be my game, it was his playfield. The war for the Otherworld would not be won with beguiling smiles and wit alone.

But despite my better judgment, my breath stole from my chest as I took in the circular ballroom. Endless white columns framed a wide, open floor made of pure obsidian, the surface glassy as black ice. Light sparkled from dozens of giant chandeliers, crystals like icicles draped from the branches of frozen trees. Across the impossibly tall walls, frescos of every shade told long forgotten stories, the rainbow of colors mirrored in the surface of the floor. And at the ceiling, domed glass curved wide, exposing the night sky littered with thousands of stars beyond.

I inhaled a sharp breath. It was beautiful.

A deep ache in my chest tore open an old wound as I studied the details of the nearest stone-laid story. In it, two lovers embraced in a field of white trees, so eerily similar to the spring.

Ronan would've loved this place.

Ronan.

Ronan.

Ronan.

I chased the thought of my husband away. I had no room for sentiment or sorrow tonight. Tonight, I shed my snakeskin to make way for my most monstrous parts.

"It's stunning." My voice quivered, unbecoming of the queen I was meant to be tonight. Arawn chose our arena well. This place was almost beautiful enough to make me forget. To make me remember.

"Would you like to see more?" His deep voice caressed the words, soft as starshine. He stood flush behind me, his presence radiating heat.

"Yes." A dangerous truth. A dangerous game.

Death laid a gentle, guiding hand on the small of my back, coaxing me to the next multicolored wall.

Three women waited in the stone, naked forms encircled by the moon shifting through her phases. The first had golden hair, her body barely budding with womanhood, a joyous smile on her face. The third, her hair silver, her skin sagging with age and wisdom packed deep in her wrinkles. The center had dark hair, fanning away from her face, blown by an unknown wind. Hands circled her middle, round and swollen with motherhood. With possibility and potential.

Our eyes met, two waiting mothers both trapped in different kinds of stone.

"How goes your training?" Arawn pivoted, blocking my view of the fresco, captivating me in his gaze instead.

I faked a smile Finna taught me, one made of moonlight and mystery. "Better."

I tunneled down into the depths of my body, to the smallest parts that stored the latent power. I opened my palms, summoning the light to my fingertips with ease. Shadows rippled around it, the seductive tango a push and pull of ego and surrender. Both were mine–shadow and sunshine, night and day. My power could be anything I wanted it to be.

I'd been secretly practicing in my room every night with Papa, envisioning my power taking shape, shifting to my will. Most days, it was simply light; possibility, untamed and unfiltered, like the ever-changing moon in my pocket. Some days, it looked like fury and starfire, a protective wall of flame designed to desecrate any that crossed my path. Others, like sea and storm, like streams of gentle water that could both heal and drown.

Today it looked like exactly what I thought Death wanted to see; polar opposites, flirting for dominance. Finding salvation and power in each other's embrace.

"Impressive," he murmured, large hand clasping around mine, extinguishing both shadow and light. He did not let go–cold fingers tucked between like they belonged there. Belonged to *him*.

He led me to the next image, one of a giant, inky tower, and my heart shuddered. This image resembled God's Eye to a frightening degree. My throat ran dry, the thought of the slaves beneath the Orwellin temples digging up a buried wrath.

"What about Connor Yorath and Morwyn Locasta?" I blurted without thinking, that anger arming my tongue with a mind of its own.

Death's brow pulled tight. "What about them?"

I sucked in a breath, leashing my anger and remembering instead my plan. My duty.

Find out what he wants from ye. See if ye can get anything out of him in return.

My voice found a foreign pocket of certainty and softness, silken as the dress I wore. "I understand more now that the Otherworld—well, it's only hell if you want it to be. But why let your devotees harm the Deyrnas?"

Arawn's hand stiffened in mine, his whole frame rigid. A different kind of darkness—a hollow, hateful kind that one might imagine belonging to the God of Death—contorted his face to a scowl. "They might claim to be my devotees, but I do not support them in return. They have found a way to corrupt and control the shadows," he whispered, the sound made of that same black smoke. "I've been keeping an eye on the living witch, but there is nothing I can do to intervene, aside from watching in my mirror. Lyr has made it impossible for me to reach the mortal lands. I have to wait for them to cross over to enact my judgment…as I did with Councilman Yorath."

"I heard you wiped his existence from the world."

Surprise cleared the smoke. He blinked, long lashes brushing his angular cheeks. "Who blabbed?"

I shrugged, staring back at the mosaic before Death could catch my tells. "Just because you don't talk to any of your servants doesn't mean I can't."

"Ah, Cythie," he chuckled, scattering any lingering tension from the air. But his voice still had an edge, made of cracked ice and cold disdain. "I'm not proud of what I did to Yorath. But what he did to you…while I am more than glad to have you here, you did not deserve that fate. I would've much rather seen you come to me one day of your own will than have your choice stolen from you by a worm."

At that, my head swiveled. I was not the only one with sharp weapons in my possession tonight. Death's words all bore arrow-tips, some dipped in poisoned poetry.

"I'm glad he's gone," I managed, a mumbling fool in comparison to Death's eloquence. "Thank you."

"As you'll come to see, I have a hard time denying you anything." He slid in front of me again, an opponent parrying my every counter. He matched my softness with his own. "I have to apologize again for the other day with the mirror…I thought it would help, but it crushed me to see you so hurt…"

Ronan.

Ronan.

Ronan.

Citrine and gold, sunset eyes and sea-blue stares.

I fought away the ugly, jealous monster muttering in my middle. I wanted to slap Arawn across his smug, sensual face. Wanted to curse his name for playing with my heart as he did; for breaking it for fun. For knowing I was that easily swayed. Ronan might be the man swimming with sirens, but Arawn knew just how to drown me in my own sorrow.

Instead, I squeezed Death's hand. Stepped closer, breathed him in. Pine and rose. Poetry and ruggedness. "It did help. I needed it. That's twice tonight I've needed to thank you."

Death tucked an errant strand of hair back into my braided crown. "I don't deserve your thanks, but I gladly accept. That makes me greedy, but I don't seem to care with you."

Blush heated my cheeks. This was the plan. The role. So far, it was working perfectly, each brushed hand and lingering gaze between us all a part of the design. But it felt dirty and cheap. I'd much rather deal my blows with sharp swords than feigned flirtations.

Except there was still a part of me—a dark corner of my heart, one I tried so hard to deny—that wasn't faking. That was enchanted by Death. By his presence and power. By his propositions. By the thought of a *friend.*

Dark and light. Life and death. Love and hate, rage and desire.

Uncle Aidan used to say the best lies were anchored with truths.

I armored the part of me that wanted this, letting it take control. If I was going to succeed, I would let sincerity lead me. Let it bring me closer and closer to the edge of no return. And when I was close, tucked away in Death's dark embrace…

I would aim for his frozen heart.

"If anyone is greedy, it's me. You've given me so much already, more than anyone ever has, and I've done nothing in return for you." This time, I reached out, tenderly touching his cheek. The warmth surprised me as it met my palm. Death was not just ice and snow. Not just darkness. He was desire and fear, heat and pleasure.

The burning behind his gaze promised as much. He pressed into my touch. "Your presence is a gift in itself."

Finna had been right, yet again. This man—no, this ancient, wrathful god—knew exactly how to stoke the fire.

But so did I.

"But if I wanted to repay you...to show my thanks..." I bit my lip, baiting him further. My thumb grazed his sharp, stubbled chin. "What does someone offer the God of Death?"

Eyes asked what words could not, forbidden fruit ripe for plucking. An arm slid around my waist, pulling me close, the other taking my hand from his cheek. He held it extended, palm to palm, as we stood face to face.

Death wanted a dance.

A brief thunderclap of panic rang through me, stormclouds signaling the hurricane on the horizon.

"I don't—" The beginnings of protest fought past my traitorous lips before I clasped my jaw shut. I could withstand whatever tempest to come. I was made of sea and storm and starfire and smiles. I feigned my favorite, hopefully faster than Death could notice my blunder.

But as always, Death saw all. Grin pulled into a frown. His hand lowered, but did not let go of mine.

"I know, you don't dance with men who aren't your husband." A laugh like bubbling champagne tumbled out of him, masking a deep, dry ache. "But it will always, *always* be worth the try."

Papa always said actions spoke louder than words. Perhaps he'd never met Arawn and his poetry. The breezy, elegant words that made even the sturdiest masts bend.

I would weaponize my words all the same. And I'd let my actions do the real talking.

Pulling his heavy arm back to position, I pressed myself closer. "I was going to say I don't dance without music."

"*Oh.*" The single syllable spilled from his mouth, so soft I wouldn't have heard it if his lips hadn't formed the shape.

He blinked twice, and by his endless magic, music echoed through the empty room. It came from nowhere and everywhere, the reedy buzz of violin strings, the warm drone of a cello, the twinkling richness of a piano's many keys. All blended together, switching partners and swelling through different tempos as they traded the tune.

Like drizzling rain blossoming into a storm, it happened drop by drop, then all at once. The sweet music, the stars above, the floor begging to be danced on…it was a spell, crafted to transport and transform me, body and soul.

It was enchanting and enthralling. My body ached to move with it, with *him*, to add the percussion of our footsteps to the chorus. I'd never heard something so beautiful in my life.

The Otherworld had once been paradise, after all. For the first time, I believed it.

Death took me in his arms, and without further hesitation, carried me away on the back of the melody. We slid across the dark floor like it was made of ice, feet gliding together in a synchronized rhythm. Our breaths mingled together, the heat of his body like a campfire in snow, the dark delight of his gaze like a starless night. It might have been minutes or hours, but he led, and I followed, my body swept up in the midnight music.

I'd planned this. My intention had been set, my costume donned and role rehearsed. I tried to hold on to my senses, to stick to the versions of me I knew best.

But nothing could prepare me for the way it *felt*. The euphoria of a dance with Death, triumphant darkness itself our dance floor and the songs of ice and fire our orchestra.

Here, I was more than a girl. I danced and danced with Death until the parts of me that were mortal fell away. Until I forgot my last name and my life before, thoughts drowned out by the voice of the violin.

Arawn and Ariannad.

Here, I was a goddess. The Silver Wheel. Turning in time with the symphony of Death's snow-kissed stare.

"Twirl," he commanded, and I obeyed, spinning out so my dress flared around my ankles.

Death stopped moving, the music cutting out altogether.

I stumbled to a stop, sweat licking the back of my neck, heart hammering in my chest like the last lingering musician. Not just from the exertion, but from the sheer weight of his eyes on me. Obsidian and fresh snowfall. Endless night and pine. Unanswered prayers and unspoken promises.

"What, did I do it wrong?" I heaved between ragged breaths, air dragging from my lungs. He shook his head, and my cheeks heated. "Then why are you looking at me like that?"

His answering smile lit the room better than any crystal chandelier. "Can you fault a man for staring at the stars? You make even the God of Death feel alive."

Alive.

The word hurtled into me like a meteor, blowing apart all other thoughts as it made impact. Dancing with him, the music carrying me away on a daydream, sweat on my back and heart racing in my chest...

I felt alive. Even in the depths of the Otherworld. Even with my heart still left behind in the realms of man.

Real.

Real.

Real.

Alive and powerful.

The parts of me that were Branwen raged against it. Parts that were Mathonwy and mother, parts that were sailor and Captain. I could hear them all, an angry, surging chorus of naysayers screaming for me to return to my senses. To break whatever spell his song had cast on me. To show him the blade I kept beneath my dress, to snatch the crown from his head and take my throne.

But what if there was another way? What if instead of theft and betrayal, instead of the sabotage and backstabbing that got me here...

What if I struck a deal with Death?

I loved Finna, but she had been wrong about men before. Had her grudges clouded her perception of Arawn? I loved Papa, but he'd been gone for five years and was no longer Captain. Did he see the full scope of the situation we were in?

I loved my husband, but he wasn't here. He had a life to keep on living.

And I had only myself to rely on to keep me and my daughter safe. Perhaps making Arawn my dance partner instead of my enemy would serve us all well.

After all, I had no more lives I was willing to sacrifice.

"Speak your mind, *Caraid.*" He brushed a stray hair away from my face, one that must have broken loose from its braided prison during our dance. Perhaps I could break free too, not with weapons or warfare, but with compromise. With compassion.

I held my crowned head higher, as the Queen Mother of the Otherworld would. "If I were to accept your offer, as a *friend*," I emphasized, "what would you expect of me?"

Surprise shattered across his face like cracking ice, practiced expression giving way to the flowing emotions underneath. Joy and desire swam together in the depths of his dark, smile-crinkled eyes, his grin wider than the river of souls.

"Follow me."

And despite the game I set, despite the plan I'd perfected...

I did.

Death led me not to the garden for a walk, or the mirrored room like I might have expected, but instead to the kitchens. Tall countertops made of obsidian bore a resemblance to the rest of the estate's decor, but the russet stone walls and worn wooden table looked starkly out of place. Dried herbs hung from the rafters among pots and pans of every size and shape, a mismatched variety that cried of whimsy. A wide hearth baked the small room in delicious warmth, the playful fire licking the bottom of a deep black cauldron. Something rich and herbal simmered in its stomach, a familiar stew perhaps a reminder from Reina of just how stupid I was being.

I wondered if he brought me here to break bread, or to feast on the prey that willingly walked into his trap.

The intoxicating effect of the music had worn off some on our walk down, the heady buzz receding from my ears, allowing clearer thoughts in once more. But still, a strange wanting tugged at me, a reckless temptation that begged me to explore this *what if* just a few moments further.

Death discarded his suit jacket, tossing it over the back of a nearby chair to roll up his sleeves. Veiny forearms protruded from the white fabric, far more dangerous than any of the weapons I'd ever wielded. He sifted through the tall icebox with a surety that suggested he had his bearings, finally pulling out a long glass bottle filled with bubbling golden liquid.

"Champagne?"

"No, I'm fine, thank you." I shifted in the doorway, discomfort nipping at the back of my heels. Every time I tried to understand him, to anticipate his movements or guess his agenda, he threw me off his scent, masking it in another unexpected surprise.

He smiled, either entirely unaware of the way his presence disarmed me, or all too knowing. He pulled out the chair with his jacket on it, patting the tall back with his broad hand. "Come sit, *Caraid*. No need to be a stranger."

I let that troublesome temptation carry me forward, taking the seat, ignoring the shiver that ran up my spine as his hand brushed against it.

He didn't notice, busying himself immediately. From the icebox, he pulled a handful of bright carrots and a long, magenta-colored fish, its dead eyes staring at me. He slapped it on the table right in front of me with a satisfying flop before handing me a carving knife.

"Filet that into a few steaks," he ordered with an authority born of experience before turning his focus on the carrots. He pulled out another, smaller knife and quickly chopped the roots into small, even slivers, folded knuckles guiding the blade with precision despite the speed.

I tore my eyes from him before I could be impressed by the knifework, instead studying the long blade in my own hand. Silver glistened bright orange in the firelight. Death had handed me a sharp weapon, had trusted me with a blade in a room not built for easy escape.

Instead of driving my knife through Death's heart, I turned it on the vibrant fish.

I knew my way around a filet, and within minutes, had it cut and de-boned, leaving only one strip of skin on each portion for cooking. Yet, by the time I had it done, Arawn was already tossing the carrots in a large, iron pan, honey and fresh herbs sizzling in a way that made the most uninteresting vegetable in the world suddenly mouthwatering.

He picked a small slice from the pan with careful fingers, unbothered by the heat, and held it out to me. "Try a bite of this."

Again, against the warning whistle blaring in the back of my head, I did, letting him pop the morsel directly into my mouth. I tried not to blush as my lips grazed his fingertips.

Food was a language of love, something I learned directly from Reina's kitchen and plenty of nights sharing meals on Papa's ship. It was a unifier, a shared experience that anyone could connect to, no matter their coat color. It brought crews and families together, the simple act of service nourishing far more than hungry bellies.

I'd never tasted anything so delicious in my life. Sweet and salty and tangy, it was clear the tiny bite was cooked not just with expert hands, but something more.

And it was a rutting carrot.

I was in so much trouble.

I stifled the moan that threatened to break free, swallowing the bait and instantly wishing for more.

"Is your plan to avoid our talk by shutting me up with food?" I wiped the sticky honey from the edge of my mouth, licking the lingering sweetness from my thumb. "Because if so, it's working."

Arawn watched the action, eyes flicking from my mouth to finger, before reaching for the salmon steaks I'd cut. He placed them skin down in the pan with the carrots with a satisfying sizzle. "I find difficult truths are easier to unearth over delicious meals."

A stiff drink and a hot meal make every problem easier to solve.

So strange, to hear Papa's words on Death's lips. I hoped a full belly might help me find my way out of the mess I was making. "Did you cook our first meal together?"

He shrugged, the gesture so human, it was almost easy to forget who he was. Who *I* was.

Arawn focused on the frying fish, sprinkling fresh herbs and squeezing a ripe lemon over it, a master absorbed in his craft. My mouth watered, hunger rising in my pit…not just for the salmon.

"I know you have questions…" He wiped a bead of sweat from his forehead with the back of his hand, a rare, shy smile quirking up on the right side of his face. "I want to answer them, but I need a promise first."

Here it was, Death's trap. I slid the carving knife from the table to my lap, making note of the single exit behind me. Still, I kept my voice to a calm curiosity, ignoring my heart's rapid beat. "Depends on what you're asking me to promise."

"Promise you won't run." Death grabbed a wide silver plate from the cupboard above his head, and in one swift motion, he flipped the contents of the pan onto it. Steam rose in tender tendrils from perfectly cooked faire as he placed it in front of me. A peace offering for a promise. "Promise you'll let me finish my story before you decide."

Perhaps it was the gloriously sweet scent of the food in front of me, or the way his dark eyes captured the glowing embers of the hearth, or the last sparks of hope that I could see this plan through, but I smiled at him.

"I can't run in this dress." I shrugged, sticking a fork in the flaky fish. An offer accepted. I popped the morsel in my mouth, the luscious honey and citrus combination all the convincing I'd ever need. My eyes may have rolled back as I chewed, but I was too consumed by the flavor to notice.

"I know the story the mortals tell of me," Arawn chuckled, but a shyness crept across his expression. He sat in the chair across from me, hands steepled on his lap like a devotee in prayer. "That I was supposed to sit in the Otherworld and fend off the powers of war and darkness, but I got power-hungry. That I stole Dan–your mother's heart and cast her out in a fit of jealousy and greed."

I slowed my chewing, ice creeping back along my spine. "Or so they say."

I'd heard the story, from my husband's mouth. But I also knew how legends grew and distorted–had seen Ronan himself craft the tale of the Rydha with wit and will alone. Stories were not truths, but powerful, ever-changing tools that could shape the world without more than a word.

I set my fork down, ready to hear Death's version.

"The truth is, I loved her. More than myself." He stared down at his hands, an uncharacteristic quiver in his voice. "This *was* paradise once, green and teeming with life, and she–she was my everything. We ruled together, creating a space for all the souls that crossed over, fighting back the ice and torment together. We had children, a life. Nef, Cerridwen, Gwynn, Bris, Bridget…they're all *ours*, you know. Not just hers. It was perfect."

I absorbed his words, a picture dancing in my mind's eye. Arawn and Danura, dark and light, strolling through the rose garden together. A crewful of tiny gods, children still, running around their feet.

It wasn't the strangest story I'd ever swallowed.

I leaned forward, coaxing him on. "But then…"

"Then she left." The short, clipped words clinked together like metal against glass, cold and discordant. "They all left."

I knew little about Danura other than she kept her secrets closer than her freckles hugged her face. She could change women into sirens, could cleanse and remake…but she could also abandon and hide. Could speak in riddles instead of revelations.

I'd assumed, as had the whole world, that Danura left Arawn with good intentions. But in reality, she could have left him with just as little love as she left me.

And here we were, two wandering souls in the Otherworld, still waiting for the Goddess of Life's attention.

"Did she say why?" the forgotten, lonely girl within asked with my voice.

"She ran away with Lyr."

I blinked, words failing to register. "Ran away…aren't they *siblings?*"

"Ah, how the mortals have twisted the details," A dry, humorless scoff, then, "Gods, no. We were all friends once. In the beginning. I *thought* of him as a brother, and I thought that's how she saw him, too. But I was wrong. I caught them sneaking off together in the night, plotting how to write me out of the narrative and claim the Otherworld and the lands of men for themselves."

I opened my mouth to speak, but no words came out. A buzzing filled my head as time-frayed edges finally weaved back together, as the picture finally focused.

Arawn stared into the hearth, the fire casting grim shadows on the wide planes of his face, similar darkness as his eyes told of memories long lost to legends. "I'm not proud of how I reacted that night. I became the monster they made me, and I was harsh with her. But I would've taken her back, would've forgiven her and begged for her forgiveness in return if they hadn't…"

He trailed off, his voice taken by the smoky pain choking back the final notes.

"If Lyr hadn't used his powers to separate the realms," I finished for him, remembering the story whispered on a worn shipdeck. Told with a very different tone, by a boy kissed by the sun and the sea, not the orphan of darkness before me.

His throat bobbed heavily, no other confirmation needed.

I pushed the barely touched plate away, my appetite gone, chased away by the taste of Death's sorrow. It had been millennia, thousands and thousands of years, and yet the gravity of his grief still crushed his broad frame. It filled the air around us, tangible as the rot and ruin of his estate, the despair latent in every dusty banister, every cobwebbed corridor.

Not that I blamed him. I'd only known grief for a few years, and I could never imagine the empty nothingness carved in my chest being full again.

"Do you still love her?" Again, the forgotten girl asked, this time left behind by that sunbaked boy, separated by the vast sea.

"A part of me, maybe. But it's been ages, and I see what a fool I was." Arawn laid another truth on the table, another offering of peace between two heartbroken gods. "Nothing would ever be enough for her. Life is never enough. She always wanted more, and she hated sharing. And when she got tired of things, she cast them off, already searching for something new."

A long-jilted anger dragged its way through my gut, outcast heart pounding in my chest.

"And what do you want of me?" My fingers fell to the knife still in my lap, the metal of the blade reminding me of my own serrated parts. Parts made from shards of a shattered little girl, one cracked by her mother's apathy. Still, if I was a blade, only I chose who wielded me. "My power? So you can finally hurt her back?"

My accusation fell flat against his unbothered facade. "I won't lie and say I hadn't considered it."

His blunt honesty doused my rage in cool water, sizzling until it fizzled out altogether. As if I'd been any better. I was sitting here on a well-calculated mission to do exactly that. To find out what he wanted, and to use it against him. And here he was, giving me all the ammunition I'd need. The betrayal he felt towards Danura and Lyr. The loneliness and misery of a life spent frozen in forsaken paradise.

"But now I know you, and I finally know what I want." Arawn ripped his gaze from the fire, instead turning its full, molten heat on me. "*Caraid*, you are so much more than she could ever hope to be. Living a human life...your heart is not greedy. You are so selfless and *good*."

Selfless enough to sacrifice my life for my family, to marry a man I thought was a monster. Selfless enough to run away again when he needed me most.

"I don't know about that." Guilt rattled around my empty middle, made of splintered promises and calamitous choices. "I'm a monster too."

We all are monsters. Some just hide it better than others.

Death stood from his seat, crossing to me in long strides that devoured the small space. I hid my knife beneath my thigh as he stood in front of me, loosened strands of long hair falling forward as he towered over me.

"You are not a monster." A broad hand cupped my cheek, and I caught a whiff of the remnants of honey and citrus. A new sort of chill sent a shiver down my spine. "You are the Queen this realm needs. Someone with a brave heart. Someone to help melt the ice and restore paradise. Someone who can shift the tides, who can reunite the realms again."

The Otherworld was not the paradise of legends. It was a wasteland. It was ice and numbness. It was nothing.

But perhaps I—*we*—could make it into something more. Could restore paradise for all the souls stuck here. For Papa and Reina, for Finna and Owen and Lochlan...

For my future daughter. For me.

There's more than one way to sacrifice a life.

But I had sacrificed mine in every way I knew how. I had nothing left to give. Perhaps, finally, I could take just a piece of paradise back and build it into something my daughter and I could thrive in.

"I'm not a queen, nor am I a pawn."

"No, you're a goddess." His hand traced a path of ice and fire from my cheek, down my arm, to my tattooed hand. He enveloped it in his. "But even if you were a mere mortal, even if you favored your father's lineage instead of your mother's...I would love you all the same."

And at that, Death knelt before me. Both knees kissed the stone floor, a devotee at an altar, ready to offer his prayers.

A goddess kneels to no one.

And yet, Death knelt to me.

The obsidian of his round eyes bore into mine as he offered the answer to our unending torment.

Such beauty in those cruel eyes.

This was the plan. The role. Lure him in with batted lashes and half-truths, with beauty and kindness.

And yet.

Ronan.

Ronan.

Ronan.

"I can't offer you my heart. It's not mine to give."

Even now, after he'd discarded it. Even in the Otherworld. The universe had tried to cleave us apart twice. Had never wanted us to be together in the first place, really. I should've accepted Fate, should've taken it as a sign that I was never meant to love Ronan Mathonwy.

But even if he stopped loving me one day—even if it was wrong and selfish and stupid—I did. Body and soul, I loved him.

Tears stung my eyes, and Arawn jumped to his feet, collecting a salty droplet on the tip of his finger. "Shh, *Caraid*, no need for tears. I know it all feels broken right now, trust me. I know you truly loved him, and you aren't like your mother—not so easily swayed to disloyalty." He hooked a finger beneath my chin, tilting my face to meet his. That same, soft dark watched me, scanning for unseen scars. "But I can be patient. And I will offer you paradise, if you'll only allow me the key."

"I can't offer you my heart. Maybe not ever." I stood, our faces only a few hairsbreadths apart. I swallowed hard, wincing at the taste of my salt-and-sorrow tears. I would not let my defeated parts define me, nor would I waste my time trying to put the shattered pieces back together. Instead, I would take each shard and mold them together into something new. Broken and beautiful. Dark and light. I looked up at Death through my wet lashes. "But my friendship…that is already yours, despite my better judgment."

A friendship for the forgotten. A partnership to redeem paradise.

This close, I could see the faintest hint of blue beneath the blackness in his eyes. So close, only a small choice away. A small sacrifice.

"May I?" His voice was husky as his rosebud lips parted. Eyes asked what words could not, forbidden fruit ripe for plucking.

A peace offering. A promise. It was not love, but an alliance. A friend. And because I needed that too, I allowed the tiniest, whispered word to seal my fate. "Yes."

Death's lips brushed against mine, softer than snowfall at first, then in a blizzard of his need. His mouth captured mine, the taste of him like honey and citrus, pine and snow. Desire and darkness, fire and ice. His hands held my face, and mine found purchase on the planes of his muscled chest, his heart beating against my fingertips.

Then Death pushed further, parting my lips not to concede, but to conquer. To take. I tried to close my mouth, the peace between us shattered with this crossed boundary…

Arawn pulled back, ripping us apart, gripping my shoulders. A single moment passed, barely enough for me to catch my breath. Eyes blew wide with his desire–and shock.

Then.

"You're pregnant."

"What?" Reality crashed into me as the air flooded from my lungs, the floor bottoming out, leaving me floating and falling. "No, I–"

"Don't lie to me," he hissed, a new frenzy fracturing his cool facade as he licked his lips. "I can taste it on you. Life. *Him.*"

"I didn't know," I lied, a hand flying to my abdomen. Fear pooled there, blood rushing and heart pounding, drowning out the sound of my own voice. "Why does it matter?"

His wicked grin widened. "You've just made me the happiest god in the universe, Keira." His fingers pressed bruises into my shoulders. "But I'm afraid this changes *everything.*"

"Let go of me, I–" I swatted him off, stumbling back. My hand fumbled for the knife I'd left on my chair, for a weapon that wouldn't fail me.

But before I could close my fingers around the metal, before I could protect myself, shadows snatched my wrists, pulling my hands behind my back. I tugged against them, burrowing down into my pit, summoning the light, the burning inside, anything to save me from myself…

"Keep struggling, and I'll snuff out your families' souls like I did Yorath's."

The threat stilled me faster than the cage of ice ever could, and the power in my veins winked out.

Finna had been right. Papa, everyone. They had risked everything, and I failed them again. I'd played right into Death's hand and given him my last remaining ace. Now, they'd pay the price for my mistakes.

Again, I was frozen.

I was nothing.

I stared at Death, sending every ounce of hatred and heat his way. Hatred for him, and for myself. "You really are a monster."

Death winced, but shadows still snaked their way around my limbs, tightening to discomfort. "I'm so sorry, my love, but I need to keep you safe. *Our* baby, safe. I'll need her even more than I need you. Now I can finally end them *both*."

And then he plunged us both into darkness.

19

Mountains and Monsters

GRIFFIN

It was a shame that I was rather fond of my nuts, because they were about to fall off. My teeth chattered like castanets in my skull as we trudged up the Pysgoddian mountainside, one that looked like every other mountain in the Spine.

Lifeless. Freezing. Entirely void of misplaced gods.

My crew of jesters and I were getting unfortunately used to fool's errands, but this one was particularly perilous. We were built for sun and sea, for saltwater spray and seaweed swims. For sparks of trouble in hearth-warmed inns and adventures born on the backs of summer winds.

None of us were suited for snow and ice. For squinting against the endless white expanse, plodding through the dagger-sharp winds that threatened to skin us clean. For throbbing, numb toes or eyelashes frozen closed.

Damn Danura and her half-baked help. I should've known not to play games with a goddess, no matter how charming she was or how expertly she stroked my Lyr-forsaken ego.

At least we'd finally managed to dump our supplies to the appropriate place. Even if we froze to death, the Deyrnas would live to eat another day. Agatha Amos and Councilwoman Tommins had intercepted us in Dynas Fir, Pysgodd's one and only port not completely blocked by ice. We'd gotten a quick chiding for being a few weeks behind, and for letting some of the produce spoil on the way, but we made up for it in the haul of fresh crops of fruit we'd 'borrowed' from *Hiraeth* before Danura sent us packing. The refugees were enthralled by the exotic delicacies.

But now, as we climbed the steep side of yet another ice-slick summit, I wished Agatha had just run us through instead. At least the Otherworld would be warm.

"Griffin, this is useless," Reagan stuttered through chattering teeth, wrapping her thick furs tighter around her tiny frame. She pulled up the rear with Vian, the pair of orphans huddled together and finding their footing in the tracks the rest of us made.

"Then go back down to the village," Rhett grumbled from his place in the front of the pack with Saeth, his patience thinner than the mountain air. "Vala and Reese are down there. They'll tuck you in. Maybe Weylin will even read you a bedtime story."

"I'm not a child, you meat-head." Reagan rolled her eyes.

"Then stop whining like one." Rhett shivered, pulling his meager scarf in front of his scowl for warmth.

He'd been surly since Drystan and Weylin boarded our ship. It had been a gods-send—literally—to have a few more seasoned sailors in our midst, but Rhett only noted Drystan's dazzling presence as a plague, cursing under his breath and dragging his feet the whole way. And his mood had only darkened when Drystan, now only a few steps behind him, insisted on helping us track Nef down.

Tarran interrupted the squabbling from beside me, shaking snow from his ginger hair. "I'd rather freeze to death than listen to you two bicker anymore."

"Then die already," Saeth snorted at her twin, blunt and brutal as the frigid mountainside. She'd been even grumpier with Weylin's presence, but there had been a shift. Though the rest of us were frostbitten and fatigued, Saeth never looked more alive in her life. Saeth was made of stone and ice, of mountain and dagger-sharp icicles. Crimson kissed her cheeks as the wind tousled her copper hair, like a defiant torch in the middle of the winter's storm. She pushed ahead of us all, stomping through the calf-deep snow with ease. "Lyr below, you're all—"

"As useless as wet towels, we know." Tarran threw his hands up, throwing in said soggy towel. We'd all had enough of the frosty insults. "Get some new material."

"Enough, all of you," I called, flexing my fingers in and out to make sure they were still there. Lyr below, we were in over our heads, and worse for wear. If I didn't put a stop to the fighting, we'd all kill each other before the mountains had a chance. I locked eyes with the shivering Reagan. Ice air rasped through my lungs as I sucked in a deep breath, my exhale misting in front of me. "Air is too thin to waste our breath up here. Anyone that needs a rest can head back now and warm up in the village. No questions asked, no judgment. But if you choose to stay, you better bring your best behavior."

The crew stared back at me like I had a foot-long pecker strapped to my forehead.

Maybe I wasn't the model of morality and good moods either.

"I'd be happy to escort you back, Miss Reagan," Drystan said earnestly before my crew could give me a tongue-lashing, pausing to offer Reagan a hand. "You're not a child, but this is no place for a young lady, either."

Reagan took it as she stepped over the next snowbank, already rosy cheeks reddening further. "I'm fine. I'll stay."

Rhett rolled his blue-and-silver eyes so hard, I thought the good one might pop out, too.

"The wind says we are close anyway." Vian brushed past them both, adopting Rhett's grumpiness to bump Drystan's broad shoulder. He skipped up the side of the snowbank, lanky limbs putting him in front of even Saeth in a few long strides. His mumbling voice somehow carried against the howling wind. "This is the place, I know it."

"Oh, what a relief." I fought the sarcasm that longed to loose from my tongue. Vian might have been kissed by Trouble, but he'd also been bedded by crazy. Then again, so was I for following *his* plan, ending up on this gods-forsaken mountain. I shook my head as he hopped up on the next crest, a small divot between two taller spires of rock.

"Huh, that's strange." He quirked his head to the side, peering precariously over the ledge. He bent at the waist, curiosity piqued at whatever waited beyond. "The wind didn't mention this."

Triumph sang the warning in my ear before I could put voice to it, "Vian, watch yourself–"

Too late.

Limbs flailed as he toppled over the edge, disappearing behind the ridge.

"No!" Reagan screamed first, her inhuman cry echoing as she hurtled past us, frantically floundering through the snow.

My stomach punched up my gut, panic lighting my limbs with fire against the cold. I sprinted up the slippery slope, catching up to Reagan before she could reach the edge. I snagged the back of her coat as she crested the embankment, before she could fall, before it happened again…

Crimson against ivory. Blood against stone.

"I'm okay!" Vian called out just as I reached Reagan. She exhaled at the sound of his voice, going totally limp in my arms. My heart pounded in my ears, but the fire in my nerves eased, a warm campfire instead of a blazing inferno. I crawled to the ledge carefully, surveying the drop. The other side was steep, dark rock, practically vertical in pitch, but it only stretched a few meters deep, maybe two tall men high. Vian sat at the bottom, a grin on his face despite an open cut on his knee that tore through his trousers.

"Look what I found!" He gestured broadly to the space behind him. The broad canyon stretched at least two-ships lengths wide. As if a giant had scooped a chunk out of the mountain, the deep gray rock–somehow free of snow and ice–carved into the ground. A natural gate of sharp spires lined the far edge, like teeth jutting from the earth.

And Vian was not completely alone. A shiver unrelated to the cold ran through me, blood turning to ice.

Hundreds of animal skeletons littered the clearing, white bones graphic against the charcoal stone.

"Hold on, we're coming, kid. All hands!" I flagged the crew behind me, beckoning their worried faces to follow. I handed Reagan to Drystan, and the girl somehow managed to move without a snarky remark. Something dark rumbled in my gut, a fear Truth and Triumph repeated as they buzzed fervently on my back. Swinging my legs over, I jumped down, hissing as the impact rattled up my legs. I crossed to Vian and pulled him back to his feet. He limped as he tried to put pressure on his blood-crusted knee, but he would be fine. "What is this place?"

"Some kind of den?" Rhett hurtled over the edge only a second behind me. His sharp silver eye scanned the space, every muscle in his body coiled and ready. His strong jaw worked hard with worry. "A *blaidd* maybe, or some kind of large mountain cat?"

I gnawed my lip as I studied the bones again, closer this time. Something with antlers, nearly twice my size, decayed nearby, picked clean. I caught Rhett's eye, swallowing a new lump of fear in my throat. If it was a *blaidd*, it was enormous.

I didn't want to find out exactly how huge. I preferred to keep my limbs and loins intact.

"Everything all right?" Drystan called, still standing above us, his arm draped around a shivering Reagan.

"Yeah, stay with her." I shifted so Vian could wrap his arm around my shoulders, distributing his weight off his bad leg.

"Thank you." He beamed, a stray wind tossing his long hair.

Lyr's ass, these kids would be the death of me.

"At least it's warm." Tarran slid down the side of the ridge, pulling off his gloves. He rubbed his hands together, reviving his frozen fingers. "You know, despite the bones."

He was right, even if he was stupid. It was considerably warmer here–the ground itself beneath my boots heated my numb toes, tingles working their way up my calves. Another wave of fear rocked through me, the buzzing a blaring alarm now.

"That's exactly what its last meal said," Saeth crouched down on the rock before I even realized she had jumped. She brushed her fingers along the stone, a thick layer of dark soot coating the tips. She shot back to standing, eyes flying wide with warning as realization hit her. "This is ash. We should get out before–"

A deafening woosh drowned out the end of her sentence, followed by a sharp gust of wind and an earth-rattling crash.

My head snapped to the sound, grip tightening on Vian.

The world went still for a breath. For two, as I blinked, processing the behemoth before me.

It stood taller than any ship mast I'd ever seen, even crouched on four talon-tipped legs. Its long, snout-like nose puffed clouds of smoke, fangs poking from its black lips. Spikes sprouted from the crown of its head and trailed all the way down its spine to its barbed tail, mirroring the mountain ridge behind it. Scarlet scales glistened against the snowy backdrop like blood on fresh linens. Slanted gold eyes narrowed in our direction as it unfurled its massive, sail-sized wings.

Rhett swore a string of creative curses under his breath as the dragon breathed us in.

A gods-damned *dragon*.

Reagan took a dazed step forward, mouth falling open. "Lyr's asscrack, is that a–"

"Well, that is definitely *not* a blaidd," I cut her off before she could finish, then uttered my solitary command. "Run."

All at once, chaos descended, bathing us in Trouble's stench.

My instincts kicked in as I dragged Vian away from the creature, breaking into a full sprint despite his weight back towards the ledge. Saeth swooped in on his other side, helping him hobble over the uneven ground. My heart hammered in my chest harder than a blacksmith forging steel, banging against my ribs in quick strikes.

"This way!" Rhett bellowed, scaling up a slanted part of the rocky ridge in expert strides like it was rigging. Tarran careened up after, hot on his heels, his lanky legs carrying him up.

The dragon roared, a blood-curdling, guttural sound that tore from its throat, one last warning as it curled back on its haunches.

"You first!" I launched Vian upward with adrenaline-born strength, handing him off to Rhett's outreached arm. Rhett hauled him up over the edge, Vian scrambling to push up with his good leg.

I spun to Saeth, ready to give her a leg up, to get us all the hell out of this shithole and far away from the beast breathing down our backs–

Another boom, as the creature lifted from its perch, the ground shaking as it soared into the air. Saeth stumbled, twisting as she lost her footing…

And landed wrong, *so wrong*, on her ankle.

A cross between a groan and a cry escaped her chest, her hands flying to the mangled, twisted limb. *Wrong, wrong, wrong.*

The monster roared again, this time high above, circling us. Wings flared wide as it prepared to dive.

Trouble's trance washed over me, an eerie calm fighting back the fear burning through my veins. I sucked in a deep breath.

Breathe in. Breathe out. Repeat.

"Rhett, get them out," I thundered, whipping my head to my partner. Silver-and-blue eyes burned with fear and rage, a protest ready to fire back, but I shot first. "That's an order, love. *Go.*"

Rhett hesitated for one long second, staring me down with even more heat and danger than the dragon's gaze. "Don't you dare die."

Then he swept Vian up in his arms and sprinted out of sight, the crew on his tail.

"Leave me, you idiot!" Saeth hissed despite the tears springing to her eyes, her teeth clenched in pain.

The air froze around me, everything colliding to complete stillness.

Saeth, a siren made of sea and ice.

Saeth, who had kept us all together even when we were falling apart at the seams.

Saeth, who had killed every last weak part of herself to make room for the cutlass we needed her to be.

Saeth, willing to die as dragon-fodder to save the rest of us.

"Not a chance, Sharky." I scooped her up like a toddler, wrapping her arms around my neck and bracing her weight with an arm coiled around her waist. For someone so sharp, she was surprisingly light—*fragile.*

Crimson against ivory, blood against stone.

Silver eyes, ushering a silent command.

Not again. Not another cousin.

She shifted uncomfortably, hissing as she tied her tormented ankle around my waist. A fresh wave of pain had her bucking out of my arms, sliding down to the ground too fast for me to catch. Her green eyes blew wide, molten fear creeping into their normally metallic hue. "Griffin, go, please—"

Truth and Triumph both sang a war cry on my back.

Right as the creature dove.

And landed six feet in front of us, snarling.

Up close, it was even more menacing, its fangs serrated and harsh, the heat from its steaming nostrils warming my face.

"Shit." I held my hands up, tense stillness trapping me in the dragon's gold-eyed stare. Dread trumpeted through my head, a disorienting clamor as I tried to remember Uncle Cedric's lessons about facing a predator—was I supposed to make myself look bigger? Or was I supposed to play dead? I chose neither, fear feeding my foolishness. I kept my voice low, trying to hide the surging panic. "Easy there, big boy."

It was a shame I was rather fond of my nuts, because they were about to be burnt off by dragon-fire. A low growl rippled from its throat, one taloned foot stepping closer, cracking the stone beneath it. Steam surged from the broken earth, the canyon *breathing* with the massive beast before us.

"I don't think that's working." Saeth skittered behind me on her hands and knees, avoiding her disfigured limb.

I had to get us up the wall. The predator hadn't attacked yet—either playing with its food, or unsure if we were a threat. I highly doubted it was the second—we were totally useless.

Still, I would take advantage of its hesitation. Maybe if we moved slowly, we could climb up the hill and hide behind one of the larger snowbanks until it got bored and left us alone...

I drew Truth with slowness, every muscle in my body shaking with the effort. "It's fine." I took one tentative, snail-paced step back toward Saeth. Sweat beaded on my brow, the billowing steam creating a veil of heat between us, much to our advantage. I crouched down, ready to grab Saeth with my free hand and go. "Shhhh, there, there. Nice dragon."

"You're just pissing it off." She climbed into my embrace without hesitation this time, whispering the warning through clenched teeth.

I shook my head, gathering her weight as best as I could, ready to stand. The plan wasn't perfect, but it was something. If we moved carefully, if we made ourselves as unintimidating as possible, I could haul her up the wall, could escape to tell the tale...

The beast shifted its weight between legs, sniffing the air, lips pulled back to expose the full row of fanged teeth.

And then it reared up on its hind legs, letting loose a reverberating roar. Fire—bright and orange and *hot*—gathered in the monster's mouth, ready to spew.

"Fuck." I flew to action, stashing Saeth behind me, pressing her back to the stone wall despite her yelps. I didn't have time to get her out, but I could shield her, could buy her time...

An arrow sliced through the misty steam, lodging itself deep in the beast's left eye. An ear-splitting screech shattered the air, the creature twisting in agony. It fell back, wagging its massive head, blood pouring from the wound, before curling up on itself and crashing to the ground with a massive thud.

At that, the arrow's master jumped down into the clearing in front of us, giant bow cocked with another round. Strong muscles strained against the tight white fabric of his long-sleeved shirt, a thick, white fur cape adding to his already-tall frame. He stood bold against the ash, but a perfect match for the wintry landscape.

Instead of the expected relief, a deep disquiet settled over me, still pressed against the stone wall.

"Get up, both of you," he grunted over his shoulder, weapon still trained on the unmoving dragon. Eyes the color of fresh-turned soil glared at us from the shadow of his strong brow.

I'd known Trouble intimately my whole life, but I'd never met him face to face. This man did not just wield a weapon—he *was* one. A pure hunter, far more deadly than any dragon or beast known to man.

I gripped Truth tighter, heeding her caution for once. I jutted my chin at the stilled dragon across the canyon. "Did you kill that thing?"

His stare darkened, matching the deep brown stubble that framed his sharp jaw. "No, my single arrow did not just kill a dragon. Even if it is just a cub." He lowered his bow, facing us full on. He was not conventionally handsome—not in the effortless, flaw-free way Rhett and Drystan were. But there was a ruggedness to his face, a power to his presence that made my pulse race. His deep voice ricocheted off the stone like it was made of the same material. "I just bought you time, now let's move."

He did not wait for us to follow, hoisting himself up the cliffside.

"That was a *baby?*" I gaped, finally processing his words, not just how attractive he was. I lifted Saeth again and stumbled after the hunter. I'd rather follow Trouble down a dark road than wait for the dragon to stir—or worse, for its *mother* to burn me to a crisp.

"Questions are a waste of time. Follow me." The hunter reached down, offering his hand to Saeth to help her scale the wall.

My cousin paused at his outstretched hand, disinterest painted across her face despite our very recent brush with death. "Who are you, exactly?"

Lyr below, we were screwed. At least the Otherworld had better company waiting.

"I'm the person that just saved your asses." His gaze narrowed, loose strands of his long, umber hair falling into his face.

Saeth met his stare, steel against stone, sea against earth. Predator versus hunter.

My cousin lifted *herself* up the wall, pushing from her one good leg and pulling up with her twigs-for-arms, without even a single wince. She scooted back onto the snowfall gracelessly, yet nothing eroded the cutting edge to her tone. "Right, and if I were to write a thank you note, whom should I make it out to?"

The hunter grimaced, but a twinge of respect danced in the corner of his mouth.

"Gwynn," he said, and Truth and Triumph hummed an impossible, resounding testimony. "Let's get your crew. My sister is expecting you."

My stomach did a somersault before rising up my throat.

Gwynn, the Great Hunter of the North. The White Wolf of legends old, in the flesh.

And then the God of War walked down the mountain without dismissal, knowing we fools would follow.

20

Gates and Ghouls

RONAN

I'd always loved to read.

Stories of grand adventures and forbidden romances, stories of gods and monsters and faith and trust. Stories of families found and forged.

In one of my favorite tales—a novel about a lost warrior princess reuniting with her family to save the man she loved from certain death—the gods of the land stole mortal bodies as hosts. These deities meddled with human affairs, stoking wars between nations and rivalries between siblings. When their chaos came for her lover's life, the young heroine sacrificed herself, trading his life for hers.

When I'd first read the book, I sobbed. Angry tears for the injustice, the pain. Pitiful tears for the star-crossed pair, for the single soul cleaved into two. I'd read it cover to cover dozens of times, each one praying that somehow, the end would come out differently. That the lovers would live happily ever after, that the greedy gods would be vanquished and families would prevail.

Now, as a man, I saw the beauty in sacrifice. Saw the power of reading an old tragedy and hoping it might fare better. Saw the unmovable love in the girl's heart, the untaintable worth of her gift to him. And I was ready to make the same one.

The gate to hell slept deep below the surface of the water.

As the sirens and I stared into the abyss, so dark that the light barely carved out the outlines of our colored tails, I could feel its icy tug at the very center of my chest.

Come find me. Come closer.

I knew how this story might end. It would cost me dearly, and there was a chance we would not live happily ever after. But it didn't matter. My wife and child would be free. My sacrifice would have meaning.

"Once we enter, the gates will try and send us back." Danura's voice gurgled through the water as Nelle held tight to the goddess to help her stay submerged. Luckily, she was still able to breathe despite her very human form; a gift we assumed connected to the scales that housed her powers. "It is a trial. Not Arawn's or mine, but something *other*. Something that came long before gods."

"That's really reassuring, thanks Danura." Sarcasm dripped from my fangs as unease sank to the tips of my fins, lighting them with the overwhelming urge to swim back to the surface.

But the day my wife died, a darkness was born within me. Darker than the gates of hell, a rage and ruination waiting to be unleashed upon the world that took her from me. To be pointed directly at the Dark God that held her captive.

I would withstand whatever trial or test the cosmos threw my way. I'd best them all, and then I'd test Death's darkness against mine.

Danura swam closer, voice carrying despite the water so the rest of the girls could hear. "The Triad will not harm you physically. But they will look into your mind, your heart…your fears and desires. Don't stray away from the path. Keep moving, don't speak to anyone, and you'll get through just fine. We will meet on the other side, and we can reassess then."

The uncomfortable thrum of fear numbed my clawed fingertips, the last human parts of me smart enough to be wary. But the beast within was ready. He'd been caged for too long and needed the sweet release of action. I stared into the blackness, ready to take whatever the path ahead offered.

"Anyone that does not want to come can turn back," I called to my crew, to the people that had gotten me this far. This was not their battle to fight, not their beast to vanquish. But they'd swam all the way to the ocean floor with me, ready to risk their tails in the

Otherworld beyond. A family found in the isle of the lost. "I will not fault you for it, either."

A silence seeped through the frigid water, a stillness discordant against the usual ebb and flow of the currents. My friends looked at me, gemstone eyes somehow glowing even in the endless abyss, sturdy and strong.

"Anyone that deserts us now is a guppie," Marina sang, swimming closer to the edge of the gate, the darkness devouring more of her crimson tail.

"We're with you to the end, Captain." Siobhan followed, the warrior ready to lead the charge. "Let's get our girl back."

"Ellian?" I turned to the shifter, who paddled awkwardly next to Laureli. The giant metal helmet he wore filtered out bubbles of air through the small vents he and Laureli had designed into it, his face visible behind a pane of round glass in the center. He was the picture of a fish out of water, despite our currently wet environment. "You have people. You don't have to come. Someone could stay on the ship…"

"And give you all the glory?" He raised an eyebrow, floundering closer to me. Emerald eyes misted behind the glass. "You *are* my people, brother. Keira is my people. I made a vow to protect her, and I will. The Deyrnas can wait."

I nodded, swallowing down the ball of sentimentality that rose to my throat. The road ahead had no room for kinship or gratitude. No space for the words left unsaid, for thank yous that would have to wait. We'd come to the end of our narrative, the very end of the *world*, and all that was left were the soulless parts that might survive beyond.

"Danura, if you would do the honors."

The goddess dove first into the gates of hell, unlocking Death's domain.

And I followed, ready to write my own story into the cosmos. Ready to resurrect my wife.

The gate was not a door, but a portal. The absence of life and light, turning me inside out and around. My body screamed in a flash of pain, tail tearing into two legs, head spinning with the dizzying weight pulling me down and through and under…

Until it spit me out on the other side, my knees and palms scraping the cold ground.

My eyes filled with fresh tears, squinting against brightness. Not darkness, but blinding light. I blinked, focusing on the frozen nothing in front of me. Not fire, but ice.

I stood, ignoring the blood rushing to the crown of my head as the whirling white wilderness slowed to a stop. Somehow, I was dressed—a plain beige tunic and linen trousers hanging loose on my form. I shivered, cold creeping easily through the parchment-thin material, a chill sinking into my fading scales.

The Otherworld was nothing but an endless stretch of frozen waste.

Except, on the distant horizon, three blurred forms stood harsh against the blanketing ivory.

A smarter version of myself might have waited, might have assessed the situation better. But a rumbling instinct in the very center of my being urged me forward, that same icy pull beckoning me closer.

Come find me.

A tentative step, then another, as I found my footing. I rushed toward the figures, ignoring the bite of the cold against my skin and the pricks of pain against my bruised knees. As I moved, a path cleaved itself into the ice, a straight line of dark rock that stretched right to my destination. My bare feet pounded against it, picking up speed as the road bit into my heels, my breath raw in my lungs. My eyes narrowed, fighting to make out details, splashes of color morphing into streamlined strokes of features….

I stopped in my tracks, sliding to a halt.

Blobs against the brightness transformed into three women, standing tall in long black robes that hid their shapes.

I'd recognize the center person anywhere, her likeness carved into every chamber of my heart. The spattered mess of freckles across her pale skin, the dark arch of her brows, the midnight mane flowing in gentle waves down her back…

Keira.

Keira.

Keira.

My goddess. My heart. *My wife.*

Yet something was wrong, *other*. Her eyes were a void of pure black, hollower than the gate I'd journeyed through. Her smile was a rotten twist of her ruby lips.

To her right, her *mother* matched her expression, her hair white again, but her eyes the same shade of onyx. Somehow in front of me, instead of where I'd left her minutes ago. And to her left, a young blonde I had never seen before wore Keira's same freckles and cruel grin, ebony eyes trained on me.

"Keira?" My breath misted in front of me in ghostly plumes as I staggered back, the *wrongness* of them all blaring through my veins. "Danura?

Together, three mouths moved in unison, a chorus of a thousand voices razing the bare tundra. "We have no given name that your tongue may taste, *Manawydan*."

As they spoke, their words scented the air with an ancient power, the smell of chaos and charcoal, of order and salt. Danura's instructions drifted back to the forefront of my mind as I assessed the women–the creatures–power rippling from their presence.

It is a trial. Not Arawn's or mine, but something other…they will not harm you physically. But they will look into your mind, your heart…your fears and desires.

"Who are you?" My own voice sounded an ocean away, distorted and twisted and inside out.

"They call us death, or sometimes truth," all three answered together in a sound that rattled through my bones. "Life, or sometimes the lies we tell ourselves at night. We are the world."

"As it was," Danura's double cooed a solo, graveled and rough as the rock I stood on.

"As it shall be," the young girl laughed, shrill as the scrape of metal against glass.

"As it is," the one who stole my wife's face finished, matching the soothing waves of her voice to perfection.

If this was a test, I was failing. Danura had warned me not to speak, not to stray, but that thing in my gut told me I must. My heart slammed against my ribs, head pounding and pulse thrumming a wicked rhythm. Standing in their presence was like swimming against a current or holding a mountain on my shoulders, the weight crushing me beneath and dragging me to the abyss.

I took a brave step forward, legs like rubber, cold wind scalding my cheeks. "What—"

"No," the single word interrupted from all three mouths again, stealing the air from my lungs and silencing the end of my sentence, "the question, boy, is what are *you?*"

Faster than a northern wind, they rushed me, a pack of wolves moving in a synchronized swarm—too fast to process the wave of fear washing me head to toe, the curiosity quickening my pulse. All three faces stopped only a few icy breaths away, eyes tunneling beneath my skin, measuring me from the inside out.

"Eyes like the sea, a gift from the god that bore you." The white-haired creature plucked one of my eyelashes in a quick strike. I swatted her away, stumbling back, only to bump into her partner.

The imposter Keira pinched my leg, that rotten grin festering wider. "Tail of gold, a gift from the god that loved you."

"Watch it," I warned, though my bark had no bite. Breath shallow as a puddle in my lungs, I swiveled again, my gaze meeting the blonde's head on. While her eyes were lifeless black, there was something familiar in the tilt of her head, the dimple on her left cheek....

She smacked her palm flat against my chest, right over my tattoo. "Heart of a dragon, a gift from the god you've yet to meet."

At her touch, my heart shuddered to a stop, a soul-deep ache seizing my chest in a viper's hold. The world around me squeezed like a black hole, pain imploding inward, deeper, carving new paths as it folded me. A scream might have worked its way from my mouth, but it was drowned by their siren's song.

"If you want to save her, you'll need all three," the trio sang together again, and the pain stopped like a string had been cut with their words. I fell forward, crumpling to the rocky earth.

If you want to save her.
Keira.
Keira.
Keira.

I coughed, hot with the taste of blood. "Do you know where he's keeping her?"

"We are knowledge itself, sipped straight from the source." The one wearing her face held out a hand, and in her palm, a tiny golden bowl appeared. Black liquid lapped the sides, specks that looked like stars swirling in its inky current. "Will you sip, boy?"

My throat ran bone dry, like unwatered soil. I stared at the reflective surface, thirst ravaging my cracked insides.

"What's the catch?" I croaked, dragging my desert tongue across my chapped lips.

"Truth has no catch, but always a cost." She held the rim closer to my lips, dark gaze mirroring the contents. The scent of lavender and cedar enveloped me–*Keira's scent*–the taste of a memory budding at the back of my mouth. "Take our trials, and then decide."

Danura's warning grounded me to the last shards of my resistance and sense, a diluted drop of unease running down the back of my neck.

Don't stray away from the path. Keep moving, don't speak to anyone, and you'll get through just fine.

But then another, louder voice at the forefront. Keira's voice, bright and clear as daybreak against a snow-covered shore.

Come find me. Come closer.

"And if I don't? If I just keep going on the path?" I rallied my wavering strength to lift a weak finger, pointing on the straight, rocky path through the center of the frozen field. It would be so easy to push on, to find the sirens and keep moving. A primitive instinct verified the truth, that my friends waited for me just beyond.

"The straightest course is often the safest." The dimpled blond stepped out of the way, an invitation for me to pass.

"But rarely the most satisfying." Danura's twin gestured broadly to the road, a dare for me to deny the desperate curiosity clamoring in my ribcage.

"Drink." A shrug, my wife's forged signature from the false goddess as she handed me the smooth gold. "Or don't. Choice is yours, *Manawydan*."

My reflection met my gaze in the star-spattered blackness, sapphire eyes shining as I decided. Then I lifted the bowl to my lips and guzzled the contents like a sailor lost at sea, or perhaps a man found.

Together, the three witches smiled. Not-Danura took a graceful step forward, lips pulling back to reveal a toothless smile, hollow and empty as the wasteland surrounding us. Her hand jutted out, clasping around my throat, robbing me of air. "Me first, boy."

And the world disappeared into darkness.

21

Dens and Dragons

GRIFFIN

"Oh, thank Lyr," Rhett's voice broke first as we rounded the side of the nearest peak, meeting our crew in a dense forest of towering evergreen firs. He lurched forward, tripping over hidden roots, nearly knocking over an injured Saeth at my side to crush me in a tight hug. "I would've killed you if you died."

I stilled for a moment before my hand pressed him closer. His long hair tickled my cheek as I breathed him in, citrus and leather, fresh and worn at the same time. A foreign, forgotten laugh bubbled out of my chest, adrenaline finally giving way to euphoria in his embrace. "Don't worry, Blondie. Only I decide what hurts me."

Rhett pulled back in surprise, blue eye filling with glassy tears as the words—*his words*—sank in. A smile brighter than sunlight on snow lit the shadowed glade. "I knew that meager dragon was no match for my Swordsinger."

Something greedy and gluttonous rumbled deep in my gut at the nickname, a wanting that was not weakness, but pure, unadulterated power. It lassoed my heart and pulled tight, ribs straining to contain the wild beating.

My Swordsinger, he said.

Rhett Mathonwy had the power to make even mortal men feel like gods. I brushed a strand of his wild hair out of his face before pressing my lips to his in a hungry kiss, desperate for that taste of my partner's lethal love.

"Get a room." Saeth hopped away from us on her one good foot, as I broke away from Rhett, and Tarran swooped in to grab her.

"Welcome back, brat." He grinned as he carried her, the relief on his face palpable.

Her grimace wavered into a smile. "Good to see you, too, pubes-for-hair."

A throat cleared, interrupting the heartfelt reunions, the *literal* god waiting to lead us on our next quest tiring of our public affection. I reluctantly pulled back from Rhett—squeezing his hand once to assure him we'd finish *that* conversation later—before facing the deity's dark glare head-on.

Rhett's brow furrowed as he took in our white-clad savior. "Who—"

"I'm Reagan Mathonwy, and I'm practically in charge here." Reagan sauntered up to the God of the Hunt, her arms crossed as she sized him up. If Rhett bestowed godhood with his belief, Reagan stole it with her swagger. She had to tilt her head all the way back to meet Gwynn's high gaze, but the little dragon merely sniffed the air around him like he had shit on his shoe. "Who are you, arrow boy?"

"By the gods," Drystan swore, breath stolen in a white wisp of mist as he put the puzzle pieces together. Orwellin was Arawn's island, but the temples there had homages to all of the gods' likenesses. He kneeled, hissing as his knees kissed the frost, metallic eyes opening wider than a whore's legs. "You're—"

"Yes, yes, Gwynn, at your service," the god grunted once, strapping the bow to his back again in a swift, fluid motion. He stared at me over Reagan's head, unfazed by her fire. "Let's keep moving."

He marched through the thick trees, the impatient immortal crunching through snow like a man on a mission.

Reagan stared after him like she was planning something stupid, but the rest of my crew looked to me, a chorus of eyebrows raised and arms crossed. I shrugged. I might be Captain now, but I was just a man, not a myth, and I'd had more than my fair share of legendary encounters today.

So instead of answering, instead of uttering a command or feigning certainty, I simply followed the god into the wilderness, hoping it might bring us closer to something akin to salvation.

My crew, loyal and foolish as ever, stomped through the frost and pine needles beside me. Rhett's hand slipped its way into mine, cold fingers clasped in a welcomed cage, one a stray cat like me never thought I'd yield to.

Gwynn led us through snow-bowed trees for a few hundred paces, to where the forest met the sharp incline of the peaks' north end. In the face of the mountain, a cavern yawned open, a hidden portal to what waited inside.

"Come in," he called over his shoulder, the white wolf swallowed by the dark entrance.

"I knew we were close," Vian muttered under his breath, crossing the threshold first, a still-pouting Reagan to his right.

"If you mean close to being breakfast, then yes," Saeth spat, still bitter as burnt coffee despite her injury. She hung off Tarran's back like she was the queen of snow and he was her noble steed.

Rhett and I exchanged a quick glance, and my partner shrugged. No fear or hesitation left, we followed Gwynn into the dark, scary cave.

We're all so fucked anyway, what's the harm in trying?

The hollow interior was massive, rows of flickering torches struggling to light the space. In the amber glow, looming stalagmite rocks stretched toward the ceiling, stone sentries guarding the grotto beyond. Within their natural enclosure, there was no mistaking the giant beast taking up nearly half of the clearing, its black scales blending into the shadows.

This time, as its fanged face locked eyes on us, a laugh startled from my mouth. It was all I had left, the ridiculousness of the last few weeks rewiring my nerves and normalizing the insanity.

"Dragon!" Tarran shouted as if it helped, voice ricocheting off the damp rocks. He staggered back, nearly toppling Saeth again before she tugged one of his curls, a jockey reining in her unruly mount.

I laughed harder, clutching Rhett's hand like a lifeline, hoping it would pull me back to my senses. My partner looked at me as if I'd grown a tail, but it did nothing to quell the nervous snickering bursting from my clenched lips.

The dragon—three times the size of the last one we'd seen—shot us a bored look before curling up and settling down like an oversized mutt.

"Don't worry, that one is tame." A hint of amusement twitched Gwynn's lips, his rust-colored skin warmed gold in the light. "*Ish*. He belongs to Nef. His name is Awyr."

"Lovely to meet you," I snorted between heaving laughs, bowing to the giant dragon that could easily fry me and feast on my charred flesh like toast, "Awyr."

And I swore the dragon *winked* at me with one gilded eye before shutting both and huffing a plume of smoke, a kitten ready for its midday nap.

Trouble was toying with me now, content to play with its meal before devouring me whole.

"Are you sure it's safe?" Tarran's voice quivered as he took a single, hesitant step closer.

"Let's get you all inside." Gwynn's focus zeroed in on Saeth, ignoring her colt entirely. "Nef will look at that ankle."

"I'm fine, it's just a sprain." Saeth dismissed the god like a petulant fly in her food, sliding off Tarran's back for emphasis and bouncing forward, fueled by her own fury alone.

Again, steel clashed against stone. Their expressions locked in a silent war, somehow so much more terrifying than the dragon warming the cave.

Gwynn's brow furrowed, muscles in his jaw working hard over whatever curse he fought to swallow. "Is that one always this stubborn?"

"Yes," the crew answered in unison.

Gwynn huffed and turned on his heel, a man of few words. We followed him deeper into the mouth of the mountain, the rumbling snore of the sleeping dragon vibrating the ground beneath our feet.

Our pace was slow to accommodate Saeth's half-limp, half-hop, who adamantly refused to be carried any longer. As the clearing narrowed into a small, earthen tunnel, lanterns replaced torches as the air tightened around us. A damp chill settled over us, cold sweat licking the back of my neck and pits. I peeled my furs from my torso, wearing only my thin tunic beneath despite the icy clime, but even so, the deeper we went, the more the moist air clung to our skin, blanketing us in humidity. Rhett tied his hair off his head, droplets of mist hugging the few dangling strands at the back of his neck.

Finally, the tunnel widened once more, revealing the source of the moisture. A deep, bubbling pool of crystal blue water steamed the grotto, a hidden hot spring in the depths of the mountain.

A pang of homesickness cleaved between my ribs, thoughts of the spring we'd left behind in Porthladd stirring my stomach. Our sacred space, desecrated by the blight that was Morwyn Locasta.

I was far from a holy man. I was a pretty-faced slut and a lying scoundrel, Trouble's favorite courtesan. But even I had lines I could not cross, morals etched into my essence, passed down from generations before. And even if my family had fallen to corruption and chaos, even if the smear of betrayer's blood would permanently stain the Branwen name, there were still some things worth saving.

Perhaps there was a chance to make allies of these gods yet. Perhaps they too had springs they wanted to stay clean.

I forced myself to look away, instead studying the rest of the space. The walls here were different, too, sanded down and carved, the imprint of intentionality in every crevice. A series of smooth, rounded doorways lined the perimeter, giving the hideaway a lived-in look.

A den of gods and dragons, buried beneath rock and ice.

"You're late," a tall woman lectured as she stepped through the doorway nearest us, her white-suede tunic bright in the lantern-lit space. Sunlight-gold hair—so bright it was almost white—flowed in long waves that scraped the small of her back, angular eyes staring down at us over the severe ridge of her nose. "And you brought us our visitors."

"This is Nef." Gwynn jerked his head at her before disappearing through the archway. Nef watched him with the attention of a hawk as he retreated before flicking her sharp blue stare back at us, tilting her head. Not a single bead of sweat sullied her brow. She looked no older than Reina had been, her pale skin still tight to her face, but there was something ancient in the way she stood, strong and tall as a Pysgoddian pine. A cool breeze kissed the back of my neck, relief from the condensation gathered there. I peeled the hem of my soaked tunic up as embarrassment flushed my cheeks pink.

Vian stepped forward first, sticking his hand out for a shake. "Hello, I'm—"

A wide smile breached her sharp features. "I know who you are, child." She reached out, ruffling Vian's mop of dark hair. "Look how big you've grown."

A beat passed, then another, as I struggled to grasp what was happening.

"I missed you." Vian mirrored her grin, a perfect match in shape and intensity, before wrapping his long arms around her in a familiar hug. Before she returned the gesture, burying her face in his shoulder. "*Mama.*"

Vian, the songbird trapped in Locasta's cage.

Vian, the wind whisperer without a pot to piss in.

Vian, our adopted little brother, who wound his way into our hearts like a hymn on a breeze.

Vian, son of the goddess Nef herself.

Born of a god. *Duweni.*

Lyr's hairy pits, we were so in over our heads.

"What the—" The end of my sentence died on the gust of air that tore through the spring, Rhett gripping my hand to remind me to scrape my jaw from the cavern floor.

Nef broke the embrace first, still holding Vian's shoulders, meeting our eyes one by one. "Come inside. We have a lot to discuss."

Another understatement. My head spun like a tornado as I tried to find my footing in some certainty. If Vian was Nef's son, then he had the blood of a god. We didn't need Keira back to end Locasta or Arawn. We didn't need Danura or Gwynn or any of the others.

Then again, he was still just a boy. A little nightingale still learning to fly. It was unfair to put the weight of the Deyrnas on his back alone, no matter his bloodline.

No, we didn't need some inexperienced virgin. We needed well-seasoned gods, ones that had fucked and fought their way into this madness in the first place. The same bastards that had been avoiding their messes for centuries now.

And thanks to the little songbird's clever scheme, we'd found some.

We followed Nef through the first archway, which opened to a study. A polished pine table occupied the center, cluttered with maps and mismatched arrowheads. Tall wooden chairs surrounded it, upholstered in more white fur. Various bows and spears hung on animal antlers, decorating the stone walls from floor to ceiling, a hunter's paradise. The glassy, dead eyes of an eight-point stag met mine, the stuffed head the pride and glory of the den.

Gwynn sat directly beneath the deer's mantle, sharpening an arrowhead with the distinct off-white of bone. He looked up at us as we entered, perhaps considering exactly where he'd mount *us* if we got on his bad side.

"Sorry I didn't tell you about my ulterior motive," Vian whispered as we shuffled into the room, nudging my side.

"It's fine, kid, I get it." I didn't, actually, but I knew from firsthand experience that I'd do or sacrifice anything for my mama, too. And no matter his motives, he'd led us right to our desired goal.

Now all I needed to do was to convince them to join our cause.

Nef reached for a bag on the table, rolling out a healer's toolkit; vials of herbs and small, tiny metal apparatuses shoved into specific pockets of the brown leather pack. Her sharp focus narrowed in on Saeth. "You with the bum ankle, come here. The rest of you may sit."

To my surprise and relief, Saeth hobbled over without complaint, plopping into the chair next to Gwynn and propping her disfigured leg right on the table. Nef carefully removed Saeth's worn boot and rolled up her ash-covered pant leg, revealing deep purple bruises already forming against the misshapen limb.

Saeth barely winced, but the rest of the crew made faces of varying degrees of disgust as they too took to the fur-lined seats.

"That's gross." Tarran blanched, taking the seat farthest from Saeth and the gods.

"You're gross," she spit back.

Reluctantly, I unwound my fingers from Rhett's, stepping forward not as a lovesick cad, but a Captain. I was Trouble's footstool, but today I'd sit on his throne.

"We've been searching for you. Danura sent us from *Hiraeth.*" I took the closest chair, directly opposite them both. I forced myself to sit tall, Truth and Triumph poking at my back. If other families wanted any chance at reunion, the Deyrnas didn't have time for us to dawdle over revelations. I set my intention clearly, as Keira and Cedric had always done, Captains who knew exactly what was theirs for the taking. "We need your help."

Nef frowned as she examined Saeth's leg. "I know why you came, but I'm afraid there is nothing we can do for the Deyrnas."

In a swift, effortless motion, she set the bone, so quickly my cousin could barely react to the pain. A single hiss escaped her lips as she jerked forward before falling back into the chair, a murderous look trained on the goddess.

"I just watched *that* one–" Saeth gritted out, pointing a long needle from Nef's pack at Gwynn like it was a rapier, somehow swiping it without any of us noticing, "shoot a dragon in its eye. What do you mean there is *nothing* you can do?"

Nef finally looked up from her ankle, incredulous stare plastered across her open-mouthed expression.

I stifled a smile. I might have been vying for Trouble's title, but Saeth was already the Queen of Needles and Ice. Siren or god-born, injured or not, she was the sharpest dagger in this room. Even if I was supposed to be Captain, I would relish having such a formidable weapon at my side.

"We can't interfere with human affairs." Gwynn stopped his carving, pointing the arrow at Saeth, mirroring her hostility tenfold. "It's the code we made for peace with the other gods. Arawn promised not to attack if we didn't do anything to upset the balance of life and death. So we do our jobs–we help the seasons shift, we keep magical beasties in check, make life possible–but we don't directly intervene in *politics*."

He spat the last word like it was dipped in dragon shit, so fiercely even Nef grimaced next to him.

A forgotten fire lit in my belly, heating my veins as it pumped through them. It was better to be pissed off than pitied, and I would not let our past be minimized by some prick of a god who barely deigned to pay us any mind.

Crimson against ivory. Blood against stone.

This wasn't about politics or promises long dismissed. This was life or death for the Deyrnas. For Tolio and Amilee, who never made it out of Bachtref. For Papa and Finna, victims of Connor's treachery. For all the refugees camped at the base of this mountain range, frightened and freezing and fighting for resources. For my crew, my family.

I leaned forward on the table, purposefully nudging it into Gwynn's knees. "Arawn isn't holding his side of the bargain. There is a plague in Bachtref. And Morwyn Locasta has used some sort of puppet magick to steal bodies for her army. I don't know your definition of *politics*, but genocide and mass starvation sounds like it should be your business."

"And they took Keira Branwen," Rhett added at my side, folding his thick arms across his chest to emphasize their size. "She's technically your sister, isn't she? That should be a declaration of war in itself."

Gwynn's glare darkened as he twirled his bone-carved arrow in his fingertips. "Half-sister, I guess. Danura is our mother, but Arawn is our father. To cross either of them would be betrayal. War, more horrific than you mortals could even imagine in your worst nightmares."

Nef nudged her brother before she reached for a wooden splint, setting it against Saeth's ankle gently. "I'm very sorry to hear about the tragedies you've all witnessed. It isn't the first time mortals have gotten their hands on dark magick." Not pausing, she tied a long white bandage around the limb, using the splint as a brace to keep it straight. But her frown only deepened, a different worry clouding her features. "But it's not Arawn's doing directly. We can't help. Our hands are tied."

In my ear, Truth murmured a reluctant authentication.

A silence filled the cavern, dead and hopeless as the mounts on the wall. Rhett and Drystan exchanged a look, former foes somehow united in their frustration. Tarran's head fell to his hands, even his sunshine extinguished in the darkness of the mountain. Saeth gripped Nef's needle so tightly, it nearly broke, tension rippling across her frame. Even Vian stared at Nef—at his *mother*—with a look akin to disappointment clear in the furrow of his usually smooth brow.

The fire that had fueled my last parry died out, as useless as a single torch in a blizzard. We'd been too accustomed to foolish quests, too drunk on our luck to anticipate the reality. Fights were easy. Fights, I understood. But bargains and treaties, politics and allies...

I'd failed.

No one was coming to help. Gods or monsters, they were just as useless as the rest of us.

"I get it now," Reagan breathed on the other side of Rhett, arms folded. A wicked grin curled the side of her mouth upward. "You're both cowards."

Nef's head whipped to her faster than a northern wind. And for the first time since meeting her, Gwynn looked directly at her, a hunter locking his sights on his prey. "I don't expect a little girl to understand the contracts between gods."

"No, but I understand fear." Reagan crumpled a paper on the table in front of her. She threw it at Gwynn's head, the hunter swatting it away with ease. But still, Reagan threw another ruined parchment at him, her teasing tone grating like flint on metal. "*The big bad white wolf, afwaid of daddy getting angwy at him?* Pathetic."

Truth and Triumph both hissed at my back, dread leadening my limbs. My pitiful flame had been extinguished, but Reagan's was made of dragon-fire. It would devour even the snow-heavy evergreens of Pysgodd, hotter than hell itself.

And the great hunter god had just become the next victim of the little dragon's fury.

"Watch your tongue, girl." Gwynn drove the arrowhead into the table like it was made of butter, growling at Reagan from his perch. "You have no idea what we have lost."

Reagan clutched the table's edge with white knuckles, ready to spew her fire with renewed force, when the Ice Queen intervened, matching her heat with impossible frost.

"I've heard your story before, you know," Saeth sneered at the hunter. "Always amazed me that you fell for the doe, and not the arrow. What was her name again, Silvia? *Sinead?*"

At her name, Gwynn went impossibly still, every muscle in his body ready to attack. As always, the needle-wielder had worked her way under his skin, pricking and poking the beast awake. Her smile had razors in it. "Sounds to me you only prey on the helpless. I wonder what she'd think of her great hunter now."

I swore to Lyr, Gwynn *flinched.*

"Reagan, Saeth–" I warned, but it was too late. A tornado of fire and ice, the two feral women were already onto their next victim, a path of destruction in their wake.

"And you! Some dragon tamer you are," Reagan hurled the accusation at Nef, standing from her seat. She pointed a shaking finger at Vian, the fire burning her from the inside out. "He's your son, and you left him to rot. He was in a dungeon for *years*. Alone, afraid. A *child*. And the best you could do was whisper in his ear? When you literally have a fucking *dragon* as a pet? You make me sick."

Tears sprang to the goddess's eyes, like stormclouds covering the blue sky. She shook her head, crossing behind Saeth to take Vian's hand. "It's all so much more complicated than that, Vian. I gave you to the temples thinking they'd protect you, but I knew if I kept you,

Arawn would find out and try and take you. You were safer away from me, and I didn't think they'd *enslave* you. I loved you the whole—"

Reagan shoved back her chair and stomped up to the goddess, the dragon on the warpath. "My mother *died* to keep me safe. *That* is love." Her words sucked all the air from the room, sealing it in silence again. She stared up at the goddess, throat bobbing once. Twice. "All you have are excuses."

Raindrop-sized tears slipped down Nef's elegant cheeks.

It was better to be pissed off than pitied, and Reagan had mastered the art. Whether this rage was directed at the woman in front of her, or the bodies she'd left behind, I'd never know.

She breathed in the sobbing woman one last time before turning on her heel and storming out of the small enclosure.

"Where are you going?" I ran a tired hand over my face, calling after her.

"Fresh air," she fired back, voice already echoing a distance away.

It was easy, sometimes, to forget she was barely a teenager. Easy to remember her powerful parts, to forget the orphaned little girl she hid behind masks of confidence and contempt.

"Go with her, please, Drystan." I sent the handsome guard after her, hoping his effortless charm would help, or that his talent with a sword would at least protect him against her scorn. He nodded, bowing to each of the gods before hastening out the archway.

Nef wiped stray tears from her smooth skin with the heel of her hand, straightening her shoulders again. "I understand you all must be hurt. We can't help you directly, but that doesn't mean we want to leave you empty-handed. There are... subversive ways for us to support you."

"Like?" Rhett's silver eye swiveled, the enchanted object searching for signs of trickery.

"If what you say is true, and you're working against a death magick-user, you need godly items," Gwynn snorted, finally finished licking his wounds. He pulled his arrowhead from the table, sharpening it again like Saeth hadn't castrated him with a few words. "Each god has only one or two, as they are imbued with a part of their power. Use the item, and it can break through any spell cast by mortals, clean or unclean."

Saeth opened her mouth, ready to finish the job she started, but I interrupted before she could. "And where do we find said items?"

"You have mine strapped to your back." Gwynn pointed the arrow at Truth and Triumph, a growl breaking through his grimace. "I've been missing those swords for a long time, mortal."

The swords sang in unison, recognizing their master in a chorus. I pressed my back into the chair, trapping my friends behind me. Gwynn might have made them, but I'd won them fair and square. Or at least, fair enough.

"They've been helpful more than once, thanks." I flashed him a winning grin, the same I used to swindle the swords out of a game of cards. "But nice bow!"

"That's mine, actually. Though he uses it more than I do now." Nef extended her hand, and Gwynn removed it from his back grudgingly. She clasped the long bow to her chest, pressing a kiss into the dark wood before laying it across Vian's lap. "You may borrow it. It never misses its mark."

Vian lifted the weapon and shrugged, head tilted. "Thanks. I guess I'll have to learn how to use it."

"That's terrifying," Tarran muttered out loud, before clapping his hand back over his mouth and sitting back in his seat.

I couldn't tell if Triumph's whisper in my ear was a celebration, or a warning.

"Any others we should keep an eye out for?" Rhett gripped my thigh beneath the table, pulling me back to the task ahead. If this was the only bone the gods would give us, we'd have to take a page out of Gwynn's book and carve it into something sharp enough to skewer our enemies.

"Lyr's compass, Bris's sickle, Cerridwen's cards, Bridget's crown of coins," Gwynn rattled off, the hunter's jealous gaze still fixed on the bow in Vian's lap. "And Arawn's pistols."

The dizzying firework of hope shot through my center as I clawed beneath my tunic for another lifeline I didn't realize we had.

"We have another one of those already." I pulled the compass from my neck, the slim needle spinning wildly, Cedric's old bronze trinket somehow more valuable than all the jewels in Ir'de. Even if it didn't work. "Though I think it's broken."

Both gods stilled; Nef's eyes went wide as an owl's while Gwynn licked his lips like a hungry wolf in front of a lamb.

"The compass leads you where you are meant to be, not where you *want* to be." A reverence shimmered in Nef's cerulean stare. "As evidenced by today's encounter, I would imagine."

At that, my grip on the bronze tightened, realization stirring in my stomach uncomfortably. In all of our adventures, all the chance meetings and fateful standoffs—it had all been Lyr's doing, the sunken god steering our ship even from the depths.

I opened my mouth to speak—to ask a question that hadn't really even formed yet—

The metallic click of a pistol's safety ricocheted around the small cavern.

Saeth's smirk was dipped in wickedness as she pointed her father's silver pistol—*Arawn's* gun—at Gwynn. "And what does this do?"

Gwynn shot from his seat, beads of sweat forming on his brow. He swallowed hard, neck straining with the action as he stared down the barrel of the silver death note. My swords screamed at my back, a deep dread tangling my stomach in sailor's knots.

"Put that down immediately." Nef's voice trembled as she lifted her hands slowly, taking one hesitant step away from the seated assailant. "Where on earth did you find it?"

My gaze locked on the silver pistol, the harbinger of so many deaths, friend and foe. I'd thought it was lost with the fall of Porthladd. Thought Keira had dragged it with her to the Otherworld, had returned it to its maker, thought Weylin had buried its twin somewhere in Orwellin or *Hiraeth*...

Where Saeth had snatched it from, I could only guess.

"Only a god can kill a god, right?" Saeth flipped the loaded gun back and forth between her hands, tempting Death for the second time today. "So if their objects possess some of their powers...will this do the trick?"

A newfound flurry of hope swirled in my chest, like the winter's storm outside. The pistols were made of destruction and death, but perhaps they would herald salvation. Perhaps we could repurpose them to revive the Deyrnas instead of end it.

"Yes," Gwynn breathed the single syllable, an admission and a surrender. "So be careful where you point that thing."

Saeth's finger stroked the trigger. "Then be careful of what you say, hunter."

The Ice Queen knew how to flirt with Trouble and Death, but I'd had enough. We needed the gods' help, whether or not they were willing. And the only god who would taste that pistol's lead already waited in the Otherworld.

"Stand down, Saeth." I let the cool metal of Cedric's compass endow me with a sliver of his authority. "That's an order."

The room chilled as she shifted her frosty stare to me. A breath passed, and then another. Finally, she clicked the safety in place, stuffing the gun back into her waistband.

Nef and Gwynn exhaled in unison, Nef crumpling into the seat next to Vian. Gwynn crossed his arms, leaning on the wall below the deer's head, the hunter still on high alert.

"Where can we find the others?" I cleared my throat, letting Rhett's hand on my leg steady my racing heart.

"The more you can gather, the better your chances are against Arawn. Bris's sickle was rumored to be destroyed ages ago, when Bris died. It makes sense why Bachtref was affected by this blight first. No one is there to keep the balance," Nef sighed, smoothing out her tunic. "But I know Cerridwen and her cards are still around somewhere. They give you a glimpse into a possible future—the most likely one. And Bridget's crown is where it always was—in her old jewelry shop in Ir'de. She's gone, but it brings luck to whoever wears it—so Cerridwen has kept it under lock and key. It's not as useful as a sword in battle, but you'll want the luck on your side."

Rhett snorted. "Great, that should be easy."

Again, we were passed off to the next quest, mortals meddling with affairs we had no business in. More gods, long forgotten, to petition their aid. More danger, for us and the Deyrnas, as time ticked forward. We did not know when Locasta would strike again, only that she would.

"We better get moving then. The Deyrnas might not have time." I stood up, sheathing Cedric's—no, *Lyr's*—compass against my chest. Hopefully it would lead us to the next stop on destiny's grand map for us. The others stood with me, securing their belongings, already content to follow me back down the mountain, onto our next mad mission.

Tarran was already halfway to the door, the curly-haired coward content to leave the gods behind for good. "If we leave now, we could make it back to the village before supper."

Only Vian stayed seated, the longbow still splayed across his lap.

I sighed, clapping the boy on the back. "Vian, if you want to stay and catch up–no one would blame you. We will come back eventually, and Vala and Reese are staying down in the village and would be happy to keep you in the loop."

At that, the boy stood, looping his head through the bowstring so it hung across his frame. He took a quiver of bone-tipped arrows from the wall, his gaze just as sharp as it met mine.

"I'm coming." He tilted his chin, a boy ready to take his first step into manhood. "I owe Morwyn Locasta a blood debt."

I couldn't help my smile, pride beating against my ribs. Nef might have been Vian's mother, but we were the young god's family now. And maybe, just maybe, he would be our salvation.

"Good riddance," Gwynn spat at us, glowering against the wall.

Nef pushed back from the table, pressing a loving palm to the boy's cheek. "Vian, please stay. I would love to–"

Vian clasped her wrist in his long fingers, silencing her while gently tugging her hand away. "In all my years in that cell, I never questioned your choices. Don't judge mine, Mama."

Nef blinked, whatever protests the goddess had next dying on her lips.

Footsteps thundering against stone shattered the moment, just as Drystan's booming voice reverberated through the room.

"Help! I'm sorry, she–" The guard panted as he skidded into the room, his normally slick bun frayed into a wild mess of curls, horror coloring the bronze of his round eyes. "The dragon–"

My heart dropped to my toes. Adrenaline poured into my veins, and I was moving before Drystan even finished his sentence. I tore into a full sprint, legs aching beneath me, sweat licking my limbs. Up the humid tunnel, back through the winding burrow, Rhett hot on my heels. The others may have followed, but I didn't care.

Dancing with Trouble had consequences, and Reagan was about to meet hers.

I stumbled into the large cavern first, eyes scanning the ground for Reagan, for any sign of a struggle or worse...

Until my eyes finally found her. Not cowering behind a stalagmite, or caged within the dragon's claws...

But sitting proudly on the monster's scaled back, right between its mighty wings, hands gripping one of its spikes like a saddlehorn.

"Reagan?" Rhett managed to form her name first, somehow training his tongue to move. Mine was still lame with shock. "Reagan! What are you doing?"

"Get down, please," I finally found my voice, shaking with fear. Not a captain, a coward.

"Awyr!" Nef roared as she and Gwynn rounded into the room, horror evident in both of their pale expressions. "Get off him right now!"

"Thanks for all the help, turdheads!" Reagan called, patting the creature's neck. It stretched its head back to her, a deep rumble that sounded like a cat's affectionate purr echoing against the stone. A wild smile cut her round face. "I promise I'll bring him back in one piece."

And like he was a mild mare, not a legendary beast of prey, Reagan kicked her heels into Awyr's side. The dragon spread his massive wings, rearing back on his powerful hind legs, and *flew*.

Legs commanding me forward, we ran after, winter wind assaulting us as we exited the warm respite of the cave, but we were too late. The dragon's form was already a small splotch against the white sky, taking my cousin and charge with him.

Lyr below, we were so incredibly screwed.

"Shit," Rhett kicked a tuft of snow, running his hands through his long hair. He stomped back to me, mismatched eyes blazing with fear and fury. "Griffin, we have to go get her."

Pain and panic scratched through my lungs like the bitter cold air, scraping with each ragged breath. "I know, I–"

"Meet us for dinner!" Vian cupped his hands around his mouth to shout after her, a square smile stretched across his slim face. "She'll be fine. The wind says so."

"Lyr's tits," I swore under my breath, spinning around to meet two furious godly faces. "Don't worry, we'll go get her and your dragon."

I promised them, and myself. Trouble clearly hadn't had its fill of me yet, its favorite fuckup to toy with. But if anything happened to Reagan, if she was hurt or worse–

I would run my swords right through Trouble's sorry ass.

"If you don't find her, I will." Gwynn stepped to me, the threat as fiery as his hot breath warming my face. Made like a mountain, the God of the Hunt made me feel small.

I nodded once, no longer willing to test Trouble's mercy.

"You'll get your dragon back when we're done with him." Saeth patted Gwynn's stubbled cheek as she hobbled past him, snow crunching beneath her braced foot. She leaned casually on my shoulder, picking her fingernails. "Come and find us if you dare, oh great hunter."

22

Cages and Consequences

KEIRA

Rage was an old friend I'd long abandoned. I'd buried it under mistakes and regret, storing it in a tightly locked chamber beneath my ribs. But now it gurgled in my stomach, vicious teeth ready to smile at me again. Fangs ready to sink into whatever pour soul—man or *god*—dared stand in my way.

In the mirror room, Arawn stood sentry in front of the one exit to the small space. Candlelight from the black candelabras flickered across his stony features, casting the room in shadows. What once looked like a palace now revealed its true nature: a prison cell, built from ice and stone.

"What are you doing?" I hissed at Arawn, who faced his wall of ice, an unbothered reflection staring back at him.

"This is for your protection, *Caraid.*" His impassive voice filled the void, souring the air and stoking my fury—oxygen to a flame.

Trapped for my protection. A bird of prey shoved in a pretty cage. A goddess in a gilded jail. Anger rose to the tip of my tongue, hot and heavy as dragon's breath.

"I don't need protecting." I stomped to him, my silly heels clacking across the floor, until I could breathe him in. I might've been dressed as the damsel, but I was distress embodied. I stood straight, Papa's sage advice strengthening me. *Think tall, you'll be tall.* "I need honest answers. I *deserve* that much."

Dark eyes met mine, a flicker of his own ancient fury mirroring my own. "You want to lecture *me* on honesty?" An ice-edged cackle croaked out of him, his imposing frame somehow wider in the doorway. "You *knew*. But just like your *mother*, you didn't trust me to help you. Well, now we are doing it my way, whether you like it or not."

Instinctively, my hand flew to my middle, to the secret I'd accidentally sacrificed to this tyrant. Still, my old friend warmed my core, that delicious wrath pounding in my chest with my quickening heartbeat.

"I didn't know before I came. Before I was taken here, *against my will*, if I must remind you," I seethed, breathing in his snow and pine scent and spitting back the ashy remains. "I only found out recently, and I didn't know if it was even real—"

"It is very *real*." He cut me off, ice against fire as he placed his palm on my cheek. I smacked him away and stepped back.

"Do not *touch* me," I warned, the goddess within speaking through my lips. The ground beneath us rumbled, the Otherworld sounding the alarm with me. "You will never touch me again."

Dark eyes solidified, warm coal hardening to impenetrable obsidian stone. He took a single step back, shadows kissing his heels and swirling around his frame.

For the first time since being trapped in the ice, I saw the Dark God for what he was. A beautiful beast. A lovely, wicked villain. The God of Death and darkness, of deception and disaster.

"Fine. Have it your way." His voice carried, rose-colored lips curving into a curse of a smile. Lips that had whispered sweet nothings in my ear. Lips that promised redemption instead of ruination. Lips that had kissed me, that had tricked me into believing a fantasy. "I have to move quickly if I'm going to prepare for the baby's arrival."

He turned to go, broad back blocking out the light, ready to run up the steps and shut me behind, in this dungeon…

No, I was not a prisoner anymore. I was the predator, primordial chaos and cruelty too. And I demanded answers.

"What does that mean?" I snatched his wrist, spinning him to face me. Eyes widened at the unexpected force. "If you hurt her, I swear I'll—"

He ripped his arm away, but he scoffed, shaking his head. Slowly, he circled me, a beast baiting its prey. "You really do see me as a monster. I would *never* hurt that child. She is redemption itself."

His hand circled my waist, possessive and protective as his broad palm flattened against my slightly rounded belly. Revulsion rocked through me like I'd sniffed old milk, bile rising up my gullet.

"I won't let you use her, either." I dug my nails into his hand, earning a sharp wince as he wrenched away from me. My disgust settled, renewing my rage. No more flirtations or careful machinations. No more disguises or chess matches. If I had to, I would use the weapons I knew best—my fists and my unending fury. As if summoned by my anger alone, light burst from my fingertips, bright and hot in my hand. "If you want her, you'll have to kill me."

Arawn's eyes narrowed at my power, hungry gaze drinking in the light, before he swallowed once. Twice. Then, his mask slipped back in place, impassive and cold and endless ice. "Don't be dramatic, *Caraid*. This is all for you two."

He climbed the stairs in long, easy strides. I chased after him, ready to let him taste my rage. But I crashed into an unseen barrier, my face stinging with pain. I banged hard against the invisible forcefield, my fists cracking open across the knuckles, but it wouldn't budge. Panic fought for purchase in my chest as I slammed again against the hardened air, my heartbeat a wild war cry in my veins.

"Where are you going?" I screamed after him, voice tearing out of me.

He paused at the top of the steps, turning ever so slightly to stare down at me over his shoulder. "I have much to ready. Tomorrow, you and I are going topside."

A stone settled in my stomach. Ice ran down my spine, threatening to freeze over any determination I had left in fear.

But Arawn continued, Death not done dancing with me yet, "You're going to split Lyr's seas with that power of yours, and we are going to build our paradise on the bones of Danura's precious Deyrnas."

The air fled the room, and my breath froze in my lungs.

I was not the predator. I was the weapon, one he'd forged for his own use with soft smiles and well-practiced patience.

He left without another word, shutting me in his personal prison, trapping me.

He'd planned this. To trick me into doing his bidding. To use me against my own people, my home. The Deyrnas.

And I had believed him. I had been a stupid, selfish girl, so consumed by her own grief and fear that she'd swallow whatever illusion the shadowmaster summoned for her.

But not anymore. Like dry kindling to an already burning flame, it heated my core, my limbs shaking. I had been the weapon, but I would rather cast myself back into the fire and melt myself down than let him use me. Use my daughter. I would destroy him, and myself in the process, if it meant Rhiannon and the Deyrnas would be free.

And that's when the burning started.

Deep in that forgotten fury, it set me ablaze from inside out. It ran through my limbs like wildfire, all the way to my fingertips, where it ignited in the chill air.

I would burn it all to the ground. Burn him to the ground.

Before I knew what I was doing, I placed my palms on the ice wall. It sizzled beneath my touch, thawing and melting and dripping as I pressed harder.

Brighter and brighter.

Hotter and hotter.

Until it was gone, just a pool of steaming water drowning his precious room like he'd tried to drown me.

And from the depths, I rose.

23

Trials and Tribulations

RONAN

The darkness faded to a scene I could paint from memory. Ship planks groaned under my feet as I shifted weight, blinking to fight the illusion. Not-Danura stood at my side, the frigid Porthladdian wind waving her long white locks like a Jolly Roger against the dark night.

A night I'd replayed over and over again in my nightmares, in the lanternlit hours of quiet that always stretched too long. A night that poked and prodded harsh reminders at the back of my skull every time I saw the black spot on my wife's shoulder. A night that burned crimson every time I shut my eyes, every time I opened them to wake alone in the aftermath.

And just as it was that night, Aidan stood in front of Keira on the *Ceffyl's* deck, Arawn's silver pistol pointed at her face.

"What is this?" I seethed, tearing my eyes away from the moment I knew all too well, focusing instead on the ruthless creature to my right.

It was a useless question—one I knew the answer to. This was my darkest memory, the night Keira had to save me in the spring, forsaking herself. The night that rocketed us on our current path, the night Death first claimed my wife as his prize.

"A past that cannot be changed." The crone watched with a flat expression as Aidan stepped forward, as he clicked the bullet into its chamber. "A regret unsettled."

"I'm not watching this." I shut my eyes, a phantom ache pitting in my stomach, as if remembering my wound for me. "This isn't real."

And yet, I still heard my memory-self stomp forward, boots a war drum against the deck. Heard the second gun click into place. Heard my voice carry across the empty docks, *"Drop the gun, Aidan."*

A warning I should never have given him.

"You can turn away, but it still won't shift the wheel of fate," the witch whispered, pinching my side. My eyes flew open again, locking onto her empty sockets. "And while this is just a memory, the failure festering inside you is very *real.*"

Pushing past the stone lodged in my throat, I swallowed, turning to the scene again.

And I watched as Aidan pulled the trigger.

As I collapsed to the ground like a puppet with his strings cut, red blood and black ooze pooling around me.

As my wife fell at my side, an unearthly scream thundering out of her.

"I could've saved her if I'd just shot first," I whispered as the guilt prickled beneath every inch of my skin, an itch too deep to ever scratch. I clutched my abdomen, hands remembering the sticky heat of my life force seeping from my insides, the impossible, numbing cold as my blood drained from me. "If he hadn't hit me, no one would've needed the spring or a cure—"

"*If.*" The creature's impassive expression broke into a curved, cruel grin. "A tricky little word. Tell me, what might have happened if you killed him on sight? Do you think she would've thanked you, or hated you?"

She jerked a gnarled thumb in memory-Keira's direction. Keira, who crouched in front of me like a lioness protecting her pride. Keira, whose silver eyes sparkled despite the impenetrable night surrounding us, alight with rage and salvation.

The NightMare of the Four Seas. The Silver Wheel.

The Goddess Ariannad.

I'd been both shielded by and subject to that rage, the searing heat she stored in the most sorrowful corners of her soul. But it didn't matter. I'd take a thousand years of her contempt if it meant even just one more day of her life unmarred by Death's mark. "I don't care if she hates me if it means she'd be safe."

"Safe from what?" The creature snorted, facing me head-on. She gripped my shoulders, fingers digging into my flesh like the claws of a creature far larger. "Boy, *she* does not need protection. She is not a little sparrow to be locked in a cage and kept."

I stuffed my hands into the linen pockets of my borrowed threads, an uncomfortable shame clawing its way back out of the deeply buried hole I'd stuffed it in. "I know that. She's always been so strong, I just–" I trailed off, the end of the phrase tangling my tongue in knots.

Keira didn't need protection. And Keira didn't need me.

Not-Danura tilted her head, studying me with an ancient scrutiny that turned my stomach inside-out.

Then she flicked my nose.

"Ow." I rubbed the tender spot, but the creature's brow furrowed.

"It is not her you don't see clearly. I can taste it in your memories–you see her as the creature she is." She poked my chest, right above my heart again, so hard I knew it would bruise. "It is your own self you do not know yet. Tell me, boy, who were you on this night?"

I forced myself to look again. As Keira embraced her traitor uncle, burying her head in his shoulder. As he pressed the pistol to her back. As I laid there, an adder bleeding in the grass, too afraid to strike.

"I was a hesitant fool. I thought my masks made me a man, but all my cleverness and calculations didn't make me bulletproof."

"You see a fool?" The creature scoffed, walking closer to the memory. She crouched next to my still form, swiping two fingers through the blood staining the deck. With another twisted smile, she brought it to her lips and sucked the crimson from her skin. I shuddered as she spoke again, "I taste a fighter. A man willing to give his life for the woman he loved."

At that, past-me sat up beside her, his pistol aimed straight, and the gunshot rang out as the spot of red marred Aidan's forehead.

"And yet, I'm still alive, and my wife is beyond your gate." No matter what choices I made, no matter what I offered, it had gotten me here. Had gotten Keira kidnapped.

It was never enough.

I wasn't enough.

The creature stood, sauntering again across the deck. "Tell me boy, what are you willing to give this time?"

I met her consuming stare, letting the last of my regret dissolve in the black holes of her eyes. I had nothing left to give, and yet, it didn't matter. This time, it would be enough. It had to be.

"Everything."

She waved her hand, the memory disappearing into shadow once more.

"My sister waits."

When the darkness cleared, Danura's face no longer stared back at me. In its place was a face that consumed my soul. A face I knew better than my own.

"You look just like her," I mumbled before I could catch myself, resisting the urge to brush a strand of her wild raven hair behind her ear. I focused on the parts that were wrong, the dark eyes instead of silver, the wicked grimace instead of her normal scowl.

"I look like whatever you choose to see." She ran her fingers through my wife's locks, tossing the mane over her shoulder. "Though it's been a long time since I've taken a form this lovely."

I forced myself to look away, the homesickness squeezing my heart too painful to bear. Instead, I studied the strange surroundings. We stood in the center of a dark room, floors made of pitch-black stone, tall walls lit with wrought-iron candelabras, their candles made of black wax. An ostentatious velvet throne and a small table with blood red roses were the only pieces of furniture in the strange room, equal parts ridiculous and ominous.

And on the far wall, a sheet of black ice stretched from the floor to the ceiling. Shadows danced in its glacial face, both beckoning and off-putting, sending a wave of dread sloshing through my gut. "Where are we now?"

"A present you cannot see alone." Keira's face spoke as she walked to the threatening wall, placing a hand on the icy surface. At her touch, the shadows bucked and twisted with frenzied force. "A fear inescapable."

The swirling burst into an image, clear as a window.

Massive pine trees cast their shadows onto an untouched blanket of white snow, fat flakes still falling through their needled leaves. A lone figure sat against a tree trunk, blowing on her shivering, ungloved fingers. Her chestnut hair was a mess, tangled and tousled, pine needles and sticks poking out from the knots.

The world fell out beneath me, dragging my heart to my toes with it.

"Reagan." I crossed to the ice in two long strides, bracing both hands against it. She was alone and unarmed in what looked like Pysgodd, tears streaking down her round face as she hugged her knees to her chest. "Where are the others?"

The others, who I left in charge of my ward. The people who'd been fighting my battles for ages now. My crew, who I couldn't blame for my absence and shortcomings.

No, this was my fault. My responsibility to fix.

"She has chosen to run from her fear, as have you." The creature stroked the image, a snicker rumbling in her chest. She cocked her head, fingernails tapping against the ice in a spine-tingling rhythm. "Tell me, do you remember what you said to her the day before you left?"

The words carved through me like a knife scraping at the frozen ground.

I wasn't the one out of place on the deck, and I wasn't the one that missed.

"I—"

"Cruel words for a young girl." The woman cut me off, silencing my shame before it could tumble from my lips. "And yet you stand here, watching from afar again, unable to take a single shot."

She might as well have fired a bullet straight through my heart. I gaped at her, struggling to find the words, to convey both my regret and resolve—

When another figure crossed into the image, towering over even the larger pines. Scales black as night coated the beast's body, its massive wings blocking out the sunlight.

Fear blotted out any other emotion that might have fought for purchase in my chest, washing me in a limb-leadening, heart-stopping dread.

"A dragon." My teeth chattered as if my whole body had been encapsulated in the ice.

Swirls of smoke filtered from the dragon's fanged snout, its nose larger than my cousin's whole frame as it sniffed her, inching closer—

The image cut out, blackness snatching it away from beneath my fingertips.

"Reagan!" I scraped my claws—not even realizing when they materialized—against the wall. I snapped to the woman, rage melting the jagged edges of my fear. "Bring that back, witch! I need to see her—"

She shrugged, dark eyes unstained by even the tiniest flicker of concern. "I can't bring it back. The moment has already passed. The present is the only truth that exists." She twirled a lock of her midnight hair around her finger, sick glee lighting her grin. "And in this present, you chose to chase your pretty wife instead of protecting your cousin."

Again, impact, as the truth crushed me beneath its weight.

I chose to leave her. To send her off with Griffin rather than help her heal myself. Rather than face my failures and fix my family.

"I can't protect everyone at once." The protest lacked sincerity, the bland excuse as useless as a siren without scales.

"No, you can't protect *anyone*," the false Keira sneered, a set of her own long fangs appearing between her lips. She stepped closer, breathing me in like the dragon ready to fire on my cousin. Ready to gobble my petty excuses whole. "That's the fear that keeps you up, right? Slithering in and out of your brain like a worm, no, like *maggots*, like you—"

"Stop it—"

"No, *you* stop, boy." Her hand jutted out, grasping my face, her thumb and fingers smushing both cheeks together. She forced my gaze her way, the black abyss pulling me deeper. "Stop running from the fear."

My chest squeezed tighter, the remembrance of the same voice uttering a similar lesson, her hair swept up by the wind as she watched the sun shrink beneath the horizon.

I think I've been running for too long. And if I keep running, I'm never going to catch my breath.

I shouldn't have listened to her then. I should have thrown her over my shoulder and swam her back to Ir'de myself, putting Porthladd's stinking form behind us for good. I should've let her aunt and everyone else die so she could be safe, so we could survive—

No, that was the fear again. The part of me that knew I never stood a chance in that fight. Worried that even now, I wasn't enough.

"How?" The lonely syllable slipped through the cracks of my grief.

Fake Keira let go of me, squaring her shoulders as she stood her ground. "Say it. Say it out loud, the consequence of your choice."

"Reagan might die," I gasped, the witch tugging the terrible truth from my traitorous tongue. "Reagan might die, and it is my fault."

"*Your* fault," the creature taunted, voice filling the room like smoke. She leaned closer, her lips an inch from mine. "Like Keira was your fault. Like Reina and Cedric and everyone else, it's your fault, because you ran. Because you keep running away. Because you *failed.*"

If I keep running, I'm never going to catch my breath.

I was a failure. In many senses of the word. But I could also be a fighter. Could use my wife's gifts to be *more* this time. I had to prove myself, otherwise everything she and my family had sacrificed would be in vain.

"No, I'm not running away. For once in my life, I'm running toward the fire. Toward the fight." I stood straighter, staring at the witch over the bridge of my crooked nose. She wore Keira's face, but she was not my wife. Not my salvation. And I would not yield to her commands. "You want me to stand up to my fear? Fine. I'm not afraid of you. And I'm not afraid of failure. Not anymore."

"Then what will you do in this present?" She snapped her fingers, and the ice revealed my cousin once more, paused in an eerily still picture. The little dragon stared at her namesake, not an ounce of fear in her frozen expression despite the worry wrinkling mine. "I could send you to Reagan. You could rescue her from the dragon breathing down her neck, could make sure she finds her way off that mountain. I promise you, you will succeed. It would be a guarantee."

I could save her. I could *do* something. Could be the guardian she needed me to be, could finally right the wrongs I'd left festering between us.

And if I left, it would seal my wife's fate. And the fate of the sirens that waited for me on the other side of this test.

I rooted myself to my cause, to the journey I had to see through.

And to the crew I trusted to pick up the pieces.

"I'm here for my wife. I'm not leaving without her."

The monster pretending to be her smiled again, tongue tracing the tips of her pointed fangs. "So be it."

And then she pushed me through the ice.

Instead of blinding white or endless dark, my eyes opened to lush, vibrant green.

Flowing grass–blown by a phantom breeze–kissed my ankles, gentle caresses beckoning me forward. A small, brick-built cottage simmered a burnt red against the clear blue sky.

And in front of the structure, at a white-painted picnic table, waited the blonde third sister, her black eyes stark against the quaint scene.

"You're late." She leaned her head on her hand, mischief in her smile. "And early."

I stomped up to her, bare feet tickled by the grass, to take the bench opposite. I sat with my arms crossed. "Save me the vagueness. I take it this is the future?"

Past, present, future. Regret, fear, and fantasy.

Their test was more effective than it was evasive.

"Clever boy," she giggled, like birdsong. Here, her presence was far less intimidating, as kind as the steady breeze tickling her locks. "This is *a* future. One possibility of many, depending on how Fate spins her wheel and how you weave your tale."

Another riddle, another test. One last obstacle between me and my wife. But like the future always was, this was far less clear than the past or present.

"Who are you supposed to be?" I pried, meeting her abyss-like stare head-on. "The Danura and Keira lookalikes are obvious, but I don't know you."

"Not yet, silly boy," she teased, but she shifted. Formless black robes melted into a plain red cotton shirt and black leather trousers. Wry smile softened to sweet. Smoky eyes cleared to reveal a perfect, sterling silver. "Does this make it any clearer?"

My heart shuddered in my chest, squeezing like a cobra around the ball of realization.

Blonde hair like gold thread. Warm freckles like constellations. A dimpled smile that spelled trouble. Silver eyes like starshine.

She was us. A perfect blend between each parent.

Our daughter. Our *baby*.

"You're—"

"Your wife has already taken to calling her Rhiannon," the creature finished, the last syllables a symphony.

Rhiannon Mathonwy. The new queen of my heart and soul.

Tears blurred her image before I could fight them back, my smile wide as the sea. "It's fitting. I like it."

"Will you two come inside?" A commanding voice broke the soft tether between us as she stomped through the open door to the cottage. Stray strands of black hair curtained her face, pale cheeks and dark tunic both smeared with flour, but neither softened the sharp look in her silver eyes. "The food is getting cold."

Keira.

A phantom again. A facade, a test.

But to see her, eyes clear and sharp, head held high and stance strong…

Every muscle in my body tensed, ice running down my back and stilling in my core.

The girl—*Rhiannon*—spoke instead, that mischief-laced snake-smirk sliding onto her mouth. "Sorry, Mama, but frankly, I think that helps."

"Smart-mouthed brat." Keira chucked a dirty dish towel at the girl, a wave of giggles echoing through the grassy plain. Then her gaze fixed on me, eyes meeting mine. Like she could see me. Like I was there. "You're going to let your daughter talk to me like that?"

Your daughter.

I sat speechless, watching the illusion of Keira cross her arms, as she had a million times in my memories and dreams. Watching the way her dark hair caught and tamed the wind. As her brow furrowed.

"Ronan?" The name—*my name*—two gentle syllables like a song on her crimson kiss. But worry clouded her stormy eyes. "You all right? You look like you've seen a ghost."

She spoke *to* me.

She could see me.

Keira.

Keira.

Keira.

For once in my Lyr-forsaken life, words failed, lost to time and space. I just sat there, gaping at my wife, the deafening beat of my heart roaring in my ears.

"He's probably just horrified by the poison you're about to feed us," the girl whined, hopping up from the picnic bench and hurrying over to her mother. My wife. *Keira.*

Keira threw back a look that could declaw a dragon, but then let loose a sigh, her form sinking into the doorframe. "Fine. We'll go to Griffin's for supper. Vala will have cooked something edible."

Rhiannon squealed, pressing a quick kiss to Keira's cheek. "Thanks, Mama."

Mama.

Warmth spread from the center of my chest to the tips of my fingers, lighting every nerve from the inside out. Keira's cold expression thawed too, a rare sunlight smile softening her harsh features. She stroked the girl's cheek, accidentally leaving a trail of flour in the wake of her thumb. "Go get dressed, and find your brother, you little devil."

"Fine." She rolled her silver eyes–her mother's eyes–before winking one at me. "You two have fun."

"Brother?" The word broke through, a single sob escaping. "I have a *son?*"

Before she could answer, the image of him swam into my head, real as rain. Lanky and long for his age, with wide blue eyes and his mother's dark hair. A dimple on his right cheek, but not his left, though you never could tell with the scowl he always sported…

Keira chuckled, shuffling over to the bench and plopping down across from me. "Funny, but like it or not, Rhydian gets his attitude from you."

Rhydian.

Yes, I remembered–or at least, *knew,* somehow. Fire and rage, strength and courage. We chose the name before we met him, but he grew into it like a weed. He had his mother's temper and his father's wit, a dangerous combination under the wrong circumstances, but he had a good head on his shoulders, and his siren of an older sister always helped keep him in line…

"Seriously, Ro, are you all right?" Keira broke me from my trance, looking at me in *that* way she did that always felt like peeling up my scales. Still, I relished it, her attention an addiction.

"I'm fine." I cleared my throat, meeting my wife's gaze. Somehow, she was just as radiant as always in this future, not a single wrinkle in her skin. Though I would've loved her just as fiercely even if she were old and gray. I reached out, slipping my fingers into her rough, working hands. They fit together perfectly, just as they always had. "I just missed you."

"Missed me?" An eyebrow rose, but she squeezed my hand in return, thumb rubbing circles of flour across the back of mine. "I've just been inside all afternoon trying to cook those biscuits. If you missed me that much, you could've *helped* me."

I fought the tears that threatened to spill, my heart swelling as my whole body flooded with joy. Gods, this moment–it was so peaceful, so boring and normal and *perfect.*

"I'll cook tomorrow, I promise," I managed, a vow I hoped to one day keep. I'd do a thousand ordinary tasks for her if it meant I could keep her close, if it meant she'd one day be safe and our children would be healthy. Her hand was an anchor, holding me to this moment, and I never wanted to let go of her again. "Gods, you're so beautiful."

Keira rolled her silver eyes, but I savored the tint of red that colored her cheek.

"And you're acting like an idiot. Less than a week on land, and you lose all your salt. What's gotten into you?" She stood and sauntered around the table so she was hovering over me, my Captain ready to usher her next command. Her eyes narrowed, scanning my seated frame for any tells of whatever trickery or witchcraft consumed my tattered brain. Slowly, the left corner of her mouth tilted upward. "If you were drinking with Griffin again, I told you...if you're going to have a good time, you're not allowed to do it without me–"

In one quick motion, her sentence died as my kiss consumed it. Our lips met as if they'd never parted, puzzle pieces sliding together. My arms wrapped around her, desperate and delicate, as her hands found their familiar purchase on my chest.

Her gentle press over my heart signaled pause, and I broke away.

"What was that for?" she breathed, pupils wide, that glorious blush blooming across her face.

I wanted to tell her. How much I missed her, how hard it was without her all these months. Like my limbs had been hacked off, and

I was forced to stumble throughout life without a crutch. Like my heart had been carved out, with nothing to fill the hollow hole left in my chest. I wanted to bury my face in the crux of her shoulder, to cry and rage and let it all out, to hold her close and never let go, to sit in this blissful paradise for forever.

I leaned forward, resting my forehead against hers, our breaths mingling. "Does a man need a reason to kiss his wife?"

Keira smiled, and somehow, that alone made it all right.

"No, he doesn't." Her hand slid to my face, warm palm cupping my cheek and restoring my broken, shattered heart. She leaned in, lips only a hair from mine. "Come here, Mr. Mathonwy–"

She halted, frozen in time, lips parted, eyes shut.

Behind her, Rhiannon–no, the *creature*, clothed again in darkness–fixed her night-black gaze on us. "If you want to stay, you can."

I paused, staring at my frozen wife, savoring the last moments of her touch. I could stay. I could live out this fantasy forever, the blissful embrace of this patch of paradise more than enough to sustain me for eternity. I could choose this happiness, could swim in this delusion until Death came for us all.

"Is it real?"

"Not yet, but it's nice, isn't it?"

It was a test. A trial.

A promise of what was to come if I made it through. Nice was an understatement. This moment was everything I'd ever wanted. I'd sell every scale on my tail for another taste of it.

I couldn't stay. Not now.

But I would come back. I had to come back.

"How do I get here on my own?" My voice was stronger than it had been in months, fortified in the certainty of my new quest.

I'd save my wife, and one day, years from now, I'd show her this moment. I'd find this grassy knoll, this paradise to return to in between sails, and we'd raise our family together.

"I can't tell you that." The creature clicked her tongue, shaking her head as she stepped forward. As she came closer, Keira disappeared, the vision vanishing around us. Grass became ice beneath my feet, the cabin fading into white nothingness. My arms ached with my wife's absence, soul plummeting to the pits once more.

But a new kernel of hope rooted itself in the cracked, empty spaces of my soul, filling in the gaps and promising the bud of a new dream. "What do I do next?"

The blonde witch shrugged. "You just have to choose which path you're going to follow. But I will promise you–this future is out there. It's unlikely, but possible."

Possible.

That's all I needed. For Rhiannon and Rhydian, for Keira...

For me.

My throat threatened to close around the emotion swelling to the surface, but I croaked out my gratitude, the gate giving me more than it took after all. "Thank you for showing me."

"Don't thank me yet, *Manawydan*," her warning rippled through me with that ancient, preternatural power. "The real trial has only just begun."

And again, I fell.

Through the bottom of the world.

Through the twisting, winding void.

All the way through to the other side to the gates of hell.

To the Otherworld.

To save my wife.

24

Flights and Falling

GRIFFIN

We caught up with Reagan halfway down the second mountain, *cuddling* with Awyr against some toppled pines. The girl nestled against his long neck as the beast purred, eyes shut, the deep sound rumbling the ground around us. Gentle tendrils of steam rose from his nostrils, melting the snow around them.

"Sorry I flew off the handle." She shrugged, fighting the smile tugging at the corner of her mouth.

"It was worth the look on Gwynn's face." I ran a tired hand over my stubbled jaw, slumping against Rhett to my left. My partner wrapped an arm around my shoulders, laughter shaking his frame.

"Yeah, I'd break both ankles just to see it again," Saeth snickered from where she hung on Drystan's back, arms twined tightly around his neck. Her ankle looked fine thanks to Nef's healing, but I wouldn't dare come between her and whatever prey she'd marked next. She scrunched her face up, mocking the hunter god's deep scowl. "*If you don't find her, I will.* What an ass."

Gods above and below, we were such lucky idiots. How we'd survived was a mystery and a miracle.

Then again, with night closing in around us, there was still plenty of time for us to eat shit or die.

Vian walked straight up to the cozy creature, thick snowfall crunching beneath his boots. His dark eyes lit with wonder as he stroked the beast's snout as if he were no larger than a pup. "What now, Captain?"

The title still grated beneath my skin, a deep itch akin to the more uncomfortable venereal diseases I vaguely knew of. But relief washed over me as I took in our crew, whole and healthy enough, ready to ride onto the next adventure.

"We have a dragon to return, and then we camp in the village overnight." My voice felt stronger than it had in weeks. Months, maybe. "Tomorrow, we set sail for the south. Either we find the rest of the godly items and give ourselves a better chance, or we at least grab more supplies to ferry back here."

A chance; that was what we'd been given. Not a god to fight our battles for us as we'd hoped, but a chance to manage them ourselves. A chance to protect the Deyrnas enough to make it out alive, to bring Locasta down without any deities.

I'd taken greater bets with worse odds.

Still, Reagan pouted, the expression almost enough to remind me how young the little dragon really was.

Almost.

"Do we have to give Awyr back?" Her lower lip wobbled in that practiced puppy-dog look as she scratched one of the giant beast's scales. "I think he likes me."

Quickly, Vian jumped to her defense, nodding so hard his dark hair fell into his eyes. "The wind says we can keep him."

I crossed my arms, trying to mimic that look Keira gave the brats that could somehow leash even their unruly tongues. "No, the wind doesn't, you're not pulling that shit on me. *The wind* was about to rip my dick off and let Gwynn mount it like a trophy on his wall."

I shuddered at the thought of Gwynn's fury, of the sharp kit of medical instruments Nef displayed that would make his work all too easy. Not that he needed tools to…well, to take mine.

"Don't worry, we can't have you losing my favorite part," Rhett mumbled low in my ear, breath caressing the shell, hopefully deep enough none of the kids could hear it.

I shuddered again, this time not with fear or cold.

Lyr's massive member, only Rhett Mathonwy could get me excited in the middle of a frozen shithole with a dragon breathing down my front and two gods hunting my ass.

"Let's put it to a vote," Reagan announced, her piercing tone enough to sober me completely. Her words were well-placed blows, each sharper than the last. "Keira always used to let us vote."

The mention of my cousin sliced through the heady relief buzzing through me. I sized up Reagan once more, the true monster in this clearing. As always, she knew exactly which heartstrings to manipulate and tug, which bruises to flick and prod with her little dagger.

I pulled away from Rhett, rising up to my full height. This wasn't the first time Reagan and I had sparred, and I wasn't foolish enough to go easy on her. "Keira isn't here, as you so often like to remind us."

Reagan's eyes flared with fire. But it was Rhett—*Rhett*—who shrugged, staring at the dragon like it was a stray cat they were begging us to keep. "I vote the dragon stays."

My head whipped to my partner faster than a northern wind, outrage rising up my gullet like a tidal wave. "What?"

Rhett wore a frown—one that spelled out a half-assed apology—but continued, his silver eye narrowed as if it saw beyond the present threat. "One of two things happens: the beast either helps us protect ourselves and the Deyrnas, or it baits those lazy fuckers to come get him, and maybe help us while they're at it."

Tarran—thank Lyr for that little welp—threw his hands in the air. He'd been quiet for most of our interaction with the gods, but he had hit his limit. "Or three, it eats us and burns down our ship!"

"Since when is Tarran the only one with sense?" I muttered, stepping away from Rhett and closer to the anxious redhead. A grateful, proud smile swelled on the twerp's face, but the dragon enthusiasts were content to deflate his ego.

"Look at this guy, we wouldn't hurt a fly," Vian scoffed, and to emphasize his point, he climbed Awyr's scales like they were the ship's rigging. Lithe limbs carrying him up the smooth surface, he hauled himself to the top, standing between the two large horns on Awyr's head—horns that were nearly half his body size. "I vote we keep him."

"Me too." Saeth shrugged, sizing up the wind whisperer like this was the first time she was seeing him.

Maybe it was. After all he'd hidden about his lineage, perhaps there was more up the sprite's sleeve.

Still didn't stop me from wanting to strangle them both.

Drystan cleared his throat, strong chin held high. "Rhett has a point, so me three."

The fact Drystan was agreeing with Rhett almost had me doing cartwheels, but I shoved down the instinct, instead nailing myself to the last of my resolve. "This isn't up for a vote."

"Too bad, the yeas have it," Reagan yelled over me, sticking her hands to her hips in her signature victory pose. "Awyr is officially a part of the Rydha's Rebellion."

I opened my mouth to protest, to override this foolishness…then shut it. I had a bad habit of walking into fights I couldn't win, but I knew I'd met my match. I dragged a hand through my hair, freeing the tangles in it like the knots still in my gut. Resistance would get me nowhere. Trouble was the only master I bowed to, and she stood before me, chestnut eyes alight with certainty. I plastered on a tired smile. "Is that what we're called?"

"Yup." Reagan patted Awyr's neck, stirring the beast, his gold eyes winking open. Without further resistance, she climbed up his side, settling herself between two proud spikes along his spine. "Anyway, hop on, everyone. Grab a spikey thingy and hang on tight."

Vian slid down from the crown of the dragon's head and straddled his back just behind Reagan, claiming the prime spot for himself. The others hobbled up, Rhett giving Saeth a boost and tucking himself behind her for support, Drystan awkwardly throwing himself behind the pair–careful not to touch Rhett as he held tight to a spike.

Only Tarran and I still stood in the snow, Awyr's gold eyes blinking at us.

"We are *not* getting on that thing." Tarran's face blanched. His expression matched how I felt, my stomach already stirring like I'd had a few too many sips of spirits. Still, I squared myself off and marched over the snow to the waiting dragon, doing my damndest not to flinch at the smooth texture of his scales beneath my palm.

"This beats walking to the village. It's almost night," I told Tarran–and myself–as Drystan hoisted me up. I adjusted on Awyr's back, the wide spread of my legs uncomfortable. I gripped the spike in front of me tightly, ready to lift off.

Tarran sighed, then trudged up to the beast, swinging himself on without further protest.

And then, with a kick of Reagan's heels, the dragon stood. The girl turned and offered one last vicious smile, her teeth gleaming in the fading sunlight. "Hang on."

And then we *flew*.

Flying made me sick.

I was a sailor that could weather the roughest seas, my legs and gut infallible in even the cruelest tempests. But after the first two minutes on Awyr's back, my nuts and my stomach had been fighting for the prime spot in my throat.

Never mind the fact we were atop a dragon, with no safety gear or harnesses to speak of. But the *heights*, the massive mountains and pines reduced to small, swirling white masses beneath us. The weightlessness, the rolling and diving and bucking...

Just thinking about it had me painting the ceramic toilet in Mama's guest-cabin with fresh puke. It had only been a half-hour journey, but it was the longest of my whole life.

The heavy wooden door to the plain washroom banged open, and I could rutting smell the smirk on Rhett's face before he even spoke. "Hey, *Captain*, feeling any better?"

I shot him a dirty look as I flushed the mark of my shame down the drain. Grabbing my discarded tunic from the floor, I slumped against the birch wall, desperate for the support. "Don't call me that, please."

My usually abounding patience had been purged with the rest of my gut. I'd been in here for the last hour, forgoing dinner in the main cabin with the rest of the crew, Mama, and Councilwoman Agatha Amos. Normally, that would've been everything I needed to recover from today's encounters: a hot, homemade meal from Mama, some of Agatha's better booze, and a laugh or two to dull the ache in my chest.

Not today. Not with gods and fucking *dragons* to contend with. The nausea and worry lingered longer than any scar I'd ever earned, the ache bone-deep.

But Rhett just crossed his arms, either oblivious to my tattered nerves or purposefully tugging at their frayed edges, a devilish smirk gracing his handsome face. "Do you prefer lover? Swordsinger? Sexgod?" He stepped closer, brushing a strand of my wind-matted hair from my face, his gaze trailing down my bare torso. "*Sir?*"

Normally, that word alone would've poked the beast and I'd have Rhett bent over the nearest surface, his pretty face flushed, daring him to utter the title again. But even my finest, most vital parts had been shaken beyond the point of performance today. I brushed past Rhett, unwilling to watch the disappointment strike, stumbling into the small adjacent bedroom we were meant to share tonight. "Lyr's piss-hole, I can't believe I'm saying this, but I'm not in the mood."

A rare, near impossible occurrence. We had a whole cabin to ourselves, something I'd never had in my whole life. Despite the cramped quarters, a plush mattress occupied the center of the space, covered in fur-lined blankets that could fight off even the deepest Pysgoddian chill. A fire crackled and popped in the hearth across, kissing the dry air with balmy warmth, made better yet by the two high-backed chairs and small table to the side of it, adorned with a tumbler of amber liquid that would chase away any lingering cold the room could not weather-proof.

Any other night, I would've relished the privacy, the intimacy. Would've seen how loud I could make my partner squeal and moan without anyone hearing, his howling drowned out by the wolves that prowled the outskirts of the small, forest-laid village.

Not tonight. No, I could feel that *itch* beneath my skin, the trembling in my fingers I couldn't steady. Whether it was the flight back or the adrenaline crash or the sight of Saeth's blood on the ground...

The nightmares would come for my throat tonight.

I plopped onto the soft mattress, burying my face in a feathered pillow that somehow smelled like lavender. The blankets tickled my bare chest. At least I'd be comfortable when I awoke swallowing a scream.

"I'm sorry." Rhett's voice trailed behind me until his weight shifted the bed. An unassuming, unpressured hand stroked my spine, like he was stitching me back together. "I should've known how hard today was for you. I didn't mean to make light of it. I just thought you could use a release."

The thoughtfulness and tenderness in his voice stirred something else in my dragon-tossed stomach, a gratefulness that rose up faster and hotter than the sick, soothing the raw lining of my throat.

I lifted my face from the pillow to stare at the saint before me. Sitting carefully on the edge–not too close, giving me room to breathe–his blond hair tinted pure gold in the firelight, cold silver-and-blue gaze warmed like heated metal.

Warm enough to melt my armor down. I smiled despite myself, my mood shifting like the tide. "We are so royally stupid."

A quiet laugh as Rhett brushed his knuckles across my cheek. "Aye, we are. But the dragon is an asset. We'll get used to it."

I rolled to my side, propping my head up on my hand to face him better. Rhett exhaled, sinking into the bed and stretching his long legs. He slid one of the larger fur blankets up, covering both of our lower halves with it.

Silence had never been my friend. I'd avoided it like the plague, filling the gaps in conversations with my snark since I was old enough to babble words. All my life, silence was an invisible, sharp dagger, ready to carve unseen scars into flesh. A space where harsh truths screamed in a language of their own.

Fool. Whore. Fuck-up.

Your fault.

My fault.

But with Rhett, silence was a blanket, warm and soft as the furs that covered our toes. I didn't need to be the court jester with him, always armed with a sharp joke or a quick trick. I could just breathe it in, letting the silence fill the ache in my lungs, let it clear my head and steady my heartbeat.

Breathe in. Breathe out. Repeat.

Finally, when the air stopped tasting like vomit and the smell of the burning wood had done its work uncoiling the pit in my stomach, I reached for Rhett's hand. Fingers fit together, our hands rested between us on the mattress. "The gods are going to come for us, and it'll be my ass on the line."

My ass.

My fault.

"Don't worry, I'll protect you." Rhett's voice dipped low, a darkness clouding his bright gaze, but he forced a smile. Then, the shadows shifted, danger and unrest softening into a darkness I knew well–desire. His smile turned to seduction. "Your spectacular ass is mine."

Maybe it was the offer of protection, so true and wholesome from my knight in shining armor's lips, that blazing devotion enough to get any man drunk on it. Or maybe it was the way his eyes lingered on my rear, the pure possession in the word *mine* that gave me a heady buzz…

But my stomach flipped twice. Not in the same unpleasant way I'd felt earlier.

A silly, girlish laugh fizzled from my lips. Flirting and fucking were both art forms I'd mastered by my late teens, and yet Rhett Mathonwy still managed to make me giddy as a virgin. "You're insatiable, and that's coming from me."

He let go of my hand to trail a gentle touch up the length of my arm, absentminded and lazy. I could *smell* his ego inflating as gooseflesh rippled in the wake of his touch, his smirk deepening. "You've rubbed off."

Two could play this game.

And surprisingly enough, I wanted to play. Wanted to slip back into the role of Swordsinger and spar with my partner, my friend. Wanted to put the gods and monsters far behind me and instead focus on the brawny blond inching his way further onto the bed.

Wanting was weakness.

But hell, I knew I was weak. For this man, I was feeble as a fucking flower in a rainstorm.

"Stop talking about rubbing," I grumbled, but didn't try to disguise the edge of amusement from my tone. "You're making it hard to stay grumpy."

"Ah, my master plan is working then." Rhett waggled his eyebrows as he scooted closer, and the game was over and done, a different playfulness roping us both in. Another genuine laugh rumbled from my chest as he forced a wink. "Sorry if it's rubbing you the wrong way…I'd be happy to rub you the *right* way."

"That one was too punny, even for me." I scrunched my nose at him, both of us shaking the bed with our laughter.

We laughed for a few long moments, trying to catch our breaths as the ridiculousness of the day rolled off us in waves. Then, when we'd finally grabbed hold of ourselves, all it took was a single look in the others' direction, and we'd be cackling again, a frenzied cycle until our sides were sore and our breathing ragged.

Finally, as the laughter died, that same silence settled—gentle. Somehow, Rhett had ended up on his back, my head in the crook of his arm, my cheek pressed to his chest.

Built like a mountain, I rarely felt small. And whenever I did—it was more often than not an insignificant kind of small, the one that makes a man feel like a little welp of a boy again.

But hearing Rhett's heartbeat, hearing the soft sigh of each inhale and exhale, the smallness and silence felt friendly. A cozy, comfortable small.

Safe.

"Are you excited for Ir'de?" Rhett muttered into my hair after a long stretch of that intimately safe silence. His fingers fiddled with mine, our matching callouses brushing against each other. "I know we have to find some secret trove and steal from another god, but it *is* your favorite island."

At that, I pushed up onto my elbows to look at him. Again, it was like my first time seeing him—another side of him revealing itself and managing to surprise me. "How did you know it was my favorite?"

A snort. "Are you kidding? It was practically made for you." Rhett toyed with my hair again, twirling a strand of red between his fingers like it was made from the same Ir'desian silk he envisioned. "The gambling, the brothels, the city and people and the *life*. It fits."

I stilled, holding my breath. This was always the part where I ran. When that silver eye of his caught a glimpse behind the masks and armor, when he saw the jester without his makeup, truly saw *me*...I always found a way to slip his grasp, to recover and protect and deflect before he could find the many flaws hiding beneath the surface.

The instinct tensed through me again, the part of me that was a fighter first ready to duck and cover.

But instead, I took a breath. In and out.

Rhett had given me space and silence and softness. Tenderness and understanding. And in return, I'd been dodging him since that night on the *Ceffyl* when things got a little too vulnerable. When I let him see me at my worst.

Rhett *saw me*. He saw me and didn't run or hide or spit in my face. And I would let him look his fill if that's what he wanted.

All of you. I love you, and I'm here for you when you're ready to let me in.

I'd been an asshole not to repay him in kind, even if it was at my own expense. I inched closer, my fingertips brushing the soft fabric of his tunic. "I dunno, I haven't felt the need to wander into a brothel in a long while."

Rhett perked up, hearing the unspoken subtext in my words.

I haven't wanted anyone but you.

Another smile broke across his face, this one full of something I still didn't have the stones to name. "You know, as long as I'm included, I wouldn't mind if you did."

Again, surprise lifted my brows, each new revelation like trading blows. After his history with Maddox, I'd assumed Rhett the jealous type. Lyr's ass, even looking at Drystan or Nelle for a second too long still earned me the bad kind of tongue-lashing. But there was no lie in Rhett's expression. No nose scrunches or fluttering eyelashes. He would be open to explore and to taste what life had to offer, as long as he was with me.

Another punch that stole my breath.

"You're full of surprises, ya know that? You're the one built for Ir'de. Every day, there is something new and exciting to uncover about you, Rhett Mathonwy."

He watched me carefully, delight in his sparkling gaze, but hesitation edged his voice. Like I was a sleeping babe he didn't want to wake, or a feral dog he was feeding from his hand. Like he didn't want to startle me or send me running again. "Maybe–maybe when it's all over, when *this*," he waved his hand vaguely, "is just a bad memory we laugh about…maybe we settle in Aechnad City. Buy a small flat right by the spice corridor. I've got some savings."

For a traitorous second, I let myself picture it. The scents and sounds of the bustling spice corridor pouring in from an open window in our little, finely-decorated apartment, the gauzy curtains swaying with a salt-aired breeze. Over the noise of the market, we could still hear gulls cawing from the docks in the distance, the ocean just a short walk away. We'd spend the morning in bed, too lazy or lustful to do anything but worship each other, but in the afternoon, we'd explore, tasting whatever new delicacy the land of a thousand silks and spices offered. Then at night, when the colorful paper lanterns were lit, when the city bathed in crimson lowlight…we'd drink from every sinful cup we could find, watching the dancers and entertainers in our favorite taverns work their magic, maybe even participating in a few private performances…

"I want that," I whispered, locking eyes with him. "So badly, I want that. But—"

But all I could see before me was the path of blood and despair we'd chosen. The war we fought from all sides, the hunger and misery we beat back every day. The gods ready to ruin us for simply surviving. The feral dragons ready to devour us the second we stumbled into their horde.

"But you don't let yourself want things to avoid disappointment," Rhett finished for me. Still, his gaze didn't waver, that devotee's faith fortifying him even in the weakest moments. "I know. But even if you won't get your hopes up, I will. For both of us."

Something in me snapped. The chains I had on the cage that held my heart, perhaps. They'd been rusted and ruined for a while now, and finally, they gave under the tender weight of his words.

All of you. I love you, and I'm here for you when you're ready to let me in.

Tension scented the air, as ripe and fragrant as the spice corridor. Not the gut-clenching, heart-stopping tension I'd felt in droves all day. No, the alluring, core-tingling tension of a moment that inspired and sated.

I didn't speak, not wanting to shatter that precious silence. Not wanting to spoil any second of his moment with my fat mouth, of what was happening in the warm embrace of this bed.

I loved Rhett Mathonwy.

I fucking loved every inch of him, from the scar that decorated his princely face to the very tip of his crooked little toe.

I loved his tenacious heart, his unshakeable certainty and faith in a world that had done nothing but scorn him. His patience, his kindness, for a man that should've been his enemy. His voracious, hungry appetite for life. His inability to lie without scrunching his nose, his pure talent for grumpiness. The masks he showed the world; the cold, grumbling, tired version of himself; and the adventurous, hopeful parts he saved just for us. For *me*.

I loved him.

So I kissed him, rising up in a swift motion to greet his lips. There was nothing tender or soft about the kiss. No, there was nothing sweet about me that I could offer. All I had was my grit and drive, my rough, brutal edges. And yet, he accepted every uncut, unrefined piece of me like it was a precious gem.

My ferocious, claiming kiss devoured his mouth, and Rhett matched my tempo, as always, rising to the occasion. Meeting my expectations, and then far exceeding them.

He broke the contact first, pressing his forehead to mine to give our hungry lips necessary distance. A slow, teasing smirk twisted his swollen mouth. "I thought you weren't in the mood."

Two could play this game. And Rhett was the only person I ever wanted to play with.

I loved him.

"Moods change." I fisted my hand in the mane of silken hair, tugging his head back to expose the strong column of his neck. A small gasp escaped his mouth, a pretty blush rogueing his cheeks. "Kiss me."

A small, breathy moan. "Yes *sir*."

He moved to comply with my command, but I held him in place with a gentle tug at his hair.

"You have a wicked mouth." Lyr below, this man would be the end of me. The familiar beast I favored snapped and snarled in my center, ready to consume him whole...

But I wanted this time to be different. Not just base needs and blistering lust. Not just desire and distraction, charged thunder and lightning as we smashed together like warring storm clouds, but...

I moved first, bringing my lips to his with the gentleness of the sweetest summer wind. They brushed together, barely touching, a whisper of a kiss that stirred the wanting deeper. Rhett matched my pace, and I released my grip in his hair, instead trailing my fingers softly along his soft tunic.

I didn't want to fuck him. Not tonight.

Lyr end me, tonight I wanted to make love.

"Please," I murmured in between feather-soft kisses, and Rhett went utterly still. The 'P' word was as foreign on my tongue as the 'L' word I barely managed to hold back. Our foreheads pressed together, the sacred space between us buzzing with a different sort of energy.

The charge of that unspoken *thing*, so strong it chattered my teeth. "Rhett, I–"

He cut me off with another kiss, his hand cupping my face as he swallowed the words I didn't know how to say. Like he knew them all the same.

The kiss deepened, but not in our feral, frenzied way. Rhett kissed me like he wanted to explore, to know every part of me, to lay me bare and learn my every secret. I let him, lowering the last pieces of my armor.

A shift, and he was on top of me, pressing me back into the bed. The weight of him was a welcome pressure, his legs settling around mine, his arms braced above my shoulders as his kisses moved from my mouth to my jaw, my neck.

Lyr below and Nef above, *this man.*

I'd never surrendered like this to anyone. Never had my back to the wall without an exit, never just let myself submit and let go. But as each caress of his mouth claimed me, tingles erupting from every point of contact, I allowed myself the pleasure of losing. I sank further into the mattress, into each of Rhett's tantalizing ministrations across my body.

He kissed down my chest, sinking lower, careening toward the aching need below–

I halted him, fingers gently pressing into his arms. His gaze shot to mine–pupils wide with desire to match the impressive hard-on outlined in his trousers. But he stopped, blinking it away, concern icing his expression instead. "Everything all right? Did I do something wrong?"

"No, as far as I'm concerned, you're doing things very, *very* right," I chuckled, brushing his hair back from where it dangled over my chest. "But–"

"But what?" His brow furrowed as he sat back on his heels, hovering above my thighs. Fuck, if I was a painter, I'd capture that pose in every color I could name. But I hated the distance, a chill running through me with his absence despite the delicious fire heating the room. I sat up, bringing our faces closer once more. Still not close enough. Not to satisfy the deep emptiness I felt without him.

"You first this time." I tugged up the hem of his tunic, splaying my hand across the hard abdomen beneath. Gods, he was so fucking beautiful, carved from something finer that any statue in Orwellin. I drank him in through heavy lids, ready to let him have me in ways I'd never let anyone else. "I want you first."

Rhett stilled again, hearing the hidden meaning in my words. His hoarse voice was the only indication of his want, his need. "Are you sure?"

I nodded once, and that was all that was left.

Rhett was more than gentle as he slipped my pants off and removed his own attire; he was reverent. His mouth whispered prayers across my body as he readied me, each kiss and lick and caress more heavenly than the last. His hands prayed over me, inside me, each touch and intrusion delivered with such care, he had me moaning a string of vile curses that would've made any other holy man blush.

And when he slipped his stunning cock inside me—so carefully, pressing my legs up to my chest—I nearly saw stars. Not from the slight pain, the pressure and stretching that was uncomfortable at most. But from the sheer pleasure of being held by him, filled by him...

Loved by him.

If loving was lethal, I'd gladly die by Rhett's hand. Or more accurately, his impressive member.

And when he moved; *gods.*

I'd always loved sex, and had plenty of talented partners that had me howling for more. But nothing, *nothing* compared to this feeling. The tightening, rising wave of pleasure that had my favorite part twitching against my stomach with each thrust and deep grunt from him. His steady, even pace pushed me farther, closer, *higher.* My fingers desperate for something to latch onto, to tether me to this earth, I fisted his hair again, tying myself further to him. Moans tumbled out of me with abandon as I surrendered myself fully, to the hot, heady rapture that rose and rose and rose...

I spilled all over myself first, a cry erupting from the depths of my fucking soul, faster than I'd ever admit to anyone. Rhett's eyes darkened at the sight, and with a few more powerful, soul-rocking thrusts, he followed me over the edge with a roar.

Rhett collapsed on top of me, the Otherworldly weight of him so delightful I didn't care about the mess between us or any ruined sheets. I held him, arms and legs caging him to me lazily, my head still spinning with ecstasy.

Mine. He was mine.

And gods, I was entirely his.

After our breathing settled and smoke cleared from our heads, Rhett rolled off me, padding to the bathroom on quick feet. My stomach dropped to my toes and I sat up, a small, abandoned part of me rising to the surface—

Fool. Whore. Fuck-up.

Your fault.

My fault.

But he returned in the doorway a moment later, a damp washcloth in one hand and a glass of water in the other. He handed me both, a pretty blush creeping over his cheeks. "Here you go. Staying hydrated helps with any discomfort after—"

His eyes traced every inch of my naked, messed form with that same worshiping stare. But this time, I did not balk. I didn't shrink back within myself, behind the armor I'd made out of every hurt and failure I'd ever carried. This time, I sat there unguarded, staring back at him with the same veneration I didn't know I was capable of.

I cleared my throat, setting the washcloth and water—his simple gifts of care and adoration—on the bedside table. I looked into his eyes—my favorite shade of blue and silver, and grinned. "I love you."

The smile that broke across his face could summon sunshine even in the depths of hell. It chased away the dark shadows of the fear and frustration that followed us back from the mountain. His voice shook, but his hands were steady as they clasped mine. "I love you too."

Gods and monsters and dragons be damned, there was nothing more powerful in this entire world than that.

We cleaned up in that same comfortable silence, letting it wrap around us, preserving this moment of peace. Of love. Then we tucked ourselves beneath the soft furs, our shield against the world, Rhett's chest settled against my back, his arm around my waist.

And for the first time in ages, I slept like a baby.

25

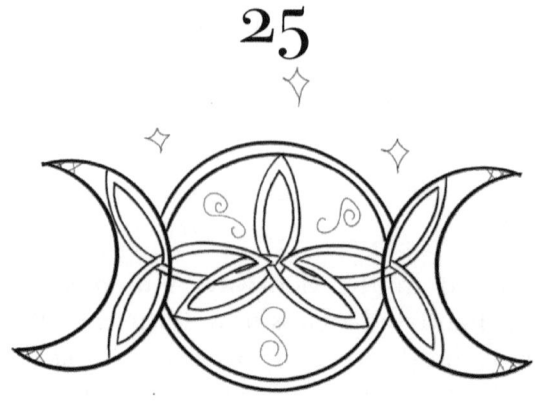

Floods and Farewells

KEIRA

I burned and burned and burned, hotter and hotter, nothing stopping me. No ice could withstand my heat, a star stolen from the sky now blazing beneath the ground. A sun, ready to suck everything into its heat and light.

Destruction and despair.

Rage and ruination.

Fate both furious and victorious.

"Keira, stop it!" A single voice cut through the roaring in my ears, past the monster I'd unleashed and piercing the heart of the little girl inside. A little girl trapped within the goddess's claws and teeth. A girl that just wanted to go home.

Even beyond the veil, through the burning, I was obedient to that voice.

Papa.

I spun, my heat flickering and sputtering out as it sucked itself back inside my fingers. The whirlwind still raged in my chest—storm and star and sea, heat and hatred and chaos all in one. All in *me*. But my hands stopped glowing, the power receding in my veins, knotting again into a deep pit buried in my heart.

Papa splashed through the scalding pool—once a great wall of ice, now a puddle to my waist—hissing as he waded deeper into the near-boiling bath.

No Branwen left behind. Not ever.

"No, what are you doing?" I snapped back to my senses, panic rising with my words. "Get out, it's not safe!"

My father did not slow. His sunset eyes stayed fixed on me, his tailored waistcoat soaked as he trudged further, closer.

"Enough, Keira girl." His hands gripped my shoulders, a lifeline in a hurricane. The touch anchored me back to my body, back to myself. To the hundreds of moments on the *Ceffyl* in this same stance, the same command gentle on my father's lips. Back to time, to space. To the reality of where and who I was. To Keira Branwen.

Keira girl.

"I—" Oh gods, what had I done?

The mirror was gone, Death's favorite room flooded with the debris—and above us, the whole estate *groaned.*

Because I'd just taken out half of its foundation.

Papa squeezed my frame, diverting my attention back to him again. He stared at me long and hard, a true Captain calculating his next move. A father figuring out how best to protect his child. Then, a long-held sigh. "We should've done this from the start. Time to break ye out."

Out of hell. Out of Arawn's reach.

"Papa, we can't. There is no—"

"We *always* find a way." He silenced me with an efficient slice of his words, killing any protest I might have conjured. The last of my rage died out, leaving only the emptiness behind. The crushing weight of my failure. The terrifying scope of that killing power slumbering again in my pit.

My skin suddenly felt too tight, the air in the room burning and blazing, just like the fire, as I sucked and heaved in and out. I was so stupid, so worthless, a weapon without a seasoned wielder...

"I'm sorry. I'm so sorry. I should've believed you all, I should've—"

"Should've and could've are poisonous words, Keira girl. They'll eat ye alive if ye keep drinking them down." Papa softened, pulling me to him. Strong arms wrapped around me. Even though I was almost his height, now, even though I had just unleashed a star inside a basement, I still felt small. Just a little girl, safe in her papa's arms. He kissed my cheek, stubble scratching at the skin. "Look forward, girl. It's the only direction you can go."

Forward and up. Through Arawn's gates and out into the world beyond.

To the Deyrnas, where my daughter would have friends and loved ones to help care for her.

Where my people still suffered, seduced and then screwed over by the same Dark God that had ensnared me.

We are going to build our paradise on the bones of Danura's precious Deyrnas.

"I'm going to ruin him." The words sizzled on my tongue with that burning starlight, surging up again, ready to melt down every last inch of Arawn's frozen domain…

"*Forget* him. Focus on ye and yer daughter." Papa's gaze darkened, sunset finally dipping beneath the horizon. I nodded, slamming the fire back down my throat and sliding the heavy lid over it. Later, I'd let my power loose on him. But now, I had other things to think about. A gate to somehow cross. A crew to reconnect with. A daughter to protect.

Papa's grip tightened on my shoulders, lips pressed to a thin line. He spread his feet slightly—a ready stance I knew all too well. But he gnawed the inside of his cheek—a rare sign of nervousness from the infallible Captain Cedric. "Now, this is going to feel awful. Close yer eyes and hold yer breath."

As always, I obeyed, shutting my eyes tightly—

Then the world faded away, and we were falling.

No, not falling—twisting, lurching. Inside became out and up became down as we spun, like debris lost in the eye of a hurricane—

Until we stopped, hitting the ground with a sharp impact.

My stomach emptied itself on the ice—

Ice. Vast, endless ice.

I spun—too fast, nearly vomiting again—to see the estate, miles and miles behind us, a small black blip on the horizon.

"I'm glad that worked." My father shrugged, wet clothes dripping to the cold ground. Papa had somehow misted us out of Arawn's keep. All that surrounded us was bright, white ice, stretching for eternity in every direction. The deep chill of the Otherworld settled into my bones. The soaked, skimpy dress clung tightly to my skin, frost already forming on the trim.

The Otherworld was not the paradise of legends, nor was it the prison of Death's estate. It was nothing. It was frozen, ferocious nothing, ready to scrape away and devour the flesh from my skeleton with each gust of sharp, icy wind.

Another spurt of black mist, and panic surged back up like bile—

Until friendly faces emerged from the darkness.

Finna's crimson mane was like blood against the white background, her black frock a stark shadow. Next to her, Reina's expression was painted with pure concern as she narrowed her eyes at my flimsy attire, my bare feet and chattering teeth. A sharp exhale passed through her clenched jaw, and she materialized a pile of fabric from thin air. "Here, put these on."

I didn't protest as I fluffed out a pair of fur-lined tan trousers and a long-sleeved white tunic that was thick enough to fight back the cold. I peeled off my sodden dress—Papa turning away for some shred of privacy—and shuffled into the warm garb, hopping between my feet to fight off the frostbite already nipping at my toes.

"These too." Finna rolled her eyes and tore the stiff black boots from her own feet, chucking them at me. I caught them with fumbling, cold fingers, a protest rising like the tide in my chest, when she silenced me with another jade glare. "Don't worry, I'm already dead. I don't think I can get frostbite."

"Thank you," I muttered, slipping into the warmth. They were a smidge tight, but they'd do. I sucked in a deep breath of the chilled air, letting it steady me, the ice coating my lugs, my veins, my soul. I could be just as sharp and frozen as this damned place, and I would use every frostbitten part of my soul to crawl out of hell.

Straightening my spine, I stared at my family. Papa and Reina and Finna. My saviors in the world beyond and this one. They'd always been there to challenge and support me, to push me and then prop me up. To test my limits and then teach me how to move past them.

I wouldn't fail them again.

Forward and up.

I fought the quiver in my voice. "You should all go back inside. I have to go."

Reina snorted—so different from her normal poise and politeness. "Not a chance, girlie. We'll see ye to the gate, not a step before."

Heat lit my eyes as tears formed, but my 'thank yous' died in my mouth before they could take shape, as mist once again swirled and shuddered before us.

Three tall figures emerged, black uniforms covered in a fine layer of gray dust—

No, not dust. *Ash.*

Roland, Owen, and Lochlan were covered from head to toe in ash.

"Sorry it took us a minute, we were making sure the Dark God was distracted." Lochlan ran a hand through his curls, sending a plume of that powdery substance into the wind.

"Ye did an excellent job in the basement." Roland winked at me, brushing off the evidence from his waistcoat, despite the dark gray smudges on his leathered face. "So we thought some fire in the rose gardens might add to the atmosphere."

My stomach sank to my thawing toes. I spun on my heel, squinting in the distance, focusing on the palace beyond.

Clouds hovered above, dark and ominous, marring the view of the palace jutting up from the ice—

Not clouds. Smoke.

Fire.

The Otherworld was burning.

"What did you *do?*"

Owen shrugged, a sly smirk slinking onto his normally honest face. "Honestly, I just thought to myself, 'What would Griffin do?'" His grin matched his younger brother's mischief, strands of his copper hair falling out of his neat ponytail as if Griffin himself had mussed them. "I think it's a cozy touch."

True dread settled like stone in my stomach, fear freezing my limbs just as efficiently as the cold.

As if he stood behind me, the Dark God's voice rippled through my skull, dark and dangerous as the abyss.

Keep struggling, and I'll snuff out your families' souls like I did Yorath's.

No, there was no going back for any of us.

"He'll kill you." Fresh tears stung my eyes, not born of relief as they had been for a moment before. This time, my vision blurred and burned with horror, with the irrevocable shift of fate that carried like smoke in the wind. My hands shook, not from the cold. "He'll know it was you."

The crew before me did not so much as blink. Papa's lips just curved upward, humor dancing in his amber gaze. "Death must be a grand adventure. No one comes back."

No. *No.*

Not again.

My father's bloody corpse staining the deck of Ronan's ship, Ronan's hands the same crimson, the knife ripped from my father's neck...

Another decaying body splayed before me. Bloated, pale, fish-eaten. Shark's teeth razor sharp in his mouth. Chestnut hair tangled as sailor's knots.

"We've made our peace." Finna's smile was bright and warm as her hair, like the fire burning steadily behind us. Owen and Reina both nodded, Lochlan and Roland wearing twin grins. My cousin pressed a quick kiss to my cheek, sharp jade eyes softening to grassy green. "Go find yours."

Red hair against stone streets, blood the same color. A body disintegrating to ash as the light burned, my light. Chestnut eyes, lifeless as the bloodstained deck of the ship. Screaming that pierced the night. Mama, no. Mama, please.

No. I couldn't lose them all again, couldn't leave them behind to die. Not just die, but vanish. To be obliterated from existence, no paradise waiting beyond, no Otherworld to cradle their memories...

"Come with me," I begged, falling to my knees. Sobs tore through my middle, the air thin and cold as it clawed the inside of my lungs. "I'll figure out a way for you to cross the gate, we can go to Reagan and Ronan together—"

"Keira girl, we don't have real bodies. We can't come. Yer wasting time." Papa lifted me up like I weighed nothing, sticking me back to my feet. "Yer the fiercest thing on two legs, and we need ye to keep moving. Keep going forward, and don't look back."

"Papa—" I choked on another sob, my legs shaking beneath me.

I couldn't leave him again. I wouldn't.

His warm palm cradled my cheek, love and light burning in that sunlight stare. The same stare that had always given me strength, that was branded in my memory whenever I needed guidance.

A howl pierced the air, echoing through the wasteland.

Then another, and another, until they became a dissonant chorus.

Every hair on the back of my neck stood taller than a Pysgoddian mountain. Papa's eyes blew wide, smile falling.

"The hounds." Lochlan's deep skin went pale as he spoke, the first to whisper the warning we all felt blaring in the back of our heads. "Move, now!"

26

Tundras and Tolls

RONAN

When the world righted, ice greeted my knees as I fell. But there were no misty figures on the horizon, no soul-crushing power pressing into me. Instead, my gaze found my friends waiting, standing in front of the obsidian black doors.

My head spun as I remembered where we were.

The Otherworld. This was no longer the illusion, but the destination.

Hell.

Frozen and lifeless, I was here to…

To…

What *had* I come here for? Something important. Something so dire it kept me up at night, that it ate away at my soul every time I thought about it…

I winced as the ache in my head squeezed tighter. I blinked, dislodging the discomfort, instead squinting at my surroundings…

I couldn't remember, but perhaps my friends would.

Like the colossal black gate, Ellian towered over me. His curls pointed every which way, but instead of the ridiculous helmet, he sported a smile, his hand extended. An anchor again back to my mission. Our mission.

Something important. Something worth everything…

"Took you long enough," my brother sneered as he hauled me back up. He tossed me crumpled clothes from his pack, saving me from the blistering chill with a smirk. "Good to see you."

I pulled the soft clothes on—magically dry thanks to an old spell Laureli placed on the pack to waterproof it. I didn't dare ask where she learned it—especially when I was so grateful for the warm tunic and leathers.

Shrugging into the attire, I let myself don my favorite mask of confidence and calculation. My friends were counting on me to lead, to be their clever Captain, to be the Serpent Prince I'd promised them…

Even if I had no memory of what I was leading them to.

Later. I'd remember later.

"Everyone accounted for?" I surveyed the rest of the crew, counting the right amount of heads; Willow and Cassryn closest, both scouring over a parchment—presumably trying to map out what they saw. Danura and Siobhan whispered next to them in hushed tones, the goddess shivering despite the warm clothes, the warrior's face drawn. Nelle crouched in front of Marina, whose back was turned to me, an equally ashen expression on her already-pale face.

No one appeared wounded from first glance, no blood or gore to mar the fresh white ice, but I knew not all scars were visible. I wondered what horrors they'd faced in the black gates. "Is everyone all right?"

What had *I* faced?

"For the most part." Ellian cleared his throat, lips pressing tightly together. His emerald eyes darkened, confirming my suspicion. "Big Red is here, but…"

Hearing him, Marina shot up from where she sat, spinning away from Nelle. Her crimson stare—usually clear and clever—blurred with frantic tears, deep scratches purpling the skin beneath the sockets…

As if she'd tried to claw them out.

"The truth will set us free, but it also will be our cage," she giggled, a terrible laugh that grated against her hoarse throat. Her words clanged around in my head like a bullet in a glass jar, noisy and distinct, as if begging me to think, to *remember*… Marina fisted her auburn locks, tugging strands loose from her scalp with another harsh snicker. "The truth is death and life, the truth is—"

Nelle intercepted, shackling the siren's wrists in her gentle hands before she could inflict any more terror on herself. "Shh, Marina, it's okay. You made it out," she cooed, pressing her forehead to her friend's. "We're right here, love."

My stomach knotted, souring like month-old milk. Marina had always been the most engaging and least bothered of us all. Like she was made of stream-water and sass, she flowed and danced around trouble with the grace of an Ir'desian performer. She never faltered or tripped over earthly cares, always moving forward.

Danura met my gaze, the goddess's worry reflecting mine, her jaw tightly clenched.

"Can you fix her?" I whispered, to both the deity and Nelle.

And me. The silent thought was alone in my head, no memories rising to the surface.

The dove's violet gaze flicked between Danura and I, as if deciding which leader she'd disappoint first. I held my breath as she spoke. "I'm not that kind of healer."

"Truth-teller. Star-eater. Story-weaver!" Marina twirled out of Nelle's grip and launched herself at me. With a shriek, she grabbed the collar of my shirt, pulling me closer. She took a deep inhale, sniffing me, then scrunched up her nose like she'd smelled something foul. "Three gods, one body. Who will claim him? Maybe only Death."

Ice ran down my spine at her words, cold and frozen as hell itself. I steadied her, bracing my hands on her shoulders, searching for any sign of my friend in that crimson stare.

None. Only bloodshot eyes stared back, unseeing and unaware.

I swallowed back the fear that tainted my taste. "Danura?"

She shook her head, a solemn admission. Ghosts haunted her gaze. "The gate requires a price. Everyone makes a sacrifice."

A sacrifice, to ensure safe passage. The cost of salvation.

What had I given, again?

What will you give this time, boy?

Everything.

And the Crimson Witch had given the sharpness of her smirk, the knowing-mischief of her ruby gaze. Her *sanity*.

Nelle wrapped an arm around Marina's shaking frame, pulling her off me. "Don't worry about her, I've got her."

Siobhan nodded, the warrior aware and ready as always, a quality even the gates couldn't strip her of. She looked ahead, to the horizon. "We need to move. It won't be long until Arawn knows we're here."

Arawn. The Dark God.

Something finally stirred in the depths of my mind. Something important.

We were here to rescue something from the Dark God. Perhaps *someone?*

Siobhan set the pace, lifting her pack and trudging across the ice without a single misstep. Gratitude swelled in two parts; one, that Siobhan knew where to go even when I didn't, and two, that no one asked questions. My friend's authority was preserved in the amber of her eyes, an uncompromisable beacon. The rest of us followed dutifully, careful to repeat her footsteps on the treacherous ice.

Except for Marina, who skipped at Nelle's side as we traveled, an out-of-tune song on her lips. "The hounds and the hunter, hurry hurry hurry."

"Keep her quiet," Cassryn snarled with a tone too harsh even for her, her stone face scrunched in concentration. "We're trying to listen."

I stared at her for a moment, the way she clung to the parchment, the way her hand shook as she sketched. I'd never seen her so rumpled...so unnerved.

I didn't dare ask what the gates took from her.

Marina sang on, the melody scraping against every nerve. "'*Awooo*' sing the hounds, their song a funeral dirge to any who hear."

I walked closer to Ellian, nudging his side. "Is everyone else intact after their trials?"

Was I?

"We'll make it work." My friend shrugged, but his jaw muscle still overworked with tension. He tucked his hands under his armpits for warmth, slowing his pace to put some distance between us and the rest of our pack. "What did you offer the gate to pass through?"

"Hmm?"

Ellian's eyes raked over me quickly, as if inspecting me for scars just as I had. "The first test—everyone had to pay. Marina tried to get away with tricking them out of it, I guess, and they took—well, you can tell." His voice dipped low, a dark rumble in his chest. "But I had to offer all the claws on my back paws."

My gaze flicked to his feet. Sure enough, the toes of his boots were darker than the rest, the tan stained the deep red-brown of dried blood.

Shifters were rare creatures, mostly because of the way they'd been hunted through the centuries. It was a dark, brutal history—the way the *faoladh* were made slaves and sold for their parts. For him to have lost any piece of himself, what that stood for…

Emotion lodged in my throat as I thought of all the ways my friend had given himself over to this cause. Our very important, essential, unforgettable cause…

Something about a rescue.

I shoved down my frustration and gratitude, instead slipping back into the Serpent Prince. Cold and calculating. Clever and cunning.

"What about the others?" I kept my chin high despite the unease churning in my pit.

"They took Laureli's orb—the Kraken eye—and Nelle hasn't been able to use her healing magick." Ellian's frown pulled downward as his voice dipped. As if it would help—the sirens could hear just as keenly as he could. Still, the furball had always been as polite as he was dense. "Siobhan offered her physical strength, and they took Willow's sharp eyesight and Cassryn's hearing…not all of it, but enough to dull all three of their senses and gifts."

"Shit," I said out loud before I could catch myself. I stared at the back of Siobhan's curls, tight to her head. She moved with her normal grace and power, but there was a snag to her step, a fatigue in the slight slack of her shoulders.

The sirens were more than their gifts—they were a team, and even with handicaps, they'd make do. They always did. But to imagine them stripped of their sharpest weapons, to see them practically de-fanged and flayed…

I shuddered, the chill finally getting to me.

"So what did they ask of you?" Ellian's question sliced through me with the precision of the swords he forged. That pit in my stomach clenched further, hands shaking at my sides, my body remembering the horrors my head could not.

What will you give this time, boy?
Everything.

I swallowed the sick that rose to my tongue. But I painted on my favorite snake smile, a mask even shifter-eyes couldn't see through, and shrugged. "I can't remember."

A truth disguised as a lie.

Truth-teller. Star-eater. Story-weaver.

Ellian watched me a moment too long. I shoved my hands in my pockets, the weight of his scrutiny salting a wound I couldn't quite place. But before my friend could respond, Willow shuddered to a complete stop, claws digging into her sister's arm.

"Hear that?" she hissed, the wispy woman suddenly straight and sharp as an arrow. Cassryn stilled, wide eyes scanning the misty distance.

And as if in answer, howls rose against the silence, distant but distinct.

My blood chilled to match the air around us, freezing in my limbs. I couldn't remember why we were here, who we were here for...but I remembered every brutal horror story about Arawn's legendary hounds. Even a pack of sirens, a goddess, and a shifter would have to be at their best to face them, and given our current circumstances, we were not.

I assessed the crew—Siobhan's lopsided gait, Willow's squinting eyes, Ellian's bloody toes...without Nelle's healing and Laureli's foresight, there was a good chance we'd be dog chow if we waited for the howling to come closer. I pinched the bridge of my nose to fight the headache still pounding between my eyes. "Should we turn back?"

The sirens' heads whipped to me faster than gunfire, like I'd threatened to bed their mothers.

Oh right, our mission. Our very important, earth-changing mission.

I straightened my tunic, avoiding their accusatory gazes.

Willow's face went white, her focus shifting away from me, thank Lyr. "No wait, I hear running—"

Again, as if summoned by her will alone, I heard it too—several sets of pounding footsteps, coming closer. In an instant, my claws sprang from my fingertips, the siren parts of me ready even if my human parts struggled to catch up. I fell into a ready stance, one mirrored by the rest of my friends...

Until the runners crested over the nearest hill, forms clear against the white backdrop, and my heart threatened to stop. Cedric and

Owen and Finna, all three with ginger hair just as vibrant as I remembered. Reina and Roland and Lochlan, my *family*, somehow there too, faces flushed from running, smiles blindingly bright as they beheld us…

And at the front, a woman with jet black hair and pale skin led the charge.

Until she stopped.

And stared.

"Keira?" Ellian gasped at my side, reverence and desperation in his tone. Then again, louder, like it was a victory song. "Keira!"

But it was not his name the woman called back, tears in her eyes. Not his name that echoed through the frozen wasteland like a war cry.

"Ronan," she screamed, and then ran again. Stumbling and desperate, those silver tears blurring her vision. "You came for me."

I'd never seen her before in my life.

27

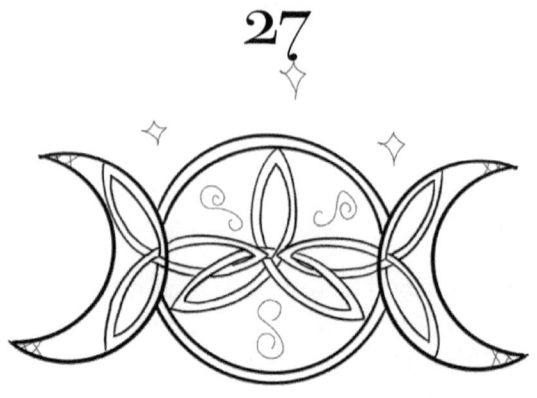

Runs and Rescues

KEIRA

There would be no time for goodbyes, no time for begging or bargaining. My family had made their choices, and there was no time left for discussion. Only survival.

Later—we'd argue about Fate's plans for us all later.

We broke into a sprint, the ghostly howls propelling us forward, farther, instinct taking over. We slipped and slid as we went, the Otherworld clawing at us to stay, to become hound food.

But still, I ran.

A thousand paces. Two.

I ran from Arawn and his deception. Ran from the parts of me I wanted to leave behind, an offering to the grave.

Never slowing, despite the cold air carving our faces, the hot metallic taste of blood on our tongues. Even Reina and Finna kept pace, their phantom forms pushing on despite the ragged breaths they drew.

Another thousand paces.

I ran toward the gate, toward my family waiting beyond it. Toward the freedom I hadn't dared to crave since my first day in the ice. I had no idea if I could even make it through, no idea if the people waiting on the other side even *wanted* me alive, after all I'd done. But that would be a question for later, too.

My footsteps cracked the ice in a steady rhythm, syncing with my beating heart. The percussive song pushed me forward as I slipped into that place where I just *was*. The girl made of sea air and thunderclaps and starshine. The girl forged from the elements, my breath like a hurricane in my aching chest, my legs like strong steel with every painful step.

Another thousand. Two.

The hounds' cries never died, gaining instead. We couldn't see them in the glances we threw behind, but we knew they were there, hunting us in the mist and snow. Waiting for just one of us to fall, to skid on the ice, to stop for a fraction of a breath—

We pushed on, closer and closer to the gates, their black doors stretching up from the white. A small kernel of hope burrowed its way into my chest, stoked like a fire with every harsh breath I sucked past my chattering teeth.

We were close. So close.

We'd make it to the gates, and I would pay whatever price they demanded. They could take my gifts, every last ounce of power stored in my veins. Or, if they would not yield, I would get my family out myself, even if it meant I had to burn the doors down too.

Another hundred paces.

So close. Close enough to see forms blotted a only a thousand paces in front of the massive doors, streaks of red and blue and gold and orange—

I skidded to a stop as they took shape. *Eight* bodies, two of them tall and harsh and decidedly male, the rest soft and curved. But one my eyes locked onto without will.

A blond head, his curls brushing the collar of his red jacket.

His mouth hanging open, arms limp at his sides.

Not real.

Not real.

Not real.

"Keira!" Next to him, Ellian's baritone voice carried like the wolves' howls, and my whole chest collapsed at the sound, my heart crashing and stopping. Blood roared in my ears, drowning out the frozen world around me.

Ronan stepped forward, closer. Every other thought eddied out of my head, every other color blurred from my sight. All I could see was him, as I had a thousand times in this hellscape. His lean, steady body. His crooked nose. His wide eyes.

So close. Barely a hundred paces now.

Not real.

Not real.

Not real.

"Is this a trick?" Someone nearby–a soprano voice I knew, *Finna*–asked the others. "The mind games…"

Papa shook his head in my periphery, breath heaving out of him as he slowed. "No, that's–"

"Ronan!" The word was enough to shatter the world as it broke free, and then I started moving. Running.

I ran toward him, one arm outstretched.

Real.

Real.

Real.

I'd know the real him no matter what deception Arawn used to delude my brain. His aura called to me, unforgettable and unforgeable, a tether between us crafted from the same material as the cosmos.

"You came for me." The hoarse words cleaved from the empty cavern in my chest, a flood of love and gratitude filling in every crack. Ronan came for me, through trial and tribulation, through the gates of hell–

Closer.

Closer.

Closer.

Close enough to see his knotted brow tight with confusion. Close enough to see the horror as he clasped his chest, like his heart too was beating too hard, too loud. "*Who*–"

The hound was a white blur–too fast to make out–as it slammed him into the ground.

He was there.

Ronan was there, strong and sure and just as breathtaking as I remembered him.

He was *there*.

And then he wasn't.

The hounds came at us from all sides. Enormous–nearly the size of a *blaidd*–ghostly figures circled and lunged with incredible speed and precision. Claws tore at flesh, and one by one, the sirens went down.

I was unarmed, but that didn't mean I couldn't fight. My power rose from my center, hot and ready with rage, tingling at the tip of every finger. Waiting, *wanting* to be unleashed.

The first hound jumped at me—its white fur blending with the snow, its red eyes locked onto my throat—before I shot a burst of pure light at it, blinding it on impact. My palm burned as the creature yelped and jerked away, skidding across the ice and swerving from me. The wind carried the scent of burnt flesh and blood, and I tried not to gag.

My breath caught in my chest as my gaze flicked to Ronan. He was against the ground, a giant hound snapping and snarling on top of him. He held the creature by its throat, arms shaking with the weight, but the beast's claws dug into my husband's shoulders, his crimson blood staining the snowfall.

Blood, pooling in his middle, staining the deck.

Sapphire eyes dimming, skin pale and pasty as the life drained from his veins.

No, not again.

The cry that tore from my middle wasn't human. It was the monster's voice, not my own.

I didn't care if Ronan feared me or hated me for it. The raw power in my middle took shape as blazing light. It singed my palms again as it flew at the beast, burning its white fur to ashy black. A gurgled scream erupted from its throat as it thrashed and bucked off Ronan, rolling to the ground to try and extinguish the flames.

I sent another beam its way, right at its head, and the sound came to an abrupt stop.

Ronan scrambled to his feet, face pale and sapphire eyes wide as I ran to him.

Fear, again.

I fought back the insecurity that twisted my gut into knots. My power was horrifying, even to me. Even when it saved us.

Don't be sorry for what you are. That power is a glorious gift. It should be celebrated, not shamed.

I shook off the Dark God's false flattery, banishing the very thought of him from my head. He could spout all the pretty words he wanted, but his actions had spoken louder.

As had my husband's. He was here.

He came.

"Are you all right?" I grabbed his shoulders—oh gods, he was so sturdy, *so real*, it was an effort not to sob or launch myself at him. I inspected his bloodied frame quickly. The claw marks cut deep, his beige tunic shredded and red, but he was already healing, the blood slowing and clotting—a benefit of his sirenhood. Tears welled in my eyes again. I stroked his cheek, relishing the familiar stubble, the soft skin beneath. "Gods, I was so worried. I missed you so much."

Ronan stilled beneath me, eyes as unreadable as the stars in a thunderstorm. He gripped my wrist—gently—and pulled my hand away from his face, lips flattening into the start of a frown.

"Thank you." His voice was colder than the Otherworld, colder than the cage of ice I'd been trapped in. "Keira, was it? I'm fine."

He stepped back, the strong column of his throat working hard as he swallowed.

"Ronan, that's not funny." The light burning bright in my chest winked and snuffed out, an icy void instead consuming the space between my ribs. I scanned his face, searching for signs of trickery or witchcraft, waiting for my sweet, smart-ass husband to peek through again. To tell me it was all a joke, another Mathonwy con. To tell me he loved me and was happy to see me, too. That he hadn't stopped for even a second—

"A little help!" Ellian snarled to our left, dragging me back to the chaos. He stood over an unconscious Siobhan, Laureli cradling her limp form. Siobhan, whose gift of instinct and superior strength allowed her to never lose a fight. Who was made of feral ferocity unmatched by even Arawn's prized pooches. I swallowed hard as Ellian swung his broad ax at an incredibly large hound, pushing it back with each mighty slice.

The beast crouched, ready to pounce.

This time, my power surged as darkness, the shadows dancing across my fingertips nearly as black and brutal as Death's. My shadows were not absence, but vengeance, a manifestation of the darkest parts of my gift. I was Fate, and I decided how my gift settled the score. I squared my stance, ready to unleash the anguish of hell onto the hound—

But Ronan moved first, his fangs and claws at the ready. To save the shifter and the Seer.

And Siobhan.

He slammed into it, his long arms capturing the hound around its middle as he squeezed. A crack rang through the clearing as the canine's ribs broke, its fierce growl dissolving into a pained whimper.

Without hesitation, Ronan sank his fangs into the creature's neck and tore, silencing the beast forever.

"Well, shit," Laureli muttered, still hugging Siobhan close to her. Blood trickled from a wound above her left eye, staining her cheek.

Ellian stared wide-eyed for a long moment before blinking, falling into a crouch next to Siobhan again. "Thanks, brother."

Ronan wiped the blood from his mouth, his chin still stained red. His gaze trailed over Siobhan, the hardness he'd shown me melting as he looked at her. "Don't mention it."

I shoved my feelings back down my gut and focused on the madness around us, at the ghosts and sirens fighting tooth and nail, claw and fang to stay alive against Arawn's murder-hounds. Willow and Cassryn fought off two at once, their backs pressed together. Imprecise and slow, but they were holding on. My crew—Papa, Reina, Lochlan, Roland, Owen and Finna—fought nearly a dozen, misting in and out of reach easily. They wouldn't suffer flesh wounds the same way the rest of us would; they just had to avoid capture. A few paces to the side of them, a dark-haired Danura wrestled a beast on her own, an uncharacteristic feral grin drawing across her pale face.

Lyr below, even my *mother* came for me. I swallowed down the ball of emotion that choked me, no time to process what any of that meant.

But to my far left, Marina *cowered* behind Nelle, a healer, not a fighter, who swung wildly at the two hounds circling them like easy prey.

Adrenaline filled every crevice of my limbs. I cleared my throat, finding the Captain I'd buried inside of me. "I'll get to Nelle and Marina, you go—"

"On it." Ronan cut me off, running toward Willow and Cassryn without a single look back in my direction. I tried not to let it sting, instead moving toward Nelle and Marina, ready to protect them.

"We'll get Siobhan out." Ellian grabbed my wrist, halting me before I could run off to the sinking sirens. Emerald eyes burned with a swell of a dozen emotions, fear and relief and joy and sorrow all flecked in the bright green. "See you on the other side, Keira Branwen."

Laureli nodded, hefting Siobhan up without another word.

My starved heart swelled again as I pressed a quick kiss to Ellian's cheek before running as fast as my legs would carry me toward my other sisters.

Ronan came, but so did all of them. My friends. My family. My Lyr-damned *mother*.

They came to save me. And I wouldn't let them down.

No Branwen left behind.

I skidded to a halt in front of Nelle, sending a blast of angry shadows toward the closest hound. The black whip of energy wrapped itself around the beast's neck, choking it and bringing it to the ground where it thrashed before falling completely still. The second hound snarled, but hesitated, sizing up the new threat in front of it.

A premature, triumphant smirk worked its way onto my face. I pushed Nelle and the quaking Marina behind me, eyes trained on the creature. "Everyone okay?"

"The gate demanded a price of us all, but we'll live." Nelle's voice trembled at my back. "Marina isn't feeling well."

"Angry hounds, *awooo*. They come for me, they come for youuu!" Marina sang an off-kilter melody that sent a shiver down my spine.

Lyr below, what *price* reduced the most self-assured siren in the world to this half-mad mess?

I shook off the worry—we'd help Marina once the beast in front of us and the rest of Arawn's hounds were all fur rugs to decorate our floors with.

"Is there a price to go back through?" I kept my gaze on the snarling hound ahead as I tried to prepare for our next steps in this deadly dance.

"No, I don't think so." Nelle's voice came stronger this time. "Our way out is clear."

Relief flooded my middle. Both my family and my crew had carved a path to safety for me and my baby. Even when I had lost hope and vision, they hadn't, steering the tide of fate in my absence.

I crouched low, shadow and light both dancing in my palm, hope and darkness mixing and swirling, ready to be weaponized. "Get her out now, then. I'll hold off the hounds."

"We came here for you," Nelle protested, tugging my arm as she stepped next to me. "We aren't leaving without you."

"Trust me, I'll be on my way. But you all are powerless right now, and I'm not letting the hounds chase us through that gate." The power in my hands flickered in response, proving my conviction and capability. I straightened my spine, remembering the parts of me Arawn had tried to strip away. "Go."

Nelle squeezed me tightly before dropping her hands, silver tears brimming in her gaze, a grateful smile lighting her face. "Be safe."

Without further ado, she ran, scooping Marina up from beneath her armpits and dragging her toward the gate in the distance. Keen gaze tracking them, the hound lunged, deciding on the easier prey.

I blasted its furry ass with light as my shadows snared its hind legs, trapping it in the range of the fiery blow. It whimpered in pain and thrashed against its phantom chains to no avail. I sent more of the infinite, unrefined magic at it, ending the poor creature's life as quickly as I could. That would be the only mercy I would afford today.

The Silver Wheel took no prisoners. Not with my family on the line.

I sprinted away from the creature's charred corpse, rounding about to where Papa and the other ghosts sparked around almost a dozen of the beasts. They'd managed to kill one or two, but they were mostly unarmed aside from Papa's small dagger and a handful of broad kitchen knives stolen from Arawn's collection. Papa wielded his with the grace and ease of a lifetime of practice, a laugh bubbling in his chest every time the metal clashed with a large hound's sharp canines. Reina and Lochlan both made jabs at two hounds each, cutting small slices into their white fur, sending the creatures into a vicious rage as they stumbled and collided with each other, fumbling toward Roland, who finished them with brutal strikes and a crooked grin.

Next to them, Finna cooed at another, baiting it to chase her while Owen crept closer, ready to sink one of the knives deep into its flank. But the hounds still snapped and swiped at them, unable to distinguish between them and the flesh-and-blood sirens, making them a brilliant distraction.

Pride bloomed across my whole chest, tightening my heart in an uncomfortable, wonderful squeeze. This was who I was, who *we* were; half-wild pirates up for any adventure. Sailors staring Death straight in the face and laughing, our next trick already stuffed up our sleeves.

This was the legacy my daughter would inherit. This was what made me, more potently than the moonlight or shadows creeping beneath my skin, more truly than the sea or sunshine in my veins.

"Ye all right, Keira?" Papa called, smoking out of the way just in time before one of the hounds could swallow him whole.

"Aye, Papa." I grinned as I ran into the fray, lassoing the beast in place with a rope of darkness so the next swing of Papa's dagger could strike true, a line of red staining the beast's neck as he slashed it. "A little busy?"

Papa beamed at me, his expression echoing the feeling lodged in my heart. "Aye, now use those fancy gifts of yers to give an old man a hand. I need my lucky charm."

I obliged without further protest, striking out just as I was taught. The beasts went down, one by one, as I synchronized my attacks with my family's, just as I'd been raised to do. My magic twisted and shifted in their presence, each attack reflective of the love they poured into me.

Because my power *was* me, whatever I needed it to be, and always had been. A small whirlpool of water that sprang free faster than a canon blast, blasting a hound off its balance so Papa could finish it off. Shadows in the shape of tangled, thorny vines that trapped another and pricked its flesh in a tight hold, just in time for Reina to deliver the final strike. A ray of light, hot and bright as sunshine, blinding another as Owen tackled it to the ground, stabbing it with an equally radiant smile.

One by one, they fell, bodies littering the ice, the sweet taste of victory coating my tongue. Behind us, the sound of fighting ceased as Ronan helped Willow and Cassryn finish their load.

As the last hound crashed at my feet, dead eyes staring into nothingness, I let loose a cry, howling to the sky like *I* was the wolf. A *blaidd*, made of power and nurtured by purpose. Filled with that same relief and fury, my family joined in, their voices echoing to the heavens all the way from the depths of hell.

As we came back to ourselves, I surveyed the survivors. Willow and Cassryn stood together, the first leaning on the second for support, Ronan tending to them. He didn't bother to look my way, but he was busy enough. We would talk when we got out of here, the last leg of our journey so close, I could taste it.

Between us, Danura stood still, eyes blown wide.

"Cedric," she breathed as she stepped over the nearest fallen hound, a wild wind sweeping her dark hair behind her. It was strange how similar we looked without her white mane. Blood spattered her dress, and an angry wound seeped more from her left shoulder. But her face wore a broad smile to rival every star in the sky, her eyes lined with shining tears. "You look good for a dead man."

I swear to Lyr, my father blushed, his hands dropping to his side as his dagger clattered to the icy ground. Slowly, he took a step toward her, breathing her in. Then he stood taller, running his hand through her matted locks.

"Love what ye did with the hair." He grinned, voice dipping. Danura leaned into his touch, silver eyes sparkling. "We can catch up later, darlin'."

My heart shuddered and seized in my chest with a whirlwind of emotion. A part of me ached against the sheer force of their obvious love, somehow unbroken despite the years and worlds between them. They stared at each other like they'd only said goodbye yesterday, two souls finding their mate again.

For a moment, I let myself dwell in that feeling, imagining what it might have been like to have them both growing up, to see that love up close and personal, to be fostered and sheltered by it.

Another part writhed with jealousy, so sour and unsettling it churned in my gut. I cast a glance at Ronan, who stared on impassively, his finest mask secured tightly in place.

This was not the reunion I imagined for us. Not the man I knew, all smarmy looks and golden smiles, even if he had come for me.

"Keira, ye need to go." Papa pulled back from Danura, his hand trailing down her arm, his sunset stare tugging me back to the moment. "There will be more coming, I can smell 'em."

My blood froze, reality crashing into me with the weight of the moon. This was what we'd been racing toward, the secret hope I'd been holding since I first woke in the ice. Freedom. Home. A life topside with my daughter and husband, my crew.

But going through the gate meant leaving Papa and the others. Meant losing them all over again. My eyes filled with tears, blurring Papa's visage as I took a step toward him. "I won't leave you."

Papa tilted his head, a smirk pulling at his whiskered face. "Yes, ye will. We aren't helpless, ye know."

Danura laced her arm through his, scanning the vast wasteland around us. A somberness sagged her regal shoulders as she leaned against Papa. "This was my home once. It looks like I need to redecorate again. I told the gate that I would stay this time, to make it all right." Finally, her metallic stare settled on me, lined with tears to match mine. "I need you safe, you hear me? I promise I won't let *him* hurt anyone here. This is my price."

Relief and regret battled in my chest with equal ferocity. I wanted to trust Danura, to hand the world over to the goddess's capable hands and move on with my life. My family. But I knew what a life without Papa looked like. That grief already fought its way back to the forefront, snaring me in its heavy chains. Now, without Reina's warmth too, without my newfound peace with Finna...that grief would be a dagger, stabbing me through the ribs with every shuddering breath I took.

Still, the grief of walking away from Ronan again...even if he didn't need me. Even if he didn't want me...

I couldn't bear that pain twice.

Papa laid his hand over Danura's, nodding once in the way that meant he was laying down the law. "Yer mother is right. Get yer boat in motion, girl."

I didn't have it in me to protest. Not when Ronan stood so close, stoic as he was. Not when my crew waited beyond the gates. Not when new life grew in my womb, deserving a chance.

I gazed on my parents, together at last in the Otherworld where they belonged—and I didn't. "Thank you both. For everything."

I tossed myself at them, wrapping them both in a tight hug. Messy sobs wracked through me as I buried myself in their embrace for one gloriously long moment, Papa's whiskey and wood scent blending perfectly with Danura's tropical floral. I held tighter as Papa's whiskers brushed my cheek, a tightness in his normally relaxed voice. "Yer our greatest joy, Keira girl."

"You'll understand soon, love." Danura kissed my cheek as her slender fingers grazed my stomach, a spark of her energy connecting somehow to the life within.

For one last held breath, I let myself be the little girl who wanted to make them proud. Who longed for their love above all else, who needed them both to show her the way forward. I inhaled deeply, fighting back the piece that wanted to stay here forever, safe in their embrace. "I love you both."

I forced myself to let go, turning away before I got lost in their love forever. They didn't stop me, knowing what I needed without words.

Look forward, girl. It's the only direction you can go.

I set my sights on Ronan, who stood with Reina, Lochlan, and Roland, the three sharing a tear-stained smile as Lochlan hung his arm across Reina's shoulders.

Reina reached out to stroke Ronan's cheek. "I love ye like my own. Tell our little one we love her, too."

"Aye." Ronan took her hand and placed a delicate kiss on his auntie's knuckles, a gentleman as always. Some parts of him would never change, no matter the trials he faced or the choices he made. "She knows, but I'll repeat it."

Reina's chestnut stare swiveled to me, secrets hidden in their depths, so similar to the day we first met. I could never thank her for all the ways The White Snake and the Rydha saved me. *Liberated* me. But I would use every breath I had left in this body to try. "Take care of my family, Keira dear. And yers."

"And tell my boy to always bet on red." Roland winked, his wicked grin and love for a good bet never faltering, even beyond the veil.

Ronan's narrowed gaze flicked between us, as if he was trying to piece together a puzzle with the image face down, but he said nothing.

"Go. I won't tell ye again!" Papa called, and I dared one last look back. Danura, Finna, and Owen smiled and waved behind him, like dock-dwellers at a maiden voyage. Like we were simply going for a sail, and we'd be back before sunset.

I blew a final kiss to my family.

I would be back one day. But not yet.

"We have to move. Before he sends more hounds." I cleared my throat and looked to Ronan. Hesitant, I reached out, brushing the backs of my fingers against his. A spark crackled between us, the hair on my arm standing upright.

Ronan's brows flew up in surprise for a second, but then he schooled his features back into submission and stuffed his hands in his pockets.

Guarded. Hiding.

"Fine." His jaw flexed as he averted his gaze to the last of the sirens. "You two ready?"

Willow and Cassryn hobbled closer, both looking worse for wear as they leaned against each other, blood staining their clothes. Willow's eyes glazed over an eerie, milky white, and they looked toward the horizon, unfocused as her brow furrowed. "We have to go fast. I hear more coming."

My gut clenched, power rippling through me as dread and bloodlust steadied my limbs.

"Which direction?" Cassryn said just a smidge too loudly, head jerking around as she searched for signs of battle.

"South—" Willow started, but a chorus of howls alerted us all that we'd dwelt too long on goodbyes.

Ronan swore under his breath just as another pack of hounds— this time tripled in number—crested over a not-distant-enough hill.

I let the power fill my palms again, bracing for another fight. I would burn every threat Arawn sent my way to cinders. "I'll cover the frontline, you all pick off the stragglers and get going."

"No, Keira, you and the baby have to get out." Cassryn shook her head violently, horror uncharacteristic on her normally stoic features. "We can handle this."

At that, Ronan's attention whipped to me. "*Baby?*" His eyes flicked to my abdomen quickly enough to be polite. A frown carved his handsome features, cold and calculating. The Sea-Snake in his truest form. "If you're pregnant, you should leave."

Hurt flashed through me, quickly chased by a lethal combination of adrenaline and anger, both making me just as venomous as he could be. I was a Mathonwy too, and while we had a lot of catching and cleaning up to do, I would not be dismissed. My voice growled low in my throat. "As if I'd ever leave you behind."

But I had. Twice.

I turned away before shame could capture and distract me, scanning the approaching horde.

But from the east, another figure on the back of a brilliant black horse raced toward us at a fiery speed, auburn hair burning like a lantern as he bellowed over the howls. "Keira! Cedric!"

I blinked twice, not believing my eyes as Aidan fucking Branwen gained on us, closing the distance faster than the hounds could.

"Ah, Aidan!" Papa waved his arm wildly, a wide smile on his wrinkled face. "Thought ye'd never show! Good to see ye, brother."

Uncle Aidan.

All of the hurts and words unsaid rushed through my already dizzy head, mixing with an unexpected relief clutching my heart.

No Branwen left behind. Betrayer or not.

But his eyes were wide with horror as he smacked his horse's flank in a punishing rhythm, the hounds not far behind. A single word shaped his lips, sound lost beneath the thundering of heavy paws and hooves across the ice, but I'd been learning to read lips.

"*Run.*"

I took a step back, ready to do just that, when I slammed into a hard body.

Arawn's eyes were pitch dark as I turned into him. "There you are, *Caraid.*"

28

Gods and Goodbyes

RONAN

While I still struggled to figure out exactly who Keira *was*, there was no mistaking the man holding her close, his fingers biting into her flesh hard enough to bruise.

The Dark God.

Arawn.

I'd seen him in dreams, a horrible familiarity swimming in the back of my mind. He'd choked me, face brimming with anger…but over what? When had *I* crossed the God of Death?

I tried to shake the sick feeling clawing at my gut, straightening my posture.

"Don't touch me. We're *done.*" Keira tried to shove back from him, those strange glowing palms of hers burning the shirt on his chest, the smell of singed cotton and flesh assaulting my senses. But he didn't so much as flinch. His hands only gripped her tighter, red splotches coloring her pale skin.

"Not this time."

On instinct, I snarled at him, a feral part of me rising to the surface as I dropped into a low crouch. I didn't know this woman–to my knowledge, at least–but the beast inside of me twisted and snarled at the mere thought of her in danger. Perhaps it was the knowledge that she was pregnant, the creature that ruled my emotions primed to protect the young and helpless. My voice spilled out without my command. "Let. Her. *Go.*"

"Ah, nice to see you again, *boy*," Arawn spat, his impossibly dark gaze snapping to me, a smirk crawling along his features. His grip on Keira softened, one finger trailing down her arm in a possessive caress. "But I'm afraid she's not yours to protect anymore."

The beast inside roared, but I stilled, struggling to piece it all together again. His joke was at my expense, but I was somehow missing the punchline. Keira snarled at him and jerked away, but he held firm.

"Let her go, Arawn." Danura's command was armored with ancient authority, and my back straightened as her voice pierced through the clearing.

Arawn stilled as I did, instinctively letting Keira go. She ducked out of his reach before he could snag her again, shuffling to my side, but he made no move to catch her. Still, I took a shielding step, my feet moving again by will of the beast within. Aidan and Cedric Branwen shifted closer too, the feuding brothers somehow allied around protecting this girl.

But Arawn didn't so much as look our way, instead staring at Danura—this woman's *mother*, from what I could gather—a war waging in his eyes.

"Danura. I knew you'd come crawling back." His insult was sharp as the ice around us, but the strain in his voice revealed his weakness.

The goddess lifted her chin. Even with the kiss of mortality blackening her hair and dimming her shine, she stood with the presence of a queen, her crown unshakeable, born of the universe itself. "We have unfinished business."

Arawn's composure broke as he stepped forward with a snarl. "You're nothing but a washed-up scrap of power from some useless island. We have no business. But Keira, my future child, and I have a world to change. Now I will offer you all this grace once." His voice dipped low as he regained his air of certainty. I tensed, hand snapping to Keira's as his threat echoed through the clearing, his gaze tracking over all of us. "Leave now, and I will not erase you from the world. Keira and I will go about our reign, and we'll never bother any of you again."

"I will *never* help you." Keira stormed out from behind us, tearing away from my grip, palms blazing again with starfire. Tears streaked her cheeks, but a feral smile graced her face. "You'll have to kill me."

Lyr below, this woman was either incredibly brave or wonderfully stupid. But bold or brainless, my crew had sacrificed far too much on this journey to save her to let her play the martyr today.

"Don't." I snatched her back with my siren speed, placing myself firmly between her and the God of Death. Maybe *I* was the idiot.

Arawn's black stare flickered with amusement, his hands twitching at his sides.

"Fine. I'll settle for them first." He nodded to the rest of the crew amassed on this rescue mission. "How about mother dearest?"

Before anyone could move to stop him, a burst of daggered black shadows shot from his hand, barreling toward Danura. She lifted her hands, eyes flying wide.

There was a single moment to react, but my limbs leadened, fear snaring me in place...

"No, *Serenhi*!" Willow cried out, moving first. She flung herself between Danura and the oncoming spears.

My stomach dropped and then rose to my throat as they sliced through her with the ease of arrows, riddling her body with bloody holes. She collapsed between Arawn and Danura, her blood pooling on the ground, eyes glassed over as life fled from them.

An inhuman, animal scream tore at my eardrums, the pain and horror in the sound twisting my heart.

"Willow!" Cassryn loosed a guttural shout. But Willow did not move, not even a flutter of her eyelids or a single beat of her pulse. Her eyes stared lifelessly across the expanse; there would be no coming back. Not even as a ghost to haunt the Otherworld. Sirens did not have souls.

Willow wasn't just dead. She was *gone*.

Danura winced, the connection officially severed with the girl she remade. My own heart seized, the finality of her sacrifice stabbing at both my grief and fear. My sweet friend, soft and kind as a breeze through tree branches, silenced forever.

Arawn laughed, a mirthless sound that ran up my spine like claws. "Foolish child."

Cassryn bared her fangs at the Dark God, trembling at her sister's side, a blazing rage that shook her whole frame. "You vile bastard. That's my *sister!*"

And as she lunged for him, the world descended to madness again.

Cassryn slammed into a wall of shadows that Arawn manifested with a bored flick of his wrist. She crumpled to the ground, blood trickling from a wound to the head, her eyes just as unseeing as her sister's. My gut twisted in a tight knot; at the same time, Danura flew around Arawn's flank, tackling him to the ice with a loud smack. Where they crashed, the ice cracked and melted, creating a pool of water larger than the Porthladdian Spring around them.

Arawn's surprise lasted only a second before he shot at Danura again. The two gods wrestled with vicious vengeance as the whole ground shook around us.

At their maker's mark, the pack of hounds pounced.

"Run to the gates, don't look back!" Cedric shoved Keira toward me before he snatched his dagger from the ground. Determination glinted in his eyes like the steel in his hand. "Aidan, go with them. You and I will talk when they're safe."

Aidan's jaw tightened, but then he nodded to his older brother, his former Captain. I vaguely remembered there had been bad blood there, a *betrayal*, a blademark across the throat and a bullet wound to the head...but the details were fuzzy, like trying to look at my reflection in muddy water.

I couldn't waste time trying to remember now. Two of my siren sisters had already fallen, and I would not fail the others waiting beyond the gate for us to finish this fool's mission. Whoever Keira was, she was worth everyone I'd ever respected throwing their lives on the line for her.

Cedric raced toward the nearest hell-mutt, driving his dagger into it as the rest of the ghosts formed a blockade against them. Aidan and I both grabbed Keira's arms at the same time, pulling her toward the gate, but she thrashed against us, pain and rage swimming in her silver eyes as she watched the brutal scene behind us. "But Cassryn—"

"Go!" Danura hollered as she pressed Arawn's head below the freezing water, her wet hair plastered to her face, someone's blood—*hers*, by the scent—smeared across her cheek. The Dark God thrashed beneath her, and another tremor vibrated the earth beneath our feet, the ice cracking in a hundred deep fissures.

I cursed under my breath. I would not fail; for all the things I didn't know, I was certain in my very bones that we needed to save this woman, whatever the cost. And we were fresh out of time for her heroic, self-sacrificing tears.

I shot her a dark, warning look before using my siren's strength to drag her forward. "Let's go, lady."

To my delight and surprise, she didn't protest this time, breaking into a sprint that matched mine.

"I'll see ye through," Aidan panted as he ran beside us, casting glances over his shoulder to make sure we weren't followed by hounds. "I *wanted* to see ye, to say–"

"I know, Aidan," Keira cut him off, shadows writhing across her palms, her jaw set as our feet pounded across the ice. "We're all sorry."

She blasted the magick behind us just as a few hounds broke through the blockade. The attack fell short of the beasts themselves, but instead hit one of the deep cracks in the ice dead on. The world rumbled again as the ice tore apart, a wide gap separating us from the horde, the crack running across the valley as far as the eye could see. Two of the dogs fell forward into the cavern, yowling as it swallowed them. Their companions barked and snarled, skidding to a stop as they met the ridge.

I stole another look at the woman sprinting next to me, more than a little impressed. I was starting to get an idea of why she was so valuable to us. I imagined that ever-changing power trained on Morwyn Locasta and glee danced beneath my scales. This woman could singlehandedly turn the tides of our fate.

We didn't stop running until we met the gate, air sharp in my lungs, the tang of metal pooling in my mouth. But we couldn't slow, not yet. Not until we were on the deck again sailing straight for Pysgodd, putting the frozen fearscape of the Otherworld–and our fallen friends–far behind us.

I hoped this woman could sail well enough to make up for our dwindled crew.

Aidan tried to tear open the tall, obsidian door with a grunt, but it wouldn't budge. A frown pulled at his mouth, but Keira shook her head and pressed her palm to the structure. A faint glow emitted from the place she touched, the stone groaning as it widened for us. Aidan huffed a sigh of relief and awe before schooling his features once more. "Get through as fast as you can. Don't look back. We'll all guard the door while you pass through, and we'll try to close it. But it's a two-way street. Once the prices are paid, anyone can move in or out. Including him," Aidan warned as he squinted back toward the chaos, trying to catch a glimpse of who'd taken the advantage. But it was no use, too many blurry forms moving faster than light, hard for even my siren's sight to make out.

Keira nodded as she stared into the abyss of the doorway. "We can't let him follow us. What he plans for the Deyrnas...it's unimaginable."

Aidan clapped her shoulder, and she winced, but fought not to pull away. A sadness flickered across Aidan's features, but then he stuffed it back down, his expression solidifying with a small, confident smile. "Yer mama will hold him off. Just go so we can close this thing."

Her throat bobbed once. Twice. "Aye, Captain."

"Goodbye, Keira girl." He patted her cheek before she stepped back, sights already set on the gate. "Live well."

I cleared my throat, pulling both of them away from the strained moment. As touching as it was, it was a waste of precious moments the Deyrnas didn't have. "Let's go."

I didn't wait for her confirmation as I tugged her wrist and dragged her through the portal. It wasn't very well-mannered of me, but I'd rather ask forgiveness than permission with so many lives on the line, so many friends already lost.

I spared one last aching thought to Cassryn and Willow, my chest squeezing, before the portal tugged us into its embrace.

Falling, twisting, the darkness consumed and remade until we stared at an open field of green. I breathed it in, a familiar tug at my mind suggesting I'd been here before, that I knew this stretch of grassy land...

Three cloaked figures stood before us, hoods masking their faces, but their voices triggered an instant recognition that yanked and scraped at my very core.

"Reunited at last, goddess and servant," the first laughed, a weight pressing into my chest as the sound bore down on me. I shook it off, grabbing Keira's hand again and walking forward. I had to keep moving, had to keep to the path, or else...

"Tell me, boy, was it worth the price?" The second hooded figure sneered, and my head pounded as the sound rang in my ears like a warning bell. She stepped in front of us, breath like rotting death filling my nose. "Or can you not *recall?*"

"Shut up," I gritted out, sidestepping her, half-dragging Keira forward, onward, out...

"Stick to the path you're on, Ariannad," the last figure sang, reaching out to brush Keira's arm as we passed them. She skipped away, black robes swishing around her ankles as her discordant melody soured the air. "But beware of who may follow."

They disappeared as quickly as they came, leaving us to the green paradise around us. A forgotten part of me longed to dwell, to crash into the grass and let it tickle my skin, to laugh and stare up at the open sky while the breeze danced around us...to hold the woman at my side here, too, both of us trapped in this beautiful cage, the rest of the world falling away...

No, we had to keep moving. Had to get to the others...

"Who were they?" Keira whispered, trudging through the tall reeds, silver eyes darting around on high alert. I could feel her pulse in her wrist, hammering fast with fear. My fangs ached in my mouth, the feel of her blood beneath my fingertips calling to me...

"The gate keepers. They gave us all tests..." I answered, searching for the knowledge. I had been here before, a small, blonde girl in that cloak teasing me, tempting me...letting me stay for something, *someone*...but the rest blurred and mashed together, stray images undistinguishable as they misted away in my mind's eye. Frustration bit at my heels as I gripped Keira's arm tighter. "I don't remember mine. I don't remember why I'm here."

I pushed forward, ready to be rid of this mission, but Keira dug her heels in, coming to a firm halt.

I spun to snap at her, but my protest died on my tongue as I caught sight of the tears budding in her eyes. She swallowed thickly as one ran down her cheek, carving a wet line across her pale flesh. "Do you...do you remember me?"

Shame rattled through me, tying my tongue in tight knots.

I stared at her, willing myself to understand, to remember. Her dark hair, her spattering of freckles, those unique silver eyes...all of them begged to be noticed, as if they'd once meant something, meant *everything*, perhaps…

But nothing came to the surface. Like lines in the sand wiped clean by the tide, any trace of this woman in my life had utterly vanished like she'd never been there in the first place. I stammered as I finally found my voice again. "Who am I to you?"

She inhaled a shuddering breath, one that stole the air from my lungs as I waited.

"Ronan…" My name was a somber psalm on her lips, both reverent and mournful as her pretty lips formed around it. "You're my…you *were* my husband."

The word slammed into me with the force of a gale wind, knocking me back.

Husband.

She was my wife.

"What?"

It wasn't possible. I'd never seen her before, never even knew of her existence…

But no, that didn't make sense either. I knew her family, her father and her mother both despite them representing two very different parts of my life. I'd sailed with her Pa as a boy, and Danura had taken me in when I washed up after…after…after *whatever* happened to me. Another gap that didn't make sense. Besides, my crew and kin knew her, too, were willing to *die* for her, even…how could I have not noticed someone so essential, so central to every path of my life? Logically, I had to have known her somehow before my memories had been taken.

But my lover? My *wife?* I couldn't forget that.

Could I?

And did that mean…was the baby growing inside of her…*mine?* Or was it the Dark God's spawn, as he had claimed?

"Ronan…" she breathed again, tears falling freely now, her scent souring with grief and pity. I pulled from her touch again, hating the way she looked at me, like I was some wounded, broken thing, like I was damaged…

I stuffed my rage and confusion deep down, pulling on my impenetrable mask again. The Sea-Snake didn't need pity. He didn't need *anyone*. He thrived on trickery and cunning alone.

"You're lovely, but you'll have to buy me dinner before you propose next time." Hurt flashed across her features, but I ignored it, instead yanking her toward the exit. I had a mission to finish. I'd deal with missing memories and wayward wives later.

We crossed the rest of the field without issue until I felt that deep, twisting void again, the other side of the gate just a step away.

I offered her one warning. "Hold your breath."

And then I plunged us through the space between worlds.

Again, the pulling, swirling, sinking enveloped us, and I was only mildly aware of our hands clasped together, anchoring us despite the way the void tried to wrench us apart...

It spat us out into the dark depths of the sea.

My fins and gills burst forth in a single second of burning pain, and I sucked in a breath through the slots in my ribs, water filtering out. I turned quickly to Keira, expecting her to flail and panic as the pressurized water pressed into us, crushing her aching lungs...

Instead, her silver stare met mine, shrouded with an eerie calm. She held her breath, no bubbles escaping her clamped mouth. Utterly relaxed, she floated, every muscle loose, like she was born of the sea just as certainly as I was. A soft glow emitted from her skin, warmth spreading through the icy waters and kissing my cold-blooded scales. I shivered at the sensation.

Before I could linger in that ridiculous feeling, her gaze shot topside and she kicked her feet, paddling us upward.

Gripping her hand tighter, I sped toward the surface with a powerful thrust of my tail. A small part of me–the beast, perhaps–wanted to rile her, to get under her skin just as effectively as she had crawled beneath mine. But instead of screaming or thrashing in panic, she laughed, the bubbles racing with us as her wide eyes flared in wild glee.

I gritted my teeth together and swam faster, breaching the water just beneath the waiting *Madyn*, Keira's head bobbing up a single second after.

"You'll have to try harder next time," a breathless laugh escaped as mist against the cool air. "I'm never scared of anything when I'm with you."

Something familiar and forgotten in the back of my mind ached at that, like I heard it before, perhaps on another moonlit swim...

The tinge of the memory faded fast as I watched her free-swim to the hull of the ship, leaving me in her wake. I shifted back, my human legs freezing without her glowing warmth, the icy water biting into my skin in a punishing cold. But I relished it as I paddled forward, letting it sober and focus my whirling mind, bringing myself back to the task at hand.

"Oh, Nef's breath, you're all right!" Nelle cried as she helped Keira over the rail, crushing her into a hug as I flopped back onto the deck.

Laureli tossed me a pair of trousers, her jaw tight as I pulled them on. "Where are the others?"

She might as well have thrown a dagger at me, her words slicing me up in a million slivers all the same.

"Danura is staying behind," I spoke through the grief wrapping itself around my throat, thinking of the twins. I missed their bickering already, unable to process a world without them, but the loss would be even deeper for Laureli and Nelle. The sirens were a family, every last one of them. I stared at the wooden slats beneath my feet, unable to face the truth reflected back in their eyes. "Cassryn and Willow didn't make it."

"No," Nelle whispered, pain straining her voice, and I wished with all my heart and soul it wasn't true.

Tell me, boy, what are you willing to give this time?

Everything.

"Arawn killed them," Keira growled, shaking beneath the blanket Nelle tucked around her frame. Not from the cold, but from the rage that smoldered in her eyes, burning hot and ready to be unleashed against the Dark God.

The heat there forged my resolve, too. This wasn't over, not yet. The Dark God had stolen from me, from all of us, from the Deyrnas. And his followers, Morwyn Locasta and her puppets, still had their ropes tied around our necks.

They would pay for Cassryn and Willows' deaths with their own. My fangs would taste their rancid blood.

"Your deaths will be avenged, my sisters," Laureli whispered to the sea, her words echoing the promise in my heart. The dark water churned against the ship, the wood groaning in solidarity.

"The dark one eats the light like hearts." Marina crawled out from belowdecks on her hands and knees, crimson hair knotted and sticking up in every direction like she'd been tugging at it. Her bloodshot eyes stared at nothing as she flopped onto the deck, a shrill giggle tumbling from her. "Always *hungry*."

Nelle and I caught each other's eyes, a warning look passing between us that unsettled my stomach.

"She's still out of it?" Keira hedged, stepping up to the siren. She brushed a lock of Marina's red hair from her face, and Marina sighed into her touch.

"Ah, the Silver Wheel, here to heal!" she sang again, nuzzling into Keira's hand like a puppy greeting its master. Keira's brow pulled tight as she let the woman stroke and cuddle her, practically shifting herself into Keira's lap.

"We have another problem," I admitted to Nelle and Laureli. I watched Keira embrace Marina, her face drawn in a frown. She was easy to look at, her features lovely even when robed in concern, but I still couldn't remember a single moment of our life together, our supposed *marriage*…I stuffed my hands in my pockets, forcing myself to look at Nelle instead. "My memories are…wrong. Fragmented. I can remember almost everything, but I have no recollection of who *she* is. Like someone just plucked her out of every memory."

Nelle and Laureli shared a long look, pain and pity warring for dominance between them. Nelle gnawed at her lower lip, hands fisting into her skirt. "Ronan, I'm so sorry. But the Gate demands a price. And it often takes what is most valuable."

I fought a grimace. Mine and Marina's muddled minds were too much for me to handle with the weight of loss still pressing hard on my chest, so hard it was difficult to breathe. We were all still missing pieces. I just hoped we'd find a way to get them back. I cleared my throat and my head, desperate for a problem I could *fix*. "How's Siobhan?"

"Resting below, Ellian's taking care–" Laureli started, but stopped, blue eyes glazing over in hazy white. I stilled, every muscle in my body tense as the vision swept over her, her jaw slack and brow tight. Then, she blinked, urgency clearing the mist. "We'll figure it all out, but we need to get moving. Something is still *off*, and my visions won't let me see. It's all veiled in shadows, and without my orb there isn't much I can do to pinpoint it."

My stomach tugged at the truth of the statement, the wrongness of the moment hanging in the air.

"He follows the light, always needing more," Marina lilted as she rolled off Keira, playing with her dark hair instead.

I ignored her, instincts prickling at the warning. The sun had just started its ascent into the sky, the morning already warming, but the air was stale, the sails limp with the absence of any wind. I clenched my fists at my sides as the panic dragged its claws through my veins, trying to hold on to the Captain's mask I'd been wearing the last few weeks. My crew needed me to deliver what was left of us to safety.

I ran a hand through my hair, trying to tame the wet curls as I fought to calm my nerves. "We're a few sailors short, but we're going to have to row."

My back ached at the thought, but the horror in Laureli's expression was enough to motivate my muscles into motion.

"I think I can help with that." Keira scooped Marina off her and stood, staring up at the sky. She closed her eyes, dark hair falling behind her in a curtain as her freckled face tinted gold in the sunlight. She took a steadying breath, her palms turned upward she whispered, "Please let this work."

A moment passed, and she took another breath. Then she opened her eyes.

In the same second, the water around us rushed with a loud *woosh*, sea spray splashing against the hull as the ship lurched forward, propelled by the motion. I staggered to catch my balance, and a fierce wind picked up around us, nearly knocking me back a second time.

Keira's hair snagged in the wind, but she stood perfectly still, focus falling on her features as we picked up the pace.

I somehow found my sailor's legs beneath me, moving to the rigging to secure the sails in place as they ballooned with the breeze, filling to the brim and dragging us forward at a punishing pace.

"That's a new trick. Otherworld teach you that one?" Laureli crossed her arms as the wind whipped her dark hair into a crow's nest, the start of a smile cracking her serious features. She moved to the helm, turning the wheel to point us where her Sight directed.

A smirk quirked the side of Keira's mouth as she kept her hands steady, the wind and water both picking up. "Something like that. Apparently, my magic is malleable to whatever I want it to be."

Nelle brushed a hand across Keira's cheek, violet eyes glassy with tears. "We'll find a way make it right. We're just so glad you're back, dearie."

Keira grinned, but it didn't meet her eyes. Those flicked to me for a moment, so fast I almost missed it. "Me too."

Somehow, it sounded like a lie.

I climbed higher into the rigging, securing the last few knots in place, ignoring the way my gut tangled whenever I looked at her. I shouted over the howling wind, my voice more certain with our turn of fate, "Let's get back to Griffin and the rest of the crew. We need to reconvene fast, before whatever is wrong comes to bite us in the ass."

"To Pysgodd, then?" Nelle called up, wrapping her arms around herself. It had been ages since she'd seen her home island, and I could hear the edge of hope in her voice. I opened my mouth to confirm, setting my sights northward, but Keira cut in.

"No. Ir'de." Keira shook her head, a panic rising with the pitch of her voice. "Griffin will be there. I can feel it. And something is...*wrong*."

My heart hammered in my chest at the prospect of yet another disaster waiting around the corner. I hopped back to the deck, ready to argue or demand a better explanation...but the fierce determination in the set of her jaw and the certainty in the square of her shoulders silenced all thoughts of protest.

I might have been Captain, but this woman was a goddess. Fate kneeled to her, and if I wanted any chance of saving the Deyrnas, so would I. "Lead the way."

Laureli swung the wheel at the same time Keira's wind shifted in our favor. "South it is, then, Captain."

And we put the Otherworld and our fallen friends behind us like a bad dream.

Fires and Foreboding

GRIFFIN

We set sail for Ir'de early in the morning; while flying was my least preferred mode of transportation, something about Awyr soaring above the *Ceffyl* as we sailed made my soul sing. As Reagan rode him, his mighty wings cast a vast shadow over the deck and he often dropped down to splash seawater at us like some overgrown otter.

Lyr's left ass cheek, the whole crew had a pep in their step as we worked beneath the belly of the beast. Tarran had taken to Gennevieve again like fleas to a dog, following her around and 'showing her the ropes' like he was her personal shadow. Not that the little duck seemed to mind, her pale cheeks flushing as red as my cretin cousin's hair every time he scooted up to her.

But it wasn't just them. Reagan and Vian both took turns flying with Awyr, sometimes riding together, their laughter and squeals of joy mixing with the gulls' squawking. And when they were on deck, they moved through their work quickly without complaint, both on their best behavior to keep their dragon-riding privileges. Drystan and Rhett were under the same spell, working next to each other in the rigging without sneering at each other, even *laughing* whenever one of the kids said something ridiculous.

Gods above, even *Saeth* had taken to humming, a nasally, off-key tune filling the air whenever she took to sharpening the arrows from Nef's quiver.

But whatever enchantment had tamed my half-wild crew into this happy band of little workers, I didn't care. I just soaked it all in, letting it settle the deep dread that had been sloshing in my own gut since we set sail. Truth and Triumph sang warnings in my ear, but I tuned them out, instead relishing the streak of good luck we'd managed to fall into. It was enough to make a betting man like me want to risk it all, placing all my chips in their capable hands. Maybe, just maybe, we could fix everything wrong with this stupid world. Maybe, with just a few more godly items and a bit of this upbeat mentality, we could change our own fate. And the fate of the Deyrnas.

Rhett stood at my side as I took the helm on the eighth day of sailing, Ir'de's outline finally forming along the horizon. And as I took it all in, that little streak of hope dashed.

From the distance, ominous columns of smoke billowed into the sky, darkening the clouds with ash.

Ir'de was burning.

My stomach lurched at the sight, but I took a swig of my flask to wash the unease away, trying to hold on to the last strands of optimism. The never-ending party-of-an-island had festivals every other day. It was winter now, and even though the chill barely touched the southern isles, maybe the locals were all burning bonfires, keeping warm and dancing in the heat. After the weeks spent trudging through the Pysgoddian everfrost, I was ready to warm my ass in front of a flame while some pretty Ir'desian performers heated my blood.

"Does that seem off to you?" My partner stilled at my side, his jaw flexing as he looked at the dark tendrils reaching to the heavens.

"The wind has a warning." Vian popped down from the rigging, his wraith-like face drawn in severe lines. "I can't understand, but I have a bad feeling."

I pursed my lips, knowing just how accurate Vian's bad feelings tended to be. I patted the boy on the shoulder, but couldn't find the words to comfort him.

Above us, Awyr let out a deep growl, circling back and dipping lower. The sound sent a shiver down my spine, the beast's warning clear as a bell. He swooped down, Reagan sliding off his spiked tail and landing on the deck beside us before the beast took to the sky again, banking hard west toward Hud. My fantasy died fast, worry eating away at the hope I'd stored in my chest.

"He'll be back, but something is wrong." Reagan frowned, staring after her giant pet. She nudged Vian, the wind whisperer relaxing slightly in her presence, but not enough to soothe my doubt.

Tarran dropped down from the foremast, a spyglass in his hand. He raised it to his eye and squinted, but quickly shook his head. "The smoke is too thick to make anything out." He forced a tight smile. "We're a month to yule. Maybe everyone here just burns their logs early?"

My swords sang the familiar melody of war at my back, their unheeded warnings all like scars in my mind. I faked a smirk for my cousin's sake. "Let's hope."

"We should prepare for the worst." Drystan folded his arms across his chest as he stepped close to the rail, his posture straight as he scanned the horizon with his golden eyes. While he was mild and friendly most of the time, he was also a former Colonel of the Orwellin Guard. Danger was written into every muscle of this man's body, and they all tensed as he gritted his teeth at the smoke. "I've seen enough burnings in Orwellin to know what a house fire looks like from a distance. And that looks like *several* housefires."

My stomach rolled as I looked again at the dozens, if not *hundreds* of individual lines of darkness, all of them amassing in the swirling cloud of ash above.

The last lingering threads of denial snapped inside my head, reality sinking into my soul like the smoke curling into my nose and filling my lungs.

Saeth pursed her lips at Drystan's side, her hands tightly clasped around Nef's bow. "We need to see this through."

As much as the pit in my stomach said otherwise, the part of me that belonged to Trouble was fast to agree. Griffin Branwen didn't run from a fight. I *started* them. And today, I would end one if I had to.

"Everyone stay sharp and armed." My voice slipped lower as I uttered the command, drawing my swords from their sheaths. I hoped Gwynn's luck would be on my side, but if not, I had his weapons and a tinge of his bad attitude.

The crew readied to disembark as we docked, the thick clouds of smoke clawing at our throats and lungs. Genni fashioned scarves out of scraps of clothes for us to wrap around our faces to keep the ash out, but it still stung our eyes to bloodshot. I cursed beneath my mask, glad that no one could see me grimace.

Something was *beyond* wrong. The oppressive smoke clawed at us like it wanted to reach into our mouths and lungs and suck out our very souls.

We stalked off the *Ceffyl*, anchoring her in the North Port dock farthest from the main streets of Aechnad city. If we had to turn tail and run from whatever lurked beneath the ashy haze, we would. And we sure as shit wouldn't risk the *Ceffyl's* structural integrity by introducing her to fire.

The crew stayed close behind me as we moved through the shadowy fog, the normal light and life of Aechnad entirely still and silent. None of us spoke as we traveled from the outskirts toward the main city, outside of a few low curses whispered as we took in the maze of horrors. Around us, the ruins of homes and shops and buildings crackled as last embers of the burn died out, nothing left to consume. But aside from the groan of buildings ready to collapse and the hiss of dying fires, there was nothing. No screams for help or cries of pain or relief. No life at all murmuring beneath the rubble. Ir'de was a ghost town.

"How the fuck did this happen?" Rhett's voice was muffled by the cloth covering his face, but his fear was as potent as my own. We'd been crawling deeper into the abandoned, ruined city for nearly an hour, the once beating, bleeding heart of the Deyrnas, now deader than the Otherworld.

"I don't know." I had no idea what could have possibly razed such cruelty across this land, but I was not keen on finding out. My swords had not stopped screaming their cries of warning and terror since I'd stepped foot on the Ir'desian soil.

My heart threatened to stop in my chest. Aechnad wasn't just the Jewel of the Deyrnas; it was my future. My unspoken wish. We passed the buildings that once held so much promise and laughter: Madame Markins' famous smoke bar, which had the best rum in the south. Mr. Dugal's Dance Hall, which always featured the most talented– and half-naked–dancers the Deyrnas had to offer. Old man Hastings' apothecary, home to the best hangover cure ever invented.

Though I'd never admitted it out loud, this place felt like hope. Like home.

And it was *gone*. All of it.

Wanting was weakness.

We worked our way through what had once been the Spice Corridor, the hundreds of stalls all crumpled and burned. But instead of the bustling city street I knew and loved, I found it just as abandoned as the rest of the wasteland.

Until two silhouettes across the long avenue caught my eye, blurry through the curling smoke, but moving toward us.

People.

My heart soared for a moment before crashing again. We didn't know if they were friend or foe, victim or victor of whatever chaos had devoured this city whole.

I stilled, my swords at the ready as they slinked closer.

An old, withered woman stepped through the ash first, her silver hair marred with dark soot, her bloodshot stare sharp and cunning as ever. And to her left, a face I knew better than the bottom of a whiskey bottle grimaced at me, her dark skin and long, tight braids blending with the shadows.

"Madame Hedd?" My gaze darted between the two, trying to piece together just how they were here. "*Councilwoman Amos?*"

Madame Hedd's wrinkled face pulled into a deep frown, ignoring my confusion as tears lined her crow-footed stare. "Yer too late. We're all too late."

My gut lurched at the truth, not needing either of my swords to confirm. The devastation was clear, but how the hell this happened was still a mystery. And I didn't want to assume ill of the Magicka in front of me, once an ally, but her powerful presence couldn't mean anything good. I gripped the hilt of Triumph tighter to steady my pounding heart.

Rhett focused on the more familiar face among the two, his silver-and-blue stare narrowing on Agatha. "How in Lyr's name are *you* here? We just left you in Pysgodd…"

The barkeep waved him off with an eyeroll, like she hadn't just outpaced the fastest cutter in the four seas and turned up in the heart of a destroyed metropolis without explanation. "I have my ways. I left as soon as my cards showed me what would happen…" Her lips pursed, as if she warred with how much information to give us, before a flat expression masked whatever secrets she hid. "But I was late too."

I pushed down the flurry questions that rose to my lips about her presence here, instead focusing on the more pressing, immediate concern.

"What *happened?*" We needed to know what we were up against, no matter the cost. I was not above smacking the sense into these two hags if that's what it took.

"Morwyn Locasta," Madame Hedd answered instead, uncharacteristic fear and hatred flashing across the witch's features at the very name. Smoke swirled around her as she spoke, like the ghosts of the fallen urged her on. "Those of us in Cerridwen City could see it over the bay, but there was nothing any of us could do to stop it. The dark arts are not to be toyed with. It's the same in Werth. Her puppets swarmed both cities, setting fires everywhere, and the fighting was brutal, but then–"

She stopped herself, looking away as the horrible memory consumed her. She wrapped her arms around herself tightly, the old woman suddenly looking as fragile as her age suggested.

My heart twisted, looking to Agatha to continue the story, but her expression was made of impenetrable stone, hard and sharp and unfeeling as she shut down whatever secrets she held.

"Tell us." Rhett eyed her, his brow still furrowed. But the normal scowl he wore around the others slipped, revealing a glimpse of the tenderhearted man I knew dwelled beneath. "Please."

Madame Hedd blinked at him, swallowing hard as she continued, "Then the giant black gate rose out of the sea, somehow already opened, and he…he…"

The old woman shook as she stammered over the words, a darker fear encasing her whole body, her eyes wide and her pupils blown. Every muscle in my body turned to lead as her fear filled the air, capturing us like the smoky fog closing in. Something had scared her worse than Morwyn Locasta and her puppets, something darker and more dangerous…

Agatha finally did us all a favor and put us out of our misery, naming the terror that had torn into our minds and hearts. "Ir'de is gone. And he is risen." She tilted her strong chin up, but a shiver shook her frame despite her best effort. "The Dark God has returned to the land of the living."

Mother of the Moon

30

Sorrow and Schemes

GRIFFIN

By nightfall, the crew huddled together in the *Black Cauldron*, covered in soot and shame as we sat on the stiff benches with Agatha. Rain battered against the stone building, slamming into the windows with rage, as if the sky itself ached to wash away the stench of ash and death that still reached us even here. But while the Huddians could do nothing to stop the God of Death's rampage, the very bones of their island were steeped in old, protective magick, and we'd be safe. For now. Drystan and Genni escorted Madame Hedd back to her shop to gather supplies for spells and more protection charms, but before leaving, the old crone warned us that this moment of peace would be temporary at best.

The rest of the Deyrnas was still vulnerable.

We'd been too little, too late. The Dark God walked among us.

Whenever I'd faced a crisis before, I managed to find the silver lining, a joke in the rough to lighten the weight of pain and worry. It was a survival mechanism, one that had saved my ass more times than I could count. Laughter kept the darkness away, like a shield against the brunt of every tragedy. But there was no humor in what happened to Ir'de. Not a single punchline or snarky spin or hopeful perspective.

No, this was hell on earth.

We'd spent hours scouring through the rubble and debris and found nothing but the dead. Those that died by the mercy of the fire instead of the other painful punishments the Dark God and Locasta's minions had doled out were lucky. Some were burned to dust, but others were mangled and mutilated, their deaths beyond gruesome. Gennevieve worked to dissolve those that hadn't burned as the rest of us pulled them out—men, women, fucking *children*—lining them up and saying prayers over them before the siren used her gift. It wasn't a proper burial, but it was the best any of us could do. Mass graves took too long to dig, and there was no kindling left to burn for a pyre.

None of the Huddians or Tannians came. They just sat on their sister islands, letting us scour through the wreckage of what had once been the soul of the Deyrnas. Not that there was anything left for them to search for.

Silence blanketed the inn, no one even bothering to chew. It'd been a full day since we'd eaten anything, yet we all barely picked at the stew the innkeeper served. None of us had any semblance of an appetite, still covered in ash and soot and grime, none mustering the energy to clean ourselves. But the real mar was on our souls, burned into the dark space behind our eyelids, the horrors of what we'd seen ready to haunt us as soon as we closed them.

The God of Death walked among us. And he'd killed an entire island before the morning tide.

Reagan spoke first, the little dragon rising from beneath the ashes before the rest of us. "We have to fight this. Or he'll kill us all, island by island."

Rhett turned to his youngest cousin, brushing a strand of her messy braid out of her eyes. He grimaced as if it physically hurt him to see the scowl on her face, the darkness churning in her gaze. "I know you want to fight, little dragon, but what can we do? We don't have the rest of the objects, and this is beyond dangerous."

She smacked away his wrist as the stone wall of her will cracked, tears budding in her eyes as her voice quivered. A part of her still managed to care, despite all the ways she tried to prove she didn't. Despite all the terrible things she'd seen to prove it wasn't worth it. "We have enough of them to *try*."

My heart squeezed at her determination, the foolish fighter in me admiring her tenacity. But I said nothing. Because for the first time in my life, I'd been truly defeated.

There was no fighting death and walking away. We could only submit.

Tarran lifted his head for the first time since we'd entered the inn, soot covering his freckles, painting him in uncharacteristic darkness. There was no joy or hope written in his features, only despair caked on like grime, his face drawn and hollow. "We'd all die before we can even get close."

"Would you rather die sitting down in some run-down piece of shit inn?" Saeth snapped at him, sinking her dagger into the bench just an inch from his thigh. But Tarran didn't flinch as he usually did, his fear and fight drained. Saeth snarled at the lack of a response, ripping her dagger from the wood and pointing it at her twin's chin. "You're a coward. I refuse to wait to die. I want a say in when I go and how it happens."

"Enough, please," I groaned, rubbing my forehead to try and combat the forming headache. Rhett nestled closer to me, but it wasn't enough. I couldn't form a single thought over the bickering. I needed the silence, the darkness, an escape. Lyr below, I'd never wanted a drink more in my life, but I knew even whiskey couldn't wash away the trauma that had lodged itself into every nook and cranny of my soul. I sighed, leaning into Rhett for comfort. "I'm trying to think."

"Don't hurt yourself, big guy," Saeth sneered at me, plopping down into her seat again with a wicked smirk.

"Fuck off, Saeth," I spat back before I could think, my rage and sorrow bubbling over. I knew she was like me–that anger was easier than the anguish. But still, I needed one second to breathe, to rest, to try and outrun the brutal images my mind was throwing at me….

A white nightdress stained red. A swollen stomach punctured and poured out like a skin of wine. A blue eye, rolling across the cobblestone. A scream in the distance, clawing up from my throat.

Bodies piled in heaps, ash everywhere. Shadows and smoke filling my lungs, choking me, reminding me I'm next. No screams, just silence. Endless emptiness.

"Sorry." Saeth drew me back to the stone walls of the *Black Cauldron*, her voice consumed with pain. She rubbed her eyes with the backs of her hands, spreading the soot across her pale cheeks. "I just–"

"I know." We were all in foul moods. It would be more unsettling if she wasn't her prickly self right now. I sat back, the shoddy wood biting at my ass, but I let myself feel it, glad to feel anything at all. My body had gone numb hours ago, even though my mind was still an aching whirlwind. I let loose a laugh, one born of instinct and repetition, but there was no mirth to the sound. "This is all so messed up."

"Yer not alone in this anymore. We all have to come together, or we risk extinction," Agatha cut in, her presence demanding authority. We still hadn't heard even the slightest of explanations from her, but all the same, her warrior's will was welcome right now. I'd spent enough drunken, disastrous nights in her bar to trust that the shrewd woman knew her way around a tight situation. And I didn't have the stones to stand up and lead. Her brows furrowed, but there was a certainty in her square jaw that made me sit up a bit straighter. "Ye can't have my cards, but I'll use them fer ye. And I'll snag Brigid's crown, if it managed to survive the attack."

I blinked at the woman, trying to decipher the meaning of her words, but they all blurred and rammed together in my dog-tired mind.

Agatha was a barkeep. A businesswoman. How in Lyr's name did she know about the cards and the crown? A lot of legends had probably tumbled from loose lips at her barstool, but for her to bring that up now, of all things...

I stared at the woman like I was seeing her for the first time in my life.

"What do you mean *your* cards?" Rhett growled, leaning forward. He hated surprises, and after the day we'd all experienced, I doubted he was in the mood for Agatha's secrets.

"They work best if I use them." She shrugged, as if he was simply asking about the weather, not magical cards designed by a long-lost goddess. A hint of a smirk graced her dark features. "I made 'em, after all."

My head spun like the witch slapped me, a trickle of surprise managing its way through the body-wide ache of hopelessness that weighed me down to the bench.

"Lyr's stinky bits," I cursed out loud, sizing up Agatha with a fresh perspective.

Her dark braids clung to her head and trailed down her back like snake-tails, the metal clasps fastened at the bottom twinkling in the lantern light like beady eyes. The midnight blue dress she wore wrapped loosely around her, hiding most of her frame, more mysteries tucked away in its folds. Her inkblot gaze held mine, swimming with secrets. She'd always had an aura of strength about her akin to a warrior princess, but a goddess? Not just any goddess, but the magick weaver herself, who legends said stole magick from the realms beyond and brought it to the isles of man...

"You're–" Tarran stammered, figuring it out. "I'm sorry, you're telling me *you're*–?"

The door to the tavern flew open and banged against the stone wall before Tarran could finish his sentence, a cool wind stirring the stale, charred air. And in blew another surprise—and though we'd already been saturated with enough upheaval for one day, our heads all snapped to the direction of the newcomers.

"Cerridwen." Nef waltzed in first, still clad in dark furs, her sunny hair spilling in loose waves behind her. A strike of lightning highlighted her silhouette in gold. My nuts leapt into my throat, fear prickling across my back as I remembered the teeny tiny *dragon* we'd stolen from her, but she didn't make any note of me or my crew, wholly focused on Agatha. She held a terse smile as she drank in the barkeep. "It's great to see you, sister. It's been too long."

Sister.

Her Lyr-damned *sister*.

Cerridwen.

"Not long enough, Neffy." Agatha blinked at the sky goddess, face impassive as if she barely registered the intrusion. I fought the smirk that twitched at the corner of my lips.

Gwynn shoved in after Nef, his frame darkening the doorway as his sister stepped deeper into the *Black Cauldron*. The hunter's gaze instantly found Saeth's, and my cousin stiffened in her seat, heat flaring in her pale, ash-smeared cheeks.

"Told you I'd find you again, Ice Queen." After a too-long moment, he looked away, stepping between the two goddesses present, a broad smile aimed at Agatha. I didn't think the surly bastard *could* smile, but his sharp white teeth glimmered against his skin in a genuine expression that captured his whole face. "I can't believe you were *in* Pysgodd and didn't bother to say hello."

"I can't believe you didn't know." Agatha's mask cracked, a hint of a smirk pulling her lips. But she still crossed her arms, not looking away from Nef. "I didn't think I had an open invitation."

The rest of us sat in perfect silence, staring at the standoff with wide eyes and clenched asses. Even I had better sense than to get involved in whatever family drama was unfolding in front of us.

"So I guess you're my auntie, then?" Vian broke the quiet first, his head tilted to the side as he addressed Agatha from his perch on the table. He shoved a hulking spoonful of stew into his mouth, carrying on while he chewed noisily, "Nice to re-meet you."

"You have so much explaining to do, Agatha," Rhett muttered under his breath, silver-and-blue eyes darting between all three gods, his knuckles white as he gripped my thigh. Not that I minded the contact, but I was pretty sure he'd cut off the bloodflow to my toes with his anxiety.

Agatha turned to us once more, finally remembering that we were still here, putting her back to the other gods like they were nothing. A growl built in the back of Gwynn's throat and Nef raised her eyebrows, but Agatha remained unbothered. She ran a dark hand through her braids, tossing them behind her. "Please call me Cerridwen. Or Cerri. Agatha is a terrible name. If I wasn't in hiding, I'd have ditched it long ago."

My crew looked at her again like she just admitted to eating dog shit for breakfast before their heads all turned to me. And waited.

Breathe in, breathe out.

I had no patience for any of this madness anymore. No answers, no plans. No explanations for the three gods suddenly gracing us with their presence, no idea how to face the sea of sorrow waiting outside of our stone-walled safehouse. I was spent, body and soul, out of chips to bet and short on luck. It was high time I turned in my cards and cut my losses like a respectable man.

But I wasn't a respectable man. I was as foolish and flagrant as an unpaid escort. Even when the world was on fire, I still hadn't learned my lesson. I was still willing to get burned.

"Lyr below, does anyone else have any life-altering information to share? No more hidden gods, right?" I cracked a grin, stretching my arms behind my head with a wink to Aga—Cerridwen. I had no idea what a good Captain would do in this nightmare. I probably should have offered my prayers at the gods' feet and begged for salvation. But an idiot like me could wring a joke from even the driest of moments. And if I couldn't offer my crew safety or security or any of the things that mattered, I could at least shoot for consistency. I leaned further into the familiar role, nudging Tarran's knee with my dirty boot. "Tarran, you're not secretly a fair-folk rabbit-shifter, right?"

"Why, you want to boil me in a stew?" he snorted, the sound chasing back some of the burnt taste of sorrow still lining my dry throat. Rhett coughed a laugh, covering himself as he patted Tarran's back with false pity.

Reagan lifted her head, dark eyes gleaming with mischief as she snickered. "No, you would be too chewy."

Vian nodded excitedly in conspiratory understanding. "The wind thinks he'd be better fried."

This time, the laughs weren't guarded or muted, but free and full, enough to clear some of the tension from the air. Even Rhett's constricting hold on my leg loosened with relief. I dared a deep breath, my first one in hours. Days, maybe. And as the oxygen filled my smoke-scarred lungs, it swept away more of the debris from my soul.

Hope, apparently, could not be destroyed by fire and shadows and ash.

Only I decide what hurts me.

The Dark God would have to try harder next time.

"So you all decided to come out of your cozy little caves now that an entire island is dead?" Saeth spat at the gods like they were servants, not deities incarnate, bursting the little bubble of ease we'd fallen into. "Great fucking timing."

Nef and Cerridwen both grimaced as her words struck them, staring at the dirty floorboards, grief and guilt written across their faces plain enough for a blind man to read. Saeth stood, the shark scenting the blood in the water, unable to back down from the taste. But Gwynn kept his head high, his broad shoulders straight.

"You're right." He did not balk beneath my cousin's gaze, taking her fury and malice on the chin. His voice was softer than I'd ever heard it, but strong all the same. "I'm a hunter, not a hider. I'm sorry it took a few smart-mouthed brats stealing my sister's dragon to remind me." He smirked, nodding to Reagan, a lightness in his dark eyes I must have missed during our first encounter.

Saeth opened her mouth like she had a retort, no doubt one that would've made all of us wince, but on cue, Reagan popped up next to her, sticking a hand to her hip without the slightest trace of fear or reverence. "Better to be a smart-mouthed, bratty thief than a stupid cave-dweller who bathes in dragon shit."

I stilled, heart racing, my hands twitching nearer to my swords with every slow second that passed. But then Gwynn reached his hand out, and instead of smacking Reagan into oblivion, he tousled her hair like she was the family pet.

And for the first time all day, Saeth managed a grin, her icy stare melting just a little.

Lyr below, maybe these gods were capable of miracles.

Curses, too, the flattened island across the river a brutal reminder to any of us that dared forget. I shifted closer to Rhett, his steady presence the only anchor I had in the storm of conflicting emotion battering against me.

"We take full responsibility for the carnage that occurred here. We should have heeded your warning," Nef spoke up as if reading my thoughts, her head still bowed to Saeth like my cousin was a queen and they were her faithful followers. She cast a glance at Gwynn. "We've gotten complacent in the mountains."

The hunter god's throat worked hard as he swallowed down that truth, his stare finally dipping from Saeth's eyes to her toes. Shame burned his cheeks scarlet, and for the slightest moment, the overwhelming presence of him dimmed. Perhaps, beneath the power and muscle and ancient understanding, he was just a man, too. One plagued with the same affliction of guilt I'd been carrying for months.

Crimson against ivory, blood against stone.
Silver eyes cast in sorrow and understanding.

"You're not responsible." I stood, tossing both arms around Saeth and Reagan, wiping some of the soot off Reagan's face with my only clean finger. None of us were truly good or right; we'd all have our regrets to sort through at the end of this dark path. But regret only served as a reminder of lessons learned, not blame for what we'd endured. And there was only one creature in this universe that could shoulder the fault of what happened here. "Arawn will pay for what he's done."

Gwynn's head flicked up, his dark, steely gaze acknowledging me for the first time since he strode into the place. But an unspoken respect passed between us, a truce against the real enemy. He nodded, his voice dipping into a low, nearly animal snarl. "It is time we remind him of his side of the pact and hold him accountable."

"How?" Tarran shifted, a plea in the strain of his voice. "You saw what happened…the *whole island*…"

Gwynn plopped down onto the bench next to him, stretching out and spreading his legs like he owned the whole tavern. Tarran stiffened and turned beet-red next to him, but Gwynn nudged his side like they were old buddies, eyeing me like I was his next victim. "Well, if your Captain wants to hand me my swords back, I can show you all how to use them."

The swords sang at my back, and I frowned, a possessive, stupid piece of me unwilling to part with them. Saeth snickered in agreement. "Go ahead, Griffin, I can think of quite a few places you could shove them…"

"Enough," Rhett grumbled, and I wanted to kiss him right then and there. The crew and the gods all went quiet at his command. I settled for offering a grateful look as he stood at my side, ready to help me carve a path forward. "An island is dead. Keira is still missing, and somehow the gate to hell has been opened. We don't need jabs and bickering. We need a Lyr-damned plan."

"So what do you suggest, Captain?" Vian pulled his mother's bow from his back, determination stretching his wire-thin frame tight. Nef pursed her lips, watching as he barely paid her any attention, but said nothing, instead looking at me with the same deference her son did.

I glanced at Rhett and Saeth, wishing I could siphon off some of their easy confidence or authority, but this was my test. I couldn't keep passing the torch anymore. The longer I denied my leadership, the more time Arawn had to bury another island in ash and darkness.

You remind me of Cedric.

It was high time I started acting like it.

"Where do we think he's headed next?" I kept my voice even and raised a brow at the gods, hoping one of them could shine some divine light on his moves. If I was going to lead my crew into a suicide mission to stop the God of Death, I needed insight, and the lazy deities that finally swaggered into the inn were going to deliver it.

"I'll consult the cards, but my best guess is he is going to make camp in Orwellin now that he's topside. The obsidian is basically a conduit for his power, and even though he managed to get out, he's going to want to stay where he's strongest and where Lyr's influence is lessened," Cerridwen sighed, sinking into the bench next to her brother, her eyes glazing over in a milky white for a moment. Her brow tightened before she blinked the haze away, lips flattening into a tight line. "But that doesn't mean he won't try and take out the other islands one by one. I can't see any of his movements specifically."

My gut knotted at the thought, a chill running down my spine as I remembered the massive black temples in Orwellin, all amplifiers to his already-mighty power. If he could wreak this kind of havoc without the boost, how would Pysgodd or Hud stand against him *with* the assistance?

"If we were to use all of the items against him at once, how would we fare?" Rhett rubbed the stubble on his chin, blackening the blond hairs with dark ash. His eyes screamed the same worry gnawing at my nerves.

The gods exchanged a similarly tight look.

Nef huffed a breath first, violet eyes darkening as she joined us on the bench. Even sitting, her posture was straight as an arrow, her birdlike gaze sharp and cutting. But there was a fear there, too, hiding just beneath her polished exterior. "Hard to say. Morwyn Locasta's dark magick poses a threat. We can cut through it with the items, but my guess is Arawn is prepared to let her take the brunt of the hits for him. We would need to take out Morwyn and her puppets first and then maybe, *maybe* we have a chance at him if we combine objects and our powers."

Fear prickled at the back of my neck at the mention of the shadow puppets. I'd never run from a fight, my sense of self-preservation inherently lacking, but up against those mindless beasts, I tasted true terror. There was nothing in any of them. No fury or hope or any natural motivation. Just bloodlust. Death.

The thought of facing them again sent my stomach flipping upside down. Morwyn was a monster in her own right, and with Arawn behind her...

There was no easy path forward. No way to circumvent the inevitable battle against darkness itself.

And this might just be a fight we had no hope of winning.

"We need to find a way to bypass Morwyn and strike Arawn first. Take him by surprise." Saeth's voice was barely above a whisper, but it carried, eyes hunting for an answer as they flicked between us. Heads perked up as she spoke, the idea fanning the flames of hope that had all but died down. As always, the queen of needles thought in pinpricks and loopholes, anything to burrow beneath her enemy's skin and pry it up from within.

I rubbed the spot on my chest that housed my tattoo, thinking of Finna. She'd be so proud to see how cunning our cousin had become under her tutelage.

A deep ache sank into my limbs, but I fought the weight threatening to drag me under.

Cerridwen shook her head, dashing our dreams with a scowl. "It's very hard to sneak up on him. He can scry through obsidian and ice…there's a good chance he'll see us coming."

Saeth sank into her seat, disappointment evident in her clenched jaw, but her partner in crime was already there with a parry on her behalf.

"Not if he's distracted." Reagan nudged Saeth's side, and she sat straighter again. "If we can create a large enough diversion with Locasta, he might not focus on a smaller group sneaking past his defenses from behind."

"Or below," Vian chimed in, his boyish face harsh with shadows and ash. "He's going to make camp in God's Eye. It has the worst energy, and he'll probably love that. If he does, I can get us in through the hidden passages."

I looked at the three of them for a long moment, my brain blank with all but awe. Saeth's brutal cunning, Reagan's voracious passion, Vian's eccentric daring. Fire and ice, earth and wind, they were unstoppable forces of nature, and they were still only *children*. At their age, I could barely tell my head from my cock. But even in a room full of warriors and deities, they stood untouchable. Since the start, they'd been the thinkers, the mischief makers, the planners. They'd carried us through to find the gods, meeting challenge after challenge with unwavering grit, and now they were already outpacing the king of Death himself.

Lyr help any poor soul that ever crossed their paths.

I would not be one of them.

I cleared my throat and my head, throwing in my support before anyone else could question their initiative. "We'll need more people if we're going to distract Daddy Death."

Rhett slid his hand into mine and squeezed, my fearless partner already rallying to my aid before I even had to ask. "Drystan can send word to his comrades in Orwellin. He still has spies from the defected guard."

My brows flew up at the casual suggestion of relying on Drys for help, but he shrugged, a grin toying with his pretty mouth.

Cerridwen nodded. "Madame Hedd and I will help gather some Magickas. Perhaps there are those in Hud that would be willing to cast protections or counter spells against Locasta to keep her busy."

My heart soared, treacherous, dangerous hope blooming through my whole chest before I could stop it. "The more fools willing to follow us, the better. The Dark God won't know what hit him."

"Councilwoman Tommins would send hunters from Pysgodd if we asked," Tarran piped up, running a hand through his mess of curls. "She said she'd throw her support anywhere we needed it."

"The hunters, maybe, but no civilians. They'd be fodder to buy us time, and I've had enough of that." Gwynn patted Tarran's knee, and my cousin shrank again, but the hunter god held no contempt, a dark challenge instead rising in his glare. "We can handle Morwyn without them."

The taste of brewing trouble coated my tongue, and I lapped up the familiar warning, a kinship spreading as my respect for the surly hunter instantly doubled. No more dead innocents was a policy I could get behind, even if the prick rubbed me the wrong way most of the time.

"It's Arawn I worry about," Nef interjected, folding her arms across her chest as she shivered despite the sticky heat of the inn. "He sired the three of us, so there is a sway. His gift is absence, shadow. He can amplify others, but he can also weaken our influence. So we would still need all of us at once to manage it."

I looked to Cerridwen and Gwynn, hoping one of them would deny Nef's claim, but the truth was apparent in the matching frowns they wore.

"So Vian would need to take all three of you to him with the objects while the rest of us handle Morwyn," I spelled out the uncomfortable imbalance. We'd fared fine the first time we went up against Morwyn, but without Keira, Ronan, and the sirens, I didn't want to imagine how long a handful of mortals and a few Magicka were going to last against a dark magick witch bitch without some aid. "Is there anything else that can help us against Locasta's tricks?"

Cerridwen ticked her fingers against her chin. "Anything imbued with pure magick. Siren scales, *faoladh* teeth, dragon-fire…"

My gut sank, the list almost as daunting as the task itself. Again, if Ronan and his crew were here, we'd be more than all right, but without them we were severely lacking. Shame spread through my middle like wildfire, the all-too familiar feeling of failure rattling around in my hollow heart.

Again, I wasn't enough on my own. Never enough.

"I can help with that." Nef burst from her seat with the speed of an arrow before I could finish feeling sorry for myself, a broad smile spreading across her effervescent face. "Why don't we take a look outside?"

I narrowed my eyes at her as she strode from the room, her long hair swishing behind her on a phantom breeze. Gwynn followed tight at her heels as he fought a smirk, his cheek twitching with the effort.

My crew looked at me, waiting for my signal. I shrugged, anticipation building in my veins. I had no idea what the gods had in store, and I was well beyond trying to sort it all out in my tiny head.

We all crammed through the door without further hesitation, the sweltering heat and humidity smacking me the second I stepped outside. But as the rain pelted against our faces in large droplets, the scent of ash subsided, today's terrors washed away by the water. I squinted against the crying sky to see what Nef pointed at, her long arm extended. Thunder clapped above, and I jumped, whirling to the sound.

No, not thunder.

Wings. Booming as they carried the massive beasts higher and higher…

"Holy dragon dicks," I swore as I took them all in, standing closer to Rhett. Diving in and out of the clouds, proud wings beating loudly, dozens of dragons soared overhead. They all swooped up, swallowing down clouds of ash to clear the smoky sky, their multicolored scales gleaming as the rain trailed over them.

"Awyr!" Reagan pointed at the gigantic black dragon circling closest to us, larger than any of the other beasts by far. As if he heard her, the creature flicked his tail and dove fast, gold eyes trained on us like prey. My stomach rose to my throat, but before he could crash into us, he spread his wings wide, banking up to the clouds once more.

I barked a shocked laugh, covering my brow from the rain so I could watch the horrifying, magnificent beast careen toward the others, snapping at a jade dragon's tail like an overgrown mutt.

"The Dragon Horde always flies together," Gwynn explained, his smugness returning with a vengeance.

"And as his horde, they will fall in line with Awyr wherever he goes," Nef added, sticking her hands to her hips. Somehow, despite the rain, her hair still billowed around her, untouched, while it drenched the rest of us.

I grinned at her anyway, not caring if I looked like a drowned rat right now. This rain would help clean the southern isles of Arawn's path of destruction. And the dragons would help us rid the world of Morwyn Locasta, her puppet army, and the Dark God once and for all.

"I have an idea no one is going to like." Vian stepped forward, soaked, his head tilted back so he could watch the dragons with a wild gleam in those keen eyes. "But it might work."

This was hell on earth, and there was no silver lining to these rainclouds. But as thunder roared above in tandem with the dragon horde, I couldn't help but let loose another bubbling laugh, my voice joining their chorus.

The Dark God walked among us now, and we were going to give him a proper Deyrnasian welcome before sending him back to the Otherworld in pieces.

"Tell us what you've got, kid."

3I

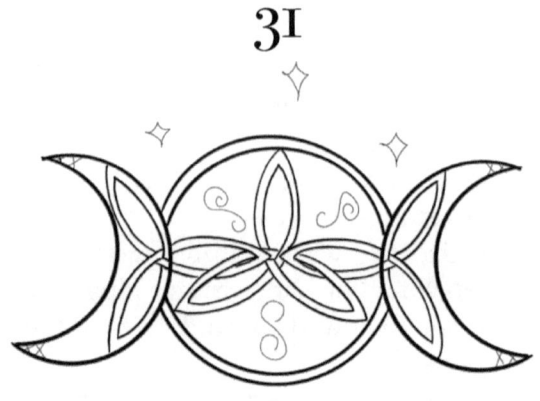

Memories and Magic

KEIRA

My husband had no memory of me. Of us.

Not a single moment of our life together. Not the faintest hint of the blood and banter between us, nor a mention of the love and loss we'd endured. He had promised the gates everything, and they'd taken it all without mercy.

I'd made no such promise, but the gates ripped my heart out all the same. I'd come back from the dead only to have my life stolen.

Now all that was left were the curious, confused glances of a complete stranger. Those sapphire eyes that once looked at me like I was the whole world, narrowed with scrutiny as he sized me up. Those bow-shaped lips that had once kissed me with passion and whispered promises of tomorrow, pursed as he decided what to make of me. Hands that once held mine, shoved into pockets or made busy with work. Heart that once beat only for me, guarded behind layers of masks once more.

I'd escaped Arwan. Ronan had not.

He was never less than polite about it, responding easily whenever I spoke to him first, or offering casual, courteous greetings as we passed each other throughout the day. But it felt like a punch to the face all the same, when every strand of my being ached to throw myself into his arms, to kiss him until he remembered, until he felt the bone-deep longing I felt...

We'd been sailing for three full days, my gifts helping us cut through the tempestuous sea at a voracious pace. But with our crew halved and healing, we all needed more frequent breaks than normal, and we were still a day or two from Ir'de. A day from my family, my crew. From the only people in the universe that might be able to understand, to comfort me. I was desperate for Griffin's ridiculous but reassuring presence, for Saeth's blunt acceptance and Tarran's sunshine smile. For Rhett's steady quiet, Vian's wild whimsy and even Reagan's fiery rage. I was ready to take accountability for it all, to serve my penance and repair what I'd broken.

But even if I was reunited with my kin, there would be no returning what was lost all over again.

Ronan.

Ronan.

Ronan.

Papa once said a good sailor needed a home to come back to. I'd just never realized that home could be a person. And mine had been torn down without my consent, leaving me banished once more.

The very thought of Papa sent a shiver up my spine despite the warm sun licking the back of my neck. A deep ache settled in my chest as I missed him with a fury as painful and potent as the day he died. He would've known what to do about Ronan. He and Reina, Finna and Owen and Roland...they would have fought for a solution, for hope, just as they had against Arawn. They would've swaddled me in love and light until the black pit in my heart was no less than a few lingering shadows.

But they weren't here. Not anymore. I'd left them behind.

For the first time since that black night on the *Ceffyl*, I was truly alone.

Past noon, the sun already hung like ripe fruit in the sky, the southern heat rising in waves from the dry wooden deck. It was so strange, to be warm again after so many weeks of ice. My body had forgotten what it was like to sweat, to work. To *live*.

It all felt wrong. The rope in my hands as I climbed the rigging too coarse, too rough. The salt water on my skin too cold, the sun on my cheeks too hot.

I hefted myself up onto the first beam of the mizzenmast, sighing as I settled onto the wood. I worked at the knots to free the heavy sail, my fingers trembling like a new sailor's legs. I didn't know the *Madyn* as intimately as the *Ceffyl*, but still, I should've had more tact than this. Lyr below, perhaps it was best Papa couldn't see me now.

"Do you need a hand there?" Ronan called up from the deck, brow knotted as he watched me fumble about. His voice sent chills down my back, my flesh peppering into goosebumps as the familiar velvet of his tone enveloped me.

This was worse than being separated. To have him so close, so *real*. And to be barred from him all the same. Strangers.

"No, I could do this in my sleep," I scoffed back, my eyes on the knots I failed to untie. I couldn't look at him for too long without my chest threatening to cave in, grief crushing me like a breaking dam.

"Still, you're pregnant," he sighed heavily, the way he always did when his mind was torn. I spared myself a glance at him, though I immediately wished I hadn't. His blond curls shone pure gold in the sunlight, his eyes sparkling with concern as he rolled back his sleeves and climbed into the rigging.

Concern, not for me, but for the baby, I reminded myself. My mouth went dry at the bronze of his forearms, thicker than they had been before I left. A new tattoo of a proud dragon cradling a crescent moon inked his flesh, his skin remembering what his mind forgot. His saltwater gaze trailed to my middle.

"I doubt that this is appropriate for someone in your condition."

My hand flew instinctively to my abdomen, the urge to cover and hide welling up. My cheeks flushed with embarrassment, tears stinging at the backs of my eyes with a much deeper hurt.

"I've done far more dangerous things in my *condition* without your permission, thanks," I snapped before I could catch myself, turning back to the knots in front of me while letting my hair fall forward, a curtain between us. He didn't deserve my anger after all he'd been through to save me, but hurt flashed through me all the same.

My condition, he'd called it. Not our baby. Our future.

Taming you would be like taming the sea.

I was unbidden, pregnant or not. I was a sailor, a sea-born, salt-forged fucking pirate. A goddess, my power pure and unrefined. Yet he'd tamed me body and soul. He'd made me his in every way possible. And then he'd sacrificed it all. For me.

I should've been grateful. I was, somewhere deep down. But more than anything, I was hurt. Hurt that he hadn't traded something else. Hurt that the gates demanded so much.

Hurt that I couldn't fix any of it.

A single tear betrayed me, spilling from my eye and splashing onto the dry wood of the mizzenmast. I scattered to try and cover the spot, but Ronan was faster, his hand brushing against mine as he moved to wipe the tear away, smearing it into the oak.

He pulled his hand back a second later like I'd branded him. My heart sank. *No*, he'd branded *me*, right on my soul, and there was no cutting the mark away. My heart remembered him even if his did not.

"My apologies, Captain. I didn't mean to overstep." Ronan cleared his throat, his tone all cordial and contained. None of the dangerous wit I loved, none of the semisweet sarcasm I savored. Cold and calculated, like I was nothing to him anymore.

I supposed I wasn't.

But he was everything to me.

I groaned, finally whipping my head up and meeting his eyes. My face likely told the full story of my feelings, but I didn't care. I didn't know how to shield my thoughts from him any better than I knew how to shield them from myself. So even if he couldn't remember any of his own mind, he would be subject to mine. Because I couldn't take it all alone anymore. "Please, for the love of Lyr, just call me Keira. I know you don't remember and you're adjusting, but it just feels cruel to call me *Captain*."

Surprise lifted his brows for a brief moment, the corner of his mouth twitching with amusement before he schooled his features again. Ever the snake, shedding one skin for another whenever it suited him. But still, my heart leapt at the brief glance of the real him.

"I imagine this is all hard for you too," he leaned back, twisting his head to the side to hide his expression. His hand still grasped tightly on a rope, the muscles in his glorious arms straining as he held himself aloft. Lyr below, I'd forgotten just how breathtaking he was, blinded by Death and desire. Since my return to the land of the living, whatever false feelings I held for Death had disappeared entirely. But it was too late to change what I'd done. What I'd lost.

Ronan's head fell back as he soaked up the sun, his tan skin glowing as he absorbed the warm rays on his cheeks. "I've been trying to remember, watching you work and whatnot, and I swear it all feels familiar, like I *should* know…but I don't."

My heart skipped a beat, not just from his effortless beauty, but his words dripping life into the dried-up well of hope in my chest. I leaned closer, scanning his face for truth. Memories could be taken, but perhaps *feelings* couldn't be erased entirely. All that we'd been through together, all that we'd shared–it had to have left a scar, a stamp on his heart as it had mine.

"I was thinking, we should try and see if you can jog his memories!" Nelle called from the deck, and I jumped in surprise. Panic rattled my head as I scrambled, veering so far forward that I nearly fell off the beam, but a strong arm caught the crook of my elbow, pulling me upright.

His touch sent pure electricity through my veins, reanimating parts of me I thought dead and left in the Otherworld. My heart raced, fear easing, only to give way to a different sort of alertness that quickened my pulse.

Ronan tracked my face with predatory precision, searching for signs of harm before letting go, blush reddening his cheeks. My skin chilled at the loss of contact, but a heat crept up my neck and face with the realization that our semi-private conversation had been privy to at least one set of siren ears.

Ronan recovered first, hopping out of the rigging and onto the deck with ease. He stuffed his hands into his pockets, full attention trained on Nelle. "How could we do that?"

The siren pursed her lips and looked to me, waiting for me to join them. With a sigh, I followed less gracefully, slowly walking myself back down the rope ladder, the slight roundness to my middle throwing off my equilibrium just enough to make me clumsy. I hadn't noticed in the Otherworld, and even as the faint curves of my midsection had started to show, my body hadn't felt *altered* in any way. Then again, I hadn't felt much at all, aside from the tricks and illusions Arawn wanted me to experience. But here, the reality of the physical change stood out like a sore thumb. Or a sore back, really. And sore feet. And swollen, skill-less fingers and the overwhelming urge to piss every twenty minutes and nausea that mimicked the worst seasickness every rutting morning.

Nelle had warned that things would start to get worse. According to the math, I was likely seventeen weeks along, and I would naturally start to experience more symptoms anyway, though there was no real knowing how my time in the Otherworld had affected the timeline or development. Nelle had a theory that the magic was somewhat like *Hiraeth's*, slowing down time in a way that also slowed growth. But the female body was already a mystery and a miracle without the little thing of a few months in the realm of gods to add an element of surprise to it.

I finally met the deck, my stupid, aching feet pinching in my shoes as I raised a brow at Nelle. This information had better be worth me looking like an overfed seal trying to climb down in too-small boots. I panted as I stuck my hands to my hips. "What's the plan?"

"Danura used to do it whenever sirens came in with trouble remembering what happened to them...before." Nelle toyed with the end of her long braid, anxious fingers matching the fluttering beat of my own heart. Violet eyes flicked between Ronan and me as she explained, words tumbling over themselves to get out, "Laureli is brewing a simple memory draught from the supplies we have left, but I thought that maybe, if you added your power, we might be able to trigger *something*. Since you made him a siren after all, there might be a connection we can tap into."

My hope snapped in half like a bowstring pulled too tightly, the tension recoiling through me so hard I winced. Arawn had taught me to shape my gifts into different elements, my control over my power the only benefit I'd earned in hell. But wielding power as a weapon was very different from using it as a tool. The last time I'd tried to heal instead of kill, I'd barbequed Finna. The scent of her burnt flesh still haunted my memories, even after the recent weeks we'd spent bonding.

I eyed Ronan, the picture of pure health. It had been worth the risk when he was on Death's doorstep, but to put him in that place again while he was well made me cringe. "I don't know, that might be—"

"Worth a try," Ronan cut me off, shrugging like it was a hand of cards to bet on, not his life. A smirk worked its way across his face, and I had to fight the urge to smack it off. "What's the risk? I'm not going to turn out like Marina, right?"

I shuddered at the thought. The siren hadn't spoken outside of the nonsense riddles since we boarded, and at night, her dreams tore her from her chambers with abstract screams none of us could decipher. Nelle had been drugging her since just to help her stay calm and quiet. Ronan's fate was already terrible enough, but to addle his mind further…

No, we needed him sharp. Safe.

Nelle placed her hand on my arm, her thumb tracing soothing circles into my skin like she could taste my fear. "It might be uncomfortable for you, Ronan, but nothing too severe. We'd stop before anything gets rough."

Ronan nodded again, folding his arms in the way that meant business. I knew that look—the burning, sizzling thing that would not be easily swayed or satiated.

I rolled my eyes, huffing out a resigned breath. He might not remember who I was, but he sure as rain hadn't forgotten himself. "If you're sure."

"Absolutely." He tucked his hands in his pockets, his wicked grin spreading. "Mostly."

I jerked my head to the cabin, shoving down the fear that still gurgled in my gut. I had gotten stronger in the Otherworld, Death's tests fortifying my control, and Nelle was here to guide me if I needed it. There would be no more mistakes. "Let's try now while the wind is low anyway."

I took a decisive step toward the deck, straightening my shoulders as I led. If Ronan was willing to try, I had to be willing to let him. I wanted my husband back, and I wouldn't let fear own my footsteps. I made my own fate.

Or so I thought until I stumbled over my own feet, nearly faceplanting into the gray wood.

Ronan caught me around my middle, his sturdy embrace gently righting me. "Careful, Cap—Keira," he corrected, his hold lingering for one blissful moment before he uncoiled himself from me, mask tight to his expression.

"Sorry, I'm not used to this." I looked down at my useless, clumsy feet, the heat of his gaze too much for my already burning cheeks. But my hand held my abdomen, a small rush of love banishing the embarrassment. Already, the life inside me was as mischievous and unsettling as her parents, able to rock me like a wave with her tiny existence. I blinked back up at Ronan, wishing he could know this force of nature in my womb like I did. "In the Otherworld, I barely felt pregnant. Or anything, really. The magic is strange…my external senses were heightened but my sense of self wasn't. But I do feel her. Even there, with Arawn toying with me, her presence was palpable. She'll be something incredible one day."

Ronan's eyes lit with wonder as they met mine before falling to my middle. The wickedness of his grin washed away, a softness only I'd been allowed to see finally making an appearance in his expression. "She already is."

Slowly, he extended a hand, an offering. My heart beat faster, just as uncoordinated as my legs as I took it. This time, I was ready for that jolt of electricity, and I let it center me to myself as he led me down into the belly of the *Madyn*, his presence steady at my side.

The walk to the Captain's quarters was not long, though walking past the Galley where Ellian huddled over Siobhan sent a pang of longing through me. He hadn't left her side in days, the bags under his eyes a deep purple, watching as she slipped in and out of consciousness, healing from the hounds' attack. I had no idea when he'd fallen so deeply for her, but there was no calling him off her scent now that he'd gotten a whiff of it.

I needed this memory spell to work. Needed my own better half at my side again. Needed my Ronan.

We pushed through the gray door to where Laureli commandeered the space, turning it into her own little workshop. Ronan dropped my hand as we entered, and I fought a frown, instead taking in Laureli's transformed space. Pillows lined the floor in softness, the tapestries hanging from the rafters coloring the dull space in a rainbow of silk and soft cotton. A black cauldron sat in front of the siren, her dark hair wrapped in a silk scarf to keep it back from her face. The smell of rotten eggs and some sharp spice wafted from the tendrils of smoke swirling from the mixture, turning my already-queasy stomach.

I gagged aloud, unable to swallow the disgust that crawled through me. At that, her head snapped up, a smudge of something green on her left cheek. "You look like crap. Have you slept at all?"

I pinched my nose, settling myself onto a deep sapphire pillow furthest from the stinky potion. "Thanks for the compliment, but no."

Ronan grimaced as he took a seat next to me, crossing his legs and leaning far from Laureli's cauldron like it was going to bite him if he got too close. Even Nelle covered her mouth with a hand, suppressing a few coughs as she took my other side, all of us hugging the wall like ivy.

Laureli rolled her eyes at us, reaching behind her and snagging a vial of plum-colored liquid from her messy collection. She rolled it toward me across the rug, jerking her chin in a no-nonsense command. "Drink it."

I fingered the vial with distrust, holding it far from my face as I studied the purple concoction. "What is it?"

"The less you know, the better." She shrugged, turning back to the vile concoction she was brewing, stirring the contents again. "But it will give you and the runt in your belly some energy. And it smells better than this."

I popped the cork and took a swig without further coaxing, desperate for some kind of boost and salvation from the stink. The liquid slid down my throat easily, the taste of blueberries and something sugary coating my tongue in a blissful escape. I groaned as I swallowed before drinking the rest of the bottle greedily. Almost immediately, a buzz tingled through my veins, the colors in the room brighter, my back less sore.

"Thank you," I said, and Laureli nodded, sitting back and wiping sweat from her brow as she finished her brew.

Ronan eyed me warily, a flicker of concern passing through the impassive facade. "Are you certain you're up for this?"

"Absolutely." I crossed my arms, the energy zapping through me making me bold. I grinned at him. "Maybe."

Ronan smiled at the joke. At the first new inside memory we had together. My heart soared, the potion giving wings to the hope in my chest. Maybe we could do this. Maybe we had a chance, but even if we couldn't restore all of it…maybe we could build something new from the rubble.

If, of course, Ronan survived Laureli's cooking first.

Laureli produced a ladle and scooped a whopping serving of the thick, green potion into a cup, handing it to Ronan with a wry smirk. "Drink up, boy, and then we begin."

Ronan pursed his full lips, swirling the mixture in the goblet twice before tilting it back into his mouth and swallowing. His face blanched as he belched, patting his chest to encourage the odious drink to stay down. "Gross."

I bit my lip to stifle a laugh, but Ronan shot me a look that killed the sound in my throat. And also stirred something else much deeper, a desire I wouldn't dare name.

"What do I do?" I cleared my throat and my head, turning to Nelle instead.

She offered a small smile. "It'll take a few minutes for the potion to start working. Then, when it kicks in, you'll touch him wherever you feel the tug, just like when we turned him. I'll be here, my gifts guiding you again. I can't heal anymore, but I can still observe."

I swallowed hard. Touching Ronan right now was no easy feat, despite the way my pulse quickened at the thought. Worse, I knew his siren hearing would pick up on the syncopated rhythm, baring my embarrassment clear as sunshine on the sea.

"Then what?" I continued, eyes never leaving Nelle's, unable to face Ronan yet. Lyr below, I was worse than Griffin right now. I wondered if the heat building steadily in my core was a symptom of the pregnancy. Had to be.

"Dunno." Laureli shrugged, sitting back and thankfully putting a lid on the cauldron that lessened the repugnant smell. "But we'll see."

"That's not very reassuring," Ronan scoffed, uncrossing his long, muscular legs so they stretched out before him. I tried to avoid ogling them…and failed, appreciating the way the tight linen trousers he wore clung to his thighs. Ronan continued on, thankfully unaware of my leering at him. "It reminds me of the time when I was two and my mother scolded me after I wet the bed and told me that if I did it again, monsters would eat my toes off in the middle of the night."

The silly story pulled me straight from my trance. I raised an eyebrow at Laureli. "Potion working?"

Laureli crossed her arms, smugness radiating pungently from her like the smell from the cauldron. "Like a charm."

Ronan's eyes went wide. "I don't know why I said that. It's like that one time I blurted out to my cousin River that I was the one who stole her chocolates from beneath her bed–"

"Hush before you embarrass yourself, boy," Laureli interrupted before Ronan could finish his story, and he clamped his hand over his mouth to stay his tongue.

"Where is the tug?" Nelle asked, redirecting us all to the task at hand. I exhaled, settling back into the role I needed to play, noting the edge of fear creeping back up my spine. I shook it off. I was creation and life, Fate's Silver Wheel. I could do this.

I had to.

I closed my eyes, imagining my power rising to the surface, the molten heat spilling from my heart into my fingertips. Furrowing my brow, I concentrated further, pushing my power outward, searching for a thread, for the untamable thing to take shape…

My eyes snapped open again as I felt *it*, that piece of myself that still lived and breathed in my husband, the bit of power that called back to mine like a duet, singing with one voice.

"His heart," I murmured, and Nelle gently placed my hand over Ronan's heart, right by his tattoo. I hissed as the electricity passed through us again, and Ronan's eyes fluttered shut for a moment as if he felt it too. It was ecstasy and torture, pleasure and pain, the tingling thing that pulsed between us. I sucked in another breath as I let myself get used to it, the bond strengthening.

Nelle shifted closer as her hand gripped my wrist tighter. At the point of contact, the gentle guide of her power flowed through my skin into my palm, my own power molding into a clearer, defined shape in my mind. Nelle's voice dropped to a command, the healer made from starstuff slipping into her role. "Now imagine that you can see all those memories swimming around in his head."

I closed my eyes again, following the path my power carved inside, latching onto that energy that lived in his heart. An image popped into my head as I sought it out.

Ronan, hiding under a bed in Mathonwy Manor, belly flat to the dusty floorboards as footsteps creaked in the hall outside. Anticipation building in his chest as he held his breath, the figure drawing closer, the hunt afoot…

"I can see it," I breathed, shutting my eyes tighter as I tried to hold onto the image. "You were a cute kid."

Ronan's voice rumbled low in his chest, the sound buzzing through my palm. "My father used to say–"

"Shh, I need to concentrate," I chuckled, peeking one eye open and pressing a finger to his mouth to quiet him. Shock swallowed his expression for a moment, but I didn't balk, shutting my eye again and focusing in. I watched as the memories changed and flowed together, like streams of a great river feeding into one large pool.

Ronan's father, a rare smile on his face as he stood next to Eleri, the two of them tickling Ronan's sides until he nearly peed with laughter. Ronan and Rhett in their early teens, wrestling in Reina's rose garden, each of them covered in thornpricks but all smiles. Ronan holding a baby Reagan, her giant eyes staring at him while her little hand wrapped around his finger, pride and love blooming through his chest...

Tears pricked at the back of my eyes as I relished this glimpse into my husband's heart. His life before me. His family.

Nelle's voice was an anchor as I swam through the memory pool, mooring me to my body and the task at hand. "Now try and think of some of the memories you want him to remember. See if the tug can lead you to them. They might be blocked or hidden..."

I nodded and conjured the image I wanted to find. Ronan and I on the deck of the *Aife*, our wedding night, the silent sea our backdrop as we said the first of our vows to each other. The memory was clear as glass in my mind's eye, the way his golden hair shone near white in the moonlight, the long cloak that emphasized how tall he'd gotten...

The energy in my chest snagged onto the thought, somehow knowing to seek out its counterpart in the web of streams that connected our memories. I felt the tug, like the undertow of a current, guiding me up, through, until...

A dry, cracked space, where the memory should have rested. Dried up. Not a drop left in its wake.

"It's gone," I breathed, a cavern opening in my chest. Our wedding night was not an inherently pleasant memory, and there had been several times that I myself wished I could just forget about it. But it had forged us into who we were today, our story starting that night on the bloodstained deck.

And it had been stolen from us, from him, the bare, empty space like a missing limb.

I felt it as Ronan's presence surged, his own energy seeking, scanning with mine, exploring the streams next to that gaping hole. "I remember coming back from *Hiraeth*, and going to Esme's ship to...to..."

Nothing.

"There's no block. It's just gone, like someone tore a page out of the book." I gritted my teeth, rage spearing through my middle.

Laureli swore under her breath from my periphery, and my chest deflated further. "Look for another one. Maybe something less important?"

I nodded, determination sparking against the flinty fury, my magic pressing again inward, deeper. I brought the memory to my mind first: sparring on the deck with Papa while Ronan watched on, the summer sunshine hot against our skin. We were ten at the time, just two kids learning to fight. Learning to lose with honor. And while we were both there, we still barely knew ourselves, let alone each other. Perhaps the gate would have spared that simple, secondary detail.

My power sought it out in Ronan's head, taking shape with brutal efficiency and pressing hard against the current.

Ronan released a shuddering breath as the thought formed, painting the picture I could see with his words. "I swabbed the deck on Cedric's ship, and we sparred, and then after my turn, it was someone else's, but then…" The image died as quickly as it came, the small, trickling stream going bone dry in an instant. Ronan groaned, doubling over so far it was hard to keep my hand firm on his chest. "*Ow*. My head."

Fear and panic flooded my veins, a dark, ancient something rearing up against my power and shoving it back.

"Pull back, Keira," Nelle warned, but it was far away, the overwhelming surge of darkness drowning out the world around me. But my power flared in response, the light searing beneath my skin as it burned through the shadows until they recoiled with a hiss.

"There has to be something. One of them," I ground out, pressing my will firmer against that ancient shadow. I brought another memory to my mind, this time sharpening it like a tool.

The gate might have taken his memories, but they could not have mine. And I was willing to part with a few to help him remember.

This time, I willed the energy not to seek, but to strike, to plant itself in the rockbed of his mind and take root. Ronan moaned as the pain intensified again, and I willed him to remember, pouring my power in with my memories.

A trip to Pysgodd when we were young, both of us laughing as the wind brutalized our faces to pink. A night on the *Ceffyl*, stargazing as he held me to his chest and spoke of stories old. A morning in bed, our bodies tangled together in the sheets, sweat and sleep coating our limbs.

Our history, our friendship, sweet and painful and long. Our love, flawed and perfect and real.

Real.
Real.
Real.

Ronan shook, a cry tearing from his lips as my magic overwhelmed and invaded, a foreign enemy behind his defenses.

"Keira, enough!" Nelle commanded, withdrawing her hand from my wrist with a vicious hiss. Without her touch, my power spiraled, lashing out in uncontrolled strikes against Ronan's mind. But I couldn't let go, couldn't give up. I needed him to return to me. Needed my sweet and sincere and snarky husband, needed our perfectly imperfect love…

"Stop, please," his voice was barely above a whisper, but the desperate plea cut me to the bone.

My eyes flew open as I dropped my hand from his chest, my power snapping back into me, crashing down into the depths of my soul. In its absence, dread spread through my veins, guilt ensnaring my heart in thorns.

Ronan clutched his chest, his expression twisted with pain, and my stomach lurched. This was wrong. I was wrong, my power a cruel, useless thing that only hurt those I loved most.

"I'm sorry, I'm so sorry," I sobbed, tears that I didn't realize had gathered spilling onto my outstretched hands. Hands that had hurt. Hands that ruined.

Ronan's fingers wrapped around mine, his other thumb lifting my chin so I met his gaze. Sapphire depths swam with worry, not for himself, but for me. For the monster that had harmed him. For the selfish beast that put him in this situation in the first place. At his small, guarded smile, my guilt only doubled. "It's all right. I wanted you to try."

I pulled my hand away and scooted back before I could hurt him further. Before I could lose control entirely and throw myself sobbing into his arms. Something flashed across his face before he sank his hands into his lap.

"Did it work at all?" Laureli inched closer to us, offering Ronan a vial filled with blue liquid. He eyed it warily before Laureli nudged his hand with it, and he accepted. With one fluid motion, he uncorked it and tossed it back, his strong throat bobbing as he swallowed.

He coughed once before answering, his voice thick with an emotion I couldn't name. "No. Nothing. Just some heartburn."

I wiped my tears with the back of my hand, shoving my guilt and greed down with the power that had almost cost me everything. Ronan might have been willing to give himself to the gate to save me, but I would not take any more of him than he already lost at my expense. And I would not let my emotions get the better of me anymore. Wouldn't let my desperation and desire put him or any one in harm's way ever again.

"Maybe we give it some time and try again. Perhaps the magic is too fresh right now," Nelle reassured sweetly, but her eyes never left the floor, the lie too apparent to meet my face. She reached out to both of us, taking each of our hands in hers, her palms clammy. "Keep spending time together and see if it triggers anything in the meantime."

"Yeah. That's a good idea." Ronan nodded, a glimmer of the enthusiastic, wholehearted man I knew and loved peeking out from behind the mask. Even when he didn't remember me, even when he didn't owe me, he was still willing to try. To sacrifice himself, because he was kind and *good*.

My husband had no memory of me. Of us. And perhaps he was better for it.

32

Devotions and Deities

RONAN

I woke to the sound of screaming.

I jumped from my cot, torn out of whatever dream I'd been having–something to do with the spring…something *good* according to the uncomfortable bulge in my pants–but any lingering excitement was doused as the screams pierced the otherwise quiet morning again.

I sighed, rubbing my eyes with the heels of my hands as I fell back onto my cot. After four mornings of the same startling alarm, I'd resigned myself to inaction. As per Nelle's orders, Keira's nightmares were hers to handle, and they were just that: bad dreams, destined to disappear with the rising sun. Nothing a goddess like her couldn't manage.

Still, there was a deep ache in my chest whenever I heard the sound, the urge to run to her practically maddening as each shrill cry settled beneath my scales. Spots of light sparkled across my vision as I pressed my palms harder, trying to stifle the need to wrap her up in my arms and promise to take away every bad thought that dared enter her pretty head.

It had been unbearable the last few days, watching her work hard on the deck, the sun kissing her skin in a sheen of sweat. Every time I found myself looking at her, my body threatened to take over, coaxing me to offer her a towel or water, or to stay by her side in case her clumsy feet failed her again. I wanted to help her, to *serve* her, even. To count her freckles and run my hands through that messy mane of hers.

It was a bad idea. It would only hurt her more if I gave into those instincts. Hurt me too, maybe, to acknowledge those feelings and not know anything of what they meant to us. To her. To lead her on when I had no idea if she even still wanted me. Or if I wanted her, for that matter, outside of the tug in my gut that told me I did.

I'd been turned by her, after all. There was an innate loyalty the sirens all felt towards Danura because of the magick of the shift. Perhaps I too had a primal need to please her, my maker, just as they did.

Then again, maybe she didn't want to be back at all.

She may have made me, but she'd also discarded me.

With another huff, I sat up, pulling on my tunic and boots, readying for the day. The soft blue material hugged my skin, helping me pull myself together. I'd always preferred red, but the color like a gentle sky calmed the beast scratching away at my insides.

I ran a hand through my hair, untangling the long curls before I strode out the door, not bothering with a morning shave. My feet carried me up the first hall to the left, to a bunk only three doors down from Laureli's renovated Captain's quarters. When Keira had chosen an empty room instead, my heart had swelled in an uncomfortable strain. She was pregnant and had been trapped in the Dark God's keep for months, suffering only Lyr knew what, and yet she still sacrificed simple luxuries for the good of her crew.

I told myself I wasn't going to bug her. I was just going to politely knock on her door. Pretend I hadn't heard her scream, and maybe just invite her to breakfast. Yes, that was it. Just one former Captain greeting another, discussing business and schedules over a meal before the sun climbed too high.

My fist rapped against her door and my heart jumped in my chest as I waited. I was glad she didn't have siren hearing, or she might read into the sprinting beat. I told myself it was just the lingering effects of her magick that had me so anxious. Nothing more.

Whatever delusions I tried to convince myself of died a swift death the second she opened the door, peeking out from behind it with those giant silver eyes. Hollow bags of blue bruises rested beneath them, her skin tainted with seasick green hue. And yet my pulse doubled at the sight of her, like she was the most gorgeous creature to ever walk the seven isles.

I closed my gaping mouth and cleared my throat. "Good morning, Keira."

Her chest rose and fell in uneven breaths as she stared at me, something dark haunting her gaze. I wondered if it was the lingering nightmare, or if *I* was the phantom she feared. Her hoarse, curt word made my heart sink. "Morning."

I swallowed down my wounded pride, painting on my best Mathonwy mask. Confident and clever, instead of the deep-seated insecurity snared like barbed wire around my stomach. I leaned onto her doorframe casually with a smirk. "I was thinking we could try the memory thing again today. Maybe if the other sirens are there, we can try and go deeper. I can handle the pain, and you can draw on their power."

The suggestion was far from nonchalant, but I delivered it as if I was asking about the weather, a trick Pa had taught me before I learned to lace my boots. Negotiations always went best when you asked for something like it was already yours.

Keira's pale face blanched even further, so white it could rival clean linens, and I fought a wince. The pain toward the end of the ritual had been terrible…but her power itself was rapture incarnate. Lyr below, the second I felt her presence press into mine, something lodged in the depths of my soul sprang free, shuddering with waves of pleasure as the bottomless well of energy coursed through my veins.

I could suffer a little torture if it meant another taste of that eternal light. I waited with anticipation, biting my tongue as she decided.

She inhaled sharply, silver eyes falling to my boots. "Honestly, I don't think it's a good idea. But thanks for trying."

Instinct propelled me to grab her chin and direct her gaze back to mine, to tell her it was worth the risk, that I wanted this for myself, and that this wasn't her fault. I could smell her guilt on her like week-old trash, the emotion just as rotten.

I stuffed my hands in my pockets instead before I could do something too brazen.

"Have you eaten yet?" I blurted out with the tact of a big toe, shifting my weight between my feet. Of course she hadn't eaten—

she'd just been screaming in her sleep, her long tunic unbelted as it brushed against the bare skin of her thighs…I didn't let my gaze linger too long on that fact.

Lyr below, this woman had me tied around her finger and I barely remembered her *name.*

Kind as she was, she answered my downright stupid question with a soft smile. "No, I haven't."

This time, my returning grin was not a mask. "Well then, throw some pants on and let me accompany you to the galley, Captain Branwen."

Her smile fell, and so did my gut.

"Actually, it's–" she hesitated, opening and shutting her mouth twice as she wrestled with whatever shadows darkened her gaze. "Never mind."

I stepped closer, that same primal part of me pushing my feet forward before I could stop them, crossing the threshold of her doorway as I scanned her tight features. "What is it?"

Her shoulders slumped as she shyly kicked the door with her bare toes. So different from the Captain I'd seen take command without a single moment of hesitation, or the goddess that wrangled the sea and sky to abide by her will. Perhaps she wore just as many masks as I did. "Technically, it's Captain Mathonwy. But now that I think of it, Branwen is probably best. I just have to get used to it again, that's all."

My stomach did a somersault that would've rivaled the most talented Ir'desian acrobats. I hated that I'd been so careless and forgetful, yet again, wrenching and twisting the knife I'd already stabbed her with. But I *didn't* hate how my name sounded from her mouth.

Both notions were equally disorienting.

I shoved them aside, instead crossing my arms and raising a brow at her. "Pants first. Let's put some breakfast in you, *Captain Mathonwy,* and then we can sort the business of names and titles."

Shock splayed for a flash across her face before she nodded, pushing me back with a gentle shove before shutting the door on me.

By the time I recovered from the surprise, the door flew open again, and she was dressed from head to boot. Black trousers hugged her legs and cinched around her middle, the soft roundness of her stomach emphasized even with the loose-fitting maroon tunic that covered her upper half.

I did my best not to stare. I failed.

Our synchronized steps were the only sound as we trudged up to the galley. The warm, spiced smell of tea wafted from the room as we approached, making my mouth water, but I didn't smell anything of substance yet. We turned the corner into the large space and found it empty of both company and food.

I wondered where Ellian and Siobhan had gone off to. The two of them had been holed up in this room all week, Ellian tending to Siobhan with a fierce protectiveness I'd never seen from him before. Perhaps if Siobhan had woken, they'd gone to Nelle's workshop to finally give her a proper bath and change her bandage dressings.

I shook my head, clearing it of the thoughts. It was so strange how vividly I remembered everyone else in my life, even with the missing chunks of information where Keira used to be.

I strolled over to the pantries as Keira moved to pour tea into mugs, both of us falling into a comfortable routine without a word, as if we'd practiced it a thousand times. I supposed we had, even if I didn't remember. My body knew the motions, muscle memory unchangeable, like riding a horse or wielding a sword. But despite being entirely alone with her, enveloped in the quiet, I was far from uncomfortable as I imagined I would be with a stranger.

A dangerous thought crossed my mind before I could halt it: it almost felt like home.

I slammed that intrusion down into the depths before riffling through the cabinets, pulling out a few stale rolls of hardtack from our stores. Our rations were meager, as we hadn't seen port in weeks. Not that it mattered, since most of us got the majority of our nutrition from fish blood these days, and despite Ellian's rich-boy attitude, he was more than fine nibbling on jerky and hardtack for most of his meals.

I eyed Keira as she poured water from the kettle, the pot somehow already steaming. Her hair fell into her face, hiding her expression, and I ignored the prompt to tuck it behind her ear again. But my stomach twisted with a different unease. Sure, she was a sailor, one who'd probably seen far rougher seas than I ever had. Yet a foreign part of me felt wrong feeding this lifeless, flavorless paste to Keira. Maybe I was worried about the baby's health.

But I was not useless, either. I had many talents outside of forgetting. I searched again through the cabinets, grabbing the jars of honey, cinnamon, and the last hunk of hard, sweet cheese we had. With my knife, I slit the rolls in halves, leaving them open-faced on the gray countertop. Then, slicing the cheese, I adorned each half-roll with a slice before drizzling a generous amount of honey over them and finishing it with the cinnamon.

"Did Reina teach you that?" Keira broke the silence, staring at me as I sprinkled the last of the spice over the food. She set a cup of tea on the counter next to me, steam rising in gentle tendrils from the deep brown liquid. I nodded as I handed her a piece, watching *too* closely as she fit it into her mouth, the honey wetting her pink lips.

"Yes. It's so strange…" I cleared my throat and looked at my own portion, wiping some of the sugary nectar off the side and bringing it to my mouth. I needed something to occupy it before I lunged to lick the honey directly from her tongue. "I remember everything else in better detail than I have in forever. I could tell you every recipe I watched Reina make, could recite the plot to books I haven't read in years. But then there are giant gaps that I feel soul-deep. I know something important is supposed to be there. That *you* were somehow there. And I can't recall any of it."

The truth slipped out before I could catch it, viscous as the honey dripping from my roll. My cheeks heated as I took a bite, silencing myself before I could say anything more foolish. Despite the flavor I'd anointed it with, I barely tasted anything, every sense in my body still entirely focused on her. At the bob of her throat as she swallowed. At the rainclouds that sprang to her eyes, dark and ready to spill. She looked at me for a long, heavy moment, setting her own roll on the counter again.

"We have a long history." She gnawed at her full lower lip, and again, I wanted to catch it with my own teeth, steadied only by the pain in her tight voice. This was already so hard, so complicated for us. I didn't need my base desires making it worse. Her silver eyes finally met mine, and her grief shone so bright it became my own. "I'm so sorry this is happening to you. You did it to save me, and I…well, thank you. But I understand if you no longer have the same motivations. I know we need to save the Deyrnas and our families, but if, after that, you want to go your own way…"

I reached out, grabbing her hand. To steady her, or myself. To lessen the anguish in her eyes and my heart. Her brows lifted gracefully in surprise, but she didn't pull away, and the beast in my chest roared with the small victory. I huffed a breath, trying to make my voice as strong and unchangeable as the current. "I know I can't remember. But I swore loyalty to you. I said my vows. I'm not the kind of man to go back on them."

A strange concoction of emotions swirled in her expression, her pulse quickening. I tucked my fingers through hers, trying to read every mystery in the mix, but she finally pulled away, leaving my palm empty and cold without her heat.

"I wasn't loyal to you." Her voice fell to a passive and passionless depth despite the whirlwind in her gaze. "In the Otherworld…Death got into my head. He's a master manipulator, and I fell for it. I thought he was my friend. And then he kissed me."

Shock stabbed my chest first, sharp as a cracking whip. But it wore off fast, giving way to something uglier, a beast biting back.

Jealousy.

I could not remember this woman, and for all intents and purposes, had only met her a few days ago. Yet there it was, bitter, burning jealousy, the dragon inside turning green with envy.

I looked at the floorboards, stained with flour and salt. My voice rumbled low in my chest, my heart thumping loudly in my ears. "Do you still want him?"

"No. I never did, not really. I wanted to feel less alone, and he used that. But I feel guilty that I ever considered it at all." I let go of the breath I'd been holding, my shoulders unknotting; Keira continued, hands wringing in front of her. "Your devotion was a gift I didn't deserve before, and I certainly don't deserve it now. I won't ask it of you."

At that, my heart threatened to stop.

This ache, this need, grinding incessantly in my chest, churning and pulling at my ever fiber…

It was something tangible, a promise to the goddess before me, good and kind and somehow feeling guilty for the things she had to do to survive. But devotion? Could I devote myself to this woman, *worship* her? The thought both terrified and inspired something deep within, a fire catching in my center.

"I can't promise something as intense as devotion. But you have my attention, Captain," I whispered, letting that heat reawaken parts of me I'd thought forgotten. Her silver eyes met mine, and I found another name for the thing inside of me. No, I wasn't some blind devotee worshiping at the altar of a goddess I'd never meet. But she was a Captain, through and through, and I could give her something far more potent and practically earned. "And you have my *respect.* The way you treat the crew, your work ethic, your admittedly captivating eyes...I can see why I fell for you the first time. Vows or not, I'm willing to see where it goes again."

A smile broke across her face that lit the whole room. Her eyes were still guarded, secrets forged into the silver, her hands still folded in her lap...but that smile felt like a forgotten memory come to life, a nostalgia I couldn't name wrapping me up and holding me close.

"That seems like a good place to start over." Her voice was low, hesitant, like she didn't want to rip this tentative tether we'd tied between ourselves again. But it was not made of something flimsy or cheap. It was new, but durable, forged of iron and starlight and bone and shadow.

It would endure beyond the gates of hell, beyond memory loss and death itself.

"To new beginnings, then, between forgotten friends," I lifted the mug of steaming tea she poured me in a toast, an offering to the god of simple pleasures. Of home and hearth and happiness.

Mirroring me, she lifted hers as well, the ceramic singing a satisfying clink as we rapped them against each other. A soft chuckle escaped her lips. *"Lechyd Da."*

My returning smile was not faked, not a mask or a character. *"Lechyd da*, Captain Mathonwy."

For a breath, we just stared at each other, neither of us sipping our tea, my eyes unmoving from her mouth, our faces leaning ever so slightly closer. She was so near, I could smell the honey on her breath, a feral part of me still longing to sample it.

It was a bad idea. A terrible one, really. And yet, the beast within was absolutely famished for just a single taste of her...

The door to the galley banged against the wall, and I nearly spilled my hot tea on myself as Ellian and Siobhan burst through. Last I'd seen them, Ellian's white shirt was crumpled and dirty, his curled hair skewed to the side like he hadn't combed it in days, and

Siobhan was even worse for wear, her bloody bandages and undergarments the only thing covering her too-thin frame. But now, they were both washed and dressed for battle. Ellian's fine, long-sleeved tunic was tucked tightly into crisp cotton trousers, his axes strapped to his back, while Siobhan wore her black battle scales, the gashes in it patched with metal. They sported matching expressions, brows pulled tight and mouths drawn in thin lines.

Ellian spoke first, his voice booming through the closed space, "Captain, we have an issue."

Keira jumped from her seat, setting down her tea as she strode up to them. "What is it?"

"Ellian and I have to go to Tan," Siobhan answered coolly, features set in stone; but the scent of fear rose from our companions, their heart rates leaping to an alarming rhythm. I could still smell the blood seeping from Siobhan's wounded side, the metallic tang souring the air.

"What?" I snapped before Keira could respond, my own worry rising to the surface like a tidal wave. Nothing good ever came from Tan. The only worthy warriors on the whole island were the ones who managed to escape. "*Why?*"

Ellian squared his shoulders, tall frame straight with false confidence as his palms slicked with sweat. "We need to convince the assassin clans to help us."

"That's madness," Keira breathed, eyes narrowed, voicing my thoughts exactly. "They would never help. We have no coin to offer them, and they have to know that Locasta would be the higher bidder anyway. They wouldn't dare cross her."

Siobhan looked to me, eyes pleading as she pressed a fist to her chest. "Ronan, it's my *instinct*. We need them for something, I don't know what, exactly…"

My stomach leapt to my throat. Siobhan's instincts were her gift from Danura, infallible as Marina's truth-telling or Laureli's sight. But the gate had taken so much from us, it was hard to trust even the most consistent tools. I stuffed my hands in my pockets, my claws aching to be set free as anxiety spiraled through me. "Are you sure it's still intact?"

Siobhan nodded once. "I wish I wasn't sure. But yes."

"Why do you think the Tannians might help us now?" I countered, folding my arms as I thought to all of the unanswered letters we'd sent.

Siobhan only raised her chin, the morning light gleaming against the slight sheen of sweat on her bronze skin. "I can be very persuasive."

Keira stepped forward, eyes narrowed. "What aren't you telling us?"

Siobhan blinked twice as the question caught her off guard before she regulated her expression once more. But I could still smell that shift in her, the slight tinge to her scent that spelled deceit.

Finally, she sighed, "I was a princess before I was a siren, you know. The heir to the Rhyfelwr clan, actually."

I tried not to let the shock register on my face, but my jaw dropped. I'd known bits of Siobhan's pain, but never the depth. The truth. My mother had spoken of the Rhyfelwr people. They were the largest clan in all of Tan, the keepers of the Anial Wastes. They weren't just nomads like the rest of the Tannian clans; they'd created a kingdom beneath the rocky, sandy terrain, threatening any and all who happened to discover it. And they had the rarest line of shifters in the world, the Basilisks. According to legend, they were few in number, but beyond powerful. One poisonous bite of the giant snakes' fangs meant certain death.

I finally gathered my senses, clearing my throat as I urged Siobhan to continue. "What happened?"

She shrugged. For a woman born of the desert, she sure had a way of freezing out her emotions. "I was not one of the *faoladh*. So they sold me off."

"Bastards," Ellian growled at her side, the *blaidd* showing his bite.

I struggled to rein in my own rage, boiling hot on behalf of my friend. She was a warrior, but she'd been stepped on and wounded in ways I could never understand. I shoved my hands in my pockets, anchoring myself to my clever parts. The parts this crew needed to survive. "What makes you think they'll help you now, given that?"

Siobhan shook her head. "I'm finally what they wanted me to be. A shifter. A siren, no less. A beast of legends. I knew they'd accept me back the second Danura changed me. But I didn't want to go back, to deal with the monsters I called family." She placed her hands firmly at her sides. She may have been inches from death just a few days ago, but the strength of her will billowed out of every limb, filling the small space with her unconquerable presence. "But now, it doesn't matter. If it means protecting my true family, I'll do it. We lost Willow and Cassryn because I wasn't there."

Keira looked to me, her eyes boring holes in my skull as she opened her mouth to speak, but another shrill cry down the hall captivated our attention. "Captain!"

Keira didn't hesitate a second before hurtling out the door, the rest of us hot on her heels as we answered the cry.

Laureli waited in the hallway, her milky white stare haunting as she leaned against the wood. The sight was so agonizingly familiar, an unnamed panic hammered through my chest with my heartbeat.

"Are you all right?" My voice sounded like it was coming from beneath the seafloor, far away and drowned with fear.

Laureli blinked and her eyes cleared, her hand flying to her chest. She clutched her tunic so tightly her knuckles turned white, her face blanching the same shade. "We have to shift course, straight to Orwellin. The rest of your crew are headed there already." She looked at Keira, tears springing to her eyes and carving wet, messy paths down her ashen cheeks. "Arawn followed us out. He's here. And..."

Laureli trailed off, but the words she already managed were enough to drown us all straight down into Lyr's keep. At my side, Keira went completely still, and I didn't need to know her well to read her thoughts as my own.

The Dark God walked. The image of his endlessly black gaze haunted me, the cruelty and emptiness there unimaginable.

But he'd followed us out of the Otherworld. Did that mean the ghosts we'd left behind to fight had failed? Were Danura and Reina and Lochlan and the others...were they all just *gone?*

And now, if he was headed to Orwellin....he was on a collision course with everyone else we loved. If we didn't do something, *anything*, would they all be fodder for his cruel appetite?

My stomach sank all the way to my toes, numbness crawling along my limbs as they froze over, icy and lifeless as the Otherworld itself.

"Say it, Laureli." Keira broke out of her trance first, shuffling forward and placing a hand on the siren's shoulder.

Laureli looked up, light blue eyes almost as colorless as Keira's swimming with phantoms. With the horrible truths only she had seen.

"Ir'de is gone," she whispered, but the words still sliced through me with the same brutality of her claws, replacing the numbness with pure agony. Her lip quivered as she continued, "I'm so sorry, without my crystal ball, I didn't see it right away, but I've been drinking that damned potion all week to get my Sight to start working again…"

"It's not your fault, you did the best you could." Keira hugged the siren to her chest as the older woman sobbed, grief scenting the room with a potent rot I couldn't ignore.

Ir'de was gone.

The Dark God walked.

And he would kill us all if we let him.

Siobhan strode forward, half-limping, but not a single speck of fear in her straight posture. "We need to hurry. If we're going to stop him, we'll need the assassins. This is what my instinct warned me of."

"You trust them too, Ellian?" Keira throat bobbed as she asked the shifter coming to stand at Siobhan's side.

He shook his head, expression already schooled into the readiness of a warrior. "No. I trust *her*. And my mother was a Tannian refugee. Of the Chi clan. I hope to sweeten the deal."

I watched on, my fear still sticking my voice in my throat, my legs heavier than lead welded to the floor. Watched, as Keira and Ellian and Laureli planned, as they shoved past their fear and put it to work.

No, Ronan, you did nothing.

Reagan's accusation was as true then as it was now. My inability to rise to the occasion when the straws were drawn. My lack of leadership when others needed it most.

"We're still two days from Tan," I managed to get past my swollen, dry tongue, my voice weak but logic sound. This, I could do. Had to do. Because I didn't want to just revere Keira one-sidedly. I wanted to earn her affection and respect in turn. I cleared my throat again, my words coming out with more certainty. "And if we're going to reach Orwellin, we have to shift east now. We can't afford the detour."

Keira looked between Siobhan and me, lower lip sucked between her teeth. Finally, she sighed, pinching the bridge of her nose. "We can't afford to face them on our own, either. Look at us."

Before I could formulate a response, something slammed into the side of the ship. Something *big*, pitching the whole structure to the portside.

I stumbled forward, catching Keira around the waist before we both slammed into the nearest beam. Pain flared across my back and side as I took the brunt of the fall, Keira's sharp elbows digging into my ribs as she groaned.

The ship swayed back to right, a grumble escaping my throat as I steadied Keira. "You all right?"

She nodded, calloused fingertips caressing the skin of my forearm as she held onto me. I swallowed hard.

Laureli brushed off her long skirt and cracked her neck as she straightened herself out. "What in Cerridwen's Cards was that?"

"You're the Seer," Siobhan sneered, shaking like a leaf in Ellian's strong arms. It was so disconcerting to see a tiger tremble like a fawn, but her stare was still all predator. "You tell us."

"All crew on deck, *now*," Keira commanded, splashing out the squabble before it had time to brew. She straightened her shoulders, leading the way toward the stairs to the deck above.

I caught her elbow just as her boot kissed the first step, shooting a glance at her round belly. "You should stay below, it's dangerous for you both."

Firm fingers pried my grip from her skin, silver eyes rolling. "Stop manhandling me, Ronan, or I'll jog your memory on just how hard I hit."

She climbed the rest of the stairs without a glance back, knowing we'd all follow, and I watched with my mouth hanging open, words failing. A twinge of something familiar twisted my gut, a subconscious reminder that went beyond both imagination and remembrance. That same tug that transcended thought or cognition, but instead based itself in the deepest, instinctive parts of the animal in my chest.

"Is it always a threat from you?" I muttered as I hurried after her like it was just as natural as breathing.

I swore *something* flashed across her face as we stumbled onto the deck. But any other thoughts or feelings were dimmed by the giant black shadow cast across the deck, and the imposing beast blotting out the blinding sun snarling down at us.

Lyr below, one rotten surprise after another.

A *sarffymor*, its black scales and gold eyes glimmering, raised its massive head high above us. I had claws and teeth and scales of my own now, but a pit of fear lodged itself firmly in my gut nonetheless, cold sweat slicking my palms and neck.

Nelle clambered onto the deck after us, blood that I guessed to be Siobhan's smeared across her tunic. She swore violently under her breath. "Nef's breath, that's—"

And just as suddenly as it appeared, the sarffymor dissolved, thousands of bubbles bursting from its form and carrying through the air. I blinked twice, missing the trick, only to find a very different monster staring back at me.

She appeared decades younger than when I'd last seen her, silver hair warmed to gold, wrinkles flattened and smoothed. But her violet eyes and gunpowder scent were unmistakable, as was the wicked gleam in her smile.

Keira's voice uttered the impossible question first. "*Esme?*"

Esme Rhiamon. In the flesh.

"Did ye really think I'd just keel over, girlie?" She strode across the deck of the *Madyn* like she owned it, her chin high and her back straight. Before anyone could stop her, she wrapped both Keira and I in a hug. Her single arm lassoed me down to her height with a chain-strong grip. Storm and sea and gunpowder enveloped my senses as she pressed quick kisses to each of our cheeks before releasing us, gaze raking over us in appraisal. "It's good seeing ye love birds up close."

"You're the *sarffymor*." A wild laugh bubbled from Keira, both frantic and relieved. "Of *course.*"

Esme shrugged like Keira was simply mentioning the clear weather. Like she hadn't just emerged from the dead as a giant, fearsome sea-monster. Like she hadn't defied the very laws of age and time. "Anyway, I've got someone I'd like ye to officially meet."

Keira and I both gaped at her, but she smiled without care, snapping her fingers with mischief dancing in her ancient gaze.

Another flash of light and seafoam burst from the nothingness at her right. A second later, a man materialized astride a dripping wet horse.

No, not a man. Not a horse.

"Oh, we all know each other quite well." He shook out his long blond mane as he dismounted the *ceffyl dwr*. Standing, he was somehow just as tall as the creature, his broad frame towering over us. He wore no shirt, only dark trousers, so his shredded, muscular physique was on show as he patted the animal's neck with a firm hand. The beast whinnied and nipped at him playfully before he turned our way, unleashing the full weight of his crystal-blue stare on us. A stare that was a near perfect match for my own. "Good to see you both on this side of the gate again."

My mouth went dry, and my head went entirely blank as I tried and failed to piece together what I was seeing. "Lyr below—"

"Not quite. More like at your service." The God of the Sea bowed at the waist, a warm smile breaking through his trimmed beard. "We have important matters to discuss."

33

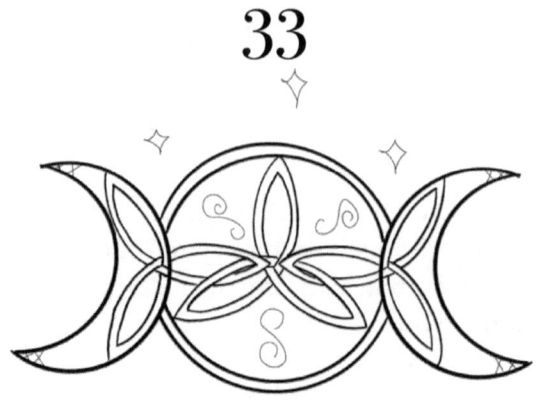

Legends and Lineage

KEIRA

The God of the Sea stared at me with eyes a shade of sapphire I knew better than my own name. Golden blond waves of hair rustled in the wind as he stroked his scruffy beard. He sighed as he leaned back on the rail of the *Madyn*, nestling closer to Esme beside him. My gut clenched, as if they might dive over the edge and dissolve into sea mist once more if I took my eyes off them for even a second.

Lyr had come to us. The sunken god, risen from the abyss, sitting on the rail of my ship in all of his gilded glory. And Esme too, back from the dead, breathing in front of me like not a day had passed since our night in the spring, given life by the sea-god's gifts.

I was a goddess in my own right, born to the mother of all things, but I had worshiped Lyr before I knew how to say my own name. Had loved him like he was kin, even without seeing his face. Papa would've shit an anchor out of pure joy if he could see me now, playing hostess to the father of waves and warriors.

Now he was here to answer my prayers, *finally*, after so many years of waiting and wanting.

And my faith in him had never felt more fragile.

I wished I had my crew beside me. Griffin and Saeth would somehow know what to say, even in the presence of legends. Hell, I'd take Tarran's awkward stuttering or Reagan's bold confidence.

But even with Ronan at my back, I felt entirely alone. The sirens and Ellian had gone below to begin preparations, and I was left to fend for myself with the sea-god and the sea-witch.

"What took you so long?" I whispered as I sat across from the drowned deity, sea-salt spraying my cheeks with every dip and bob of the ship. The wind had picked up since Lyr came aboard, bringing with it the misty scent of trouble to come. Still, I couldn't help the tears that stung my eyes, fueled by the wounded girl that still lived in the recesses of my soul. "All these years, you spoke to us but did nothing to help. Why?"

"Watch it, girlie." Esme narrowed her eyes at me, their hue flashing dangerous red, but Lyr placed a hand over hers to soothe the sea-monster's rage.

"I always wished I could help more. But the gods had a treaty," he answered in the voice I knew as well as my own, deep and vast as the sea itself. A voice that had kept me company in the darkest nights of my grief, that had been there through the fear and uncertainty. The voice that abandoned me to Arawn and his guns. Sapphire eyes crinkled as a sad smile graced his tanned face. "Arawn would keep the Otherworld, and the rest of us would live here and take care of the isles of man. We could not directly prevent people from going to his keep, and he could not do physical harm in the human lands to unwilling participants. But when he left the Otherworld, he broke his side of the bargain first. It freed us to retaliate."

My stomach sank as Lyr confirmed Laureli's vision. This was the beginning of the end, whether we liked it or not.

Death had risen.

"Why is he doing all of this?" My husband—no, just Ronan now—asked beside me, running a worried hand through his locks that shone the same gold as the sea god's.

Lyr pursed his lips and looked to me again, both an answer and a question in the action that set my stomach to flopping.

"In the Otherworld, he told me…" I ignored the discomfort that squeezed my chest thinking of Arawn. Of the sadness in his eyes as he spoke, of the false sincerity in his voice as he lured me deeper into his dangerous trap. Instead, I focused on the god in front of me, both wild and gentle at once. "He said you and Danura ran away together."

The God of the Sea and Sail *snorted*, elbowing Esme on the rail next to him. "I'm not surprised that he thinks that, but he's even more deluded than I imagined." His smile soured to a grimace as he turned to watch the waves, the sea and sky both darkening with his mood. "Your mama and I are so close, we're practically siblings. She really only had eyes for Arawn. But she was unhappy, too. He loved her, but love looked a lot like control to a man like Arawn, and he wouldn't listen. So she asked for my help to get away. He made his assumptions."

"Damned fool," Esme hissed, the sea-witch losing none of her bite even in her human form.

I swallowed, this telling of the story adding another piece to the puzzle. Papa always said the truth was an illusion of perspective. 'Right' and 'wrong' were as subjective as right and left; it only mattered which way you were looking.

Perhaps Arawn was so stuck in his own direction that he'd gone blind to any other possibilities; and now he was willing to kill entire islands of people rather than look at himself and his own failings. I'd been so foolish to believe him outright, to not take a step back and look at things from other angles, too.

Just as I'd been so willing to believe that the god in front of me had abandoned me, not thinking of all he'd done to protect me from the monster sitting on the throne in Orwellin. Of what he'd done to protect my mother, too.

I stared at a knot on the wooden railing, trying to untangle the snags that had tied themselves in my heartstrings. "That's why you spoke to me when I was younger? Because you were close with my mother?"

This time, Lyr's smile was all sunshine, rainclouds clearing from the sky above. "In part. I also liked watching over you. Only the godsborn can hear us, so it was nice to have someone to chat with. And your Pa was a good man, too. Danura loved him well." He leaned back into Esme again, the sea-witch stroking his hair. A piece of my cracked soul healed ever-so-slightly at the fondness in his tone, but the mere mention of Papa and the simple act of love gnawed at the raw edges of my own grief and jealousy. A reminder of how lonely I was.

I yearned to hold the man pacing next to me with such casual closeness. Or to be with my father, my good luck charm, safe on the deck of the *Ceffyl* where no sadness could touch me.

Lyr looked at me with those painfully blue eyes again, nodding like he knew.

You're not alone anymore, little one. His voice eddied into my head like the morning tide before he spoke aloud again, "But when you went and got that mark, I couldn't risk talking to you without having him find out I'd been nudging you along."

I nodded, my shoulders slumping with relief. Even his absence had been to protect me.

But Ronan did not relax, his hands stuffed in his pockets as he narrowed his eyes at the sea god. "How did you speak to me, then?"

Surprise leapt through me, and I stared at my husband again.

Lyr had spoken to him? When? And why hadn't he told me?

The bitter taste of betrayal coated my tongue. Ronan might have forgotten me, but had I ever really seen behind his masks?

Lyr tilted his head, his expression a mirror to Ronan's. Every instinct in my body prickled at the familiarity, the resemblance the two bore to each other. Gold and sapphire, sea-salt and scales.

Then Lyr leaned forward with a smirk I'd seen in my dreams time and time again. I blinked, my eyes playing tricks on me. "Do you want to know why Arawn wants your child? Why the Council wanted your bloodlines to come together?"

Ronan's jaw worked hard as he swallowed down whatever anxiety plagued him, his snake's mask slipping into place. Another lie, another coverup.

"Enlighten us."

The ship swayed as Esme shifted her weight from foot to foot. Even in her human form, her presence was a force of nature. Storm-cloud eyes narrowed at us. "Did ye know the Mathonwys were one of the founding families of Porthladd?"

"Yes. The Branwens too," I replied flatly, less interested in ancient history and more concerned about the very real danger waiting in the present.

"Very true, but they came after. The Mathonwys were first." Lyr folded his well-muscled arms across his bare chest, the whole look of him vast and untamable as the sea. His voice rumbled like thunder, with an edge to it that had goosebumps prickling across my flesh. "Headed by Esmerelda Mathonwy, who originally set sail from Pysgodd in search of new land to conquer and landed on Porthladd's soil."

Lyr and Esme shared a long, loaded look in a language all their own, storm and sea clashing and caressing in the space between them. My heart lurched, envy boiling so hot it blinded me.

I knew that kind of love, once. Violent and soothing, dangerous and comforting in the same breath.

I couldn't bear to look at Ronan right now. Not when he'd almost kissed me this morning, the poor creature so broken and confused that he felt guilty enough to want to appease me even after I'd betrayed him.

Not when he'd lied to me in turn, hiding important truths from me behind serpentine smiles.

"And?" I pressed again, trying to focus on the story over the rage tingling in my chest.

"Esmeralda…that was the name of the woman Lyr fell in love with," Ronan answered, his mouth falling open in surprise. For a moment, the masks fell away, the little boy with big blue eyes staring at Esme like she could reach up and grab the stars. "You're my–?"

Esme reached out and patted his shoulder, kinship sparkling in her violet stare. "There are too many 'greats' in my title fer ye to count them, but I suppose ye can call me Granny."

My heart both leaped and sank in one twisting motion. I looked at the three of them, finally piecing it all together. Ronan and Lyr's twin-like resemblance, aside from Lyr's rugged beard and slightly larger build; Esme's sea-serpent swagger, the mischief and mockery in her every wild gaze. Ronan's connection to the spring, Esme's plotting and planning in the earliest days of our marriage…

Only a Mathonwy snake could have lied to us like she did.

It ran in the family. *Ronan's* family.

My husband was a child of Lyr. The truth spilled from my lips as everything I knew to be true shattered around me, yet again. "You're godsborn, too. *Duweni.*"

"The bloodline was diluted over the centuries, so your power has lost potency, but yes. The Mathonwys are my kin. Our descendants. Once you came to the spring, I was able to form a connection," Lyr spoke cheerily, but I still gaped at Ronan and Ronan alone.

Ronan, who looked just as confused and concerned as I felt. Whose hand reached out ever so slightly, as if he wanted to touch me, to hold me for support.

Ronan, who collected secrets and deceptions for sport. Whose cunning was second to none.

Ronan, who was made of godstuff long before I gave him claws and scales and fangs.

"Our baby…" he whispered, and the softness in his tone threw me for another loop as his gaze drifted to my middle. Sapphire shone brighter than starlight. "She has both Danura's blood and Lyr's. Two of the three original gods."

At that, all my thoughts pivoted abruptly. Both mine and Ronan's past transgressions mattered little in comparison to the innocent creature growing inside of me. She was unmarred by any stain or sin, by secrets or stumblings like we were.

She was the legacy of two great families. Of the two most powerful gods. She would be sea and stars and storm and sun. She was salvation itself.

And she was in danger for even existing at all.

"She'll be the most powerful creature ever to walk the earth," Lyr confirmed, and a rotten dread roiled in my gut, worse than any sea or morning sickness I'd ever endured.

"And if Arawn got his hands on her…" The blood ran from my cheeks, hiding from the dark truth I could not admit.

If Arawn came near my daughter, he wouldn't just try to ruin her. He'd chain her in ice and never let go. He'd use her to throw the entire world into his darkness.

Fury found its footing in my chest, heat and rage building through my veins and concentrating in my palms. My power ached to be unleashed, to destroy any threat that even dared breathe toward my daughter. I met Ronan's gaze again, shoving down every mixed emotion about us and finally focusing on our mutual responsibility. "When Arawn found out I was pregnant, he forwarded his plans. He wanted to control her through me, wanted the Deyrnas gone so we couldn't rise up to challenge him."

Ronan's expression darkened, sapphire dimming to near-black as a growl sounded low in his chest. "I'm going to *end* him."

I rarely got a glimpse of Ronan's monstrous streak, but I didn't recoil from it. Rotten and wicked, we belonged to each other. Violent and vicious. And all the lies and fights, the betrayals and abandonments that lay between us were part of that imperfect, powerful partnership.

But our daughter still had the chance to be good. To be better. We would be the villains of this story if it meant keeping her safe.

"There is more." Lyr's low voice tugged me back to the moment like the tide, washing us onto the *Madyn's* deck.

Ronan flashed his fangs at the god, venom dripping from them. "What could possibly be more pressing than the God of Death wanting to control our unborn daughter's power?"

"What he plans to *do* with her power," Esme snarled, and thunder cracked overhead. A similar stroke of electricity ran down my spine. "The Branwen curse."

My tongue thickened in my mouth, dry and clumsy. "Finna mentioned that. Something about the blood of an innocent."

I cursed myself for not remembering better. For not heeding Finna's warning. My hands shook with both fear and rage, at myself and at Arawn once again for his trickery.

Lyr reached for my trembling hands, scooping both up in one large palm. His skin was as coarse as the sandy ocean floor, but my breath eased in my lungs. Lyr continued, steadying me like an anchor, "When Danura left him, Arawn was so jealous that he never wanted her to have love again. He cast the blood curse. He couldn't absorb her power, so he scattered it, and vowed that anyone else that falls in love with her would doom their whole family to betrayal and ruin forever."

A stone sank to my toes.

My Papa had loved Danura well. Growing up, he'd never spoken a word of ill about her, even if he'd kept so many of her secrets from me. And even after decades apart, the way they looked at each other across the frozen expanse, like two lodestones drawn together despite the test of time and space…

Papa loved Danura. He'd stolen her heart.

And my family…Aidan and Donnall, Finna and Weylin…

They bore that love as a curse. Arawn's curse.

"That's terrible," Ronan muttered, gazing out to the horizon like he could see it all playing out before him. Perhaps he could, the storyteller in him needing nothing but his mind's eye to keep him company.

I was glad I could not envision such a nightmare. Though I didn't need to; I'd watched my family fall apart at the seams, had watched Aidan's intelligence turn to cruelty, Weylin's loyalty to bitterness.

Watched Finna's cleverness sour to envy, Donnall's strength crumble to insecurity.

And I'd witnessed Arawn's coldness and cunning up close. Had seen him tearing at Danura's flesh in a frenzy, had seen his shadows cut and snare and kill without hesitation. "He's not afraid to be the monster."

Lyr stroked his golden scruff, his proud brow furrowed. "It's old, dark magic. It requires the blood of a betrayer. Then the soul of an innocent, then the heart of a god. That's how he bound her to *Hiraeth*. Danura didn't truly love him, so he offered his own heart the first time. And that cursed him to stay in the Otherworld, and the Otherworld became a wasteland since it was heartless. He can't escape unless someone else carved a path for him."

Ronan let loose a feral growl, the siren swimming to the surface of his skin, his claws poking a hole through his pocket. "Until we went and opened the gates for him. Lyr belo–I mean, gods, we *helped* him."

My gut lurched like I'd been punched.

We'd let him out. Come to his aid and given him access to the Deyrnas. Moreover, I'd been his pawn in the Otherworld. I'd let him tease me and dance with me and kiss me, let him fill my head with fairytales of a brand-new world with us smiling down at it. I'd believed him.

The blood of the Deyrnas was on my hands.

Mine and his.

Lyr gave voice to the odious truth, his words javelins through my heart. "Aye. My guess is now, he wants more than the Otherworld. He wants to absorb Danura's scattered power for himself and regain his 'heart' and total control."

My power surged beneath my palms as he spoke, a vengeful monster begging to be let loose. "My uncles, and Finna's baby...he was trying to complete the ritual then. All he needed was my heart...until Finna ruined the innocent life."

Again, a bell rang in my ears, sharp and shrill and cold.

Death.

Death.

Death.

I was a monster, my soul blackened by the choices that led me down the road to hell. But Arawn drew the map. He'd been the one to ruin everything I'd ever loved. My family's love and loyalty,

Ronan's memories, my home, my people, my identity. He was darkness incarnate, devilry and deception hidden behind a dazzling face and a dash of charm.

I'd almost fallen for it.

But he would fall at my feet instead.

I met Lyr's gaze again, starlight singing in my veins to end the Dark God's blackest night once and for all. "Tell me what to do to stop him."

No one escaped the God of Death. But my daughter would be the first. And on the powers above and below, on the life brewing inside me....

I'd make him bow to me.

Lyr shook his head, and every fiber of my being threatened to burst like a pus-filled, rotten blister. "It's already started. He already has plenty of betrayer's blood, and if he can't have your heart, he'll steal your daughter and raise her to love him. But he clearly needs you too for that, at least until she's born, so he'll take the entire Deyrnas hostage."

Ronan's claws burst free from their sheaths, tearing the pockets of his pants entirely. His voice rumbled low, and I swear to Lyr, his eyes flashed *gold*, something ancient and terrifying swirling in their metallic hue. "We won't ask again. *How do we stop him?*"

I watched Ronan for a long moment, emotion lodging firmly in my throat. My wicked, dangerous creature. Maybe I didn't know all his secrets, but this beast had once been mine. Even if I was no longer his.

We would stop Death together.

So faintly, I wasn't sure I heard it, Lyr's voice slithered again into my mind. Or perhaps, this time, it was Papa's, a phantom lingering from beyond the veil. *Small victories, Keira girl. What do you want, and how can you get it?*

"We take away the ingredients. We make sure he can't have any god hearts, for one," I replied, letting my power and passion armor me in confidence. The Goddess of Fate was the goddess of small victories. Step by step, choice by choice, win by win, we would defeat Arawn. And that started by tearing away at his plans just as viciously as he had ours.

Lyr stood from the rail, rising to his full height. The God of the Sea was taller than a tidal wave as he looked down at me, a smile carving his wild features. "And two…someone else absorbs Danura's power before he can."

I stilled, my heart thudding loudly. If we could rob him of all opportunity, if we could pirate his plans and sink his ship from within, if we could walk away with his treasure before he could even lay a single finger on it…

We'd send him back to the depths without a doubt.

Small victories, indeed. My voice was just above a whisper when I found it again. "Who, though?"

Lyr patted me on the head like I was no more than a child. Knowing sapphire eyes stared deep into my soul. "Someone who already possesses the heart of a god and has been spattered in betrayer's blood time and time again."

I shook my head, hope falling out from under me. I couldn't take my mother's power from her. I barely had space enough for my own, the ancient, raw energy inside of me barely reined in. "I can't—"

"Not you," Esme cut in, licking her lips as she looked at me. No, not at me. Past me. At Ronan. "My sweet grandbaby."

34

Drinks and Deliberations

RONAN

We'd convened in the galley again as the sea-god and the sea-witch dangled a carrot of hope in our faces. Laureli and Nelle stood sentry on either side of the door, both sirens staring with awe and abject horror as the God of Tempest and Tidal Waves sat with his feet propped up on our small oak worktable. Even Marina had come out of her hiding spot, her skin wan and her crimson hair limp. But she exhaled for the first time in days in his presence, her head quirked to the side as she watched him.

His supposed-to-be-dead-lover perched on a stool next to him, her massive beast somehow contained in the hazy cage of her wraith-like frame. Without the wrinkles and age-whitened hair to mask her in mortality, the sheer savagery and power of her presence was overwhelming. She was the same salt-worn sailor we'd grown up with, but she was other, too. Or, perhaps the same.

Duweni.

Like Keira.

Like *me.*

I took a deep dreg of rum straight from the bottle, the liquid burning down my throat as it coated my insides in flame. I wanted to spew it all out, exhale the fire raging within like dragon's breath, my fury and fear too hot to swallow any longer.

A week ago, I didn't even know I had a wife. Never mind a child, growing in her belly, a tiny goddess ready to save the whole world with her goodness.

But today, I'd take on the God of Death with my bare hands if it meant keeping her safe. Keeping them both safe. I'd swallow the stars and steal from the gods and bathe in the blood of a thousand betrayals if that was what it took.

I took another long drink of rum. I'd need it. I licked my lips before looking at Lyr again, his golden image bathed in bronze in the lowlight of the cramped kitchen quarters. "Tell us again how any of this is supposed to work?"

Esme tapped one of my claws. I hadn't managed to retract them since they'd boarded, the beast within chomping at the bit to be unleashed. Still, the witch only smirked at me, one sea monster sniffing out another. "Yer body has already been transformed by the love of a goddess, Mr. Knives-fer-fingers. Keira can't give *anyone* her heart, because ye already own it. Yer even able to harness Danura's power in your scales, and you have *Duweni* blood in your veins. If anyone is built fer this, it's *you*, boy."

I took a steadying breath, the scale stone hanging around my neck burning at the mention. The sirens shared a narrowed-eyed look, all three of them witness to the wonders and mishaps of that night. That ritual. I'd flown in blind on that one, and still, we'd managed to summon Danura. Managed to siphon her power into a few stray scales, plucked from our own tails.

Before we sank *Hiraeth* to the depths and abandoned her to the Otherworld, of course.

I might have had the build for her power, but did I have the will required to wield it?

"What about the soul of the innocent?" I gnawed my lower lip so hard the skin tore, the metallic kiss of my own blood on my tongue grounding me back to this body. *My* body, made by gods old and new. It was a weapon, but I would choose how it was wielded. "I will not kill someone without due cause."

Keira's gaze shot to me, and I swore something warm melted the hard silver of her stare. She'd been angry at me before, cold and sharp…but perhaps I'd only imagined that, too.

Lyr let out a long sigh, swiping the bottle of rum from my hand and taking a deep glug for himself. The amber liquid dribbled from the corner of his lip and into his beard as he guzzled down the last of the precious stuff. When he finished, he looked at me again, cheeks ruddy and eyes bright. "Rules and rituals can be changed. My guess is we won't need the old magick if we learn to harness the new. You've already done it."

Keira, gods bless her, ran a tired hand over her pale face. "What does that even mean?"

Lyr's stare did not leave my face, his gaze so focused it had me squirming in my skin.

"When you summoned Danura, you spoke in the ancient tongue. One long forgotten, even by Arawn himself. I heard the call too. You used it to bind her power in a meager handful of scales." Lyr swung his feet off the table and leaned forward on his forearms, shadows dancing across the planes of his sea-hardened frame. His voice held the power and quiet of the darkest abyss, the pressure relentless even though he barely spoke above a whisper. "How did you do that, *Storyspeaker?*"

The dragon in my chest squirmed with discomfort, a call and an answer both sounding in the back of my skull. "I don't know, I just—"

I trailed off, the memory of the ritual skimming to the surface unbidden.

Focus and fury buzzing in my palms. Parts of me that were both siren and storyteller. An ancient truth fused to my bones, one married to the novel power coating my scales.

Then I sang, the melody bubbling up from the depths. Answers sought and remembered.

A self-fulfilling prophecy authored by the power pulsating within. My tongue tied with truth, each word of my song weighty under the magick that caressed them.

A song of past and present. A song of curses and cures.

A song long forgotten and remembered by all.

A song of caution and triumph.

A song to the universe that made both monsters and men.

How had I summoned the power to pull Danura from *Hiraeth?*

"Sirens always get gifts from their makers," Nelle chimed in, voice quivering with her signature mix of fear and fascination. Violet eyes stared through my soul like she was seeing me for the first time.

Laureli nodded at her side, crossing her arms as she too surveyed me like a new spell or riddle to be solved. "Some more potent than others."

Marina giggled, the sound soft and free of pain for the first moment in days. "The *Ddraig Aur* is both fixed and fluid, God of Truth and Lies!"

I opened my mouth, piecing together Marina's riddle, but Esme tossed her nest of blonde curls over her shoulder with a feral glee, smacking me in the face with her wall of long hair. "And when Keira gave ye her heart and remade ye, it must have combined with the dormant power ye already had…"

"My guess is you have the power to use the old language to speak things into existence. New *spells*, even," Lyr finished for her, and my mind swam with the onslaught of information. "You've made yourself into a god, Storyspeaker."

My head struggled to wrap itself around the information, but the beast in my chest shuddered with relief. That thing, both ancient and just beginning, stirring and singing with the realization. With the name for what it was–what *I* was.

The Storyspeaker. A man turned siren. A siren forged a god.

"So how do we use that now?" Keira cut through the whirlwind, her sweet soprano a siren's call beckoning me back to her, to myself. To the task we still had to see through. "What do we have to do?"

"Arawn has taken Orwellin." Laureli's voice rang steady, but her hands shook. Nelle laced her fingers through them, and with Marina's, standing in solidarity with her sisters. Broken and battered, the last of Danura's sirens would not balk beneath the weight of the war to come.

Lyr gave them a gracious nod, a grimace pulling his mouth at the mention of our mutual enemy. "Aye. Your crew is headed there with some of the lesser gods, but it will not be enough. Arawn has too much sway over them, since they all hold his blood. And even with the tools they carry, it will be useless unless we come with reinforcements."

My stomach dropped so low, it almost fell through the floor all the way to the abyss. My crew was still out there, headed straight for the monster's open maw. Griffin and Rhett, Saeth and Vian…

Reagan. The little dragon, fierce and angry enough to walk straight into trouble. Still grieving, still raging.

I would never forgive myself if something happened to her.

No, Ronan. You did absolutely nothing.

Not this time.

My claws snagged the edge of the worn table, carving into the wood. "We have to save them."

"Aye, we do. Not just because we want to, but they've got the pistols," Lyr growled, his energy matching mine. I looked to my ancestor with renewed respect as he continued, the odious words only stoking the fire that licked through my every limb, "If Arawn gets hold of his guns again, even if we take Danura's power, he can just shoot Ronan and take it all back for himself."

I snarled under my breath, the beast barely contained beneath my flesh. As if by instinct, Keira grabbed my hand before I could absolutely shred the table, her cold skin soothing as ice on a summer's day. I shuddered at her touch, but she didn't let go, instead staring at Lyr with that impenetrable Captain's focus. "How long do we have to get there?"

Laureli cleared her throat, answering first, her words piercing deep beneath my scales. "Two days, at most three."

Marina shook again, nestling deeper into Nelle's side. "Hurry hurry, to outrun the hounds of hell."

My gut sank and twisted again, a pit of snakes squeezing my insides with panic. We were still so far from Orwellin, at least three days. We'd be cutting it way too close for comfort. Especially if the *Ceffyl* had a head start, and the superior speed to boot. "That's not enough time."

At that, Lyr unleashed a booming laugh that rumbled through the table, so loud Marina jumped with a yelp. His shoulders shook like a ship in a squall. "Child, I'm the god of these seas. We will make it enough time."

Esme leapt from her stool, a feral purr rocking through her as she stretched like a cat. "I'll escort yer friends to Tan to collect some assassins to assist us as well."

She shot a wink in my direction before sauntering out of the room, off to fetch Siobhan and Ellian for an adventure all their own. Tan was dangerous, but it was no match for the *sarffymor*.

Relief flooded my limbs, the snakes releasing my gut from their grip, but my heart still ached, a larger worry gnawing at me from the inside.

"What happens when we get to Orwellin?" I stood, needing to stretch my legs before they shifted into fins against my will. If I was going to absorb Danura's power, I had to start acting like a god that could handle such a gift. "How do we protect Keira from him?"

Lyr's answering smile was eel-like, electric and slippery. He turned it on Keira, and my instincts prickled uncomfortably. "Maybe I'm just an old fisherman, but…"

"Bait." Keira crossed her arms around her middle, but she matched the storm-tossed god's smirk with a wicked glint in the silver of her eye. "You want to use me as bait."

The ancient deity stood, clapping Keira on the shoulder and squeezing. "Aye, atta girl. Get close to Arawn, let him think he has you, while Ronan completes the ritual and takes Danura's scattered power." Then, the sunken god's gaze found mine, the beast rising to meet him. An unspoken alliance between the old gods and new. "And when he realizes he's lost, we can end him once and for all."

Songs and Send-offs

GRIFFIN

My final night aboard the *Ceffyl Dwr* was filled with song. The gorgeous, glorious music of drunk cousins and comrades chanting battle hymns as we prepared for the coming war. The clink of kissing mugs, the sharpening of swords. The frightful, frenzied giggles of excitement and anticipation. The soft, heavy sobs we failed to hide. It was music to my ears, the grand finale of Trouble's finest symphony.

The plans were set and settled, this last week spent rehearsing our individual parts. Cerridwen's ravens had delivered our desperate pleas for help across the four seas in record time. Reese had sent word that the *Ddraig* was armed to the teeth and teeming with Pysgoddian hunters, ready to heed their deity's call. In our own hull, two dozen cramped Huddian magickas waited, their charms and spells brewing as we sailed to our final destination. And above our heads, the war drum of booming dragon wingbeats propelled us onward, keeping time with the song in our hearts.

Two ships, three gods, and a handful of dragons to take on the Dark God and his shadow army.

Our odds were terrible. Worse than any drunken bet I'd ever placed. But we sailed on, against all odds, Trouble guiding our course anyway.

"Come drink with us, Griffin!" Tarran's freckles stood stark against his bright red cheeks in the torchlight on the deck, ale dribbling from his chin. Beside him, Gennevieve let loose a sparkling laugh as she wiped at his bottom lip with a gloved finger, staring at him like he was the moon and stars. Tarran's blush deepened as he looked her way, forgetting me entirely.

My heart swelled at the sight, the pretty little siren and the simpleton enjoying one last moment of hope and peace before battle tore it from us. I'd trade every freckle on my ass to ensure that Tarran and Genni had a life after this.

It reminded me of the company I really wanted tonight. A different blond, whose soft-as-silk hair would feel perfect between my fingers right now. Whose blue and silver eyes would also see straight through my bullshit in less than a breath.

"You two lovebirds have fun without me." I saluted the two as I turned away, seeking out my next target. There were little pockets of mirth all around the ship tonight, each an addition to the song. Plenty of people to keep me occupied. *Distracted.*

Saeth and Gwynn sat at the bow of the ship, Gwynn's hands flying around as he animatedly spoke, Saeth's posture rigid as a priestess's starched panties. An interesting pair indeed. The god had assigned Saeth to his assistance from the moment he'd arrived, employing her to help him take stock of the weapons and keep inventory. I'd never seen her take an order that eagerly, though I supposed the chance to have access to all her favorite sharp things probably sweetened the deal.

Or perhaps the sharp hunter god had her attention.

I sauntered up to them, not knowing if I'd be welcomed or stabbed, but figuring either option was better than boredom.

"I'm telling you, it depends on the wood." Gwynn's voice carried as I neared, the growl in it rougher than a drunk's stubble. "If you use hollow arrows, they're easy to split. You just need godly aim like mine."

Saeth didn't notice my arrival as she cut down the God of the Hunt in brutal, efficient strokes. "I think you're full of horseshit. The chances of hitting an arrow dead on and splitting it the whole way?" She tsked like he was a petulant schoolboy. "Impossible."

I crossed my arms, soaking in the scent of Trouble that wafted from them both, my swords screaming at my back like spectators at a boxing match, egging them on with me.

Gwynn grinned wildly, bracing his hands on the rail next to her to lean closer, strong arms flexing as he put his weight on them. "I'm the God of the Hunt, little girl. Nothing is impossible for me."

Saeth grimaced, breathing him in without a flicker of fear. "So the bad breath is a choice, then?"

Gwynn scoffed, leaning away, a blush filling his tanned cheeks. "Clever, but you don't want to pick a fight with me, dear."

"Why, afraid you'd lose?" Saeth's smile was full of razors.

"You're just a little girl playing with my father's gun."

"It's *my* father's now." Rising to the challenge, Saeth brandished said weapon. The silver of the pistol glinted cold in the warm lanternlight as she pressed the barrel right up to the stubble on his neck. "And you're just *afraid.*"

The god's throat worked hard as he swallowed, but his smile was all delight and desire.

"And I thought this would be the fun crowd." I finally voiced my presence before Saeth could remove–or worse, *fondle*–the hunter's balls. Both of them snapped their heads to me, annoyance dripping like blood from their fanged smiles. "I was clearly wrong."

Saeth rolled her eyes so hard they nearly leaped from her head. "A habit of yours, cousin."

"Touché." I raised my hands and bowed, stepping away from whatever weird foreplay I'd stumbled in on; Saeth had a taste for dangerous men that paled only to her love of sharp weapons. The God of the Hunt was both, and I preferred to spend my last night on my family's ship without his sword up my ass.

I wandered over to the mizzenmast, staring out to the dark sea. Normally, a night like this would inspire fear, but there was none tonight. There were no worries lurking in the shadows, no beasties ready to emerge and drag me down into the deep. All of the monsters were already here, waiting for tomorrow in the bright light of sunrise. I leaned against the *Ceffyl's* broad backbone, the dented wood of the old girl as precious to me as any kin.

I'd miss her when the sun rose.

Without warning, a head popped down from the first beam, a curtain of black hair nearly smacking me in the face as it blocked my view of the dark horizon. "You look nervous."

"Lyr's puckered pooper, Vian!" I swore as my heart considered growing legs and walking straight out of my ass. Maybe there were some monsters still lurking in the dark corners of this ship. Monsters I'd invited aboard. Monsters that spoke to the wind and rode dragons. "What are you doing up there, you little imp?"

"Reagan and I are shooting paint pellets at the dragons and seeing who hits the most." A full-toothed grin skewed his features as he hung from the rafter like a baby monkey. "Wanna join?"

I leaned my head back against the mast and shut my eyes, wishing the beam above would fall and knock me out of my misery. It would take everything I had to survive the coming storm, but Vian and the little dragon were determined to take me out first. I opened one eye a crack, the songbird still staring at me, his head tilted, waiting for an answer. "Can't you two just wait to tempt death until tomorrow like the rest of us?"

The lopsided smile fell to a frown. Vian twisted from the beam, landing gracefully on his feet and crossing his arms. "Is that a no?"

I opened my mouth to respond just as Reagan climbed down the rigging, plopping down by the wraith's side, a scowl on her paint-smeared face. "Vian, he can't join our game. He needs to see Rhett." Her hands met her hips as she tilted her chin at me. "You're avoiding him."

The little monster saw too much, yet again. Her chestnut glare wore down even my strongest armor, each and every word as heavy as a blacksmith's hammer. Guilt scratched at the back of my neck, but I rubbed the spot with a warm palm and ignored it. "I am not."

"Are too." She scrunched her nose, but her posture softened, shoulders relaxing as she played our familiar game. The corner of her mouth twitched upward. "Go, or I'll sic Awyr on your ass, old man."

Reagan knew better than any that I'd rather be pissed than pitied, even by my own hand. She would not allow me to sit and feel sorry for myself rather than savor the last stolen moments of happiness I could.

I pushed off the mizzenmast, ready to face my fear. I ruffled her head as I passed, messing up her braid. "Tiny tyrant."

She whacked my hand away, smearing blue paint over my arm, but she chuckled anyway. "Overgrown man-child."

Young as she was, she was right. I was a little boy still striding around in his papa's oversized boots and his uncle's Captain coat. Hoping I didn't make the same mistakes as the first. Pretending I could live up to the latter.

But with a pep in my step thanks to the little dragon's nudge, I walked down the familiar steps of the *Ceffyl* to go see the one man that made me feel bigger and better than a god.

If this was our last night this side of living, I'd make him feel just as powerful, too.

When I opened the door to see him waiting, my breath fled my chest. He sat on the edge of my bed–no, *our* bed–his warm skin glowing in the flickering light, his blond hair the color of the sun's first brave rays. *He* was the god among men, every scar and blemish a story I wanted to hear, every hill and valley of his marbled form a land I wanted to explore.

I'd run out of time for both. But Lyr below, I wouldn't waste another breath.

The door creaked, and his eyes pivoted to mine, the metallic-and-blue instantly sending heat straight to my core. My voice was husky when I finally managed to speak. "You're all alone?"

Rhett's lips twitched. "I was playing cards with a few of the magickas, but they're all worse cheats than my father was."

"No way, that man was the best of the best." I snorted a laugh as I sat beside him, our thighs brushing slightly. I stifled a groan at the contact, my woefully unattended dick pressing against the uncomfortably tight leather trousers I wore. Lyr below, how this man managed to get me so excited without even a kiss was a mystery and a miracle in itself. But I would not have to wait much longer. I leaned close to his cheek, waiting for him to turn so I could capture that wicked mouth with mine...

But Rhett's smile didn't reach his eyes when they finally flicked to me. "Who knows, maybe I'll get to play with him again soon."

"Rhett..." My arousal was doused like a match in a rainstorm, my cock practically shrinking in on itself as reality reigned once more. My voice was a strangled thing as I placed my hand on his leg, the touch pious as a priestess's. "Listen, tomorrow will be–"

He silenced me with the calloused pad of his forefinger as he pressed it to my lips. "Don't sugarcoat it with me, love. You don't need to hide here." The hand strayed from my mouth and buried itself in my hair, tugging me closer. Our foreheads bumped together as our breath mingled in the silent space between, until Rhett spoke again. Sorrow stained the crack in his voice. "We aren't making it out of this, are we?"

"No, probably not," I exhaled, unburdening the truth from my tired tongue. I'd been holding it in too long. "There is a plan with Drystan and Reese to get the kids out safely, but it would involve us covering for them."

Rhett pulled back, and I missed the closeness. His eyes glassed over, but he smiled wide enough to crinkle the vicious scar across his cheek. His palm trailed down my face again, all the way down my shoulder until it rested above my heart. "A necessary risk. You're an incredible Captain. It will be an honor to go down with you."

I covered his fingers with mine, unwilling to let go. It was unfair to take him down with me. Unfair to bring him into this mess at all. But wanting was weakness, and I was utterly frail without him by my side. I would need his faith and strength to succeed tomorrow. Even if loving each other was lethal for us both.

I cracked a grin, tasting the salt of the stray tears leaking down my cheeks. "I'm sorry you bet on the wrong hand."

Rhett chuckled, stealing each lingering drop of water away with a quick kiss. "No, Griffin. It's always been you. And even if tomorrow is the end, every second was worth it. I bet right, against all odds."

I stared at my lover, the faithful, grouchy, good-hearted boy that dared to love a disaster. I could lose a thousand hands or take a hundred blows right to the gut, and it would still all be worth it for every moment I had with him.

Tomorrow I would lose, but tonight, I'd already won. For once in my gods-forsaken life, I was free of regret and disappointment.

The fear was gone from my voice, my heart laid bare to the man who'd healed me. "I love you."

And like he always had, he met me right where I was, toe to toe, heart to heart. "I love you too."

We both sat there a moment longer, soaking in the sweet silence, before Rhett leaned back, tucking an arm behind his head with a raised eyebrow. "So, Red, how do you want to spend your final night on this beauty?"

An errant spark of Trouble lit in my chest. I was Griffin fucking Branwen, the Lyrs-damned Swordsinger. The cad of the east, the fire-crotched man-whore of Ir'de, the Rydha's right hand rebel. If tomorrow brought only death, I'd go out with a bang, my final notes on this earth loud as blaring trumpets.

I snatched Rhett's hand with a grin, ready to make some noise and start trouble. "Not here. Follow me."

Rhett obeyed, letting me tug him out the door and down the hall. Then another. Then down the stairs and to the left, a path I could walk with my eyes closed and my hands tied behind my back. As we jogged, the sounds of the rest of the crew's merriment fueled our steps, the symphony coming to its natural, magnificent end. Drumbeats banged in my ribs, my heart keeping tempo as excitement and nostalgia traded the melody back and forth.

We stopped finally outside the familiar cold bars, water pinging against the metal, the smell of rotted hay and regrets stinging my nose hairs. Rhett raised a wary brow as he surveyed our surroundings. "The *brig*?"

I nodded, admiring how handsome he looked even in the dim dampness of my family's ship. It wasn't some nice inn in Pysgodd, but it was me. *Us.* This had been my home, the belly of the beast that was the *Ceffyl*, where I didn't have to pretend or play nice. Where I could think and stew for hours in my own trouble without worrying who might see or care. And it's where Rhett stole my heart and made it his, even if I hadn't recognized it then. "It was always my place to reflect. And it's where you and I…"

Rhett didn't let me finish as he trapped my mouth in a kiss. I melted in his touch, my hands digging into the hard flesh at his waist, our chests glued together. His lips danced with mine to the rhythm of our quickening pulses, our tongues trading jabs and blows. His hand fisted in my shirt, nearly tearing at the material, the taste of his urgency intoxicating. When we finally came up for air, his expression was hot enough to chase the chill from the bare brig. "Wanna finish what we started that day?"

I gripped his face tightly, relishing the scratch of his stubble against my palms. I'd follow this man to the end of the world and beyond. And if this was our swan song, we'd sing it together. "Aye, Blondie. Let's see this thing to the end."

And as he laid me down in the hay, worshiping my body with his, my final night on the *Ceffyl Dwr* was filled with the song of love.

36

Farewells and Fires

GRIFFIN

The silence that wrapped itself around the *Ceffyl* was not the comfortable, soothing nothingness I'd come to love with Rhett. There were no gentle, slow breaths or soft gull calls echoing in the distance. The ship did not even groan as it drifted into the Orwellin docks, the shallows kissing the bottom of the hull without a whisper, as if the vessel itself knew the urgency of our errand.

No, the silence was hollow, much like the ship itself. Everything of value had been emptied out or left behind, the only contents still remaining the dozens of abandoned cauldrons, brewing still in the belly of the beast. Like my stomach too, after I'd heaved up my meager attempt at breakfast.

It was the silence of oblivion, of endless, blackest night. The promise of what waited if I failed my sole task.

The others had cleared off in the earliest hours of the morning, when the moon still hung pregnant in the sky, the chill clawing its way across our spines. As my crew and kin took to the skies on the back of dragons or to the sea in the small lifeboats, they'd been quiet too, our plan prioritizing stealth over sentimentality.

There were no softly spoken goodbyes, no fanfare of farewell. Just sunken eyes and shaking hands. Sharpened swords and loaded guns. Waiting with held breath for war. For the signal to begin.

My signal.

As the first rays of sunlight bled purple and pink in the sky, it was time. There was no more waiting in silence. It was time to bang the first drum of battle.

I kissed the mizzenmast of the *Ceffyl* once, running a hand over her smooth wood.

"Thank you, old girl," I croaked out to this ship—a part of my family. Part of me. I thought of all the memories etched into the wood and ropes of this beast. The countless swordfights with Keira and Tarran, playing heroes in the rigging while our Pas yelled at us to get back to work. The drunken tales told belowdecks on the coldest nights, all of us huddled together to keep warm. The hours in the hot sun swabbing her deck to the merry tune of a shanty. The quiet, hungover mornings woken by the gentle rock of waves and the distant call of gulls. The damp chill of the brig. The cozy perch of the crow's nest.

It was wrong, that I was the last Branwen she'd see. Trouble's tarnished toy, sinking the fastest cutter in the four seas with one of his terrible ideas. But it was all I had left to offer—the cursed, troubled parts of me that knew how to fight and win before all else. Parts I'd learned to cultivate on this very ship. And somehow, I'd make it worth her sacrifice.

I did not look back as I finally strode off the deck, ready to set my whole world ablaze just for a chance to feel the warmth. My boots began the rhythm of the fight as they thudded across the gangway and onto the wooden dock.

Breathe in, breathe out.

The puppet guards were waiting for me in a swarm, black hoods covering their faces. We'd been quiet, but we knew Arawn would be watching for approaching ships, and Locasta's creatures were ready, swords drawn for a fight. I would oblige them. A dark smile curled across my face, Truth shouting at my back as I unsheathed her. She was desperate to rejoin her twin, Triumph waiting somewhere on the other side of Orwellin with Rhett, and I would not deny her much longer.

The puppets raced forward, passionless and feral, ready to cut me down.

Breathe in, breathe out.

I bid them closer, closer, striking and swiping my mighty sword, cutting them down if they got too close. Blood spattered the dock, the gangway, not a single scream exiting their lifeless lips as I cleaved into them with reckless abandon. My heartbeat thundered in my chest, the call desperate, feverish.

Not yet. Almost.

Breathe in, breathe out.

Back up onto the deck of the *Ceffyl*, a whole buzzing host of puppets following, charging me.

Charging straight into my trap.

They clustered onto my family's ship, onto the only home I'd ever known. Truth rang out in my palm, breaking the silence. Telling me it was time.

Just as the sun cast the morning in glowing, orange fire, I lit the wick waiting on the rail. The rope caught fire, the burning traveling faster than sound to where the cauldrons waited belowdecks, their contents both potent and flammable.

I jumped overboard into the shallows as fast as my legs would carry me, Trouble dragging me forward, not yet done playing.

And as I hit the cool water, the *Ceffyl* exploded with a ferocious, ear-splitting bang.

A warning. A signal. A battle cry.

War was coming for Death itself.

37

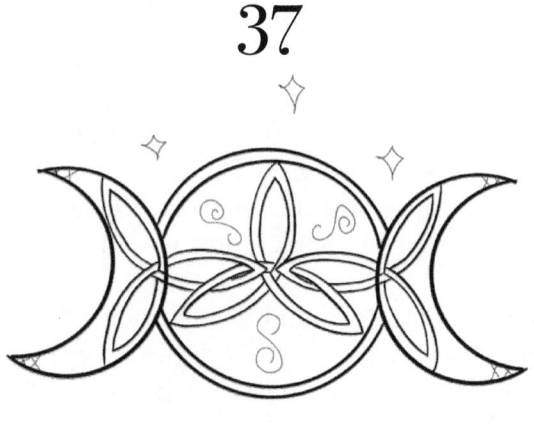

Vows and Vengeance

KEIRA

The God of the Sea made good on his promise.

It only took us two days, and Orwellin's form appeared on the horizon, the first rays of morning blotted out by the black colossus of God's Eye tower.

Arawn would be there. Waiting. Ready for me to walk straight into his trap.

But I would be ready this time, too.

Ronan's hands were stuffed in the pockets of his black leather trousers, fashioned to match the billowing black tunic he wore as he stared at the tall monstrosity looming over us with contempt. "You promise you're certain about this?"

I nodded, crossing my arms against my own dark battle suit. Dark enough that the God of Death wouldn't see me bleed. Nelle had worked the whole night to tailor Marina's scaled battle garb to fit my unbalanced frame. Armored in siren's scales, the well of ancient power pooling in my veins, and my husband standing tall at my side...

I'd never felt more powerful or sure.

Papa once said it was better to know your enemy than to let them know you. And I was armed with all the knowledge I'd gathered on Death. What he wanted. What he'd kill for.

I was about to dangle it in front of him while my husband snatched it all away.

I tore my eyes away from God's Eye, dismissing it to take one last deep breath of air before I sank into the deep. I looked to Ronan. To my lighthouse in the storm, my anchor in the tide. Even though he didn't remember us, he still stood with me. Still fought with me. *For* me. No matter the hurts and lies between us, no matter the truths unsaid, he would always be there. And I would always come back to him.

"I've only been more certain once in my life." My voice did not quiver or quake. It carried over the crashing waves, given wings by the lightness of the truth. "And that was when I decided to marry you the second time."

Ronan quirked a brow, a twitch in the corner of his pouting lips. "The *second* time?"

I thought to that moment again, letting it lift my heart. Us, on the *Ceffyl*, in front of our closest kin. The bright sunlight, the taste of adventure in the air. The hard-won love in the warmth of his palm as he took my hand and my heart. As he offered his in return.

Perhaps I'd only been allowed that brief moment, our paths meant to diverge as Fate often did. But small as that peace was, it would be enough to last my whole life long. It would carry me through the pain to come.

"It's a long story. I'll tell you when we survive this, if you'd like."

"Keira–" Ronan grabbed my hand, electricity shooting through the place of contact. I met his gaze again. His mouth pressed into a tight line, stormclouds of worry in the horizon of his eyes. "I–"

"I'll be okay." I placed my hand over his, working to memorize the feel of it. Soft and strong, calloused and comforting. We'd been here before, on the precipice of change, waiting for the wind to blow us over the edge. But this time, I was ready to let go. Ready to fall into the waiting depths below, no matter the sharks in the water. My tattoo stood dark against my skin, a reminder of what I fought for. What I'd bleed for today, if that was what it took.

The Silver Wheel. The Hand of Fate. The promise of the future in my middle.

My smile was not faked as it stretched my cheeks with a welcome effort. "I'll keep her safe, I promise."

Ronan blinked, his soft lashes brushing away gathering saltwater tears from his eyes. The emotion made me pause, made the breath stick in my chest. His free hand reached out, tucking a loose curl back into my intricately braided hair. No matter how tightly I pulled the untamed strands, they wouldn't stay. Nothing ever did, no matter how hard I'd held on. But Ronan tried, time and time again, despite it all, to put things back together.

"I need you safe, too." His thumb swiped my cheek, as if he was trying to wipe away my freckles…or commit them to sensory memory. The sea of his eyes somehow burned as he held my face like it was fragile. Precious. "I may not remember us, but I know my own heart. I know how I *feel*. I won't let you slip away again."

I leaned into his touch against my better judgment. I'd spent so long keeping him at arm's length, protecting him from me, from my mistakes, I'd forgotten the simple, sophisticated pleasure of his warmth. If this was our last moment together, our final goodbye, I would not waste it on pride. If we managed to somehow survive, and he went on to regret this moment of affection, he could walk away. I'd let him, too. But I would follow. Until I forgot my last name, or my feet fell off, I'd follow him home. "I'm not going anywhere this time."

"Good." He flashed his fangs in a wide smile that made my heart want to leap straight from the cage of my chest. He was both monster and man, feral and polished. A contradiction of themes that set my soul ablaze. "How many men get to say they've had the privilege of falling for their wives all over again?"

The air fled from my lungs as I searched for the truth to his words. And there it was, in the deep blue of his eyes. In the gentle but insistent caress of his thumb across my cheek. In the dimpled stretch of his lopsided smile.

Again, on the precipice. Ronan fell for me.

Fate was cruel and twisted, but sometimes, she was fair. Sometimes, she was the patron of unlikely victories, big and small.

And when my husband kissed me, his lips molded firmly with mine, the taste of saltwater and citrus and something *other* on my tongue, I knew I'd won. No matter the result of the bloodbath to come, no matter the pain or suffering we'd have to endure to ensure humanity's survival. I'd won, because in this tiny moment, I had hope.

Small victories, Keira girl. What do you want, and how can you get it?

If we survived this, I'd make my husband mine again. I'd give him my heart willingly on a platter made of finest silver. And together, we'd raise the little girl blooming in my belly.

I lingered in the kiss a moment longer, my power surging as the god before me gave me his heart in exchange for my own.

And when our mouths finally parted, our breathing fast and our hearts pounding in time, I readied myself to war. "Let's end this."

Ronan pulled back but did not let go of my hand. A promise fulfilled. Another vowed. My favorite smirk snaked onto his expression. "We're only getting started."

At his words, the boom of fireworks echoed from Orwellin's shore. Black smoke billowed into the air, a thick cloud marring our view of God's eye.

No. Fireworks didn't produce that much smoke.

Ronan's hand flew to the pistol at his side, tense stance a mirror to my own. "What was that?"

I ran to the spyglass on the portside, peering through the tiny lens. I waited as swirls of smoke and ash cleared from view, revealing the source of the noise beneath their dark fingers.

My gasp got stuck in my throat as the world tilted.

Tucked into the docks of Delm Arawn, less than a league away, rested the burning corpse of a ship I knew as well as my own name.

The *Ceffyl Dwr* was burning. *Sinking.* Her wooden frame torn to bits, her remnants devoured by the famished fire.

"No."

Oh gods, was my crew still on board? My stomach rolled at the thought, leaping straight to my throat.

No. They wouldn't be so foolish. Sailing straight up to the front door of Arawn's territory sounded like an obvious, terrible plan that not even Griffin could've come up with. This had to be a diversion, or a trap.

Still, I pulled away from the spyglass, and with long, steady strides, I grabbed my sword and dagger from where they rested next to the mizzenmast.

"Stay with the sirens," I commanded my husband, the plan already set and secured. I had to get ashore, had to get to my family. If they needed a distraction, I had a few tricks up my sleeve to give them just that.

"Be safe," Ronan called back, already shooting into action.

I nodded. I was owed another dance with Death.

This time, I'd lead.

Lyr bounded up from belowdecks, his wild mane of gold hair blowing behind him on a phantom breeze. He wore tight armor made of shells that hugged every jagged muscle of his godly frame, a vision of the tempestuous sea that had guided me all my life. His stormy gaze met mine. "Are you ready, girl?"

My answering grin was wicked. I was the NightMare of the Four Seas. Ariannad, the Goddess of Fate and Fury. I was born of the sea and salt, of the Branwen Clan and Porthladdian soil. Of the wild *Hiraethaen* river, of my mother's starshine and the sandy beach of the isle of the lost.

And I was carved straight from the ice of the Otherworld, rescued by the Serpent Prince and molded by the God of Death.

Now, I'd end him.

"More ready than ever."

Dewy jumped onto the *Madyn* from the water, his dark mane glistening with cold seawater. He knelt before me, red eyes wide, ushering me onto his back. I slid on easily, letting his powerful form flex beneath me. I patted his neck, and he exhaled an excited whinny.

Without any further stalling, I kicked my heels into his flanks, urging him onward. And with the God of the Sea behind me, I rode the last remaining *ceffyl dŵr* to claim my victory.

38

Tales and Transformations

RONAN

Mama used to warn me that a single story held more power than an entire army. When I was a child, it was a mere fairytale. A starry-eyed boy's daydreams, to imagine his favorite heroes and let their lessons lead him through a rose-colored life.

Now, I needed it to be the truth. I saw stories for the weapons they were, spells and spears against the shadow of Death. If the cosmos willed it, the very fabric of the Deyrnas could be transformed and turned upside down with one whispered tale, one legend made reality.

I no longer underestimated stories. Instead, I would wield them. And I would become a living legend if it meant I could rescue my wife and child. I would tell the tale and write my own part, would craft and cast whatever magick brought Death to his knees.

My stomach turned in time with the ship as it rocked against the lapping waves. Even from a league away, I could hear the clamor of fighting already beginning, the cries of swords and screams of terror and pain. The smell of blood carried on the salt breeze, the darkening sky overhead matching my mood.

Was Reagan in the midst of the chaos? Was Keira? Was it their blood marring the black streets of Delm Arawn?

I couldn't think about the fight, not yet. I caged the instinct begging me to run, swim, fucking *fly* to their aid. And I would. But first, I had to swallow the stars, to forge myself anew.

I tuned it all out, listening instead to the beating hearts around me, their rhythms steady and sure and united. Laureli, Marina, and Nelle stood in a tight circle with me, our hands all locked together in the center as we tilted our faces toward the black sky, the sun and stars fully hidden behind the thick ash and angry clouds. A chill ran down my spine, anticipation and fear prickling as the beast within rose to the surface.

Nelle's gentle timbre blanketed me in a veil of comfort, the charge between our clasped palms electric as all four of our magicks melded together. "Close your eyes and focus, love. We are here to amplify."

I shut my eyes, letting the chilly breeze swathe my exposed chest and face in goosebumps. It absorbed into my skin, feeding the part of me that was *other*, the creature stirring and stretching within. This was what it desired, what it thrived on. Power and persistence. Wind and salt and secrets. Stories and myths and mist.

I shuddered as the dormant thing surged, scratching to be let loose.

"Oh universe, keeper of the gods above and below," I fumbled through the words Lyr had given me, fighting to keep my voice level. Sweat slicked my palms and my brow furrowed as I concentrated, trying to manage the *thing* within. "I, Ronan Francis Mathonwy, claim what is mine. I claim the stars in the sky, the power over life itself, as designed by the Mother Donn."

I conjured the image of Danura, of her white hair and effortless grace, her sharp silver stare and steady force. I was a storyteller, and if that was the role I was meant to play next, I would wear her costume as my own, remake myself in her image. I held my breath, my claws stinging in my knuckles to be let out, my fangs scraping against my tongue. The siren, the predator, grew impatient, wanting to devour and claim as I spoke.

But nothing answered, not even a shift in the wind. An emptiness rattled through me, the air in my lungs suddenly stale and unsatisfying. I took a fresh breath, burrowing deeper into the stream of power waiting within, but it felt stagnant. Like a putrid, abandoned well, dirty and dingy with disuse. I tried to access it, to stir it once more, to push it upwards and outwards, a channel to the stars I summoned. But no matter how hard I focused, it remained out of reach, untouched and uninterested. The dragon in my heart flicked its tail in aggravation, ready to dive in and splash around.

"It's not working," I gritted out, eyes flying open, frustration boiling in my belly.

"Try again?" Nelle's lips pressed together in a thin line as she shot a worried glance to Laureli, the seer mirroring her concern.

I swore under my breath, grasping their hands tighter, pulling more of their power—Danura's power—into me. Jasmine and herbs and healing light. Brine and incense and dark possibility. Both twined around me and twisted into one, baiting the feral thing within.

"Speak the truth you do not know," Marina whispered with a shudder, her voice warm and steady for the first time in days. Her power overshadowed the others' as it slid deeper into me, a curious crimson thing that lit my veins in ruby recognition. The phantom fingers of her gift folded over my beating heart, tugging the truth up from my center, like a twitching muscle ready to be used and exercised. "Surrender to the beast."

"She's right. You have to make it your own. You're not taking her power the way she used it, you have to believe it's yours," Laureli encouraged, eyes white as a vision consumed her. Connected like this, a flash of the image blasted in my own mind.

Talons and fangs. Golden scales and starfire breath. Fins and fury and…
Oh gods.

I stood straighter, sweat now drenching my brow and back despite the chilly sea air. I had to do this. For Keira, for Rhiannon, for the Deyrnas. I had to be more.

No more failures or shortcomings. No more missteps or forgetting.

My legs shook and my knees wobbled, but the sirens held me steady as I wrangled the words once more, my voice booming with the echo of the beast. "I claim my birthright, as a son of Lyr and a tool of the Goddess Ariannad. As father of the promised Rhiannon."

Above me, and somehow within, I felt something unlock. Something fracture and fuse together all the same. A shift, as if the universe itself winked open one eye, peering at me with a mixture of curiosity and expectation.

And then, just as it did when I'd summoned Danura, the very ground gave out below me, and I dove into that deep, ancient pit within.

Magick tasted like fire as it spilled from my throat, onto my waiting lips.

"Eyes of the god that bore me, vast as the sea.

Scales of gold from the goddess who loved me, ever changing and ever present as the moon in the sky.

Heart of the goddess I've yet to meet, the Queen Rhiannon, regent of love itself."

My song was ancient and all-knowing, new and limitless. It carried all the way to the sky, to the heavens, a prayer and a reply. My legs trembled and my heart beat a furious, fascinated rhythm against my ribs so hard they nearly cracked. But I did not stop as I belched up my tale, the story I was destined to tell.

The cosmos had both eyes open now, fixed on me. Nowhere and everywhere at once, as the clouds rumbled and shifted. A hole opened above as it did below, light shining on our circle. Warmth and fire. Energy and change. Every hair on my body stood at attention as it poured over me, *into me*, as alive and alert as I was.

"Keep going!" Someone—Nelle—shouted, but it all sounded far away, the thunder overhead and within drowning it out like the mighty roar of a great, forgotten monster. My story twisted and shaped itself with it, spreading its wings and readying to take flight.

"Eyes of sapphire. Scales of gold. Heart of diamond strength," I growled with the same power, my body vibrating as it sucked in every drop of pure energy. I would drink the starlight and make it mine. Not Danura's, not life and balance and light and beauty. No, it would be both wicked and wonderful, monster and man, just like me. It surged and soured in my belly, but I swallowed it all anyway, burning like whiskey and whispered triumphs. *"I take what I've been given, and sacrifice what I've already lost."*

Another flash of bright, and my legs gave beneath me entirely. I crashed to my knees, palms scraping the course deck as I caught myself. The sirens broke the circle, crowding me, concern laced in their stares. I shuddered and shivered, my body fighting to contain it, to capture it all.

No, it would not be caged or controlled.

Stories needed to be told.

It needed to be *freed*.

"I am the Ddraig Aur, *the Golden Dragon!"* I yelled to the sky, a promise to the heavens that had fed and grown me. My truth expelled from my lips like fire, carving a path in their wake for every

god and monster to see. *"God of transformation and truth. Of life reshaped and reborn."*

On my command, by *my* will, my flesh tore and ripped at the seams, the beast finally unchained. Legs stretched and reformed, back broke and repaired, until I was greater. Bigger. Stronger.

And with my scaled wings and starfire, I took to the skies in my dragon form to save my wife and daughter.

39

Wars and Witches

GRIFFIN

I hoisted myself out of the water on the other side of Delm Arawn, the black city named for the god himself. My lungs burned from the breath I'd held too long, scratches from the blast littering my freckled skin. Saltwater stung the open cuts, but I didn't have time to care. A deafening ring in my ears tuned out the chaos of the fight before me, my tired legs carrying me forward on staggering steps.

The streets of Delm Arawn had once glistened like stars; now, they burned red, blood running through the stone in hundreds of streams. The carnage was well underway, the time it took me to swim from the docks to the north side of the city more than enough for a battle to get bloody. The bodies of soldiers in both colors—black, Locasta's men, and gray, Drystan's sleeper agents—were strewn about the city like fresh decor.

I tried to keep my stomach settled as I noted the civilians scattered among them.

A woman, wilted like a flower, a sword driven through her middle, her blue frock stained deep red.

Crimson against ivory. A stomach punctured like a sack of wine.

A man, reaching for his house, an arrow through the back of his skull, his unseeing eyes tilted skyward.

Silver eyes, ushering the unspeakable command in our silent language.

A little girl, trampled. Arms and legs sticking out in all the wrong directions.

I did not stop. Couldn't.

This was only the beginning. I had to keep moving, had to find my family and Locasta to end this madness once and for all. The gods would handle Arawn, and us mortals would burn the witch.

I trudged forward, Truth crying in my palm as she brought me closer to my targets. Soldiers clad in black dove at me from left and right, but I sliced through them, ignoring the burn in my arms and legs as I pressed onward.

Breathe in, breathe out. Slice and strike.

Repeat.

Repeat.

Repeat.

Through the hive of puppets, to the front line of Huddian magickas casting protection charms. They were bruised and battered, gauzy garb torn and plenty of them bloody. But they held their arms high, chanting the ancient words fused to their bones, eyes burning for their brothers and sisters and Ir'de. Madame Hedd offered me a nod, a signal to the others to let me pass. I gave her a tight-lipped smile in return.

They did not stop as I walked past them. Couldn't.

I didn't either, weaving through their lines to my destination.

My breath stuck in my chest again as I saw Rhett and Tarran pressed together, back-to-back, fighting off four soldiers by themselves. Their silver breastplates and leathers were smeared in every shade of blood, but they were still standing. Still fighting. Still *alive*. Relief and rage flooded my veins.

The soldiers would not be much longer.

With a lunge and a swipe, I felled two, slicing through their middles. Their tops halves toppled from the bottom, insides spilling onto my boots. Another spin, and my blade sang across another's neck, relieving him of his head.

The fourth twirled and raised his sword at me, black hood masking his face so I couldn't see where he'd strike. I crouched, holding Truth tight, readying for attack…

Triumph's tip glistened crimson as it poked through his chest. The guard dropped his own weapon as his body went limp, slumping to the ground without a sound.

Rhett met my gaze as he freed his blade, tawny skin stained red from the blood of his enemies. A wide smile broke across his face. "Took you long enough!"

For a moment, the world went still, chaos falling silent as I stared at my lover, my heart pounding in my chest with a mix of adrenaline and an emotion I still hesitated to name. "Sorry, I had to swim a league." I wiped my blade on one of the fallen guard's black cloaks, the thick material absorbing the dark blood.

Tarran strode to us, pushing his sweat-and-gore matted curls from his face. "Pssh, excuses."

Rhett waved him off, his own chest heaving in heavy breaths. They must've been fighting for over an hour straight at this point, but still, his gaze raked over me with efficient scrutiny, lips a fine line as he scanned for signs of harm. "You all right?"

I stood straighter, twirling Truth with a flourish. "Better than ever. Where are the others?"

"Drystan and Genni are pushing through to the tower while Madame Hedd holds the line." The deep wrinkles across Rhett's brow crinkled his scar. "Morwyn has to be here somewhere, but she hasn't shown herself yet."

My stomach sank at that. No sight of the wicked bitch herself, and yet, we were already staggering under the might of her forces.

This was exactly as Nef had warned. The Dark God would not offer us a fair fight. He would hide behind his shadows and Morwyn's mannequins until we were good and spent and barely hanging on.

Then he'd strike.

Unless we did first.

I wiped the sweat from my brow with the last unbloodied scrap of my soaked tunic. We had a plan, but we needed all three legs of it to work if we had any chance of success. Of *survival*. "Any word from Delm Duwei?"

Rhett nodded, and my heart skipped a step. "The smoke signals have gone off, so Reese and the hunters have to be there."

Another pang of relief. The hunters would have to manage against whatever forces protected the south side of the island. If we could just keep pushing inland, if we could corner Locasta and send them scrambling back…

I raised my gaze. Even in the ash and smoke, the black giant of God's Eye tower peered down at us. Somewhere in its hold, the Dark

God waited. And hopefully, so did the most important members of our crew. Saeth and Gwynn, Nef and Cerridwen and Vian. Gods and a half-siren, the last hopes of the Deyrnas. "And the tower?"

Tarran grimaced, following my line of sight. "Nothing yet."

I had no time to let my disappointment settle as two figures sprinted toward us, fear smeared across their blood-marred expressions, a mix of gray and black clad soldiers on their heels.

"Fall back!" Drystan waved his sword above his head as he bellowed, running full speed toward us.

Genni was hot on his tail, her gloves off and her claws out. A growl escaped her small form that could rival a dragon's. "She's here!"

My stomach lurched. I exchanged a quick look with Rhett before hefting my sword back up despite my protesting muscles.

Breathe in, breathe out. Repeat.

Repeat.

Repeat.

This was what I was made for. Fights, I knew. Fights, I won.

"Magickas, on me! Locasta is coming!" I hollered as Drystan and Genni drew closer. The magickas followed rank, pulling their circle tighter around us, the charms they cast raising the hairs on the back of my arms. I held Truth at the ready, scanning the oncoming stampede for Locasta's sunken form. "Stay sharp!"

The puppets descended, crashing first into the wall of magick the casters wielded. A few grunted as the soldiers slashed at the invisible shield, but it held firm.

I sighed a breath of relief, again looking out for Locasta among the ranks. She had to be there somewhere, and I would fight until she bled at my feet. For what she did to the Deyrnas. To my father, turned betrayer at her hands. To Finna, to Keira.

But as shadows licked at my legs, wrapping themselves around me, I knew I'd been foolish. Trouble's toy, yet again.

The Queen of Shadows did not play fair.

"Hello gentlemen," she crowed behind us, her frigid voice sending a chill up my spine.

I spun to face her, Truth screaming in my palm as I took in her dark form. She stood within our magick barrier, dressed from neck to toe in a veil of shadows, a cruel, twisted smile on her gaunt face. Blackness stirred against the pale flesh of her palms. "Did you really think it would be that easy?"

"Morwyn," Rhett growled as he stepped closer to me, his heat at my side fighting the chill of the shadows misting around our legs. Neither of us needed a reminder of what her shadows could do, weapons in their own right.

Still, I shot an irreverent gesture her way, shoving down the fear that scratched away at my insides. "Well, well. You look like you just rolled in hellhound shit, Councilwoman."

A grimace pulled at her gaunt features, the shadows around my legs wrapping tighter. I stilled as they snared me, phantom chains that I'd never truly escaped the first time. Heart pounding, I shot a quick glance to the rest of the crew, distress and determination written across their features as her power touched each of us.

Morwyn folded her hands together, darkness gathering where her spindled fingers met. "I've let you all run around and play your games for far too long. Let you play heroes in the north and south, let you sail your ships to try and feed the poor refugees, let you *think* you were doing something. But now you've become bothersome little gnats, starting fights on *my* island. The Dark God is not pleased. So I've come to exterminate you."

Her threat punched straight through me, fear climbing up the back of my neck as her shadows worked their way up and around, tighter and tighter.

Crimson against ivory. Blood against stone.
Silver eyes, uttering an unspoken command.

No, not again. Not this time.

I was Griffin fucking Branwen. I was the Swordsinger, Trouble's favorite chewtoy. I was the final Captain of the *Ceffyl* fucking *Dwr*. And I would not let Morwyn Locasta take anything else from me ever again.

Not without a fight.

And fights, I won.

I stepped forward, away from the others, ignoring the pain that shot up my legs as the black ropes cinched against them. I pointed Truth forward, my friend and weapon ready to taste the shadowmaster's blood. And like the asshat I was, I laughed right in the queen of darkness's face. "Funny, the only bugs I see are the ones that crawled up your ass and died."

Locasta snarled, taking my bait. Her eyes went wholly black as the abyss, all traces of humanity vanishing from the witch's expression. "Enough. *Laddaf.*"

A single command.

Kill.

At her order, the soldiers surged, the blackness bursting from her palms a beacon to her hive. The chains tightened around my middle, holding me in place, a fly caught in the spider's web.

But I had a command of my own. A final pass to a sparring partner that would make the God of Death himself wish he'd never been born.

My smile brimmed with dragon-fire as I tugged the flare from my waistband.

As I pulled the trigger, aiming high at the sky.

As the red flash lit the ashen clouds in a crimson to match the bloodstained streets.

As Reagan and the dragon horde descended.

40

Bait and Bindings

KEIRA

Papa used to say I was the fiercest thing on two legs. Riding astride Dewy through the small strip of wild land in the middle of Orwellin, it had never felt more true. Here, amid the tall oaks and crunching undergrowth in the center of the Nightless City, I was power and destruction and untamed contradictions. Here, I had a purpose. Kill and create, devour and remake.

The NightMare of the Four Seas had made landfall, and I would not stop until I made things right.

I could feel my family in the distance, the hair on my arms standing straight as the charged energy washed over me in waves. Somewhere in the fighting, they still lived and breathed. My ever-changing power acting as a beacon, I could feel every one of them, their fates pricking at the back of my neck.

Griffin, Rhett, and Tarran… alive, but struggling as they swung their swords in tandem. Reagan, further *above*, somehow, rage pulsing through her like dragon-fire. Saeth and Vian, shrouded in some type of darkness, fear masking them from me.

They were running out of time.

But I was not the same girl that fell to the Otherworld. I'd been reborn, the Goddess Ariannad.

Time would bend to my will, and Death would follow.

A goddess kneels to no one.

But Death would kneel to me.

I kicked my heels into Dewy's flank, urging him faster. With an annoyed whinny, he complied, his strange webbed hooves slapping against the rocky ground as he barreled ahead.

Flares shot off in the distance, but I couldn't let myself be distracted. I hoped they were signals of small victories instead of cries for help, but I could not be their divine intervention today. I had a single task.

Get the Dark God's attention. Keep him busy.

Wait for my husband to swoop in and end him.

Again, I coaxed Dewy faster, the wind biting at my face as he sprinted with the speed of a hurricane. We'd need every last second we could wring from this plan. Lyr was supposed to meet me at God's Eye tower, coming up from the bay on the other side of it. We'd find a way to manage Arawn until Ronan could absorb every last drop of Danura's gift. And then, together, we'd send Death back beyond the veil.

As my faithful steed moved onward, the black shadow of God's Eye consumed more and more of our path, casting us deeper into darkness. Trees shrank to carved marble statues. Rocky terrain shifted to smooth, obsidian-laid paths as the forest dissolved into cityscape. I let my power rise to my skin, the glow of starlight brightening the way. The energy buzzed in my veins, every ounce I'd stored over the last few days itching and scratching for a chance to be released.

I only hoped it would be enough.

The True Fire burned brighter as we closed in on the tower. Heat and power scorched along my nerves, desperate to finish what I'd started in the Otherworld. I let it consume me, blinding white radiating from my every inch, a defiant cry against the umbra outline of the monolith.

A beacon. A call to arms. A gauntlet thrown at Death's front door.

I burned brighter and hotter still, Dewy's excited whinnies urging me on as I did him.

Faster, flying through the streets, until only the tower and the sea beyond were visible.

A dark form burst through the colossally tall doors, the shadows at his heels the same onyx as the stone. His eyes met mine, as they had so many times in the space beyond. Black like night and nothingness. Cold like ice and apathy.

A moment passed, teeming full of all the time we'd spent together. Trapping and teasing. Dancing and deceiving. Cooking and calculating. All the games we'd played in the frozen wasteland, each of us smiling and seducing and striking at each other with gentle caresses.

I tugged at Dewy's mane, and the beast halted so abruptly, he nearly threw me from his back. But I straightened my shoulders, my gaze unwavering from Arawn's.

Here we were again, at the end and the beginning. At the precipice of every choice I'd ever made or failed to follow through on.

Today, his beautiful form was encased in white robes, matching the bright smile he'd weaponized so many times before. Ebony eyes were glassy with crocodile tears. His deep purr carried, the shadows behind him twisting and turning with the rumble of his words. "Good day, Ariannad, my darling. Are you here to fight me, or beg for my forgiveness?"

"What are you doing, Arawn?" My voice did not shake as I called him by his name. He blinked at the causal title, long lashes fluttering like raven's wings. I dismounted Dewy, swinging my legs over with ease. It had been so long since I'd stood on real, solid ground. So long since my legs were not sliding across ice in the Otherworld or swaying with the waves. I planted my boots like roots, ready to stand just as tall and strong as the tower looming above. For my family, fighting in the distance. For my daughter, growing in my belly. I masked my next question in gentle tones, just as I had during our every dance and parry. "This is madness. The people here have done nothing to harm you. You had your quarrel with my mother, I get it. But she's back in the Otherworld. You don't have to be a monster anymore."

His dry chuckle clawed at the back of my neck. "This is not about your mother. This is about us, *Caraid.*" He took a soft step forward, posture relaxed, as the darkness behind him whirled faster. Intimidation and intimacy in a perfect blend. His eyes slowly drank me in, and I fought the flush of revulsion that crept up my spine as his gaze landed on my abdomen. "And our sweet baby."

My instincts begged me to run, to fight, to scream. Lyr had not yet arrived, and I worried that something had gone terribly wrong for the sea god to be late. But I planted my stance firmer into the unyielding earth and wove a mask that could rival my husband's best. "You expect me to be with you when you destroyed half of my home? When you put my family at risk?" I let my lip tremble for effect as I stumbled closer, letting myself wilt like a flower starved of sunlight. But even the prettiest roses had thorns, and I could be fierce without being violent. I held his stare like I needed coddling—Finna's favorite tool. "This is not the paradise *we* wanted."

His throat worked hard as he swallowed and his-rosebud lips fell open on a sigh. For every part of this facade that was fake, there was no falsifying the desire that hooded his eyes.

Real.

Real.

Real.

But wrong. Distorted. Frozen in ice and thawed out in a time that was not his own.

"Fear not, our darling child will have paradise once I take this land back. It will be our paradise, and when our baby is old enough to learn to use her power, she will rid us of Lyr and Danura once and for all." He breathed me in, a bright smile dressing the smooth planes of his face. Warning stirred in my gut, unease sloshing around at the flicker of light in his dark eyes. "But I have a gift for you. Some of your precious pets that I'll let live with us in our new home. Consider them a peace offering."

With a wave of his hand, the living, breathing shadows at his back disappeared, pulling back like a curtain and revealing the truth.

Saeth and Vian sat back-to-back, bound together in ropes of his creation, mouths gagged as their muted screams pierced my heart. Panic and pain burned in their eyes as they both struggled against the ties. Someone's blood smeared across Saeth's angular face.

My heart shuddered to a stop, and the starfire in my veins burned hotter than sunlight. It poured from me, my limbs trembling from the weight of my own power. All diplomacy and deception fled from my tone, Fate turning her wheel to favor to the vicious bloodlust clawing at my insides like hunger. "Let them go."

Arawn strode up to them, brushing his hand gently through Saeth's ginger hair. I swallowed a growl as she shook him off, her eyes narrowing to dagger-sharp slits, but Arawn only grinned. "Don't worry, I won't harm them. A half-siren and another *Duweni* child? They will make great servants to our little one, one day."

My blood ran cold, icy sweat licking the back of my neck like the Otherworld itself had breathed on me.

"Let them *go*," I repeated, focusing my power to my palms, conjuring water instead. Tempest and storm and salvation. I didn't know how to free them without also hurting them if I let the light out unaltered, but I had other arrows in my quiver.

But before I could attack, Arawn flicked his hands again, and three new forms appeared, two trapped and one unbound.

I did not recognize the blonde woman with a bow on her back thrashing against the shadowy ropes, nor the gigantic man with dark hair, but his eyes were wholly black, the whites devoured entirely. Saeth's muffled screams loudened as she kicked and tugged at her restraints with renewed vigor, but the man stood eerily still. *Enchanted.*

But I did know the third figure, her dark braids framed in a glowing crown, her black eyes screaming with fear as they met mine.

Agatha Amos.

"You know one of my prodigal daughters already, though I believe Cerridwen has been moonlighting as a barkeep. Isn't that right, Nef?" Arawn asked the blonde, who let lose muffled swears against her gag. Fear leadened my limbs as Arawn then patted the huge man on the shoulder, a master hunter displaying his prized hound. "And this is my son, Gwynn. Another one of your half-siblings. I caught them all trying to sneak up on me from the tunnels, and we can't have that, can we? So, Gwynn here will protect us from any other intruders trying to ruin this."

The world spun at a dizzying pace.

Gwynn, the God of the Hunt, one of the most legendary warriors in the world. Nef, the Goddess of the Wind and Sky, Keeper of the Sun.

And Agatha—no, Cerridwen. The magick maker herself.

My siblings.

My *friend.*

Arawn flicked his wrist again, and the empty husk of Gwynn's form walked behind my cousin and Vian, placing one hand on each of their heads. Arawn's grin turned sinister, and every instinct in my body begged me to wipe it off his face, to unleash the growing well of power stirring in my soul.

But if I did, I might hurt Saeth and Vian. Or Gwynn could strike first before I could react.

Or I'd get too close, and Arawn would take me, my *daughter*, and the whole Deyrnas would fall prey to my selfish whims.

Here I was again, Fate herself powerless in the face of Death as he took hostages. I hated the pleading edge that took hold of my voice. "This has to stop. *Please.*"

I had a single task.

Get the Dark God's attention. Keep him busy.

Wait for my husband to swoop in and end him.

Arawn took his sweet time as he sauntered forward. A tender hand reached out and tucked the wild strand of hair behind my ear, as he had time and time again. "Why won't you let me stop?"

He said the same thing every day. In my frozen prison, it had always been like this.

Once upon a time, I'd have stayed silent.

Today was different.

Today he played with my family. My daughter.

Today I said, "Fuck you."

Arawn frowned, his shoulders slumping. "Wrong answer. Unfortunately, I don't think we need all five pets for our dear girl."

Death clenched a fist at his side. The shadows tugged.

A scream lodged itself into my throat as the shackles snapped Nef's bow in two.

Then her neck.

Then Agatha's.

The God of Death discarded his dead daughters back onto the ground, their bodies crashing in a lump. A cruel, dark laugh rattled his frame, and as the taste of their dying magick blanketed the air—Cerridwen's cinnamon and sage, Nef's sunshine and icy wind. I could feel every ounce of it as it flooded the clearing.

Arawn inhaled a breath, like he was drinking it in. A shudder ran down his back, his dark eyes rolling into the back of his head...

He looked down at his daughters' bodies with tears in his eyes. "Thank you for your sacrifice."

His daughters. My *sisters,* that I'd never get to embrace.

Agatha's—no *Cerridwen's*—unseeing eyes met mine, and my stomach heaved at the sight.

Vian let loose a cry of agony, his roar practically shaking the tower as he fought his restraints, and Gwynn lunged.

Not at me. Not at Arawn.

At Saeth.

All other thoughts and plans died in my head, and the starfire that burst from every chamber of my heart was hot enough to melt Death's bones.

41

Monsters and Martyrs

GRIFFIN

Reagan let out a whoop of victory as the dragon-fire melted the guards into dust and guts. The stench of burned flesh and fear turned my stomach, but my heart flew. Atop Awyr's back, she banked into the sky again, the horde following her lead. The boom of giant wings sounded like triumphant cannonfire, the merry revelry of turning tides.

Diving and soaring, blasting the world in fire and then taking to the skies once more. Over and over.

The dragon queen's cover let us retreat to safety, taking refuge in the rubble of the once proud city, catching our breath as the dragons spewed theirs with the force of the sun.

But the puppets descended the moment Locasta's command left her lips. They surged against our forces with renewed vigor, fearless despite the dragons decimating their ranks.

Locasta's shadows were another problem entirely. With a flick of her fingers, the dark witch sent blast after blast of the horrible stuff at us and at the horde flying above, aiming to pick us all off one by one.

A giant red dragon nearly the size of a house dove at her, smoke building between its bared teeth as it snarled with warning–

A sharp whip of death magic, and Locasta cut the creature in two. Dragon blood and ash spilled over the roofs of the nearest buildings, staining the city in her victory.

If I'd had anything left in my stomach, I would've painted my boots with vomit.

"I will end every last one of you!" Morwyn cursed to the skies. Twisting her hands together, she cast a shadow beast shaped like a dragon hauling after Reagan and Awyr.

"Well, shit, we just pissed her off more," Tarran whined as he sliced through another soldier, his height a warrior's advantage even if he complained like a little prince.

"She has a talent for that." I shrugged between blows. I worried for Reagan, but Awyr would keep her safe.

Another fighter jumped at Tarran, but Genni caught the man by his neck, her palm disintegrating his whole frame into dust before he could raise his sword. The weapon clattered to the ground, and the blonde launched herself at her next mark with a fierce cry.

I had no time to be impressed as I shoved my blade through the heart of another, tearing it out and swiping behind me before a third could strike at my legs.

Breathe in, breathe out. Slice, strike, parry.

Repeat.

Repeat.

Repeat, until the whole world bled at my feet.

I hopped over my fallen foes and ran, Rhett following as I pushed closer and closer to God's Eye, hoping to concentrate our forces closer to Saeth's team. I had no idea if they'd made any progress against Arawn, but my faith had to remain unwavering if I wanted to focus.

Or survive. We couldn't last much longer if we didn't cut the beast off at the head.

Out of the corner of my eye, a whip of black magick snaked through the line of magickas still casting counter spells. Truth buzzed feverishly at my side, the sound matching the anxiety ringing through me. I shouted a warning, but my voice was buried beneath the loud, sickening crack that reverberated through the ground as the shadows shot up.

Skewering them all.

My jaw went slack and my stomach churned as I met eyes with Madame Hedd. Hers were glassy, unblinking, tears of blood pouring from their corners. Her head tilted at an unnatural angle to accommodate the spear of darkness tearing through her.

The golden glow of her protection magick died as she did.

Before I could mourn or mount my revenge, a spurt of shadow shot past me. Rhett let loose a cry of agony, doubled over, as Locasta's aim proved true. He fell to the ground.

"Rhett!"

The world shuddered to an abrupt halt, the fighting tuned out around me. My legs moved on their own to his side, tunnel vision painting everything else around us in black.

Crimson against ivory. Blood against stone.

Not again.

Not *him.*

Rhett held the seeping wound on his side, just beneath the cover of his armor, drawing shallow breaths as he winced. Red coated his fingers, but he waved me off with his free hand, determination in his twisted brow.

"I'm fine, go! You have to get to the others and get out!"

"No way in fucking hell am I leaving you," I growled as I crashed to my knees next to him, ignoring the bite of stone against the leather. My hands replaced his, pressing into the flesh, and I let out a sigh of pure relief as my palm met the hard wall of muscle beneath his soiled tunic. A nasty cut, but shallow. Survivable. I dragged him to standing, my heartbeat loud enough to drown out my words. "Keep pressure on that, and let's move."

We were going to live. We were going to win.

We had to.

For Madame Hedd and the others that died to buy us time. For Finna and Papa and Keira and Cedric.

The pain that shot through my chest disagreed.

For a moment, everything stopped. I stopped. Time crashed to a halt.

Then agony like fire erupted from within. I clutched my chest as I pitched forward. The ground rose to meet me, blinking pain smacking on impact.

Had I been stabbed? My fingers tainted red, vision blurring black at the edges. But no, there had been no blade. No arrow. The shadow that pierced me evaporated in my hands like it'd never existed at all, fresh blood oozing in its absence.

Rhett leaned over me, silver and blue eyes lined with tears as he said a word over and over again, his pink lips forming the same shape...

My name.

"Griffin!" Hands against my heart, saltwater tears seeping into the wound. "Griffin, please. *No.*"

A cough sputtered from my core, sending another wave of fire through me. My tongue coated with a strange taste, metallic and rich. I swallowed it back, sitting up with a groan, taking his hand in mine. "I'm fine. It's a scratch."

The fire burned, but I was the fucking Swordsinger. This was manageable. Survivable.

In the hazy edges of my eyesight, a thin line of a woman stepped forward, shadows wrapping around her arms like snakes. I staggered to my legs, holding onto Rhett for support, the last scraps of my survival instinct armoring my veins in electric perseverance.

Breathe in, breathe out.

Locasta narrowed her eyes, the shadows slithering around her, ready to strike. "I've had enough of this."

I drew my sword, spitting a fresh wad of blood on the ground. I was the Swordsinger. Trouble's tool. A little flesh wound was not enough to kill me. And I would not let Morwyn Locasta take another easy breath ever again.

Not without a fight. And fights, I won.

My smile was born of adrenaline and arrogance. "I'm only getting started."

Breathe in, breathe out.

Repeat.

Try not to fall. Or die.

Locasta licked her lips, hungry for the taste of my blood and steel. The shadows slowly slinked forward, taunting. "Everyone you've ever loved will die for your insolence. I will enjoy killing them all slowly."

Witty retorts died on my tongue as the world swayed, the flames stoked as I inhaled sharply. Instead, I offered a vulgar gesture and winced against the flash of pain.

Rhett stepped in front of me, the broad lines of his sweat-soaked back obscuring my bleary vision. He held something in his hand, two small orbs the size of coins. A chuckle shook his shoulders. "You'll have to catch us first."

I blinked as recognition settled. Fire breathers. One of Madame Hedd's ingenious–and horrifying–inventions. Each little glass contraption had enough firepower to mimic cannonfire. Even in death, the witch was saving us.

I remembered to tuck my head and cover my ears just before Rhett tossed them both at Locasta.

The flames singed the hair at the back of my neck, smoke choking me. But strong hands found my arms, pulling me out of the debris. *Rhett.* I stumbled over myself, trying to keep up, but my legs wobbled like rubber. After a few sluggish half steps, he gave that up with a frustrated curse.

I was surprised with how easily he lifted me, tucking one arm beneath my knees and the other behind my back like I was a blushing bride as he ran. The world shifted in and out of focus around us, my head heavy where it smacked against his shoulder, over and over again as he ran across the rocky terrain.

He finally put me down as we ducked behind the crumbling frame of a stone house. The others crouched next to the structure– Drystan and Tarran and Genni, all safe. Covered in grime and cuts and bruises. Clothes torn and armor dented. Sucking in air, barking out coughs. They were run down and exhausted. But it was all temporary. *Survivable.*

I exhaled a shallow breath that tasted like iron, slumping against the rugged stone. The fire licked its way from my chest all the way to my toes now, the extremities so cold they burned.

But my comrades were all right. We would survive.

Breathe in, breathe out.

Tarran's freckled face went paler than a virgin's bare thigh. "You're hurt."

"Wanna kiss it all better, Tare-bear?" I scoffed at him, reaching out and ruffling his ginger curls. The red darkened to deep burgundy.

Breathe in, breathe out.

But each breath tasted more and more like steel, just as heavy and immovable.

Rhett's sharp tone cut through the pain, clearing some of the mist from the corners of my eyes. "Drystan, get the kids out now."

My chest deflated. I looked at Rhett, then at Drystan. At the silent understanding passing between them. I'd seen that look before, the resignation. The surrender. On Roland's face, and Finna's, before they succumbed to the otherside.

On Keira's.

Silver eyes, uttering the unspeakable command in our silent language. A nod in return, when I should've protested.

I guessed I'd see them all again soon.

The guard's jaw went slack, and then he nodded. Tarran shook his head, voice cracking over a ball of an emotion I didn't want to explore. "We aren't leaving you two."

But they were. They had to. It was the only way any of them would survive.

Breathe in, breathe out.

Repeat.

Repeat.

Repeat, until my lungs gave out and my heart stopped.

Just a few more inhales, a few more moments to finish what I'd started. Trouble's final prank.

"Go find Reagan and Saeth. Get to Reese's ship," I stammered, my heavy tongue moved by sheer willpower. "We'll meet you when we're done with *her*."

The lie tasted like stale whiskey and blood, but for once, not regret. Perhaps I'd be a martyr after all, remembered not for my failures, but my fealty to my family. They would survive, even if the price of their lives was mine.

Uncle Cedric used to say there was more than one way to sacrifice a life. But I was a dense motherfucker with a bad habit of taking things too literally.

Genni tugged Tarran's arm with a gloved hand, her lower lip wobbling as she fought back her blubbers like a brave little soldier. "Tarran, let's go."

My cousin let loose a cry of rage, pulling away from her with an expression that mixed a snarl with a sob. "We aren't leaving!"

I opened my mouth to say something inspiring or comforting, but neither happened. I wasn't made for words of wisdom. I was a below-the-belt-joke on my best days, usually made at Tarran's expense. So

I grinned instead. "Please, go. I don't want your ugly mug to be the last thing I see."

My cousin sniffed, shaking as the sobs wracked through him. "Griffin, I–"

His words died on his tongue as Drystan smacked him across the back of the head with the pommel of his sword. Tarran went limp, eyes rolling in the back of his skull.

"Sorry, kid." The guard frowned as he lifted my youngest cousin like a sack of potatoes. He shot a teary-eyed wink at Rhett. "Learned that one from the best. It was an honor fighting with you two."

I saluted my handsome friend, lifting my useless arm across my chest. I'd never earned his friendship, but I'd treasure it until my rapidly-approaching last breath. "Get them out, Colonel."

He didn't hesitate before tearing off with Tarran flopping over his shoulder, Genni covering his flank with her talons and fangs extended. I watched them go, the image muddier as the black threatened to take over.

Breathe in, breathe out.

Just a few more. Just a little longer.

I turned to my last remaining ally, my partner in pain and pity. I would not dishonor him by asking him to leave with the others. I knew he wouldn't, just as I couldn't. We'd promised to see this through together. But I did offer a lopsided smile, reaching out to run my fingers through his silken hair one last time. "Are you sure you don't want to change your mind yet, Blondie? I'm a bad influence."

Rhett kissed my palm before drawing Triumph once more. Our work was not done. He tore his gaze from mine to peer over the rubble, eyes scanning for the final foe we had to face. "Locasta is still alive. She's wounded, but still coming this way. I know you're in no shape to fight." His throat bobbed, but he kept his voice low. "But if you can distract her, I can get to her."

He didn't need to say the rest. That he'd probably give his life, and mine, to make it happen. But it didn't matter. We were just men in a story of myths and monsters. Our lives meant nothing.

Maybe our deaths would.

For Finna and Papa. For Roland and Owen and Cedric and Keira.

Somehow, I found my legs again, falling forward into an awkward crouch. I ignored the hot, sticky substance rolling down my stomach. I'd lost too much of it already to care. "My middle name is Trouble. I'll manage."

Rhett bit his lower lip to steady it, silver-and-blue eyes staring straight into my soul. "I love you."

I took two more borrowed breaths, shutting out how they seared my lungs, shunning the icy prickles that ran down my back. Two more breaths, just to let myself look at this man a moment longer. This cranky, kind-hearted, dutiful man who'd taken a chance on a second-born fuckup and turned him into something worthy. Something that would make his mama proud. A Captain, willing to sink with his ship.

In and out.

Repeat.

Repeat.

"I love you, too. Against all odds."

My lips were too numb to feel his as they met mine, the kiss sealing our fate. But my heart soared, leaving behind the pain of my body. With Rhett, I was flying. With this man made of iron will and cloud-soft compassion, I was untouchable. Limitless. He broke away, but he'd given me the breath of life I needed. His smile thawed the ice. "See you in the Otherworld, Red."

And when he ran in the other direction, Triumph glinting in the sunlight, I stood.

Fights were easy. Fights, I won.

I wasn't done fighting yet.

"Oy, Mor-witch!" I bellowed, my breathing shallow and my voice shaky. But I was the Swordsinger. The last standing Captain of the *Ceffyl Dwr*. Trouble's brutal blade. I always had another crass trick up my sleeve. I clutched the bleeding wound on my chest and flipped her another vulgar gesture. "Thanks for the new hole, but next time, shove it up yours!"

Standing on top of a pile of rubble, the body of a Huddian Magicka dead at her feet, Locasta whirled on me. She glowered as she spotted me, shadows shooting out and tying me up, tighter than a seasoned sailor's knots. Again, my body screamed against the pain, but I kept my mouth wired shut with a forced smirk.

"You're still alive? I'm going to enjoying shredding you to bits. Then I'll pack your parts up in a pretty box and send them to your cousin." She lifted me up with the ghostly ropes, dangling me in front of her like bait on a fishhook. I supposed I was, skewered and bleeding like chum in the water. A distraction to lure her away from the real predator.

Behind her, Rhett prowled between fallen debris, his sword singing to me.

Breathe in, breathe out.

Triumph was near.

I snorted, taunting her attention to me. Using my last words wisely. "How'd you know I like it rough?" Another shadow lashed out, piercing through my leg like it was made of soft cheese. I groaned as the fire spread, consuming everything in its path. My head spun, vision blurring again, but the sparkle of light against steel fortified the last of my nerve. "*Harder*, please."

Breathe in, breathe out.

One last time.

Here I was, Trouble's puppet, on a string and ready to dance my final jig. But the laugh that stole my final gust of air was made of light and love.

"But I warn you, my lover is the jealous type."

Rhett blew me a kiss before he raised his blade. Breathed in, breathed out.

Strike and slice.

Locasta's head rolling across the stone street was the last thing I saw before the world went black.

42

Stars and Sisters

RONAN

Dragon eyes tinted the world in shades of red.

Or perhaps that was the blood running rampant through the streets. The blood of my friends, my enemies. My family.

From above the clouds, the island looked so small. So tiny, just a little clump of land, even with God's Eye jutting upward. A speck of red and black against the sea of blue, insignificant to the eyes of the heavens.

And yet, it was everything. Humanity's last stand against the Dark God. A moment where fate and life and death all converged, coming together in a small, singular moment to decide the future of the Deyrnas. Of peace as we knew it.

The stars twinkled around me, calling my name as I flew through them, absorbing their light into my golden scales. Energy buzzed around me, their anticipation and anxiety bright as my own. As they filled my belly with their fire, they told me stories of the world below. Of the choices my friends and family made to save their tiny home.

Of Ellian and Siobhan, racing towards Delm Duwei with nomads from the north and south alike, the two most opposite islands standing as one for the common good. My red eyes zeroed in on their blurred forms, watching the action unfold from my spot in the skies. The ground trembled as the pack of shifters, assassins, and Esme guarded Ellian's furred flank, Siobhan atop his back like a warrior Queen. *Blaidds* and Basilisks, and Lions and Leopards. Three dozen strong, the deadliest clans come together, united against Death himself.

Together, they rounded the corner of a tall bronze temple–this one built for the goddess Cerridwen–and skidded to a halt, claws scraping at the stone of a wide clearing of rubble . Even from above, I could hear Ellian's warning howl to those who followed his lead .

White fur stood stark against the ruined streets, deep snarls rumbling through them as they snapped at the prey cornered in the center of their circle.

Hellhounds.

A lot of them.

The stars whispered as the *blaidd* and siren lunged at the hounds, their people at their sides. Bite and tear and claw. Snarl and snap and devour. Cut and slice and claw.

Over and over.

The stars spoke of my father, Reese swinging his sword valiantly from where the hellhounds had him trapped. Blood streaked down his arm, sullying his coat, but a smirk to match my best twisted his lips. Behind him, Weylin Branwen stood with a dozen hunters. Each held drawn bows or swords, wearing deep furs from Pysgodd.

Branwen and Mathonwy. Pysgodd and Tan. North and South.

Life or death.

I spotted a woman–Councilwoman Tommins, I figured–her braided white hair a flag flying against the wind. She shouted as she loosed an arrow, the mark hitting a hound straight between the eyes.

Her expert shot launched the world into chaos again as the hounds attacked. As my father and friends countered with wicked, wild pride in their veins.

On the other side of the island, the stars sang of Griffin and Rhett, standing together against Locasta and her puppets. Of the love that linked them even as they risked their last breaths to disperse her dark plague.

The stars cried for their fallen sisters, for Cerridwen and Nef, who'd already winked out against Arawn's darkness. They cheered for Keira as she faced down her former captor, the Silver Wheel returned to earth to steer us all toward victory again. They sang and spoke and sobbed as I collected them all, specks of power tucked away in my heart for what I was meant to do next.

My human parts urged me to swoop down and save them. To find my friends and unleash my starfire onto the devil hounds. To swallow Morwyn Locasta whole and spit out her charred, cursed bones. To protect Keira from Arawn's darkness.

But I was the *Ddraig Aur*, the Storyspeaker now. The stars had a purpose for me. A power, greater than my desires and loyalty.

Movement in the clouds below pulled me from the stars' whisperings. A black dragon as large as I was, rolling through the gathering storm, trapped in an embrace with a beast made entirely of shadow. But this hold was far from loving. The creatures snarled and clawed at each other, the shadow beast unwavering in its attack, the black dragon's belly exposed and bleeding as it protected the rider on its back...

Chestnut hair and eyes that could level grown men with a single pointed look. A small dagger in her hand as she swung at the creature, trying to slice through shadow like it was flesh and blood.

Reagan.

A strangled screech left the dragon's maw as the shadows ripped him open from stem to stern, his red blood showering the earth below in gore.

A moment later, the shadow beast was gone, evaporated into nothingness. Rhett and Griffin must have won, must have silenced Locasta once and for all.

But the dragon was falling. Reagan scrambled for purchase on his back, tears streaking down her face as she begged him to fly, to live...

The creature was still. I didn't need the stars' scrutiny to know he'd been vanquished.

Reagan tumbled through the clouds, her form like a single grain of sand. So tiny, so small in comparison with the cosmos.

I was the *Ddraig Aur*, the Storyspeaker now. But I'd always be Ronan Mathonwy first. No matter how many memories were stolen, or how many stories I was fed.

And there was Reagan, falling toward the tiny dot like a shooting star. My tiny tyrant. My little dragon, wingless and fangless, but still the most fearsome thing to have ever existed. So small, but larger than life.

The stars screamed another warning in my ear, of help needed in the world below. Of my father, pinned as the hounds closed in. Slipping past his sword. Going for his throat.

I did not think before I dove, my broad wings tucked tightly to my sides to better glide through the air.

Not to save my father. Not to defend my people.

I'd left Reagan before to fend for herself. To handle her own grief and guilt, to wage her own wars. She was just a child, but I'd forced her to grow. I'd abandoned her time and time again.

No, Ronan. You did absolutely nothing.

Not again. Not this time.

Down and down, the little dot of Orwellin below growing larger and wider as we plummeted. A growl left my lips as I straightened out, willing my mass to pick up speed to catch her.

The stars rallied around me, urging me faster. Begging me to save her, the dragon raised in a rose garden, the firebreather forged in familial love and sacrifice. I flew faster, even as the stars cried for my father, bleeding to death in the jaws of a hound, a wicked smirk still on his face as he crossed to the Otherworld. The truth cleaved through my heart, an agony I knew too well, but I did not slow.

Down and down, to save my little sister. My best friend. My biggest regret and greatest victory.

Finally, she spotted me, eyes wide as she screamed my name. Recognition, even in this altered state. One dragon calling to another. Her tiny hand reached for me, fingers outstretched. I pushed harder, swimming against the sky, the black and red stain of Orwellin rushing up to greet us.

A thousand feet.

Five hundred.

One hundred.

Twenty.

When my claws finally wrapped around her, my leathery wings expanded automatically, catching the air and pulling us back up to the skies.

"You came back." Reagan shook in my grasp, sobs wracking through her. So little, like a baby bird in my hand. "You saved me."

Soaring above, I lifted her up, letting her crawl up my neck and onto my back. Just like our piggyback rides up the stairs. Back when the world was easy and stories were all we needed to survive.

My voice was strange in this form, gruff and low like rocks sliding against each other. But my message was clear, one I'd needed to deliver for far too long. "No, little dragon. You've always saved me."

Reagan was quiet for a moment, holding tightly to the spike she straddled along my spine. The stars watched us as we floated above, awaiting our next move. Like this moment, too, held power, a choice only the gossiping cosmos could see.

When Reagan finally spoke, the heavens exhaled a breath. "Is Keira back?"

"Yes."

The little dragon patted my back, and the stars let out a triumphant cry. "Then let's go help her kick some Otherworldly ass."

43

Challenges and Choices

KEIRA

Everything happened at all at once. Moments stretched to infinity, and yet it all flashed forward faster than I could blink.

The power billowing from my fingertips knocked Arawn to the ground, a cry tearing from his mouth. As he fell, the shadows holding Saeth and Vian faltered, the *Wynnaid* slipping from his restraints easily, jumping to Saeth's aid. Gwynn lunged for them, black eyes unfocused and absent, as Saeth bared her literal *fangs* at him. But before he could make contact, a pillar of water blasted him to the ground.

A warm voice slid into my consciousness. *Hold him, Keira. I've got Gwynn.*

My heart soared, the small victory rocketing through me. Lyr was here somewhere. I was not alone.

I leaped onto Arawn before he could tell the water wasn't my doing, straddling his chest and holding my burning palm to his neck. His eyes flew open, and he hissed as the light singed his throat. The scent of burned flesh assaulted my senses and knotted my stomach, but I bore down harder, giving Vian and Saeth a chance to escape. Giving Lyr a chance to get into place.

Bait and trap.

Despite the pain, Arawn's face lit with a grin.

"Such spirit, as always, Keira." He squirmed beneath me, large hands biting into the flesh of my thighs to keep me in place. His husky voice dipped with seduction. "I did say I preferred you mean. Let out that monster, Keira. Let me see my true mate."

Repulsion rolled through me at the possession of his grip, his long fingers the chains I'd been so desperate to shake. But he would not shackle me again. Not with shadow or ice or pretty words meant to disorient and disguise.

My *true mate* was out there somewhere, the greatest pickpocket and swindler in the Deyrnas stealing the stars themselves to save us. A sailor and snake, he'd slithered across the veil to the Otherworld for me, sacrificed everything to give me safe passage away from this monster. He'd always been my equal in selflessness and wickedness. He'd freed me from the binds of my past, had given me a future I never imagined for myself.

Ronan.

Ronan.

Ronan.

The god at my feet had nothing on him. Ronan was something greater. Something *more*.

I squeezed Arawn's neck tighter, and his smirk fell. "I should've known the day I stepped into your palace that you are rotten and destroyed to your core. I wanted to save you, to help you," I growled at him, anger boiling my insides. He clawed at my legs and bucked beneath me, trying to throw me off, but I held firm, stealing the breath from his lungs with wrapped fingers. I met his obsidian gaze, wide with terror and panic. "But there is nothing of your soul left to salvage."

Perhaps Arawn had once been something more, too. Perhaps the man beneath layers of ice and shadow once had a heart, broken and bruised from loss and regret. But he'd cut it out on his own accord to save himself from the pain. There was nothing left to heal.

It was time someone put him out of his misery.

His eyes rolled to the back of his head as his consciousness wavered. My power flared again, Fate ready to finally put Death to rest, but a flash of silver pulled my attention, a scuffle breaking loose in front of God's Eye.

Saeth stood, unbound, over a half-drowned Gwynn, a familiar silver pistol drawn.

Weylin's gun.

Arawn's gun.

My heart beat faster on instinct, fear creeping along my spine. Her finger clicked the safety as tears fell down her cheek, her hand shaking as she pointed it in the enchanted god's face.

Seath, who never cried, not even at her mother's funeral.

Saeth, who was made of brutal efficiency and bluntness.

"Saeth, shoot him!" Vian shouted from behind her as he crawled toward them both, a scratch on his cheek gushing blood.

But Saeth, the queen of needles and battle-axe accuracy, hesitated. Saeth, the arrow-sharp ice princess, lowered her weapon. Her voice quivered as she looked down at the hunter, her steel gaze melting down into something soft. "I can't, I—he's—"

Lyr's alarm blared in my head a moment too late. *Stay alert!*

Strong arms launched me skyward before snaring me in shadows. I hung suspended in the air, writhing against the bonds as Arawn pushed to his feet, an ugly, charred mark on his neck in the shape of my hands.

"Saeth, shoot!" I cried, the light building across my flesh smoldering the shadows, but not fast enough.

"Clever imp, that does not belong to you!" Arawn roared at Saeth, casting a black gust of his power her way. She yelped as it knocked the pistol from her hand, the weapon flying through the air and clattering to the ground. But she did not scurry for it, instead crouching over Gwynn, flashing her fangs and tugging a dagger from her boot in a defensive position. *Protective.*

Arawn's focus snapped to the gun.

Not again. That weapon had taken enough from me.

Keep stalling. We're almost there! Lyr sang in my ear, though I did not need urging. My restraints melted, and I fell. My knees sang in protest as I landed, sprinting toward the gun. But I was too slow, too clumsy in my changing body. I tripped, just managing to catch myself, the rock biting my palms.

Arawn was faster. Steadier. His fingers reached out, lengthened by more ropes of darkness, so close to the pistol…

A gust of wind carried the weapon up, out of reach. And then swept it away entirely, as if by magick.

Not my magick.

Arawn and I both blinked at the careful trickery as Vian offered the Dark God a crass gesture that would've made Griffin proud. His angular grin captured his whole face as he stood, the breeze tangling his dark hair. "That was for my mother."

For a moment, as the two stared at each other, a cold realization settled over me. Ice ran down my spine as I noted the similarities. The same inky hair, the same high cheekbones and dark eyes…

Vian, my kindred spirit. The songbird with clipped wings who longed to taste the saltwater breeze, the boy raised in the belly of an Orwellin temple. The warrior who swam in the river of *Hiraeth* with me and emerged reborn, a dark phoenix ready to take flight…

Not just Nef's chosen speaker, but her *son*. My eyes trailed to the crumpled body of the sky goddess.

I am Duweni, son of the wind and sky. One day I will be their reckoning.

Arawn's grandson.

Duweni. Godsborn.

Arawn must have made the connection as I did. He stalked toward Vian, shadows rippling around him in agitation. They lashed out at Vian again like whips, striking him across the face and chest. "My *daughter* lacked both the power and conviction to make anything of herself. You're just as useless, *son*."

Vian groaned in pain, his tunic cut open to reveal his mutilated chest. Blood seeped from a fresh lashmark, a new scar to accompany the many that already marred his pale skin.

Something shattered in my chest as I pushed to my feet. Something shaded and vengeful, like the darkest side of the moon. Vian was the night sky, a descendant of shadow and Death, son of the wind and breeze. But I was Ariannad, the balance between all things. The Liberator, the Writer of Fate.

And *no one*, not even Arawn, touched my kin without consequence.

Strands of my own darkness shot from my fingers, my power manifesting as wisps of revenge and ruination clawing at Arawn's back. Victory roared in my veins, my vengeance sweet as I relished the red staining his white robes. He howled as he spun to face me, his shadows crashing against mine like the arms of two warring krakens.

"As useless as a god picking on a boy half his size?" I sneered at him, poking holes in the hull of his ego. "Pathetic."

Anger wrinkled his perfect face, but then Arawn chuckled, the sound drenched in dangerous delight. A wall of pure darkness descended over us, hiding both Vian and Saeth from my view. Worry speared through my ribs, my heart beating a frantic rhythm, but I held firm, the wicked parts of me relishing the chance at revenge for all I'd suffered.

"This anger is the best of you, *Caraid*," Arawn said, reading my thoughts across my face even in the near-blackness of our bubble. His power tugged against mine, a push and pull, a call and response that teased and taunted. That begged me to unchain the wicked thing in my middle. "These little insects can do *nothing* for you. And here you are again, in the same place as always. Fighting to save your lessers, unable to do anything because you can't bear to see them hurt. Because you can't bring yourself to finish me even when I give you the chance. Imagine what you'd be if you let loose."

A part of me wanted nothing more than to do just that. To explode. To tear him limb from limb. To show him who was truly *lesser*. Not my family, who'd fought and struggled and sacrificed at every turn; but him, this pretty-faced bully who thrived off manipulation and subversion, who did his dirty work in the dark of night, who stabbed from behind instead of facing his opponents head on.

But he was *right*. I always ended up here, with a choice in my hands. A choice between darkness and light.

Between revenge for my father or killing my uncle.

Between abandoning my family or risking myself.

Between murdering Connor or saving my cousin.

Between committing horrors in the name of nobility or sacrificing my pride for a chance at forgiveness. At redemption.

Perhaps it was foolish to always back down from my monstrous parts. Perhaps it would always lead to this.

The same voice that steadied me in every choice echoed through my head once more, the tide turning me back towards my goal. Towards myself. *You're doing so well. I almost have Gwynn free of the enchantment. Ronan will come, and we will make our stand together. Just hang on, Keira girl.*

My duty was clear as placid water in a warm spring. Clear as stars in the cloudless night sky.

"That's what you want, right?" I stepped away, withdrawing the blackness back within me. Arawn's surged without resistance, but the light buzzed again across my skin. Not a blade, but a shield. His tentacles of darkness bounced off me, colliding with the light that wrapped me in a warm blanket. A friendly reminder of who I was, swaddling me in the love that had dragged me back from the Otherworld. My voice carried with that same firm gentleness, brightness chasing away Arawn's lingering stain. "I won't let my power run rampant. I won't do the work for you so you don't have to get your hands messy. Just like you let Locasta wage war while you hid here in your tower like a *coward*."

The light was harsh against the sharp lines of Arawn's face, blanching his features. But a darkness crept into his gaze, black pupils spreading outward, consuming the last of the white. The last of whatever small piece of restraint he had. "You mistake me again, *Caraid*. I am not afraid of being a villain or blackening my soul. As you aptly pointed out, I no longer have one. Though I have devoured many. Let me show you."

At that, the wall of darkness crashed.

It swirled around us, a whirlpool of night, threatening to drag me into the void. Panic rose through my limbs as the shadows tugged me closer, like a current drawing me right into Death's hand. Saeth and Vian both screamed as it sucked them in, knocking them off their centers and dragging them under like the backtow of a wave.

Death laughed as I struggled to stay upright, the gravity of his magick pushing and pulling me deeper, buckling my knees and pressing against my back.

But a single thought kept me standing. A call to my other half. A promise I made and sealed in the Otherworld.

Ronan.

Ronan.

Ronan.

In the back of my mind, a voice deeper than the ocean floor chuckled a final warning. *Brace yourself, Keira girl.*

Everything happened at all at once. As a tidal wave of water rose up from the shore, stretching all the way to the gathering clouds in the sky, higher than God's Eye.

As Gwynn vaulted from the vortex, eyes clear of spellcast, with Saeth and Vian tucked under each arm.

As the giant golden *dragon* swooped from above and rained pure starfire from his mighty snout.

44

Struggles and Starlight

RONAN

Dragon eyes were sharp, but Reagan spotted Keira first.

"There she is, at the base of God's Eye!" she yelled over the howling wind, its swirling gusts picking up pace. Thunderclouds gathered around us, bumping into each other as they grew heavy, threatening rain. Like the sky had become lawless, bathed in the same chaos as the fighting on the ground. I beat my wings harder against the zephyr to keep us steady, scoping out the base of the tower like Reagan commanded. "Saeth and Vian too!"

Shadows danced along the obsidian stone, creating the illusion of a pool of black. But within the writhing sea of night, something glowed bright as day. A small, riotous star. A beacon, pulling me in.

Not something; *someone.*

Not just anyone. *Her.*

And in front of her—a creature that blended with the inky swamp. Not someone, not anymore. Just the phantom of a god, the heartless, living corpse of a man whose mind was wholly lost to the Otherworld.

Heat gathered in my lungs, the taste of ash on my tongue.

Death would not be offered a burial today. But I would light his funeral pyre with the fire in my belly.

My thunderclap voice challenged the roaring wind. "Hold tight, little dragon. We're going in."

Reagan clung tighter to my spikey back, little fingers digging into the scales for purchase. But lightning laced her words, a buzzing energy I knew like my own. "You're letting me come?"

I nodded my giant head. I'd left her behind too many times to count for her protection, and where had it gotten us? Nowhere. I'd locked her in Mathonwy Manor with her mother, stowed her belowdecks with Saeth and Tarran. At every sign of danger, I'd sheltered her. Shielded her.

Stifled her. Lost sight of her.

Not this time.

Now, I would be right by her side to protect her, my fangs and scales and firebreath enough to keep us safe. And with her at my side, I'd stay sane. Stay human, despite my beastly bits. "I need you too, little dragon."

I couldn't see her, but the warmth in her voice told of the smile on her face. "Come on, golden boy. Let's fly."

With a grin stretching my snout, I did. I circled high, above the tempestuous wind, before diving toward the ground in a flash on the opposite side of the tower. Reagan let out a whoop of excitement that died against the updraft of air.

A thousand feet.

Five hundred.

One hundred.

Twenty.

At the last second, I opened my broad wings to soften our landing. My claws scraped against the obsidian, my considerable weight cracking the stone beneath me. But thunder above masked the resounding boom, the wild sky on our side for one moment longer.

I stretched my neck and turned so I could see her out of the corner of my eye, lowering my wing so she could easily slide off. "Get off here. Stay close and wait for my signal."

"Aye, aye, Captain." Reagan somersaulted off, landing gracefully on the stone with a flip of her hair.

Chestnut eyes met mine, lighter than I'd seen them in ages. I held her stare for a moment as all of the things I'd longed to say since I'd left her behind in Hudd tangled my too-long tongue. Words were harder in this form. Then again, the tiny tyrant always had a way of stealing them from me even when I walked on two legs.

Bold as ever, Reagan winked, saving me from whatever fumbled apology I'd have come up with. "Go save your girl."

The fire in my belly burned brighter, fueled by something far more potent than revenge or rage. I took to the sky again, my heart beating with one less crack in it.

It almost stopped its rhythm entirely when a deep voice rumbled through my mind, loud as the thunder overhead.

Are you ready, Storyspeaker? They both need you.

A growl rippled through my chest as the fire rose up my throat, resting in wait on my tongue.

I was more than ready. I was *hungry.*

Lyr's wave surged upward unnaturally from the bay, a tsunami ready to crash at his command as I plunged myself into the fray, breathing flame down onto the black pit. I would burn every shadow into ash, would cremate every last remaining fiber of Arawn's power into dust.

The Dark God cowered beneath my starfire, shielding his face. But I did not yield. I burned and expelled, drawing on the well of the stardust I'd gathered in the clouds. I burned and burned until my throat went raw, until every injustice me and mine had suffered had been paid for, until there was not a drop left.

When there was no more fire to spit, I closed my tired jaw, ready to use all the other weapons in the Serpent Prince's arsenal.

My limbs folded in on themselves as I transformed, fangs and claws shrinking, snout morphing to my crooked nose, arms replacing wings. But my gold scales still covered my skin from my chest to my ankles in hard armor, fortified by the starlight pulsing through them.

Arawn crouched in front of me, hands over his head, burns covering his forearms in ugly scars to match his soul.

I planted a firm kick into his side, casting him nearly twenty paces away. Lingering smoke curled around my words as I spat them at him: "Stay away from my wife."

My wife. My daughter.

My future.

A dragon protected his horde.

"It's about time. I missed you." Keira blinked away the silver tears resting across her dark lashes, and the dragon almost burst free again out of sheer pride. She had scrapes on her knees where her black battle scales had torn, and her hands were red, like she'd just stuck them in steaming hot water. But aside from that, she was unscathed. Safe.

"I missed you too." The words were truer than I could express. I did not remember our lives, but I missed it with every rotten part of me.

"What is this?" Arawn hissed, righting himself again, his dark stare flicking between me and my wife.

I stepped in front of Keira, blocking her from view. She'd already done more than her share, throwing herself into the fray as bait and shield. But now, it was her duty to herself and the Deyrnas to keep her and the little one safe.

Now, it was my turn.

Lyr's voice echoed the sentiment in my head. *On your word, I drown the fucker.*

I barked a dry laugh, calling the starshine to the tips of my claws. "All of this to gather Danura's power, right?" I tilted my head at the bastard, every wicked part of me craving the taste of his blood. I might have been a dragon now, but my smirk was all snake. "Well, it's mine now. But I'm generous, so why don't you have a taste?"

With another flick of my fingers, a bullet of starlight shot from the tip of my claw, smacking him across the face. Blood dripped from the mark below his left eye. He wiped it away with the back of his sleeve, eyes blown wide. "No. How did you–?"

Another discharge of light from my finger, this one aimed at his shoulder. The Dark God stumbled back as it made impact. "You took *everything* from me. I had to take something back."

"Now, Ronan!" Keira cried, sprinting toward Saeth and Vian on the outskirts of the clearing. A huge boulder of a man stood with them, tucking their wiry frames behind his broad back. "We've got them!"

She didn't need to tell me twice.

Only a god could kill a god.

This time, it took no effort at all to reach down into that part of me that was other. Into the old, preternatural thing living inside my chest, made of mist and mystery. I settled into it, brighter and stronger and laced with stardust and secrecy. I took a deep breath, letting the words flow from me like a melody.

"Stars above, let me take again what I've been given, and sacrifice what I've already lost." I sang in the ancient language, feeling the draw again. Not to Keira this time, but to Arawn. To the dark emptiness where his heart should be. *"Grant me power over death. Let this light erase the shadow from the world."*

My power surged to the surface, my neck coating in sweat as the heat radiated from my every pore. I tugged again, commanding the thing to absorb, to take. To suck the Dark God dry of every last drop of his power, to finally silence his song of terror.

But there was no response to my call. No answer. The cosmos watched on, expectant and anxious, as they had before. But no matter how hard I focused, my knees wobbling and back straining, there was nothing to take.

He was vacant.

He was the void.

Arawn chuckled.

"I don't know what you're mumbling, boy, but you cannot take my gift from me. I am absence. I am Death. I am a hunger that cannot be satisfied. I am ice that cannot be thawed," Arawn growled, backing away from me, closer to God's Eye. His back hit the obsidian, cornered in my trap like a mouse beneath a dragon's claw. Still, he smirked, condescension dripping from every word. "Your words have no power over nothingness."

I gritted my teeth, reaching deeper into the thing the stars gave me. To what my wife gave me, when she made me more. To what Lyr and Esme gave me, when they joined together centuries ago.

To my very essence, the Sea-Snake, the Serpent Prince, the *Ddraig Aur.*

To Ronan Mathonwy.

To my very heart. To everything I'd ever loved and ever would.

My melody was strained with effort, but I sang it anyway. *"I am power itself. Transformation and turmoil. I will take what is mine."*

I heaved against his power again, trying to make it mine. To carve space in my own scales to hold all of *nothing.* I cried in agony, and around me, the stars echoed my screams, worry and warning in their many-voiced chorus.

Arawn winced for a moment, but the connection was severed again, consumed by the void where his heart should be.

"Again, a neat trick. But I have one too. This whole place is carved from obsidian." He flattened himself against the stone of the tower, palms caressing it like it was a long-lost lover. A shudder ran through him, his eyes hooded as he taunted me. "Tell me, oh wise little boy. Do you know what happens when a star dies? What happens when you amplify *infinite* nothingness?"

Something snapped within me, and a chill colder than death ran down my spine. My starlight sputtered out, the power in me yanking the other way, wrestled *away* from me...

Run! Lyr commanded in warning, and the giant, hovering wave groaned as it collapsed. The water rushed forward, our last resort to wash away the darkness.

But Keira ran *toward* me, silver eyes blazing with fear.

My name on her lips. "Ronan, stop!"

"A black hole." Arawn's lips curved over the words as he smiled, drawing his final ace to play. "A lighteater."

Behind him, the tower *dissolved*.

And in its place, a *Melthith* spot big enough to blot out the sun swallowed the wave flowing toward us.

A black hole.

Keira grabbed my hand just as it sucked me in.

45

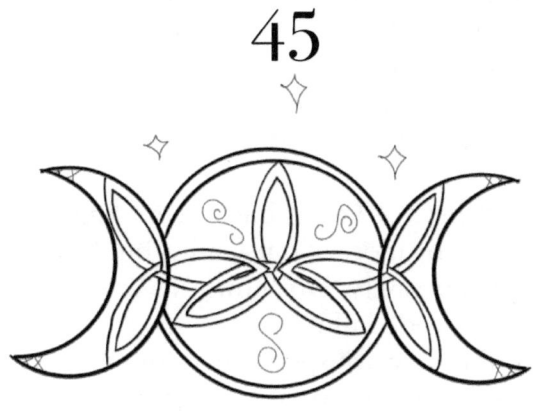

Blackholes and Bullets

KEIRA

My fingers locked onto Ronan's just before the giant cavern of shadows could suck him in. Like the mouth of hell had opened itself, the blackness towed us closer, a beast ready to swallow us whole. I held on tightly, palms sweating and tired, but I would not let go.

I would never let go again.

"Get out of here!" Ronan cried, sapphire eyes ringed with brilliant gold. He was light and love and fire. He was change and transformation. He was wicked and wild, compassionate and controlled. A snake constantly shedding his skin to make room for growth, he'd somehow manifested himself into a god.

And he was mine.

I would never let go again.

My power tethered me to the obsidian stone, my own shadows anchors against the heavy pull of the hole. Every muscle in my body screamed at the effort, but it didn't matter. I was Fate. I was fury and forgiveness, I was a goddess of victories big and small.

I was his.

The whooshing of hollowing air deafened us, but I screamed against it, a riotous bellow against the tide: "I'm not leaving you! I'm never leaving you again."

He shook his head, untying his fingers from mine. I grabbed with both hands at the base of his wrist, refusing to let go. Tighter than any rope I'd ever tied, tighter than every single heartstring wound in circles in my chest. His voice laced with acute pain as he shouted over the roar of the vortex, "Reagan is out there somewhere, you have to—"

"Vian will find her," I yelled back, tears blurring my vision. I couldn't bear to lose any more of our family, but I would not sacrifice Ronan to ensure their safety. Not now. Never again. My daughter needed her father. I needed him.

And I trusted the wind whisperer to grant me one last favor.

Ronan opened his mouth to protest again, but the sound died as a shape appeared behind him.

My stomach sank to my toes.

Arawn's face stole my breath, this time in a horrified gasp. He'd doubled in size, grotesque muscles tearing through the white fabric of his robes. Blackened veins wound up his arms and necks like the vines of decayed ivy, even the rose of his lips smudged over with that same inkiness. His long hair went from shiny to wilted, strands of sinew and cobwebs hanging from his head, horns protruding from the top the color of old bones.

But it was his eyes that were the most different. The most wrong.

They'd always been that dark, but this blackness did not promise the soft embrace of dreamless sleep. Their empty pits were the darkness of nightmares, the chasm of damned souls and eternal suffering.

I might have pitied him. Might have cried for him, even, this monster cursed to wander that lonely abyss for eternity.

But when he wrapped his long, bone-thin fingers around my husband's ankle, I threw all the mercy he might have earned into the maelstrom trying to envelop us.

I tightened my hold on my husband. Light met light in the space that we met, our gifts a mutiny against Arawn's madness.

This time, that piece of myself that still lived and breathed in my husband answered my call like a duet, his power old and new rising to the surface and melding together with mine, both singing with one voice. The electricity passed through us again and again, back and forth, stronger together than it was apart; ecstasy and torture, pleasure and pain, an infinite loop of past and future and right and wrong between us. I sucked in another breath and held on, letting it consume us in a shield.

Arawn hissed as our light burned him, but he did not let go of Ronan's leg.

"You two will not last. You're powerful, I'll give you that," he laughed, his voice raspy and hollow like a last breath rushing out of tired lungs. "But I have ended powerful gods before. I have drunk every last drop of their gifts. And I will do the same to you. You'll stay trapped in my kingdom until that baby is born, powerless in the pit, and then I'll eat both of your hearts as I take her from you. She will end the others, and I will be her master. I will rule *everything*."

With that, he jerked back, throwing his considerable weight toward the vortex with Ronan still in tow. I held on for dear life, crying out as Ronan's claws bit into my flesh for better purchase, his screams mixing with mine as the God of Death and I pulled him in a tug of war.

Sweat slickening my palms, my fingers slipped.

But another wave of seawater crashed into Arawn, knocking Ronan free.

"Long time no see, brother," Lyr's greeting was colder than the Pysgoddian bay as he surfed into the fray, his shell-plated armor glistening with saltwater. He stuck his hands on his hips like I'd seen Reagan do a thousand times, apparently the whole family inheriting his bad attitude.

The sea-god had not abandoned his chosen children. I'd never been more grateful for the Mathonwy heritage in my whole life.

I scrambled to Ronan's side, catching him in a cocoon of shadows before the vortex could suck him in. Using the dark side of my gift, I rooted us to our spot, sending my shadows deep below the earth. I dragged Ronan to his feet, anchoring him to me as I fortified my stance.

I'd never let go.

Sapphire-and-gold eyes found mine, the tears lining his thick blond lashes filled with all the words neither of us could find.

"Lyr," Arawn purred, snapping my attention back to him. The Dark God shook out his wet, lifeless hair as his misshapen face pulled into what once might have passed for a cruel smile. "I should've realized these *children* couldn't have done this themselves."

The God of the Sea ran a hand through his own voluminous mane, the picture of vast confidence and untamed power. "They would've bested you ten times over if you didn't hide behind your toys and little witch soldiers."

Arawn scoffed. "I'm not the one that cowers behind sea-urchins."

I'm buying you time. You two need to close that hole. It traps power, so you'll need a lot of it. Lyr's deep voice rattled off in my mind with an unexpected urgency, like frantic waves tossing a ship in a tempest. His cockiness was a mask, his hidden fear matching mine.

How?

Figure it out.

I breathed in, letting the air fill every tattered pocket of certainty I still had. Small victories, indeed. What did I need next, and how would I get it?

I looked to Ronan, my partner until the end. He nodded like he'd heard Lyr's command, too.

Small victories, Keira girl.

Close a black hole and end the Dark God. No big deal.

Ronan jerked his head to the vortex, a silent command to get us closer. I unrooted my gifts from the obsidian, my shadows working like spider's legs to inch forward while Lyr held the Dark God at bay.

"She's dead, by the way. Your Councilwoman," Lyr called aloud, baiting him with a snort.

"No matter. It is a pawn's nature to sacrifice for a king," Arawn wheezed back, his voice decaying with the rest of his rotted form. I shuddered at the truth of him, at the monster that lived beneath his skin. I should've believed him when he admitted what he was. "Meanwhile, you always walk around like a peacock with its feathers out, thinking you're the most clever and powerful of us all…and what do you have to show for it?"

"An unbroken winning streak, old friend."

"Not this time."

The two gods dove at each other, sea and storm against rot and ruin. Powerful bodies crashed together like colliding stars, and a boom rang out that vibrated through my bones. But despite my chattering teeth, Ronan and I made a break for it. My power still our only anchor, we flew closer to the wide opening stretched out before us. My limbs were heavy from the strain of resisting its pull, the lighteater desperate to devour us both.

Voices whispered from the bottomless, swirling pit; voices I'd heard before, in this world and the next. Vicious, hungry souls, made of gloom and dread and regret. Violent, hurting dead filled with fear and hateful words.

Join us, some beckoned.

Feed us, some growled.

End us, others pleaded.

My blood ran cold, but the energy in my middle buzzed to life. An answer to the call. A light in the darkness.

"We need to do this together," I whispered to Ronan, working my fingers through his.

A solemn nod. "I'll follow you to the Otherworld if that's what it takes."

Again, that charged, intoxicating energy pulsed in the space where our hands met. Light burst forth, pure and warm. The untapped source of all, the starfire and soul dust that made the universe. I focused in, my breath grounded and my heartbeat steady as my partner's pulse matched mine. As we dove deeper into that limitless gift that resided in both of us now.

Another bang behind us, as Arawn launched Lyr back in a flash of dark power. Lyr screamed as he flew past us, into the vortex, disappearing fully into its depths.

"Don't you dare stop!" his voice echoed from the cavity.

Panic surged in my stomach like bile, but I heeded his command. I clutched Ronan closer, letting his strength fortify mine. Letting our power meld and radiate and riot against the vortex.

Small victories.

Arawn stalked closer, tendrils hugging close to his body. "Now, where were we?"

I kept my gaze glued to my husband. My Ronan. "Don't let go."

His smile held the brightness of a thousand suns.

"I won't," he lied.

And hand in hand, heart to heart, we exploded.

The pure energy burst out of every pore, blinding us as we huddled together. My legs buckled, my skin burning with the painful, pleasurable intensity of the raw, unfiltered blast. Ronan's hands shook in mine, but I held. I endured.

The vortex wavered as our power slammed into it, and Arawn let out a brutal bellow of frustration. Shadows tried to devour us, the pull increasing, but I did not waver.

I was the NightMare of the Four Seas. Mother of the Moon and Wheel of Fate. I controlled the balance, the cycle of all things. The turning of the tides and the shifting of seasons.

Bren Arriannad.

Queen of the Silver Wheel.

Queen of the Lost.

Queen of the Deyrnas.

Queen of the Otherworld.

I held. I endured.

So did the darkness. The void yanked and tugged, the whispers frenzying into harsh screams.

Come to us.

Nourish us.

Kill us.

They drained at our power, the clash between light and dark near impossible to withstand. My body crumpled to the ground under the pressure, knocking Ronan with me. Eyes drooped as exhaustion threatened to take hold, the life leaving my limbs slowly as the void consumed more and more of the energy we expelled.

But I held. I endured.

For my mother and father in the veil beyond. For my cousins and aunts and uncles, waiting for me in the afterlife. For the ones that still lived, that learned and fought and survived for the good of others.

For the precious hands I held in mine. For the life born of that love, still kicking in my middle.

"You have to leave, Keira." Ronan's voice wrapped around me. So sweet and gentle, like honey and cinnamon on bread made with loving hands. So *tired*. "She has to live."

His power caressed mine, a gentle invitation for me to give him more. To let him carry the weight for a while.

But I heard the unspoken surrender in those words. The fatigue that hollowed out his bones, too, the pain that weighed his voice.

She has to live. I have to die.

Big sacrifices. Small victories.

Somehow, I still had tears to shed. They slid down my cheeks one by one, each a different memory of our life together. Of our love. Of the night spent on my family's ship, flirting and laughing before the weight of the world was so heavy. Of days spent in the spring, hurting and healing in the balmy waters of renewed connection. Of lonely twilights in the empty expanse of the Otherworld, missing and mourning the life we had and the one we wanted.

I'd let go before. I would never let go again.

But if I didn't, my daughter would die with me. The world would be devoured by the black hole of Arawn's misery and monstrosity.

I was the Goddess of Fortune.

But Fate was not always fair. She was a tricky mistress, the keeper of the balance between salvation and sacrifice. Give and take.

Here I was again, at the precipice. At the choice between having some or losing all. On the verge of saving my soul or risking my heart.

She has to live. I have to die.

Big sacrifices. Small victories.

"Ronan Mathonwy, loving you has been the greatest honor of my existence."

Gemstone eyes bore into mine. "I'll love you in every world, in every life." He reached his trembling hand to my face, brushing away my falling tears. "The ones I do remember, and the ones I can't."

Our power blossomed like the roses outside of Mathonwy Manor as he took more of it from me, ready to transform it all into something good. Something *more*. The God of Change, willing to sacrifice his own heart to put a stop to Death.

It would work. Certainty centered in my gut, a knot too tight to untie.

It would work.

He would die.

Big sacrifices. Small victories.

"Arawn, please," I begged, one last desperate attempt as Ronan let go of my hand. A petition from one lonely, broken god to another, as I took a step back. One last offer of potential paradise. "It doesn't have to be this way. We can work it out. No one has to kneel. We can do better. Let us spare your life and ours."

His hoarse, humorless laugh punctured the last of my hope. "You will spare *my* life?"

Another voice answered before I could, cold and sharp. A small voice, so much darker than the last time I'd heard it.

"I won't."

The gunshot peeled through the world like a death knell.

One single shot. One silver bullet.

Arawn fell to his knees. The God of Death, kneeling at last. A bloody wound seeping from his heartless chest. He gripped the bullethole, lifeforce pouring out of him like the power sucked into the blackhole.

He doubled over, grotesque hands catching himself. His eyes cleared, the dark edges eddying back within the confines of his nightsky irises.

Two small words formed on his rosebud lips. "Thank you."

And everything stopped. And started.

The lighteater folded in on itself, a snake eating its own tail. The screams from within cut off as the black spot winked out of existence as quickly as it came.

It spat out a familiar blond mass, Lyr tumbling from the void with wide eyes in surprise and horror.

Ronan's light flickered as he burned out, his golden skin wan and sticky with sweat. Still, a smile slithered across his face as the taste of victory lined his tongue. The taste of life.

But standing above Arawn's deformed corpse, the silver pistol smoking in hand, a tiny form stuck her hands to her hips.

And Reagan Mathonwy, the youngest living descendent of the sea-god, the little dragon herself, looked down at her fallen foe with rings of black lining her chestnut eyes. "For Mama."

46

Stories and Salvation

RONAN

The day the Arawn died, a legend was born.

Every battered survivor in the Deyrnas sang the battle cry turned victory hymn. Word of the Dark God's ending spread like pollen on a warm breeze, thawing the seven isles like spring come early. It took less than a week, and every hungry belly and broken heart, every wounded soldier and homeless refugee–they all added *her* name to their nightly prayers.

They did not pray for her. They prayed *to* her.

But to the chagrin of those who knew her best, it was not Reagan's name on their lips. Nor the Little Dragon, the Tiny Tyrant.

Bren Morgawse.

Queen Morgawse.

Conqueror of the Otherworld.

Protector of the Deyrnas.

Victor over Death.

The day the God of Death died, a new deity was born. One who'd marched through hell on earth to meet the Dark God's challenge. One who carried the Deyrnas out of the darkness on the back of a dragon. One who'd saved us all with a single bullet from the same gun that killed her mother.

But while we'd survived, none of us had made it out of the battle unscathed. My power still hummed beneath my flesh, but it was muted, resting. I'd gotten too close to the edge of the precipice, too close to burning out like an imploding star, and I'd pay for it in time.

And I was one of the best off. Saeth and Vian both had vicious cuts and bruises from Arawn's mishandling of them, not to mention the unseen scars they bore after watching Agatha and Nef killed before their eyes. Keira and our unborn daughter were by some miracle alive and healthy, but she'd been so tired since, the bags beneath her eyes nearly as dark as her hair now. Ellian had a limp that would probably never go away, Tarran broke three of his fingers, and little Genni had a gash on her arm that would definitely scar.

Even Gwynn and Lyr, both full-blooded gods, still fought the aftereffects of Arawn's attack. The blackness that temporarily claimed them both haunted their gazes, something about them both so wounded and *mortal*.

But they'd all live.

Griffin was still unconscious.

Huddled belowdecks, Nelle and a handful of the surviving Huddian magickas tended to him day and night to keep him breathing. She'd stitched up the gaping hole in his chest the second Rhett had dragged him all the way back to the *Madyn*, but he'd lost a lot of blood. He still straddled the gate between life and death, Rhett monitoring every breath like it might be his last.

Then there were those we'd lost. Madame Hedd and Agatha. Nef. Too many of the hunters and assassins to know by name.

My father.

The day Arawn died, so did my father. They did not sing Reese Mathonwy's name across the Deyrnas. They did not mourn the life of a washed-up pirate.

But I did. He'd never been much of a parent, but he'd tried. He taught me how to cheat and swindle and smirk. He'd handed down my favorite mask like our hair color. So I mourned the man he was, and the man he might have been. The potential of the relationship we could've had if he hadn't been snuffed out by Arawn's hounds.

Reagan mourned him, too.

Sitting next to me on the *Madyn's* deck, the wind tossing her chestnut hair, Reagan cried with me for all the members of our family we'd lost. Lochlan and Reina. Eleri and Reese. Roland and Auntie Astrid.

And for the family we'd found, too. For Keira and Vian and Lyr and Esme. The sirens and the rest of the crew. Those who would hold us together when our world crumbled.

At some point, they joined us, quietly shuffling across the wood floor, surrounding us with their unshakable presence. Vian stretched himself across Reagan's lap, long limbs pointed in every direction as he soaked up the sunlight like a bird in a happy bath. Nelle and Laureli tucked Genni between them, Marina and Siobhan on either side, the last sirens swaddled together like a tight school of fish. Gwynn and Saeth lounged on the rail, their shoulders brushing against each other, like they were too afraid to let anything bigger than a fly between them ever again. Even Lyr and Esme sort of joined our little huddle, Lyr laying across Esme's sea-serpent back as they both floated alongside the ship. Only Rhett, Tarran, and Ellian remained below, the first duo taking a turn tending to Griffin, while Ellian sorted things with Councilwoman Tommins for later.

Keira found her way to my side, leaning gently against me for support. Not that I minded—with her here, everything felt a little less hollow. A little more whole. Like the grooves in my mind where the memories of us had been still remembered her shape. Like she was there to fill the gaps of me that I'd never replenish on my own.

No one said anything. No one needed to. We just sat and cried and breathed, unleashing all that we held from the world in our little private place of healing. Anchored in the shallows of Orwellin with too much to do to move on yet, there was no rush to leave. There was still so much we had to fix, to rebuild.

But first, we needed release. We needed rest. Recovery.

When my tears finally dried in salted crust against my cheeks, I stared at the black spot crawling across Reagan's arm. It rested on the opposite shoulder from her white-ink tattoo, like light and dark fought on either side to claim her. Another scar, another price to our victory. Another problem still left to solve.

Reagan frowned at whatever expression I'd offered, folding her arms. The Queen of the Deyrnas broke the silence, a catalyst of change as always. "I don't understand all the fuss. It's just a spot."

The day Arawn died, a curse was born. One there was no escape for, no matter how strong of will or pure of heart one was.

I sighed, looking instead at the knotted wood below my boots. "It's a *Melthith* spot, little dragon. You used his gun. It's a curse that marks you as the Dark God's."

"But Arawn is dead." Reagan smirked. "I killed him, remember?"

"Not like anyone will forget," Nelle chuckled, voicing my thoughts, but her violet eyes narrowed with worry. She shifted closer to Genni, tucking the little duck under her wing. "But my guess is the gun isn't tied to the god, but the Otherworld itself."

"Could we do a Carthu? Clean that thing right up?" Laureli leaned forward, her forearms resting on her knees as she eyed the black spot like a puzzle she was trying to solve. I prayed in every language I knew that she'd crack the code.

"We could try." Keira shrugged, silver eyes lighting with the challenge. Lyr below, this woman never took a break, jumping from one adventure to the next like she ate them for breakfast.

I had a funny feeling I'd spend the rest of my life trying to keep up. Not that I minded in the slightest.

But a faint tingle down my spine alerted me to the stars watching distantly. They wanted something yet again, a yearning in their gaze. An answer that I didn't want to hear.

"It won't work. She belongs to the Otherworld, all right," Lyr announced as he hoisted himself over the rail on a torrent of water, splashing us all in a mist of his sea spray. My gut clenched like he'd speared me through it, the stars overhead twinkling brighter in taunting confirmation. Unbothered, Lyr strode over to Reagan, ruffling her hair with a smile. "But the Otherworld belongs to her, too."

Silence rippled through the crew again, this one not born of quiet comfort, but of edged anticipation. The icy hellscape of the Otherworld haunted my mind's eye, sending a chill running down my spine.

"What does that mean?" I pressed, holding Keira closer. Her warmth thawed the frost in my chest, allowing my lungs to expand fully again and take a much-needed deep breath. For a moment, I wished they were gills, wished the deep silence of the sea could swallow me and all my problems for a moment longer.

But winning battles was only half of the art of war. It was simple to burn the world to ash.

It was harder to rise from it. Harder to create than destroy. Harder to *live* than survive.

I looked to the sunken god for an answer. Perhaps he had a treasure map that might lead us to something other than misery.

"I didn't want to spook anyone, since I thought it would be Keira or Ronan…but she's the Otherworld's ruler now. The code is if you kill a god, you gain their title," Lyr explained, blue eyes fixed on the little dragon. On the god-killer. *Bren Morgawse.*

Queen of Death.

Queen of the Otherworld.

Reagan straightened her back like the regent she was as my sails deflated.

"She's *fourteen,*" I protested to deaf ears.

Reagan flipped her braid over her shoulder, confidence unwavering. "Practically ancient, if you ask me."

"The Otherworld sees us as we see ourselves," Keira mumbled, metallic eyes glassy. Her hand tightened around mine, steady and certain, the silver wheels in her head turning with the outline of a plan. Of a future. "She's the only one of us that has a half decent chance at making it something good."

"And she won't be alone." Vian sat up, the wind whisperer riding on my wife's current as he twined his fingers through Reagan's. "I'll go with her."

The way my cousin blushed the same crimson as her tunic was almost enough to win my vote.

Almost.

"You're both too young." Gods, I sounded like a middle-aged father already. By the time Rhiannon came around, I'd be a professional scolder. I imagined trying to raise my daughter without Reagan there with us, and that thought alone was enough to almost bring tears to my eyes again.

Almost.

"Danura and Papa are there too, to help." Keira's silken soprano pulled me out of my masochistic musings. The wisdom to her words gave me pause, even as they slashed through my heartstrings. "And Lochlan and Reina."

My whole chest cramped at the mention of my aunt. At the thought of her last words in the Otherworld before we left them behind.

Take care of my family. And yours.

Maybe I was kidding myself to think I could take care of her the way she needed.

"That doesn't sound half bad." Reagan's confidence cracked with her voice, a sadness ancient as the sea itself working its way into her tune. "But what about everyone else…here?"

I followed her gaze as it raked over our assembled, patchwork family. At those of us that had been here from the beginning, and those we'd adopted along the way. Saeth and Gwynn. Laureli and Nelle. Genni and Siobhan. Tarran and Rhett and Griffin belowdecks. Ellian absent as well. I'd rather rip my heart out of my chest and stomp on it before losing any more of them. It was a price too steep to pay.

But what would it cost if she didn't rule? What would happen to the souls that called the Otherworld their sanctuary? Reina and Lochlan, my father and Keira's…

"Considering most of us can cross the veil without sacrificing our souls, it doesn't seem to be a problem," Saeth piped up, the Ice Queen somehow always two steps ahead and three tiers above the rest of us. "Griffin is the only full mortal."

My head snapped to her so fast I gave myself whiplash, realization straightening my spine. Of course, the blunt little redhead was absolutely right. Everyone aboard the ship was either part siren, a god, or a descendant of one. The Otherworld wasn't just safe for us, it was built for us. *By* us.

Gwynn smirked. "And if Reagan's in charge, the passage will be safe. We'll make sure of it."

A chill careened down my spine at the mention of the gate. Even if the Otherworld was safe, the gate was its own entity. I could not recall what I'd seen there, but the absence of what it had taken from me still ached like my insides had been carved out.

Tell me, boy, what are you willing to give this time?

Everything.

"Won't the Gate demand a price?" I looked to Lyr, still perched on the rail, dripping seawater everywhere without a care in the world. I'd inherited his arrogant mask, but mine was made of paper and his of steel.

He crossed his powerful arms, but his saltwater-and-storm stare softened. "You've all already paid it. We are the only living gods left. We get to rewrite the rules. Right, *Storyspeaker?*"

The little bud of power left in my chest flickered in response, the stars above peering closer so the hairs at the back of my neck stood straight. Ancient, powerful words etched in my belly, ready to fly from my tongue. Ready to rearrange the stars to my liking, to shift the tides to better suit my course.

Keira squeezed my hand, her heartbeat racing like she could feel it too. Like fate and change were finally in harmony, both of us ready to write the ending to our own story as we wished it.

A shout belowdecks made me jump. I nearly shifted as the creature in my chest rose to the surface on pure instinct. My siren ears strained as I listened to the commotion below.

"Sounds like Griffin's awake," I announced, and the crew went silent. "We'll finish this conversation later."

No one needed further prompting. Saeth shot up first, dragging Gwynn by the wrist toward the cabins with the focus of a sharpshooter. Reagan and Vian followed hot on their heels, matching smiles breaking across their faces that chased away some of the lingering doubt in my mind.

The rest shuffled behind, the sirens and even Lyr burrowing through the door to check on one of his favorite sailors. I held back a moment, waiting for Keira.

"We can't go back to before, Ronan," she whispered as she pushed to her feet, her silver eyes glistening with tears. "Not even we can turn back time."

She squeezed my arm once before brushing past me, off to see her best friend safely returned to the land of the living. But her words hung back with me, lingering ghosts even after she'd moved on. I wondered how many phantoms she hid behind her freckled facade, how many hurts she still covered.

We couldn't turn back time. Couldn't go back to who we were before, kids without a care in the world. We couldn't regain the memories lost, couldn't save the lives already sacrificed.

But maybe we could make things better. Maybe we could move on and grow up and find something special in that once in a lifetime opportunity.

Or Reagan could.

I shrugged off the heaviness resting across my shoulders and marched myself down to the captain's quarters where Griffin waited. There was no use worrying when a small victory needed celebrating.

"The Otherworld isn't half bad. But why do I still hurt?" Griffin's strained voice carried as I rounded the corner, stopping in the doorway of the cabin. The room was not built for our numbers, especially with all of Laureli's trinkets littering the space, but no one seemed to care as they all huddled in the room, cramped and on top of each other. Reagan and Vian shared a small floor pillow for a seat, while the sirens stacked like sardines in a corner. Lyr and Gwynn had to stand hunched over, Saeth wedged sideways between them, as Rhett and Tarran both balanced precariously on either edge of the cot assembled in the middle of the room. They all held their breaths, heartbeats thundering in a chorus as they waited.

Griffin propped himself up on the cot with several bloodstained pillows, a woven blanket covering his lower half as his bandaged chest flashed us all.

He scanned the room, stopping on Keira, who stood slack-jawed in the center.

"*Shrimpy.* You're here. So, I did die, then."

Keira closed her mouth and opened it again. "You didn't die."

Griffin tilted his head, blinking away the surviving exhaustion crusting his eyes. "But you're here."

She nodded. "Yeah. I'm here."

A moment passed between them as they held each other's gaze, silent words the rest of us would never hear somehow filling the room.

"You're *here*," Griffin repeated, hoarse voice cracking as his whole face pulled into a smile. He sat straighter, but winced at the action, his head lolling back as he groaned in pain. "Ugh, I *survived?*"

The tension in the room dissolved, everyone sharing a collective exhale as the Swordsinger finally returned to himself.

"Why is surviving a bad thing?" Saeth scoffed, throwing a look at her cousin that could stop his heart all over again.

Griffin flipped her a vulgar gesture right back. "Because! That was my last chance at a truly heroic death! I'm never gonna top *that*."

"Keep talking like that and I'll kill you myself," Rhett warned, but he beamed anyway.

Laughter–real and hearty–rippled through the room, everyone healing just a little bit as Griffin's wounds had. But the too-crowded space suffocated me, the air thinning and my lungs struggling to take in a deep breath. Griffin had survived, thank the gods, but we'd gotten so close to losing him. So close to paying the ultimate price for our victory.

Would I have to ask Reagan to do the same? Would I have to cage her again, this time in a palace of ice and darkness, because she made the choices I couldn't? Because she saved the world when I'd failed?

I took a step back out of the room before the walls could cave in on me, before the world could crumble again. Once in the hall, I flattened myself against a wood beam, desperately trying to tune the world out. I closed my eyes, sinking into a crouch, wishing I could just disappear into the wood like a ghost.

I inhaled, letting the air soothe the jagged, frayed edges of my nerves. Maybe I had some wounds to heal myself, festering beneath my flesh, out of sight but not out of mind.

Creaking floorboards alerted me to my company before her voice did.

"You're moody," Reagan stated, a hint of taunting in her tone that scratched beneath my scales. Since Arawn's fall, we'd spent nearly every waking hour together, either in quiet mourning or comfortable companionship. I'd missed it, that bond between us, more than words could express. The rift that had divided us before I left had carved giants chunks out of my soul that I'd finally stitched back together. But the closer we were, the better she knew how to push the boundaries of my patience.

The more she saw through my bullshit.

"I'm not moody, I'm worried," I grumbled back, hanging my head between my legs. She didn't deserve my attitude, but then again, she was the only one who might get it. "It's different."

Reagan shuffled closer, sliding down the beam to sit next to me. She wrapped her arm through mine, another wound closing at the contact as she rested her head on my shoulder. "Ya know, I think it's time for you to start worrying about yourself for once. You're always running after someone or trying to save something."

I pressed a quick kiss to her scalp. "That's my job, little dragon. I take care of my family."

Little fingers reached up and flicked me on the nose. I jumped up, ready to unleash dragon-fire on her, but her soft smile unlocked something else in my chest. "Ronan, you've got a kid on the way and a wife to re-woo. I can handle myself."

I blinked at my cousin. Wisdom reigned in the dark soil of her eyes, always seeing far beyond her years. Her fighting spirit dwelled within, indomitable as she'd saved the world from the brink of ruin. But there was comfort there, too, a soothing presence that tended to my most vulnerable hurts. A rose despite her thorns. I'd been kidding myself to think I was just her caretaker.

She'd always taken care of me, too.

A lopsided gait on the stairs halted whatever comeback or compliment I might have thrown at her. Ellian appeared in the doorway, his long hair swept up in a bun, his finest tunic hanging neatly from his broad frame. He offered an apologetic smile, the Councilman ready to come collect me for the show I had to perform. "The others are ready, Ronan."

It was simple to burn the world to ash.

It was harder to rise from the rubble. Harder to create than destroy. Harder to *live* than survive.

And the rest of the Deyrnas needed leaders to step up and show them the way.

"I'll fetch Keira."

The hull of the *Ddraig* had never been so full of life. Through my childhood, it had been an empty shell, filled with goods but never love. My family's ship was a vessel of war and commerce, built on the principles the Mathonwys valued most: money, power, and dominance. But anchored in the docks of Orwellin, packed full of Deyrnasian refugees from every corner of the seven isles, it became the epicenter of a new beginning. The birthplace of the new Deyrnas, to be founded instead on the *Ddraig's* antithesis; community, rehabilitation, and justice.

We sat stalwart around the table in the galley, a feast before us as we penned the new contract of what the Deyrnas would become. Cured venison from Pysgodd, bathed in salvaged spices from Ir'de. Porthladdian shrimp tossed over potatoes grown in Tan, of all places.

Huddian whiskey poured into ornate glasses donated from the Orwellin's surviving kitchens.

I sipped the amber liquid, letting it fill my belly as I dipped my quill in the black ink, the parchment before me brimming with potential. I had the honor of acting as scribe, as both the Storyspeaker and Serpent Prince. My sword might have been lacking, but my pen would always be one of my mightiest tools.

"Mr. and Mrs. Mathonwy." Councilwoman Tommins sat at the head of the table, gnawing on a chunk of cured meat. Her white hair hung loose around her shoulders, but the three jagged cuts across her cheek painted her face in severity. Another mark of what had been sacrificed. "As the heroes of our little collective, I suggest you start us off."

Keira grabbed my hand under the table for support. It was strange, this comfortable contact that sent electricity up my spine every time we touched, but I relished every moment of it. She cleared her throat. "Turns out, we did very little. Our crew deserves the full credit."

I smiled as I squeezed her fingers. This woman had stood against the Dark God, had survived his cage and then held him off on her own, all while pregnant, and she still managed to be modest.

I didn't know if I wanted to shake her or kiss her for it.

"Still, the Deyrnas owes you and your crew a great debt, *Mr.* Mathonwy. Let us flatter you," Madame Katrin chimed in, her sultry voice dipping low as she made direct eye contact with me. A blush crept up my neck, and Keira stiffened at my side.

"Or what's left of us," Madame Neirida interjected, distracting us from Katrin's unapologetic flirtations. I'd never much liked the siren witch of Porthladd, but I sure as hell was grateful for her presence now. "Which is why we are gathered here, to form the new High Council of the Deyrnas."

I looked around at the medley of misfits ready to right the wrongs of the world. The new High Council. Councilwoman Tommins of Pysgodd sat next to Madame Katrin, the brothel owner and businesswoman from Ir'de. Ellian and Siobhan perched beside them, along with Siobhan's mother, Queen Anlisa of the Rhefylwr Tannian clan. Her hair was almost purely white, soft wrinkles sagging her deep skin, but her eyes were the same sharp citrine as her daughter's. Keira and I came next, flanked by Drystan, Madame Neirida, Rhett, Greyson Leary, and Weylin Branwen.

It was a wild assortment, one no conman worth his salt would've bet on. But we were all that was left. Beggars couldn't choose, and the Deyrnas needed whatever help it could get.

We'd have to be enough.

I pressed my quill to the parchment, titling the page.

"I volunteer as delegate to the Tannian nomads." Siobhan stood from her seat, placing her hand across her heart in a formal salute. "Along with my betrothed, Councilman Ellian Llewelyn."

I nearly broke my quill in half. Keira's brows flew up, like this was news to her, too.

"When were you going to tell me that?" I whispered to Ellian, nudging him in the side.

Emerald green eyes danced with real, honest-to-gods happiness. "Never. It was the agreement that got the queen to come with us." He winked, then stood, seamlessly slipping back into the role of Councilman. It suited him like fine-made clothes, his chest puffed with a pride befitting a newly engaged man of authority. "My fiancé and I pledge our service not just to Tan, but to the whole of the Deyrnas. We also wish to support the Ir'desian and Huddian rebuilding efforts. The Southern Isles need a united front."

Siobhan smiled like I'd never seen before, her whole face relaxing into the expression that for once didn't hold the slightest hint of aggression or condescension. Warmth spread through me, the sight of my friends happy almost enough to heal over the open wounds in my own soul.

Almost.

Ellian and Siobhan's motion was approved unanimously, a short series of 'ayes' confirming the *blaidd* and the siren as the newest–and *first*–members of the Deyrnas's highest honor.

My elegant script swirled their names onto the parchment carefully, my friends more than deserving of every respect I could offer them.

"I'm not qualified to be a councilman, but my partner Griffin and I would love to offer our sailing expertise to all the islands that need rebuilding. Once he's recovered, of course," Rhett spoke next, straightening the lapels of his long blue coat with shaking hands. He'd even tied his long blond hair back in a slick ponytail, the Red Fang of the Deyrnas turned respectable gentleman.

Councilwoman Tommins clapped her hands together as she settled deeper into her chair. "Duly noted, Mr. Mathonwy. I'd like to then formerly appoint you as a trusted advisor to the Council."

Rhett's shoulders relaxed as his scarred eye crinkled with a broad smile. I tried not to think of the resemblance to my father, to an old scar I'd never see again. Rhett cleared his throat, interrupting my downward spiral of grief. "I'd also like to suggest Colonel Drystan Farchos to serve on the Council for Orwellin."

Drystan spat out the sip of whiskey he'd just taken.

I raised a brow at my cousin. Last I'd seen them together, Rhett had gladly smacked Drystan across the back of the head with a sword for simply *existing* near Griffin. But we'd all changed beyond recognition in the last few months. Rhett shrugged. "They need good people to lead. Drystan is the best candidate."

"I–" Drystan wiped his mouth, a blush coloring his warm skin. His amber eyes gleamed with tears. "I'd be honored."

Councilwoman Tommins raised her glass high. "All in favor?"

"Aye," the room said in unison. Drystan's smile didn't fall the rest of the night.

I scratched his name across the page with the same care and a prayer he'd be better than his predecessor. Assuming he didn't commit genocide, he was already more than halfway there.

"Good. Now to Bachtref and Porthladd. Without puppets in control, both islands can return to the hands of the refugees stinking up my island," Councilwoman Tommins trudged on, and her sharp violet eyes landed on Keira and me. I shifted in my seat, holding Keira's hand tighter under the weight of her gaze. "Mr. and Mrs. Mathonwy...since most of the Porthladdian Council is dead or otherwise occupied, and since yer godly folk, the Council members think you'd be the logical choice to fill their place–"

"No." The word rolled off my tongue faster than I could think it through.

All eyes in the room shot toward me faster than a bullet from Arawn's gun, everyone falling uncomfortably quiet.

"Is something wrong?" Keira rubbed her thumb across mine beneath the table, and I took a deep breath.

My heart smacked against my ribs in a vicious rhythm. Why did I hesitate? We'd given so much to the Deyrnas already, what was the use of backing out now?

Tell me, boy, what are you willing to give this time?

Everything.

Perhaps I had nothing left I was willing to give. Perhaps I wanted to keep what I had left all to myself, to enjoy and rest and recover for the first time in my life.

My cousin's words echoed through my head, an anchor back to the parts of me that needed the most love. Rotten, wicked, selfish parts that needed to be accepted and cared for. That needed *time.*

I think it's time for you to start worrying about yourself for once. You're always running after someone or trying to save something.

I looked up into the deep silver pools of Keira's eyes. I wasn't willing to give anything else to a noble cause. I just wanted her. To get to know her all over again, to explore every side of her I'd yet to meet. Wanted our family, the little life waiting to be started, the new role of fatherhood I'd have to step into, an adventure in itself. And Lyr below, I wanted *rest.* Wanted a small, brick cottage in the *Dubryn* Hills to return to after a long day, to raise my family in the quiet shelter of the white willows and whispering spring.

My voice was steadier than it had been in weeks. "My wife and I are expecting, and we have quite a bit of work to do with my cousin's recent changes." I scanned the rest of the room, drawing my line in the sand. "We need a break."

Keira's throat worked hard as she swallowed, lips twitching up at the side. "But my Auntie Vala might be the perfect woman for the job," she said, voice firm with the authority of a true Captain. The Goddess Ariannad, willing to turn the tide in my favor. "She never left, even when things got hard. And I'm sure Captain Leary and my Uncle Weylin would love to help out."

Sitting across from us, the last living Branwen brother perked up, rare droplets budding in the corners of his eyes. His ginger hair had been combed for the first time in years, his eyes clear and skin bright. *Healthy.* And maybe, once he found his way back to Porthladdian soil, he could be *happy* too. "Aye, my loyalty is to our home."

Grayson shrugged, his expensive gray coat shifting. "I gave my ship up, so it's about time I looked into other career options."

Relief and something akin to joy spread through me, reanimating parts of me I thought long gone, stolen by the gate and the pain I'd been through since. "And we will of course still fulfill our duties along with the other gods to keep things moving."

To keep things balanced, to make sure history didn't repeat itself. No, my work was not done. Lyr below, we didn't even know how long gods *lived*–Keira and I could have an eternity ahead of us, and the Deyrnas would surely call on us again.

When they needed us, we would answer. We would not abandon people to madness, would never let despots like Connor or Locasta or Arawn rise as we watched from the sidelines.

But for now, we had time to just be. Not just survive, but to *live*.

Councilwoman Tommins sighed, an understanding in her expression. She raised her hand, calling it to a vote. "Aye. All in favor?"

And again, the new leaders of the Deyrnas lifted their voices in a unanimous, "Aye."

The Otherworld stretched out before me yet again, both unchanged and entirely different than it had been before. Ice still blanketed the expanse, but there were places where soft green grass broke through like the threadbare patches of a well-loved, woven quilt. My breath still swirled in wispy tendrils of mist around me, but the cold did not seep into my bones. Instead of silence, birdsong greeted us as we stepped through the tall black gates.

There had been no trial. No test. No *taking*. No portal to turn us inside out and spit us back into the world. No misty figures with empty eyes and outstretched hands, ready to lead us astray.

Just a door, like stepping through the threshold of an old friend's house, no need for invitation or inquiry.

Like coming home.

Relief held my hand as I breathed in. A part of me feared I'd lose myself all over again, that the gate would demand the few precious memories I'd made since my last visit.

But a small, wistful part of me fell, longing like hunger scratching at my gut. The gate hadn't taken any more, but it hadn't returned what I'd lost, either. No memories flooded the empty ravines in my soul, no recollections stitched my tattered mind back together.

Like coming home, yes, and finding someone had rearranged all your furniture while you were gone.

Reagan cleared her throat and redirected my attention. There was no use mourning a loss I'd never remember. She surveyed her new kingdom, hands planted on her hips like the conqueror she was. "This place isn't nearly as bad as you made it seem."

I shrugged, tucking my hands in my pockets. "Now that we know it's safe to cross, I'll have to fetch Vian. And then you two will have to make it your own."

Reagan nodded, a plan already brewing behind her eyes. But before she could voice it, Reina winked into existence next to us, blonde head popping in first, followed by the rest of her. Instead of a black frock and a servant's apron, she wore a flowing red dress that swished around her calves as if blown by an invisible breeze, her unbound golden hair mimicking the motion. "We've been doing some redecorating. Wait until you see the palace."

Reagan's arms fell at her side. Then, a sharp intake of breath as tears watered the dark soil of her eyes. "Mama."

Reina opened her arms, her smile warm enough to thaw the rest of the frost from the ground. "Are ye too old and powerful to give yer ma a hug?"

Sobs shaking her frame, the little dragon melted too, launching herself into her mother's waiting arms. Reina held her to her chest, pressing kisses into her hair over and over again, one for every day they'd been apart.

I had to swallow back the emotion rising to my own throat. I'd been against this, not wanting to see Reagan suffer an eternity of darkness for my failings. But there were no shadows clinging to the edges of Reina's smile. No darkness misting around our feet, ready to drag us under. Just a tender reunion, like the first buds of spring after the long winter's night.

Like coming home.

"I could get used to it here." Reagan finally pulled back–just a smidge–to beam up at her mama. She was a queen now, but she was still just a girl, who after every grand adventure, craved the safe embrace of her mother's arms.

A tiny, jealous thing wriggled in my stomach, the envious musings of a forgotten little boy that never had a real parent to run home to. For so long, it had been the three of us, Reina, Reagan and I, a little ragtag shelter hidden in the den of snakes. Now, it would be them and me, separate entities, no kitchen in Mathonwy Manor to all somehow find our way back to.

I stuffed that unsavory feeling back in my pockets as I sheathed one hand, ruffling Reagan's hair with the other.

"Don't get too comfortable," I teased, glad to just be her cousin and not her Captain for a moment. I doubted I'd have the chance to be either again. "You're going to have to visit us topside now and then."

Reagan unwound from Reina's embrace to swat me away. But a smirk to rival my own crawled across her face. "Only if you promise to visit me here, too."

Reina nodded, tucking Reagan beneath her arm, like she'd never let her stray too far again. "And tell yer wife to bring that baby when she comes so her great-aunt Reina can shower her in some love."

My heart did somersaults in my chest, the little lost boy hidden beneath the dragon peeking his head out.

I looked at Reagan, my breath held. There'd been so much hurt between us, I didn't know if I deserved to still heal at her side. Sure, we'd connected in the days after the battle of Orwellin out of necessity, out of the stalemate of kinship and mourning that brought even the worst of enemies together for a moment of respite. But that didn't mean she still could see past my monstrous parts.

My voice washed in putrid self-pity as it spilled from my lips. "Do you want me to?"

She lifted her chin, a true dragon staring down at me from over the bridge of her nose. But in her chestnut eyes—eyes that had seen too much—the little girl who'd once looked at me like I was the sun still hid behind walls of dragon-fire and steel. "Just because I'm this all-powerful goddess doesn't mean I'm too old for stories, ya know," she teased, but I didn't miss the way her throat bobbed, the way she clutched the end of her tunic with white knuckles. "If you wanted to practice for when the baby gets here, I mean."

Something unlocked within me. Something bright and strong and sacred. A fusion between the little boy who loved to tell stories, and the man who'd do anything to make them come true. I smiled—

a real, unfiltered smile—my heart lighter than it had been in weeks as that *something* healed a little more. "I'd tell you Airid again, but you've already made that story come true."

Reagan smiled back, her face so much younger with the action. So tiny, so bright. But that unerasable mischief still flickered in her dark eyes like fireworks, ready to burst. "You used to say that stories were living memories. I could tell you some, too."

At that, I lifted a brow. I'd told Reagan many stories over the years. Stories about love and change and sacrifice. Stories of pain and forgiveness and family. Mama always said that a single story held more power than an entire army. What Reagan would do with that gift was both terrifying and awe-inspiring. "About what?"

Reagan looked out across the landscape again, at the story she'd have to finish writing. "When I was little, before you left for *Hiraeth*, you told me so many stories about Keira that when she walked through the door years later, I knew exactly who she was." She turned her head to me, an unspoken offering in her eyes. A story of forgiveness and recovery and a family broken and found. Of memories lost and meaning restored. "I could probably remember a few. You're not too old for stories, either."

"Oh?" I croaked as the hollow spaces in my heart swelled, and for the first time in my life, I was at loss for words.

There was no going back to before, no remembering what I'd freely sacrificed. I was a god made man, the *Ddraig Aur*, and even I could not replicate or replace the missing pieces.

But Mama always said a single story held more power than an entire army. And now, Reagan offered me a piece of that inalienable power, a chance to listen at her feet with stars in my eyes, the fire in my chest alight with wonder and mystery as she whispered her tales.

Stories that could make me, teach me, cultivate me. Stories that could cure all ills, could fix all problems. Stories of silver eyes and freckled cheeks, of salt and sea and summer love.

Stories that could give me back what I'd lost.

Tears blurred my vision as I wrapped my cousin in a soul-crushing hug.

A moment passed before she wrapped her slim arms around my waist and squeezed.

"You know, Keira was only my age when she made a name for herself as the baddest female sailor in the Deyrnas," she murmured against my chest, the first words of the narrative that would heal us both vibrating through my bones, gilding them in starfire. "The NightMare of the Four Seas, they called her. And you, apparently, were her faithful little sidekick. Until she thought you killed her father, that is."

I imagined it clear as day, as if she'd painted the words across a canvas in rich oil hues. Then, as if summoned by her speech, the images danced across the blotted ice, like a mirror into my past. Keira at Reagan's age, her dark hair as wild as the gleam in her silver eyes. My long, lanky form following behind, a lopsided smirk across my face. A stormy night and a silent sea. A glittering spring and a signature on a worn contract.

The day the Dark God died, a goddess was born. One that would reimagine the world in happier colors, one that could harness a story and write a better ending than the rest of us ever could.

Queen Morgawse.

Queen of the Otherworld.

But I would always know her as Reagan Mathonwy. As the little dragon, the tiny tyrant.

As my little sister, through heartache and happiness.

I kissed the top of her head before letting go, her faithful servant until the end of this story and the next. "Tell me everything."

47

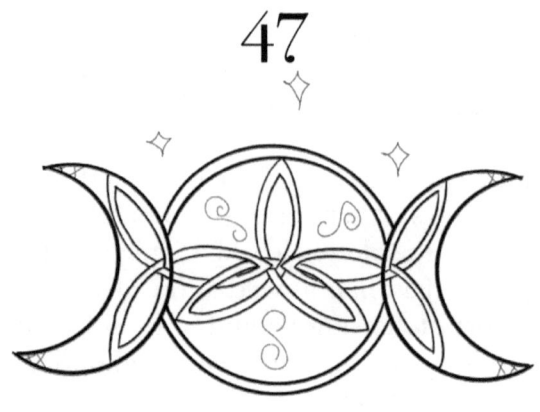

Havens and Happiness

KEIRA
ONE YEAR LATER

The Otherworld was not the paradise of legends. Nor was it the hell of nightmares past.

It was more, now. Imperfect and incredible all the same.

Green fields dotted with wildflowers stretched for miles, as far as the eye could see, every shade of the rainbow sparkling in the morning sunlight. A gentle breeze licked my cheeks as it greeted me, a friendly hello.

As it did every time I visited, the beauty stole my breath. Reagan and Vian and the others had made this place a sanctuary for souls, lost and found.

The lost soul behind me needed such a haven. The old woman slid from Dewy's back first and drank it all in with awe, mouth hanging open. Her frail frame wavered, swaying with the wind, a reed ready to plant herself in this field of dreams and tranquility.

We'd found her in Bachtref, just skin and bones, too weak to sip the water we'd offered. Too tired to *chew*. Her soul was fatigued, ready for the warm embrace of the endless sleep. Or whatever else she chose to make of her afterlife.

"This is the Otherworld?" she whispered, pointed edges of her frame softening and filling out as she took a deep breath, the healing magick washing through her.

I hopped off Dewy's back, careful not to snag the hem of the calf-length dress I'd stuffed myself into. I placed a gentle hand on her arm, my tattooed hand stark against her skin. "Aye, dear. Enjoy your rest."

"Thank you." Dark eyes watered as she took her first hesitant step into the field that would give her space to grow and soak in the sun and nourish her weary heart. Dewy neighed softly, nudging her forward with his nose. She patted his head as her face lit in a warm smile. "Bless ye, *Bren Ariannad*."

Bren Ariannad.

The Silver Wheel.

The Hand of Fate.

The Ferrywoman of Souls.

For all I'd done to fight my fate, it embraced me like an old friend as I grew into my title and duty. I watched the woman walk away until her form was just a speck in the distance, the sunlight blurring her silhouette as she became one with the Otherworld.

It had been a year since the Dark God's fall. A year of stitching wounds and rebuilding cities. A year of ferrying souls to paradise beyond the veil and working to create one above. A year of funeral pyres and birth announcements, of loss and celebration. A year of rekindling relationships and letting new ones bloom.

I smiled at myself as I straddled Dewy, clicking my heels to urge him forward. He trudged slowly along the dazzling glass path to the palace, the sparkling walkway so reminiscent of the ice it replaced, yet new all the same. We meandered through the maze of bright red rose hedges, regrown from the ash of the old ones, their petals yearning toward the affectionate sky. Though I'd been here nearly a dozen times in the last year, the ever-blossoms never failed to amaze me. Seasons changed topside, life beginning and closing with every new day, but here, the peace was forever. Eternal.

And yet, somehow, not frozen or stagnant. It shifted like the wind, grew like wildflowers out in the fields. Fixed, but fluid. Perfect, but always in progress. In *motion*.

Much like the two teenagers running through the halls of the palace, caking the dark marble floors in dirty footprints as they blew through like a tornado. The massive doors opened wide to welcome the breeze, the chaos inside spilling out like laughter. Danura and the others had done a marvelous job at renovating the palace, washing away the decay and despair Arawn had left behind, but it seemed the young rulers made it their personal mission to make a mess of it daily. To *live*, even in the realm of death.

Vian led the charge, his fine tunic rumpled and untucked. He took the grand stairs in twos with his long legs, dangling Reagan's rose-laid tiara from a single finger over the polished banister. The little dragon laughed as she gave chase, kicking off her expensive golden heels, scattering more mud across the room.

A third small figure followed after with hurried footsteps, panic in her squeaky voice. "Mistress, Master, please! Cythie just washed the floors this morning!"

I didn't need a clear view of her face to hear the eyeroll in Reagan's voice. "How many times do we have to tell you, Cythie, you live here now. You're not a maid, and you don't have to clean!"

Cythie stomped her foot and opened her mouth to protest, some things absolutely unchanged, but slammed her jaw shut when she noticed my presence. The little girl fell into a deep curtsy, the top of her tight black bun pointed at the floor. "Oh, Madame Ariannad! You're here early!"

"Hi, Cythie," I chuckled as I dismounted, giving Dewy a good pat before leaning against the tall doorway that led to the foyer. I feigned irritation on Cythie's behalf as I fought a grin. "Are you two menaces ready to go? We can't be late, or Rhett will have our heads."

Reagan frowned and straightened the hem of her light pink gown, the ruffled silk fabric clearly Reina's doing. She snagged the tiara from Vian, setting it on her head with a huff. "Hold your horse, I'm a very busy ruler, you know."

"I can see that." I peaked an eyebrow. "You can tell that to Rhett yourself, then."

"Don't listen to her, I'm ready!" Vian tucked his light blue tunic back in and brushed the dirt from his rump, his long dark hair still unbridled as he rushed back down the stairs, looking *past* me to Dewy in the courtyard. "Is the baby here?"

I shook my head, my heart melting at the mere mention of the baby. It had been almost six months since Rhiannon was born, my little starbeam a light in all of our worlds. "She's already sitting up on her own, but she still isn't *quite* advanced enough to ride the horse by herself, Vian. She's on the ship with her papa."

My heart and soul, together on my ship. A paradise in itself.

Vian nodded, grabbing Reagan's wrist and dragging her toward the waiting steed. "Let's go, Reagan! I want to play with her before the ceremony."

The little dragon rolled her eyes, the whites of them flashing bright, but followed. "Fine, fine. I don't get all the fuss for a little thing that still shits itself and mumbles, but whatever."

Vian snorted. "You're just jealous because she's everyone's favorite now."

I bit my lower lip to stifle a laugh, but Reagan whirled on him, a cruel, wicked smirk carving her face. "You're just butt-hurt that you were *never* the favorite."

"You're short."

"You're strange."

I kneaded the pressure point between my brows. Even in the comfort of the afterlife, these two still were agents of chaos. My kindred spirits in both ferocity and infatuation always kept me on my toes. I strode past them with a deep sigh. "You're both going to give me a headache if you don't stop squabbling like an old married couple."

The blush that colored Reagan's cheeks rivaled the roses. "Ew, Keira. Did childbirth rot your brain?" she spat, tossing her perfectly curled hair over her shoulder.

But I didn't miss how she still let Vian help her up onto Dewy's back, a tender hand on the small of hers. How the wind whisperer's square smile became a fixed point in space and time, unashamed, as he sat behind her.

I opted to walk rather than burden Dewy further, enjoying the use of my legs. It slowed us down, but the journey was worth it as I let the cool breeze caress my skin.

By the time we got to the gates, a small gathering formed, ready to see us off. They dressed in finery, as if they were coming with us, Reina in a lovely sage dress that matched the tall reeds of grass kissing her ankles, Finna in a soft blue that brought out the lightest flecks in her jade eyes. Papa and Reese wore their Captains' colors, both metallic crests glittering in the warm orange sunlight, Danura's opalescent gown shimmering between them like a star. Lochlan,

Aidan, and Owen, on the other hand, all wore plain tunics, but they'd washed and combed their hair back, while Donnall sported the most grotesquely ornate gold jacket I'd ever seen, the fabric struggling against his burly arms.

Cedric and Reina, Finna and Reese, Lochlan and Owen, Donnal and Aidan and Danura. Branwens and Mathonwys together, united in the new Otherworld. Entwined in celebration and sacrifice. Above and below.

I supposed in a way, they would be with us tonight. Though they could not cross the gate, we carried them in our hearts. In our souls.

"Tell the boys we're proud of them." Roland's graveled voice choked on the emotion he did little to hide.

Donnall straightened the lapels of his absurd coat as he stuttered through tears of his own, "And that we miss them."

"Get it together, man," Aidan smacked his second mate on the back of the head, his clever grin tugging his cropped ginger beard.

Finna twined her arm through her pa's, tugging the blubbering boulder closer with a soft nod. "And that we're sorry we can't be there."

I swallowed hard, moisture prickling in my vision. "They know."

Papa broke from the pack, tugging away from Danura's hold, his sunset eyes sparkling as he wrapped me in a tight hug. His cedar and cinnamon scent filled my lungs, a piece of him I could always take with me. "Remind them anyway. No Branwen left behind."

I squeezed tighter, ready to pass it on to my cousin.

Reagan and Vian waved goodbye to the others before Dewy carried them through the gate. I took one last deep breath of Papa's scent before letting go and marching myself through the portal.

In the year since the Dark God's fall, I'd been to the Otherworld and back a dozen times. But it never got easier to say farewell to my family, even if it was just a 'see-you-later.'

The greeting on the other side always softened the blow.

Reagan, the clever little witch, with Danura and Ronan's help of course, had managed to place the Otherworld's main entrance rather conveniently in the hull of the *Ddraig*. It took getting used to at first, especially when Reagan and Vian both had bad habits of popping onto the deck in the middle of the night to stir trouble. But as I stepped out of the threshold, the familiar view of my crew made my heart leap in my chest.

"Glad to see you, Captain." Saeth noticed us first, as she always did, hopping up from Gwynn's lap and flattening the silver jumpsuit she wore. Her bright ginger hair was styled in soft curls, but it did little to dull sharp angles of her face. "And the stowaways, back again."

Reagan stuck her tongue out as she slid off Dewy. "Missed you too, Saethy-poo."

Vian ignored them all, his head bobbing around like a bird ready to catch the worm as he searched for Rhiannon. "Baby?"

"She's right here." The warm velvet tenor purred behind me, and the last of my bittersweet sadness melted away as Ronan sauntered out from the cabin. I turned, drinking in my favorite sight in the whole world with a greedy appetite I'd never satiate.

Two matching golden heads, ringlets like silk fluttering in the wind. Rhiannon curled against her Papa's chest, silver eyes wide with wonder as she took in the world. My husband smiled as he pressed a quick kiss to her tiny forehead.

The Otherworld was not the paradise of legends. That utopia was right here in front of me, my little family, the only elysian peace I'd ever need.

I stroked my little girl's cheek, bathing in the tiny giggle that scrunched her nose.

Chaos rode the back of a swift wind as Vian zoomed between us, hovering over Rhiannon like a bug to lanternlight. "Well, hello!"

I laughed as Ronan gently handed her off to him, making sure to rest her head carefully on his elbow. "Say hi to Uncle Vian, Rhi-rhi."

"Ba-ba!" she babbled as she grabbed at strands of his long hair.

"Oh really?" Vian tilted his head to the side, unfazed as she yanked at him, the wind whisperer also fluent in the language of babes. "I've never tried mashed carrots, but I'll have to."

My heart swelled, too big for my chest as he carried her over to Reagan, who rumpled her nose in pure disgust.

"Safe trip?" Ronan's arms snaked around my waist, pulling our chests flush together.

My hands trailed over the embroidered lines of his red dress tunic as I rested my forehead on his lips, breathing in the citrus and sea and starlight of him. "Aye. Another soul sent to paradise."

Both the woman I'd helped cross and my own, tucked away in this pocket of sunshine and love. In the year since the Dark God met his end, so many days had passed like this aboard my husband's ship, cuddled in his embrace while the gentle sea rocked us and our baby. And yet, the safety and goodness of it all never failed to squeeze my heart so hard I struggled to breathe.

No victory felt small, not when I'd been granted everything I'd ever dared to want and more.

Ronan shifted back far enough to reveal the pretty ring of gold that lined the center of his iris, the price of our triumph. We'd won, but there had been a cost. A sacrifice. A duty we still paid with our existence, a promise to do better than the gods that came before us. Ronan's full lips flattened to a thin line. "Gwynn says he thinks he spotted some more of Locasta's former puppets in Pysgodd. They look lost. Laureli is down below with the other sirens trying to confirm."

The wind changed, instincts pricking beneath my skin as the silver wheel turned with it. We had our happily ever after, but so many still fought for theirs. In the year since the Dark God's fall, so many Deyrnasians needed both new homes and new purpose, everything they knew and loved ripped from them. Ronan and I had taken our break, letting ourselves relearn the intricacies of each other in the safe haven of our spring for the few months before Rhiannon was born. I'd never had a home before, but we'd made one together, built from the ruins of the people we were before and on the sweat and blood of the people we wanted to become. But we still had an obligation to use our power for better. To lead others to their patch of happiness, to give them a fighting chance.

I pulled Papa's compass from my dress's hidden pocket, rubbing my thumb over the inlaid inscription.

All who are lost shall be found.

"We'll head that way to find them after the celebration, and I'll see what I can do," I sighed, letting the briny salt air of the Porthladdian docks steady me as it always had. "But after that, we might have to take a break again in a few months. Settle down on land for a bit."

Ronan's brow knotted, scanning me for signs of injury. "What? *Why?* I know it's hard to juggle Rhiannon aboard the ship, but with the sirens helping, she's thriving with all the attention."

I swallowed, mooring myself to the safe shore of his frame. This home we'd built was fixed, a truth that could never be stolen from us again. But it was fluid, too. Ever changing and growing. A perfect work in progress.

I looked over my shoulder to watch Vian dance across the deck with the baby in his arms, Reagan sidestepping while Saeth and Gwynn laughed at them both. Rhiannon would keep growing, too, a weed just starting to sprout, one day chasing them around. Perhaps with her little brother or sister in tow. "She better get used to sharing the spotlight soon. With the new baby on the way."

"Who–?" Ronan started, then stopped. Took a deep breath. Looked at my face, and then my abdomen, sapphire stare glassy.

Then he began to *glow*, the power inside of him radiating from his skin. The *Ddraig Aur*, triumphant again. His smile somehow shone even brighter as it consumed his whole face. "You're pregnant?"

My fingers squished his lips together before he could shout, my voice dropping to a whisper that could barely contain my joy. "Don't tell anyone until after the ceremony. I don't want to steal Rhett and Griffin's thunder."

Ronan nodded, and I released him, our budding little secret only ours for a moment longer. A special something shared by just Ronan and me, as it had been since our beginning.

"I love you, Mrs. Mathonwy." Ronan gripped my face gently beneath both hands, his stare penetrating every hidden part of me. Parts that were rotten and wicked, parts that were kind and happy. Ronan loved me for all of it, for all of *me*, and I loved him in return with the burning light of every star in the endless sky. "To The Otherworld and back."

"I love you, too."

When he kissed me, the world righted itself. Paradise was not in the Otherworld, but right here, in the fluid motion of our lips moving together in harmony like sunlight on the morning sea. Here, in the warm coast of my husband's strong arms, in the synchronized rhythm of two hearts beating as one.

All that are lost shall be found.

We'd found each other, again and again, through hardship and heartache, through revenge and regret and recovery.

As long as he lived and breathed, I'd never be lost.

"She spat up again!" Vian cried, shattering the moment. Ronan's deep laugh rumbled through my bones as he broke our kiss, an unspoken *'your turn'* written in the look he offered.

"Insufferable cad," I smirked and drifted away from him, knowing I'd always return to shore.

Vian held Rhiannon by her armpits as the white goo dripped down his ruined tunic, my happy little starbeam wearing her father's smug smile as she admired her artwork.

"That's what happens when you spin her around like that," Saeth admonished, wiping the baby's mouth with the edge of *Gwynn's* tunic sleeve.

"Gee, thanks, love." He shot her a look that could down a dragon, but did not stop her from puppeting his arm, the wild hunter God of The North turned to a dishrag by my cousin's steel and seduction.

"Here, come to Mama, little one," I cooed at Rhiannon as I grabbed her from Vian, patting her back as I held her to my chest. Her tiny form melted against mine as she wound her little fingers in a stray lock of my hair. "Vian, go get changed or we will really be late."

He sprinted off into the cabin without another complaint.

"Pfft, you've gone soft," Reagan stuck her hands to her hips as she studied me, a whirling mix of revulsion and respect in the dark shade of her stare that I knew all too well. "What happened to the NightMare of the Four Seas, the most vicious pirate to sail across the Deyrnas?"

I'd been the same once, a girl and goddess trapped in one, my soft parts protected by my barbed edges. I'd been afraid, then, of what Fate had in store for me. Of who I'd be.

I was no longer afraid. I was found.

I shrugged, careful not to disturb my daughter's cheek where it rested against my shoulder. I stared out over the edge of the *Ddraig's* rail, at Porthladd's proud form, an easy southern wind wrapping us both in its welcoming hug. "She found her daydream."

Ronan stood at my side, his hand fitting against the small of my back, the most important part of that dream come true. My favorite smirk curved across his face. "Anyway, let's get moving! We have a wedding to attend."

48

Epilogues and Ever-afters

GRIFFIN

The sea was noisier than a barfight the night of my wedding.

Or perhaps it was my family, half of them late as they filtered into the seats laid across Traeth Beach, throwing elbows and tripping over each other to get a better view.

Not that I blamed them. I was a sight to behold today. My white tunic had dragons and roses embroidered in gold that highlighted the lighter shades of ginger in my slicked-back hair, Truth was polished and sheathed at my side, the perfect accessory.

My family's presence helped soothe the waves rolling in my gut, a side effect of the nerves and the quarter bottle of whiskey I'd drank the night prior. I might have been a committed man now, but that didn't mean I'd given up *all* my favorite vices. I scanned the crowd, each face present a gift in itself after so many lost.

Mama and Uncle Weylin sat up front, Mama already holding a tear-stained handkerchief to her watering eyes as Weylin awkwardly patted her back in reassurance. Next to them, Tarran and Genni sat beside Gwynn and Saeth, the twins never more opposite, flanked by their dates for the affair. Keira and Ronan chose Rhett's side of the isle, evening it out, a sleeping Rhiannon tucked in Ronan's arms.

Behind them, Vian and Reagan giggled with their heads pressed together, murmuring plans I longed to be a part of.

Others gathered too, waiting in the rows further back. Drystan and Councilwoman Tommins chatted away with Marina, Nelle, and Laureli while Grayson Leary sat wedged between Madame Katrin and Madame Neirida, a happy grin on the handsome lad's face. Everyone who'd stood with us in Orwellin, who'd supported us from the beginning, all gathered to *celebrate* something for once instead of mourn.

Still, I couldn't help but miss the friends and family not in attendance. Those waiting beyond the veil, the martyrs excused from yet another event.

My hands twitched at my sides as the sun sank lower against the horizon, the time approaching faster with every breath I dragged into my shoddy lungs.

"You look great, Griffin." Keira broke away from the others, leaving Ronan with the baby, a knowing light in the silver of her stare. An unspoken reassurance in our secret language.

Relax.

I raised a brow back. *I'm trying.*

She rested a hand on my shoulder, giving me a firm squeeze. "Everyone below is celebrating with us, too. They all love you."

I swallowed down the jealousy and appreciation rising up my throat in a bile-soaked cocktail. As much as it soothed my soul to know the rest of my kin were happy in the world beyond, it still hurt being the only mortal barred from getting to see them with my own eyes. I never envisioned myself a married man, a fool like me undeserving of such an honor, but to accomplish anything without them felt hollow.

Not that I wanted to rush to see them anytime soon. I'd dodged Death too many times to risk flirting with it ever again. Especially when I had someone here who made me feel like a god even in my battered human body.

"You look peachy too," I cleared my throat, eyeing her closer. Her normally pale-as-a-dove's-ass skin had a warm glow to it, health and happiness radiating from every pore. She was in a good mood, the silver wheel turning in her favor today. "You've got that look, Shrimpy."

The same look that once spelled a bad idea veiled in good intentions and doused in adventure. A look that almost always landed me in the brig or with a bruise or two. A look I'd follow into the unknown if she still let me tag along.

A smirk twisted her lips. "I'll tell you later. It's married person stuff."

Out of the corner of my eye, I noticed Ronan striding toward us, like a magnet drawn again to his wife's gravitational pull. A bad idea stirred in my head, my mischief bidden to the surface.

"I *see*," I taunted loud enough for him to hear, another vice I'd be hard pressed to part with. "Is my good cousin Ronan not giving you the business right?"

Keira whacked my arm as Ronan covered the baby's ears, shielding her from my vulgarity in a way that made my chest swell with pride.

"By the gods, Griffin," Ronan growled as he came close, voice a lethal low. "If you don't behave, I'll never let you babysit your nephew."

"I—" I made to protest before the words died on my tongue. Realization hit me harder than Keira did.

Keira's effortless glow, Ronan's smug-as-a-hermit-crab-with-a-new-shell smile…

"You're knocked up?" I hissed a whisper, my heart pounding with joy. If Ronan hadn't been holding Rhiannon, I would've tackled them both in a hug.

Another baby Branwen. Another member of the crew to teach and watch grow and love. Another kin counted among the living.

Keira held a finger to her lips, silver eyes dancing with delight. "You're the first to know, so don't spoil it."

"First to know what?" Tarran injected himself in the conversation, red curls smoothed flat against his head. He'd filled out some more, his breadth almost matching mine now, accentuated by a robin's-egg waistcoat that must have cost him an arm and a leg.

My second mate had expensive taste. He'd grown into a man now, the boy I loved to tease almost lost from his freckled features as his jaw edged to match his stature.

"Seriously, what is it?" Tarran stomped his foot. So much for all grown up. "What aren't you saying?"

Keira gave me a sharp nod, a silent command to stay quiet. I mimed stitching my lips together and throwing away the needle.

"That you look *ridiculous* in that thing, Tare-bear," Saeth snorted, ducking out from behind him to save the day. Even if I didn't have the heart to tease him, his shark-blooded twin did. "Did you get dressed in the dark today?"

A wobbling soprano voice sniffled, "Actually, I dressed him. I made the waistcoat myself."

Genni wiped her giant blue eyes with her gloved hands, the fabric perfectly matching her partner's. Tarran's face went redder than a crab's ass, fists clenched to his sides, and for a moment, something that looked almost as human as regret flashed across Saeth's steely features.

"Hmmm," I hummed as I crossed my arms, interrupting before Tarran could blow his carrot-top and ruin my moment. "Well, Genni, your work is lovely as always. It must be the model wearing it that's off then."

Our collective laughter exploded like a firework, the tension whizzing and fizzling out. Even Genni stopped her sniffling, a small giggle instead bubbling from her. The swishing anxiety in my stomach settled, the chorus of my crew's glee a better tonic than any hair-of-the-dog I'd ever sipped.

Tarran's eyes rolled so hard they almost popped out of his head. "Ha, ha, you're all hysterical. Could we maybe get through *one* family function without bullying me?"

"Nope," Saeth said.

"Not a chance," Keira echoed.

I shrugged, my smile untamable as the sea lapping against the edge of the beach. "Consider it a wedding gift."

"We're giving gifts *before* the ceremony? That's unconventional." That booming voice preceded Ellian's arrival, the Councilman fashionably late and insufferably loud as usual. His green finery was almost as embellished as mine, bronze-inlaid stripes emphasizing his wealth. After his stint of time as an outlaw, it seemed the blacksmith was tired of roughing it with the sailors.

"We're a group of shifters, gods, sirens, and sailors," Siobhan unwound her arm from his, her burnt-orange dress swirling over her muscled body, the warrior cleaning up nicely for the wedding. The siren shot me a rare smile. "Did you expect something normal?"

No, we were not normal, this family of mine. But I loved this group fiercely, those I called kin by blood and those I'd won in battle. And I wanted to celebrate it more than I'd ever allowed myself to want anything in my life.

Not that I'd ever say that to any of them. I had a reputation to uphold. I wagged a finger between Siobhan and Ellian. "Speaking of strange, if you two pop out a kid, is it going to be half fish or half wolf?"

Ellian stopped breathing, and if I hadn't been wearing white and about to get hitched, Siobhan would've killed me.

"Or would their child be all person, the two magicks canceling out? Or maybe they combine in a weird half fish, half wolf combo?" Vian mused, appearing out of fucking nowhere in a way that only the wind sprite could, summoned by absurdity.

I jumped as my heart nearly fell through my ass, Vian almost finishing Siobhan's job for her.

"Find yer seats, ye bunch of fools. We're starting." A voice like storm and running springwater announced, the last guests finally arriving. A hush washed over the crowd as Lyr and Esme walked side by side, both of them stopping in front of the canopy of seashells Lyr had assembled as our altar.

Our officiants had arrived.

It was time.

Everyone shuffled back to their seats, the warm hum of Ellian's fiddle and the gentle splash of the waves masking the sounds of settling. I took my place standing in front of Lyr and Esme, hands shaking at my side as reality set in. No more pretending or teasing. No more running.

Breathe in, breathe out.

I turned around to watch Rhett walk in.

I'd been stabbed through the middle before, but nothing compared to the ache that clutched my chest as I laid eyes on him.

His tunic matched mine in design, white with silver horses embossed in the fabric. But it paled in comparison to the rest of him, his straw hair bathed gold in the last rays of the setting sun, his scarred face a work of fucking art.

His smile stopped my heart again.

His hand in mine restarted it.

"Hey, Blondie," I croaked as his image blurred, my eyes stinging.

His thumb rubbed gentle circles against my palm. "Hey, Red."

"We are gathered here today to celebrate two hearts coming together as one before the gods." Lyr's rolling-thunder voice echoed over us, but all I could hear was the drumbeat of my heart as it hammered Rhett's name into my bones, again and again. I tried to focus, to *breathe*, to brace against the tidal wave of wanting that washed over me. "Two lives, intertwined through sadness and joy, through sacrifice and—"

"Cut to the good part, Your Godliness." The words burst free from my mouth before I could stop them, encouraged on by the wild thing thumping inside of me. I had no patience left, no armor to protect me. Not a single moment I was willing to waste parted from his side. "I need this man to be my husband."

The sunken god looked to his wife, and the sea-witch smiled in understanding. "Do ye, Griffin Arnold Branwen, take Rhett Silas Mathonwy to be yer husband?"

"*Arnold?* I thought Griffin's middle name was Trouble." Someone—*Reagan*—snickered in the crowd, earning a round of hushed laughter, but I didn't care. I'd change my name to Ralph and pierce my dick with a rusty spoon if it made the man in front of me happy. If it gave Rhett even a fraction of the joy and love he'd already poured into my empty cup, so much so that it ran over like the tears streaming freely down my face.

"Aye, I sure do," I said with genuine pride for the first time in my life. Even if he didn't reciprocate, even if he ran from this altar here and now and never looked back, I would not regret a single moment of our story. Rhett Mathonwy had made me want to be more than a second-born fuck up. Had made me a better man, not just a harbinger of Trouble, but a soldier for peace. A family man who didn't hide from his worst parts, but loved them instead.

Lyr looked to my partner, to the man who made me feel like I could walk on water and breathe fire. "Do you, Rhett, take Griffin in return?"

A moment passed, too long, as I waited in wanting.

Then, "I do."

My hands stopped shaking, an exhale finally rushing from my lungs.

Breathe in, Breathe out, as I finally met my *husband's* sky-blue and sterling-silver gaze. He looked at me like I was deserving. Like I was loved.

And for the first time in my gods-damned life, I let myself accept that.

"Any of ye arse-hats object?" Esme threatened the crowd with a glare of her red eyes, and for a split second, the world was absolutely silent.

Save for Truth singing at my side, a gentle reminder of how truly right this moment was.

Rhett smiled, like he could hear it too.

"Then by my power, I pronounce you two as one, in this life and the one beyond." The God of the Sea set his hands above ours, solidifying the invisible bond that had already tethered Rhett and I together from the first moment we shared in the brig. "Go ahead, give us a kiss."

So I did. I kissed Rhett with every single drop of love I had in my overgrown body, with every healed wound and shattered armor, with every loss mourned and victory won. I kissed him and he kissed me back, so long that cheers erupted from our loved ones, someone—Ellian—even whistling.

When we finally broke apart, the crack in my world had somehow molded itself together again.

"Reception at the *Raven*!" I hollered, some things forever unchanged. I was a married man now, but I was a Branwen, after all. We'd revived the bar after Agatha left it behind, our new little dream while we healed. It wasn't a flat in Ir'de, but it was his and mine. *Ours.* And I planned on saluting our small victory in the best way I knew how. "Drinks on me and my husband!"

Rhett kissed the back of my hand as we took our first steps toward our forever. "Lead the way, Mr. Branwen-Mathonwy."

THE END

☿Pronunciation Guide ☿

Adolli ⤞ (ah-dOH-lEE)

Annwyn ⤞ (ahn-wEEn)

Arawn ⤞ (ah-RAH-wihn)

Ariannad ⤞ (ah-REE-AH-nihd)

Awelymor ⤞ (ah-wEHl-EE-mawr)

Bachtref ⤞ (bAHk-trehf)

Blaidd ⤞ (blAY-iht)

Carthu ⤞ (kAWR-thOOH)

Ceffyl Dwr ⤞ (kEHf-eel dweer)

Clogwynn ⤞ (klAWg-ween)

Ddraig ⤞ (trAY-ihg)

Deyrnas ⤞ (dAY-er- nahs)

Dubryn ⤞ (dOOH-breen)

Duweni ⤞ (dOOH-wehn-ee)

Dynaur ⤞ (dEE-nawhr)

Faoladh ⤞ (fohl-AHd-uh)

Hiraeth ⤞ (hih-RAYth)

Hud ⤞ (hOOHd)

Ir'de ⤞ (EEr-uh-day)

Lechyd Da ⤞ (lEHtch-ee-dAH)

Lyr ⤞ (lEEr)

Madyn ⤞ (mAH-dEEn)

Melthith ⤞ (mEHl-thEEth)

Neid ⤞ (nEE-ihd).

Orwellin ⤞ (awr-wEHl-ihn)

Porthladd ⤞ (pAWrth-laht)

Pysgodd ⤞ (pEEs-gawt)

Rydha ⤞ (rEEd-hah)

Sarffymor ⤞ (sahr-FEE-mawr)

Serenhi ⤞ (seh-rehn-hEE)

Tan ⤞ (tAHn)

Tyawell ⤞ (tEE-ah-wehl)

Tysor ⤞ (tEE-sawr)

Wynnaid ⤞ (wEE-nAY-ihd)

ACKNOWLEDGEMENTS

Well, dear readers, we've made it to the end of our tale, of a *trilogy*, and there are no more voyages left to sail with Keira and Ronan. But this series—this third installment especially—would not have been possible without my crew. My people, who've followed me to the Otherworld and back, whose passion and starfire got me out again unscathed. I have too many thank yous to possibly put into words, but here are an important few.

To Renee, my editor and dear friend; thank you for being my navigator through rocky seas. Thank you for challenging me to be indulgent with this book, and then steering my course back on track when I got lost in *what ifs*. Thank you for your gentle encouragement and masterful criticism. This series would not have existed without your support. In your edit letter, you joked that I might find a better editor for the next project, but none such exists. And thank you for always sticking up for Tarran, even if no one else does.

To Cass, my critique partner and earth sign sister; thank you for overthinking with me, for your beyond helpful feedback and adjustments that grounded me when I got sucked into the whirlwind. For always responding to my nonsense DMS without judgement, and for always just *getting it*. I can't wait for our books to be comp titles and to sit next to each other on my shelf.

To Katie M, my critique partner & audiobook narrator; thank you for helping me find these character's voices (literally and figuratively), and for knowing the first book better than I do at this point. For all the little reminder messages that helped me dive back in when drafting got hard, and for always advocating for this series. I can't wait to return the favor one day.

To Cassidy, my proofreader; thank you for crossing my Ts and dotting my Is, and for your undying support of all my side ships. I promise you'll get to read the deleted scenes before anyone else. Your friendship and enthusiasm always makes the hard days easier.

To Fran, my incredible cover designer: Thank you for giving this series its iconic look. I am so pleased with how it all came together, and I appreciate your patience for my nitpicking. Thank you for lending your talent and taking a chance on an indie author!

To my beta team, Jen, Kelly, Maddie, Shana, Lara, Jenny, Cass, Cassidy, Alex, and Jessa; thank you for the incredible feedback and help. For your ardent enthusiasm for so many of the ships, and your insightful feedback about the pacing issues. Thank you for helping me wrap up this story, and reminding me why I wrote it.

To my street team & ARC readers: your excitement and creativity is unmatched! I am blown away by what this series turned into, and I am so thankful for your support.

To my insta community: though you're my 'internet friends', you all mean so much to me. The love for The Children of Lyr helped me survive the loneliness of the pandemic, and I could never have imagined that starting a bookstagram account four years ago would've led me here. I am so eternally grateful for your presence in my life, and I hope it continues for the projects beyond.

To my family; thank you for listening to me rant and ramble about this series for the last few years. For dealing with my 'hurricane mode' whenever I had an idea I wanted to bounce off an audience. For always asking 'when is the movie version coming out?' with a wink and smile, and bragging to your friends about the series. For being the blueprint I built the Branwens from. I love you all.

To Armand, my husband and my soul mate; For being the safe shore I retreat to when the waters get choppy. For loving me not just despite my flaws, but *for* them. For listening to audiobooks just so you can talk to me about them, for folding the laundry on days I'm too absorbed in writing to notice, for learning my love languages and becoming fluent in them, and for everything else that you are. I write love stories, but none will ever compare to ours.

And finally, to you, dear reader: thank you for coming on this journey with us. For validating this part of my soul. For loving my characters. For healing and hurting with them. As Ronan says, stories have power, and I am honored to have told mine. Though this series is finished, I hope to sail with you all again one day.

And to those still finding the words to tell their stories; don't stop searching for your daydreams.

ABOUT THE AUTHOR

Growing up on the east coast in small-town New Jersey, Lina spent her early days playing pretend and making up stories for her friends and family. Little did they know, that pastime would soon turn into a lifelong passion for storytelling in all of its forms. While she's a couple's therapist by profession, she's a writer at heart. When she's not scribbling ideas about fictional worlds into the margins of her notebooks, Lina spends her time reading anything she can get her hands on, driving her husband crazy with her wild daydreams, and snuggling her adorable pups.

You can find out more about future projects and Lina's publishing label, Silver Wheel Press, at www.silverwheelpress.com or on Instagram: @Lina_Amarego_Writes.

OTHER WORKS BY THE AUTHOR

The Children of Lyr Series
    Daughter of the Deep (book one)
    Sister of the Stars (book two)

Of Fate & Fury: A Deadly Sin Anthology

www.ingramcontent.com/pod-product-compliance
Lightning Source LLC
Chambersburg PA
CBHW050843210726
48290CB00004B/1058

* 9 781734 826593 *